Fade to Midnight

fade to midnight

SHANNON MCKENNA

BRAVA

KENSINGTON PUBLISHING CORP.
http://www.kensingtonbooks.com

BRAVA BOOKS are published by

Kensington Publishing Corp.
119 West 40th Street
New York, NY 10018

All Kensington titles, imprints and distributed lines are
available at special quantity discounts for bulk purchases for
sales promotion, premiums, fund-raising, educational or in-
stitutional use.

Special book excerpts or customized printings can also be
created to fit specific needs. For details, write or phone the
office of the Kensington Special Sales Manager: Kensington
Publishing Corp., 119 West 40th Street, New York, NY, 10018.
Attn. Special Sales Department. Phone: 1-800-221-2647.

Brava and the B logo Reg. U.S. Pat. & TM Off.

ISBN-13: 978-0-7582-2866-6
ISBN-10: 0-7582-2866-X

First Hardcover/Trade Printing: June 2010
First Mass Market Printing: September 2011
10 9 8 7 6 5 4 3 2 1

Printed in the United States of America

PROLOGUE

1994, Portland, Oregon

*T*ony Ranieri sucked in smoke and fingered the tarnished
dog tags in his hand. He had no patience for mysteries.
Not in books, not on TV. Mind-squeezing, time-wasting bullshit. But there he was. In Tony's face.

He watched the kid squirt disinfectant into the bucket and
start in on the floor, staring at the ponytail of streaky, dirt-
blond hair, the thick muscles of the kid's shoulders, emerging
from the sprung out tank top of Tony's, two sizes too big for
him. The flesh-creeping pattern of scars snaked and spiraled
over the kid's skin. Those wounds had still been oozing the
night he found the unlucky son of a bitch, almost two years
ago, now. He hadn't dared to take the kid to a hospital. The
guys who'd done for him would be watching.

Tony had braced himself to see those wounds go bad.
There was internal bleeding, broken bones, too. And the kid's
face. Mother of God.

He'd steeled himself to have to hide the body, pretend
he'd never found the kid. Like he didn't have enough shit on
his conscience.

But he hadn't died. Tony sucked his cigarette, in defiance of the no smoking rule in the diner kitchen. His sister Rosa, colossal ballbreaker, was home, asleep. His young nephew Bruno had crashed hours ago upstairs. And the kid wasn't going to rat him out. The kid couldn't talk for shit. He could wash dishes, chop onions, scrape plates, and fight like a fucking demon from hell. But he couldn't say a damn word.

He wasn't a kid, really, either. He'd been twentyish when Tony found him, but Tony hadn't gotten a good handle on him yet, so he'd just stuck with "the kid." He offered no other satisfying defining characteristic, besides his silence, and his scars. The kid would be movie-star good looking, if not for the scars. He was lucky they hadn't taken his eyes. But Tony'd bet his left nut that the torturer had been working up to the eyes, the balls. Tony knew what got that kind of guy off. He knew it all too well.

But something had interrupted the torture fest. The bastard had decided to finish the kid off. Just beat him to death and dump the body.

Who knew why. Mysteries. Fuck 'em.

The kid paused in his mopping, looked over his shoulder. He wanted to say something, wanted it bad. His green eyes burned with urgency. But nothing came out. The wires were cut. He was all fucked up. It hurt to look at him.

The kid's shoulders slumped. He got back to work. Slop, dip, swab.

Tony's fingers closed around the dog tags. He stubbed out the cigarette. He was a straight shooting guy. Kill or be killed, that was the kind of motto he could get behind. Ambiguity fucked with his digestion.

Tony wound the chain round his hand til it burned his fingers. He'd found the tags in the kid's blood-soaked jeans pocket, the night he'd chased off the killer. Not the kid's own, though that was Tony's first assumption.

These tags were of an older soldier. Tony's generation. Tony's war.

Tony had nosed around, asked his Marine buddies, and heard stories to curdle a guy's blood. The name on that tag struck fear into the hearts of battle-hardened men. Sniper, killer, monster. Accused of unspeakable atrocities. Disappeared after Nam, before they could court-martial him. Probably slitting throats for the criminal underworld.

He'd be Tony's age, by now, with a team under him. Guys as badass as him, or worse. There was always worse.

Tony stared at that lost, fucked-up kid bent over his bucket, and renewed the decision he made every night. The kid was in no shape to deal with the people who had reduced him to this. They would squish him like a cockroach. He was better off scraping plates, swabbing floors. Tony stared, breathing smoke. Hating the sick feeling of doubt in his guts.

Eamon McCloud. What was he, to this kid? He cursed under his breath, in thick Calabrese dialect. He shoved the tags into his pocket.

The name on those dog tags could put the kid's broken life together.

Or it could get him killed once and for all.

CHAPTER

1

I am fucked.
The thought flicked through Kev's head, calm and detached. The roar of icy water filled his ears. The current would pull him loose in counted seconds. Seconds measured by the pounding pulse of blood through his brain. Each throb hurt like a raving motherlover, but there was nothing like imminent death to take a guy's mind off a headache.

His little angel's face flashed through his mind. His dream companion, his spirit guide. Her big eyes looked sad, and scared.

He'd known since he got out of bed that today was going to be the day. He'd had that prickle, as if someone were looking at the back of his neck. Not surprising, since he'd set the day aside for high-adrenaline sports activities, his chief joy in what passed for his life. One would think, having gotten a clue from the Great Beyond that death lurked nearby, that a reasonable, sane person would spend the day on the couch, watching reruns. Cruising the mall bookstore, reading about mindfulness or voluntary simplicity. Lying low in a multiplex, watching a nature documentary. Sipping a green tea latte. Well out of sight.

Not him. The reasonable, sane parts of himself were out in space. Along with his memories and his normal and natural fear of death. Danger? Bring it the fuck *on*. He should be dead already anyway. Look at his face. Kids ran screaming to mommy when they saw his bad side.

Cold had numbed the pain. He no longer felt his hand, clamped around the boughs of the dead tree. He did not feel the compound fracture in his other arm. His injured limb flopped in the water, sucked by the current, a few yards from the head of the falls. His broken bone tented out the nylon of his jacket, pinkish with blood. But he doubted he'd be using that arm again, once the water flung him over the brink.

Whatever. He'd been smash totaled years ago. Living on borrowed time. Half a brain, half a life. No clue at all.

Don't start with that. Just shut the fuck up. He did crazy shit like this for the express purpose of keeping himself too zapped with adrenaline to indulge in self-pity. That was why he hung off the edge of cliffs, hang-glided treacherous air currents, rafted badass rapids. When he was that close to death, he felt buzzing, connected. Almost alive.

Since Tony found him he'd had some mechanism functioning that damped his emotional volume way down. High enough for function, but no more. Probably caused by the trauma to his brain that had caused the amnesia, and rendered him speechless, back in the bad old days.

Whatever it was, he was bored with it. If he could, he'd join the military, fly fighter jets. Playing with toys like that, yeah. Talk about a coping mechanism. But the military wouldn't want a guy with crossed wires, a questionable identity and a black hole in his mind to fly their hundred million dollar toys. They'd put him to work cleaning engines. If they took him at all. No, he had to make do with high-risk sports. They kicked his ass into high gear, and he liked that gear. The color, the noise. The buzz of being awake to it, aware of it. Giving a shit.

He'd gotten what he wanted. But he was going to pay big.

He stared at the top of the falls. Clouds of vapor rose from the thundering tons of water crashing down, hundreds of feet below. How many hundreds? He tried to remember. Several. Well over three. Whoo hah.

Not that he was afraid of dying. At most, he was curious. Sorry he'd never unravel the great questions of his existence, at least not as a living man, and who knew what happened after? He'd never speculated. His present mortal existence was problem enough, for as long as he could remember. Roughly half of his life. He didn't know how old he was. Tony put him around twenty when he'd saved Kev from the warehouse thug eighteen years ago. So he was fortyish. Give or take.

At least the boy was going to make it. Kev was immobilized by tons of rushing ice water, but out of the corner of his eye, he saw activity in the trees choking the cliffside shore. Rescue proceedings were underway. Other people besides Kev had been at the point when he'd put ashore, where he'd seen the kids spin past, oarless and out of control. Only a guy with a black hole in his brain would be suicidal enough to jump in after them at that point in the rapids, but he'd taken no time to ponder that implacable truth. He just went for it.

And then, a long, hopeless wrestle with nature while the water got wilder, the roar of the falls louder.

While death approached, smiling. Happy to see him. His old pal.

Maybe he'd subconsciously wanted it. Bruno threw that death wish crap in his face a lot, whenever he got cracked up doing daredevil sports. Could be. Not worth worrying about, though. Particularly now.

The kids had capsized by the time he caught up. Kev saw a bobbing head and scooped one out of the water by sheer, blind luck. Then they plunged into a trough, the raft flipped, and they were tossed like twigs, the boy flailing, choking. He'd clamped the kid against him, struggled, kicked. He'd wanted to save that kid. Wanted it ferociously. He was played out, now, though. In fact, he felt strangely serene.

The other boy was gone, over the falls. That was fucked, and he was sorry. Rescue was on the way for the other one, but the greedy way the water sucked at the tree told him the hard truth.

He was going down. Anytime.

He forced his head to turn, checked on the kid. Sixteen or so. A drowned rat, clinging to the lucky side of the rock that split the top of the falls into two long, thin tails, hence the name, Twin Tails Falls. The weight of rushing water pinned him against the bulwark of the rock. He couldn't move if he wanted to. But he'd live. That was good.

It wasn't strength or skill that had smacked them up against that jutting rock. Just chance. And then, just as fast, *bam.* That bastard came up so fast, he barely shoved the kid out of the way before the tree trunk snapped his arm, smashed God only knew what else in his thorax, knocked him loose—and then spun out perpendicular to the falls, catching on a rock across the torrent. It formed a barrier, trapping him against a temporary dam. But not for long.

Smashing him, then saving him. When it worked loose, it would fuck him again, definitively. He'd ride that bastard out over the cliff.

The story of his life. Something inside him laughed, with stony irony. Wasn't it always the way. Like Tony, who'd dragged Kev out of his own rapids years ago, and kept him there, brain damaged, shambling and speechless. Washing dishes, mopping floors for room and board at the diner. Lying on a sagging cot, watching paint peel in the windowless mildewed room behind the diner where he'd slept. For fucking *years.*

The rope thrown out to save him. The same rope that he strangled himself on. It was almost funny. Except that it wasn't.

The tree was about to go. The branches stuck on the rocks on the other side were wavering, wild water bending the flexible limbs, teasing them loose. The tree shuddered, rolled. The water sucked and insisted.

Any time now. He composed himself, tried to pay attention, to be present for it, to breathe. Difficult. So cold. So much water. The kid's mouth gaped, begging Kev to do something. As if he could swim against that current, even if he weren't fucked-up. He had as much strength left as a broken doll. A final swell shook the tree loose. The ponderous slow motion made those last moments of clinging stretch out, infinitely long.

He struggled to stay conscious. The last wild ride. He'd better enjoy it. He wondered if he'd know, once he was dead, who he'd been before. What he'd done, who he'd known. Who he'd loved.

Probably not. This was all he got. It would just have to do.

Whoosh, the river rolled him under the tree and spat him far out into vastness. Endless space, above, below. Turning, head over ass.

The angel flashed across his mind. Those big gray eyes, so achingly sweet. A sharp sting of regret that he didn't understand. And another face, too, scowling his disapproval as the immutable laws of physics had their stern way with him. A face he saw in his dreams every night. A young guy. His face maddeningly familiar.

Kev had been having a dream argument with that guy, that very morning, he suddenly remembered. The man had been scolding him.

"*Dying is easy. You told me that yourself,*" the guy said. "*It's living that's hard. Meathead. Hypocrite. You piss me off.*"

So that was how he'd known today would be dangerous.

Part of his mind hooted and shrieked with unreasoning joy at the icy rush of air and water on his face. *Whoa. This shit is fun.* Another part pondered acceleration rates of falling objects, wind shear, probable force of impending impact on the rocks below. He calculated it down to ten digits after the decimal in that last, eternal instant—

And hurtled into a blank, white nothing.

* * *

Goddamnit to hell. Thick, stupid, useless *cow.*

Ava Cheung refocused her mind to a laser point. So much information streamed through the human nervous system to make a body move smoothly through space. So much of it was automatic. One couldn't fathom how much until one tried to provide the impulses for someone else's body, using one's own will while simultaneously suppressing theirs. Mandy was responding poorly. Shuffling, clumsy. Ava could not get the girl to shut her mouth and keep it closed. The drooling was driving her crazy, and it was all the more grotesque with Mandy's sexpot beauty, her heavily lashed blue eyes vacant behind the goggles, her pupils vastly dilated by the X-Cog prep drugs.

Ava fancied that X-Cog master-crowning required a skill level comparable to what it must take to play an instrument at a professional level. It required intense concentration to make the crowned person move and speak naturally. Unless you upped the doses, which lowered the subject's resistance, but melted their brains in a scant hour. Not cost efficient. One had to be a virtuoso, like her, and Dr. O, of course.

This rendered the X-Cog interface less commercially feasible. How many people were willing to put in the hours to hone a new skill? People were lazy, contemptible slobs, as a rule. They needed things to be easy.

Ava was committed to finding a way to make X-Cog accessible to anyone with the money to pay for it, and Mandy was the umpteenth effort to that end. But a virtuoso needed a decent instrument to play. Not a thick, dull, unresponsive piece of *shit.*

Ava yanked off the master crown and flung it onto the table, more forcefully than she should have, considering how much it cost to develop and produce. The streamlined silver cap was very different from Dr. O's heavy, clunky design, which had given her tension headaches. Dr. O hadn't bothered with aesthetics. Dr. O had been a results man.

The new design was her own graceful innovation. Everything essential was there, but the end result was a light-as-air tangle of flexible wires and sensors on a light mesh cap. Both master and slave crowns were designed to be easily concealed beneath a hat, scarf, or wig.

Ava's brilliance was wasted on Mandy. The dumb little bitch was going straight into the shredder. Mandy whimpered as Ava wrenched goggles and crown off the girl's head, yanking out long blond hair. She whipped the master crown glasses off. Stupid, talentless cow. Crowning her was like trying to send nervous impulses through a lump of clay.

Ava smoothed glossy black hair back and stared at Mandy, who swayed on her feet, gaping. The girl was dressed in the silver spandex jog bra and shorts that Ava had mandated as a uniform for X-Cog test subjects. She liked her girls to look sexy and sharp. But Mandy looked anything but sharp, with drool trailing off her chin.

The look on the girl's face disgusted her. She slapped Mandy. The girl stumbled against the table, looking vaguely confused.

Ava slapped her again, harder. And again. *Smack. Smack.* Blood trickled from Mandy's nose, from her split lip. The girl's hands crept up, tried to cover her face. Ava struck Mandy's ears, whapped the back of her head, knocking her forward. Mandy thudded heavily to her knees.

"Back off, Av. That's millions of dollars you're kicking around."

Ava spun around, and shot a poisonous look at the man who had just walked in. "Mind your own fucking business, Des."

Desmond jerked his chin towards Mandy. "She is my business."

"She's a worthless piece of shit," Ava hissed.

"Don't take your frustration out on her." Desmond's arrogant, know-it-all tone made her want to put out one of his bright blue eyes. "You thought that upping the burn would give you more direct control with the crown at a lower dose of the drug. You were wrong. Too bad. Honest mistake. We won't make it again. Grow up, Ava. Move on."

"But the basic idea is sound! Next time, I'll recalibrate the—"

"No." The curt word cut her off. "We reached the point of diminishing returns weeks ago. No more cutting, no more burning."

There was no arguing with Des when he got that tone. He was the one with the money, the contacts. He'd funded her whole show, since Dr. O bit the dust. But bumping up against the limits of her power over him made her bad tempered. She kicked Mandy's buttock viciously. The girl lurched forward with a pathetic grunt. "Don't lecture me," she said, sulkily. "I'm the one who's clubbing with the stinking masses to troll for test subjects! Wasting time I should spend on research, bumping and grinding with Ecstasy whores like her!" She kicked Mandy again, making her whimper. "I need to delegate this tedious shit!"

"I'm trying, babe, but I don't understand why you're so set on wiping them. I enjoy crowning the ones who aren't burned or cut much better. It's that inner resistance that makes it exciting, you know?"

Ava snorted. "It's not about excitement. You've never tried to crown a subject into anything more complex than sucking on your dick. Try making one of them type a string of code, and see how far you get. You can compel a girl to blow you by putting a twenty dollar gun to her head. You don't need a ten million dollar X-Cog crown. I want to market X-Cog to defense contractors. Understand? Are you with me here?"

"Fellatio is actually a pretty complex motor process." Des sounded faintly hurt. "Particularly when you're hung."

Ava rolled her eyes. "Please. Leave the neuroscience to me."

Des waved that away. "I've got good news and bad news."

"I don't want to hear the bad news," she said pettishly.

"Then I'll tell you the good news, first." He nudged Mandy thoughtfully with his toe. "We need a steady supply of high quality, hand-selected lab rats. We also need someone to deal with our disposal issue. Remember Tom Bixby, from the Haven?"

Ava grimaced. Bixby had been one of Dr. O's rich pets. One who'd survived and thrived after Dr. O's Brain Potential Program. Off to Harvard with Dessie. She still remembered his hot eyes, his groping hands. "An arrogant prick, as I recall. That's your brilliant idea?"

"He runs his own private military company. Bixby Enterprises. It's gotten huge. I think X-Cog would be extremely interesting to him. And we would have multiple layers of security, since he's Club O."

Ava's lip curled. "But he's a dickhead."

Des's eyes rolled impatiently. "Don't be a spoiled baby. Offering him a partnership would solve all our problems in one move."

"And create a lot more," she said.

Des's eyes narrowed. "I've set up a demo. You will be good, Ava."

Well, look at him. Throwing his weight around. Trying to whip her into line with his big dick. She crossed her arms over her chest. "Tell me the bad news," she said. "Maybe it'll cheer me up."

Des stared at her, nostrils distended, cheeks reddening. Anger turned him on. A fact she often turned to her advantage. "I was at a Parrish Foundation board meeting today," he said finally. "Parrish is taking over where his bitch of a wife left off. Getting rid of Linda distracted him for a while, but the party's over, everybody out of the pool. He's engaged a panel of financial forensics experts to examine every penny of Parrish Foundation money spent in the past three years. And to vet all future projects. No more cutting it close."

"Oh, God," Ava moaned. "I'm so close to a breakthrough!"

"I know, but what can you do. He's as much of a pit bull as his ballbusting wife, may she burn in hell. The Morality Police don't want anything naughty going down, after Dr. O's big scandal."

"Fucking hypocrites. 'Helix was a victim, too,'" Ava mimicked.

Des looked at the moaning girl at his feet. "This shit does not look good, Av. Save it for when we can afford a more secret facility, and that won't be until after we get control of the Foundation board."

"It can't wait! Besides, no one will miss her. She's just a whore that I scraped off the bathroom floor of a dance club. No wonder she's a dud." She kicked Mandy in the kidney. "I need better raw material to work with."

"We need reliable funding first." Des's voice was stern. "And someone to supply lab rats, and safely dispose of the garbage for us. The Parrish Foundation is watching like a hawk. It's too risky."

"Charles Parrish has been raking in hundreds of millions in medical patents for years," Ava said bitterly. "Like he cared where the smell came from before his nose got rubbed in shit."

"Thank God he's retiring. I'm giving a fawning speech for that pompous tightass at the retirement banquet. Fucking bore."

"Retiring? That's good."

"Not really. It just leaves him that much more time to be possessive and controlling about Parrish Foundation research money."

Ava gave him a big, brilliant smile. "So let's kill him."

Des looked startled. "That wouldn't solve our problem."

"No? You're on the board. You handpicked the last two board members after we got rid of Linda. If Parrish disappeared, the rest of them will do anything you want, for the 400K salaries, the skybox, the Lear jet. The paid luxury vacations. They're sheep. It's easy, Dessie."

Des grunted. "Hardly. Don't oversimplify."

"But it is simple," Ava said. "We create the perfect board. Eliminate the watchdogs. Create a perfect screen of bland, squeaky clean product development projects that they can all feel virtuous about. Siphon a percentage of the money back to the real stuff, like Dr. O did. Except we won't fuck up, and let it explode in our faces."

Des looked dubious, but he wasn't rejecting it out of hand.

"Who inherits Parrish's fortune when he dies?" Ava asked.

Des frowned thoughtfully. "His younger daughter, Ronnie. Ronnie's thirteen. Edie, the older one, was at the Haven with us, remember? Glasses, braces. Woof, woof. The cognitive enhancement program bombed out bigtime on her, as I recall. She never got into Club O. Just didn't have what it took."

Ava nodded. She remembered the tongue-tied Edie. One of the privileged ones, like Des himself. Rich kids who did the soft core version of Dr. O's dirty mind games, because Mommy and Daddy wanted better grades. Ava hated the pampered little cunt for that.

"Who inherits if Ronnie dies?" Her voice hardened.

"Av. Please," Des grumbled. "We can't kill everyone in sight."

"Who?" she persisted.

He shrugged. "The Foundation, I guess. I know that Edie's out of the will, because I overheard Dad and Charles talking about her. He'd cut off her personal funds. He was arranging to disinherit her. That was a few years ago."

"What did she do? Drugs? Partying? Fucking the wrong men?"

Des shook his head. "No, she's just weird. She embarrasses him. Charles can't stand that. She had, ah, problems. You know . . ." He twirled his index finger in a circle at his temple. "Doesn't surprise me, since she's one of Dr. O's duds. Most of them cracked up years ago."

Ava tapped her lip. "Dr. O wanted to do an interface with

Edie Parrish so bad, he was practically pissing himself," she said. "She had the perfect test results for it, but she was Charles Parrish's little baby girl. He had to keep her in bubblewrap. Stick with the standard cognitive enhancement program. It drove him crazy."

She left the rest of the thought silent. How she, Ava, had borne the brunt of Dr. O's frustration. He'd taken it out on her. She had good reason to hate that mealy-mouthed little Parrish princess bitch.

Des looked baffled. "What was it that he liked about her? What can you see from test results and MRI's?"

Ava's smile was bitter. Des was such an ignorant dick-head sometimes. "They were exactly like mine," she said softly.

Des's face was still blank. "Meaning?"

Ava sighed. "I was his best interface, Dessie. Besides Kev McCloud, of course. We were the only ones that didn't die of brain bleed. Some lasted a few days, but only McCloud and I were genuinely reusable. That's why I survived. That's why I wasn't flushed down the john with the rest of them." She brushed her hair back with a swipe of her hand, preening. "And being pretty helped, too."

Des looked vaguely uncomfortable. "Um. I see. I'm, ah, sorry."

The insincere, pat words grated on her. "No, you're not. You don't give a shit, and we both prefer it that way," she said crisply. "Kev McCloud was the cornerstone of Dr. O's research. X-Cog wouldn't exist if it weren't for McCloud. So Dr. O was always looking for test results similar to his, and mine. And Edie Parrish had them. That's all."

Des let out a dubious grunt. "Kev McCloud managed to escape and practically fuck the whole project. Looks like that perfect interface had some pretty big fucking holes in it. And his twin, Sean, forced Dr. O to slit his own throat, re-member? That should give you pause, Av."

Pause, hah. It had given her sleepless nights for years.

Wondering frantically how Sean McCloud had managed it. When she could not.

How? How the *fuck* had he done that? All those years of being Dr. O's slave-crowned dollbaby. Used like a puppet, all the while dreaming of hammers crushing, knives gouging, axe blades hacking. Gouts of black arterial blood. Her hands began to shake, just thinking about it.

She locked the feelings down automatically, so that she could function. "The McClouds are freaks. Edie will be different. She's female, artistic, creative. Shy, introverted personality. Probably emotionally crushed by her father, which is fine for our purposes. She'll be a good little girl. She won't slit my throat."

Des's blue eyes narrowed. "What is this? First you want to kill her. Then you want to crown her."

"Crown first, kill later," she said airily. "Waste not, want not."

Des shot a speaking glance at Mandy, who was rocking on the ground, sucking on her thumb. "You don't call that a waste?"

Ava's teeth ground. "No. I call that a calculated risk. So what are we going to do about Parrish?"

Des looked irritated. "Shit," he muttered. "I don't know."

Ava sighed. Des was so fucking slow sometimes. "Des. Honey. Brainstorm with me. He's about to retire, right? Dangerous age for a man. Health problems, chronic pain? Grief, solitude? And he was bereaved last year, too. Poor Linda. He must be fragile. Depressed. And his daughter, with her mental problems? Oh, dear. So sad. Plus, he disinherited her. She must be so angry with him. She must feel betrayed. Maybe even . . ." Her voice sank to a whisper. "Murderous?"

Des's face took on an expression of dawning discovery. "She might. Wouldn't surprise anyone. He's such a self-righteous, pompous tight ass. I'm surprised someone hasn't beaten her to it."

"So sad," Ava said solemnly. "All those years of staunch

service to the company, the community . . . and it has to end like this, at the hand of his own flesh and blood. It's Shakespearean in scope."

"But there's Ronnie to consider, if you're talking about the money," Des said. "Ronnie would inherit the—"

"Edie must be so jealous of her little sister," Ava cut in dreamily. "Daddo's little favorite, right? I bet Edie lies awake nights contemplating how that complacent, self-satisfied little piece of shit deserves to die. So she offs the sister—and then kills herself. It's awful. It's epic."

Des chuckled. "I love the way your mind works," he said, with frank admiration. "Your twisted genius knows no bounds."

"No bounds except for your pussy squeamishness, that is." Ava kicked the girl curled on the floor in the back of her thigh. "Get rid of this trash for me. I'm sick of looking at her."

Des's smile vanished. "I don't do wet work, Av," he growled. "Even though I know it would turn you on."

"So get us more money. That would turn me on, too. Think outside the box. Isn't that what Dr. O trained us for?" She licked her glossy red lips, a move calculated to make him hard, and strolled to the chaise. "Break the chains that bind your brains, hmm? Like Dr. O said. Think about it. Complete control of the Parrish Foundation. Parrish's personal fortune, too. All his billions, invested in X-Cog, giving us a thousand percent return. Wouldn't that be just . . . perfect?"

His smile showed off his perfect teeth. Desmond Marr, future president of Helix. Harvard man. Pampered prince. Her personal slave.

Des had been one of Dr. O's pets, too, but the Haven had been a very different place for the son of Raymond Marr, cofounder of Helix. Des had been a rich pet, a Persian cat with a diamond collar. Desmond had never experienced a slave crown interface in his life.

Ava had been in the other category of pets. The parent-less, penniless, alley cat kind. Ava had worked for her keep, like the rest of the runaways, prostitutes, junkies, and punks. The ones Dr. O could fuck with and get measurable results. Helix was built upon their backs.

Or their bones, rather. They were all dead. All but her. And maybe Kev McCloud. Somewhere, out there.

Des had been her lover for years, ever since they'd met as teenagers at Dr. O's oasis of depravity, the Haven. The spark was immediate. They had so much in common. But certain things Dessie could never understand. If you'd never been a slave, how could you truly know what it meant to dominate? A privileged boy with billions behind him could never get that. It was a gulf between them. Sad.

But look at her now. She hadn't croaked from brain bleed like the rest of the lab rats. She was special, and Dr. O had realized it. From slave crowned zombie whore, she'd become Dr. O's crowning achievement. She'd undergone the most in-tense and rigorous of Dr. O's cognitive enhancement tech-niques. He'd trained her in X-Cog master-crowning technique. He'd arranged for her advanced studies, multiple degrees in neuroscience and bioengineering. With Dr. O's mentoring, she'd developed nearly as many products for Helix's bioscience and nanotechnology branch as Dr. O himself, over the years. He'd used her hard, but he had groomed her into something extraordinary.

Sometimes, she even missed that depraved, sadistic psy-chopathic prick. It was nice, to have someone be proud of you. To own you.

Even when it broke your bones, and hacked off your limbs and sucked your blood. Crushed you to dust. Burned you to fucking ashes.

Des caressed his erection, staring at her taut, curvy body, her nipples. He cast an uncertain glance at the girl moaning on the floor.

"Ignore her," Ava commanded. "I'll give her an injection

after, and put her in the fridge, since you can't soil your lily-white hands."

His face reddened. Scolding him sharpened his lust, but going too far made the situation unmanageable. He was large, physically strong, extremely quick, and had a cruel streak that ran very deep and wide.

"No more cracks about the wet work," he growled.

"Oh, Dessie." Her voice was throaty. "I love it when you're stern."

"Do you? Turn around. I'll show you stern."

She hesitated, feeling the heavy pulse in the air. The timing had to be right. She turned, with deliberate slowness, positioning herself on the chaise. Her micro-mini barely shadowed the parts she kept shaved, perfumed, and pantiless. Ready for immediate use on demand. Old training died hard. She swayed, watching herself reflected in the shiny silver file cabinets opposite. Black hair swinging, red lips parted. She looked good, she concluded, pleased. Dangerous, unstable. Red hot.

Des undid his belt as he approached, jerked open his pants. Yanked out that horselike member of which he was so proud.

He shoved her skirt up over her ass, and parted her buttocks, fingering her pussy. She writhed and gasped with theatrical enthusiasm around his delving fingers. His ego was so big, he always bought her act, no matter how extravagantly she overplayed it. Men.

He thrust his hand deeper, growling. "You're sopping wet."

Actually, it was hitting Mandy that had excited her, but Ava saw no reason to deny him the credit. Besides, she could lube on command. She knew what nasty things to think about to get that hot rush.

"It's you who does it to me." She let her voice quaver, to hint at hidden vulnerability, calculated to puff him up, make him feel like the king of her world. Thinking he ruled her, with his throbbing scepter.

He grasped her ass cheeks, and drove inside. Ava whimpered as he started pumping. This was the tedious part. All that bucking and moaning. Des was relatively skilled, too, so the thrusting went on for a tiresomely long time before he allowed himself to squirt. Ironic, how personal politics dictated that she praise him for that quality when she would infinitely prefer it to be quick.

But she managed, defaulting to the familiar state of floating detachment where she always went to endure sex. Leaving just enough of herself there to keep the show convincing. The rest of her highly functioning mind was at work. Preparing the next X-Cog test.

Too bad the test subject couldn't be Edie Parrish herself.

The thought triggered a rush of genuine sexual heat that took her by surprise. Wow. She'd gotten Des on her side, using his weakest point, and it turned her on, too. Bonus points. "Is she cute?" she asked.

"Who?" Des grunted, his hips thudding against her backside. "What the fuck are you talking about?"

"Edie Parrish. I haven't seen her in years. Is she cute?"

His thrusting slowed. "I don't know. All right, I guess. Tall, long hair, bad glasses. She hides. Nice tits, though. Why do you care?"

Ava twisted, to fix him with a hot, wild stare. "When we take her, I want to crown her. And fuck you. Through her."

He was so taken aback, he stopped moving. "Huh?"

"She'll be the best interface ever." She rocked back, enveloping his cock once again. "Much better than all the others. I'll make her into a red-hot nymphet. I'll make her do things that you've never imagined."

"I can imagine a whole hell of a lot," he warned.

She turned her head, smiled. "Things I'd never do myself, with my own body," she explained sweetly. "Wild, nasty, dirty things."

Desmond rammed into her, so hard, she stifled a gasp of

discomfort. "You are one depraved bitch," he said, his voice admiring.

"Why, thank you." She turned, bracing herself against each jolt, making keening, catlike wails. She'd gotten him. He'd do anything to make it happen now. But she realized, shocked, as the ride thundered to its roaring finish, that this fantasy of the X-Cog threesome compelling Edie Parrish was . . . oh, God . . . it was making her come.

Explosively.

He dripped blood as he ran. Shocked faces, their mouths horrified 'O's, stumbling back. No one stopped him on his desperate race toward the guy's office. He had to tell them the truth. Make the killing stop.

But the man didn't listen. He was disgusted, terrified. Kev had thought that the blood, the burns, would be a proof too strong to dispute.

Wrong. He'd scared them to death. His gore had blinded them. He was living proof that hell on earth existed. Something to deny, forget.

He fought, but he was weak from drugs, torture. He threw one of the guys through the window, but there were too many of them. They brought him down. Dragged him out. Then he saw the little angel.

So strange, to see an angel in hell. Small, perfect, clad in blazing white like a sunlit cloud. A halo of white crowned her hair. She saw him with her fearless, fathomless eyes. Not a monster from collective human nightmares. Just him. She retreated into the distance as they dragged him away. Her compassionate eyes followed as he craned desperately to keep her in his field of vision. He cried out, but she was too far—

He gasped for air, felt the jolt, from dream to waking, but the images lingered on. His small angel. Her deep, soft eyes. The man he had begged for help, yelling at him to shut up, to go away, leave him alone. The security staff that had dragged him away. And a name. Someone was screaming a name. The monster that had to be stopped.

Osta . . . *Ostamen* . . . ?

Gone. *Fuck.* It slid out of his mind, like sand through his fingers.

He gasped for air, groped for the name. This felt like . . . fuck, it felt like a memory. Not a dream. A *memory.*

Excitement pumped through him. He tried to open his eyes. Light stabbed. The stench of disinfectant assaulted his nose. His head throbbed, his insides churned. Unintelligible sounds battered his skull.

He tried to open his eyes, turn his head. Nothing moved. His eyelids were weighted down. His body was lead. The effort to move unleashed . . . *pain.* Raw, burning pain that he hadn't known since—

His mind flinched away, like he'd brushed up against a lethal live wire. A memory. He'd brushed up against a fucking *memory.* Oh, God. And it hurt. The memory hurt. He tried to calm himself. *Breathe.*

What the fuck? What was going on? He was shit scared. So intense, the sounds, the smells. He wanted to scream, writhe, cry. Hide.

He grasped, instinctively, for the image of his little angel. His magical talisman. Her gentle gray eyes regarded him calmly. Wise and kind. He clung to her, until the panic calmed. The little angel never let him down. She had led him through his confusion, through the speechless darkness all those years ago. Back to relative normality and function. He was starting to hear now. He could breathe again. *Ah.*

Voices. Audio cut in and out. He struggled to make it out.

". . . no signs of previous physical trauma in his brain that would account for the amnesia," said a male voice. "What was his diagnosis at the time? Where was he treated? I'd like to talk to his physician."

There was a long pause. "He wasn't," said a low voice.

A voice he knew. He tried to open his eyes. No luck. Paralyzed.

Bruno. That was the guy's name. Bruno. Bruno's face, Bruno's history, slid into place in his mind. It was an exquisite relief. Bruno Ranieri. His adopted brother. Tony's great-nephew. Tony Ranieri. The diner. Rosa. OK. He had it. He knew who he was now. More or less.

Kev. Kev Larsen, that was what he was called, when someone cared to call him. He clung to his name, such as it was, like a lifeline.

"He . . . but he was obviously in some terrible . . ." The man's voice trailed off, almost frightened. "What in God's name happened to him?"

Another reluctant pause. "We don't know."

"Excuse me?" The man's voice was incredulous.

"We don't know." Bruno's voice was defensive. "My uncle found him that way. He'd been tortured, we don't know by who, or why. He doesn't either. Like I said. He couldn't talk. For years afterwards."

"And he doesn't even know what—"

"No." The guy cut him off, curtly. "He does not know diddly shit."

"So his name . . . his identity, it's only . . . ?"

"Yeah. Made up. It's only eighteen years old," Bruno finished crisply. "His previous identity is unknown."

There was a pause. "Ah . . . that's incredible. Were inquiries made? I mean, to the police, private investigators?"

"At the time, my uncle didn't want to go looking for the guys that fucked him up," Bruno retorted. "I mean, look at him."

"Well, yes, of course," the other man muttered. "Terrible."

Kev opened his eyes. Light sliced in, an agonizing red-hot blade straight into his brain. Pain, white. Bright lights, beeping machines.

Immobilized. In a rigor of burning agony. Fear built, as he hydroplaned through inner space, toward a memory that held a lethal charge. People touching him, making him flinch. Patting his cheek.

". . . hear me? Kev? Can you hear us?"

"Hey, Kev!" Bruno, again. "Wake up, man, it's me! You awake?"

Kev squinted up into the light. The babble of excited voices was hellishly loud, battering his head. The light hurt, it *hurt* . . .

Pat, pat, pat, on his cheek. The gentle, persistent slap made his head reverberate with sickening pain. He opened his eyes.

Young, good looking. Dark curly hair, close-set eyes, peering down at him. White lab coat. Smiling, pleased with himself. *Pat, pat, pat.*

Mad eyes, lit with hellfire. Wet red mouth, crazy smile, muscling inside his brain. Shoving, wrenching him. He cowered away from that shit-eating troll. Better to hide in a hole, to wither and die there, than to crawl out and be mind-raped again—by . . . by—

"Ost . . . er . . . man." He forced the syllables out. *Osterman.*

Yes. Osterman would never hurt him again. *Never.*

"What's that?" *Osterman's fanged mouth dripped blood, his hot breath sulphurous.* "Did you say something? Try again! We're listening."

Kev exploded out of the bed with a scream of rage, ripping out tubes, IVs, leaping at the guy. He bore Osterman to the floor.

Screaming. Grabbing. Punching. Cold tile against his cheek. Hands held him, pulling him from his prey, and—oh, *shit.* The sting of a needle.

Back down into that hole, fast. Only place to hide, inside his own head, in the deepest, darkest place. Lights out. Shut down.

Shovelfuls of earth rained heavily down on top of his mental hiding place, until the blackness was absolute.

CHAPTER
2

Edie Parrish scanned the entrance of the restaurant and the twilit street outside as she sipped her red wine. No sign of Dad's upright figure striding, coat flapping around his legs. She deliberately released the tension in her chest, her face, her hands. Squeeze, release. Breathe, slow. In, out. This dinner would be fine. Dad himself had asked for her to meet him. She would take that as a gesture of peace. She had to.

Because she wanted to see Ronnie, desperately. She ached for it. Dad held the keys to that tower. It was his most effective instrument for controlling his uncontrollable daughter, and he used it mercilessly, punishing her for all perceived misbehaviors by keeping her away from her little sister. The strategy was brilliant in its simplicity.

God knows, if not for Ronnie, she'd have run away years ago.

She swallowed down the bitter gall of old anger. Maybe tonight she'd have some stroke of brilliance to persuade him. Maybe Dad would have a change of heart. She had to hope.

She sank down into her chair, glanced around to make sure she was unobserved, and gave into the guilty impulse, flipping through the pages of her smallest sketchbook until she found one with some space to fill. She shook hair over her face, for discretion's sake, and resumed people watching. Her eyes softened, absorbing infinitesimal details that her conscious mind didn't perceive as important enough to notice. This would get her into trouble for sure, but she couldn't resist. When she watched people, her fingers itched for the pen, the pencil. She knew she'd pay for it, but there was a part of her that just didn't care. And that part always, always won.

An obsession, her parents had called it. And so? What if it was?

Her eyes seized on the death-of-a-salesman type across the room, the stringy comb-over, the reddened nose, the eye bags. He was consuming his prime rib and baked potato with glum ferocity. Edie rendered him with a few swift pen strokes, and then tried again, trying to capture the set of his shoulders, the defeated look.

The weirdness started to happen, like it always did. Her brain kicked into a new gear. It felt like an eye, opening up deep inside her, seeing everything more deeply, more brightly. The world outside the focus of her eyes blurred. Her perception widened, deepened, softened. Her pen went by itself. Time ceased to move. God, she freaking *loved* it.

The sounds of the restaurant disappeared as she caught the dull anger in the broken veins across his nose, the aggression in his down-turned mouth, the heavy sadness of his hanging jowls.

He was avoiding home. Using work as an excuse to stay as far away as he could from the grandson he and his wife were raising. The child was violent, hyperactive, with learning disabilities, attention deficit disorder. His wife was exhausted, desperate, at her wit's end. So angry at him for abandoning her to deal with it all alone. Again.

He fled that situation every day, just as he'd fled similar problems with the boy's mother, his promiscuous, drug-

addled daughter. He felt like shit about it, but he could not change. He didn't have the strength.

Oh, God, how sad, how awful. Edie dragged her eyes away from the unlucky guy and stared out at the lights on the street, trying to get the taste of the man's guilt and sour self-loathing out of her mind.

When she went into that place in her mind, she started picking up stuff from the airwaves. Whatever people were projecting. And there was no shutting it out. Not if she tried.

She looked around, for someone else to tune in to. Someone more upbeat, more hopeful. Like that cute couple across the aisle from her.

Yes, they looked promising. He was handsome, in a stiff, prosperous looking way. She looked sweet. Edie sketched her, smearing ink with her finger, trying to catch that glow, the shadows and curves, that unfocused, blurred look of shifting possibilities . . . oh, *God.*

Pregnant. That girl was pregnant. Just a few weeks along. It was still secret. Her dinner partner didn't know. She was planning on telling him. Tonight. Nervous about it. Smiling until her mouth ached from it, but her guy was not responding to her smile. He looked preoccupied.

Edie drew the stern line of his Roman nose, his sealed, thin-lipped mouth. His eyes, deep-set, sharp, pinched looking. Energy was gathering inside him. A storm brewing. He intended to hold forth, say his piece, present some watertight argument. He would bolster himself with arrogance, conde-scension. He thought only of himself; his freedom, his fu-ture, his own best interests. They filled his mind so completely, he didn't even really see the girl. How beautiful she was. How hopeful. The cliff she was poised upon. He was bored by her puppyish clinging. He felt suffocated. He was wondering if he could do better. Snag someone sexier, more interesting, more educated. Smarter. Richer.

He was about to to tell his girlfriend that he thought they should be seeing other people. Edie's pen faltered, digging a hole in the paper.

Maybe she was projecting. Casting this guy as another Eric. An ex who had worn a similar hateful look on his face when he'd dropped that same bombshell on her. But probably not. She was never wrong in these things. Not even when she desperately wished that she were.

Ouch. She capped her pen, laid down the sketchbook. Threaded ink-stained fingers together. Studied her wineglass. She should stick to horse skulls, stuffed birds. Drawing real people was too dangerous.

So she defaulted to the next best thing. Fictional characters. She could draw them, have intense insights into their heads, and call it creativity, rather than delusional craziness. Or obscene invasion of personal privacy, depending on your mood.

She didn't mean to do this, to anyone. She didn't want to. It was just something that happened to her, since she was fourteen. Since the Haven, and Dr. Osterman's cognitive enhancement techniques.

She'd been enhanced, all right. Practically into the mental ward.

But dwelling on that was not useful. She did some quick sketches of Fade Shadowseeker, the main character of her graphic novel, trying to catch the right pose for the part where Fade was holding the knife to the throat of the sex-trafficker villain of the fifth Fade Shadowseeker book. Demanding to know where the girls were, because his lover Mahlia was being held among them. His face was a taut mask of fear.

Drawing Fade made her think of the argument she'd had with Jamal that afternoon, while the kid was systematically inhaling everything in her fridge. Jamal was her eight-year-old upstairs neighbor and her very good buddy. He came down and slept on Edie's couch when his mother was entertaining her clients in their two room-apartment, on the floor above Edie's. Which was quite often.

The argument had come about because Jamal had been having problems separating fantasy and reality. Jamal was insisting that Fade Shadowseeker was real, and walking the streets of their neighborhood. Jamal claimed to know people who had seen Fade with their own eyes, people who'd been saved by him. Jamal knew of places to which Fade had given big wads of money that he'd taken from bad guys, after beating the shit out of them, of course. He had shown his Fade books to people who had seen this guy. They said yeah, it was him. He totally existed.

Jesus, what had she done? It gave her a wobble in her stomach. She was the one who had created Fade and put him into Jamal's mind, so Jamal's problem was partly of her own making. And it made her heart hurt, how intense Jamal's need for escape must be. It wasn't right. Reality should not have to be so bleak that the kid had to escape from it at all costs. But it felt hypocritical to scold him about it. After all, escape into fiction was one of her coping mechanisms, too. And it was a better one than most. Better than drugs, for sure.

It scared her, though, when Jamal's fantasies strayed into the realm of actual delusion. Jamal's mom was too busy with her clients and her own drug addiction to be bothered with the problem, so Edie wondered uneasily if she herself should track down Jamal's social worker, or school psychologist. Someone ought to know. But who?

She spotted her father coming through the doors. The host pointed Charles Parrish her way. She popped up, waving. Smiling.

Her father jerked his chin, waving her down. His disapproving smile said, *sit, Edith. Try not to make a spectacle of yourself.*

She sank back down, trying to be decorous. Ever since she learned to talk, she'd been trying. Though come to think of it, when she'd learned to talk was more or less when the trouble began.

She shook away that unworthy thought as he walked toward her. Her cheeks ached with tension. They were both making an effort, and that was positive, right? Being defeatist or sulky would not help her get to see Ronnie. She was going to keep it together. Oh, so good, oh, so mellow, oh, so very normal and natural. No need for meds.

She got up when he reached the table, and they did the stiff, awkward kiss and half-body embrace. Always timing it wrong, jostling the eyeglasses, bumping chins, going for the wrong cheek and hitting a jawbone, or kissing an ear. Nervous, muttered apologies.

Finally, they were safely seated on opposite sides of the table. Searching for an entry point in the seamless marble wall between them.

Charles Parrish's eyes fell on the pile of sketchbooks on the table, the pens scattered on the smudged tablecloth. Her blackened fingertips. She suppressed an urge to gather them up, mumbling apologies. She stopped herself. She was twenty-nine, a woman, a successful, well-known professional artist. Not a naughty child caught misbehaving.

The waiter arriving to bring water and take their order was a welcome distraction for a couple of minutes, but soon they were left alone, staring at each other. At a loss.

Her father made an unfriendly gesture with his hand toward the sketchbooks. "Hard at work?"

"As always. It's going well." She waited for him to ask for more details. In vain.

"Is it?" he murmured vaguely. "Is that so."

The dismissal in his voice killed the urge to pull out the sheaf of reviews she'd printed up for him, for her latest graphic novel. They said things like "ground breaking," "genre defining." They referred to her, awkward, shy Edie Parrish, as "one of the freshest new voices of a disillusioned but stubbornly hopeful generation." They used phrases like "immensely powerful," and "full of pathos and palpable yearning."

But Charles Parrish didn't want to hear about it. His oldest daughter's pathos and palpable yearning had been an embarrassment to him her entire life. Edie crumpled the printouts in the pocket of her long sweater, and scrambled for something else to say. "I, um, have a book signing this Saturday," she offered. "At Powell's. At seven p.m."

"Oh. That's nice," he said, his voice distant.

"It's for the release of my new graphic novel," she persisted. "The Fade Shadowseeker series. The fourth installment. It's doing well. It's a pretty big deal, this event. I was wondering if . . ." She clenched her hands around the paper. Let him turn her down flat, right to her face. "Wondering if you and Ronnie might come," she finished breathlessly.

Her father's eyelids quivered. "Fade Shadowseeker?" he said. "That would be the character based upon that that horrible event that blighted your whole childhood?"

Edie cupped her hands around her wineglass and stared at the liquid trembling in the glass. "I wouldn't say it blighted my childhood," she said quietly. "But yes, that's the one."

"I'm sorry to hurt your feelings, but I disagree with you about that. And I find it ironic that you would actually suggest that I come and . . . *celebrate* this unhealthy obsession of yours. Or that you suggest I let your thirteen-year-old sister witness it! What are you thinking, Edith? To ask me that? It's an offense!"

Edie felt her cheeks start to burn. "No. It's not like that, Dad."

"I understood working out your feelings about that experience through drawing, and I applaud the attempt, but this has gone so far beyond a therapeutic tool, it's . . . it's—"

"It's a fictional character, Dad," she said, her voice gentle and flat.

There was a strained silence as they both groped for a way out of this danger zone. Dad was half right, as far as it went. The event that had inspired Fade Shadowseeker had indeed been traumatic.

She remembered every detail. It happened eighteen years ago, on her eleventh birthday. Her mother had arranged a big party at the country club. Edie had been dreading the party. Her hair had been curled into a million dumb ringlets. She'd been dressed in a ruffly white thing with a scratchy lace collar. A wreath of white roses, baby's breath and lacy fluff in her hair. They'd stopped at Daddy's Flaxon office, so that Daddy could kiss her and give her his present in person, because he couldn't make the party. He'd bought her a pink bicycle. Pink silk ribbon bows on it. Pink helium balloons tied to the handlebars.

A man had burst in, and run into Daddy's office before anyone could stop him. He'd been hideously injured. His face blistered with burns, his hair singed off. His hands were black and swollen, his body bloody, covered with oozing cuts. He'd been raving about torture. Mind-rape. Kids thrown in a hole. Begging for someone to make it stop.

Her mother screamed for security, yelling that the man was trying to kill Daddy. They had come running. The enormous, shattering crash as the wounded man threw one of the security guards through the plate glass window and out onto the grounds still echoed in her head.

More security came running. The fight went on for a long time. The man was incredibly strong. It was terrible to hear, though she couldn't see most of it. Mother screamed through the whole thing.

They'd finally subdued him. It took five of them to pull him out of Daddy's office. His eyes had fixed on her as they dragged him past, still twisting and struggling. His eyes were bright green. They shone with a brilliant, desperate light, as if lit from within. She saw it in her dreams.

He'd twisted and strained to keep his eyes on her as they carried him away. He'd called out to her for help. His stark desperation haunted her. It haunted her still, eighteen years later.

She tried to grasp that fey light whenever she drew Fade

Shadowseeker, the scarred hero of her graphic novel series. She never came remotely close. But she kept on trying. Obsessively.

After they hustled him away, she'd looked down at her ruffly dress. It had been speckled with a fine spray of tiny bloodstains.

Yes, that had been traumatic. Just not as traumatic as having both her parents withhold their approval for most of her life. That trauma beat the burned man raving on her birthday to hell and gone.

"It didn't blight my life," she repeated. "It marked it, that's all."

"The hell it didn't! You were traumatized!" Dad jabbed the whispered words at her. "You've never been the same since!"

A hard point to argue, since she doubted that her father had noticed what she'd been like before. Shy and insignificant, for sure. Easy to overlook. No trouble to speak of. No problems.

It was afterwards that she'd become a problem to them.

Her mother had canceled the birthday party, pleading a stomach virus. That had marked the beginning of Edie's oddessey with child psychiatrists and endless medications, to treat her nightmares, her anxiety, her so-called obsessions. Her utter, hopeless inability to be the daughter her parents wanted her to be.

She pushed it away, and shook her head. "It's just a character. An artistic creation. It's my work, Dad. It's how I support myself."

"Oh, stop. I've lost patience with your playacting at being a starving artist in that miserable hole of an apartment. It's an insult to me and to your mother's memory, when you could live in any of a dozen beautiful properties! You could have an allowance, a car—"

"I don't need an allowance. I'm fine. I already have a car."

"You call that thing a car? It's a death trap! You know how I worry. How your mother worried! Her worry for you shortened her life!"

Edie winced. "That's not fair!"

"That's the truth!" Her father shoved out his jaw, in that self-righteous way that brooked no argument.

Not fair. Linda Parrish's death had not been her fault, but it hurt, to hear it said. To know that he believed it.

Her mother had died of an unexpected heart attack fourteen months before. No one had known she had a heart condition. She was thin, fit, excruciatingly elegant. She played tennis, golf. She was active on the board of innumerable charities. But one day, at a Parrish Foundation board meeting, she had clutched her chest, and collapsed.

Edie had known it would happen, ever since her mandatory weekly lunch date with her mother. She'd been nervously doodling on her napkin during the lecture about her clothes, her hair, her attitude, the expression on her face. She'd sketched the sharp line of her mother's profile on the napkin, felt that inner eye open . . . and realized that she'd surrounded the portrait with dozens of hearts. Big ones, small ones. And she knew that deadly danger stalked her mother.

She didn't know how, what, or when, but something was going to happen. Something that could kill Linda Parrish. She struggled as best she could to translate the symbols her subconscious threw to the surface. The hearts made her think that Mom should go to the doctor, get tests done. On her heart. That was the best she could figure.

But her revelations had been met with derision and anger. The lunch had ended prematurely, and Edie had been banished in disgrace for forcing her sick delusions on her mother. And in a public place, too.

Linda Parrish died in the ambulance on the way to the hospital, a scant week later. No chance to say good-bye, or part on better terms.

Edie had been over it in her head millions of times. She should have been smarter, sneakier. Told someone else to call her mother, someone with credibility. She should have begged her mother's doctor to suggest it. There had to have been a better way.

Edie pushed away the grief and frustration, and tried again. "OK, never mind the book signing, Dad. I don't want to fight with you. Let's just talk about something else, OK?"

Her father looked down at his wineglass, tightlipped. "You don't understand, Edith. By dwelling on that incident, you're forever flogging it in my face. I can't get away from it, no matter how I try to put it behind me. His brothers even came to harrass me! They held me responsible for that god-awful nightmare! Me, personally! Understand?"

She gazed at him, baffled. "What do you mean? What on earth? Who, Dad? Whose brothers?"

He made an impatient gesture. "Don't play dumb. The brothers of that . . . that person. The one you saw, in that incident at Flaxon."

"He had brothers? They came to see you?" Chills ran down her spine. "You mean, you know who he is? You know *where* he is?"

"No! I most certainly do not know anything about him!" her father snapped. "I am sorry for what happened to him, but I assume that he is dead. Osterman hurt a lot of people in his disgusting illicit research, and that unfortunate person was one of them. I unknowingly funded it, Edith. It's something I have to live with every day of my life! And your ridiculous comic books do not help me!"

Guilt clutched at her. Her eyes dropped. "I'm sorry."

"His brothers thought that I was responsible for what had happened to him," he went on heatedly. "It put me in a terrible position. What Osterman did to those people was despicable, but I was a victim, too, Edith. And Helix, and the Parrish Foundation. And when I think of what Osterman did to you at the Haven . . ." His mouth tightened with disgust. "God. Whatever happened there sparked these delusions of yours. If I had any idea what that man truly was, I would never have allowed him near you! I failed to protect you, Edith. I have to live with that, too. And it is not easy for me, believe me."

She stared at him, startled and moved. A flash of what seemed like genuine concern for her. Wow. That was rare. And precious.

Laying aside the fact that the delusions were not delusions, but whatever. Laying aside the fact that she had told her father when she was fourteen that Osterman was crazy and evil, but Charles Parrish was not one to take the word of a depressed, underachieving fourteen-year-old girl over that of a distinguished scientist who was generating profitable patents for Helix. But whatever. Let bygones be bygones.

She reached out, impulsively, and touched her father's hand.

Charles Parrish's hand twitched, as if he wanted to yank it back and was forcing himself to leave it, by brute effort of will.

"One of the reasons that I'm retiring is because of that," he said stiffly. "I want to dedicate myself to administering the funds of the Parrish Foundation in a conscious, ethical way, which involves scrutinizing everything that is done with that money. Nothing will ever slip by me again. I will monitor every single goddamned penny of it."

She squeezed his hand. "Good for you, Dad."

He harrumphed. "There was something I wanted to ask you. You're aware, of course, that my retirement reception is in six weeks. I would like you to attend the banquet. Your mother would have liked for you to be there, with Ronnie. To represent the family."

Edie wasn't so sure of that, but saw no profit in saying so. Her mother had been even more embarrassed by her clumsy, unpredictable daughter than her father had. She stared at his handsome, patrician face in the light of the flickering candle. He looked ten years younger than his sixty-four years. Fit, elegant, hair silvering at the temples.

I'll come to the reception if you and Ronnie come to the book signing. The suggestion hovered, at the tip of her tongue . . . and she swallowed it back. She didn't have that kind of bargaining power. It would just touch off another ugly outburst, and she didn't have the energy for it.

Besides. If Ronnie would be at that banquet, that was reason enough to grit her teeth, don an evening dress and heels, and go.

"Of course," she said quietly. "I'd be proud to be there for you."

"Good. You'll consult with Tanya and your Aunt Evelyn about your dress and hair," he added sharply, his eyes raking her critically. "And your shoes, of course."

"Of course." Edie forced herself to sit up straighter. She had nothing to be ashamed of. Her wavy mane was clean and brushed. The horn-rimmed glasses obscured her eyes, and she liked it that way. Her high-tops were comfy. She was what she was, ink stains and all. "If Tanya and Aunt Evelyn have time to shop with me, I'll be glad to—"

"They'll make time. If not, I'll have Marta help you."

She kept her face carefully blank at that unspeakable idea. Shopping for an evening gown with her father's blond, perfect thirty-six-year-old trophy girlfriend, previously his secretary, was her idea of hell. She supposed she should be glad her father had some comfort in his bereavement, if only there were something real behind Marta's bright, lipsticked smile, but there wasn't. Just the grinding gears of a calculating, self-interested machine. "I'm sure that won't be necessary," she assured him. "Please, don't bother Marta."

"See that it's not." Her father looked down at her hands, frowning at the ink stains on her fingers. "You will have a manicure before the reception? Let's not have people thinking you work in a garage."

Edie snatched her hand back. "Of course," she said.

The waiter arrived with her goat cheese, pine nut and arugula salad, and her father's swordfish filet. After a few bites, Edie laid down her fork and dabbed her napkin to her mouth. "Dad. I was wondering if I could come home this weekend, and spend some time with Ronnie."

Her father frowned. "You know the answer to that. I've established my terms. Dr. Katz told me you've missed your sessions with him for weeks now. I assume this means you're being noncompliant with your meds. So why even ask? It's a waste of both our time and energy."

She gulped. "I don't need the meds. I feel completely calm and—"

"Edie. You have hallucinations." There was a savage edge to her father's voice. "You are a danger to your sister, and to yourself!"

She wanted to screech loud enough to shatter glass. She gulped it back. "Dad, it's not like that. They're not hallucinations. They're—"

"Keep your voice down! Does everyone have to know?"

Edie pressed her hand to her shaking mouth. No. Crying.

"Your sister is already stressed from your mother's death," her father raged on, his voice hushed. "Your abandonment is the final—"

"Abandonment? That's not fair!" The words burst out. "I never abandoned her! I would do anything to see her! You know that!"

"Shhh!" He glared at her, eyes darting around to see if anyone was listening. "She's acting out lately. We had another incident, with her firecrackers. She ordered them over the Internet, had the packaging disguised as books. Dr. Katz thinks she's punishing me. Showing me how explosive and destructive her rage is. The last thing Ronnie needs now are further examples of mental imbalance and rebellion. You oppose me at every turn, out of habit. Ronnie does not need to see it."

I oppose you because I have to, Dad. To survive.

Edie didn't say it. Her father would see the words as a spiteful blow. He could not hear the anguished truth behind them.

Poor Ronnie. She wasn't acting out with her firecrackers. She just loved things that spat bright-colored sparks and went bang. It was her bizarre karma, like Edie's, to be born into the straitlaced Parrish family.

"Would you mind leaving this subject?" her father asked. "It's ruining my meal."

Edie nodded, and pushed the remaining salad around on her plate. The heavy silence was broken only by the clink of cutlery.

When they were almost finished, she saw the arrogant young man from the couple nearby striding past their table. He'd said his piece, and he was beating hell out of there. Edie glanced over at the girl. Her eyes were streaming. Her hand was pressed against her mouth. She looked like she needed to vomit, or cry. Or both. Soon.

The girl got up, lurched toward the bathroom. Edie's hand shot out, grabbing her arm as she passed. "Wait," she said.

Her father gasped. "Edie!" he hissed. "For God's sake—"

"It'll be a girl," Edie blurted, looking into the girl's wide, wet eyes. "A beautiful little blond girl. And that selfish bastard is useless to you. He's done his job. It's all he's good for. Unload him, and move on."

The girl's mouth sagged. Wonder, fear, shock, chills. The usual.

Edie let go of her hand. The pregnant girl stumbled backward, and took off, in a wobbly, stumbling run.

Well. That had been stupid, with her father watching. It would have been stupid even if he hadn't been. But she never had a choice. It had just . . . popped out of her. Totally involuntary. Like always.

Edie stared at the drizzle of balsamic vinegar on her plate, her eyes fixed on the frilly shreds of romaine and arugula that clung to it. Avoiding the look in her father's eyes. She didn't need to see the anger, the disgust. She'd memorized them years ago. They never changed.

"So. You're still suffering from your delusions." Dad's voice was cool, expressionless. "I'll make an emergency appointment for you with Dr. Katz, first thing tomorrow morning. If you do not go, there will be consequences. This is what happens when you don't take your meds."

Experience had proven time without number that her perceptions were not delusions. They had never shown themselves to be false or misleading. Not even once. But that argument was lost before it began.

"I don't need meds," Edie repeated, wearily.

The truth was, the meds did work—in a certain sense. They zoned her out into emotional flatness, and clogged the airwaves so that she didn't get private newscasts from people's heads anymore. They also, surprise surprise, killed her desire to draw. She hated the meds.

"Promise me that there will be no scenes like this at the reception," her father said.

"I won't embarrass you at the reception, Dad," she said dully.

Who knew if that was true, though. She never had a choice. God knows, she would never have voluntarily chosen this hell. Being constantly judged, isolated. Punished. Never seeing Ronnie.

Her father's eyes flicked to the table. He jerked as if he'd been poked with a pin. "For the love of God, Edith! Stop that, right now!"

She flinched. Her hand was holding a pen, which she hadn't been conscious of picking up. It hit the bulb of her wineglass, knocking it over. She'd been doodling on the open sketchpad without realizing it.

A sketch of her father's face and torso covered the page. Wine spread across it, over the sketchbook, the table, dripping onto her lap.

Edie grabbed a napkin, dabbed her skirt, murmuring a garbled apology. She'd been a compulsive doodler ever since she learned how to hold a pen, but her parents had gotten twitchy about it after the Haven. When the incidents began.

"I'll make a strategic retreat now," Charles Parrish said, rising to his feet. "Before I get my fortune told. Please, Edith. Don't do this to people! No one wants to hear it! And take your meds, goddamnit!"

"I'll try," she said. Referring to the first request, if not the last. "Can I . . . would you at least tell Ronnie that I—"

"No!" He spat out the word with vicious force. "I'll contact Evelyn and Tanya for you. Clear your schedule for them, please, and arrange to go to their stylist and makeup artist before the banquet as well, understand?"

She nodded mutely. He strode away. At least like this, they didn't have to do the stiff, awkward, eyeglass bumping hug, she thought, bleakly. He shrank from any physical contact with her.

Do. Not. Cry. Not in public. Don't even think about it. She sniffed back the tears, swallowed, blinked. Grateful for the glasses, the shield of hair, for privacy. Dad was paying, at the door. He left. No glance. No wave. Their meetings always ended this way. No matter how she tried.

The guy with the comb-over, the drug addicted daughter and the ADS grandson was chowing down on chocolate mousse cake, with the same grim sense of purpose with which he'd consumed the prime rib. Whoo hoo, she thought, staring at him. There was still more damage she could do, if she wanted to. Anything that she said to that poor guy would provoke a massive heart attack, clogged as his arteries must be.

Hah. What a fit ending that would be for an evening like this. Something else to pile up onto her overloaded conscience. As if Mom's death wasn't enough for her to bear. And Ronnie. Feeling abandoned.

She should just stop drawing altogether. Turn away from

that part of her brain. Pretend it didn't exist. But she couldn't. Like a drug addiction. She couldn't resist that free, whole, connected feeling.

It was just the consequences that she couldn't bear to face.

She sighed and started gathering up her pens and charcoal, her sketchbooks, and shoved them into her big shoulder bag. She'd go straight home, not looking to the right or left. She'd lock the door. And if she ended up crying there in the dark, who would ever know?

She picked up the napkin, thinking to sponge at the sketchbook once more, hoping to salvage at least a few sheets of the—

She froze, staring down at the sketch she'd doodled of her father, still and cold as a block of stone. The wine had run over it in such a way that it seemed as if the stiffly upright figure with the disapproving mouth and the long, narrow nose was submerged in a pool of blood.

Chills shook her. That familiar far away drumbeat of doom.

I'll just make a strategic retreat now. Before I get my fortune told. Her father's words echoed in her head. He would never listen if she warned him. She could not help him. No more than she'd been able to help her mother. She was helpless. Hands tied.

And her father was in deadly danger.

The little girl floated over the tumbled boulders of dream landscape like a butterfly, darting out of sight, flitting back into it. Barefoot, thin, long dark hair. She wore a white tunic. When she looked back, her huge eyes looked scared, sad. She stopped beside a crack in the cliff wall. She bent. In a flash of thin legs, of dirty little feet, she was gone.

Sean followed her in, bound by the heavy inevitability that came from having dreamed it before. This feeling of being locked in breathless ignorance was horribly familiar. Like a rock sitting on his brain, blacking out the center of his being. Obscuring his sense of place in space and time. Leaving him blundering and helpless in the darkness.

The tunnel wound down, then the cavern opened out. Vastness around him. Cathedral ceilings, buttressed with gnarled stalactites and stalagmites. A forest of pallid, misshapen trees, glowing like radioactive tumors in the dark. Water, slowly dripping. The stink of batshit.

Dread grew inside him, but he had to go on, to do the hard thing. The path curved, through a choked grove of dead, white calcite columns.

A clearing was before him, a slab of stone in the center. Torches flickered in a circle around it, and the reddish light of dancing flames wavered evilly upon the man who lay on it like a pagan sacrifice.

Rocks were piled on his torso. Only his sprawled legs, arms, and head emerged. He had to be dead under that weight, lungs flattened, organs crushed. His head was turned away. He wore a blindfold. All Sean saw was the jut of a cheekbone, lank strands of ash colored hair.

A hole yawned in the rocks before the altar. Something stirred inside. Rustling, a chittering rasp. The flash of some nonhuman eyes in the hole, moving before he could make sense of the gleaming shapes.

Something monstrous, something hideous. Something . . . hungry.

Then a hairy, jointed leg extended delicately, prodding with its hooked claw. The chittering rasp grew louder.

Sean's heart thudded, but he couldn't run. He leaned down to grab the first boulder heaped on his brother, and the thing burst from its hole, eyes glittering, barbed feet slashing at Sean's face like whiplashes—

Sean jolted bolt upright, gasping for air. Heart racing. Gasps racked his torso, as if he'd been sprinting. The dreams about his lost twin had been getting more frequent, more intense. He was zonked out from sleep deprivation. As if it wasn't enough for them to deal with, the fallout they'd worked through together from that horrific encounter with the mad psycho scientist Christopher Osterman. They'd been supremely lucky to get through that with their lives and their sanity intact. More or less.

They'd been doing better. Convinced they were through the worst of it. And now, here he was. Tormented by fucking nightmares again.

Liv stirred, lifted her head. She shoved fuzzy, sleep-snarled dark curls back from her face. She touched his shoulder, in silent question.

"Shit. Sorry I woke you." He hardly got the words out, his chest jerked so hard.

Liv sat up, curling her legs up, and putting an unconscious hand over her pregnant belly. "Another dream? Same one, I take it?"

His shoulders jerked in assent, and he hunched. Trying to hide, like a turtle in his shell. "I got farther into the cave this time."

"Ah. That's good."

A harsh laugh jerked out of him. "Oh, yeah? Is it?"

She shrank from his ugly tone. "Sorry. Just said that, you know. To say something."

He kicked himself. "I'm the one who should be sorry. I shouldn't snarl at you." He forced himself to go on. "I saw him, this time."

She didn't even have to ask who. "And? How was it?"

He let out an explosive sigh. "Bad. He was blindfolded. Laid out on a stone altar. Covered with a pile of boulders. Staked out in front of the lair of some gigantic insect. Could I dream up anything worse?"

"I see." She had that careful voice his brothers used. Talking Sean down out of his freakout. Let's scrape Sean off the ceiling again.

He hated it from Con and Davy. He hated it from his wife, too.

"Sounds like a picture on a Tarot card," she commented. "How did you know it was Kev, if he was covered with rocks and blindfolds?"

"I just knew. You know how it is in dreams."

"Yeah." Liv dropped a kiss onto his shoulder. "Hey. Sean? Have you considered that these dreams might not be about Kev at all?"

"What do you mean? Who else could they be about?"

He could feel her caution, how she chose her words carefully, so as not to set him off. It made his teeth grind. "It's been about four months since you started having these dreams," she began.

"No," Sean said. "I've had these dreams for eighteen years, Liv. Ever since Kev disappeared. And when we found out it wasn't him, in the grave . . ." He shrugged. "I know he's not dead."

"I know. But nightmares where you wake up screaming? These are new." She kissed his shoulder again. "I feel compelled to point out to you that they started right about when I found out that I was pregnant."

He went rigid. "You think this is about that?" His voice was so tight, it felt like his throat would implode.

"Don't be mad. Please, consider it. I've read that images in dreams are self-referential. Whoever you dream about, and whatever they do, it's mostly about you. Your own feelings, your own issues."

"Maybe for most people, but not these dreams," he said.

"No? Why not?"

"For a lot of reasons!" He stopped, tried to modulate his voice. "Kev woke me up when Gordon kidnapped you. He stopped me from walking off a cliff. That's not fluff crap about my issues, Liv!"

"I never said it was fluff crap," she said quietly. "But couldn't those incidents have been you all along? Your own awareness, your own intelligence? Just using Kev's image to get your attention?"

"No." His rejection of the idea was violent and absolute. "It is not."

"Sean, please. I just want you to—"

"You think I'm scared because we're having a kid?" His voice cracked. "You think I'm freaked out by fatherhood, Liv? That I consider myself buried under a ton of boulders? What does that make you in this dream? The monster? A giant bug who eats her mate? Jesus, Liv! What kind of coward wuss do you take me for?"

She pulled her hands away. "Well. I guess you're a whole lot braver than me, then." Her voice was clipped. "I'm certainly afraid. I keep having dreams that I'll leave the baby at a public bathroom, or the seat of a city bus. But that just means I'm a cowardly wuss, hmm?" She swung her legs over the side of the bed. "Fine. Whatever."

Sean lunged, grabbing her waist and wrapping his arms above her baby bulge before she could slide off the bed. "No. Stop."

"*You* stop." She batted at his arms, and he could feel the anger, but he just held her there, in a steely grip, taking care not to put any pressure on that precious bump.

She could pick and pry and pummel him to her heart's content, but he wasn't letting her go. No way. He knew what was good for him.

She finally gave up, with a sharp sigh of irritation. He took that as a cue to drag her back onto the bed, pulling her down, and rolling her over so her stiff, resistant body faced his.

He pressed his face against her throat, dragging in her sweet, hot scent of her skin, the silken tickle of her hair. "Please, don't be mad at me," he said, his voice muffled against her. "I can't take that, too."

He held onto her with all his strength. After a few minutes, she relaxed, with a shuddering sigh, giving in. She wound her fingers into his hair, which had grown into a shaggy mop almost to his shoulders.

"You piss me off," she said, petting him. "You big, rude jerk."

"I know. I'm sorry." He lifted his head, fixing her with a pleading gaze. "But that guy in my dream? He's not me, babe. I swear." She opened her mouth, but he cut her off. "And I'm not scared about the baby. Really. At least not any more than a normal guy would be."

Her eyes narrowed. "And what would you know about normal?"

"You have a point," he conceded, wiggling down the length of her body until he could press his face against her belly. It was something he loved to do. Just lie there, feeling the little flutters against his cheek. It gave him such a rush, imagining his kid in there. So small. Swimming, turning and spinning in the primordial soup. About the size of his fist, on their last ultrasound. A fucking miracle. An amazing little creature.

No way. It wasn't that sweet tiny thing he was afraid of. No monsters there. Just everything that was fine, good.

"I'm ecstatic about our kid," he repeated. "Over the moon. And you don't have to be scared. You won't leave the kid on a bus. You'll be an incredible mother. A freaking Titan of a mother."

She batted at his shoulders, vibrating with laughter. "Oh, shut up. It's not like I have the greatest model for mother-hood."

He winced, in the darkness. True enough. Liv's mother was one of his least favorite people on the planet. A total whack job, to put it politely. Unfortunately, Liv's impending motherhood had inspired the woman to try to make peace with her daughter. She wanted that grandchild. God help the poor, unsuspecting kid. God help them all.

"No, really," he pleaded. He shoved the oversized T-shirt she slept in up, and found her naked beneath it. Thank God, she had finally realized wearing panties to bed was just a blatant challenge to him.

He nuzzled the velvet of her skin, working his way down into the warm bush of her pubic hair, exploring all the angles and curves of her, changed by her pregnancy, but that soft, electrifying fuzz, the slick silky ringlets that adorned her pink girl parts, were as perfect in every detail as ever. No, better. Tender flower petals. Meltingly juicy, pulling at him.

"Sean!" Liv wiggled, giggling. "This is no way to win an argument!"

"What argument? Were we arguing?"

"Don't be facetious. We have to communicate."

"We are communicating. In the best possible way. And this isn't an attempt to win an argument." He slid his tongue teasingly across her slit. "This is just changing the subject."

"Yeah, right. Tell me about it." She smothered more giggles. "Your all-time favorite subject."

"Busted." He nuzzled her groin. "Now, let's see. The new subject is better than the old one. I was just going to go on about how excellent and admirable you are. What a fabulous mother you'll be. Your courage, your beauty, your character . . ." He slid his finger inside her, followed its path with his tongue, in a slow, hungry swipe that hit all her external sweet spots. "Your yummy succulent pussy. My princess, my queen, my goddess, my world. No arguments. What's to argue?"

She dug her fingernails into his shoulders. "Seriously, Sean. Don't change the subject. We're not done with this subject."

He raised his head, wiped his mouth. "We're not?"

"No." She tilted up his chin. "You make me feel like I'm one of the bad guys in this story. Trying to make you doubt yourself. Undermining you. About Kev, for all those years. You're so angry at everyone for doing that to you, even Davy and Con. And I don't deserve any part of that anger. Not one little speck. You hear me?"

The raw emotion in her voice penetrated the hot lust that

gripped him, and he lifted up, sobered. "No, baby, you sure don't," he agreed.

She stared up, blinking in the moonlight. Her beautiful eyes were shimmering with tears. Remorse bit him in the ass, and he slid up her body, kissing his way apologetically over the curve of her belly, and into the bounty of her even more bodacious than usual tits.

"I'm sorry, baby," he whispered. "Please don't cry. You'll make me cry, too, and I hate crying. Makes my nose run."

She laughed, soggily, to his immense relief. "Oh, shut up, you clown. I just want . . . I want . . ."

Her voice trailed off, and he waited, in an agony of suspense. "Yeah?" he prompted. "What do you want?" He held his breath, hoping to God it was something he was humanly capable of granting her.

She blew out a sharp breath. "I don't want you to be forever yearning for something that might not even exist, for the rest of your life. I just want you to . . . to get over it. To be whole. And happy."

Whew. Talk about a challenge.

He positioned himself carefully over her body so that he put no pressure on that precious bulge, and pressed himself inside her. They sighed, in tandem, at the throbbing clasp of her body around him. "I'm working on that," he said. "It's complicated. But I'm trying. Just keep loving me. That's gotten me the closest I've ever been. Closer than I ever deserved to get." He sucked in air, at the perfection of being so close. "Just keep loving me," he repeated, his voice raw.

"Oh, please." Tearful laughter made her body contract, minute shudders of perfection around his cock. "As if I ever had a choice."

He rocked inside her. "I'm not scared about the baby," he told her.

She clutched at him, with arms, legs, every part of her. "It would be nothing to be ashamed if you were, doofus."

"But I'm not," he protested, stubbornly. "Really. I'm so happy about that baby, it just about makes my heart explode. Believe me."

She gave him a tremulous smile. "Um," she murmured. "OK. That's nice to know. And now," she wiggled against him, and he gasped with delight as she squeezed him, deliciously inside herself. "So. You were talking about, ah, exploding? You want to elaborate on that?"

He grinned at her, and proceeded to do just exactly that.

CHAPTER
3

The guy across the poker table in the big blind position was staring at him. Chilikers. The one who'd cornered him in the men's room and begged him for a stake a couple of hours back. Chilikers had been desperate to get back into the game and make up his losses, so Kev had fronted the guy fifteen thou against his car. But he hadn't done Chilikers any favors tonight. Kev could practically smell the guy's shit luck. As bad as his foul breath. And now he was staring.

To be fair, there was a lot to stare at. It was weird for a guy to wear sunglasses at four in the morning in a darkened room. Add to that the webwork of old scars across one side of Kev's face, the redder, fresher scars that showed through the spiky ash-colored hair sticking up all over his scalp; mementos from the waterfall bashing and the subsequent surgeries. Beads of sweat stood out on his forehead. The tremor in his hands had nothing to do with the cards he held, but if his fellow players should misinterpret that as a tell, fine with him.

Chilikers snapped to attention as the dealer distributed starting hands. Kev glanced around for tells. Laker was petting a stack of chips even before the rest of the cards were dealt. Moriarty didn't like his hand. Kev felt it, from the set of his shoulders, the muscles contracted on either side of his nostrils. Chilikers's eyes had a hot gleam of excitement. Kev's eyes swept the other players, plugging in data.

He squeezed out his hole cards. An ace of hearts and an ace of spades. In a ten-handed game, pocket aces were good almost a third of the time, but the table was modestly tight. There'd probably only be three or four players in the pot, and he'd be a 3-2 favorite. He wished he could take pleasure in it, but he hurt too much. His head throbbed, and he had a heavy knot in his guts. Sensory overload. The volume was turned up to the highest decibel, and he couldn't turn it down. Whatever had damped him down before was gone. Going over Twin Tails Falls hugging an enormous tree had killed it.

And ah, Christ, how he missed it now.

Sunglasses helped, and ear plugs, and the poker game itself. But smells got him, too, and he could hardly go around with a plug on his nose. He was used to being stared at, but even he had his limits.

He could have endured the sensory overload, if that had been all it was, but the overload came from inside, too. Emotions blazed through him, leaving charred trails in their wake. He wasn't equipped to handle such violent endocrinal activity, after years of floating numbness.

Still, he preferred to call this state emotional overload rather than bugfuck insanity. Not that he could really quantify the difference.

All day, he surfed waves of rage and free-floating terror. When those eased down, aching melancholy awaited him, interspersed with jittery euphoria. And the lust was through the ceiling. He'd steeled himself to ask Bruno about that, and Bruno solemnly informed him that constant sexual awareness was more or less normal for a healthy guy, and welcome to the club, already. According to Bruno, normal guys thought about sex constantly. All night and all day, porn footage unspooled in their heads. How normal guys managed to get through their days without totally humiliating themselves was a mystery to him.

At night, if he slept at all, his dreams were turbo-charged nightmares that spat him into waking consciousness flash-fried on adrenaline. He was taking a protracted break from sleep. He couldn't take the stress anymore. All-night poker was more restful.

If he could keep his mind on it, that is. He yanked his attention back to see Laker limp in with 200. Kev raised 600, three times the big blind, breathing with his mouth so as not to smell the guy's aftershave.

He'd been in this unenviable state since he'd woken from the second coma, the one following the stress flashback. The one which had necessitated reconstructive surgery upon the face of Dr. Prateek Patil, Kev's neurosurgeon. Embarrassing, considering how hard the guy had worked on Kev's fucked-up brain. Patil hadn't deserved to get pounded all to shit for his trouble. But life was seldom fair.

He doubted that same fit would come over him if he should see Patil again, but nobody wanted to experiment with that hypothesis, least of all Patil himself. The guy had a restraining order out on him.

On the button, Stevens cold called $600. Kev wrenched his mind back into focus. Stevens's hand couldn't be that great. His normal pattern was to re-raise big hands, get the blinds to fold, and eliminate random hands that could flop big and crush a high-percentage hand.

Pay attention. Hard to calculate what kind of hand Stevens would be playing with, his head pounding like this. Moriarty folded. His $100 blind went into the pot. Chilikers squeezed his cards and studied them again before he called $400 more. He'd been an early winner, after he got the stake from Kev. He'd even gotten ahead by about thirty thousand for a while, but for the last hour he'd been taking beat after beat. He'd gotten more sullen with each one.

Laker, the limper, called. He was getting pot odds for any

two cards. That left four for the flop. Laker, Chilikers, Stevens, and himself.

Chilikers was staring at him again as the dealer burned the top card and flipped up the board. Queen of diamonds, jack of diamonds, two of clubs. Coordinated board. Sucked, for him. Anyone with two diamonds only needed one more to win, or any two connecting cards for a five card straight. His head throbbed sickeningly. He stuck his hand in his pocket, clutching the prescription bottle, but the pills would be useless now. He'd waited too long, hadn't wanted to dull his edge. He was so nauseous now, he wouldn't be able to digest them. So there was no way out of this shitty headache now but straight through it.

Besides. Seemed stupid to zonk himself into deliberate dullness after years of spending a fortune on extreme sports just to prove to himself that he had a fucking pulse.

Man, he felt that pulse now. Every heartbeat a meat mallet blow to his frontal lobe, thudding against the swelling, the scar tissue, the knitting bones of his skull. The healing process would be slow, though the doctors had assured him that the situation would improve. The pain, nausea, dizziness, the disorientation would diminish over time. And they had. He'd already gotten off the antiseizure meds. He might even regain some lost memories, they had hopefully hypothesized.

Though it was clear none of them wanted to be anywhere near him when that happened.

But Christ, it hurt. Every beat of his heart. Sometimes he wished that organ would give it a rest. Just stop, and leave him the fuck alone.

Concentrate, goddamnit. Stop whining. Self-pity is not useful.

That would be a lot easier if that bastard would stop staring.

It didn't usually bother him, but the disgust, the veiled hostility on Chilikers face bothered him a lot, in his current state. Kev met his eyes straight on, and silently invited him to state his fucking problem.

Chiliker's eyes flicked away. He checked. Stevens, too.

Kev bet $1,500. Stevens called. Chilikers, too, then Laker. The pot was up to $8,500. And Chilikers was glaring again.

Ignore the fucker. He funneled his mind by brute force into the calm detachment that he craved. He played for the express purpose of concentration, detachment, serenity. And he was blowing it because some greedy asshole was giving him the hairy eyeball? Unacceptable.

The dealer burned, and flipped the turn. Ace of diamonds.

Ah. Now that was a problem. His mind seized on to it hungrily, rejoicing in the new slew of calculations to make. He had a set, yeah, but a bunch of possible hands could beat a set of aces. His brain churned out the list, examining probabilities in a blinding inner stream of data that gave him sweet relief. As long as he could keep it up.

He'd happened upon this new coping mechanism by chance. Bruno had brought him a laptop to keep him from going nuts in the hospital, after they'd taken the restraints off. He'd discovered online poker while fucking around with it. It had taken serious effort to get those restraints removed, and convince the hospital staff that he was not going to wig out and attack them. He winced, just thinking about it.

Online poker was the first thing he found that helped. It chilled him, just that crucial bit that kept him halfway sane. He needed dark glasses to stare into the computer, and even so, the glow of the screen intensified his headaches badly, but it was better than a padded cell.

He'd played for days on end, until the doctors started talking about taking the computer away. He'd made it clear that wasn't an option, and shortly afterward found himself discharged, much sooner than hospital protocol dictated. The staff was scared shitless of him.

He didn't blame them. Christ, he scared himself these days.

As soon as he could stagger out on crutches, he'd sought out some real poker games. High-level play. Seasoned, talented players. The more layers of complexity, the better the trick worked for him. Those guys played for real money, though. They'd kicked his ass for a while. It had been an expensive coping tool while he made the adjustment.

Not anymore, though. He won, now. Almost always. He cycled through a big circuit of clubs, so that no one got too tired of that fact.

Not that he gave a shit about winning. The money in his pocket when he walked out was a byproduct. It was the process he craved. The stream of calculations in his head, blotting out the jangle of emotional overload. The game as he played it was painkiller, anxiolytic, and sleep substitute. After hours of probabilities calculation, he felt almost rested.

Patil was still pissed. There was a lawsuit pending. But whatever. If Patil wanted money to compensate his shock, pain, and mental anguish, Kev would give it to him. Of course, money didn't do shit for shock, pain, or mental anguish. He should know. He had plenty of money, and what fucking good had it ever done him?

He'd apologized to Patil, very sincerely. Bruno had gone to see the guy while he was recuperating from his surgery, to grovel on Kev's behalf, since they wouldn't let Kev himself anywhere near the man. But Patil had been unimpressed. Maybe it was the shattered orbital bone, the dislocated jaw. Kev could relate to that. He'd had a shattered orbital bone and a dislocated jaw himself when Tony had found him. He'd been too damaged to talk at the time, but he remembered the pain just fine.

It had an unsalutory effect on a guy's sense of humor.

Bummer, for Patil, that he'd resembled the troll from

Kev's nightmares so closely. *No.* Correction. Not nightmares. *Memories.*

Not clear ones, nor particularly useful ones, but still, they were memories. Not dreams, or fantasies, or hallucinations. He was sure of it. If there was one good thing about going over a waterfall and getting pounded to pulp, it was that. He had a narrow bridge connecting him to his former self, and he was clinging to it.

He no longer went out, except for the nighttime poker. He just holed up in his loft, trolling cyberspace all day, sunglasses on, shades drawn. Looking for his memories under every rock he could turn up. Since he finally had a snowball's chance in hell of finding them.

Osterman. He had a name for the monster who haunted his nightmares. He even had a visual reference, in the luckless Patil's face.

Osterman was the name of the troll that stood guard at the door where his memories were locked. And a name was something to start with. It was a seed. Entire forests could be grown from a single seed.

He had a scarce handful of other data. The date, August 24, 1992. The warehouse south of Seattle where Tony had saved his life. A man had been beating him to death, Tony had ascertained, after watching on the closed-circuit camera for a while. Tony had been unwilling to get involved, but he didn't like the look on the guy's mug. He'd been enjoying himself a little too much. A few shots with Tony's Beretta sent him scuttling like a rat, and Tony had been left with a comatose guy, soaked with blood and beaten to hamburger. No identity. None of his marbles, either. Dead weight.

The homemade tattoo on his leg that read "Kev" was as good a name as any, so he'd stuck with it. Though it seemed odd for a guy to tattoo his own name on himself. What, like he might forget it? Hah.

Then there was the fact that he spoke some Vietnamese, of all things. That, plus his combat skills had led old Tony to conclude that Kev was Special Forces, but Vietnamese? Special Forces would make sense if he spoke Arabic, Persian, Pushtu, Croatian, Spanish. He was thirty years too young to be a Vietnam vet. It didn't track.

And the math, the science. Big bodies of human knowledge he was inexplicably familiar with. Theoretical physics. Biochemistry. Computer engineering. Earth sciences. Astronomy. The physics of flight. The history of aeronautics. The migratory patterns of birds, animals, and insects. Extensive first aid and field medic skills. Carpentry. He could sew, for the love of Christ. He connected the dots and got a scrambled clot. None of it made sense. But did any human life make sense?

Since the ride over Twin Trails Falls, his dreams had gotten clearer. They lingered after he woke up, instead of scuttling away to hide. Things were shifting in his mind, tectonic plates moving. Little puffs of steam, spouts of ash, but no dramatic realizations, no floods of returning memory, no "aha!"

Nothing so easy. Just feelings, images. Teasing, poking at him. Like his tiny angel, for instance. What the fuck was she about? She was too perfect, too iconic to be a real person, in that shining dress of hers. More like an angelic doll. A divine symbol, not a person.

Maybe he'd desperately needed a benevolent presence to counteract Osterman's evil, and his brain had fabricated the little angel for protection. Maybe he'd been religious, before. Spiritual.

And then again, maybe not. He remembered throwing someone through a window. That didn't strike him as particularly spiritual.

He shied away from analyzing the angel, though. She had saved his life and sanity. Whenever he slid into that paralyzed black hole in his head, he hung on to her, and she led him safely out. She'd led him out of the first coma, the one he'd been in when Tony first found him. She'd guided him back into speech again. Maybe a psychiatrist could explain her psychological function, but no thanks. He still needed her too badly to risk spoiling her magic with clinical explanations.

The first memory that had come to him after the waterfall had been of trying to convince some guy to help him, to believe him, but for the life of him, he couldn't remember what it was that he wanted the guy to believe. He remembered the man's disapproving face perfectly. Long nose, thin mouth, curled lip. But not his name.

It was maddening. Total amnesia had been more peaceful.

He remembered Osterman gloating over him. He remembered a blond, leering man with a thick red face, too. An open flame, coming toward his face. The sizzle of contact. And pain. So much pain.

There were gentler memories. A bearded man with a seamed, unsmiling face. Boys. A weathered house in the woods. A rough table, a kerosene lamp, like a scene from another century. Maybe he was remembering a past life. Pioneer days. Hah. This life alone was enough for him to wonder about. Spare him the red tape of past lives, too.

He needed more. Frames of reference. Names, dates. Hard data.

Concentrate, goddamnit. He'd lost the thread. He stared down at the cards. They were floating, shifting. Double vision, glowing with a halo. His ears were ringing, tinny and sharp. He couldn't screen out the soaps and deodorants of the men around the table. The detergents their clothes had been washed in made his nose burn. The earthier smells of their bodies, their sweat, their breath. Chiliker's chronic lung infection, the alcohol emanating from the pores of the dealer to his left. Cigarette smoke, peeling paint, dust. Mildewy water damage.

The fetid stink made his head throb like a rotting tooth.

And everyone was waiting for him to snap out of his

vague dream, get off his ass, and bet. Chilikers had checked, so had Laker.

Kev stared at the backs of his two aces. He couldn't take this tonight. He'd play like a hothead rookie, end it fast. "Seven thousand."

Stevens blinked. "All-in, nine thousand five hundred."

Chilikers eyes darted to Stevens. He hadn't expected that. "All-in, seventeen five," he said, but his voice sounded nervous.

Laker folded, shaking his head.

Kev shrugged inwardly. What the hell. "I call. I'm all-in."

They all stared at him for a long moment. 5.5:1 pot odds didn't technically justify his drawing odds, but he wanted it to be over, and he was feeling reckless. Angry. Twitchy. Acting out, like a bad little kid.

"Two players, all-in. Turn over your hands," the dealer directed.

Kev turned his aces, and looked to his left. Stevens had flopped a set of queens. Chilikers had turned the flush.

"Pair the board," Kev said.

The dealer burned the top card, and turned over a jack of hearts.

Full house. Aces full of jacks. He'd won fifty thousand bucks. Son of a bitch.

He flicked a few fifty dollar chips to the dealer as a tip, and walked out the door with fifty-eight thousand and change. Plus the title and keys to Chilikers' 2007 Volvo, which bit his ass, but whatever. More than usual. He usually averaged ten thou a night, and that was playing more carefully and consciously than he had tonight.

He limped out into the predawn chill. Chilikers was there, staring morosely at his Volvo, smoking a cigarette. The final blow for his infected lungs, no doubt. Kev crossed the street toward him. "Hey."

Chilikers did not turn. "Two fuckin' outs," he said, teeth clenched.

"More like seven. Eight, with Steven's quad Queen draw," Kev replied quietly. "You were the 4:1 favorite. I just got lucky."

Chilikers muttered something obscene under his breath. "Asshole," he growled. "You didn't even have the fucking odds to call."

"No. I didn't." Kev gazed at him for a long moment. He fished the title and keys out of his pocket, and held them out.

Chilikers stared. "You won that," he said slowly. "It's yours."

"You paid," Kev replied. "But I don't need it. Got no place to park it. Don't want to insure it, or deal with selling it. Take it back. Please."

Chilikers looked tempted, but then his mouth hardened. He flung his cigarette down, stomped it. "What, feeling sorry for me, now? I don't need any fucking favors, freak. You won it. You keep it."

Kev held his breath, teeth clenched. Whew. Before Twin Tail Falls, that interchange wouldn't have registered on his radar screen. *Walk away.* He already had a lawsuit in course for assault and battery.

He walked away, careful not to limp. So he was driving home, with Chiliker's unwanted fucking car. He refused to let himself feel grateful. His leg was better, but it would have taken forty painful minutes to stagger home on foot with a headache like this.

He peered up at the sky as he got into his new car. It smelled like Chilikers, he noted. Not good. But he'd unload the car soon. It was later than usual, and when the sun rose, it would drive long, cruel nails of light into his throbbing brain tissue. But with the wheels, he could afford to make a detour before he holed up in his dark lair.

He parked by the battered brick front building on NE Stark. A sign by the door read "ANY PORT IN A STORM." It was a shelter for runaway teens. It provided twenty-four-hour-a-day crisis intervention, emergency shelter, individual and family counseling, transitional living programs for homeless youths, street outreach, emergency housing, help for kids who were addicted to drugs. He'd done some cyber snooping, and he liked the place. He pulled the wad of cash out, shoved it into the brown envelope he'd shoved into his coat pocket for that purpose, scribbled the name of the director, and sealed it up. He'd give them the car, too, if it would fit through the slot, but he wasn't up for anything that would require human interaction. His head hurt, his jaw hurt. He worked the envelope through the letter slot, waited for the *thud*. Saved him the bother of writing out a bank deposit slip.

He'd had some incidents, on these morning walks. He'd once brought a young prostitute to the door of Any Port, after saving her from being beaten up by her john. The john he left where he lay, moaning in the gutter. Fuck him. Punching a teenage girl in the face. Kev tried to be tolerant, but there were limits. Another time, he'd been ambushed by a couple thugs near this very shelter, but he'd flattened them with no trouble. All in all, though, his morning walks were mostly uneventful.

But Christ, his thigh hurt. And his ribs. His arm. Everything.

His reflection in the glass window in the door caught his eye. So thin, haggard, cheekbones jutting, cheeks hollowed. He stared at himself, seeking recognition in the face he saw. But it eluded him.

All he had now was what he'd made of himself since Tony found the bashed up wreck of his body eighteen years ago. That ought to be enough, but it wasn't anymore. Not since the waterfall. Memories were stirring, and his hunger to know more itched and burned, prodding him along with nasty, anxious urgency. Almost as if something terrible might happen if he did not succeed in remembering.

He parked by the unlovely brick warehouse building on NW Lenox that housed his loft apartment, an alley in the less swank, not-quite-gentrified-yet northern outskirts of the Pearl District. His hand shook with gratitude as he stuck the key into the lock . . . until he smelled Bruno's aftershave. *Shit*. He himself had taught Bruno to pick locks, back when Bruno was a delinquent teenager. Now, Bruno was a delinquent thirty-year-old, with skills more suitable for a career criminal. His own fault. He shouldn't have taught the kid to pick locks.

Bruno lay in wait, lounging on a stool and drinking coffee like he owned the place. The smell of frying bacon assaulted Kev's olfactory nerve like a wrecking ball when he stepped in the door. So did the perfumed cream that fop had smeared over himself after he'd shaved. The stink was enough to knock a brain damaged guy right on his ass.

Kev switched off the overhead, and pressed a switch that brought the shades over the high skylights. "What are you doing here?"

"Came to see you eat breakfast," Bruno said.

Kev slowly took off the sunglasses. "Breakfast," he echoed, in hollow tones. "Uh-uh." He sank into a chair, rubbing the thigh that had gotten snapped in two places in the waterfall plunge.

"Played cards tonight?" Bruno asked.

His brother's tone put him on the defensive. "And? So?"

"Win anything?"

"Some," Kev admitted, reluctantly.

"How much?"

Kev rubbed his eyes. "Don't remember," he said. "Dumped it on the way home. I don't need it. That's not why I play. You know that."

"Yeah, I know that. Mr. Pure doesn't need money. He floats above the grotty obsessions of us normal folk. That's exactly the elitist, improvident thinking that's always driven me nuts about you."

Kev rubbed his aching head, feeling the thick ropy scars

on his scalp. "I told you. It's not about the money. I do it for—"

"Yeah, you explained. I get it, insofar as a mere mortal could. You only cop a buzz when your brain is maxed to the limit counting cards. I'm not sure yet if that's technically cheating or not, but it definitely classifies you as a fucking weirdo. Not that this is any surprise to me."

Kev snorted. "Quit it with the 'mere mortals' bullshit, Bruno. I'm brain damaged, OK? I do the best I can with what I've got to work with."

"That's negative thinking, dude," Bruno said in a lecturing tone. "If you want to get your life back on track, you've got to—"

"I am trying!" The force of the words drove a hot nail of pain through his head. He held his fragile eggshell skull together with his hands until he dared to breathe again. "Or trying to get a life, period," he amended. "I've never been on anything resembling a track."

"What's wrong with your life?" Bruno demanded. "It was fine! So get back to it! You haven't worked since the waterfall, and you've been capable for months now!"

"You've got plenty of designs to develop," Kev pointed out. "When you run out, I'll come up with more for you. Whenever you need it."

"I'm not talking about what I need!"

Kev's lips twitched. "So this is to keep me busy? You think my mathematical masturbation will make me go blind?"

Bruno made an impatient gesture. "It's a waste. You need to get out, get some sun, get laid. You made us a fortune with Lost Boys. Are you going to just throw it all away to—"

"*You* made the fortune," Kev said, with quiet emphasis. "Go make the piles of money without me. I'll be OK."

Bruno looked frustrated. "But what the fuck? You're just sitting here in the dark, staring at your computer, obsessing about your past. Let it go! Start from where you are! Your life couldn't have been that good, considering how fucked-up you were when Tony found you!"

Kev couldn't deny it, but he couldn't agree, either. "I need to know where I came from," he said.

"Why?" Bruno yelled. "What would it help? What'll it prove?"

Bruno was right. There was no reason to think knowing his past would make the quality of his life better. And there were many reasons to think that it might make it worse. But curiosity was driving him bonkers. He'd always wanted to know where he came from, but since the waterfall, that want was fueled by raw emotion, like burning rocket fuel. If the truth should prove to suck ass, he still had to know it.

But Bruno was on a roll. "What's wrong with the life you've got? You've got plenty of money, or would if you'd stop throwing it at the widows and the orphans. You've got me and Tony and Rosa for family. What are we, chopped liver? Too lowbrow for you?"

"Don't be stupid. It has nothing to do with you, Rosa, and Tony."

"We're just not enough," Bruno raged on. "You're fixated on that hole inside your head, instead of the life you've built. Ever thought that what's in that hole might be a big disappointment to you? You were in shit-poor shape when Tony got you. Whoever your people were, they didn't stand by you! They left you to die! Fuck them!"

Kev gazed at the younger man. "I won't blow you off. Even if I find my former family. You'll always be my brother. No matter what."

Bruno looked embarrassed. "It's not about that."

Kev just looked at him.

"Oh, shut up," Bruno snarled. "Just shut the fuck up."

"I didn't say anything," Kev said.

"You didn't have to. It was the look on your face. Come

on. Eat this." He slapped a plate with a fried egg on a roll, bacon draped over it.

Kev swallowed back the clutch of nausea. No way to let Bruno down gently. He shook his head. "I'll take coffee," he offered.

Bruno muttered something foul in Calabrese, and spun the loaded plate in the direction of the sink like a Frisbee. The crash of breaking crockery made Kev jerk, covering his ears. Jesus. That hurt.

He took off his coat and poured coffee, ignoring the anger radiating from the broad back of his adopted brother. He tried not to limp as he crossed the room. Any show of weakness set Bruno off.

He sat at his worktable and turned the computer on.

"Don't jerk off with that while I'm talking to you," Bruno growled.

"I'm not jerking off," Kev said mildly. "And if you do, I'll talk back."

"With only half your brain? That irritates the shit out of me."

Kev clicked his browser. "Half a brain's all I've ever had."

"Hah. You could solve complicated higher math problems while simultaneously operating a nuclear missile launcher, analyzing weather patterns, and shaving a poodle. But normal folk call that bad manners."

Kev tried not to smile. "That's funny, coming from a guy who just picked all my locks. Get out, Bruno. I'm working."

Bruno grabbed a chair and straddled it. "I'll leave when you eat."

Kev sighed. "It'll be hours," he explained. "My stomach's fucked up. No digestive fluids. I'm not being difficult. It's a timing thing."

"So I'll wait til you're better," Bruno said.

Kev rubbed his throbbing forehead. "Thanks for caring, but no. I love you, man, but I'm busy now. Fuck off."

"Make me," Bruno said.

Kev exhaled slowly, dismayed. He'd managed this badly, out of exhaustion. Now there would be no getting rid of him without a fight.

He looked at the challenge in the younger man's eyes, the set of his jaw. He looked like Tony, with that expression. Scary thought.

Kev had taught Bruno to fight. Consequently, Bruno was lethally skilled, with the advantage of being ten years younger, buff as an Olympic athlete, and not currently recuperating from going over a waterfall. Kev's bones were still knitting. He was far from a hundred percent. He might prevail, but he'd pay a price he couldn't afford.

He decided to suck it up. "Whatever. Be bored, then." He put the sunglasses back on. "Don't bug me, though."

Bruno stared at Kev's face, trying to see past scars, skull, into the brain inside. Bruno was persistent. And ferociously intense. Two things Kev loved and respected about his adopted brother. They were also huge pains in the ass. But life was like that. Full of trade-offs.

"Tony's been asking about you," Bruno said.

Kev stopped in the act of lifting coffee to his lips. He took a sip, not breathing so as not to smell the stuff. "Oh, yeah? And?"

"He worries about you," Bruno said. "He's your family, too."

Kev stared at the screen, but did not see what was on it. "Ah."

Bruno cursed under his breath. "C'mon, Kev. Tony didn't take advantage of you on purpose," he said gruffly. "He was just, you know. Being Tony. He can't help himself. And besides, he thought he was doing you a favor. Keeping you out of sight."

"While doing unpaid menial labor for him, for years? Yeah. He's a real prince," Kev said. "Tony doesn't do favors,

Bruno. Nothing's for free. Not even for you, and you're his own flesh and blood."

Bruno didn't deny it, since he couldn't. "He worries about you," he repeated. "He really does. He's a mean old son of a bitch, but he does."

Kev's silence was more eloquent than words could have been.

Bruno's mouth hardened. "What the fuck do you think he should have done for you, anyway?"

"Nothing," Kev replied. "He was under no obligation to do anything. I have no reason to complain. If he hadn't saved me, I would have died. If he hadn't given me a place to be, I would have been homeless. I would have frozen to death on the streets that first winter."

"So why are you so pissed?"

Kev shook his head. "I'm not pissed," he said wearily. "Sure, I owed him. I owed him big. But I think I've worked out my indentured servitude by now, in sweat and blood."

"He never thought of you that way," Bruno said. "And fucked if you're not pissed. You're mortally pissed."

Kev didn't have the energy to deny it again. He thought of those miserable, stifled years. Lying on a cot in the narrow, smelly room behind the restaurant where Tony had parked him during off hours. Freezing in the winter, roasting in the summer. Steeping in smells of stale boiled vegetables, and the reeking Dumpster in the alley behind. Washing with a plastic bucket and rag because the squalid bathroom back there had no shower. Splitting headaches, night after night, so bad they made him vomit. Nights filled with horrific dreams.

Crying into the dingy, flat pillow every night. So fucking alone. Unable to speak, but wanting to so badly, it made him want to explode. A big rock was sitting on top of his mind, squashing him flat. He knew he did not belong there, but he couldn't get any grip on where he did belong. He couldn't think a straight thought through from start to finish. Couldn't focus, or orient himself. He was locked in a purgatory of tedium and fear. Tony had shoved a dishrag in his hand, pushed him in the direction of a pile of greasy plates, and there he stayed. For years.

Until Bruno came to stay with Tony and Rosa. He was their grandnephew. Tony and Rosa's niece, Bruno's mother, had begged Tony and Rosa to take her son for a while, to get him away from his abusive stepfather. Just until she sorted things out and got free of him.

As it turned out, she'd sent Bruno away just in time. She hadn't sorted things out, or gotten free. She'd died right after. Badly.

As soon as he arrived, Bruno started following Kev around, talking incessantly. The fact that Kev was incapable of replying hadn't mattered to Bruno. He'd had enough talk for two. Twelve years old, traumatized by his mother's murder, jerked around by his hormones, bouncing off the ceiling. He'd desperately needed someone to listen, and Kev was the perfect listener. The quintessential captive audience.

Bruno's nonstop chatter and intense emotional need had been the first chink in the wall that closed Kev inside himself. Bruno had started the long, slow process of Kev's healing. It was no thanks to Tony.

He wasn't complaining. He had Tony to thank for his life, his skin, and a place to start healing. It was a lot. He had no reason to expect more. He couldn't blame Tony for not doing more, or caring more. There was no point. People were what they were. They cared, or they didn't. He was just damn lucky to have had Bruno.

This line of thought was making his gut cramp up. Who the fuck needed it? He turned his attention back to the computer.

After a while, Bruno got up and sprawled onto one of the couches, flipping channels until he found some sports event he liked. The squawk of the TV audio soon faded from Kev's consciousness as he systematically searched the vast pseudo-space of the Internet.

His current mode was to find data on all male Ostermans between the ages of fifty and seventy. He'd ruled out most of the ones in the Northwest. One still interested him; Christopher Osterman, research scientist, recently deceased. There were thousands of references to his cognitive research, but he hadn't found a photo yet. Many references were to "the Haven," a mysterious research facility dedicated to optimizing brain function. Reading between the lines of the promo material, he concluded that the Haven was a think tank for rich kids whose parents wanted high-achieving offspring to feed their egos. The project had been dismantled after Osterman's death, three years before.

Many of the young people who had participated in the Haven had since gone on on to brilliant careers in medicine, science, or business, or so the promo material said. Further research appeared to back this claim up, but that could be more a function of wealth and connections than it was a result of Osterman's brain massages. Who knew?

Kev was currently browsing some Haven alumni he'd found on Facebook. They archly referred to themselves as "Club O," and liked to reminisce online, exchanging pictures, memories, bragging and self-congratulation. In fact, he found them oddly repellent, as a group.

He was startled when Bruno spoke up from behind him. "It's been hours," his brother said, belligerently. "Hungry yet?"

He'd forgotten that his body existed. He located his stomach in time and space, assessed its condition. Not optimal. "Not yet," he said.

Bruno harrumped, and peered over Kev's shoulder. "Facebook? What, cruising for chicks now? Is it the lust thing, kicking your ass?"

Kev snorted. "I'm looking at online photo albums. Alumni

of this place called the Haven. Dr. Christopher Osterman ran the place. He did cognitive research. Brain enhancement. Big network of alums."

"How did you get into these peoples' Facebook pages?"

Kev gave him a look, and Bruno rolled his eyes. "OK. Stupid question. Never mind. Cognitive research? Brain experiments? So you've been altered. Ah! Yes. That would explain what a whack job you are."

"It would," Kev agreed, unoffended. "This guy died a few years ago, though. A fire in his lab, they say. I want to see a photo of him."

"Excuse me? You want to look at a picture of this freak? The last time you saw someone you thought looked like this Osterman, you went into a fugue state and practically killed an innocent neurosurgeon!"

"Shut up, Bruno," Kev said absently, still clicking. "I'm busy."

Bruno subsided, grumbling. "If you freak out and attack me, I'll kick your sorry ass to hell and back," he warned. "I won't hold back just because you're a pathetic bag of bones. Be warned."

Kev clicked on yet another photo. His eyes flashed over faces, his hand already clicking to magnify them as a name in the caption registered.

The illustrious, late, great Doctor O explains it all for us.

His hand froze on the mouse. It was set to increase magnification by ten percent at each click, but with no new activity, it defaulted to one magnification per second, the center being at the cursor. The picture zoomed in on the guy in a white lab coat. Close-set dark eyes. His arms flung over the shoulders of two teenagers. Mouth open, in a big laugh.

Kev couldn't move. His muscles were frozen. He couldn't even blink. Switches were flicking on and off inside his brain, he could not control them. He observed, as the power grids in his brain started to go dark, that the guy really did look like Patil. Patil was darker, being Indian. Dr. O looked like the Greek or Italian version of the same man.

The pressure built in his brain. He struggled to breathe, to move.

Kev? What the fuck? Kev, what's the matter? Hey! Kev!

It was Bruno's voice, faraway. He couldn't answer. Couldn't look at the other man. Muscles frozen. Falling back, into the dark oubliette.

Oh fucking shit, man, no! Don't do this to me again . . .

Bruno's frantic voice faded into the distance. The photo got bigger. The face filled the screen. The mouth. Bigger and bigger.

Pop, pop. Something gave way in his eye. A hot rush of liquid down his cheek. Broken blood vessel. A haze of red obscured his vision. That red, toothy mouth stretched wider and wider, hungry to devour. The image widened still more, into a meaningless checkerboard of pixels.

Lights out.

CHAPTER
4

"Come on, you geek freak son of a bitch. It's me, Bruno. Not that Osterman turd, so don't try a fucking stress flashback when you open your eyes, or I'll rip your throat out. This bullshit is pissing me off!"

Bruno yelled the words, leaning over Kev's hospital bed, but there was no response. Kev looked like a marble statue. It made Bruno's stomach hurt. Over twenty-four hours, and no sign of waking. Another coma, or something like it. The doctors were baffled.

Fuck this shit. Fuck it in every orifice.

Tony grunted from the other side of the bed. "Ain't you just a charmer," he said. "Whisperin' sweet nothings in his ear."

Bruno blew out an explosive breath and sprawled back in his chair, drumming his fingers on the plastic table. "We tried nice last time he woke up," he said sourly. "He didn't respond well. He liquefied Patil's face. It's safer to be rude. That way, there's no mistake about who's busting his balls." He leaned over Kev again. "Not the Osterman motherfucker, hear me? It's that pain in the ass, Bruno! Anybody home in there?" He tweaked Kev's nose. "Hey! Butthead! Hello! Anybody?"

Kev's face did not change. Bruno flung himself back into the chair, muttering. Tony sat on the other side, like a stone monolith, his slablike face grim. But Tony's default expression was always grim. He was a Marine, an ex-drill sergeant, a Vietnam vet. Habitually pissed off. Most of what Uncle Tony saw around him annoyed the living shit out of him. Bruno and Kev impartially included, for the most part.

Kev in a coma again? That pissed old Uncle Tony off big-time.

Kev looked so pale and still. Like Mamma, in her coffin. The funeral parlor guys had been creative in covering up the damage Rudy had done to her face. She'd looked weirdly peaceful, lying there.

But unlike Mamma, Kev genuinely was weirdly peaceful. Even before he relearned how to talk, Kev was super mellow. He never lost his temper. Unless someone fucked with him, of course, at which point, he morphed into a demon dervish, and kicked that unlucky someone's ass to hell and back. Karate, kung fu, judo, aikido, jujitsu, all of them were mixed into in Kev's unique fighting style. He was un-fucking-beatable.

In fact, his fighting skills had inspired Kev's chosen surname. After the incident at the diner, Tony started calling him Kevlar. It stuck. And when Kev was talking well enough to want a surname, he went with Kev Larsen. It was Kev's weird, quirky idea of a joke, though it was also a bland, under-the-radar nordic name that fit him well enough. He could be a Swede, or a Dane. Tall, sinewey, lots of dirt-blond hair. A yellowish cast to his skin, rather than nordic skim-milk white, but with that stoic expression, he was a classic, battle-scarred Viking warrior. All he needed were braids, a horned helmet, and a mantle of shaggy fur.

So Kev Larsen it was, though Bruno took pains to point

out that only a narcissistic pussy would tattoo his own name on his own leg. He'd once tried to bust Kev's balls by insisting that Kev had been a gay boy before Tony found him, and Kev was actually the name of his lover.

But Kev never responded appropriately to ball busting. His grin pulled weirdly at the scars on his cheek as he grabbed Bruno's ass and made smooching sounds til Bruno ran for cover.

Teasing about Kev's gayness had ended abruptly there.

Bruno lifted the hospital sheet, stared at Kev's leg. His calf was furred with dark blond hair, sinewy and bulging with hard muscle. The tattoo was very small. The three irregular letters were a crooked, blurry bluish smudge beneath his body hair. It looked like a bruise.

He flung the sheet down. It made him twitchy and rattled. His own vulnerability, staring him down, scaring him shitless. Kev was the pillar in the center that held up the roof of his whole life. More so than Uncle Tony, more so than Aunt Rosa. Kev had saved Bruno's ass. Kev had given payback for what Rudy had done to Mamma. Some, anyway. It could never be enough. But it was a shitload better than nothing.

Kev couldn't die. Life would be unthinkable without him. Bruno didn't usually think in those squishy emotional terms, but seeing how similar Kev looked right now to the way Mamma had looked in her coffin, after Rudy got through with her—it got to him, deep inside, in places he preferred to ignore. And being aware of it made him aware of his other stupid, irrelevant feelings, too. Like, for instance, how jealous he was of this hypothetical fucking family that Kev might or might not find. No, amend that. *Would* find. If they were out there, Kevlar would find them. The guy was as focused as a freight train.

Kev's real family. Bruno could never be part of that, if it existed. This perfect family would enfold Kev to their bosoms and overwhelm him with their wonderfulness, at which point Kev would forget that the wiseass pain in the ass punk

Bruno Ranieri ever existed. There would be a pie-baking mamma, wielding a wooden spoon, a benevolent dad with a pot belly. Brothers and sisters who looked like him, understood him, knew things about him that Bruno would never know.

Take a fucking pill. Families like that didn't exist, except on TV. Families were, by definition, fucked up. But blood was blood.

It was a stupid thing to be worrying about, though, since Kev hadn't even woken up yet. He still looked like a goddamn corpse. In fact, Kev's blood family was the least of Bruno's current worries.

He hadn't felt like such hammered shit since Mamma's death. Every muscle hurt. He had a headache, from grinding his teeth. He hadn't gone into Lost Boys since Kev's episode, yesterday morning. They were managing fine without him, thank God. He'd be useless anyhow. All he would do was snap, growl, and criticize.

Truth was, he was not terribly surprised by the recent series of events. There had always been something precarious about Kev's very existence. A sense of lurking danger. The unknowns, the questions, the bizarre violence wreaked upon him. Bruno had been waiting for the other shoe to drop since he'd met the guy. It had finally dropped, over a three-hundred-foot waterfall. And the sky was coming down along with it.

Even Kev's inexplicable flashes of genius were unnerving. Just when Bruno thought he knew the guy front and back, whammo, he'd discover that Kev had some new freakishly overdeveloped skill, or rocket scientist body of knowledge. Kevlar, International Man Of Mystery, strikes again. Maybe the guy was actually a stranded space alien.

Huh. Actually, that hypothesis would explain a whole lot. Too bad that trip over the waterfall hadn't knocked some plain old common sense into his head. It was the one thing Kev lacked. So far, Bruno filled the gap, but only because Kev didn't care enough to stop him. Like with money. Kev sincerely didn't give a flying fuck about it. He'd invent some ingenious marketable thing on some sleepless night, play with it for a few hours, toss it in the closet and forget about it.

Kev's gizmos had given Bruno the idea for Lost Boys Flywear. They'd opened seven years ago as a stunt kite outfit, to exploit some of Kev's kite designs, and branched out from there into quirky educational toys. Kev provided the brilliant ideas, artistic designs, manufacturing plans. Bruno took care of the business, the marketing. The scut work. Everybody had his gift. His was for making money.

The venture worked. He'd arranged for Kev's designs to be patented, to significant profit. Lost Boys was going strong. Neither of them was hurting for dough, or had any reason to hurt for it for the rest of their lives, if they were careful. And minimally practical, of course.

But Kev just wasn't. He was as likely, today or tomorrow, to give it all away to a stranger he met on the street.

Bruno figured he should cut the guy some slack. He was brain damaged, after all. Something had to give. But it was like watching somebody set hundred dollar bills on fire. It made Bruno's ass twitch. It came from growing up on the uglier side of Newark. Bruno liked a big, wide safety net. Lots of soft, puffy financial cushions under him.

Kev was happy to dance on a wire over the lion cage.

Like those poker winnings. Tens of thousands of bucks every night, stuffed through the letter slot of whatever charitable organization happened to be on his walking trajectory. Crazy shit. But he loved the guy. Goddamnit. Right now, he wished like hell that he didn't.

"He's barkin' up the wrong tree," Tony said heavily.

The words startled Bruno out of his unhappy reverie. "Huh?" he said, grumpily. "What tree?"

"Looking for this Otterman fucker," Tony clarified.

"Osterman," Bruno corrected.

"Whatever. Looking for some lily-white scientist prick is

a waste of time. Brain experiments, my hairy old ass. He was tortured by a professional. It takes practice and a hard stomach to do what they did to him. That says career criminal. That says mafia. Believe me, I know." He glanced sidewise at Bruno. "So should you, kid."

Bruno shrugged that off. He disliked references to the mafia turf wars his mom's boyfriend Rudy had been embroiled in when Bruno was a kid. Bruno's Mamma, too, by association. Thinking about it made him feel like shit, so he tried hard not to. Tony had run away from the life himself, decades before, to the war in Vietnam. He'd never gone back.

"A scientist could hire career criminals to do his dirty work," Bruno argued. "The mafia aren't the only ones who can figure out how to hurt somebody."

Tony waved that away with a big, bolt-knuckled hand. "He should be looking through military records of special forces troops reported missing in action in August of 1992. Or checking out mug shots of mobsters operating in Seattle. I'm tellin' you, he was special ops, undercover on a domestic mission. He got on the bad side of some big criminal organization, and they decided to take him out. Simple."

Bruno grunted. "Nothing about Kev is simple. I saw what happened when he saw that photograph."

Tony made a hawking sound in his throat. "Fuckin' coincidence."

"Kev was a scientist," Bruno asserted stubbornly. "Ever seen his bathroom books? Biochemistry, aeronautic engineering?"

Tony rolled his eyes. "Come on. Give me a fuckin' break. A fuckin' scientist, trained in eight different styles of martial arts?"

This was a decade-old argument, and totally pointless, but Bruno's innate cussedness made the words pop out. "I know you think any guy who ever went to college is a pussy, but the opposite is just as improbable. It's as likely that a scientist would learn martial arts as it is that a Navy Seal or a Ranger would study theoretical physics for fun."

Tony shook his head. "That kind of fighting ain't for fun," he said darkly. "A guy doesn't train like that unless he has to, to survive. Kev ain't no fuckin' dilettante. He was a career fighter. Remember Rudy?"

Goddamn Tony. Like Bruno's mood needed another crushing blow. The last thing he needed to think about was the day Rudy had gone after Mamma. He'd gone after her a lot. But that day, he hadn't stopped.

That time, she'd died. Head injuries, a ruptured liver, a broken rib that perforated her lung. Other stuff he couldn't even bear to think about. And Rudy got away with it, on a bureaucratic technicality related to how the evidence was collected. Rudy had connections with the local don. He was protected by corrupt police. He was untouchable.

But Bruno had witnessed him hitting Mamma on countless occasions, and Bruno was set to testify at the trial. So Rudy and two of his mafioso henchmen had flown out to Portland, to simplify things.

They'd concluded that the best time to nab Bruno was early morning, at his uncle's diner, where he went to eat breakfast before school. Nobody on the streets, the uncle asleep in the apartment upstairs. Just the kid, eating his eggs with the fucked up retard who lived out back. The guy who mopped floors and washed dishes for Tony. The one who couldn't talk. How fucking convenient was that.

Bruno remembered every minute of that morning with weird clarity. He'd pounded at the door of the diner at five in the morning, until Kev got up and let him in, like always. He'd perched at the counter, talking a mile a minute while Kev cooked and served breakfast. Three eggs, over medium, with lots of pepper, grilled ham, white bread toast with big, gluey globs of grape jelly.

Then Rudy and the two other guys burst in. They grabbed him off the stool. Rudy wrenched the locket Mom had given him off his neck, the one he wore day and night. He dragged Bruno toward the door.

What happened after was like an action film sequence, viewed from an upside down artistic angle, bent over, arm torqued, screaming bloody murder. A dinner plate hit one guy with lethal precision on the bridge of the nose like the fucking Frisbee of death, and the man smashed into the curved glass of the pastry counter, ass wedged into the cream pies. Blood, glass, rice pudding, coconut custard everywhere.

Then Kev flew out, transformed. Bruno was dumped when the storm hit. He rolled under the table and watched. Big eyed. Slack jawed.

It wasn't a fair fight, even with the knives the other guys held. Those guys couldn't land a blow. Kev ducked, swerved, evaded every assault with casual grace. Sent Rudy spinning back with a kick to his face that sent him reeling over a table, arms flailing. Seized the other guy who was rushing him, flipped him like a doll. Sent him flying headfirst through the front window. Rudy's bellow of challenge blended with the shattering crash, but his headlong rush ended just like the other attacks. A flurry of motion, a flip, a twist, a thud, and Rudy was on the ground on his side, arm broken, his own knife protruding from his ass. The fork Bruno had used for his eggs was stuck in Rudy's groin, standing up grotesquely. Rudy curled in on himself, screaming and pawing at the red spreading on his crotch with his uninjured hand.

Tony heard the window. He came running down in his shorts and undershirt. He looked over the carnage, yanked the weeping Bruno out from under the table, looked him over and gave him a whack upside the head. He gave the wheezing Rudy an unfriendly nudge with his toe. He gave Kev an assessing look.

"Next time, don't fuck the window," was his laconic comment. "Them bastards are expensive. Now help me take out this trash."

Bruno and Kev helped drag the bleeding thugs though

the kitchen, to the alley where Tony's pickup was parked. Bruno timidly asked if they should call the cops. Tony gave him a look. "Got a death wish, kid?"

Fair enough, after what had happened back in Newark.

Tony ordered them to hose down the bloodied sidewalk, and hang a CLOSED FOR REPAIRS sign. Then he'd driven his pickup away.

That marked the moment Bruno stopped following Kev around out of curiosity, and started to do it out of hero worship. Tony changed his attitude toward Kev, too. He'd started staring at him, whenever his back was turned. Wondering what he had back there, quietly washing his dishes. And if it was a time bomb that might blow up in his face.

Tony's chair creaked as he shifted in the hospital chair. "You look like dogshit," he said. "Rosa sent lamb shank. And rice pudding. She thinks the smell of food will wake him up. Have some. There's plenty."

The mention of rice pudding made Bruno think of the guy wedged into the broken dessert counter, bleeding out into the cream custard.

He shook his head, and dragged out his laptop. Researching Kev's bad guy was a good distraction, and somebody else had to do it, since it was looking pretty fucking hazardous to Kev's health to do it himself.

"You researching that Otterfen asshole? I told you. You're wasting your time. Put that goddamn thing away and eat something."

"Osterman," Bruno repeated, though it was no use wrangling the point. Tony won, by seniority, loudness, meanness. A swift backhand to the mouth, sometimes, too, when Bruno was younger. He still remembered the sting, but he didn't hold a grudge. He also remembered watching Tony drive off, the black plastic tarp draped over those mobsters who had come to kill him. How grateful he'd been when Tony came back hours later, and grimly hosed down the bed of the pickup. No talk, no explanations. It was like the thing had never even happened.

Tony had just eaten a big dinner in the back of the diner afterward, and then sat there, smoking a long series of hand-rolled cigarettes. He stared, head wreathed in smoke, looking fixedly at the back of Kev's head while the guy washed a huge pile of dishes.

Then he told Bruno to stop crying, or he'd pop him a good one. Tousled his hair, violently enough to give him a case of whiplash. Went off to bed, heavy boots thudding on the stairs.

It was like Kev said. Life was full of tradeoffs. Nothing was for free.

But sometimes, even the highest price was worth paying.

Noise battered at Kev's brain. Voices, babbling, but he couldn't decode the words. He was stuck in a hole inside his mind. His oubliette.

Here, he could not be compelled. He'd blocked the connections to his voluntary motor functions. He didn't know how he'd done it. All he knew was that here, in this place, they could not fuck with him.

The flip side was, he couldn't compel himself, either. He was safe, but paralyzed. And stuck. No door in this place. No tunnel. No ladder.

It wasn't unconsciousness. His mind was crystal sharp. And he wasn't panicking. Not yet. He'd been in here before. He'd climbed out somehow. It might take a while, but he'd figure it out.

He wondered if this was a coma, but he doubted it. Most people weren't called upon to develop evasive mental maneuvers to thwart brain control. Probably comatose people were curled up in a similar oubliette, fast asleep. Not clawing the walls, like something out of a Poe story. Whoops. Wrong turn. If he kept on in this direction, he'd panic.

Just wait. The quiet instruction floated up like a bubble from the depths. Be patient, and just wait.

He set himself to calming down the turbulence in his mind with his usual techniques. A white starflower. The Milky Way, spattered out across the night sky. A monolith of black volcanic granite, stark against a snowscape. Still, his thoughts whizzed and spun. He started to get exhausted. Only then did he bring out his secret weapon.

The little angel.

He tried not to use the angel too often. Overusing his talisman would tarnish it, rob it of its protective power. Even daring to think of her too often could overlay false memories over the true, pure one.

It worked, like always. He looked into those clear, solemn eyes, and the whizbang ricochet of desperation calmed. He felt relief, an upwelling of unreasonable joy. Like cool rain on a fevered face.

His brain slid into focus. The static of noise battering him from outside resolved into comprehensible language. A conversation, ping-ponging back and forth over him. Voices he knew very well.

". . . bullshit," a gravely voice pronounced. "They don't teach torture techniques in goddamn scientist ivory towers." That was Tony's voice, that harsh, cigarette and alcohol roughened rasp.

Emotion jabbed through him, prickly and sharp. Unwilling fondness, anger, and gall. That crusty old bastard. The jolt flipped the switch, reconnected him. He could move now. His eyelids fluttered.

". . . course it is," Tony was replying, to whoever was out there. "Kid's been a pain in the ass since the day I found him."

"You should have let the guy kill me," he blurted hoarsely. "But you didn't." His eyes opened, fastened on Tony's face

Tony stared down, eyes narrowed in shadowy bags of

flesh. "Don't mouth off to me, kid," he said. "A coma ain't no fuckin' excuse."

Kev's mouth twitched. Tony stared, stone faced. No way could he give in so far as to smile back. To yield was to die. His unspoken creed.

Kev looked up at Bruno. The only time Kev ever saw any familial resemblance between Tony's ravaged face and Bruno's *GQ* good looks was when the kid was scowling, just like that.

"No more comas," Bruno warned, through clenched teeth. "Or I will kick your useless ass right into the next life. That clear?"

It wasn't a coma, but Kev didn't have the energy to explain. He attempted to move his arm, was cautiously pleased when it obeyed his command. He patted Bruno's cheek, stubbled with black scruff.

"Thanks for caring," he said.

Bruno recoiled. "Don't patronize me," he snarled.

Kev gazed at his brother. The beard scruff was stark evidence of how upset he was. Bruno was always shaved, gelled, perfumed, dressed in the best. Today, he wore a wrinkled T-shirt with coffee stains.

He felt a pang of guilt, and struggled into a sitting position, peeling off the tape that held his IV needle into place.

"Hey!" Bruno clamped Kev's hand in his own, stopping him. "What the hell do you think you're doing? The nurse can do that!"

Kev plucked Bruno's fingers off his forearm. "I'm awake," he said. "I can move. Let me get on with it."

"On with what? With looking for the monsters of your past? Great! We get to witness you die from a stroke when you find them!"

"I won't have a stroke," Kev said mildly. "Where are my clothes?"

"Lie back down, kid," Tony advised. "You look like shit."

Kev ripped the tape loose and yanked the needle out of

his hand. He looked around the room. "Give me that laptop, would you?"

Bruno rolled his eyes. "Are you out of your fucking mind? No, don't answer that. It was a rhetorical question. The answer is, fuck no, and over my dead body! Any more questions?"

"Aw, come on. Does this place have WiFi?"

Bruno's eyes narrowed. "You want to look at that photo again? The one that made you black out for twenty-eight hours?" He glanced at his watch. "And thirty-four minutes? Forget it!"

Kev blinked. "That long?" He rotated his shoulders, rolled his head on his neck. "No wonder I'm so stiff. All the more reason to get right to it. Come on. Be a pal. Hand over that laptop, buddy."

"No!" Bruno yelled.

Kev sighed. This was going to take more finessing, and Christ knew he didn't have the energy. "I've remembered some more," he offered. "About Osterman. I was right. He was doing experiments on me. That was why I jumped Patil. He looked exactly like the guy."

"I saw the picture," Bruno growled. "I figured that out for myself."

"Experiments?" Tony grunted, unimpressed. "Fuckin' scientists."

"Mind control stuff," Kev said. "Shutting down my brain was the way I used to fight the mind control thing. That's why I'm going into these comas. It's a defensive reflex."

"That's all great, but Osterman's dead," Bruno snapped. "And no one around here is trying to control your mind. So there's no point in dwelling on this guy, and putting yourself in another coma. OK?"

Kev shook his head. "There have to be other people who knew what he was doing. I'll start with the other people in that photograph. Hand over the iTouch. I know you always have your toys on you."

"Yesterday, I dragged you in here, bleeding out your eyes," Bruno hissed. "You think I'm up for a repeat performance? Fuck that!"

Kev massaged the ropy scars on his head. They throbbed uncomfortably. "It won't happen again," he assured Bruno.

"Oh, what a comfort! Guess what? I do not trust your judgment!"

"No, really," Kev wheedled. "I remember Osterman's face. It blindsided me before, but it won't take me by surprise again. I'm picturing that photo in my head right now, every last pixel, and my head is not exploding. I swear to you. It won't get me again."

Bruno harrumped. "In any case, I've already done it."

"Done what?"

"Researched the picture," Bruno said, with a long-suffering air. "I identified everyone in it. Scraped together whatever I could find on the Internet about each one. If that's what you meant to do, it's done."

Kev realized his mouth was open. "Uh, wow. Thanks."

Bruno looked uncomfortable. "Shut up." He dragged an accordion folder out of a duffel at his feet. "The guys with Osterman were Giles Laurent and Desmond Marr. Do those names burst any blood vessels?"

The names fell like stones into the deep waters of his mind, encountering nothing. No reaction. He shook his head.

Bruno opened the file. "Laurent you can cross off your list, because he's dead."

"Why am I not surprised," Tony muttered. "There'll be lots of dead guys in this story by the time it's told. Maybe one of 'em'll be you."

"Maybe." Kev was unperturbed. "Dead how?"

"Suicide. Six years ago. Software designer. Went to Stanford after his stint at the Haven. Started a company, was doing real well. Shot himself in the head. Left a wife, two-year-old kid. Real tragic."

"And the other guy?"

"Desmond Marr. Another high achiever," Bruno said. "Harvard undergrad, Harvard business. Being groomed to take over his daddy's pharmaceutical company, Helix. Medical technology, nanotechnology. Red-hot stock. They just moved down to the Silicon Forest in Hillboro a few years ago. This guy's doing great. Hot shit on a silver platter."

"Let me see that picture." Kev reached for it.

Bruno snatched the folder back. "Fuck, no. I found another picture of Marr for you. One without Osterman in it." He rummaged through his printouts, and pulled out a photocopy of an eight-by-ten.

Kev took it. Blood drained from his face. His ears began to roar.

There were four people in the photo, sitting at a table in front of a red drapery. A white haired man was beaming, holding up a plaque, but Kev's eyes fastened on the other one; the long, distinguished face, the hawklike nose. He'd dreamed that face, thousands of times. The man was older, but it was the man from his dream. The one he'd run to, pleading for help.

No. Not a dream. A *memory.* That man was real, and from Kev's past. From before the wall in his mind. And Kev remembered him.

Oh, fuck. Excitement began to build. His heart pounded heavily.

Bruno leaned over his shoulder, pointing to a younger guy in the corner. "Here's Desmond Marr, all grown up. This is from Helix's corporate Web site. I picked it because it had the best close-up of Desmond that I could find, besides the portrait in his Web site bio. This is an awards ceremony from last year, where daddy Raymond received a lifetime achievement award from the American Medical Association for his contributions to . . . hey. Kev? What's wrong?" He jerked Kev's chin up, peered into his eyes. "Don't start with that crazy shit!"

"I won't," Kev said, jerking his chin away. "Relax."

"Hah," Bruno muttered. "So you know Raymond Marr?"

Kev shook his head, and pointed at the hawk-faced man. "No. This one." His cold finger shook as it touched the paper.

Bruno leaned over the photo. "Oh, him. Another big cheese. The CEO of Helix. Founded the company along with Desmond's daddy. His name is . . . hold on . . ." He rifled through the printouts. "Charles Parrish." Bruno waited expectantly, but Kev just shook his head.

"No broken blood vessels? How undramatic," Bruno muttered. "So, is this guy a white hat or a black hat? Is he your long lost dad?"

"I went to him for help," Kev said simply. "That's all I remember."

Tony hawked, and spat into a tissue. "And did he give it to you?"

Kev squeezed his eyes shut, and shook his head. "I don't think he did. I remember pleading with him." He struggled to pull the dreamlike memories into focus. "I think he threw me to the wolves. I scared the shit out of him. That was after the torture, so I was all fucked up. He called security. I threw one through a window. I remember that much."

Tony grunted sourly. "Of course you threw one through a window. That's your specialty. Can't just be a discreet knife through the eye, oh, no. It's gotta be loud, it's gotta draw attention, it's gotta cost money."

Kev ignored him. "Tell me more about Parrish."

Bruno rifled through his printouts again, scowling, and pulled out a sheet of paper. "I don't have a whole lot on him yet. According to his corporate bio, he worked for Flaxon for twelve years, based out of Seattle. Flaxon had warehouses not far from where Tony found you. He worked his way up the ranks, and twelve years ago, he left Flaxon and founded Helix, along with Marr. They made obscene amounts of money. Guy's worth billions." Bruno handed him another photo. "Here he is again. This is two years ago. Right after the move. They'd just inaugurated the building."

Kev held the picture closer to his face. This was a snapshot, taken at a table at some other banquet. Parrish raised his glass, mouth open. An elegant, bony woman with dark hair smiled for the camera. A young woman sat on his other side, shoulders hunched. Her face was veiled with long hair. Her shoulders were bare in a beaded sheath dress. Her spaghetti strap had fallen down. That, and the long, wavy mane made her look disheveled. Her arm clasped the shoulders of a little girl.

Bruno pointed at the older woman. "Late wife. Died a year ago." He pointed at the child. "Younger daughter, Veronica. Thirteen." He touched the young woman. "Older daughter, Edith. Twenty-nine, lives here in Portland. Unmarried. She's a Haven alum, too. Funny, huh?"

Kev looked at her more closely. "Is she on Facebook?"

"She doesn't have a profile, but I found her in some photos. She was there the same time as Marr and Laurent. Only fourteen back then. She was a nerd. Glasses and braces. Back in Parrish's Flaxon days."

"What is she, a socialite?" He studied her more closely, but all there was to be seen of her face was the tip of a nose and the flash of a pale cheek. Those hunched shoulders said *get me the fuck out of here.*

"Graphic artist. I checked out her site. Just had a book come out. Some noir, urban fantasy comic book thing. Lots of hoo hah about it. Message forums, rabid fans. Her stuff's popular with the college crowd."

Kev touched the photograph with his fingertip, tracing the outline of her shoulder. As if he could shove up the delicate beige strap that had fallen down over her arm. "Got any other pictures of her?"

Bruno rummaged. "I printed out the photo on her Web site. Didn't come out real well, but here." He passed the picture to Kev.

It was black and white. Edith Parrish looked into the camera with a diffident smile. Heavy wings of hair left only a narrow strip of her face visible. Horn-rimmed glasses shadowed her eyes. Her chin rested on her fists. Pretty mouth. Soft. She looked nervous, like she'd dart off like a fawn at the slightest provocation. "Not a socialite," Kev said.

"By no means," Bruno agreed. "A Goth art nerd. Wonder what Daddy Dearest thinks of that."

Kev kept staring. Edie Parrish's photo stirred him, but gave him no hard data to crunch. Sometimes he could trace phantom emotions to their source, make something of them. Usually not. Which was why emotions seemed so useless to him. More trouble than they were worth. But this feeling wasn't bad. It felt . . . well, fuck it. Almost good.

"I want to meet her," he said.

Bruno looked startled. "Edith Parrish? What for?"

He shrugged, defensive. "I just do."

Bruno dismissed her with a wave of his hand. "Forget her. She's too young to have anything to do with what happened to you. She was only eleven years old when Tony found you. Start with the dad."

"Of course I'll go after the dad. But I still want to meet her."

Bruno's eyes narrowed. "Why?" His voice had a challenging ring.

Kev didn't answer. Bruno let out an expressive grunt. "She's too young for you, you slobbering perv. Pick on somebody your own size."

"I didn't say I wanted to sleep with her," Kev snapped. "I just said I wanted to meet her. And besides, how do you know how old I am?"

"You weren't twelve when I found you," Tony pointed out darkly.

Bruno's cell phone chirped. He pulled it out, and stared at it. His dark eyes flicked up to Kev's face. He looked unnerved.

"What?" Kev demanded. "What the hell is it?"

Bruno hesitated. "When I visited Edie Parrish's Web site, I signed up for her mailing list," he finally admitted. "It sends me an automatic SMS when she's having an author appearance in my area."

The excitement was disorienting in its intensity. "Where?"

Bruno didn't answer. Kev lunged for the cell in Bruno's hand, and grabbed the IV rack to steady himself when Bruno whipped it out of his reach. The dangling bottle of sugar water rattled and swung crazily.

"Where?" he said, more sharply. "When? What bookstore?"

"Calm down," Bruno said. "I haven't seen you this excited since you destroyed Patil's face. Leave that babe alone. She's irrelevant. You've got no business chasing her just because you think she's cute."

Kev lunged again. "Give me that fucking phone!"

Bruno darted back. "What do you think you can learn from her?"

Kev waved his arms. "I don't know. But it feels like a sign. Or the closest thing I've ever had to one."

Bruno looked worried. "What, you mean, like, from God? You mean, you actually believe in that stuff?"

Kev finally captured the telephone. "Fucked if I know. But there's one thing I don't believe in."

Bruno looked apprehensive. "And that is?"

Kev opened up the text message, memorized its contents, and handed the phone back to his brother. "Coincidences."

CHAPTER
5

Kev's legs felt rubbery as he walked into Pirelli's, the hip independent bookstore that had recently opened up downtown. He was early for the two-thirty meet-the-author event. He'd been too anxious to wait at home, and he wanted to stay out of Bruno's reach.

They'd worked out a shaky truce. Or rather, Kev had made Bruno understand that if he tried to stop Kev from going to the book signing, or if he showed up to police him there, one or both of them would end up in jail, or hospitalized. They'd fought in the hospital room two days ago, they'd fought this morning. They fought on the phone whenever they spoke. There was no middle ground.

He understood his brother's point of view. Pursuing Edith Parrish was a big waste of time. Potentially embarrassing, possibly dangerous. She was too young to have anything to do with his past. This was indisputable. But checking out Edith Parrish was not a decision. It was a compulsion. A clawing, roaring need that could not be reasoned with.

Bruno had tried, in the hospital room, but his efforts had soon degenerated into shouting, a frequent occurrence in the Ranieri household. Tony had gotten into the fray, and after the IV rack got knocked over, the bottle of fluid smashed, and a table full of medical equipment upended, two big male nurses had come in and thrown Bruno and Tony out. And Kev had been made to understand that he was no longer welcome as a patient at Legacy Emanual Hospital. Now, or ever.

But hey. A guy had to do what a guy had to do.

He looked around, gut vibrating in that weird, tight way he couldn't get used to, and strolled down the magazine aisle. Motorcycles, Men's Health, Fine Art & Furnishings. He caught sight of himself reflected in the coffee bar machine, and winced. The wraparound sunglasses looked dumb, but he couldn't tolerate flourescent lights without them, and they hid the scarlet spot in his eye. And that hair, God. He went back and forth between long hair and buzzed off, it being a toss-up which took less maintenance, but he'd worn it long before the waterfall accident. When he wore it loose, it shielded him from a good forty percent of the stares that he caught for the scarring.

But they'd buzzed him to the scalp for the surgeries. It was barely two inches long, which meant that as it grew, it stuck up in spiky, crazy cowlicked whorls that made him look like an overgrown Sting wannabe. Even the long canvas coat, chosen for bland neutrality, seemed like a costume piece, with that hair, those glasses. And he was so fucking tall. He fought the urge to slump. That didn't make a tall guy inconspicuous.

He forced himself to straighten, and noticed the cute blonde scoping him from the other side of the magazine rack. He turned his head as if checking out the bookstore map, letting her get a good long look at the scars. Her gaze darted away. She strode off. Bingo. One down, three billion to go. He weeded out the pointless ones a priori as quickly as possible.

He had discovered, to his cost, that girls fell mostly into two camps. The ones who were repelled by the scars, and the ones who were intrigued. He wasn't sure which category was worse.

He hated explaining the story to them. He didn't like to lie, but he hated telling the truth, too. Dealing with the girls' wonder, their speculation, their sympathy, their heebie-jeebies. And the worst; their tender fantasies about soothing his ravaged soul and healing his inner wounds. Hell with that shit. It exhausted him. Celibacy was preferable.

Then he saw the photograph.

The image wiped his mind clean. Those eyes, looking out from the photograph, solemn and calm and compassionate. Full of light.

His angel. The force of those eyes, the shock of seeing her there, it hit him in the stomach like a bull's head, knocking out all his air.

His lungs were sending him signals of distress. He reminded himself to breathe, got oxygen. He lurched forward. Read the name.

MEET THE AUTHOR. EDIE PARRISH. 2:30 PM.

The table was heaped with graphic novels. He locked his knees, tried to stop the drunken swaying. Another black and white headshot, but in this one, her hair was flung back and she wore no glasses. She gazed straight at him. The look in her eyes was a quiet, level challenge.

He had no idea how long he stood in the aisle. If his mouth hung open. People jostled by, inconvenienced by his large body blocking the aisle. He registered their annoyance but he was unable to move.

Edie Parrish was his white-clad angel. No wonder she'd been so small. She'd just been a child, eighteen years ago. Eleven years old.

A beautiful child. Grown up into a beautiful woman.

He stared into those eyes, his brain revving into a strange, altered state. Fear, laced with a strange, unbelieving joy. Dread, too. He would no longer have his magical talisman, so crucial for negotiating the maze of his jerry-rigged mind. If his angel was a flesh and blood person, he could not expect protection from the powers of darkness from her. He couldn't use her like a magic penny if she was a real, live woman, with her own problems, her own bullshit and baggage.

A woman. So fucking beautiful. His hands shook. He was taking this too seriously. He could see that, feel it. But he could not stop it.

How could he have met her? Where? How had he known her? Would she recognize him? Could she know something about him?

No, dumbass. Don't go there. Don't hope that. She couldn't. She was just a child. She was tiny. She could have no clue. None.

A muffled cough caught his attention, and he caught the nervous, gaze of one of the bookstore personnel. *Fake normal, butthead.* He moved closer to the table, picked up a book. He glanced at the cover, felt the delayed jolt to his system. That was a drawing of . . . himself.

Wait. What in the flying *fuck?* Kev rubbed his eyes and lifted the lenses of his sunglasses to peer at the drawing, his body thrumming.

Fade Shadowseeker, Book IV, Midnight's Curse.

Midnight's Curse. The name reverberated inside him like a gong. Whorls of spiky dirt-blond hair, pale green eyes, thin face, flat mouth. His face was scarred, on the right side. No. Not possible. Get a grip.

Hallucinations? Was he messed up enough to justify even this? Maybe he should get stronger meds. Dope his out-of-control imagination into submission. Or get checked out for schizophrenia. Only crazy people thought everything in the world referred to them. Only crazy people heard personal messages in popular songs, TV shows. Or found portraits of themselves on bestselling graphic novels.

But something in him rejected the idea, with visceral horror. He'd admit to being brain damaged, but not crazy. He'd rather be dead. He wouldn't be squeamish. He'd just quietly put himself out of his misery. Insanity was one level of hell he would not stoically endure.

But he wasn't crazy. Stressed out, yes. Sleep deprived, knocked on the head. Of course he thought it was all about him, him, him. Never mind war, famine, and plague. Forget indifference and brutality and climate change and innocent babies dying by the sword. Oh no. His own weird, twisted problems were still the center of the fucking universe.

It was just a sketch. Bold and stylized. A chance resemblance, and Edie Parrish's solemn angel eyes had rattled him. Made it too personal. He just had to get over himself. Take a breath. Lighten up.

He grabbed another book at random. *Fade Shadowseeker, Book I, Midnight's Secret.* The man on the cover had long hair, like his own had been before the waterfall. Green eyes. The right side of his face was puckered with scars, down to his jaw. He could see it more clearly in the close-up. The book shook in Kev's hands. He flipped it open, leafed through quickly, and then more quickly, so that he wouldn't have time to fixate on anything and go into a full-out panic attack.

Every few pages there was a full-page color sketch, between the black and white strips. There was Fade pushing a broom in a desolate industrial warehouse. Fade, seated on a wretched cot in a squalid room, shoulders slumped in despair. Fade, shoehorning himself into a windowless bathroom the size of an upright coffin to wash himself. Leaning over a sink the size of a loaf of bread to splash his scarred face. Staring into a cracked mirror, into eyes bloodshot with trapped despair.

Locked in his own mind, read the thought bubble over his head.

That sink, that cot, that mirror, that bathroom. He knew them like his own hands. That was the room behind Tony's diner.

How had she seen that wretched place? How could she have known? Even Bruno had never gone back there. That stifling room had been his own lonely, private hell. The knot in his belly grew tighter.

The meet-the-author event would begin in about an hour. He looked down at the table, rummaging with a clammy hand until he found Volumes II and III. *Midnight's Scion* and *Midnight's Oracle.*

He found a secluded corner, a rubberized footstool for reaching top shelves. He planted his ass on it, and contemplated his gelatinous thigh muscles while he gathered the courage to open the books.

There's one thing I don't believe in. Coincidences. The words he'd said to Bruno echoed in his head. Problem was, he didn't believe in their opposite, either. Which left him nowhere. Trapped in limbo, suspended in midair. No clue where to stand, what to feel. What he could believe in.

So what else was new.

Midnight's Oracle, Book III, was on top. He cracked it open, near the beginning, to one of the dynamic full-page color drawings. It depicted Fade clinging to a rock in whitewater rapids. He clutched a girl under his arm. The girl struggled, screaming. On the next page, the girl had been saved, but Fade was heading over the waterfall, cartwheeling.

This time, the weirdness rattled him less. Those shock-and-awe hormones could only squirt out full bore a few times, and then the reservoir ran dry, thank God. He picked out Book I, braced for the flock of birds that was going to take flight from the pit of his stomach any minute now. He opened up the book, and began to read.

"Any more questions?" Edie looked around the crowded room. Today's was a talkative, enthusiastic bunch. The ego strokes were nice, but it took energy to be smiling and chatty with a bunch of strangers.

She pointed to a tall girl with dyed black hair and black lipstick.

"Where'd you get the idea for Fade?" the girl asked eagerly. "He's so real! And so intense. Is he based on anybody you know?"

Edie felt her smile falter. "Not exactly," she lied. "He came to me in a dream once, and I never forgot him."

That, at least, was the truth. Fade Shadowseeker had visited her dreams ever since she'd started drawing him, when she was eighteen. It hadn't taken long for those dreams to turn scorchingly erotic.

A redheaded girl jumped up without waiting to be chosen. "Fade is so sexy. I love it that he and Mahlia finally get it on, in *Midnight's Curse,* but then the bad guys abduct her and everybody gets distracted. Are they ever going to, um, you know? Get together? Like, a couple?"

"I don't know yet," she said. "I find out that kind of thing as I go."

The redheaded girl looked disappointed. "But can't you just, like, make them do it?" she said sharply. "I mean, you're the boss, right?"

"Wrong. I'm not the boss at all if the story is working. It's a paradox. But I really hope that Fade and Mahlia get together, too."

"Are you Mahlia?" the redheaded girl demanded. "She looks kind of like you. Is Fade, like, your own fantasy?"

The personal question startled her, and she stuttered. "Um, I, ah . . . no. I never thought of it. I don't particularly identify with Mahlia, no."

She felt bad for lying like a rug, but give a girl some privacy. The redheaded girl subsided, looking unsatisfied. Edie's publicist made a brisk wrap-it-up gesture. They'd run twenty minutes over for the question and answer session, and she hadn't even started signing yet.

The book signing was the easiest part, though she felt silly repeating the same scrawled sentiments on the flyleafs of each book. She made an effort to chat, but it was going to feel good, to sprawl on her couch with a cold beer and a rented movie. Mutants taking over Los Angeles. She loved mutant movies. Couldn't imagine why. Hah hah.

The line was almost finished, and the redheaded girl was coming up next. Edie smiled as she took the girl's battered copy of *Midnight's Curse*. A compliment if she'd ever had one. Out less than a month, and already dog-eared. A generous impulse spurred her to open it to the blank page after the title page. "What's your name?" she asked

"Vicky," the girl said excitedly. "Vicky Sobel."

Edie wrote, *Thanks, Vicky! Here's hoping for Fade and Mahlia, and the triumph of true love. Best wishes, Edie Parrish.* Then she sketched a quick drawing of Fade, with his arm around a woman. For the face, she glanced up to sketch the redheaded girl's pretty, wide-eyed face.

The eye didn't usually open up so quickly. Usually she had a minute or so of grace, but when she looked up from scribbling the flourishes of the girl's curly hair and up into her eyes—she saw it.

Something else. A flash of double vision. Another embrace, except that the girl wasn't embracing a man. She was wrapped in the coils of an enormous, strangling snake. Edie saw the dead girl's face, superimposed over the smiling, live face. Blue eyes staring and empty.

Edie opened her mouth to speak, but her voice stopped. Her heart kicked up, a sick, vertiginous feeling, and she opened her mouth—

"Stay away from Craig," she burst out, her voice shaking.

The girl's face went stiff. "What do you know about Craig?"

"N-n-nothing," Edie stammered. "It just came to me, to say that."

"Why?" The girl leaned over the table. "Why did it come

to you? Are you sleeping with him? Do you know somebody who is?"

"No," Edie said quietly. "I have no idea who this Craig person is. Just that he's poison for you. Drop him. Run away."

"I love Craig!" The girl's blue eyes bulged. "And he loves me! So just . . . stay away from him! Shut your mouth! Don't talk about him!"

Why, oh why, did she do this to herself? Why didn't her psychic gift come with a protective mechanism attached that would let her know if there was any point in giving a warning or not?

"I'm sorry," she repeated. "It wasn't my business."

"Shut up," the girl said, her voice wobbling. "You . . . you nosy bitch." She grabbed her book, and ran, shoving people out of her way.

Edie shuddered, seeing the empty, bulging eyes. Dark marks on her throat. Strangled. God forbid. But maybe, just maybe, being warned might make a difference for her. She could only hope. It made her feel raw, helpless. A mass of antennae, and no off switch.

Except the meds. If she preferred dead calm. No pencils, charcoal, ink. That was her off switch, if she could swallow it. But she couldn't.

She pasted a smile on and looked up—

And forgot the redheaded girl, her deadly lover, and everything else she'd ever thought, or known. Including her own name.

Fade Shadowseeker stood right before her.

CHAPTER
6

Edie rubbed her eyes, looked again. Still there. Still him. He was extravagantly tall, broad, built. His face was thin, his cheeks carved deep under jutting cheekbones. The spiky hair, the flat, grim mouth. The scars. The invisible mantle of controlled power humming around him, brushing against her body like a million tiny tickling fingers, though he was a yard away, across the table.

His eyes wiped her mind blank. That piercing green that laid bare everything it looked upon. She knew that face, though she'd only seen it once. She couldn't mistake those eyes. Those scars. She'd seen the wounds that caused them. She wished that she had not.

She couldn't breathe, couldn't blink. Their eyes were locked. His eyes glowed with some intense emotion. There was an angry crimson spot in one of them. It made the green seem even more intense.

The person behind him in line began to clear her throat. Fade stepped forward and laid down his books. He held out his hand.

She took it, and dragged in a breath at the shivery feeling. It flashed across her skin, like wind rippling grass, rustling leaves. The ringing and dinging of a hundred tiny bells and chimes inside her.

She stared at her hand, swallowed up inside of his. Her publicist approached, coughing discreetly. "Edie? They need to wrap this up."

Edit tried to reply, but a dry squeak came out of her throat. The guy gazed down, unmoving. A monument, a mountain. So silent, and intense. So beautiful. Like glacial lakes, like thundering waves, piled up banks of clouds. Wild animals. The uncontrollable power of nature.

She cleared her throat. "I sign with my right," she told him, her voice thin. "You have to let go, if you want me to, um, sign your books."

He let go. She took her hand back, peeking at it as if expecting it to be somehow changed by that momentous contact, but it was just her usual thin, inkstained paw. She opened his first book, struggling to remember what she was supposed to do. Um. Yes. Signing books. She paused, pen poised over the paper. "Your name?"

Something flashed in his eyes. "You don't know it?"

She stared up at him. How could she? Was she supposed to know it? She shook her head, mutely.

"My name is Kev," he said quietly. "Kev Larsen."

She scrawled something unintelligible to Kev on all four books, and pushed them back. He took them, moved aside politely for the next person, but didn't go away. Oh, God. He was waiting for her. Oh, God.

Excitement bubbled inside her. She was so aware of his presence, looming by the table while she chatted with the last few die-hard fans.

Julie, her publicist, came marching over, and gave the guy a cold look. "Can I help you with anything?" she asked him.

The man ignored Julie. "I was wondering if you would have a cup of coffee with me," he asked Edie. His low, quiet voice was wonderfully resonant. Full of sparkling harmonics that made her body tingle.

Edie hesitated, and Julie chimed in. "Have you two met?"

"Yes," he said. The certainty in his voice brooked no argument.

Julie gave her a sharp look. "Is this true? Do you know this guy?"

Know him? As if she could be said to know him. But she couldn't explain anything so improbable to the practical, nuts-and-bolts Julie. She hadn't even grasped it herself, yet.

She nodded, jerkily. Yeah. She, uh, knew him. Close enough.

"Well, then. I gotta run. Tell me what's going on later, OK?" She shot the man a suspicious look. "You sure you'll be OK?"

OK? Such a bland state of existence, to describe standing five feet from her ultimate fantasy, Fade Shadowseeker, inexplicably made flesh and inviting her out to coffee. She managed to nod.

After Julie's heels clicked purposefully into the distance, Edie shrugged on her coat, grabbed her art bag, and risked another peek.

Sure enough, he got her again. She went blank, wordless, staring stupidly up into those eyes. Frozen by his outsized charisma.

He offered her his arm. The little smile and the courtly gesture broke the spell, thank God. She took it, and they were walking together.

He pulled sunglasses out and put them on. They passed the bookstore coffee shop, but people whose books she'd just signed were there. She shook her head at his questioning glance. "Somewhere else."

They walked out and strolled silently down the block together until they found another coffee shop, this one almost deserted. He held open the door for her, bought them both a cup of coffee at the counter, waited while she doctored hers with various sugary and creamy contaminants, and followed her to a table in the far corner.

He took off his sunglasses, rubbing his eyes. "Sorry

about wearing these indoors," he said. "I know it looks affected, but I had a head injury recently, and the daylight's too bright for my eyes."

"Oh. I'm sorry. Please, put them on if you need them," she urged.

"No, it's OK in here. Not too bright. I've been waiting a long time. I want to see your real colors," was his cryptic reply. She gave him a puzzled look, and he clarified. "I don't want to look at you tinted green."

"OK." Her gaze flicked away. It had been more manageable when he wore the glasses. It was like looking at the sun. His gorgeousness was burning a hole in her retinas. Those eyes. So shockingly bright.

"So," she began, trying to sound brisk. "What's this all about?"

"I was hoping you could tell me," he said.

That left her feeling uncomfortably on the spot. "Tell you what?"

He pulled the Fade Shadowseeker books she had signed for him out of the bookstore shopping bag, and spread them out on the table so all four covers showed. "You seem to know all about me."

Unease deepened. She stared at him. "Those books are fiction," she said. "Completely and absolutely creations of my imagination."

"Yeah?" He opened the third book, *Midnight's Oracle,* and flipped partway through. "See this? Where Fade goes over the waterfall?"

She leaned, looked. "Sure. I drew it. What of it?"

"That happened to me, four months ago," he said.

She blinked helplessly, starting and abandoning a dozen different responses to that preposterous statement. Finally, she flipped the book open to the copyright page, and pointed. "Repeat after me," she said. "All resemblance to real persons or events is purely coincidental."

"It's true," he said quietly. "A matter of public record. It happened on June 24th. Read about it in the online archives of the *Oregonian*."

She wonderered where this game was leading. Maybe into a trap she should be smarter in avoiding. "I wrote that book before that date," she informed him. "A year before. You could have read my book first."

His lip twitched. "You think I staged it? You ever look out over the top of Twin Tails Falls? I broke my arm, my thigh. I wouldn't have done that voluntarily. For any sum of money."

"Oh, and I imagine you saved a teenage girl from drowning right before you fell, right?" she challenged.

He shrugged. "Actually, it was a teenage boy, in my case. I jumped in to help him out. Ask the kid if he pulled that stunt to live out the story in your graphic novel. Might be good for a laugh."

She shook her head. "Coincidence," she repeated.

"I would buy one coincidence, or two, or eight, or fifteen," he said. "But not hundreds of them."

Suspicion grew inside her, and with it, disappointment so intense, it made her throat burn. "I see where this is going," she said. "For the record, I'll tell you right now that I know absolutely nothing about your stupid little life, nor do I want to. Everything I have written or drawn is my own pure, spontaneous invention. So if you plan on suing me—"

"Edie, no."

"That's Ms. Parrish to you, mister, and if you want to sue for plagiarism, or whatever it is you're contemplating, go ahead and try. It happens a lot. It's one of the shittier things about being the daughter of an extremely wealthy man, and you'd be surprised how many shitty things there are about that. After the third time, my dad bought me insurance. I'll give you the numbers of our team of lawyers, if you'd like to save yourself some time." She got to her feet. "As for me, I don't have time for this insulting bullshit. I don't appreciate being accused of—"

"Stop!" He grabbed her wrist, and tugged. "I'm not suing

you! I would never attack you! That's the last thing in the world I would ever do. Please. Sit. Please, Edie."

His voice had a subtle commanding quality that unknit her tension. Her knees gave way, dumping her onto the chair. She yanked her hand away and put both hands in her lap, twisting her fingers til they were bloodless. "So, if that's not it, what do you want from me?"

"I want to tell you a story," he said quietly.

She waited for more, baffled. "A story that you want me to tell in one of my novels? I don't use other people's ideas. I don't need to, because I've got plenty of ideas of my own, and besides—"

"No. I'm talking about my own personal story. Because I think, in some way or another, you already know it."

"You don't get it," she said, helplessly. "I know nothing about you! I didn't even know your name until you told me! Why are you being so cryptic? Tell me what you want! Stop hinting! Stop playing mind games!"

"I would if I could. But I'm at a disadvantage, because I don't know exactly what I'm asking you for."

She wondered uneasily if the guy had mental problems. Gorgeous and charismatic though he might be, he was making no flipping sense at all. "Excuse me?"

He let out a controlled breath, eyes fixed on his untouched coffee.

"I was found, eighteen years ago," he said quietly. "I'd been beaten, tortured. I had some inexplicable brain injury. I wasn't capable of speaking, or even writing, for years. I pushed a broom in a diner, mopped floors, washed dishes. I have no memory of who I was before."

She stared at him, speechless and openmouthed. It was her backstory setup for Book One of the Fade Shadowseeker series.

Not possible, that this man's life had followed the same . . . oh, please. No way. He had to be lying. Had to. Her mind reeled, fought it.

"But I do have dreams," he went on. "Vivid dreams. I've always thought that maybe these dreams were of the life I had before. And one of those dreams is of you, Edie." He reached out, and gently touched the back of her hand. The glancing contact made her shiver.

"Have you seen me before?" he asked. "I think you have. I saw it in your eyes, the moment you saw me. I see it from your books."

She nodded, like a puppet. She couldn't lie to him, nor could she think of any coherent reason for doing so. "A long time ago."

His fingers fastened around her hand. "Tell me."

So she told him what she had to tell; the incident on her eleventh birthday. The bleeding burned man, pleading with Daddy in his Flaxon office eighteen years ago. The security guards that came running. The guard the burned man had thrown through the window. Watching him be dragged away, to an unknown fate.

That was all. It seemed so little, in the face of his hunger for knowledge, but he didn't look disappointed. His eyes were alight with cautious excitement. "Flaxon," he said. "Interesting."

"I had no idea what you were talking about, but it sounded terrible," she finished. "Murder, torture. I had nightmares for years."

"Not my name?" he asked. "You never heard it?"

She shook her head. "I was eleven," she said. "I never heard it said, if anyone knew it. My parents refused to talk about you. I got punished for mentioning you." She paused. "My father might know more," she said. "But I doubt he'd be willing to talk to you about it."

Hah. That was a flipping understatement, if she'd ever made one.

"Christopher Osterman did this to me," he said, touching the scars on his face. "There were others, but he was the driving force."

That, at least, was no surprise. "Dr. O." The name left a bitter taste in her mouth.

"You knew him?"

She nodded. "I did the Haven program, when I was fourteen."

"You don't look surprised to find out he was a psychopath."

"I'm not," she said. "I knew he was rotten. I told my father, but Dad didn't believe me. He thought I was just trying to wiggle out of any efforts to improve myself. Being weak and whiny and defeatist."

"So he made you do the Haven program? Why? What for?"

"I was depressed, doing badly in school," she explained. "Dad wanted to fix me. Soup me up. Dr. O talked a good line, but I don't think Daddy realized exactly what the brain potential workshop entailed. Dr. O stimulated our brains with electricity and drugs, to enhance our mental function. So he said. It was . . . well, it was weird."

Kev's mouth hardened. "Did it work?"

She shivered. "I guess that depends on what you mean by working," she hedged. "You might get in touch with the liaison from Helix to Osterman's research facility, see if they have documentation on the Flaxon era. They might be able to tell you something."

"Hmmm." He looked into his coffee cup.

"I don't understand why you came to me," she told him. "I know so little. I can't help you. With anything."

"On the contrary. You're the only one who ever has helped me."

She gazed at him, blank and bewildered. "How could I?" she demanded, almost angrily. "I did nothing. It was awful to watch that. I felt so helpless."

"You did help," he insisted. "In my dreams."

"Ah! Your dreams!" She laughed, nervously. "It's funny, to get credit for how I behaved in another person's dreams. I don't even know what I did in them, so how can I—"

"You were my angel. When I needed help, you helped me."

She shut her mouth, swallowed. "Um. How?"

"By existing," he said simply.

She grunted. "That's enough? Just to exist? I didn't do anything?"

"You didn't have to do anything. You just were. A beacon in the dark. The only one I had. It saved my sanity, maybe my life. So, thank you."

"Don't thank me," she said. "I can't take credit for that. In my world, you don't get points for what you are. Only what you do."

He shook his head. "Your world is about to change."

Wow. That was bold. The quiet conviction in his voice made her catch her breath. Her toes and fingers were tingling with it.

Toughen up, Edie. "All this woo woo stuff is really spooky and interesting, and great material for a graphic novel, but it's the creation of your own overheated brain," she said crisply. "Just like my own stories are the creation of my own overheated brain. I don't want to be mean, but your dreams have nothing to do with me. So get real, and take credit for being your own damn beacon."

He shook his head. "I might have agreed with you before I read the Shadowseeker books. But I think you've been close to me all along."

She was shredding the edge of her paper coffee cup into a fringe. An unconscious thing she did whenever she didn't have a pencil in her hand. Another of Edie's little closet full of compulsions, as her mother had called them. She tried to stop, then gave into it, and started tearing again. Why not? What the hell? She had nothing to prove to him.

"I'm sorry," he said, watching her precisely tearing uniform strips in the cup's edge. "I didn't mean to make you nervous."

She kept her mouth shut and her eyes on her cup fringe.

The silence grew impossibly long, but she resisted the impulse to pump chatty filler into it. After several quiet minutes, he spoke again.

"What happened, in the bookstore? The girl ahead of me in line?"

The awful memory made her gut clench. "Oh, that," she mumbled. "Just my evil genie, poking out its head."

He waited for more, but she no longer freely confessed what happened when she sketched people. It never went over well. Her parents had gone bananas. Her therapist tried to put her on antipsychotic meds. The one time she'd confessed it to a boyfriend, he'd dropped her flat and never called again. Other friends and lovers had found out, too, when one of her fits came over her. They always had the same reaction, in the end. So she didn't go there, anymore. Not ever.

"Tell me," he prompted, gently.

She opened her mouth, let it fall out. Secrecy seemed irrelevant with this guy. After all, he was already inside her head. He lived there.

"It happens when I sketch," she said. "I sometimes, ah . . . I pick up things. From their heads. I, um, tune into their frequency, I guess."

He didn't look alarmed, or even surprised. "What did you see?"

"I saw her boyfriend strangling her to death," Edie said.

His eyelids contracted, a quick flinch. "Ouch. Jesus," he said. "How reliable are these perceptions?"

"I can't verify all of them," she said. "Of those I can verify, one hundred percent. I've had no luck in changing outcomes, but not for lack of trying. I saw my mother's heart attack, but I couldn't persuade her to go to the doctor. I sketched my father a few weeks ago in a restaurant, and I . . . ah, never mind. So what do you want? An introduction to my father? I'm not really the one to ask, with the low opinion he has of me."

"No." He patted her hand. "I don't want to make difficulties for you. I can get in touch with your father and Helix with no introduction."

"So what do you want, then?" She felt lost.

"Nothing," he said. "Just keep existing."

She narrowed her eyes. "Oh, come on. Give me a freaking break."

A shadow of a smile flashed over his face. "I don't know. You could walk with me." His voice sounded almost shy. "Just keep me company. Talk to me for a while. I like the way it feels. To be with you."

Did he? Wow. He knew all her deepest, darkest secrets, and he wasn't afraid of broadcasting something compromising to her? Was his heart so pure? Was he so fearless, so free of shame? Maybe he just didn't believe her. Maybe he thought she was nuts. That was a classic.

She was flushed, charmed. Was he coming on? She didn't have a lot of experience with come-ons. She wouldn't recognize one if it bit her in the butt. He fell into place beside her on the sidewalk, and they walked in silence. So much for keeping him company. She didn't have a thing to say. She was flustered, bashful.

She reflected on what he'd told her. He was a man who had made his peace with silence and solitude, and it had changed him, made him different from other men. She felt it. With him, silence could be as eloquent as speech. Each silence had its own tone and flavor, its own subtle tints and nuances. Each silence said something specific. And she understood each one. Or thought she did. Maybe she was projecting, or deluded. But she couldn't resist that leap of silent understanding. Raw emotion in the center of her chest. Emotion she could barely control.

Play it cool. This man is a stranger, babbled the shrill voice of reason. She knew nothing about him, except that he was more or less brain damaged, full of weird notions, and intensely interested in her.

She should not be having these trembly, hot, gooey, hope-ful feelings.. It was fatuous. Dangerous. Stupid, too. She was going to get taken for a ride, made to feel like an idiot at best, and worst, who knew?

So run, the voice of reason bleated. Say hey, it's been real. Flag a cab. Sprint. Parrish bodyguards were hovering nearby. They would pick her up, give her a ride home. Lecture her, too. Tell her dad.

He took her hand.

She dragged in air, as energy flashed through her. Every cell in her body got a sharp, wonderful little jolt of it. She tried to breathe.

Her hand liked his hand. Oh, so much. It was big, smooth. Callused skin, like polished wood. Warm and strong. She was too shy to meet his eyes. Her thoughts scrambled helplessly, here and there.

She couldn't bear to pull her hand away. Tingling right-ness flowed from him, right up her arm. It uncoiled slowly through her, swirling, pooling in the classic places. Tighten-ing her nipples. Making her thighs clench, her clit tingle and throb. Just from holding hands.

They walked, silently, hands linked, eyes down. Barely noticing where they went. Over the Steel Bridge, traffic roar-ing around them, but it didn't matter. They were struck mute. Neither was willing to break the surface tension of that huge, gentle shyness. It was a rainbow-tinted bubble. Improbable and lovely. She would just let it float along, shining bright, and enjoy it while she could. It would meet its end soon enough.

Bubbles always did. It was a natural law.

She didn't realize where she was walking until she was standing in front of her own more or less grotty building on NE Helmut Street.

She hadn't meant to bring him home.

Oh, hell. Get real. Maybe she had.

CHAPTER

7

Edie Parrish had loosened gravity's hold upon him. Kev floated beside her, lucky for the touch of that slender hand to anchor him to earth, or he'd float right off up into the sky, as light as a cloud.

He was so jazzed, he could hardly breathe. Edie Parrish blew his mind. So beautiful, so smart. Deep and strong. Thorny like a rose. The photograph hadn't begun to catch all that she was.

His memory of her child self was frozen in time, like a medieval icon, but this Edie Parrish was no icon. She was warm, soft, perfect in every delicate detail. That translucent skin made her look like a forest sylph. Big, expressive silver-gray eyes, rimmed with indigo, shadowed with delicate purple smudges. Sooty lashes. Her face was narrow and delicate, brows dark and tilted up. Her hair a mass of unruly dark waves that brushed the top of her rounded ass.

She dressed down, tried to hide, but she couldn't. Not from him. She shone like a sports stadium spotlight to him. He could extrapolate every tilt and curve from the stretch and swing of those drab, don't-look-at-me clothes. The generous swell of her tits, the length of her slender frame, the way her jeans clung to her ass. She was tall, the top of her head hitting him right at the mouth. If he embraced her, he could nuzzle her hair without bending his neck.

God, how he wanted to. His mouth watered to lean down close, and start memorizing the smells of her scalp, her pelt. He wanted to stare at her in bright sunlight, study the glinting grain of the nap of female hair on her body. Stroke and kiss the hot fuzz in all her hidden places. He clenched his jaw, mouth watering.

He could smell her, too. Every intimate detail of her, with his olfactory capacity on screaming overload. Usually, the excess of private sensory information about strangers' bodies was embarrassing to him.

Not with Edie. Her intimate scents made him dizzy. And rock hard. He'd been dogged by inconvenient sexual impulses since waking up after the waterfall incident, but this made his previous urges look like a mild itch. He'd had no idea what sexual hunger felt like til now.

Every detail of Edie Parrish was deliberately designed to please him, and he'd never even identified any particular preferences before. The hollow at her collarbone made him gulp excess saliva. He couldn't drag his eyes from the lambent glow of her skin, couldn't stop dragging in lungfuls of the honey and milk and flowers scent that hung like a delicate cloud around her. Couldn't breathe it in fast enough.

He wanted to inhale her, drink her up. Lick her all over. Make her relax, blush, and giggle, lose that worried look. She reminded him of animals in the wild; wary, but innately dignified. None of that air of easy entitlement, like so many young people who came from wealth.

He couldn't read her eyes, under that heavy fan of lashes. She probably thought he was out of his mind. Grabbing her hand, like he had the right. He hadn't meant to. He'd just done it.

"This is where I live," she said.

He looked around, surprised. He'd tried to find her address, had not been surprised to find it unlisted. Many would see her as prey.

Not what he'd expected. A shabby, grungy boardinghouse in a run-down neighborhood. He forced himself to let go of her hand, and immediately missed the bright, vibrating song of contact.

She flung back her hair. The gesture looked defiant. "Want to come up?" she asked. "For a cup of coffee, tea? Or, ah, whatever?"

"Yes," he said. Some whatever would be fine. Lots of it.

Her gaze darted away again. "Um. Come on, then." She led him through a chain-link gate, and on a cracked concrete sidewalk around the building, up a creaking outside staircase.

Her apartment proved to be on the fourth floor, opening from a common veranda off the back of the building. It overlooked a cluster of Dumpsters and an unprepossessing alley. There was a scarred deadlock and a single aging knob lock, loose and rattling in the door. He could kick the thing loose with one blow of his foot. Or maybe even his fist.

He wondered what her people were thinking, letting her live in a dump like this. Not that he had any business complaining. Yet.

"Hey! Edie!" An eight-year-old kid scampered up, scrawny and brown, with a tangle of curly black hair and missing teeth. "Will you help me with my history essay? I'm supposed to write about the Louisiana Purchase, but—" He skidded to a stop when he saw Kev.

"Hey, Jamal," Edie said. "Maybe later, OK?"

But Jamal had forgotten his essay. His dark eyes went huge with wonder. "Shit on a stick!" he breathed. "You're Fade Shadowseeker!"

Edie looked embarrassed. "We've talked about this before! Fade is just a character, not a real person! This is Kev." She turned to Kev. "Jamal's my neighbor. He's also my first reader, and my best critic."

"He is too Fade! Look at those scars! Hey, is it true, about you giving a million dollars to the runaway shelter? And beating up that asshole who stiffed Valerie? I heard you knocked his jaw practically off his face before you took her to Any Port. Shit sucking bastard is eating liquid food through a straw. And did you really jump those guys who—"

"Jamal! No! He did not! His name is Kev, and Fade Shadowseeker is . . . not . . . real! Kev is another person! Get it through your head!"

Jamal snorted, utterly unconvinced. "So what's he doing here? You never bring guys here." Jamal turned a disapproving scowl on Kev. "Are you gonna have sex with Edie?"

"Jamal!" Edie hissed, horrified. "Shut up!"

"Fade has sex with Mahlia in Book Four," Jamal confided. "But I always skip that chapter. Girls are gross. Except for Edie. She's OK."

Kev cleared his throat. "Everyone's entitled to his opinion."

"Beat it, Jamal," Edie said sternly. "Or no more computer time. For the rest of your life. I mean it. And I do not want to hear another word about Fade Shadowseeker." Edie's voice was a thread of steel.

Jamal backed away reluctantly. Edie glared until he turned the corner. Then she unlocked her door, and pushed on in.

The scent of the place embraced him right away. Dried rose petals, cinnamon, plant food, potting soil. The pollen of the big bunch of wildflowers in a jar that adorned the cheap wooden table. Scents of soap, bath salts and shampoo floated out of the bathroom, Sandalwood and lavender, at first sniff. The smell of paper, books, ink, pencils.

And Edie herself, overlaying it all. Sweet, warm and female.

It was an amazing scent. It inebriated him. It should be bottled.

Sun slanted through half closed wooden venetian blinds,

striping the walls with slashes of light. The walls were completely covered with drawings, photos, postcards, magazine cutouts. A glimpse into her mind. He wanted to sneak in there, poke around forever. Looking at what she looked at. Studying what she thought about, what she feared and dreamed and imagined. He wanted to know it all.

And here it was. Everything he craved. Laid out like a feast.

Edie closed the door, and watched him check out her humble place. A sweeping glance was all it took. A TV perched on a steamer trunk in one corner. A tiny kitchen barely existed in another corner. Spider plants and begonias dangled from the ceiling. The rest of the room was all about her drafting table, books, and wall collage. One door led to a tiny bathroom, the other to a tiny bedroom, big enough only for a single futon bed and a narrow dresser. Not a problem, since she wasn't in the habit of collecting clothes. She worked in her underwear when it was warm, and in raggedy tights and sweats when it was cold.

"I'm sorry about Jamal," she offered. "He's a really intense Fade fan, and he's having a little bit of trouble separating fiction from reality."

"Not a problem." He looked around at her walls.

"I know what you're thinking," she said.

His mouth twitched. "Do you?"

"You're wondering why a Parrish would live in a hole in the wall like this," she said. "Right?"

"No. I was thinking how your place shows what you care about." He gestured at the drafting table, the books, the shelves of drawing supplies and art monographs. "But since you said it, go ahead. Tell me. Why is a Parrish living in a hole in the wall like this?"

Edie dragged in air, hardened her belly. There was no point in trying to misrepresent the unenviable situation she was in. She'd tried that before. It always blew up in her face, sooner or later.

"This is all I can afford, with no help from my father," she said. "The books are selling well, so it'll get better eventually, but for now . . ." She shrugged. "Parrish money comes with strings attached. I'd have to be good, take my meds, not embarrass anybody, not say anything strange. I've tried, but the meds make me feel half dead. I can't draw when I take them. I don't even recognize myself. My father thinks I'm doing it to spite him." She shook the painful thought away. "So, here I am."

"Here you are," he echoed quietly.

"I'm lucky I make enough money as an artist to afford even this much," she said. "I'm not much good at anything else."

The autumn sun slanted in the window, lighting up his eyes and warming the color into the luminous jade of a glacial lake. She'd never gotten anywhere near his power with her drawings, though she'd tried for a decade. His scars just made his stark male beauty more poignant. They put it in sharp relief, a brutal reminder of his vulnerability.

He was no superhuman. He was real.

His scars made her think of that day that split her life in half. All his revelations were bringing her own long-buried truths to the surface. Things she knew so deeply, she barely thought about them. They were the bedrock of her deepest self, the underlying landscape of her mind.

Seeing the burned man, wounded and desperate, had broken something inside her heart when she was eleven. Something that could never be mended until she could soothe those wounds, and give him the help that he had begged for. She still couldn't. There was nothing she could do for him. But God, how she wanted to. She ached for it.

It was ridiculous. Pathetic. And it was the truth.

She looked down, eyes skittering around the crowded little room. Afraid of looking stupid. Of being judged by him.

She wished she were bolder, more uncaring, more fuck-you-all. But she just wasn't.

She couldn't bear to look at him, and she couldn't bear to look away. Slices of sunlight shifted on the wall as drafts from the warped window moved the blinds. The crystals she'd hung spun rainbow splotches lavishly, everywhere. The space seemed incredibly small. He just stood there. Not twitching, not ill at ease or embarrassed. A silent, powerful presence, patiently waiting for something. Who the hell knew what. She was the jittery one, hoping desperately not to screw this up.

Not even knowing what "this" was. Where she wanted this miraculous turn of events to go. Just one thing was for sure. She didn't want to chase it away. Like she'd chased away every other man she'd ever gotten close to. But it wasn't up to her. It never was.

It was out of her hands, and that made her so scared.

Well. You could ask the man to sit down, suggested a dry voice in her head that sounded suspiciously like her mother.

"Have a seat," she offered. "Can I make you a cup of tea?"

"That would be nice," he said.

"Oh, and yeah. Here." She rummaged in her cupboard, and pulled out a colorful cardboard box. Animal crackers. She placed them on the table. "I know they're ridiculous. My mother would turn over in her grave if she saw me offer these to a guest, but it's all I have at the moment. I keep them for Jamal. He stays here a lot. You know, to use the computer, and sometimes he sleeps on the couch, when his mom is, um, occupied, with her boyfriends. I leave my window open for him, the one with the fire escape, so he has a safe place to do homework when I'm not here." She pulled it shut, latched it. "But, ah . . . not today."

He gave her a smile that made her wish she'd kept her mouth shut. Babbling on about Jamal, like a fatuous fool. "Stop it," she said.

"Stop what?" His low, gentle voice sounded caressing.

She waved her hand at him. "Stop looking at me like that."

"I can't help it," he said. "It's a sweet thing for you to do for the kid. It's a total nightmare from a security point of view, but it's sweet."

"I have nothing here worth stealing," she retorted, flustered. "And I wasn't trying to get your approval, or trying to prove anything to—"

"Of course you weren't. You don't have to. It's obvious."

"What's obvious?" she snapped.

He hesitated. "Who you are," he said. "Your quality. Never mind. I don't want to embarrass you. You don't take compliments well."

"I guess not," she said testily. "Will you please sit down? Eat some of these cookies." She ripped open a box, undid the wax paper, held one out. "Here. Sit down, eat a giraffe. You're making me nervous."

"In a moment," he said. "I'd like to look at your pictures. May I?"

She huffed out a gusty breath. "Be my guest."

She shoved the giraffe into her mouth, and crunched it while he walked the walls. She'd covered the walls with clippings, magazine images, things scribbled on restaurant bills, napkins, paper towels, paper plates. A chaotic, fluttering floor to ceiling collage.

She tried to ignore him by putting the teakettle on, setting up mugs with teabags. All she had was spiced green tea chai. No point in asking if he liked it, since she could offer no alternative.

And then there was nothing to do but wait for the water to boil.

She forced herself to turn around. He was peering at the wine-stained sketch of her father, the one she'd done in the restaurant. She'd almost thrown the ill-starred thing away, because it hurt to look at it.

Then she'd pulled it out of the waste basket, and put it up on the wall. She had to learn to use the information that came to her in this elliptical way. To save people, change things. Not just be a helpless witness to disaster. Throwing the sketch away would mean that she had given in to despair. She wasn't ready for that yet.

"Your father," he said quietly, touching it with his finger. "I recognize him. This is the drawing you told me about? The prophetic one that you did of him at the restaurant?"

His perception startled her. "I wouldn't go so far as to call it prophetic," she forced out. "How did you know that was the one?"

"It gave me cold chills. The other sketches of him didn't."

No other person had ever had an independent reaction to one of her "charged" drawings before. It felt strange. Not entirely good.

He prowled her space, peering at her things and drawing his own imponderable conclusions about her. He wouldn't sit. She wanted that leopard-about-to-pounce energy to settle, so she could breathe.

"I don't know what to do with you," she blurted.

He shook his head. "You don't have to do anything."

She rushed on. "I'm sorry I don't know more about your past. The only thing I could possibly do would be to ask my father, but I'll tell you right now, that's not as simple as it sounds. He's angry at me, and defensive about that incident with you, and I have no idea what else, if anything, he knows about it. And in any case, you might have more luck asking him independently of me. He hates . . . this. This whole situation." She gestured towards the wine-stained sketch. "The drawings. The things I see, the things I say. It freaks him out, and I don't blame him." She approached the wall, and stared at the sketch. "I saw that he's in danger, but I don't know from what, and I can't warn him. It would just infuriate him. I'm useless to him, just like I was to my mom. And you."

Tears started into her eyes. "As useless as I was the first time you saw me."

"You were not useless."

She shot him an ironic look, but the blazing force of his gaze startled whatever sarcastic thing she was going to say out of her head.

"You've been in my dreams for eighteen years," he said. "You were my angel. Leading me, hiding me, protecting me. Jesus, you even had a halo. What were you wearing on your head that day, anyhow?"

"I had on a white flower wreath," she admitted. "With tinsel and baby's breath. And white ribbons."

His throat bobbed. "I remember a halo. Like a medieval saint."

"Um." She swallowed. "I'm, ah . . . I'm no saint."

"Oh." He cleared his throat. The silence abruptly got very thick, almost stifling. "Well. Ah. Thank God for that."

The teakettle started to whistle. She was pathetically grateful for the distraction. A reason to turn her burning face away. Her hand wobbled as she poured, thinking what a disappointment the real Edie was going to be to him, after his shining angel projections. No woman could live up to that, let alone an awkward weirdo like herself. He'd cop to the truth soon enough. How unsure of herself she was, how prone to sadness, how liable to mope. He'd be creeped out by the weird things that popped out of her mouth at the most inopportune moments.

It was doom in the making. No way to swerve.

And even so, she was so physically aware of him, she couldn't breathe. Couldn't think. All the oxygen in the room was on fire.

She placed his mug on the table, sat down, and sipped her own, although it blistered her mouth. Steam rose in a shaft of light that sneaked through blinds. He sat, and waited in silence for what seemed like an hour, though it was probably just a few minutes. Not touching his tea. "There is something you could do for me," he finally said.

"There is?" Her heart thudded, her face went hot. She gulped some chai, dragged in a deep breath, held it. Never before had she so desperately wished that she'd inherited her father's ironclad poise.

"Draw me," he said.

Shock, disbelief, disappointment, all jostled for place. She gazed at him stupidly. "Excuse me?"

He didn't repeat himself, just swept a look around the wall collage. "Like what you did to that girl in the bookstore."

"You want me to do that? Deliberately? For you?"

He nodded.

A breath hissed out between her teeth. No one had ever solicited that from her. As if it were a service of some kind. A desirable thing. It was as if someone handed her a baseball bat, and said, "hit me."

So. He didn't want hours of hot, pounding sex. Draw me, he said. It was nice, complimentary, gratifying. But it wasn't "Do me."

So he wasn't interested in her romantically. He wanted to use her like a human divining rod. So? At least he was honest. It wasn't his fault she was a knot of sexual deprivation. Nor was it his problem.

Neither was the fact that she'd been having dreams about sex with Fade Shadowseeker for years. Erotic dreams that made the honest efforts of real, normal guys pale in comparison, which effectively ruined any chance of a real love life. But probably Kev Larsen himself could never live up to Fade's imaginary sexual prowess. Just like she could never live up to his shining angel. That knife cut both ways.

They were just people. She had to face reality. That was what he was trying to do. It took guts to tune in to Edie Parrish's Grim Reaper radio show. She admired his bravery, in spite of feeling . . . well, stupid.

And hot. And damp. Her hair was sticking to her neck.

"It doesn't work the way you seem to think," she explained, in a halting voice. "It's very imprecise, very impressionistic. It's not like I get a clear picture of somebody's future, or their past. I just get glimpses of what's on their mind, or I see something that they're trying to suppress, like I did with the girl in the bookstore. I won't see your lost memories, because you won't be broadcasting them. So don't get your hopes up, because I don't think that I—"

"You saw me going over a waterfall fourteen months before it happened." He reached for one of the graphic novels he'd lain on the table, opened *Midnight's Secret* and leafed until he found a specific picture. He turned the book to her. "Look. See that?"

It was a full-page color drawing from the beginning of the story. Fade, languishing in his mute exile, staring at himself in the shattered bathroom mirror. "Yeah?" she said. "And?"

"That mirror? See those cracks in it? That was my mirror, in the the bathroom of the place where I lived for seven years. You drew the pattern of the cracks exactly, Edie. Right down to this missing chunk here. That angle, those proportions. They're mathematically exact."

She shook her head, but he persisted. "You might wonder how I remember details like that, but I didn't have much else to think about. I studied cracks in the mirror. I memorized the peeling paint. I remember the precise shape of the water damage on the ceiling."

"Oh." She swallowed. "I, um, don't know what to say."

"I'll take you there and show you, if you want. You can compare."

"That won't be necessary," she said hastily. "I, ah, believe you. It's just that I don't want to raise false hopes."

He let the book drop. "I wouldn't call it hope, exactly. It's just a door to knock on. Anything at all would help me, Edie. Anything."

She tore her gaze away, and the wrench felt physical. She was sick with nerves. God knows, she'd disappointed enough people in her life. All the important ones. She couldn't bear to disappoint him, too.

He waited for a long moment. "I've spent more than half my life in a room with the windows painted over," he said, his voice tight with emotion. "If you showed me one ray of light, from any direction, past, present, future, whatever, I would kiss your feet. Shower you with praise, worship at your shrine. Be in your debt forever. Get me?"

She cleared her throat. "The theatrics won't be necessary," she said primly. "I'd be glad to help. Just don't expect too much."

"Not at all," he said. "Anything is fine. And if you don't see anything, I'll be grateful to you for trying."

She busied herself by pouring her half drunk tea into the sink. Then she grabbed her pen, and the largest of her sketchbooks. Something inside her was already rubbing its hands together, eager to get to it. She craved it. Finally, she could play. No boundaries, no rules, no fear. No one would yell at her to stop. No one would be scolding her, or forbidding her, or freaking out on her. She didn't have to draw fast, to grab an image before her head started tuning into the broadcast.

She could take her own sweet time. Just go to that place and linger there, feeling so whole and centered and alive. Play there, for as long as she wanted. Let the broadcast roar. He'd asked for it.

As long as it wasn't something scary and horrible. Doubt stabbed through the rising euphoria, but the hunger was stronger. She'd been chained for so long. She couldn't even imagine how it would feel to be loose. The sense of freedom made her almost dizzy.

He looked shy. The first time she'd seen a crack in his perfect poise. "Uh . . . how do you want me . . . what do I do?" he asked.

"Whatever you want," she said. "This was your idea."

She waited, but he looked so lost, she finally took pity on him. "Take off your coat." She grabbed a chair, and set it in the middle of the room, if a room so small could be said to have a middle. "Sit here."

He got up, shrugged off the coat, held it like he had no idea what to do with it. She grabbed it, tossed it, and gave his chest a shove to encourage him to sit. The wool of his sweater didn't shield her hand from the shock of contact.

They both gasped, and stopped breathing for a second. *Whoa.*

He sank into the chair. Such long, stong legs. His thick muscles showed through his jeans. Nothing he wore was meant to show off his body, but the graceful drape and fold of fabric as it settled over him revealed it anyway. He'd look good in anything he wore. His hands were beautiful, too. Long, graceful fingers. And his chest. So wide. She'd felt the taut, coiled strength of him in that instant that her fingers had touched him. Oh, boy. Concentrate, Edie. *Concentrate.*

He looked intensely self-conscious, which gave her a flash of tenderness. She leafed through her sketchbook for a blank page and sat for a moment, letting the pencil point dance on empty air. So nice, not to have to hurry. No short-cuts. She was used to using the fewest pen strokes possible. Not today. She could indulge herself. Take her time.

Tingling rightness filled her hand as she set pen to paper, and almost instantly, the small, nervous Edie faded away, submerged in something larger, stronger. Unafraid. And perfectly, utterly happy.

She'd drawn Fade Shadowseeker thousands of time, because it made her happy to draw him. Kev Larsen was Fade's image in every detail, but drawing Kev was infinitely more satisfying. He pulsed out those macho, charismatic vibes right before her very eyes. She didn't have to dredge images up from the depths of memory, or flesh them out with hopeful imagination. He was right there, offering infinite entry points into this drawing and a thousand future drawings.

She was so accustomed to reaching, yearning. Grasping for something as fleeting as smoke. Kev was rock solid, real. Right there.

She was having so much fun nailing down the details, she hardly felt the inner eye open up. It was so smooth, a natural extension of her regular perceptions. She was concentrating on the flare of his back, the breadth of his shoulders, the elegant jut of his cheekbone beneath the mottled webwork of scars. She sketched his nose, the grooves bracketing his mouth. And his eyes, over and over. Trying to catch the luminous flash, the fabulous effect of captured light. She wanted more; the patterns of his body hair, the shape of of his nipples, the way his pants rode on his hips. She wanted these things . . . right . . . *now.*

"Would you take off your sweater, please?"

It popped out of her, in the offhand tone of an artist making a request of a professional model. Then it hit her, how provocative the words must sound to him. He was no artists' model. He looked startled.

"Never mind," she said hastily, her face burning. "Don't."

"No, no, it's OK," he muttered, but he looked lost and nervous as he fumbled for the bottom of his sweater. She opened her mouth to beg him to stop, but he yanked the sweater off with a jerk. Too late.

She choked on whatever she was going to say. And then forgot it.

He was covered with scars. He was lean, every tendon, muscle and sinew of his body on display, and the skin of his entire torso was crisscrossed with a tracery of silver scars, in eerily regular patterns. Someone had cut him, all over. Burned him, too.

She started to shake.

It was no surprise. She'd seen the shape he was in that day

eighteen years ago. Bloodied, blistered. It had been obvious, even to the sheltered child that she had been, that he had been cut and burned.

But it hadn't sunk in how badly. Not completely. Not until now.

It slipped through her guard, and stabbed deep. Her throat got hot and tight, her eyes foggy. The pen hovered over the paper, uncertain of its next stroke. He swam in and out of focus.

"I'll put it back on," he said. "I didn't mean to freak you out."

"No," she murmured, her voice froggy. Tears had fallen on the drawing, blurring the lines of his chin. She flipped the notebook over to a fresh page, wiping her eyes with the backs of her fingers. She could see from the murk on her knuckles that she'd smeared ink on her face, but she couldn't be bothered with it. "Let me, ah, just finish this."

She took a deep breath and put her emotions aside, to open herself to what the drawing wanted. And as she did, the hum of awareness suddenly reached the threshhold of her conscious mind.

The receiving tower was open. It had been for a while. But oh, my God. This was absolutely different than her usual experience.

She wasn't picking up any mental static, because he wasn't broadcasting any. He wasn't obsessing about the past, or worrying about the future. His mind was clear, sharp. As focused as a laser beam. Focused, completely and entirely upon . . . her.

Her lungs froze, her thigh muscles clenched. *Her.* That was what he was thinking and feeling. That was all he was thinking or feeling. It flooded through her, each wave higher, deeper. Her. Just Edie.

His face did not change. His mouth was flat. He did not look at her. She had a feeling he did not dare. He rested his hands on his knees, clenching his hands into fists, unclenching them. Each pulse made the taut, sinewy muscles in his arms and shoulders contract.

Desire. The burning ache of it. The awareness created a feedback loop. She was aware of herself through his eyes. Her smell, her body, her hair, her eyes, her hands, perceived through the lens of his perceptions and feelings. His hunger to touch her, seize her. Take her.

She could hardly fathom it. He wanted her. Shy, invisible Edie. She'd never seen herself as desirable. She could pass, on a good day, if somebody else dressed her. But she seldom tried to attract attention. She'd cultivated invisibility for most of her life. She had no experience navigating wild desire. His hunger triggered an answering ache, so sharp it made her want to whimper.

She tried to breathe. Her lungs were locked.

The tendons in his neck stood out. The air was cooling as the sun sank. Dusk deepened, leaching the gold glow out of the room.

His chest had goosebumps. His nipples were taut, dark. She pictured herself running her hands over his chest. Feeling those tight nubs against her palms. Bending to feel them with her lips, her tongue.

He felt it. She saw his throat bob, his fists clench. His response sharpened hers, making the loop hum, sing, surge sharply in volume.

Another shock. He sensed her feelings, too. Her eyes flicked down, to check if he was . . . oh, my goodness, yes. Most definitely.

He caught her peeking. He'd been resting his forearms discreetly over his thighs, but when he caught that furtive glance, he let his hands flop outwards, palms up, so she could see that long, thick club trapped in denim against his thigh. There could be no secrets in that field of pure, naked emotion and sensation that shimmered between them.

Well. At least there was no question about his sincerity.

No faking that. The force of his desire battered against her. In a way, it was nice. Not to have to wonder if the guy was just being, well, polite.

She licked her lips. "You can, ah, go ahead and put on your shirt," she ventured, her voice breathless and thin. "You must be cold."

"I'm not cold."

She forced out air in a jerky sigh. "OK, let me try that one again. You should put on your shirt because *I'm* the one who's getting hot."

He just looked at her, his throat working.

"I'm sorry," she said. "I didn't pick up any clues about your past, or future, or anything. All I could hear was . . . ah . . ."

"Yes," he said. "I know what you heard."

Her face was bright red. "It was, um, loud."

"I couldn't control it," he said. "I didn't mean to scare you."

"You didn't." Her voice came out savagely loud. She might be flustered, staggered, blown over backwards by him—but not afraid.

He leaned over, picked up the sweater that was pooled on the ground beside him. "I should go," he muttered. *Before I do something stupid* was the corollary thought. She heared it as if he'd voiced it.

"No, don't!" she pleaded, panicked. She dropped the sketchbook, put one leg in front of the other until she stood in front of him. She put her hand on his hot shoulder, and did not permit it to skitter off. His hot life force pulsed into her palm. Making the hunger sharper.

"Don't go," she whispered.

CHAPTER
8

Desmond congratulated himself once again as the shiny black late-model BMW with tinted windows pulled into the lot. Probably armored, knowing that paranoid son-of-a-bitch. He was fucking brilliant. Dr. O would be proud. With one stroke, he solved all his logistical problems. He just wished he'd come up with it before he'd run through his own personal fortune to feed Ava's ravenous world domination machine. But it was all right. He'd come out way ahead.

Four people got out of the car. His old Haven pal, Tom Bixby, had gained weight. He'd always been burly, but he'd packed some fat onto an already big body. His face was thicker, broader, redder. Des stood straight, feeling very good about his own fit, trim, muscular form.

Tom was accompanied by two men, whose taut, watchful faces betrayed their status as bodyguards. A whippet-slender Asian man with a gleaming black ponytail, and a huge, lantern-jawed man with a bushy mustache. The fourth was a slender girl with dreadlocks, tight jeans, a silver studded belt, multiple tattoos, and many facial piercings.

So Tom had brought his own disposable test subject upon whom the effects of X-Cog could be independently verified.

Des hoped that Tom had chosen her according to Ava's criteria. Intelligent, creative, unconventional thinker. Statistically, those qualities produced the best interfaces. And being without significant friends or family helped, too.

He approached Tom, and did the requisite manly hand shaking, half-hugging and backslapping. "Great to see you, man."

"Yeah, likewise. Looking good, buddy," Tom responded.

Des realized, as they sized each other up, that it genuinely was good to see him. Certain things only Club O could understand. The survivors. The weak ones were already dead. Drug ODs, alcoholism, suicide, even some brain tumors. Dr O's training wasn't for pussies.

Nope, just winners, bound for the very top. You had to be tough to have fun. It was a relief, to be with someone who got it. That was one of the many things that drew him to Ava. Aside from her brilliance, her beauty, and the endlessly inventive sex games. The fact that she was out of her gourd, well, it was a small price to pay. And in any case, sanity as society defined it just meant being mentally hog-tied. Ava was free. Like himself, like Tom. An elite, free brotherhood of winners.

"So. How's life in the mercenary army business?" he asked.

"We prefer to think of ourselves as a private military company."

Right. Whatever Tom called it, it was worth hundreds of millions. Private, apolitical, and utterly confidental, it offered VIP protection, air transport, super high-tech intelligence gathering, state of the art weaponry, the power to quietly influence world events, if the price was right. All apparently legal and aboveboard. Tom kept his ass rigorously covered. No consequences. It was another of Dr. O's mottos.

"I brought a couple colleagues along," Tom said. "This is Ken Wanatabe, ex-Navy Seal, and Richard Fabian, ex-Ranger, my private security team. They are absolutely discreet. And this . . ." He gestured at the girl. "This is Keira. She's my inspiration, I guess you could say."

"Really?" Des shook the girl's cool, slender hand. "How's that?"

"I've recently become a patron of the arts," Tom confided. "Keira blew my mind with her Web site. I've been trying to persuade her to sign on to be my assistant, but I haven't had much luck. I need creative people, but she's so damn independent, you know? What's a guy to do?"

"I can't," Keira said sternly. "I'm an artist, not a gofer girl." She fixed Des with a challenging glare, dreadlocks flipping. "I'm helping Tom out to make money I can plow back into my own project."

Des put on a fascinated face. "Really? And what project is that?"

"Performance art," Keira announced. "I'm doing a multimedia art installation that explores female auto-eroticism, and how it's changing in today's world of superfast communication. My project's named 'Weird New World.' I get tons of hits a day on my Web site. It's, like, taking off. And, ah, so." She shrugged. "I'm, like, busy."

"That's amazing," Des said, in admiring tones. "So is that how Tom found you? Through your Web site?"

"I'm telling you, I'm a convert," Tom said solemnly. "You should see some of the crazy shit in Keira's Web site. I'm hooked."

Des chuckled as he led the group into the the big, bland warehouse building that camoflauged Ava's secret lair. He led them through the underground tunnels, opened the door of the lab he'd run through tens of millions of dollars building and operating for Ava.

The secret room was a traditional enough looking lab, filled with X-Cog and related equipment. But one angle had a plushy chaise longue, a screen shade artfully angled against the bright glare of the lights, a stereo, a well-stocked bar. Ava liked her comforts.

"This, ladies and gentlemen, is Ava Cheung," he announced.

Ava burst out right on cue, smiling brilliantly. Her hair swung loose, her eyes were mysteriously shadowed, her lips gleamed. Her silk blouse was too tight, riding up to show off her taut belly. No bra. Her nipples poked pertly through the shiny fabric. Dirty slut. No shame.

God, how he loved that about her.

Des turned to watch the reaction. The men stared, mouths slack. Ava had rendered herself particularly stunning. In fact, he was getting a tingle in his own crotch. He shot a glance at Keira, expecting the lemony mouthed, door-slammed-shut vibe that Ava tended to bring out in women, but Keira's eyes were fully as dazzled as the three mens'.

Ava's eyes flicked to his as she gave Tom an apparently welcoming hug and the necessary it's-been-so-long chitchat. She jerked her chin in Keira's direction, asking the question with her eyes.

He answered with a nod. A new toy. Time to play.

Ava's delighted smile got even more brilliant. She shook hands with everyone, saving Keira's for last, and then hung onto the girl's, holding it with both of hers. Keira gazed back, enthralled.

"Des, why don't you show your old friend around the lab?" Ava said, without breaking eye contact with the girl. "I'll just go have some girl talk with Keira. Can I get you something to drink? Coke, Diet Coke, mineral water? Or I could brew you some coffee, or tea."

Keira allowed herself to be towed toward the cushy bar corner. Des led Tom around, explaining X-Cog while simultaneously listening to the women's conversation. Mental multitasking was one of Dr. O's many gifts to him. He tracked Ava's questions, Keira's babbling answers, Ava's admiring interjections. Hot water gurgled as a pot of tea was prepared. He heard the delicate clink of the Japanese ceramic tea service.

The moment of truth was at hand. Ava was about to administer the preliminary drug. She slanted him a questioning smile.

He turned to Tom. "I assume we're going for independent verification with your own hand-selected test subject?" he asked quietly, just to be dead sure they were all on the same page.

"As you suggested," Tom said. "I'm still wondering what happens to her after, though. You weren't real clear about that."

Here came the tricky part. "Well, I specified that you not be overly attached to the subject, didn't I?"

"You didn't explain why." Tom's voice was flat. "So, why shouldn't I be attached? What happens to her?"

"It's a problem we have, with the side effects," Des explained. "In order to make it possible to give you, a beginner, a chance to personally effect an X-Cog interface, we have to give the subject an extremely concentrated dose of the drug. To lower her resistance to the max."

"Which means?"

"It means there isn't going to be any 'after' for her," Des said, regretfully. "Too bad, about Weird New World. The world really needs a more aggressive exploration of female auto-eroticism."

"Too bad." Tom processed that with equanimity. "Tell me more."

"Another thing," Des said. "We don't have any procedure in place for, ah . . . disposal."

"We'll handle the disposal issue today." Tom waved a dismissive hand. "And if we should end up doing business, I can get something in place for you with continuity. If I conclude the project has potential."

"Of course," Des murmured. He looked forward intensely to watching Tom's jaw drop when he saw the floor show. He glanced at the two men pacing behind him. "And them?"

"They're up for anything I find necessary or convenient," Tom said. "It's in their interests to be discreet."

Des didn't enjoy letting strangers witness the X-Cog demo, but Tom knew how to cover his ass. Tom had been one of Dr. O's protégé's. Des trusted the guy, insofar as he trusted anyone.

That was why they'd hung out back in their Harvard days. They both understood the power that their augmented mental faculties and their freedom from moral and ethical limitations had bestowed upon them. Dr. O had taken away their limitations, making them . . . well, godlike, in a way. It sounded overblown, but it was literally true.

And they were always so careful, when they played their little games. Consequences were for dickheads, idiots, and losers.

But as with any great gift, this one, too, came with its burden of solitude. It was good, to be with someone who understood.

"Keira? Are you all right?" Ava's voice cut through his reverie.

He spun, to see Keira swaying on her feet, her hand to her throat. "I feel . . . I feel . . ." She choked, coughed. "I feel . . . ah . . ."

Her voice trailed off. The teacup she held dropped, shattered. Her eyes were wide and glassy.

"Oh, no! You're feeling sick? Come over here, let me see what I can do for you," Ava crooned, grabbing her arm. "You feel faint? Here, sit down on this chair." Ava plunked the girl down into one of the wheeled office chairs. "Put your head down between your knees."

Over the girl's head, Ava pulled out a syringe, flourished it for their benefit, and drove the needle into Keira's arm. The young woman squawked, her body arched. Ava accompanied her body down into the chair, forcing her to bend at the waist. *Thud,* she landed heavily.

"It will take ten minutes for me to set up the electrical

contacts," Ava said. "A little longer than usual, with those dreadlocks. Des, could you get these gentlemen drinks from the bar in the meantime?"

A tap to the brake lever on the wheels of Keira's chair, and Ava pushed the chair, rattling over the white tiles, into the viewing room.

When the door shut behind her, Des pushed the buttons to open the viewing screen, and got the men set up in comfortable chairs, frosty beers in hand. Tom watched Ava apply her master crown and don double-view goggles. On her, they looked almost stylish. She attended to Keira's crown, glancing up at the video camera from time to time to give them sunny smiles, finger fluttering waves.

"I'm ready," she called. "Did you pick out a text, Tom?" Her sweet, husky voice issued from the speakers, loaded with sexual promise.

"Sure did," Tom said. "Does Ava speak German?"

Des snorted. "Ava has lost count of the languages she speaks. Dr. O got heavy into language acquisition in the early nineties."

"Good." Tom pulled a folded piece of paper out of his pocket, and handed it to Des. "Because I know Keira doesn't speak it."

Des ran the paper into the viewing room, walking behind Keira, who was swallowing convulsively. A sign that she was conscious, aware, and fighting with every muscle that would still move. Paradoxically, that made the interface more profound. Sometimes it was clenched fists, or drumming feet, or a taut grimace. Those were the good ones. The ones that went limp right off the bat were no sport.

Keira was a winner. Too bad she'd be dead of intracranial bleeding by nightfall, if she wasn't euthanized first. Ava usually gave the girls an injection that ended it all before they started bleeding out their noses and ears. Less cleanup.

But Keira would put on a nice show before it came to that.

Des sat down and lifted his own beer to his lips, comfortably conscious of having done his part and earned his just reward.

Ava unfolded the scrap of paper and scanned it. She looked up at the camera, eyes bright with amusement. "Interesting choice."

"Get on with it, please," Tom called out impatiently.

Ava turned to face Keira. She composed herself, her beautiful face freezing into a mask of concentration.

Keira lifted her head. Her eyes were darting frantically to the right, the left, up, down, as if she were following the flight path of a crazed housefly. She began to speak. Her voice was hoarse, and pitched slightly lower than Keira's own voice had been, but the words came out smoothly. Des started to chuckle when he recognized the text of *Mein Kampf.* An odd, twisted choice. But strangely appropriate.

They quietly listened while Keira recited the first couple of pages of Hitler's manifesto in flawless German, without a pause or a hitch. There was a moment of silence after she stopped.

"Impressive," Tom murmured.

Tom was playing it cool, but Des knew the guy was hooked. Now it was just a matter of reeling him in, hammering out terms. He took a swallow of beer. "Just you wait. You haven't seen anything yet."

Ava turned to the camera. "I need a volunteer for the next phase," she said. "To demonstrate the combat possibilities of X-Cog. Is one of you three gentlemen man enough to face me? Or, that is to say, us?"

Tom frowned, startled. "Combat? What? You mean, with her?"

"Ava is trained in several martial arts disciplines," Des said.

Tom shot a glance at his men. "Richard? Ken? Any takers?"

"I'm not attacking a girl," Fabian said. "Keira can't weigh more than one fifteen. I'm two seventy. Forget it."

Tom looked at Ken, who shook his head. "Fucking ridiculous."

"Such gallant gentlemen!" Ava's voice sang out of the speakers. "How about if whoever challenges us accepts a handicap? Give Keira a weapon. Would that preserve your masculine dignity?"

Ken still looked dubious, but Tom pulled a long-bladed knife out of an ankle sheath, and handed it to Ken. "Go do it, Ken. It's an order."

Ken took the knife, shooting a final, eye-rolling glance as he jerked the viewing room door shut behind himself. Keira rose to her feet and took the blade, though her eyes still darted frantically.

Then she sank gracefully into a crouch, and lifted her arms into guard, awaiting Ken's offensive.

Ken lunged, making a half-hearted jab towards Keira's face, and grunted at her whip-quick parry. She lunged with the knife, and Ken reeled back with a shout of outrage, countering with desperate kicks and parries as Ava/Keira pressed him back, slashing and jabbing, driving him around the room.

Ken finally got in a lucky grab, and seized Keira's slender arm in a kotegaishi hold, sending her flying. She smashed into the wall and fell to the ground like a puppet with cut strings, gasping and twitching.

"Truce!" Ava called out. "You knocked the contact sensors loose and compromised the interface! Time out while I fix it."

"That fucking bitch *cut* me!" Ken bellowed, holding up his forearm. An angry gash dripped blood down his forearm.

"Sorry," Ava said solicitously. "But I had to push, or you wouldn't have gotten a meaningful sense of the possibilities. I did have the element of surprise. And if you're using another person's body for your fight, you cancel out the element of mortal danger to one's own person. It's an amazing paradigm shift. It makes you immortal, in a sense. Because the body doing the actual combat is essentially disposable."

"Take your paradigm shift and stick it up your ass," Ken growled.

"Aw. Don't be that way." Ava pulled a handful of gauze squares off a shelf, and unrolled some surgical tape. She moved closer to Ken than she needed to be to wind the tape around his forearm, and smiled at him through the X-Cog glasses. "I promise the next part of the demo will be much easier on your nerves."

"Next part?" Ken looked alarmed. "No fucking way."

"A nicer part," she said smokily. "I promise. Just let me adjust Keira's crown, and reestablish the interface. You'll see. Wait."

And Ken Wanatabe waited, docile as any well-trained dog told to sit and stay. Most men responded to Ava that way.

Des and Tom looked at each other. "So?" Des prompted, though he knew the answer. He could see from the hungry gleam in Tom's eyes.

"What's the catch?" Tom demanded.

Des chose his words carefully. "Our problem is cerebral damage due to the side effects. Keira got a maximum dose because I wanted you to try crowning yourself. She'll have a narrow window. Maybe an hour, maybe more. If Ava was the only one crowning, we could have gotten away with a lower dose, and Ava could have played her for hours. Ava says it's like riding a bronco in your mind. Difficult, but exhilarating."

Tom's eyelids crinkled, liking it. "Hmm. An hour? Long enough to do a job, if it was planned well."

"More than long enough," Des agreed.

"We'll want an exclusive contract," Tom said.

"Oh, let's work out all the gritty details later," Des said, expansively. "I just wanted to, you know. Unleash your imagination."

Tom's mouth twisted. "It's running wild and free, buddy."

Des exulted inwardly. "Ava's been experimenting with nonpharmacological techniques, too, to lower the test subject's natural resistance, both surgically and with electrical stimulation," he said. "In the hopes of making the interface less lethal. Making them reusable."

"Brain wiping?"

"Essentially," Des said. "But the results aren't promising. It seems like the better the overall function of the brain, the better the interface."

"One-time deal," Tom said. "Crown 'em, use 'em, toss 'em."

Tom did not seem overly distressed with that scenario, Des was relieved to note. "Exactly. If one should end up in the emergency room or the morgue, the results look like pinpoint cerebral aneurisms. It's the brain bleed and swelling that gets them."

Tom pondered. "Expensive. But not insurmountable."

"I'm glad you feel that way. But Tom. You're missing the good part. Ava is amazing when it comes to fine motor control, even of vestigial muscles. Take a look."

Tom glanced at the screen, and did a double take. "Holy fuck!"

Des drained his beer. "Behold, a miracle of science. Do you know how hard it is for Ava to make her do that? It never occurs to us how compex a process it is to unfasten a belt and unbutton pants, though we do it every day. And look. She's added another ball to the juggling act. Or two balls, I should say." Desmond chuckled at his own wit.

Richard Fabian was fingering his crotch, face flushed, clutching his beer bottle with a white-knuckled hand as he stared at the screen.

"Go join them," Des urged the man, benevolently. "Ava won't mind accommodating you. She's a great multitasker."

Fabian didn't have to be asked twice. He was already

wrenching his belt loose as he slapped the door to the inner room open.

"And the sex show? Is it to show me the X-Cog possibilities for high-end recreation?" Tom asked.

Des laughed as the twosome reconfigured itself into a threesome. "No, Tommy, this is just for fun. The look on your face, pal. Priceless. Oh, and by the way. I need a favor. Ava and I have a project planned this evening, to streamline our lives and liberate some funding. Nothing complicated. We need a little tactical support. Could we use your personnel?"

"What's the project?" Tom didn't look away from the screen.

"The CEO of Helix is bugging us," Des said softly. "Charles Parrish. Tonight is his retirement banquet. His daughter Edie is going to be there. She's mentally imbalanced, disinherited, disgruntled. She'll be bringing a vial of Tamlix 12, apparently, to get rid of old Daddums. We need someone who can impersonate catering staff to administer it. Your man Ken would look convincing in a catering uniform. He'd pass, as an out-of-work actor."

"Um, sure. Brief us after." Tom dragged his eyes away from the spectacle on the screen with visible effort. "Clarify one thing for me. You mentioned that you needed a supply of research subjects. What for?"

Des was taken aback. "Uh . . . well, to make the technique more cost effective. Making the subjects reusable would reduce loss of life."

"But not necessarily costs," Tom said. "I can get girls cheap, in bulk, from ex-Soviet Bloc countries. In fact, I've got a contact who has fresh meat to sell right here, locally. We'll pay more when there's a middleman, but further down the line, when we work out the kinks, we can trim that expense way down. What's the point of more research? You've got a finished product right here. All you need is a supply of disposable final executors. Just a little mind-set shift, you know?"

"Great," Des said enthusiastically, watching Tom's eyes dart back to the screen. "I knew I could count on you for a fresh take on all this." He reached down, discreetly, and turned up the volume of the amplifier connected to the mikes in the inner room.

The soundtrack swelled. Male snorts, growls. Pleading feminine gasps and squeals. A backdrop of wet, rhythmic slapping sounds.

Tom cleared his throat, swallowing hard. "Transport is the tricky part," he said. "It would be easier to set up a clearing center directly abroad. No transport hassles, no overhead. We'd deliver the girls on a case by case basis, to wherever they're needed. More streamlined."

"You can't just pick up any whore off the street," Des reminded him. "Remember the critiera. They have to be highly intelligent. And artistic ability of any kind helps, too. Artists have a statistical edge."

Tom's eyes were caught again by the frenzied, rhythmic movements on the screen. "Uh, fine," he said, distracted. "So we post some American symphony jobs in a conservatory in Minsk, or Kiev. They'll come running. You can take your pick."

"Can we?" Des's smile grew broader. "Then pick the pretty ones, Tommy. By all means, pick the pretty ones."

Tom shifted uncomfortably on his chair. The noise level in the other room swelled, in a howling crescendo. Then, silence. Amplified panting. Tom wiped sweat off his forehead. Licked his lips.

Here it was. The perfect moment.

"Why don't you go in there yourself? Try an interface?" Des offered. "Ava's only been working her for about twenty minutes. Keira's got a solid half hour left before her brain blows out. It's the best way to get a real hands-on sense of how it works. Go on, man. Give it a whirl."

Professional caution fought with hot lust, and in less than five seconds, lust won. "Uh, yeah," Tom said. "I'll, uh, give it a try."

Des lifted the communicating mike to his mouth. "Av, could you come out and set up Tom with a crown? He wants a test drive."

Ava doffed her mesh crown and goggles, popping off the sensors from her head and walking past the panting, trembling knot of humanity as if she didn't even see it. She came out of the room, eyes sparkling, color high. Excitement buzzed in Desmond's balls. She'd be wild for it. A very enjoyable byproduct of today's business.

Ava stood a little too close to Tom while she adjusted his crown, letting him look down her blouse, brushing his chest with her taut nipples while she set the sensors. Tom stared down at Ava's chest. Her rib cage was tilted so that her tits strained against the thin silk.

Tom's hands shook by the time she was done adjusting. She led Tom into the inner room, giving useful pointers in her husky, please-fuck-me-now voice. Ignoring Keira, slumped on the floor, the two men sprawled beside her, pants gaping.

After what seemed like an inappropriately long time, Ava came out, shutting the door with a sharp click. They stared at each other.

"I'm surprised you didn't just pull up your skirt and spread for him right here and now," he said.

"Jealous, Des?" she cooed. "Or did you want me to?"

"Whore," he said.

She approached him, plucking open the buttons of her blouse until one last button strained fabric across her perfect tits. "Is that what you want me to be?"

He jerked his chin towards the scene on the viewing screen. "The cameras are running, I trust?"

"Of course," she replied. "As if, Dessie. I don't miss a trick."

He licked his lips. "No, baby. You sure don't."

He traced the curve of her half exposed breast with his finger. "Happy now?" he asked. "A steady supply of fresh meat, hand picked to your exact specs. Pretty, artistically talented. And a disposal system. Was that everything on your wish list?"

She began to circle him. "Oh, yes. I'm so happy, Des. Tom Bixby is still a big prick. But hey. Big pricks sometimes have their uses."

"I'm glad you think so." He wound his fingers into the thick, glossy skeins of her hair, and pulled. "So it was a good interface, then?"

"The best," she purred. "One of the best ever. Shame, to waste such an amazing interface on a sales demo."

"You say the good ones feed sensory data back to you. Was she that good, Av? Did you feel them, inside you? Fucking you?"

"Would it turn you on, if it had?"

Her coy maneuvering made him want to hit that perfect, mocking face. His hand tightened on her hair. "Just answer me, you mouthy bitch." He jerked her closer, and put his hand between her legs.

Ava gasped. "Yes," she whispered. "But not like I feel . . . this."

He thrust his hand up into her tightly furled, narrow pussy lips. Smooth, hot, and slick. "Good." He worked her, pressing deep.

She sighed, her slender body writhing against him, around him. "You want to know what I was thinking while I did that interface?"

"Go ahead." He fingered her clit. "You'll tell me whether I want to know or not."

"I was thinking about her." She threw her head back, closed her eyes. "The Parrish girl. How it'll be when we do her."

"How do you think it'll be? Like that one?" He wrenched

the last button of her blouse loose. The button skittered across the floor.

"No. Better. A hundred times better," she said dreamily. "I checked her out. She has a crazy interactive Web site. I liked it."

"Yeah?" He fingered her nipples, not even trying to follow her train of thought. All he wanted was to fuck.

"There were photos," Ava continued. "She's not bad, you know? And she'd look a lot better if she gave a shit. Which she clearly doesn't."

"I see." He leaned down, sucked her tit into his mouth.

She moaned, whimpering. "If she's like me, we'll be able to crown her again and again without blowing her mind," she said breathlessly. "We can do anything we want, for as long as we want."

"Great," he mumbled. "That'll be just great." He sucked, nibbled.

"We'll play with her tonight, OK? Here, after the banquet. Parrish croaks, in front of flashing cameras. Wanatabe and Fabian will be ready to nab Edie when she runs away in the confusion. We amuse ourselves with her at our leisure, while the evidence comes out showing that it was Edie who poisoned him. When the manhunt is underway, we bring her out of the woodwork, have her murder the sister and commit suicide. The money goes to the Foundation. The Foundation board will be yours to command. Have I forgotten anything?"

"Nothing. You're brilliant. You evil, filthy, calculating slut." His voice shook as he slid his fingers deeper inside her.

"It's a waste," Ava said, clenching her pussy around his delving hand. "She'd be a knockout, if I pulled her strings. It's all in the attitude. And that's the missing bit that I will provide. The attitude."

Des spun the two of them around, so that he faced the screen, and shoved Ava to her knees. A brief glance revealed . . . hot damn! Tom had gotten the hang of the master crown in record time, and was already exploiting its many possibilities. Bixby always had been a quick study, that dirty bastard. Des wrenched open his pants, inspired.

"I can't wait." Ava gazed up with that crazy glow in her eyes that always unbalanced him "It'll be wonderful, to crown someone as good as me. I'll be like a goddess. It's like, I can wear her. Like a scarf."

"Sure. Like a scarf."

And Des shoved his cock into her mouth, so that there would be no more goddamn prattling talk.

CHAPTER
9

Don't go. The plea hung in the air between them.

Edie waited for Kev's response, her fingers digging into the thick muscles of his shoulder. The seconds ticked on and on.

He didn't answer. Tears prickled her eyes. This was torture.

A muscle twitched in Kev's jaw. "You don't understand," he said. "I don't know how to handle feelings this strong. Before the waterfall accident, I was numb, more or less. Self-control wasn't an issue for me. But now, I feel . . . inside out. Like I'm going to break."

"Tell me about it," she said fervently.

"You don't get it." He gripped her hand in his own, engulfing it. "I don't trust myself. I don't want to hurt you. I have to leave. Now."

"Leaving would hurt me," she said simply.

He muttered something, in a harsh, gutteral language. It sounded profane to her attenuated senses. "You're not listening," he growled.

"You are so wrong. You will never find a better listener

than me. And if you're trying to intimidate me, don't bother. It won't work."

His eyes narrowed to bright green slits. "It won't?"

"No. It won't. I'm fearless today. I could eat you for breakfast." She plucked his hand off hers, and pulled it up to her mouth, pressing her lips against it. "You think you feel exposed?" She whipped off her long green sweater and flung it down next to his on the floor. "We're even."

Kev sucked in a harsh breath. "Oh, fuck." His voice sounded strangled. "Edie. Goddamnit. This is not helping."

She reached back, struggling with the fastenings of her shabby white bra. Wishing she had a seductive scrap of silk and lace on. At least the boobs themselves were acceptable, as boobs went. "Who said anything about helping?" She flung the bra onto the sweater, chest out, shoulders back. Displaying herself. Ta da. Take that, buddy. Tit power.

He stared at her bare chest, as if hypnotized. "I can't do this to you." His voice sounded strangled. "I'm not in control. You understand? I can't . . . I don't know what I'd do to you."

"No? Well, gee. I could give you some pointers." She felt silly, being naked to the waist and still wearing glasses, so she pulled them off and tossed them onto the table. The room shifted into soft focus. Kev glowed in the foreground, like luminous marble. His dirt-blond hair had wiry glints of gold and bronze. Silver and gilt beard stubble glinted on the unscarred side of his jaw. She liked the metallic accents. They gave him a supernatural glow, like some mythical beast in an ancient tale. He glittered and shone. Colors of the sun, the moon, the stars.

She seized his shoulders, her ink-blackened nails digging into hot smooth skin, thick ropy muscle, the rasp of bumpy scar tissues. She let her breasts sway, inches from his face, in blatant invitation.

He seized her waist. "So we're clear?" His voice was clipped and harsh. "We just met, a little over an hour ago.

There are two outcomes in this scenario. I put on my shirt and leave right now, or I throw you down on the nearest horizontal surface, and fuck you hard. And repeatedly. You understand?"

She stroked the muscles of his back, shivering. "Jeez," she murmured. "You don't have to sound so unhappy about it."

He shook with smothered laughter. She pulled him closer so his face pressed against her breasts. His face rubbed against her. His beard stubble rasped delicately against the underside of her breast. His mouth moved over her skin, the hot bloom of his breath warming her.

His tongue swirled, tasting her skin, lapping. She stifled a whimper and squeezed her quivering thighs together. He pulled her nipple into his mouth, suckled her. Her legs were buckling. She wrapped her arms around his neck, clutching his head to her chest.

He pulled back, his breath short and sharp. "Fuck. I don't know if I can be gentle." His voice was unsteady. "Are you sure you—"

"Duh," she said sharply. "Don't ask me again. It's pissing me off. You think you can blow my mind with psychic lust waves, and then walk off and leave me? Fuck that, Kev Larsen." She wound her fingers into the spiky hair on his scalp, and yanked it, hard. "Fuck that."

He shook with silent laughter. She felt strange, almost possessed. She had no idea where this uncharacteristic sexual boldness came from, but she'd do anything to keep him from vanishing. Even throw her body at him. Thank God, the boobs had hooked him.

Or she was the one who was hooked, helpless, mindless. Strung out on the way his lips were moving on her skin, the tender way his hands cupped her breasts, the way his tongue swirled, turning her chest into a liquid glow, inflaming her nipples into bright, shimmering points.

She couldn't breathe. Her skin felt like it was too small

for her body, hot and fevered. Her breasts felt swollen, taut with longing.

He pulled her closer, and pulled her leg around until she straddled his thighs, and pulled her down on his lap. Settling her crotch across that throbbing club of his penis, still trapped in his jeans, so its hot bulk pressed against her most sensitive places, making her tingle, melt. Wow. So big. And not just down there. His whole body was huge. Her relatively tall five-foot-eight was nothing compared to him. He had to be six-four, minimum.

Her nipples tingled where they brushed him. She moved, rubbing hungrily against his erection, staring into his eyes. He pressed his hand against the small of her back, intensifying the contact. Making her rock and squirm and writhe against his hardness.

"You are so beautiful," he whispered.

Something rejected the words. They broke the spell, propelling her out of herself. "Don't," she said. "Please. You don't have to say that."

His face was incredulous. "You don't think that you're beautiful?"

She was intensely uncomfortable at this turn of subject. "Its not that I think I'm bad looking. But I've been lectured all my life about the tragedy of unrealized potential, and I'm sick of it. I've moved on, see? It's too late to learn to dress, do my makeup, and blow-dry my hair properly, blah blah blah. What you see is what you get."

He shook his head, his eyes intent on her face. "Who gives a fuck about the clothes, or the makeup?" He sounded genuinely curious.

"Um, the rest of the world, maybe?" Damn. She wished she hadn't opened the subject. It sounded like she was fishing for reassurance. Like a cheesy women's magazine article, she'd blurted out Number One on the list of Ten Things Not To Say To A Guy Who's Seducing You.

But Kev didn't seem put off. He studied her face, touching it with his fingertips. His touch felt reverent. "Your lips are hot pink," he said, stroking them. "Puffy and soft, like a satin pillow with a crease down the middle. They shine when you lick them. They don't need paint. And your eyes, Jesus. I can't even describe it, how they reflect light. More silver than gray, like there's crumpled metal foil behind to catch light and refract it in every direction, and that ring of dark slate gray around the outside sets off the bright part in the middle. And your breath. It's amazing. So sweet and fresh and spicy. Mint, cinnamon, and ginger?"

Oh, man. Oh, not fair. She was utterly flustered by his catalog of her charms. She tried to suppress the girly giggles, but they bubbled up anyway. "Oh, that's just the chai," she informed him. "I made you some. You were too distracted to drink it. You, too, could have mint, cinnamon, and ginger breath."

He grabbed his mug from the table, and took a deep swallow of his cooled tea. "Mmm," he said. "Good. And your teeth, too. Wow. So white and straight. You have great teeth."

She grinned, showing off her admittedly nice teeth. "Years of orthodontia," she said. "I suffered the fires of hell for these teeth."

"Your suffering was not in vain," he said solemnly. "And I haven't gotten going about your skin yet. We're still above the chin. I could go on for hours about your eyes alone. And eye accessories."

"Accessories?"

"You know. Eyelashes, eyebrows, eyelids. The purple smudges, right here . . ." He touched the hollow below her brow. "And the way your eyelashes curl at the tips. And your eyebrow hairs. I love how they sweep up at the edges. Its all just so . . . perfect. It blows my mind."

"Thank you," she replied. Her face was so hot, she felt feverish. "The compliments are just super-nice, and I appreciate you being so sweet, but the buildup is driving me crazy. If you don't kiss me now, I will grab a fork and stab you with it. Or else faint from lack of oxygen."

His laugh rang out, loud and happy. Then he seized her.

The kiss sprang into being, fully formed. No lead in, no awkward fumbling, no slow, graceful merging. Just all of a sudden, they were twined together as if they had always been, locked into a greedy, devouring clinch like they were starving to get inside each other.

His big body vibrated. The stroke of his lips was sure and perfect, the bold flick of his tongue made her melt and squirm, but it wasn't his technique that got her. What undid her was the raw need, his desperate intensity, licking through her like flames. Making her glow and sparkle and hum. Making her wet and slick and ready. Her thighs tightened around his. He was a sweet oasis after an eternity of choking dust. She wanted to give him everything. All she had. All she was.

So far in her life, the best sex had ever gotten for her was when she'd been relaxed enough so that it didn't actually hurt. The hugging and talking afterward was the part she craved. She'd always tried too hard, been hoping too much, to actually get off during the sex itself.

Not with Kev. Her mind was wiped blank. All the cataclysmic power of millions of years of reproductive evolution was clawing its way through her body, trying to get into the guy's pants. Right now would be a good time, thanks very much, and please, *please, fuck me now*.

She dragged her mouth away from his, gasped for oxygen, and scrambled off his lap, legs wobbling. "Take off your shoes," she ordered.

He looked perplexed. "My shoes? What about my shoes?"

"Just get them off," she said impatiently. "So that when I pull your jeans off and drag you to my bed, you won't be lurching around with denim shackles on your ankles. Trust me on this."

"OK." His beautiful grin made her heart bump and skip.

He kicked off his shoes, peeled off his socks. Even his feet were perfect. Graceful, long toes, square nails, elegant bones. Who ever imagined she would get off on a guy's feet? Even the tuft of glinting blond hair on the joint of his big toe charmed her. How sweet.

His smile made something swell in her chest. She turned away before he could see the tears. The doubt that she could see this thing through without disgracing herself. That she was capable of living up to her bold moves, her big talk. She let her hair swing down to hide her face, stared at the glittering crystals, wishing she could hypnotize herself out of these stupid fears.

Screw it. A girl had to start somewhere. Frantic enthusiasm had to count for something, in the absence of experience, or technique. Or whatever the hell else the mysterious secret to great sex might be.

He touched her gently from behind, making her jump. Brushed her hair off her back, and over her shoulder. "I didn't mean to startle you," he murmured. "I just wanted to see your back. So graceful."

She nodded, trying to silently sniff the tears back, and squeezed her eyes shut as he stroked her spine, ribs, shoulder blades with his fingertips. He bent, to kiss the nape of her neck, moving down her spine with his warm lips, a kiss for each vertebra. Turning each one into a shining, glowing pearl on a string. His breath was a hot, soft caress, like silk, like fur. More tears sneaked out of her squeezed-shut eyes.

His hands circled her, a caress that made her nerve endings go nuts with bright, dazzling bursts. His lips moved against her shoulder. One hand slid low while the other crept up. She quaked in his arms, making tiny, breathless sounds as his fingers slipped beneath the waistband of her low-rise jeans . . . and stopped, tracing the waistband of her panties. Back, and forth. Back, and forth. Not venturing inside. Just making her think about it. And wait. And wait.

Until she thought she would . . . just . . . *die.*

She made a growling hiss in the back of her throat, and jerked his hand inside her jeans. "You're a tease," she complained.

He laughed, his hand sliding into the front of her panties. She almost screamed when they curled around her mound, his fingertip caressing the damp seam through the veil of stretchy fabric, stroking, pressing, circling . . . and oh—oh *God* . . .

She came apart, shaking to pieces in a shivering string of lovely little firecracker orgasms. Her chest swelled, bloomed open. Her face quivered. If he hadn't held her against him, she would have keeled over. As it was, she dangled limply over the strength of his forearm.

"Oh, man," he whispered. "That was beautiful. Do it again."

She wanted to laugh, but she would cry if she let the sound out. As if it were up to her. This never happened to her. Never.

He swung her around so that they faced the full-length mirror on the bathroom door. The sun had emerged from the clouds right before going down, and the last rays slanted fitfully through the blinds, painting pagan stripes of reddish light onto her naked torso, his face, his sinewy arms. His wrist disappeared into her jeans. She could hardly believe the way she looked, the blush of heat on her face, brimming eyes, wet cheeks, her parted lips, her helpless squirming. His hand, shoved deep in her pants, petting and working her. Driving her mad.

He kissed the side of her neck, tonguing and licking, and tugged the gusset of her panties aside. Teased her tight furled folds apart, found her slick and melting. Her thighs squeezed his hand, clenching around him as he slid his finger into her hot well, finding some sweet magic place that had bloomed into being just for him. Nudging her unexpectedly right over a cliff she never saw coming until she was already in a screaming free fall of shocking sensation.

Each driving, explosive pulse of pleasure knocked her further from what she thought of as herself, into someplace new, someplace soft and wild. And wonderfully real.

When she surfaced from the aftershocks, he still held her, his arm rock hard against her belly, his erection pressed against her backside.

Her jeans had slid almost off her ass. His gold skin deepened in tone to the darker brown on his forearm, startling against the pallor of her naked belly. The stripes from the sunlight were fading, almost gone, and the swirling rainbows along with them. The warm tiger stripes of sunset color that had painted them had been fleeting.

Like everything beautiful, this would be fleeting, too. She knew it for a fact. She had to seize it, get what she could get from it.

Her love affairs were invariably short-lived. Either the guy got scared off by the doomsaying radio receiver in her head, or freaked out by the financial and personal background checks, or intimidated by the relentless shadowing of the Parrish bodyguards. Or whatever. There was always something. Usually several somethings.

If she wanted some of this, she had to grab it. Full on, before problems had a chance to start. This guy walked straight out of her fantasy, and she was going to jump on him, and enjoy the hell out of him. Before the fantasy had to end. Because it would. Oh, yes, it would.

The anger that accompanied that thought set her spinning around, yanking for his belt buckle.

"Hey," he said gently. "No hurry."

"I say there is." Her voice was low, shaking. She wrenched his pants down over his hips. His penis sprang up like it was spring loaded.

Whoa. She stared down at him, taken aback. He was so

big. Thick, long, blunt, red. Ready for action. She hadn't bargained for . . . well, this. Whew. Her dreams tended to focus on crashing waves of emotion, fountaining sensations. They didn't specify the blunt details.

And this, oh, man. This was a blunt detail if there ever was one.

She wasn't even sure if he would work, for her. In a purely mechanical sense. He certainly worked in every other way. She was so excited, she was on the verge of coming spontaneously.

She reached to touch his big, hot phallus, gasping at the contact. So solid, pulsing. He gasped and shuddered as she squeezed, the hot, velvety skin sliding, moving over the firmness of his throbbing shaft.

"Oh, God. Wait. I'll lose it," he muttered.

"That would be OK," she assured him. "I've lost it. Now it's your turn." She sank to her knees. Never let it be said that she wasn't ready to do her part.

He caught her under the armpits, and yanked her up again. "No."

She was nonplussed. "No? You don't like . . . that?"

He looked at her from hooded eyes as he pushed her into the tiny monk's cell of a bedroom. "Of course I do, but I can't let my head explode yet. Later for that. You, first. And we haven't had the talk yet."

"The talk? What talk?"

"I haven't been with anyone since well before the waterfall accident, and they did bloodwork up the wazoo while I was in the hospital, so I know I'm clean. But I don't have condoms with me. That's not an item that I carry on my person."

Oh. *That* talk. She shook herself, internally. It had been a nonissue so long, she'd forgotten the drill. "I'm fine, STD wise," she said. "And I might have some condoms. It's been so long, I can't be sure, but let me just . . . hold on." She yanked open her top drawer, rummaging in her underwear, and found the unopened three pack, left over from her affair with Eric. She brandished them. "They're ancient, though."

"If they haven't been exposed to light or heat, they should be OK."

"They've been languishing in the dark with only my panties for company," she said, ripping the foil. "Let me get one of these on you."

He slid his arms around her, nuzzling her ear. "Hey. Slow down."

He was trying to soothe her, but she wasn't soothable. "I don't want to slow down," she snapped. "I want to get on with it."

"I don't want to rush it," he replied. "I want to do it right."

Too bad, buddy. She was helpless to communicate her urgency to him without seeming crazy and desperate. She was probably well into crazy and desperate territory already. But if she didn't push this, it would slip away from her, fizzle out, or just vanish into thin air.

And she had to have this. Had. To.

She shook the condom out, relieved to see that it looked normal. She grasped his cock again, loving the way her fingers barely closed around that broad shaft, and tried to apply the condom, but the rolled latex ring wouldn't stretch around the bulb of his penis. Damn slippery thing kept snapping off, rolling back up. Finally, he pinched the condom out of her hand, and rolled it on himself, with casual grace. He lifted her hands to his lips, kissing the backs of her fingers.

She thudded her butt down onto the low single futon bed, yanking him toward her. "Get over here." Her voice shook. On the verge of tears. Crap. Guys hated that. It could be a deal breaker, too.

She fought it, tried to keep it together, but her breath hitched, sharp and audible. She dug in her nails and dragged him closer.

He sank obediently to his knees in front of the bed,

pulling her so her bottom was perched on the edge of the futon, and embraced her.

They were forehead to forehead, her thighs splayed wide. He held his cock in his fist and petted her with it, tender strokes up and down her slick divide, each brush of contact as sweet and specific as a kiss.

The tension built, a maddening roar in her ears. She dug her fingers into his muscular ass and pulled him closer, wiggling for the angle that would lodge him inside her. Definitively. No escape for him.

"Please," she whispered, almost incoherently. "Please."

"Oh, yeah." His voice shook, too. She wasn't the only one who was falling apart. He began to press inside—

Her lungs stopped working. Oh. Sweet. God. He was huge.

She gripped his upper arms, clamped down on the sounds about to escape from her throat. She didn't want to scare him away.

He shifted back, pulling out of her. "No," he muttered.

"No?" She jerked forward and yanked on him, with furious energy. "What do you mean, no?"

He grabbed her clutching hands, kissed one. "I mean, not yet."

"I'm ready now," she informed him. "I'm falling to pieces. *Now!*"

He slid his finger inside her, caressing her where his cock had been, his lips moving against her forehead. "You're small," he said. "Too tight. Wait. I'll make it better for you."

Like hell! Wait? No! She was sick to death of waiting. She'd been waiting her whole damn life. She didn't know what for, or if she'd even know it when she saw it. "It's good now!" she insisted. "It's fine! It's never been this good for me! It'll kill me if it's better than this!"

He pried the clenched claws of her hands off his upper arms, and kissed them tenderly, held her wrists as she wrenched at them.

"I'll make it better," he said. "And it won't kill you. Trust me."

Arrogant *bastard*. The command in his voice made something inside her snap. She wrenched her arms free. "Trust you? How dare you jerk me around like this? I am sick of it!" She shoved at his chest.

He swayed backward. "I'm sorry you feel that way," he said.

"You think because you're the one with the dick, that means you're in charge? Just because you're the man?" She swatted at him, flailing wildly. "You think that makes you boss? Fuck you, Kev!"

"Oh, yes. I will fuck you. Count on it." He grabbed her arms again, held them fast. "And yeah, I am the one with the dick. I decide what to do with it, and when. And I say that you . . . will . . . *wait*."

His forceful words punched through her frantic anger and made her flinch. "Who died and made you God?" she yelled. "What was all that bullshit you talked about throwing me down on the nearest horizontal surface and fucking me hard? Brave words, huh?"

"I meant it," he said. "But that was before I felt you come all over my hand. I got off on that. That was excellent."

She was startled into speechlessness. She licked her lips, hypnotized by his eyes, his delving hand. Fingerfucking her, with skillful, demanding strokes that made her hips jerk against him.

"Now I'm strung out on it," he went on, his voice a caressing rumble that dragged over her nerve endings. "I found the strength to delay gratification. Thank God."

She was embarrassed to realize that her anger was gone. She couldn't form words yet with her trembling mouth. He pressed a coaxing kiss against her lips. Slipped his tongue inside, exploring while his fingers thrust, deep enough to make her gasp, writhe, mewl. While his thumb caressed her clit. Getting it just . . . exactly . . . *right*.

"I don't just want to shove it into you," he whispered. "I want you to love it. I want you to come and come. Until the neighbors are banging the walls, begging you to stop, so they can hear their TVs again."

That made her shake with a burst of teary laughter. "I am not a screamer," she informed him. "So don't get your hopes up."

He looked skeptical. "You were screaming just now. At me."

She bristled. "Oh, bullshit! That was different!"

"Yeah? Was it?" His grin flashed. Wow, he was smooth. He'd wrangled her right through her little freak-out, with such grace and skill, she hadn't had a chance. She must be so transparent.

"You don't understand." Her voice wobbled perilously. "I can't just take this easy, like you want me to. I have to seize the moment."

"Don't worry," he urged. "You'll seize lots of moments. Hours of moments. I won't let anyone take them from you."

He pushed her down until she was flat on her back. She glanced up at the crystals that still spun above her in the window. The light trapped in their depths swirled and glittered in her tear-blurred eyes. He kissed her chest. Dropped seductive kisses, trailing lower, and lower. She sensed where he was going, panicked, and started to struggle up onto her elbows again. "Um, hold on. Wait. I can't . . . I can't—"

"You will." His voice was steely. "Relax, for one goddamn second, Edie. Let me make this good for you."

His lord-of-the-manor tone pissed her off again. "I told you how to make it good for me!" she snapped. "By getting the fuck on with it!"

"I can't. You're too small. I don't want to hurt you." His eyes narrowed thoughtfully. "Are you into pain?"

She was taken aback. "God, no. I avoid pain whenever possible."

"Good." He pushed her legs wide. "Because if you were, you'd have to find some other guy to . . ."

His voice trailed off. She jerked up, to see what he was looking at. He was staring down between her legs, rapt. His eyes so bright, she could feel his gaze, like a touch. His intense regard was a sweet lick of delicious heat. "Ah," he whispered. "God. I take that back."

Oh, please. It was just her normal, furry muff. He didn't need to carry on about it like it was something celestial. She reached down, grabbed a handful of his hair. "What? You take back what?"

"No other man touches this." He fitted his hands around her vulva, cupping it, caressing it. "Just me. This is mine. All . . . mine."

Raw possessiveness roughened in his voice. She squirmed as he slid his thumbs over her slick folds, spreading them apart. Staring at her. Every tiny, quivering detail of her. Like he wanted to devour her.

"I, ah . . ." She coughed, cleared her throat. "That's a very intense sentiment to express after . . . how long have we known each other?"

"Very intense," he agreed. "So's this." He leaned down, dragging the tip of his tongue up her slit, sliding through her folds, swirling it up and around the taut nub of her quivering clit, suckling. "Your pussy is so beautiful. I want it. It's mine."

His voice vibrated against her sensitive bits, making her giggle and snort. "Oh, please. Pussy? That's such a silly word for it. Oh, my God, that . . . that tickles. That's . . . oh, God, that's amazing."

His eyes crinkled over the dark puff of her pubic hair. "I like that word," he said, pausing to flutter his tongue across her clit, a delicate trill that sent shudders of pleasure through her. "It's the best word. The other words sound too harsh to me. Pussy is softer. Lighthearted."

She gasped with pleasure as his tongue lashed, darted,

delved. "I'm . . . I'm not particularly soft," she pointed out. "Or lighthearted."

"No?" He slid his tongue inside her. "You are, too, soft. Amazingly soft. Getting softer all the time. But would you rather use a different word? I'll accommodate you. I'll use any word you want."

He nuzzled her groin, making her shake with helpless shudders, half laughter, half breathless excitement. "Stop that," she giggled.

"Not a chance," he said. "As for lighthearted, hey. That can change in an instant. It did for me, the second that I met you."

She was sobered by his intensity, and groped for something to say, reaching hopefully for the giggling vibe again. "What word do you use for your own . . ." She jerked her chin expressively. "You know."

"My male member?" Her goofy semantic shyness made him grin. "I don't have much occasion to talk about my dick. I don't refer to it much. Got a preference? Lady's choice. Go wild. Be creative."

She was bright red. "Um. Whatever is fine. We don't really have to, um, talk about it."

"It doesn't matter a damn to him, what you call him," he informed her, solemnly. "All he cares about is what you let him do to you."

"Oh, yeah? What is he going to do to me? And when? Hah! After all my begging and yelling? I'll believe it when I see it, buddy."

"Then I'd better shut up and get to work." He shoved her thighs wide, and buried his face between them to caress her with lips and tongue; thrusting and swirling around her melting muff. It hit her all at once, along with the next shuddering spasms, how crazy she was, dragging this big, mysterious man into her bedroom. She'd have dragged him into her body, too, if he hadn't been so stubborn.

And sexy. Her body was changing into something new,

flushed with hot, wild energy. This wasn't going to evaporate on her, or fizzle out. Kev was utterly in command of himself, her body, her pleasure. All she had to do was give in, and let him nudge her expertly along to yet another shining peak, another wild, astonished free fall—

She soared, spun, dissolved. Each wrenching pulse propelling her deeper into that magic place that only he had ever taken her. Where she felt complete, and whole. She glowed, shone.

When her eyes fluttered open, they streamed with tears, but she was not embarrassed by them. It was part of the emotional intensity between them. Honest, and achingly real. Terrifying and wonderful.

He waited, poised over her, his eyes boring into hers. She blinked away moisture, dragged in as much breath as she could, which wasn't much. Tried to move, couldn't.

He'd wedged himself inside her. She gasped and clutched his shoulders as he started to move. Slow, rocking strokes. Sensual pulses, pushing that big, hard cock impossibly deeper.

"That's more like it," he muttered, his voice a harsh rasp.

She dashed the tears away, started to say something, but she had nothing coherent to say. He could feel everything she thought and felt with his body, read it in her face, decipher her every brain wave. It was wonderful to be so close. She tried to lift herself, to meet his thrusts, but she was riveted by the slow push of his heavy body into hers. Utterly at his mercy.

She grabbed a handful of the flannel sheet and dragged it up to wipe ticklish tears on her face. Noticed a smear of black ink on the fabric as she let it drop. More tears slipped out. She was drenched. Slick with sweat. Flooded with lube. His strokes deepened. Still tight, but a wonderful sliding shove inside—and a slow, caressing drag out. Plunging, rocking. Again . . . and again.

She struggled up onto her elbows so that she could see every detail. Kev grasped her arms and pulled her until she was sitting, right at the edge of the bed, his shaft deeper inside than she'd known was anatomically possible. They stared down at the hot joining, damp foreheads resting against each other, hypnotized by the wet gleam of his thick cock as it slid out. They moaned together, as he surged inside once again. Each thrust making tiny, sexy liquid sounds. Gasps. Sighs.

She was so alive and aware, inside herself. Every slide of his body was a liquid, moving kiss, petting secret inner spots of unbearable sweetness, stroking them into quivering life, waking them to desperate need. Each thrust made her crave the next. She bucked against him, desperate for more, deeper, faster. Harder.

She dragged him closer, trying to speak. He caught whatever garbled thing she was trying to say with his hungry kiss, and that was fine. Better, even, because her frenzied response was more honest and to the point than any words could be.

She wrapped her arms around his neck and kissed him back with wild abandon. She would let him take her anywhere. She wanted to toss away her fears, the barriers she hadn't know she had, blast down the walls around herself. She wanted him inside, at her core. One with her.

She whimpered and gasped as his thrusts quickened. He slammed against her, his breathing harsh and loud, kissing away each tear as it slid out, hips surging powerfully. She hung on, riding him with perfect trust into the thundering heart of a storm.

Losing what she thought was herself there. Finding something else in its place. Something precious and nameless. Sweet, and lovely. Her naked heart, glowing like a live coal.

Free as a bird soaring, and yet forever bound.

CHAPTER

10

Kev didn't want to drift back from this plane of existence. He wanted to stay there forever. Live there, for eternity. Aware only of her.

Edie. Those soft, slender arms wrapped around him, his cock still in the clasp of her juicy pink pussy, her long, graceful legs clamping his thighs. Her head lay on his shoulder, heavy and limp, and her hair tickled him tenderly, fuzzy soft whorls of midnight darkness.

She fit. Like she'd been designed for his body. Pain and tension he'd never even been conscious of were instantly relieved by her touch. Her scent dragged into his lungs, gave him something his body needed more than oxygen. Every inch of his skin lucky enough to touch her was in shock from the perfection of that soft, hot contact.

He'd had sex before. He'd never really gone looking for it, and he tended to have long dry spells, but he indulged, when the occasion presented itself. But he'd never experienced anything like this.

He'd done his best by the women he'd slept with. He'd been polite, gentle, had taken pains to be a sensitive, satisfying lover. But the act had always struck him as an end in itself, leading nowhere but to a shudder of shallow release, and then a sad, empty flatness after.

And it created embarrassing situations, too. Women wanting him to feel things that he didn't necessarily feel. Or even want to feel.

Now he was drowning in feelings. Feelings that could kill him.

Edie. He felt the name, repeating it silently against her fragrant hair. Rolling the word around in his mouth. Loving the way it felt.

He'd come like a volcano blowing, but his dick was still rock hard. Unwilling to waste a second, now that it had found the sweet haven of her body. But he had to get rid of the latex, and let her rest.

He wondered if he'd been too rough. He hoped he hadn't bruised her. That would be humbling, after his posturing bullshit about self-control, about making her wait. Strange, that impulse, but he'd sensed that she needed a rock that she could fling herself against. She needed to push, so he'd pushed back. He hoped it had worked for her. She hadn't moved yet. In fact, she seemed to have knocked herself out.

His cock throbbed hopefully in the tight clutch of her body, wanting to rock and plunge afresh into her slick depths.

He allowed himself a few rocking slides, just to feel the tight, liquid kiss of her flesh along his length, the sigh fluttering through her. Then he held the condom in place, and dragged his unwilling cock out.

He lay her tenderly down on the narrow bed, spreading her hair out behind her head like a shining, swirling fan. Arranging it, stroking it with amazed fingertips. So soft. God. She gazed up, speechless, eyes heavy and dilated. Her soft pink lower lip caught between her teeth.

He pulled the condom off, looked around. Edie cleared her throat. "There's a wastebasket under the sink." Her voice was scratchy and dry.

He nodded, stumbled into the other room, and took care of it.

He stood out there, heart clutched with doubt. He'd always avoided even thinking about the possibility of being with a woman for the long term. It was unthinkable, given the unknowns in his life. The latent violence and danger in his past. It struck him as irresponsible, to expose some poor innocent woman to that. Or so he'd told himself.

Now he saw that reasoning for the shallow bullshit that it was. Truth was, he'd never wanted to badly enough. He'd never given a shit.

But he did now. Oh, Jesus, was he ever in trouble now.

What he ought to do was quietly put on his clothes and slink out. Leaving no address, no number. It was the responsible thing to do.

But that just wasn't going to happen. So fuck it. He let the implacable force of gravity drag him back into the bedroom, to Edie.

She'd pulled herself up, clutching the quilt. Her hair was a fuzzy, dark cape, her lips red, her eyes sultry and glowing. So fucking pretty, it made his heart stop. This couldn't be happening, but it had all the massive inevitability of fate. He'd been waiting his whole life for her.

She smiled, her eyes flashing timidly down to his tireless tentpole of a dick. "Are you, ah, cold?"

He was a blast furnace. His dick was going to be in a state of permanent inflammation, now that it knew Edie Parrish existed.

"Actually I'm burning up," he said.

"Oh." She picked at the pattern on the quilt with her fingers. "Well, whatever. I was just wondering if, um, you wanted to get under the covers with me, but if you're so hot—"

"Fuck, yeah! Absolutely! I changed my mind. I'm freezing. Going into shock from hypothermia. Warm me with your body heat. Please."

She giggled, which made his heart soar. They hadn't had many smiles so far. Mind blowing revelations, sure. Thundering orgasms, definitely. But not a lot of laughs. She held up the quilt for him, and he slid his body into the narrow, deliciously warm space beside her. Not that he was complaining about the close quarters. Any excuse to touch her again was fine with him. The tighter the clinch, the happier he was.

She arranged the quilt over his shoulders, and traced the pattern of burn scars on his deltoid with her fingertip. Burns from a cigarette, he figured. It was the best he could piece together, from the nightmares.

He loved staring at her from so close. Having her beautiful face fill his field of vision. He could let his senses drown in her, and die happy.

"Sorry about the tiny bed," she murmured.

"I don't care," he said.

"Nothing else would fit," she explained. "Unless I gave up the space for a dresser, which I suppose I could have, since I don't have much of a wardrobe. But when I got that bed, I wasn't figuring on . . ."

"On what?" he prompted.

The color flared on her cheek. He loved it. Sunrise on a snowfield, but warmer, softer. He couldn't think of anything fine enough, lovely enough, to be a metaphor for her.

"On hooking up with someone," she finished.

"Good." The surge of possessive hunger made his arms tighten around her. Wow. Hadn't known he had it in him. He was flustered.

"You could come over to my place," he blurted. "My bed's huge."

She looked through her lashes, with a mysterious smile. "Is it?"

He felt himself flush, with the sharp awareness that it did not look quite as good on his scarred, raddled face as it did on her perfect one. "Not because I'm in the habit of throwing wild parties in it."

"Hmm," she murmured, her eyes dropping.

"I'm just, ah, really big," he went on. "Uh, long, that is."

"I noticed," she said demurely.

His color got hotter. "I didn't mean it that way."

She slanted a sidewise peek at him, trying not to smile. She cleared her throat with a prim little cough. "Um. Neither did I."

Aw, shit. She was enjoying his embarrassment way too much. "Anyhow," he pushed grimly on. "The point is, there's plenty of room. My apartment is a converted warehouse. It's huge. Room for lots more rooms, if I, uh, ended up needing them. I even put in two bathrooms. In case I should someday, you know. Get lucky."

She caught her lip between her teeth. "Um, are you, ah, kidding?"

He was pushing too hard. "I don't know," he said cautiously. "Tell me. What response would get me what I want?"

"What is it that you want?" she demanded.

They were stalemated in their weird little word dance now.

I want you in my bed every night. I want you to bear my children. I want to put a ring on you. Body and soul. All mine. Forever.

Uh-uh. Not yet. He'd scare her out of her wits. He shrugged. "Maybe it's too soon for this conversation," he hedged.

"It sounds like you want me to be your, um, girlfriend," she said.

His heart leaped. "Well? So? Would you like to be?"

"There are a bunch of questions that need to be answered first."

"Ask them. I'll answer, and you can move into my apartment."

She covered her mouth with her hand. "You're scaring me, Kev."

He peered at her face. It looked like she was trying not to smile, so he decided to go with the vibe rather than the face value of her words.

"I'll build you your own room," he offered rashly. "There are huge windows. Great light, for your drawing. I've got so much square footage, I could have a skating rink in there."

"Slow down, buddy. I don't know the first thing about you."

That was not true. He thought about the Fade books, and his arms tightened around her. She did know him, in ways he didn't begin to understand. She knew things he'd never told a living soul. Things he'd barely acknowledged to himself. She'd seen them, dreamed them, drawn them. Anything inconsequential thing that she didn't know, she could quickly learn. And that was part of the strange wonderfulness of this whole experience. Feeling known. Feeling knowable.

He'd always been cut off, even from himself. Half his memories, half his self, forever beyond his reach. No childhood, no parents, no point of origin, no frame of reference. No image of the person who had fed him as a baby, changed his diapers, taught him to walk, talk, read. All unknowns, even the stupid, inconsequential stuff. His favorite color, his favorite rock band, his favorite breakfast cereal, his astrological sign? Who the fuck knew? A person had to have been a child once, to answer questions like that.

He'd never been a child, as far as he knew. He had no place to stand, to form irrelevant opinions. Likes and dislikes. He held himself apart from that bullshit. Indifferent. The vote was out, on all of it. It felt foolish and false to him, to develop a baseless self-concept, just for the sake of having one. It was a dumb ego game. Why bother? Who cared?

But all that had just changed. The vote was in on Edie Parrish. The possessive desire roaring through him scared the shit out of him. He had no clue how to navigate feelings like these. There had to be a technique to it, but he did not have it. And now it was too late. All he could do now was just struggle along. Try to keep his head above water.

Edie had looked into the dark inside him, with those eerily precise drawings. When he was with Edie, he felt connected. Alive, like never before. Edie knew him, if anyone could. Edie could show him the way.

"I think, um . . ." She bit her lip, choosing her words with care. "I think you might be building up these Fade coincidences too much. I don't want to feed any illusions you might have. About my abilities."

He thought about that, gazing into her wide, anxious eyes, and twisted a thick lock of her hair around his finger. "How about you just don't worry about what's in my mind?" he suggested. "Let me have my little illusions. What's the harm?"

"I don't know," she whispered. "But I feel like it's dangerous."

So. He was coming across like a lunatic. He needed to back off. But he just couldn't. "What is it that you need to know before we can upgrade our relationship status?" he asked, baldly.

She let out a snort of nervous laughter. "Uh . . ."

"Ask me anything. I have no secrets." He hesitated. "Unless you count the stuff about myself that I don't know," he added, rigidly honest. After all, he could be anything. A killer, a liar, a thief. He hoped not, but hope was just that. Hope. He knew better than to trust it.

She shook her head. "Those aren't secrets. Those are mysteries."

"Thanks," he said. "Mystery has a more respectable sound to it."

"Sexier, too," she informed him.

He was foolishly delighted. "You think so?"

Edie's eyes fell. "Please. Duh. You're talking to a woman who draws noir graphic novels. Of course mystery is sexy.

Mystery is practically a base, bottom-line requirement. For sexiness, I mean."

He stared up at her ceiling. The scars on his cheek stung, he was grinning so widely. "Cool," he said.

"What do you do for a living?" she demanded. "There's a basic question. I should have asked it before I fell into bed with you."

He rolled up onto his elbow. "I have a business with my little brother."

She looked baffled. "Brother? But . . . but I thought—"

"Adopted brother," he clarified. "Bruno's the great-nephew of the guy who saved me from the thugs at the warehouse. He came to live with Tony and Rosa when he was twelve. A year after Tony found me."

"So you were adopted by that family?"

"No. Nobody adopted me except for Bruno. He adopted me all by himself, when he was thirteen years old."

She looked puzzled. "And how did he do that?"

Kev smiled at the memory. "He was with me in the diner kitchen. I cut myself by mistake with a carving knife, and Bruno saw the blood when I was mopping up. He grabbed the knife, and proceeded to slice his own hand open. Then he grabs my hand with his bleeding hand, and won't let go. Meanwhile, blood's streaming down to both of our elbows. Scared the living shit out of me."

Her eyes were wide, impressed. "Wow. What was that about?"

"He wanted to do this blood brother ritual he'd read about in a kids' historical adventure novel. He wanted to make it official. He wanted to be related to me, by blood. Nothing else would do."

"That's very dramatic," she murmured.

"Tell me about it. He's all about drama. Bruno was intense. Or is intense, I should say. He hasn't changed. He needed eighteen stitches. I didn't have any bloodborne diseases, thank Jesus, so it was OK. But it's not like he could've done a discreet little nick. Oh, no. He had to lay himself open down to the tendons. My nerves were shot for weeks."

He twined his fingers through Edie's as he thought about that day. It had felt good to be adopted. He could have done without the freely flowing blood and the multiple stitches, but still, the bold, crazy gesture had moved him. That was Bruno for you.

"So you got yourself a brother?" she prompted. "That's great."

"Yeah, it was," he said. "I needed him more than he needed me. He was the one who got me talking again."

"How's that?"

He waved his hand, embarrassed. "Oh, he just talked my ear off. The kid literally never shut up. I had to regrow neural pathways just to tell him to zip his lip, or else I would have gone stark raving crazy."

Edie saw right through his Bruno schtick, and gave him an approving smile so radiant, it made his breath stop. She cuddled closer, which necesitated rearranging his dick. He folded it up, stiff and wooden against his belly so he could get closer to her lithe softness.

Every detail of her was an experience of divine grace. The bones of her face, the plump, blush fullness of her lower lip, the fine grained softness of her skin. All the flares and tilts and luscious curves. A living, breathing cluster of improbable perfections. He was dazzled.

And she seemed to have the exact same look on her face as she stared at him. She touched his face like it was something precious, beautiful. Usually when he was intimate with a woman, he sensed that she was looking at a bunch of scars with a guy behind them. Not Edie. It was like she didn't see them. Or not exactly. She saw them. They were part of him, and she saw him. But that wasn't surprising. She'd been drawing him for years. She was used to it. It was no big deal.

And that simple fact just blew his mind. It changed everything.

"OK. So?" she prompted. "This business you have? Let's talk about that. Bruno's full name is?"

"Bruno Ranieri," he said.

Her elvish eyebrows tilted up inquisitively. "Not Larsen?"

"Larsen's a made-up name. We started out making stunt kites. Named the outfit Lost Boys Flywear. Then we branched out after a couple years. Educational toys, models, science kits. Stuff like that."

"Oh, my God. I know about you guys!" She jerked up onto her elbow, her eyes lit up. "I've bought Lost Boys stuff for my little sister Ronnie! She loved them! Especially the do-it-yourself firecracker kit. Although my dad still hasn't forgiven me for that. And wasn't there an article in the *Portland Monthly* about Lost Boys?"

Kev rolled his eyes. "With Bruno's shit-eating grin plastered all over it? Yeah. Portland's most eligible bachelor, yada yada. Swelled his head like the Hindenberg. He was insufferable. Still hasn't recovered."

"Why weren't you on the cover with him?"

"I'm not in the market for a constant stream of consumable babes. Bruno's the ladies' man. You'll see, when you meet him."

Her eyelids fluttered. "Oh. Am I? Meeting him?"

"It's a step in the relationship upgrading process. I'm all for that."

"I see," she said demurely. "But you haven't adequately answered my question. You guys have a business together, so why aren't you Portland's two most eligible bachelors?"

He flopped down onto the pillow. "The first reason is because I threatened to rip the guts out of the photographer if he took any pictures of me."

She blinked. "Ah." She processed that, and went on, remarkably unperturbed. "And the second reason?"

He didn't want to go there, but there wasn't much point in lying to a woman like Edie. "Eighteen years ago, somebody tried to torture me to death. Doesn't seem too bright to advertise my face, location, and my new identity. And it would be false advertising. I'm not eligible."

Her body stiffened, bending away from him. "You're married?"

He jerked. "Christ, no! I'm sorry. I didn't mean to . . . ah, shit."

She blew out a heavy sigh. "Whew. That was an unpleasant jolt to my nervous system that I definitely did not need."

He tilted her chin up. "Please," he said, earnestly. "I'm sorry. All I meant was, a guy who has no idea where he came from isn't eligible. Not in the sense that the magazine writer meant. Somebody tried to kill me, fucked up my face, took my memories, took the life I was supposed to have. I'm lucky I'm not dead, or a drooling vegetable. I can't see them coming, since I don't know who to be on the lookout for. It's not a topic for a gushy article about rich bachelors to make the ladies swoon. And besides. The scars don't photograph well."

"Rich? Are you really?" she asked bluntly.

He cleared his throat. "Well. I don't know. Everything's relative."

"To my father, you mean?" Her voice was matter of fact.

"Yeah," he admitted. "Compared to him, I'm barely scraping by."

"What does barely scraping by mean to you, exactly?"

He sighed. He deserved the grilling. "I own my home and vehicles outright. I've got some savings, some stocks, and a reliable source of income. Six figures, anually. Bruno's patented my designs. He figures I'd be begging in the streets, if not for him. Maybe I would be."

She shook her head. "He's cut me off, you know."

"What?" Kev floundered, lost. "Who cut you off? From what?"

"My dad. He's cut me off from the Parrish money. I won't get a penny of it, unless I reform, and I'm not capable of reforming. I just thought you should know. I like to be upfront about the fact that I'm actually not an heiress at all. Saves problems. Misunderstandings."

"Well, and so?" he asked carefully. "What of it? You seem to be doing fine without your family's fortune. What's the problem?"

She waved her hand at the tiny room, at the pressboard dorm room furniture. "You call this fine?"

"No," he said quietly. "I call *you* fine. Like a South Sea pearl."

She opened her mouth, and closed it. Color came and went in her face. "Ah," she whispered. "Um, thank you. For saying that."

There was an awkward silence. He hid his own emotion by hiding his face against the swirling coils of her hair, pooled against the sheet, inhaling its scent, memorizing its texture. Fragrant and silky.

"So. Um." He searched for another starting place, and re-cycled an old one. "So you read that dumb article. That's wild. Small world."

"I read the whole thing," she said. "Your brother's cute. Great dimples. I'm a sucker for an eligible bachelor story."

Was she fucking with him? He lifted his head, peered at her. A weird moment passed in which she wouldn't meet his eyes, but her lips were quivering. "Maybe I don't want you to meet him after all," he said.

The curve of her mouth widened. She poked at his chest. "Come on," she wheedled. "Can't I tease? Weren't we trying for lighthearted?"

"It's not my strong point," he confessed.

"Mine, either, but I'll make an effort if you will. And keep in mind. I haven't spent the last ten years of my life drawing sexually charged graphic novels about your little brother."

It was the first time she'd openly admitted to their myste-rious bond. He wrapped himself around her and tried to let himself believe that this was really happening. He actually did feel this good.

It scared him. The better he felt, the deeper and vaster the abyss into which he might plunge. Even so. It felt good, to be known, to be seen. Who knew. He was more egocentric than he'd ever dreamed.

"Kites and toys," she mused. "I've been buying Lost Boys science sets for Ronnie for years. Great stuff. Mind candy for smart kids. Fun for adults, too. Strange, though. You don't strike me as the playful type. Have you always wanted to design toys? Since you can remember?"

He shook his head. "No. It was just something I did with my hands, to keep busy. Bruno had the idea to turn it into a moneymaker. It would never have occurred to me."

"But you're so good at it," she said.

He didn't answer, unwilling to sound arrogant or ungrateful. Truth was, he felt the same cool detachment about Lost Boys that he felt about almost every other aspect of his life. Floating, indifferent. It wasn't the work he was supposed to have been doing.

It was honest work, and Bruno had made it lucrative. No complaints there. But it was busywork, not real work. He could do it half asleep, blindfolded, with his hands tied. Sitting on the john.

He longed to throw himself at something bigger, harder, thornier. Something complex, that kicked his ass, drove him nuts. Something he could flog his brain against for years before he reached a conclusion.

What that something might be, he did not know, but he figured it had slipped away from him forever, even if he did get his memories back. He'd lost a huge chunk of his life, and his professional potential along with it. Whatever tight competitive window he might been aiming for before his life broke in half, he'd have missed it by decades.

Whatever. Designing toys was a way to keep his hands busy and bills paid. He didn't want to seem as if he were belittling Bruno's remarkable accomplishment. It was due to Bruno that Lost Boys was a thriving business. That was talent, too, of a different type, a type he did not have, and he respected it. He'd throw toy designs at Bruno for as long as his little brother cared to develop and market them. Easy money. It made life smoother. He was grateful for that. He truly was.

"I don't know what I meant to do with my life before . . . what happened to me happened," he said quietly. "But it wasn't making toys. It's great that they sell. But it's not my . . . I'm not at peace with it."

"You're bored," she said quietly.

She'd nailed it, but he declined to accept or deny the truth of that statement. "I haven't been to work for months," he said. "Bruno's producing from the overflow stockpile. I've been too busy since the waterfall. First recuperating. Then trying to find clues to my past."

She propped herself up onto her elbow. "How did you find me?"

He quickly told her of waking from the coma, the flashback that led to Patil's misfortune, and the name he'd remembered. Osterman.

"I did some research, and found a picture of Osterman on Facebook. Desmond Marr was in the picture, which led to Helix. And the Helix site is where I saw a picture of your father. I recognized him, from my dreams. But I was nowhere with it until I found his name."

"Until now," she finished. "You're somewhere now."

"Yeah," he agreed. Incredible, but true. He was somewhere. But amazingly, this somewhere had nothing to do with his past. And everything to do with what was happening right now. This perfect, precious second. Edie. Sweet and warm. He could forget all of it, the ghosts and the nightmares. He was tempted to just leave the past alone. Concentrate on just being with her. It was enough for this lifetime.

God, it was enough for all eternity.

He buried his face in her hair. "Do you have any more condoms?"

"I think it was a three pack," she murmured, laughter in her voice. "There should be two left. Was that an idle question?"

"Are you sore?" he asked, nervously. "Did I hurt you?"

She stretched luxuriously in the clasp of his arms. "Fishing for compliments, are we?"

"No. Just rock bottom, baseline reassurance."

She grabbed his face, jerked it around so it was inches from her own, and kissed him, her fingers holding his jaw. "I have never in my life dreamed that sex that good existed," she said. "Are you reassured?"

The scar tissue on his right cheek was burning again. He didn't smile that big very often. "So where are the condoms?" he demanded.

"Top drawer, right side, way in the back," she said.

He bounded up like he was on springs, and rummaged through delicate, feminine scraps until he found what he sought.

No power games this time. He was buzzed up on a wild, manic high. He needed to get as close to her as a man could get to a woman. To look into her eyes, make her sigh and buck and heave against him.

He rolled on the condom, and poised himself over her, waiting for the invitation of her body, arms reaching, legs parting, hips canting to accept him. She wiggled to find the best angle. Embracing him as he squeezed himself inside her, in one slow, deliberate shove. He stopped, breathless with effort, holding his weight off her. "You OK?" he gasped.

She nodded, her hips jerking against his, her pussy clenching tight. Pulling him into that delicious suckling kiss of acceptance.

He wished he could feel it without the latex. But there

would be time enough for that. The thought of a future with her gave rise to a surge of terrified joy. His body took over. He went at her, bed squeaking, breath rasping, hips thudding against hers. Whimpers jolted from her throat, but she clutched him, egging him on. Her nails stinging his skin.

Slick, hot. So beautiful. Those delicate pussy lips clung, bathed him with lube. He pulled her up and rolled over, setting her astride so he could watch those amazing breasts bob and swing, her hair brush his chest when she sagged forward, swirling when her head flung back. Riding him frantically straight into a shuddering mutual climax.

He lay there, blasted and shaking. Destroyed.

He was so unused to sleep sneaking up on him, he had no chance to fight it. It grabbed him, and yanked him under.

CHAPTER

11

Edie clambered off Kev, taking care not to wake him, but there was no need for such stealth. He was out for the count. Strange, to see him like that. He was usually the embodiment of mindful attention. The energy radiating from him was so intense, so concentrated. Seeing him sprawled and totally unconscious reminded her of his vulnerability.

He was no superhero. She'd worn him out. She almost laughed. Make way for Edie, femme fatale. Men swooned when she drew near.

She snorted. Hah. Or fled, rather.

She knelt, stared at his scars. It was almost inconceivable that someone would deliberately hurt another person like that. Her eleven-year-old imagination had not really grasped it. Which was a good thing. Her childhood traumas had twisted her quite enough already.

He was so beautiful. Greek-god beautiful, scars or no scars.

The thought sparked the urge to draw, never far from her fingertips. He'd given permission, after all. He'd asked her to. Begged her, even. She didn't have to feel guilty about it. Or even particularly sneaky. Who knew? Maybe if he was asleep, their mutual lust vibes wouldn't be clouding the airwaves, distracting them. She might even sense something that could be helpful for him. She'd never drawn a sleeping person before. Maybe she would see his dreams.

She tiptoed into the other room, avoiding the squeaking floorboards. She grabbed her big sketchbook, and some pencils. Big man, big page. Lots of space. Her fingers twitched with eagerness.

She'd drawn naked men in her classes back in school, but this was no exercise in human anatomy. He was so long and lovely, every fluid line of him. The picture grew and changed as she lost herself in it. The lines of his sleeping face looked so different in repose. Younger.

She tried to capture the muscles over his ribs, the muscular swells and dips of his flanks. His prodigious member was draped across his thigh, still sheathed in latex. She'd take the condom off herself, but she might wake him, and she didn't want to miss the chance to catch the details. There were newer scars on the swell of his thigh. Bright red, crosshatched from stitches. Surgical scars. The waterfall incident.

She realized that she'd started drawing a background behind his reclining figure, but it wasn't a room, or a landscape. It was a web of interconnecting lines. She'd filled the page before she recognized it.

A spiderweb. Oh, God. Chills began to shake her, but she did not stop drawing. He'd asked for this. She had to see where it took her.

She could always rip it up before he woke. If it was really bad.

Her pencil was going faster. Sketching quickly, filling in the huge ovoid shape, the hairy, jointed legs. A spider, gigantic in proportion to his sleeping body. She lurked, black abdomen gleaming, the image of gloating malevolence. Kev stretched out before her, unconscious. His face, in her inner vision, was deathly pale, but he did not seem dead.

He seemed drugged. Helpless. And doomed.

As a graphic artist, she knew instinctively how to make the the picture work. The light, the shadows, the proportions, the perspectives. She knew how to make it spooky and evocative, how to invoke dread. Her pencil worked fast, did its job. She finished the horns of the spider, the hot, mad gleam of its little eyes, and the pencil dropped from her cold, numb hand. The sound of it hitting the floor woke him.

Kev jerked up onto his elbow and read the scene in one quick glance; the sketchbook, the fallen pencil, the stricken look on her face.

"What did you see?" he asked.

She closed the sketchbook. What she'd just drawn would send any guy with half a brain running to get away from the spooky, possibly psychotic girl. "Nothing much," she hedged. "Just, you know, the usual hooey. Disaster, scorched earth, apocalyptic doom. Standard, for me. I didn't see anything in particular."

"Bullshit." He swung his legs over the bed. "I saw the look on your face. It was a bad one, right? Come on. Show me."

He seemed so unperturbed, for a guy who'd just gotten his fortune told in the worst possible way. He held out his hand.

She shook her head, clutching the sketchpad to her like a shield.

"Don't be upset," he urged. "Try not to worry, Edie."

The words, juxtaposed against the image of a gigantic venomous spider made her shake with hysterical laughter. "Don't be upset?" she gasped out. "What, does doom just not bother you?"

He shook his head. "It's not like it's a surprise. Somebody's out there gunning for me. It's written all over my body. I wish I knew who, and why, but I don't, so I don't bother worrying about it. They'll find me, or they won't. They'll finish the job, or they won't. Why sweat it?"

"So you just don't mind pesky issues like mortal danger?"

"You get used to it." One smooth lunge brought him from the bed over to her, on his knees. He plucked the sketchbook out of her hands.

Yanking it back would be a losing battle. She braced herself as he rifled through the pages. He found the picture she'd just drawn.

She looked away, dreading the look she had seen too many times before. The look that said, *this chick is more trouble than she's worth.*

But he didn't look up. He gazed at the drawing, brow furrowed.

"Hmm," he murmured. "A giant spider. And I'm her lunch. Yeah, it's creepy. I can see how that might upset you. Sorry about that."

The shudders were edging closer to a screaming sobfest. She'd been weepy enough during the sex, and thank God he'd been mellow about that, but enough, already. "You're the king of understatement," she snapped. "And why should you be the one to apologize? You're not the one who drew it!"

"Yeah, but I'm the one being hunted by the spider, right? I wonder what the spider vibe is all about," he mused. "Looks like a black widow. The dangerous ones are female, so is it a female to look out for? The danger comes from a woman? Strange. What I remember of the stuff that happened to me didn't involve women. Only men."

His tone astonished her. Calm, practical. Is it going to rain today and should I take my umbrella. Trying to logically analyze the giant spider she'd drawn for him. To extract conclusions from it.

After all the thundering drama she'd taken all those years for her psychic drawing, it knocked her right on her ass. She burst into tears.

Kev tossed the sketchbook aside, alarmed, and reached

for her. "Oh, God! Edie, I'm sorry. I didn't mean to upset you!"

"You? Upset me?" That made her laugh and cry at the same time. "I'm just . . . it's so strange, that you take it so well. This is the part where everybody's yelling, and I'm climbing out a bathroom window and shimmying down a drain pipe before I get hauled off to the psych ward."

He dropped a warm kiss on top of her naked thigh. "I asked you to do it for me," he said. "Hey, are you hungry?"

It was such a weird non sequitur, she stared at him stupidly for over a minute before she could organize her thoughts to reply. "Ah," she said at last. "I don't know. I hadn't thought about it. Why do you ask?"

"We could go out," he suggested. "Dinner. Like a normal couple."

That phrase made her shake with giggles. "A normal couple? How do normal couples act? You'd have to coach me. I don't get out much."

"Me neither, but we could fake it. It would be nice. Hell, it would be fun. We can . . . I don't know. Find a nice restaurant? Catch a movie? Find some music, in a jazz club? Whatever you want to do."

A date. Wow. It did sound nice. It did sound like fun. In fact, it sounded incredibly, supremely wonderful. She was so moved, it prompted another surge of tears, which she fought down savagely.

"That's sweet, Kev, but I can't," she said, with huge regret. "I have to go to this hellish corporate banquet for my dad's retirement from Helix tonight. I hate these things, but I can't afford the price I'd pay if I didn't go. Plus, it's a chance to see my little sister, which I'm usually not allowed to do. So I can't miss it."

He looked crestfallen, and then glanced up again, a speculative gleam in his eye. "What about after?"

"After?" She was startled. "It'll be late. After midnight, at least, by the time all the speechifying and schmoozing is done. I'll have to stay to the bitter end, since my dad is the star of the evening."

He shrugged. "So? I don't sleep. I certainly won't be able to tonight. Especially not if I have a chance in hell of seeing you again." He hesitated, looking uncertain. "Of course, if you need sleep yourself—"

"No, I don't," she said hastily. "Not at all. It's not like I have a day job, or anything." In fact, she usually worked at night, when the air waves were least polluted, and it was easiest to concentrate.

He grinned. "Excellent. I'll pick you up after the banquet."

She wiped her eyes, and gave him a tremulous smile. "And I'll try to find a moment to ask my father about your—"

"No," he said firmly. "Don't."

She was taken aback. "But don't you want more information?"

"I don't want to make trouble for you. You've got enough problems. I'll take care of it. We'll keep our thing separate, and private."

She hesitated, but there was no point in not coming clean. "There's something you need to know," she said. "Nothing is private in my life. My father is probably studying photos of you as we speak."

He looked startled. "How's that? We just met!"

"He keeps tabs on me, 24-7," she said. "I'm so used to it, I barely notice anymore. My dad is heavy into control."

He digested that. "Your father will recognize me if he sees photos."

"I imagine so," she agreed. "If I did, he will. He'll be hysterical. In fact, now that I think about it, it might be tricky for me to slip away and meet you tonight. I'll try, but don't take it personally if I don't show up. It just means I'm trapped in a limo, being scolded and lectured."

He smiled. The heat in his eyes made her reach up and give him a playful shove. "Stop smoldering at me," she said.

"I have to go to the salon to meet my cousin and my aunt. Wild sex is over. Duty calls."

He jerked his chin toward the dress that hung from the wall sconce, wrapped in billowing yards of clear plastic. "Is that your dress?"

She nodded. He touched the finely pleated champagne pink chiffon frill at the hem. "It's pretty," he said.

"Thank you. I have a closet full of these dresses in my bedroom at my family's house. Used for one night, and then into the closet. God forbid anyone photograph me in an evening dress that's been seen."

"I like it." His voice was a sensual rasp. "Put it on."

She was charmed, but suspicious. "Don't get any ideas, because it wrinkles if you frown at it. And it won't fit without the strapless bra—"

"By all means, model the lingerie, too. Can't I just watch you dress? Watch you do your hair and makeup?"

"I'm not dressing here," she said, regretfully. "I'm not trusted to do my own makeup and hair. In about, let's see—" She leaned over, and peeked at a clock on her bookcase. "Holy shit! I'm thirteen minutes late! The car's waiting already, and my aunt's going to kill me. I have to jump into the shower. Excuse me." She lunged for the bathroom.

Once alone with the latch hooked, she tried to release backed up emotion in a sigh, but her chest was too full, too tight, to let air in or out. Her legs shook. Her tender inside parts were so sensitive, sending shockwaves of pleasure down her legs with every movement.

She twisted her hair into a loose, fuzzy knot and anchored it with a hair-stick, since Philipe the stylist from hell would insist on washing it himself even if she came in dripping wet. But a shower could not be foregone. Not after the marvelously juicy events of the last hour or so.

He was waiting patiently, fully dressed, when she came out, swathed in the towel. She forced herself to be businesslike about being naked in front of him. He'd seen everything she had. At close range.

Still, it was hard to pull on the cream colored thong while he watched every move like a hungry cat watching a mouse. She hocked her C-cup boobs into the strapless bra, engineered to immobilize cleavage to discreet china-doll firmness, and control indecorous bouncing not fitting for a Parrish, and he didn't miss a move. A flush was burned onto his cheekbones. A visible, prominent erection pressed against the jeans that he had discreetly redonned. What a scorching turn-on it was, to be a turn-on for someone else. Who knew. Revelation after revelation. She reached for her jeans. Kev looked betrayed.

"Wait a goddamn minute!" he protested. "What about the dress?"

"Kev, I'm already so late—"

"Please, humor me. Just slip it over your head. I want to be able to imagine you there. All dressed up. Your hair, swirling down."

The intensity of his gaze made her fingers clumsy, and her breath catch. She heaved up the billowing sheer plastic to pluck the gown off the hanger. Slid it over her her head, let it slither over her torso.

She turned her back to him. "Fasten the hooks for me, OK?"

He was on the task before she finished saying the words, deftly doing her up. He turned her back toward the mirror, and loomed behind her, his big hands spanning her waist, his body heat burning through the delicate fabric. His eyes burned. She gulped, shivered.

"A princess in a fairy tale," he said. He swept her hair to the side and tenderly kisssed her throat. "I wish I could sneak into the ball and abduct you." The seductive touch of his lips made her shiver. Pleading silently with his body, for something he knew she could not grant him.

Manipulative bastard.

"Don't," she whispered. "Please. I'm already late, and I'm going to pay for it in chunks of bleeding flesh."

"I'll write you a note," he suggested.

Giggles burst out before she could stop them. "I can't risk messing this dress up. Maybe later we can, ah, use it. As a prop."

He grasped the skirt, and hiked it up, over her knees, her thighs. "You'd let me fuck you?" he asked, sounding fascinated. "In this dress?"

"Why not?" She plucked the fabric from his hands, let the skirt drop. "I won't be allowed to wear it again. Would it turn you on, to toss the skirt of an eight thousand dollar evening dress over my face?"

His eyes widened. "Eight thousand? Really? Holy shit!"

"Really," she said, glumly. "Egregious waste, I say. I don't approve. I was bullied into it."

"Ah." He shook his head, as if trying to clear it. "Yeah. OK. Just, ah, tripping out on erotic footage in my head. The part after I abduct the princess and lock her in my apartment. Maybe we should forget going out tonight. Just go straight to my place, and order in."

Her face must be red as a plum. "That would be fine with me."

"But I won't throw the skirt over your face," he said. "Talk about an egregious waste."

Aw. What a sweet thing to say. She couldn't bear to look at him, she was so flustered. "Unhook me, please."

"Wait." He held up his cell, and snapped a picture of her. Then he slid it back into his pocket. "To keep me company while I wait."

He took his time unfastening the hooks, fingers lingering over her back, each touch of his fingers echoing through her nerves.

She hung up the dress and threw jeans and a loose sweater over the lingerie. Aunt Evelyn had opted to keep her niece's stole, evening bag and shoes in her own possession, since Edie lived in such a dangerous, disgraceful dump. Edie only had the dress herself because it happened to have required fittings. A necessary risk.

She shrugged her sweater jacket on, and abruptly remembered her contacts. Oh, God. Her hideous horn-rimmed glasses were persona non grata at family functions. She shoved the bottles that held the lenses and the saline solution into her purse, and turned to Kev. "So, um. If you want to avoid the bodyguards, go around to the back—"

"Why would I want to do that?"

Her mouth worked. "Well . . . I . . . I—"

"I want to check them out," he said. "I want to see if they're worthy of the job of protecting someone as special as you. I'd like to take note of their faces, their cars, and their license plates. Here, I'll carry the dress down for you."

He grabbed the garment bag, and opened the door for her.

Wow. That was a shift in focus. Talk about accentuating the positive. The happiness blazing out from deep inside her was scary.

Calm down. She had to put this experience in perspective. She'd had a one-afternoon stand. That might be all. He might disappear. She had to be prepared for it. It had been worth it. He'd been wonderful.

She was a big girl. She could handle it.

They exchanged numbers, established meeting plans, and he slid his arm through hers. Floated her out her door. Wafted her down the stairs, inches above the ground. Puffy pink clouds bore her feet along.

The limo was waiting. Paul was driving, as luck would have it. A humorless, three-hundred-pound ex-Ranger, Paul was Daddy's man, through and through. He considered Edie to be an ungrateful, pinheaded piece of fluff for not toeing the Parrish line.

When Paul saw Kev, he straightened up, put his hand under his coat. His face was openly hostile as he jerked the limo door open.

Edie slid into the limo, took the garment bag Kev handed to her, and watched the silent showdown after Paul slammed the door. Paul, swaggering and scowling. Kev relaxed and alert, taking it in.

Paul lifted his cell, framed a shot, and snapped a couple photos of Kev. He got into the car without a word. Edie stared over her shoulder as the limo pulled away. Kev lifted his hand, smiling at her. The look in his eyes was so soft. He looked so . . . God, he looked so happy.

An impulse seized her, swelling into something uncontrollable.

"Stop!" she yelled.

Paul jerked to a stop. Horns blared. "What is the matter with you?" he snarled.

Edie shoved open her door, leaped out of the vehicle and almost fell on her face. Kev caught her headlong rush, looking startled.

"Hey," he said. "What's wrong?"

"There's something else," she confessed. "I didn't want to say anything, because I don't have any info, or proof, and I was afraid to get your hopes up and then be dead wrong and make things worse for you, but . . . but I just want to . . . to . . ." Her voice trailed off, in an agony of doubt. "To give you something," she finished.

Kev's face looked stark and taut, braced for anything. "Tell me."

Paul slammed the limo door shut, with the force of pure disgust.

Kev's eyes flicked up and looked over her shoulder. He lifted his hand in silent command, indicating that Paul keep his distance.

Amazingly, Paul stopped.

Edie glanced around, startled. Paul looked like he'd swallowed a lemon, tricked into obeying an unspoken order, but he stayed where he was, shifting from foot to foot, beefy arms folded over his big chest.

The words came out in a rush. "I had dinner with my father a few weeks ago. He told me three years ago he got a visit from some men who were looking for you. They said that they were your brothers."

Kev's hands had been resting on her shoulders. They suddenly tightened, to a painful grip. His lips went white. "Brothers?"

"Your brothers," she repeated. "They're out there, Kev. Looking for you, thinking about you. Missing you. My dad said they were very, um, intense. The way they questioned him. He had nothing to tell them, but he said that one of them actually, ah . . . threatened him physically."

Kev let out a sharp breath, and put his hand over his eyes. "Thank you," he said, hoarsely.

She stood on her tiptoes, tilted his head down, and kissed him, but his face was stiff, his eyes distant.

"He didn't say their names?" he asked.

"Not to me," she admitted. "Sorry."

He nodded, and swayed forward, placing his forehead gently against hers as his hand cupped her face. "Thank you," he said again, in a whisper she could barely hear.

"Anytime," she said. "I just hope that it's true. And that it works out for you." Her throat bumped over a painful lump. "I would hate to disappoint you, and hurt you even more. That's why I hesitated to tell you. But I just . . . I couldn't wait."

"I'm glad," he said. "And it wouldn't matter. Even if nothing comes of it. Thank you anyway. You're very, very sweet, Edie."

He kissed her temples, her cheek, and then suddenly they were kissing each other again, clinging, hanging on like it was the end of the world and the only way to survive was to get closer, tighter.

Paul cleared his throat, a loud, hacking sound. Then the wet *plop* of a glob of spit hit the sidewalk, insultingly close to them.

"Ms. Parrish," Paul said. "You're forty minutes late already."

Edie detached herself, stumbling, and backed toward the car.

Paul opened her door, helping her in with a little more force than pure professionality called for. He slammed the door shut.

He turned to Kev, and snapped three more pictures on the cell, then baldly tapped into his device, e-mailing them.

Kev did not appear to notice.

Edie craned her neck as the car pulled away. He stood on the sidewalk as if he'd been turned to stone, staring back until the car turned and he was lost to sight.

"Who was that guy?" Paul demanded, glaring over his shoulder.

Like it was any of his goddamned business. "A friend," she said.

Paul grunted. "Friend, huh?"

"That's right. Watch the road, Paul."

He screeched to a stop at the light. "Doesn't matter," he said. "We'll find out about him. I have a team following him right now."

The man's pointless, hostile arrogance made her feel sick and tired. "Leave him alone," she said, knowing the order to be useless.

Whatever she did would be stomped on, messed with, corrupted. After Paul's team caught up with him, Kev might well conclude that the down side of hanging out with Edie Parrish outweighed the up side.

But nothing could take away what had happened that afternoon. And if that was all it could be, for whatever reason, she'd still be grateful. Goddamnit. For every wonderful, perfect, shining crumb of it.

No matter what happened. She hugged herself, tried to breathe.

Tried to believe it.

CHAPTER
12

Brothers.

Brakes squealed, horns blared. Kev jerked away from sudden death in the form of a red Toyota FourRunner.

Pay attention. Lack of vigilance will get you killed. There it was, that stern voice floating up from the depths of memory. He assumed that it was memory. Since Tony found him, nobody had ever lectured him about vigilance, or lack thereof. This voice was from before.

Brothers. He stopped just short of braining himself on a light pole.

Fuck, maybe he should take a cab the rest of the way home. Except that he was too wound up. He'd bust an artery, cooped up in the back seat of a taxi. Better to keep moving.

Calm the fuck down, bozo. Right. After hours in the angel's arms? And what an angel. Complicated, seductive. Wounded and wary. So gorgeous, she made his eyes sting to say nothing of his throbbing dick.

His mind was bouncing around like a pinball machine. Overloaded, lights flashing, bells dinging. Edie. Brothers. It was a long walk to his neighborhood, but he had wild energy to burn off. And he needed to talk himself down from this dangerous euphoria.

Not the Edie component. That part he didn't have a chance of suppressing, nor did he want to. He was entitled to that euphoria, and he'd goddamn well enjoy it. Edie was a miracle.

He wasn't sure how to sort it all out yet. Finding out that his magical talisman had been a sad, lonely little girl, dressed up for her birthday party. He'd clung to his angel for so long, used her to such good effect, he was convinced there had been real power in it. His angel wasn't just a self-induced head trip. She'd saved his life and his sanity, many times over. There was grace in that, and he would honor it.

But now he'd traded it. For another kind of grace. A different miracle.

Brothers. God.

He couldn't allow himself to get all intense about these possible brothers til he knew more about Parrish's agenda. What Parrish knew, what he was hiding. The guys who claimed to be his brothers could be the ones who'd tried to kill him in the first place. Edie said that they'd threatened her father, so these men were no strangers to violence.

But then again, neither was Kev himself. He made an effort to keep his relationship to the world polite and respectful, but when the world kicked him in the teeth, he kicked back. And he kicked hard.

Parrish could have been wrong. Or just lying. But why? Why invent something random like that, out of the blue, eighteen years after the fact? And to Edie, too? There was no reason for it. No sense in it.

But the intensity of his desire for it to be true could bend his perceptions, make him blind to things that were stupidly obvious. The only way to protect himself from that danger was to stay cool, detached. To wait quietly for the muddy waters to clear.

Brothers? Holy shit. Holy . . . fucking . . . *shit.*

He was almost home when it happened. Like divine punishment for letting himself get so distracted. The guy was built like a fucking refrigerator, and he didn't even notice the clown until he did a dance step to block Kev's way and got right in his face. "Excuse me, sir," he said. "We need to talk to you."

Another one seized his arms from behind. His Fade Shadowseeker books fell. He was in motion before they hit the sidewalk, whipping to head butt the arm grabber. Cursing himself in that instant of grace before the pain hit while he took advantage of the man's loosened grip.

It hit. *Fuck,* that hurt, but he ignored it as he loaded the meathead onto his hip and sent him hurtling headfirst into his buddy's midriff. They skidded, bounced off the brick, tripping over garbage. Savage back kick to the nose of the guy who had spoken, *whap.* Side kick to the knee of the one struggling to get up, *crunch.*

He heaved the first guy headfirst into the brick wall of his apartment building. Damn. One would think he could come up with a defense strategy that didn't involve using his own healing skull with its bruised, long-suffering brain as a club. Like the headaches and nausea weren't fucking him left, right, and sideways already.

Anger at himself loaded the kick he aimed at the guy's coccyx and sent him stumbling once again into the mold-slimed bricks. "Who the fuck are you, and who sent you?" Kev snarled.

The guy whose knee he'd smashed was whimpering, curled into a comma around his fucked up leg. The other one coughed, splayed against the wall. He peeked around, spat out a tooth.

Kev grabbed him by the shirt collar, and yanked him back a few inches. "Want to kiss the wall again, asshole? No? Then talk!"

"Charles Parrish," the guy gasped out. "Security staff."

Blank dismay flooded him, fizzling out the combat buzz. "Oh, *fuck*," he muttered savagely. "Why didn't you say so before you put your hands on me? You morons! I wouldn't have broken your nose! I wouldn't have broken his kneecap!"

The guy coughed wetly. Blood spattered from his mouth. "We were, uh, supposed to take you in," he rasped. "Boss's orders."

Kev rubbed the back of his aching meat mallet of a skull. He dropped his head back and stared up at the strip of cobalt-blue evening sky that showed between the buildings, cursing in Calabrese dialect. He'd learned it from years in the diner kitchen with Tony. Tony's principle mode of communication was virulent profanity, and Kev had had lots of opportunity to learn. Years of silent, intense listening.

Great. What a way to open a dialogue with the guy who held the secrets to unlock your whole life. To say nothing of being your new girlfriend's father. What a calling card. Maim one of his employees, why didn't he. Shatter a kneecap. Knock out some fucking teeth.

Sweet, as Bruno would say. Awesome first impression. Stellar.

He sighed, dug in his coat pocket for his wallet, but couldn't find a pen. Goddamn things were all over the place until you needed one.

"You got a pen?" he asked the guy, gruffly.

The man peeked around his shoulder, eyes wide and white-rimmed, blood reddened lips trembling. "Huh?"

"A pen," Kev repeated, patiently. "I need one."

The man fumbled in his leather jacket pocket for a moment, and produced a sleek, heavy gold pen, liberally smeared with blood. Kev dragged out one of his Lost Boys Flywear business cards, and shoved the guy against the wall. "I need your back to write against. Hold still." He scribbled for a moment. "This is my home phone, cell, and personal e-mail. Take this, and give it to your boss, if he wants to get in touch."

The other guy didn't seem inclined to move, so Kev jerked the man's shoulder around and shoved the card into the guy's hand. He dug in his pocket for the pack of tissues he had stashed in there, since his eyes tended to water in strong light since the waterfall incident.

He handed one to the man. "Here. Mop yourself up."

The guy held it against his streaming nose, and dabbed, wincing.

"Give me one of your business cards," Kev said.

The other man stared at him, stupidly. "Huh?"

"I gave you mine," Kev pointed out.

"Why would you want—"

"Why would that be any of your fucking business? I might want to get in touch with you. You're my new best buddy, right?"

The man shrank back as he dug into his pocket. He handed Kev a blood-smeared card. "The first one's the main number of the security service," he said. "The one below is my personal cell."

Kev peered at the card. "Max Collier. That's you?" The guy coughed, and nodded. "OK, Max," he went on. "Tell Mr. Parrish I'm sorry I fucked up his employees." He tried to leave it at that, he really did, but he was so fucking irritated, the impulse to scold outstripped his self-control. "But you guys were assholes to jump me like that! I would have been happy to talk to you, or to Parrish himself, at any time! Just call me. Make an appointment, like a civilized person, OK? I don't like getting jumped on the street. It's rude. It makes me tense. It also makes me spout pompous lectures, which is embarrassing. OK?" He waited for a moment. "OK?" he prompted, more forcefully. "We clear on that, Max? For the next time?"

The guy nodded, jerkily. "Crystal clear."

"Good." Kev collected the graphic novels scattered on the sidewalk, and gazed at the guy groaning and rocking in the garbage. "How far are you guys from your car? Need some help moving him?"

"No, thanks, I'm good," Max said hastily.

Kev shoved his hands into his pockets. "OK. Get that guy to Urgent Care before he goes into shock. And, uh, have a good evening."

"Thanks." Max Collier's voice shook. He seized his colleague under the armpits, and started to drag him.

Ay yi yi. Kev winced, and gritted his teeth at the gurgling shriek of pain that came out as the man's injured leg bumped and dragged over the scattered bags of garbage. The guy's patella was probably in several small, bloody pieces. That had to hurt.

Kev waited, making sure the guy got his buddy safely loaded into the back seat of the black SUV that idled half a block down the street before he unlocked his door. Then Edie and her revelations rushed back into his mind. He promptly forgot the incident as he ran up the steps, springs in his feet. He was enjoying the springy sensation so much, he got blindsided when he opened the door and flipped on the light.

"Where the *fuck* have you been?" Bruno spun around in the computer chair to face him.

The graphic novels exploded out of Kev's arms. "Sweet Jesus!" he yelled. "Don't do this to me! My nerves can't take it."

"Your nerves? Yours?" Bruno got up. "I've been sitting here for hours, waiting for a phone call from an emergency room, or a prison—"

"You knew where I was going! We discussed it! At great length!"

"You fucked me over! We had a deal! You were supposed

to drop into the bookstore, discreetly check her out, and then call me!" Bruno roared. "But you turned off your fucking phone!"

Kev felt a twinge of guilt. He had promised that, to get Bruno off his back. And the second he'd seen those angel eyes, he'd forgotten everything. Nothing existed but Edie. He tried not to smile, but Bruno was quick at reading faces, even a deadpan scarred mask like his own.

"What's so fucking funny?" his brother snarled. "Did you talk to her? Where did you go? What happened to you? You did something dumb, didn't you? I can tell. I can smell it on you."

"Jesus, Bruno. Calm down."

Bruno opened his mouth, and then stopped. "You're smiling," he said. "What's up with that? Are you on some new type of pain pill?"

Kev shook his head. Bruno stepped closer, his eyes narrowing.

"Wait. You saw that girl, didn't you? You approached her. You talked to her. You promised you wouldn't. You goddamn lying *dog!*"

Kev had never told Bruno about his little angel. Now didn't seem an opportune time to explain that he and Edie had already met.

He shrugged off his coat. "Leave me alone. I'm tired."

Bruno's eyes lit up. "Oh, my God. You got laid, didn't you? You didn't just talk to Edie Parrish, you dirty bastard. You nailed her!"

Kev flinched. What had happened between himself and Edie could not be reduced to that crude phrase. "Don't speak about her that way."

But Bruno was capering and crowing like the twelve-year-old that he truly was. "I can't believe it! So why didn't you bring her back here?"

"I tried," Kev snapped. "She's busy tonight. A Helix banquet to honor the big cheese dad who's retiring. I've got a date with her after."

Bruno blew out a breath, like a stallion. "You're making me dizzy. You meet Edie Parrish, dance the horizontal tango with her, get the shit pounded out of you by her daddy's security, and now, you're taking her out on a date? All in a day's work for Kevlar, the mystery man."

"I told you not to talk about her that way," Kev repeated. "And they didn't pound me. I pounded them."

"Whoa!" Bruno blinked. "So, ah, how was it? How is she?"

He frowned at his brother. "That's private," he muttered.

Bruno waggled his eyebrows. "Lest my filthy mind skulk too near your shining goddess? Soiling her with my nasty— *mmhph!*"

He pinned Bruno to the wall. His brother struggled, clutching at Kev's hand, which was clamped over his throat. "I meant it," Kev said, his voice steely. "Be respectful, or I'll beat you to a bloody pulp."

Bruno made a theatrical gagging sound, but an uncontrollable grin was carving out the very dimples Edie had so admired. "You've got a lot of energy today," his brother croaked out, looking impressed.

"You have no idea," Kev held Bruno clamped to the wall for a moment, and decided to keep Edie's brothers bombshell to himself for now. No need to get Bruno into a jealous snit until Kev knew more.

He let Bruno drop. His brother rubbed his throat, his face thoughtful. "It occurs to me that you're probably the one guy on the planet who might be a halfway decent boyfriend for this Parrish chick."

Kev was startled, the Fade Shadowseeker books flashing through his mind. He crouched to gather them up. "Why do you say that?"

"Because you genuinely do not give a fuck about the money."

Kev laid the books on his desk, and frowned, genuinely puzzled. "What does money have to do with anything?"

Bruno rolled his eyes. "Hello? Helix heiress? Multiple billions? Never crossed your mind? Of course not. That's Kevlar for you."

Kev shook his head. "She lives in a two room, fourth floor walk-up on NE Helmut with a broken knob lock, Bruno. She's not rich."

"You don't even know what I'm talking about, do you?" Bruno shook his head. "You are one crazy-ass son of a bitch."

"I'm not crazy," Kev said, irritated. "I just think it's irrelevant."

"Hah. God help me, but I don't think I could do it," Bruno said.

"Could what?"

"Look at an heiress of billions without seeing the money first," Bruno said baldly. "Ching ching. I'm not proud of it, but there it is."

Kev shrugged. "You've never seen Edie Parrish," he said softly.

Bruno looked charmed. "Aw. That's just sweet, bro. Check you out, man. You're in a class all your own. You get the gold star."

"Could we cut out the bullshit?" Kev asked plaintively. "You have to help me out. Since you're trespassing, make yourself useful."

"Useful how?"

"With the date," Kev said. "You're the ladies' man. Where do I take her? Is there a place in town that's good after midnight?"

"What kind of place?" Bruno's eyes narrowed.

"All I know is that she'll be in a floor-length, eight-thousand-dollar evening gown, so it has to be nice. Mellow. Good music, candlelight? A table someplace in the back where we can talk, hold hands?"

"Hold hands? The man wants to hold hands?" Bruno went bug-eyed. "Fuck me," he breathed. "You are in love."

Kev decided he didn't want to discuss that emotionally loaded issue with Bruno. "Don't know. Never been in love. Got any food?"

Bruno's eyes widened even more. "What's this about food?"

"For months, you've been bringing food here, and trying to shove it into my face. You mean to say you didn't bring some today?"

Bruno bounced up and down on the balls of his feet, punched a code into his cell, and waited, humming. "Yeah? Take-out order. One beef taco, one chorizo sausage quesadilla, an order of steak fajitas, an order of enchiladas, four chicken tamales, extra guac, sour cream, and extra spicy fresh salsa." His eyes flicked thoughtfully over Kev's body. "No beans," he said. "Not tonight. But put in a quadruple order of fresh tortilla chips, and a six-pack of Corona. And a lime. Got it? Great." He rattled off his card number and the address, and broke the connection.

Kev was taken aback. "Holy shit, Bruno. That's a lot of food."

"You need to tank up, both after sex and before it," Bruno said knowledgeably. "And I'll help you eat it. Getting a clueless slob like you ready for a hot date is going to give me an appetite."

"But I don't want to wait for food delivery," Kev complained. "I want to get going, find a parking place near the hotel. In case she gets bored, or wants to leave early. I don't want to risk missing her."

Bruno's eyes swept over him contemptuously. "In that? You're looking to escort a woman in an eight-thousand-dollar evening gown in those rags? Those jeans look like you slept in them. And what's on the shirt? Blood stains? Dude. Gross. Your blood, or the other guy's?"

Kev peered at the front of his sweater. There were brownish smears on his chest. Physical violence was hard on a guy's wardrobe.

"It's the other guy's blood," he said. "And get out of my face. We can't all be George Clooney."

Bruno rolled his eyes. "Get into the fucking shower," he directed. "I'll pick out your clothes. Just wash your hair. I'll gel it myself. Shave, too. Looks weird when the beard starts coming in only on one side of your jaw, and you look weird enough as it is. Put on the aftershave I gave you. Chicks love the stuff. You haven't even broken the seal."

"Stop snooping in my cabinets, punk," Kev grumbled as he headed for the bathroom.

He had to laugh at himself as he got ready. Primping for his date like some crushed out teenage boy. Not that he had any memory of being one of those, but he could imagine it. Sex on the brain. Young, dumb, and full of come. Shaking inside, with terrified joy.

He hadn't known sex like that existed. He'd never dreamed how deep it could cut. How hot it could burn. He was wide open to her now.

She could slide those slender, cool fingers in between his ribs, grab his heart, and squeeze it out of existence. And he didn't care. He'd found his angel. She was his. Or more precisely, he was hers.

And he was cooked.

CHAPTER

13

Sweet Jesus. It was freaking bedlam in there.

Sean leaned on the doorjamb of the kid's playroom and took a pull on his beer. Sveti had been on duty, having offered herself up as usual. She seemed to think being hosted by Tam and Val to go to high school in America meant she should babysit like a bounden slave. So far, nobody had been able to persuade her any differently. But she'd roped him into temporary kiddie coverage to run to the bathroom. He was counting the seconds til she came back. Christ, he was so tired.

He stared at the giggling, shrieking knot of kids, rubbing his eyes. Rachel was the ringleader, Val and Tam's four-and-a-half-year-old fireball with fuzzy, bouncing black ringlets. She was absorbing through her pores at a tender age the manipulative power of beauty, and who could expect less of Tam's kid. Blond Kevvie, Con and Erin's oldest, was almost three. He was attempting to dislodge Rachel from her perch on the rocking horse with the toy pistol and a yellow plastic hammer, a blatant attempt at hijacking, but Rachel held her own, batting him away with a rubber fairy wand. Davy and Margot's daughter Jeannie, five months younger than Kevvie, was jumping up and down, flopping her red mop like a muppet and screaming, apparently for the pure joy of it.

And this was nothing. Considering that Seth and Raine's ten-month-old son Jesse was only crawling, Becca and Nick's five-month-old daughter Sonia was just starting to wiggle on her belly like a snake, and two-month-old Madeline, Con and Erin's youngest, was asleep in the snuggle pouch against Erin's chest. In two or three years, the decible level would be tripled for these gatherings. So would the tantrums, owies, squirted beverages, flung food, and various other disasters.

And his and Liv's own little Eamon would be in the thick of it. Flailing around, hopefully holding his own in this many headed hydra monster of The Cousins. Risking life and limb on rocking horses and tricycles. His little boy. His son.

It gave him goose bumps. A thrill of excitement, but it weakened his knees, too. He sucked on his beer, trying to banish the shivers.

It was true, what he'd told Liv. He wasn't afraid of fatherhood. It would be hard, but he would love it. It was just that he hadn't slept in months. Those nightmares kicked his butt out of REM phase every time he got near it, leaving his nerves jangling, his temper ragged as a bullet wound. And from what his brothers and Seth and Nick had said, new fatherhood wasn't going to do anything for the quality of his sleep.

He'd gone a long way toward normal, after that experience with Osterman that ended up with his skull sawed open, under the surgeon's knife. They said that depression was normal, after a severe head injury. But he had no reason to be depressed. Everything in his life was going fine. Work. Love. Family. Kids. Great.

Except that he was haunted by his brother, more relentlessly than ever before. Maybe it was like Liv said, just the metaphor his brain chose to represent any stress or anxiety. Or maybe it wasn't.

One thing was for sure. He wish he'd insisted on making those assholes at Helix squirm harder before letting them off the hook. They could have made every last filthy, bloody detail of Osterman's work public, as well as how much Helix had benefited from it.

Davy and Con had looked at the whole picture, like the super-righteous dudes that they were. They'd considered thousands of people worldwide who could lose their livelihood if Helix went down. They had concluded that it wasn't worth it. Who would it help? Kev was still gone.

He himself wouldn't have been so forgiving. But he'd been in the hospital, hooked up to machines. Comatose and incommunicado.

The screams were getting louder. He tried to analyze the situation. Out of female solidarity, Jeannie had come to Rachel's aid, and was whacking at Kevvie with what looked like a rubber pirate's cutlass, while Rachel continued to belabor him with the fairy wand. Kevvie's small face was one huge screaming mouth, surrounded by a narrow, beet red border of a face, wet with tears of outrage.

Sean rubbed his bleared, sandy feeling eyes, wondering if he should intervene, but Kevvie opted at that moment for a strategic retreat and barreled between Sean's legs, making a beeline for his mother. Rachel calmly resumed her perch on the rocking horse. Jeannie spun, babbling and slicing at the air with her cutlass. Resolved without bloodshed or time-outs. Score one for the girls. Those two took after their Amazon mamas. Watch out, world.

Yeah, poor Kevvie had his work cut out for him. He'd have to wait for years for tactical support from Jesse and Eamon, poor little squirt.

Sveti came back, smiling her thanks, and he wandered back into the living room, relieved. Kevvie had been consoled by the bowl of potato chips on the coffee table. In fact, the kid had dived into it bodily.

Davy's front door opened, and Miles and Cindy came in.

Kevvie launched himself at Uncle Miles with a pretty good roundhouse kick, which Miles parried, responding with a careful neck chop. Then Miles whipped the little kid around, clamped his head and proceeded to tickle until Kevvie was shrieking with delight.

"Yo. Miles," he warned. "Don't tickle that kid too hard. He's going commando today. No pull-up pants."

Miles grinned, unintimidated, and kept tickling. He could afford to be cavalier about baby piss, being the only one left of their bunch that was not in some stage of procreation. He and Cindy were going at it like minks, night and day, but for purely recreational purposes.

Those were the days. Frolicking in the daisies, just for fun.

Not that he was scared of fatherhood. They were going to be just fine. It was amazing. The online pregnancy journal kept them up to date on when Eamon's bladder formed, when his testicles descended, when his eyelashes appeared, when he got fingerprints, tooth buds, toenails.

It blew his mind. What little was left of it.

"Hello, Sean." The low, perfectly modulated bell tones of Tam's voice made every muscle in his body contract. "I see from your bloodshot eyes that you're in training for your son's first year of life."

He turned, bracing himself. Tam looked incredible. Her dark hair was slicked into a long, thick braid. She was wearing elaborate, baroque drop earrings and a black turtleneck that showed off her slim, curvy figure. Tam had softened slightly since hooking up with her true love, ex-super-spy and man of mystery, Val Janos. The operative word being slightly. She was still an unapologetic bad girl; hell on wheels, utterly secretive, with only marginal respect for the law. And the guys weren't quite comfortable with Janos yet. Something about the way the women eyed his movie star good looks and giggled about his perfect ass, his perfect legs, his perfect everything. They hadn't gotten a fix on Val.

But Tam had saved their collective asses in various ways, on various occasions since they'd met her years before. If Tam vouched for him, that was good enough for them. Right now, she was giving him the dazzling smile that said that she was going to fuck him up. It was Tam's way of showing affection. If she wasn't fucking with you, it meant she didn't like you. And if she didn't like you, well, that was plain bad news.

"Yo, Tam," he said. "Your daughter has been assaulting my nephew with a rubber wand. You gotta civilize that kid."

"It's best she learn early to keep men in their place," was Tam's cool rejoinder.

Sean snorted. "That's cold. Kid's not even three yet."

"Law of the jungle," she said, with a flutter of her blood-tipped nails. "I hear you're having nightmares again."

His jaw tensed. "Oh, did you hear that? Is that so?"

"Don't be mad at Liv. I overheard a chance remark, and pried the rest out of her using a poisoned hairpin to her carotid artery."

He nodded, grimly. "I see. And so?"

"And so. Have you tried drugs?" she demanded.

"Have you tried minding your own fucking business?"

She blinked, her topaz eyes unreadable. "This is what I'm worried about," she said. "You're losing your sense of humor, and this is a matter of some concern, since it's one of your defining charactistics. Outside of your ridiculous outsized libido, that is."

"My libido's none of your concern. I never inflicted it on you."

She harrumphed. "And a good thing, too, bucko, or you'd have been worm meat long ago. My point is, you're going to need that sense of humor when your son is born."

"I know that," he ground out. "And I do not need a lecture."

"Sean." She hesitated. "I had chronic stress nightmares." She instantly looked like she regretted the confession.

"About people I lost. I . . . I didn't sleep for years. It practically drove me crazy."

"You were crazy to begin with," he pointed out.

"Fair enough," she agreed. "But drugs might help. Liv said you guys already tried therapy. She also told me about the restraining order the psychologist put out on you, after the, ah, incident."

"I'm going to go have a little talk with Liv," he said, turning.

Clawlike nails dug into his shoulder and yanked him back around. "Don't blame her. She's worried. She needs to vent. You're being hard to live with, right when she needs you to be strong for her—"

"Shut up, Tam, and don't butt into my—"

"*You* shut up," Tam hissed back savagely. "We are not going to let you fuck this up. It's not an option. Take a deep breath. Calm down."

He glared at her, but her worried look was so unusual, it made the tirade he'd been building up to drain away, leaving him sad. Scared.

Like anyone had ever been able to stop him from fucking up before, no matter how motivated they were. His fuck-ups had the grand, massive momentum of a tsunami.

"Don't scold a pregnant woman," she scolded him. "It's bad for the little . . . the shrimp thingie in there."

"Shrimp thingie?" His voice rose in outrage. "It was a shrimp thingie months ago! Now, it's more like a . . . like a . . ."

"Space alien?" Tam offered, ever helpful. "Outsized head, huge staring, lidless eyes? Flippers? Gills?"

"Shut up," he grumbled. "Don't kill the poetry. Have some respect for the goddamn miracle of life, already."

"Oh, but I do. That's why I won't let you go scream at your wife right now. She doesn't deserve it. And you would regret it." Her hand shot out, and clamped around his wrist, like a steel manacle.

Sean stared down at her hand, at his own fist, struggling with the urge to shake her off and bounce her off the wall. He was much stronger than she, and they both knew it. She also knew that the fact that she was female inhibited him from using his superior strength.

He just couldn't, no matter how annoying she was. Not on a friend. That evened the field. And Tam knew it.

But her rant wasn't over yet. "Liv is worried about you. She's thinner, and she's supposed to be gaining weight! She's got circles under her eyes. She's sleeping badly. It's bad for the baby!"

"Tam, this lecture is not—"

"Get yourself together, shitbrained idiot." Her nails dug into his wrist, deep enough to leave crescent moon shaped holes.

"Hey! Sean!" Miles's cheerful voice was a godsent distraction. He handed Sean a fresh, cold beer, which Sean accepted gratefully. Miles offered a beer to Tam, who declined it with a delicate wrinkle of disgust on her perfect nose. Miles cheerfully took a swig himself from the bottle he'd offered to Tam. Sean looked him over with proprietary pride. The kid was a far cry from the puny, pallid computer geek he'd been years ago when they met him, pining hopelessly for the sexpot sister of Con's wife Erin. He was filled out, bulked up, well dressed. Regularly laid.

"I've got something to show you," Miles said.

"What's that?" he asked, absently.

He utterly failed to follow the thread of Miles's rambling discourse, while Tam's fingers tightened, grinding his bones and cartilage. Her eyes were narrow, promising punishment should he fuck up. As if he'd notice Tam's punishment, were he so shitbrained as to mess up his thing with Liv. She was everything to him. The sweetest life had to offer. And the little alien space shrimp was just going to make it better.

". . . amazing, the resemblance," Miles rattled enthusiastically on. "Cindy and I were dragging our chins on the ground when we saw it. So then we had to go out and buy the whole series, and you know what? We're hooked on it now. It's totally great. You have to—"

"Wait," he cut in. "What resemblance? Resemblance to who?"

Miles floundered, cut off in midramble. "Uh . . . uh, to you," he said, bemused. "The guy looks exactly like you. Except for the scars all over the right side of his face, that is. Otherwise, it's you. To the bone."

His stomach dropped into the void. He saw the dreamlike vision he'd had while doing the crazy mind duel with Osterman, trying to reverse the X-Cog dominance. He'd found the kite mandala in the blue sky, and followed the cord down to the man who held it. Kev. Older, harder, the right side of his face covered with scars. But it was Kev.

". . . hold on, Sean! Shit! That hurts!"

Jesus. He was gripping Miles's shoulder, in a white-knuckled death hold. "Who?" he demanded. "Who looks like me? Who has scars?"

"Calm down!" Miles looked scared. "It's just a fictional character!"

"What fictional character?" His voice shook. "Show me."

"OK! Just chill. You're wigging out." He yelled over his shoulder. "Hey, Cin! You brought the Fade Shadowseeker books, right?"

"Just a sec, I'll be right there," Cindy sang out.

She came bouncing over, hair swinging, a vision in low-slung jeans and a T-shirt shrunken til it was two sizes too small, straining around her perfect little figure. She rummaged in her bag and pulled out a book. "This is the third one, *Midnight's Oracle*. It's really—hey!"

Sean snatched it out of her hands, stuck his beer into Miles's free hand, and opened it. The hole inside him deepened, widened into a whistling void. He heard voices around him, discussing, asking questions, repeating his name. He ignored them. In shock.

It was Kev, as Sean had seen him in the vision, while Osterman had performed the X-Cog interface. He saw it clearly in the deceptively simple, fluid drawings. The subtle differences between his own face and Kev's. Hard to grasp with the eye. More a thing to be sensed.

"It's him," he said, interrupting whoever was speaking. "It's Kev."

The small group fell silent, cast each other worried looks.

"Sean," Tam said, in the careful voice that made him want to wrap his fingers around her neck and squeeze. "It's a graphic novel."

"Holy shit!" Miles's big brown eyes were wide. "I never even thought of Kev. I just thought he looked like you. Wow!"

"The scars." Sean looked wildly from Tam to Miles to Cindy. "I saw them. They're exactly the same."

"What are you talking about?" The deep, disapproving voice was Davy, scowling over Cindy's shoulder. "What's going on? Should I put the steaks on, or have we got a crisis happening?"

"Hold off on the steaks," Tam advised. "It's crisis hour."

Davy scowled at his brothers. "What crisis? What scars?"

"Kev's. The scars. I saw them." He knew that sounded crazy, that he had to rephrase, to explain so they wouldn't flip out, but that touched off a loud, confusing interchange in which Davy was brought up to date on the graphic novel, and then Connor arrived, and they did the whole damn thing again. Then Erin, then Margot, and so on.

Some minutes later, Sean found his ass planted on the couch in the living room, the rest of the group ranged around him in a circle that felt vaguely accusing. The Fade Shadowseeker books lay on the coffee table. He couldn't stop staring at them.

"So, once again. From the top," Davy opened the proceedings, his voice heavy. "You saw what? And when?"

"Twice," Sean explained wearily. "In dreams, I guess

you'd say, or maybe they were visions, since I wasn't asleep.
First when Osterman was doing the X-Cog interface. I didn't
think . . . I mean, I saw Mom, too, and Dad. They talked to
me, tried to help me, so I figured Kev was just another ghost
in my head, trying to help me out. But he wasn't like I remembered him. He was my age, hair buzzed off. Flying a kite.
And he had scars. Exacly like these." He pointed at the
books.

"And the second time?" Connor asked.

"On the mountain, when I was climbing after I got out of
the hospital," he explained. "I was about to go off a cliff in
the mist, and Kev stopped me. Scolded me. He had scars
then, too."

Connor's head fell into his hands. "This is all we need."

Sean stared down at his clenched fists. "I know this woo
woo stuff sticks in your craw," he said, his voice rough. "But
please. For the love of God. Just swallow it down, for once in
your life."

Liv came forward, her hands cupping the swell of her
belly, and sidled in beside him behind the coffee table. She
picked up one of the books, frowned at it thoughtfully. "I've
come to a decision," she said.

Her voice had a challenging ring to it. Everyone felt it.
The silence that followed was absolute, but for the background noise of happy babbling and screeching from the
backyard outside.

"And you have decided exactly what?" Margot asked quietly.

"I've been thinking about this for a while now," Liv said.
"For years, Sean has been suffering because he believed
things that everyone else thought were crazy. But you know
what? They weren't."

"We know that, Liv," Davy said.

"Not once has he been off target," Liv continued, as if
Davy had not spoken. "He was right that Kev wasn't crazy.
That he hadn't killed himself. He was right about the foul

play. The bomb that almost blew up my car. Gordon kidnapping me on the road that night. Every time, it was his own pure, naked instinct, against all of the evidence."

Davy cleared his throat. "I'm with you," he said warily. "And this entails . . . what?"

"This entails getting real. Accepting the real, compelling statistical probability that Sean is right about this, too. That Kev is alive, out there, and needing to be found. And it's time to get off our asses and do it." She grabbed Sean's hand. "I'm behind him. All of you need to be, too." Her blazing glance swept the room. Daring them to contradict her.

No one did. Liv was an Amazon, too, when the spirit moved her.

Sean was so grateful, he had to fight the urge to burst into tears. He enveloped Liv's hand in his. "Thanks, babe," he muttered, thickly.

She shot that blazing glance at him, too, and the heat of it flashed straight to his groin. Jesus, what a woman. Amazing.

He'd been waiting for this for years, and now that he finally had her behind him, if not the others, he had no fucking clue where to start. So much for his dead-on instincts. "So, uh . . . so what now?" he asked.

She smiled, encouragingly, her fingers tightening around his hand. "Remember that kite you saw on the beach years ago? The mandala that was the same one Kev had painted? Let's start there."

"Sure!" Miles piped in. "We can comb through the online sports catalogs. You guys got an image of Kev's mandala painting around?"

"It's Davy's computer desktop wallpaper," Margot told him.

Liv gave him an encouraging smile, and picked up one of the Fade books again, glancing at the back cover. "And I think you and I need to go to . . ." She scanned the author bio on the back, ". . . Portland, Oregon, and talk to this Edie Parrish about the font of her inspiration."

"Excellent idea," he said, a rush of relief going through him. "We can crash in a hotel in Portland tonight."

"No," Liv said softly. "Not tonight. We have an ultrasound tomorrow afternoon, remember?"

He gulped. "Uh. Yeah. Well, then. We'll go tomorrow night, then."

"Wait a second." Davy's voice was sharp. "Did you say Parrish? The author's name is actually Parrish?"

There were harsh, audible gasps. The three brothers and Miles all stared at each other, mouths open.

"No way," Miles breathed.

"Could be a coincidence," Connor offered, without much hope.

"When is it ever, with us?" Davy got to his feet. "Let's go to the computer and see if this woman is any relation to Charles Parrish."

Half the room, the male half, headed toward the studio to peer over Miles's shoulders while he hacked. The female half, sensing the way Liv and Sean were looking at each other, started slipping discreetly out of the room. All except for Tam, who stood there with her arms crossed. "Don't you dare fuck this up," she warned.

"Piss off, Tam," Liv snapped.

"I won't fuck up," he said. Then he looked into Liv's beautiful eyes, her shining face. Full of faith and trust. His heart overflowed.

He grabbed her, and forgot that Tam or the rest of it existed.

CHAPTER
14

No one around the table would meet her eyes. Edie felt the wrongness in her stomach. Churning like some indigestible food.

In fact, it was threatening to . . . oh, no. She got to her feet, her hand to her mouth. "Excuse me for a moment," she murmured.

Her father's hand shot out, clamping her wrist. He gave her a flinty smile. The smile was for the room. The flint was all for her.

"I don't think so," he said.

Her stomach lurched. "But I feel nauseous."

Charles Parrish's eyebrow twitched up. His iron stomach never suffered anything so weak and contemptible as stress nausea. "Then Tanya and Evelyn will accompany you to the bathroom, and Paul will wait outside to make sure you all get back safely." He glanced at his watch. "My speech is about to begin, as soon as Desmond introduces me, and only Ronnie will be here to hear it. Humiliating, to have my family table empty for my farewell speech, but if your self-indulgent little fits are more important to you, then so be it."

She sank into her chair, already visualizing the gossip

headlines: *Helix Heiress tosses her shrimp puffs on her plate at Daddy's retirement bash. Too much champagne? Bulimia blues? Time for rehab? Preggers?*

She glanced around the table. No one would meet her eyes, except for Ronnie, who kicked her ankle under the table and gave her a quick, guilty wink of support. Thank God for Ronnie. So tough. And sweet.

She stared around the glittering ballroom of the Ridgemont Grand, trying to get air into her lungs. This was miles beyond the normal tension she suffered in these situations. Beyond the scratchy boning that held up the bustier of the dress, the pinch of the peep-toe Jimmy Choo sandals Aunt Evelyn had bullied her into buying. Beyond the frozen smile on Marta's face. Marta, resplendent in oyster-toned silk and a blinding diamond collar, was being given the cold shoulder by Aunt Evelyn, who didn't approve of her brother's sordid affair with his ex-secretary. Tanya followed her mother's lead, as did the other society matrons who had been Linda Parrish's friends. Icy drafts were puffing around the room. That left Edie with the thankless job of trying to compensate by being extra nice to Marta. She'd tried, but Marta had drawn her conclusions about Edie years ago. Every attempt Edie made to chat was coolly rebuffed.

And her father was in a cold white rage. Which could only mean one thing. He knew where she had been all afternoon, and with whom.

She'd sensed it from the second he'd laid eyes on her, scrutinizing every detail. Dress, shoes, hair, purse, makeup, nails. Dangerous, nonparentally approved boyfriend.

Just a little bit longer. Her hand twitched for a pencil, a pen. For refuge in that safe place where she was in the groove, centered and strong. Knowing who she was. Happy to be that person. The way she'd felt with Kev. Oh, God. She couldn't believe she felt this. Crazy happy.

In any case, it was over. She wasn't going to see him

again. They were going to lock her up. It wouldn't be the first time. She'd been here before. The long, fuzzy tunnel of enforced medication. Useless therapy sessions with the doctors Dad chose. The slammed-shut-doors in their eyes. They never heard what she said. Poor little rich crazy girl.

She should never have come, knowing that her father was sure to find out what had happened, but she couldn't pass up the chance to see Ronnie. And she'd been flying so high. Not thinking straight. She'd wanted to love everybody, make peace, forgive the whole world.

The world wasn't going to forgive her back. She was in the doghouse, and the choke chain was going on.

She put her shoulders back. "Dad, I wish you'd just tell me what you're so angry about, instead of—"

"Your timing is unbelievable," Dad said, through a smiling grimace. "You pick the most public moment of the most public event of the year, cameras trained on us from all sides, to ask me this question."

"I just want to run to the bathroom, and I—"

"You cannot be trusted to do the simplest thing on your own. You demonstrated that today." His whisper punched into her ears.

"But I—"

"I know who you were with. I know what you did with him. I am disgusted, Edith. Revolted."

She shook her head, bewildered. "Why? What do you know about him, other than what Osterman did to him, which wasn't his fault?"

"I don't need to know more. He was damaged by that madman. And I know that he's dangerous, Edith, because he attacked me, personally, and I remember it very well. He holds a grudge, and he's found the ideal way to humiliate, punish, and control me. Through you."

"No." She shook her head, wildly. "No, it's not like that. It's—"

"I am not going to allow him to do it. This stops, here and now."

"But you've got the wrong idea!" she protested. "He isn't—"

"Bad enough that you've been advertising for years in a public forum for his attention, through those damned comic books. It was just a matter of time. And now that he's found you, I have to protect you from him. Since you appear to be incapable of protecting yourself."

"I wouldn't be surprised if he taped the whole thing," Marta offered, her eyes glittering with unpleasant enthusiasm. "We could have your dirty little adventure posted on the Internet, for the world to enjoy."

She stared at one, then the other. "That's not true! That's a disgusting thing to say! He would never do that to me!"

"Keep your voice down," he hissed. "You slept with him! How could you have been such a goddamn idiot?"

Her back straightened, as something inside her turned to ice. "I did nothing wrong," she said, with quiet dignity. "And neither has he."

Her father snorted. "No? Well, I'm done trying to let you work your little fits out in your own way. I am going to get you the help you need, once and for all. Now *smile,* goddamnit."

But she couldn't. It was one of the things her father hated most about her. Her feelings, written on her face for all to see.

One of the catering staff leaned in front of them, a strikingly handsome Asian man. He scooped up her father's wineglass, filled a new one. Marta's eyes roved over the man's broad shoulders and trim ass as her glass was filled, eyes glinting in her Botoxed mask.

Edie took advantage of the distraction to pull her cell out of her purse, holding it under the table. She texted without looking:

> trouble. going 2 lock me up
> it was beautiful. thank u. good-bye

Wine gurgled into her glass. Edie looked up. The waiter's dark, inscrutable eyes met hers. For an instant, she felt a yawning emptiness in the pit of her stomach, as if she'd stopped short of walking off a cliff.

Then the waiter gave her a professional smile, and turned away.

Overimaginative, unstable, fanciful Edie. Just one of her little fits, her mother would have said. Let it go and move on. Don't dwell.

Less than forty seconds later, the phone gave a quiet burp in her trembling hand. She clicked open the message, glanced down.

> fuck that shit
> waiting 4 u in lobby outside

Her heart leaped up, frantically. As if it were bumping against the lump in her throat.

"Edith! Are you texting?" Marta said sharply. "With that person?"

Edie popped open the case of the phone with her thumb, and pried out the SIM card. She felt Ronnie's waggling fingers, dropped the card in her sister's hand and snapped the shell back on. "No."

Her father held out his hand. "Give me the phone, Edith." His voice seemed all the more angry, for how controlled it was.

"Dad, I—"

"Give it to me, or I'll have security deliver you to the psychiatric clinic right now, with everyone watching. The more outrageous this soap opera becomes, the less I care about the bad publicity."

"Charles!" Marta flashed a blinding smile. "People are looking!"

"The phone," he repeated, louder.

There was no reason not to oblige him. She wasn't going

to have a chance to use it again anyway. She handed him the phone.

He tried to turn it on. "What's the code?"

She shook her head, and his eyebrows tightened. "Do not play games with me," he growled.

"You've already done your worst, Daddy," she said quietly. "You're all out of threats. What are you going to do now? Break my legs?"

Aunt Evelyn gasped with outrage. "Edith! How could you?"

Dad opened his mouth for a reply, but cut off when Marta nudged his arm. He glanced up. Des Marr was on the dais, starting his intro speech. No one would guess from Dad's genial, smiling face that an ugly family drama was playing out at the table. Unless they looked at Edie.

Fortunately for everyone, that didn't happen very often.

Dad lifted the wineglass to his lips, but Marta nudged him before he took a sip, whispering in his ear. Edie focused on the bulb of the wineglass in Dad's hand. Burgundy sloshed, viscous and dark, like blood. It made her think of the spilled wine on her drawing.

The wine.

Desmond Marr's voice came to the forefront of Edie's consciousness. ". . . sure you're ready for me to button my lip and get to the good stuff, but it's really hard to stop talking about Charles's remarkable accomplishments. Almost as hard as it is to contemplate Helix without the benefit of his amazing leadership . . ."

Funny, how she hadn't even heard the guy's smarmy speech, she was so absorbed in her own predicament. Hypnotized by the wine sloshing in her father's glass. Every line of her sketch burned in her mind's eye. Her father's face and torso, drowning in a pool of blood.

The wine.

Her father lifted his glass once again to his mouth—

"*No!*" She had no idea how she moved so fast, but she

found herself sprawled headlong across the table, the stem of Dad's wineglass in her shaking grip. Wine had sloshed over their hands, her father's cuffs. It splashed his chin, the front of his tux. Water glasses wobbled and tipped, flower arrangements and candles toppled. Gasps, murmurs, shocked exclamations. Marta's red mouth dangled open.

"Edith?" her father's eyes were white-rimmed with shock. "What on earth . . . for the love of God, let go! Sit down! Sit . . . *down!*"

"Don't drink that, Dad!" Her voice shook. "Don't drink it!"

Her father peeled her wet fingers off the wineglass. Aunt Evelyn grabbed her from one side, Tanya from the other. They pried her up, off the table, and set her down in her chair. Everyone was looking.

". . . the upshot of it is, Charles Parrish has set the example for us all," Des yapped blithely from the dais. "And he's set the bar high. Not only for his innovative business practices, his rock-solid ethics and his plain good sense, but also just because he's just so damn elegant. A real class act. So please, everyone, welcome Charles Parrish!"

Desmond Marr put down the mike, and clapped enthusiastically.

Her father dabbed wine splatters over his tux, and gave Edie a look that froze her inside. Edie bit her shaking lip. What had come over her? And she thought she'd been in the doghouse before.

She stared up at Des's grin. She'd never liked Des, though she'd known him since forever. They'd been at the Haven together, but he'd been one of the cool kids, one of Dr. O's favorites. She'd been fourteen, geeky, out of it. Wanting desperately to be someplace else.

Since she could remember, Des Marr had been held up as a perfect progeny. Handsome, athletic, socially adept. Lucky Raymond, Daddy's Helix cofounder. At thirty-three, Des was poised to take over for Raymond and run a corporate empire worth billions. He wasn't leaping across tables in public, spilling wine, blurting grim prophecies.

Des couldn't be blamed for showing her up for a decade. But she still didn't like him, even making allowances for her own resentment. Something about the way he used people's names repeatedly. He'd taken too many people management seminars. It creeped her out.

Aunt Evelyn and Marta were glaring. She wrenched her attention back. *Shit.* She was supposed to be clapping for Dad. Lost in space.

She clapped til her hands tingled, smiled til her face ached. Her father was halfway through the room. He slowed. Then he stopped, swaying slightly. There was a sheen of sweat on his forehead.

The applause tapered off, uncertain of its cues.

Desmond picked up the mike, and spoke again. "And now, what we've all been waiting for . . . some words of wit and wisdom from our guest of honor! Come on up, Charles! We're waiting for you!"

Applause surged. Charles grabbed the back of a chair, as if he were afraid to let go. Fear lurched in Edie's chest. She jumped to her feet.

Her father's glare made her butt thud back down onto the chair. Ronnie grabbed her hand, squeezed. Her eyes were big and worried.

Charles's flare of anger at his clueless daughter seemed to focus him. He started weaving his way through tables. Des clapped and smiled, but it took Dad so long to make his way to the dais, the applause from the room started to slacken again. Replaced by murmuring.

She felt a tingle, and turned. The gaze of the Asian catering guy slid away so fast, it was impossible to be sure the guy had been staring at her. He walked away, his blue-black ponytail gleaming in the light of the ballroom chandeliers. The memory lingered, the pressure of his eyes pressing against Edie's skin. The contact did not feel friendly.

". . . honored to be here, and greet old friends and new." Her father gripped the podium, mouth working. Her urbane, articulate father, who was never at a loss for words. "Ah . . . thank you for your kind words, Desmond. They, ah . . . they mean even more to me, since I've known you since you were a hell-raising teenager."

Polite laughter reverberated through the room. Charles Parrish mopped his brow. "It has been my privilege to . . . see you grow and develop." He slumped over the mike. Speculative murmuring swelled.

Desmond put his hand on Charles's shoulder. "Charles? Is everything all right?"

"It's fine. Everything is . . . *fine*." Charles shook off Desmond's hand and flung his shoulders back. "It will be difficult for me to leave the wonderful . . . ah, people in this unusual organization. We've grown together, and accomplished so much. But I . . . I, ah . . ." He stopped, hand pressed to his throat, like he was trying to swallow.

"Are you all right, Charles?" Desmond asked. "What's going on?"

Her father gasped for breath, clutching his throat.

"Good God," Evelyn murmured. "What on earth . . . ?"

Marta jumped to her feet, her hand to her mouth. "Charles?"

Edie leaped up, too, but Tanya and Aunt Evelyn yanked her back down. She'd never seen Dad altered in her life. He never drank more than a single glass of wine at any social event, ever conscious of his heart, his arteries, his waistline, and now, his girlfriend, who was thirty years younger. And his immense need to maintain control, of course.

He made a choking sound, and fell backward. Des caught him, with a shout of alarm, accompanying him to the ground.

He wrenched the microphone out of her father's hand. "Is there a doctor in the room?" he yelled. "Please come up immediately!"

The room was buzzing with alarm, people shouting. Security personnel and tuxedoed doctor guests swarmed the podium. Marta plunged into the fray. Ronnie burst into tears, and scampered after her.

Edie stood on her tiptoes, peering over shoulders. Frozen in place. She was missing something. She couldn't move until she figured out what it was. Something important. Something right in her face.

What, like, her chance to run away during the distraction? Before they had a chance to tighten the noose? Run. This is your chance.

Wait. Her eyes focused on her father's wineglass. The candlelight glowed tenderly against the bulb of the glass. A half an inch of the blood red burgundy still remained. The Asian waiter reached for it.

Edie's hand shot out. She grabbed the stem. The waiter grabbed the bulb. Wine splashed over both their hands.

"Excuse me?" The guy gave her a what-the-fuck-do-you-think-you're-doing-lady smile. "Let me just take this, OK?"

"No, that's fine," Edie said. "I'll just, ah, keep it."

He looked confused. "But I'll get a fresh—"

"No, I'll keep it," Edie repeated. "Don't worry about it. Leave it."

"Edie! What on earth are you doing?" Aunt Evelyn hissed.

Edie kept struggling, her eyes locked with the waiter's.

He let go. Wine sloshed, in a long, unlucky arc that just happened to splatter all over the blue chiffon of Tanya's dress. Tanya shrieked.

"I'm keeping this." Edie shoved her damask napkin into the glass, to soak up some of the liquid. "It needs to be analyzed."

"You're the one who needs to be analyzed, Edith! Leave it, and let's go to your father!" Aunt Evelyn hissed. "Do you want people to think that Marta is the only one who cares about him?"

Who gives a fuck what people think? Over the years, she

had acquired the good sense necessary not to voice the thought out loud. Edie shoved the glass with its wine-soaked napkin into her purse, shoved the purse under the table, and hurried after her aunt.

By the time they had shoved their way through the crowd, her father was already on a stretcher, unconscious, an oxygen mask over his face. Marta presided next to him with queenly grace. She informed Evelyn and Edie that she, Marta, would accompany Charles in the ambulance to Legacy, since only one could go. The rest of them could get to the hospital by other means, if they cared to.

Her attitude made Aunt Evelyn sputter and fume, but Edie couldn't be bothered to get her feelings hurt. She grabbed Ronnie's hand, headed to the table to grab her purse and bolt.

The purse was gone.

Tanya and Evelyn exchanged glances as they watched Edie's frantic search. Their expressions changed to alarm when she grabbed the arm of one of the waiters, and demanded to speak to his supervisor.

Evelyn waited until the man was out of hearing range. "Edith, are you actually this self-absorbed?" she hissed. "Your father's just been rushed to the hospital, and you're making a fuss about your *purse?*"

"Just cancel your cards," Tanya lectured. "There are services to help recover your cell phone contacts. You're embarrassing us!"

A statuesque woman with frizzy red hair marched up before Edie could reply. "Ms. Parrish? I'm Gilda Swann, manager of the wait staff. You had some sort of problem, they tell me? A missing purse?"

"Yes! I need to speak to a member of your staff, who was serving this table," Edie said. "He was young, twenty-five to thirty, and Asian, with long black hair that was pulled back into a ponytail."

The members of the staff who had gathered to hear what was going on exchanged looks. The woman shook her head.

"We don't have anyone who answers to that description currently on our staff."

"But he was here!" Edie wailed. "Whether he was on your staff or not, he served this table! Aunt Evelyn, don't you remember? The guy who fought me for the wineglass, and sprayed wine on Tanya's dress?"

Aunt Evelyn's lips were tight. "No, Edith, I was actually busy noticing other things, like my brother having some sort of an attack in public. I don't think I should be called upon to remember the wait staff."

"And it was you who threw wine on my dress," Tanya said. "To say nothing of Uncle Charles's tux. You really outdid yourself tonight, Edie."

Edie's teeth clenched on the shriek of frustration she didn't dare let out. It was years in the making. It would bring the damn building down if she voiced it. "I swear, there was an Asian man with a—"

"Is this the purse, Ms. Parrish?" The guy who had found his boss for her held out her purse.

Edie wrenched it open. She was not surprised to find glass and napkin gone. "He took it." Her voice shook. "He took the damn glass."

Gilda Swann folded her arms. "Your purse was open on the floor. The glass could have rolled out, gotten picked up, and carried back into the kitchen. I don't think there's anything else we can do for you, Ms. Parrish, so I hope you don't object if we all go back to our jobs."

Edie clutched the purse in shaking hands. "That son of a bitch," she said. "He took the goddamn glass."

"Edie, maybe you should take some of my Valium," Aunt Evelyn said, her voice sugary and coaxing. "You seem very agitated."

Edie shook her head. "Don't you understand? Someone took my purse from under the table in the confusion! It was closed, latched, and someone took the glass out of it! Does that not strike you as strange?"

"Not really. What I think is strange was that you put a wineglass and a soiled napkin into your purse at all, Edith," her aunt replied.

"Probably one of the staff assume you're one of those rich kleptomaniacs, stealing the crystal," Tanya offered, with a tad too much enthusiasm. "Common among overprivileged youth. Helix heiress, caught stealing the glassware. I can see the headlines."

"Shut up, both of you." Edie's eyes were flooding, but with her father being rushed to the ICU, at least she was publicly justified in having a meltdown. She spotted Ronnie's lavender dress, swirling in the wet blur, and went for it. She and Ronnie collided in a tight hug.

"You better run while you can," Ronnie whispered.

Edie was desperately grateful to her sister for understanding that. "I'm so sorry I can't stay with you," she mumbled back. "So sorry."

"It's not your fault." They were both crying, but tough, practical Ronnie was the first to recover. She tucked the SIM card into Edie's cleavage and shoved her. "Go," she said sharply. "Now. Quick."

Edie plunged into the crowd, trying to blend, but those crazy high heels and her billowing champagne-pink dress put her at a disadvantage. She could only hope that her father's security staff would be temporarily rudderless and confused.

"Edie? Just a moment." A hand on her arm stopped her. She turned, wiped her eyes, remembering too late the encrustation of mascara that thickened them to superhuman lengths. Now she had raccoon swirls around her cheekbones, too. "Yes?"

Des Marr. Fricking great. Absolutely peachy. He grabbed her hand, and held it. His hand was very hot, his fingers tight.

"I'm just so sorry about your father," he said earnestly. "It must be such a shock. He's always, oh, you know. Such a rock."

"Oh, yeah," she muttered. "That he is, for sure."

"Maybe it's from the grief over your mother's death, or—"

"Maybe," she cut him off. "Look, Des. Sorry, but I need to go."

"I just want you to know that I'm on your side. And Charles's side, too, understand? Please, just tell him that, as soon as he can listen. He's like another father to me. I just want him to know that."

She fumbled for a tissue. "Ah, OK. I'll tell him you said so. When I get a chance." *If he doesn't spit in my eye and throw me out first.*

"Look, Edie, I know it's a crazy time, but would you come with me for a second?" Des pleaded. "There was something important I wanted to talk to you about. In private, if you don't mind. It won't take long. We could just slip over there, into the conference room, and—"

"No, Des," she blurted. "Not now. I have to go. Call me later."

His big, earnest blue eyes blinked. "Oh, God, yes. I'm so sorry. How insensitive of me. Look, if there's anything I can do to help, anything at all, please, don't hesitate to ask, OK?"

A light went on in her head. She grabbed his arm. "Ah, actually, there is. Lend me your cell phone for a sec, would you?"

"Certainly." He dug it out of his pocket.

Edie punched in Kev's number, which she had memorized at first glance, like a crushed out thirteen-year-old, and hastily texted:

kitchen exit hurry

She passed Des his phone back, and set off with long strides, following the wait staff toward the door from which they swarmed.

Des strode beside her, his face puzzled. "What's going on?"

"You wouldn't believe me if I told you," she said.

"Try me," he coaxed. "Please. I really want to help you."

She shot him an exasperated look. "Des, I have to go. Now."

His eyes were soulful. "But I'm worried about you."

Strange. He'd never given a flying fuck about her before. All this concern was unnerving. Then it occurred to her that the door to Kev's past had been slammed in her face by her father. Des Marr was another door. The only one she knew. And here he was, offering to help.

Her stomach fluttered. She steeled herself. If there was a door, she ought to knock on it. Kev deserved help, after what he'd been through. And there was nothing in the world she wanted more than to be his angel for real. To give him tangible help. Real-world help. In this earthly, physical dimension. Not just the wacky woo woo dream world.

"There is something else you could do for me," she said.

His eyes lit up, all eager. "Anything, Edie."

She chewed her lip, thinking of a jumping-in point in this story. She had to keep it simple. "Remember that scandal, when they found out about Dr. O's illegal research on those runaway kids?"

His eyes widened. "How not? It's the worst thing that ever happened to Helix. It's amazing the company survived at all."

"Yeah. Well, anyway, eighteen years ago, there was a guy who got experimented on, by Dr. O, like those runaways, except he got away. He got to my father, at Flaxon, and begged for help, but Dad didn't believe him at the time. He thought it was just, you know. Some crazy. No one would have dreamed that Osterman was . . . well, you know."

"Of course." Des murmured, eyes bright with interest. "Don't worry, you don't need to justify anything to me, of all people. Go on."

"They'd done horrible things to him," Edie continued. "He's scarred, and he had some brain damage, which gave him amnesia. All he remembers is some horrible mind control thing, and being tortured. But nothing from his life before. It's a complete void to him."

Des's face was blank. "Oh, my God."

"Yeah, it's wild," she agreed. "Anyway, the upshot of this—"

"You are in contact with this man?" Des demanded. "Personally?"

"Are you going to hear me out or not?"

"Of course," he said, charmingly abashed. "Sorry. Go on."

"My question is, who can he talk to who could help him go through Dr. O's old research archives? There might be info that could put him in touch with his past. His name, his whole family. He really needs a break. Could you give me a name? Someone he could call?"

Des looked thoughtful. "Yes, I think I could. The records are confidential, however. Your father ordered the archives to be destroyed."

Dismay curdled her stomach. "Oh, no!"

"But don't give up hope. I don't know how much of the disposal has actually been done yet. These things never move fast. There might still be something. Did you ask your father if—"

"No! Leave Dad out of this. Not a word to him. He's falling apart as it is. He blames himself, for what happened to those kids."

"I see." Des took out his cell, and clicked briskly. "Can you give me this guy's phone number? And your number, too, Edie."

She looked up into his bright, opaque eyes, and found herself backpedaling. "Ah . . . I don't have my phone. My dad took it. I'll, um . . . give his number to you when I get in contact with him again, OK? And now I have to run." *Before they lock my ass up for life.*

"I'm glad to help." Des whipped out his wallet and a sleek gold pen, pulled out a card, and scribbled a cell phone number on the back. "Take this. Look, Edie, I'm happy to help your friend, but do you need anything for yourself? Are you in some kind of trouble?"

Hah! If he only knew. "I'm great," she said briskly. "Just need to hook up with my ride to the hospital."

"I'll take you!" he offered hastily.

"No, thanks. Bye, Des. You were a prince." She backed away, knocking into one of the caterers. The woman's tray of glasses tipped, tumbled. Glasses crashed, tinkled. Clattering, cursing, shouts. Glares of outrage. Business as usual. She was so out of this madhouse.

She loped for the exit, wobbling on the terrifying peep-toes.

"Edie? One last thing," Des called out.

She turned, exasperated. "Yeah?"

"You look amazing tonight," he said. "Never better."

The look in his eyes. As if those blue depths had flashed an ardent red, like a burning coal. She felt an urge to cover her cleavage. Wrap the shawl around herself, hide her bare shoulders and throat.

There she went again, with her silly fits and fancies. As if Des, who could have any woman he wanted, was going to seize her in a fit of fiery passion, after totally ignoring her all her life. Puh-leeze.

"Ah . . . ah thank you," she said. And sprinted for the exit.

Kev was waiting outside the door. He caught her when she barreled through, and it was like running into a wall. But not many walls were so warm and resiliant and sexy. And well dressed, she noted, when she lifted her face from his snowy white shirtfront.

No longer. It was now streaked with brownish smears of mascara.

"Oh, no!" she cried. "I got makeup on your shirt! I'm so sorry."

"It's OK," he said. "I offer myself freely up as a mascara rag."

She giggled, almost hysterically. "It's too bad! You look so nice."

"Ms. Parrish?" It was Paul. "Stop, please! I have to talk to you!"

"Oh, God," she whispered. "Quick, get me out of here."

They were moving before she finished speaking. She sprinted beside him at a speed she'd never dreamed of. She heard Paul's bellowing pursuit over the pound of her heart, the gasp of her breath.

Kev beeped open a shiny black Jeep Wrangler. "Jump in."

CHAPTER

15

She dove into the passenger seat. He leaped in, started the motor with a snarling roar. A few deft maneuvers that tossed her all over the cab got them out of the tight parking place. Tires squealed as he sped toward the exit. Paul pounded after them, yelling. His gun in his hand.

Holy bejeezus. Everybody needed to lighten up a little.

She buzzed down the window when Kev braked, before pulling out into the street. "Don't worry, Paul!" she yelled back at him. "It's OK! I've got my own ride to the hospital. See you there!" She flopped back onto the seat as the car surged onto the street and picked up speed.

"What's this about a hospital?" Kev asked. "And this crazy shit about locking you up? Jesus, Edie! You scared me!"

"I'm scared too," she said. "It's a long story."

"Let's have it," he said.

So she told him. By the time she was done, her eyes were streaming, and his face, in the light of the storefronts and streetlights, was grim and hard. He pulled off the main strip and into a residential area, thick with trees. He pulled into a narrow alleyway that divided a block of modest houses. He parked the Jeep between an untrimmed rhododendron bush and a garage, and killed the engine.

She mopped at her goopy eyes with her hands. "Where are we?"

"Nowhere," he said. "Just a house my brother owns. He keeps meaning to renovate it and rent it out, but he's too busy. It's empty."

The dark and calm were disorienting, after all the action and drama. She was starting to shiver.

"I wanted privacy," he said. "No one followed us. I made sure of that." He reached out to her. "Get the hell over here."

She scrambled into his arms. "I should never have gone to that stupid banquet. I should have predicted how he would react."

"It's a mistake you won't make again." His voice was steely.

Edie lifted her head. "But I have to go to the hospital—"

"Why? They're jerking you around. Threatening you, abusing you. Walk away. Don't look back. What the fuck do you owe them, anyway?"

"But . . . but my little sister is—"

"They don't let you see her anyway. You burn yourself at the stake for nothing."

She struggled with that. "But my father is in danger," she said. "Someone tried to poison him. And someone has to tell his doctors, because nobody believed me at the banquet."

"Use the phone." His voice was uncompromising.

Kev had a point. No, more along the lines of an irrefutable argument, and all she had to counter it was dread. And duty.

She tried to frame it so that he would understand. "If I just disappear, they'll assume that you've kidnapped me," she said. "That's how it'll look. To them, I'm just the spoiled, mentally unbalanced heiress who's uncompliant with her meds. They've put me in the mental ward more than once, so they have precedent. They'll have pieces of paper proving

I'm incapable of being responsible for myself. They'll assume that you're using me to punish my father. They'll come after you with everything they've got. Which is a lot. Believe me."

"Let them come." He sounded unconcerned at the prospect. "I'd welcome the opportunity to tell them exactly what I think of them."

"Ah." She cleared her throat. "You're very brave, but I don't think you quite realize—"

"I realize perfectly. But I'm not the one who needs to do some realizing. Your family needs to take a fucking turn at that."

The situation was slipping in a direction that scared her to death. "You'll get in trouble," she said, her voice shaking. "You could get hurt."

He shrugged, his shoulders shifting in the dark. "I've been in trouble before. I've been hurt before. It passes."

"You don't understand." She pounded his chest. "That would hurt me! If they hurt you, it would hurt me, and I've been hurt enough!"

He went still for a moment. His arms tightened around her. "I'm sorry. I didn't know that you, uh . . . that you'd care that much."

"So get it through your head," she scolded him, and buried her face against his chest. His white shirt being by now a lost cause.

He stroked her hair, his fingers tracing lovely patterns over her back. "Call the hospital," he said. "You'll feel better."

"My dad took my cell phone when he caught me texting you."

Kev let out an eloquent grunt and he dug in his coat pocket. "So that's why you texted me from a different phone."

"Yes. Des's phone. Oh, yes. I have to tell you about that, after." She punched in 4-1-1 for directory assistance, and got put through to the ICU unit. A tense fifteen minutes went by, intermittently waiting on hold and trying to explain to a long series of doctors and nurses that whoever was attending Charles Parrish should be on the alert for the possibility of poison. The interchanges left her with the maddening sense of not having been taken seriously. Just a hysterical, know-nothing family member who thought the medical staff on duty wasn't capable of doing their jobs. But she'd tried.

She gave Kev his phone back, and hid her face against his shirt. It felt so hot and strange and shaky. Shimmering.

"Well," she said. "That was probably useless."

"You try so hard to do the right thing. And they treat you so badly," he said.

"He's still my dad," she said. "Such as he is. He and Ronnie are all I've got, since Mom died. And I can really see how all this looks, from his point of view. He genuinely believes that he's doing the right thing."

He didn't reply, but she felt his thought waves lapping over her mind. "What?" she demanded, testily. "Just say it, already."

"You'll be embarrassed if I do."

"Really? And why is that?"

"Because you don't take compliments well," he said. "I was thinking how brave and selfless and understanding you are."

"Oh, shut up. Don't make fun of me."

"I'm not," he said. "I was just thinking what a turn-on that is."

Her fingers twisted into of the now-grubby fabric of his shirt. Her hands shook from gripping so hard. She wanted so badly to hang on to this sweet, yummy guy who said such lovely things about her. Just drag him closer, never let him go. He liked every part of her. Her eyes, her face, her body. Even her character.

Of course, he was still under the delusion that she was his angel. That was a chilling little reality check. But she still wasn't letting go.

"I'm sorry, if that's inappropriate right now," he offered, his voice uncertain. "I know you've had a stressful time. I don't mean to—"

"Shut up," she said. "I can't stand it any more."

He froze. "Huh?"

She jerked him closer. "I mean, shut up and kiss me."

She didn't even give him a chance to obey her order. She just wrapped her arms around his neck in her very best strangling kudzu vine imitation, and kissed the guy herself.

Her hasty, awkward assault was met with hungry welcome. She abandoned herself to it, hardly believing it could be real, but she could feel his heat, his hunger. He wasn't faking it. He couldn't. Not to her.

This intense, beautiful man was holding her like she was the most precious thing he'd ever touched. Worshipping her with his mouth, tasting her tears. Hungry to just lay her down on the car seat and . . .

Oh. Boy. Images flashed through her head, erotic, explicit. What he wanted to do to her. The way he wanted to make her feel. Writhing, begging. Offering herself to him, in total, melting, wide-open surrender.

She was tuned to the wavelength of his desire. It was so loud and clear it practically deafened her, and she wasn't even drawing. Now that she'd felt it from him, she could never be deaf or blind to it again.

It shimmered around her, a sea of warmth, marbled with a lusty, sharp male urgency that made her squirm with eagerness on his lap.

Kev threw his head back, dragging in air. "I can't do this!"

She was dismayed. "Why not?"

"We're in public, parked in an alley! I'm supposed to be protecting you, not ripping off your clothes and fucking you in my car!"

"But . . . what if I begged you to?" she asked, timidly.

"Would that make it OK? I mean, this place, it's hardly public. It's pitch-dark."

"Your dad's bodyguards—"

"Won't find us," she wheedled. "They'd have made a move by now if they'd followed us, and you said yourself that they didn't."

"No," he said flatly. "My attention would be compromised. And that's a big fucking understatement. And besides. I don't have condoms here. " He flung the words at her, almost triumphantly.

Edie sagged forward until her forehead touched his: "God, Kev. Do you never learn?" she complained.

"I have condoms at home!" he flared. "I had, and still have, every intention of fucking you all night long, in the safety and privacy of my own apartment. With its multiple locks, state of the art alarm system, and my own personal arsenal at hand. No way am I letting my guard down like that in a car, in an alley. Fucking forget it. So *stop*."

She reached for him again. "Please," she coaxed. "Please, Kev."

She scratched her unnaturally clean, French manicured nails down his chest, making his breath stutter audibly.

"You are crazy," he said hoarsely.

She stopped short, mouth open, and started vibrating in helpless, silent sobs. Laughter, tears, she couldn't tell. "Crazy Edie," she forced out. "Oh, yeah. That's me."

Kev grabbed her, and squeezed. "Aw, shit. Edie. I didn't mean—"

"It's OK. I know you didn't." She cradled his face in her hands, covering it with feverish kisses. Trying to memorize his face, like a blind woman. Committing the texture of his skin to memory, every detail. The shiny, mottled skin of his scarred side, contrasting with the supple velvety heat of his unmarred skin on the left. He'd shaved. He was smoother than he had been this morning. He'd put on some delicious smelling cream, to please her. It made her heart thud with delight.

But something kept whispering the truth. No way were they going to let her keep this. This was stolen time. Precious counted seconds, and she was goddamn well going to make the most of them.

She kissed him, feeling the tickle of his eyelashes against her cheek, her lips, feeling the sweep of his eyebrows. "I don't know how long I'll have, before they get me," she said. "But they will get me, Kev. I have to make this count. Do it. Please. Do it right now. Right here."

He grabbed her shoulders and gave them a sharp little shake. "I am not going to let them do that to you."

Tenderness swelled painfully in her chest, for how valiant and well meaning he was. How innocent. He was just one guy, no matter how exceptional. He didn't have a private army, a vast network of social and political connections, a bottomless budget.

"I love you for saying that," she said softly. "No matter how it all shakes down."

He stiffened, outraged. "You don't believe me."

She stroked his face. He was so sweet, it made her heart hurt. "That's not it. I just have a lot of experience with these people."

"They don't have any experience with me. They're in for a shock."

Anger throbbed off him, in hot waves. Different than the anger she'd sensed before. Outraged fury, bright and hot and purifying. Not toxic or festering. It was the first time that furious anger didn't close her down. On the contrary. His fierce conviction heated her blood. She could almost let herself believe that he actually could protect her, defend her. That he could fearlessly face off with Charles Parrish, and win. Just because he was such a fine and righteous dude.

But that would be foolish, irresponsible. He had no idea

what he was dealing with, and she had to protect him as best she could.

Just a little more of this perfection first. One more time. Call her selfish. She slid her leg over his so that she straddled his thighs, pressing that damp, hot ache of longing against its perfect, throbbing opposite. She set her teeth to the damp skin at his throat, and licked away the savory tang of his sweat against her tongue.

He seized her hips, grinding her harder against his pulsing erection. "Believe it, Edie. I will protect you."

She threw her head back, flaunting her cleavage, inviting him to bury his face in it. "Show me how you'll look after me, Kev," she challenged. "Make me feel it. I need some serious convincing."

The grinding rasp that came from behind his clenched teeth sounded barely human. "I'll give you all you want when we get home."

"Now." She wrenched his belt buckle loose and struggled to get her hands into his trousers, but they were cuddled into too tight of a knot. So she slid down his thigh, and petted the hard, hot length of him, trapped in his pants. Gripping it.

"Goddamnit, Edie," he groaned.

She had him now. She could feel it. They'd topped the crest, and were tumbling down the other side. She hauled up masses of pink chiffon, and scrambled off his lap for just long enough to balance on one toe, clutching the back of his seat with one hand while she snagged the elastic of her panties and whipped them down off one leg. Almost tumbling onto her ass on the center console when the thing snagged on her stupid spiky heel. She wobbled, corrected. Left the panties rolled up around her thigh like a garter, forgotten. Climbed astride him again.

"Feel me," she pleaded, tossing up what felt like endless, billowing yards of fabric to get to his hand and grab it. "Feel this." She pulled his hand up between her legs. "Feel how wet I am."

He groaned, rubbing his face against her cleavage, petting her slick pussy tenderly, as if it were a fragile, delicate thing to be protected. She waited, breathless, and tried again. "I need you." Her voice broke.

He cursed, in that weird language that she couldn't quite place, but he couldn't resist her. He teased her folds apart, and delved, boldly. Stretching her, opening her. Spreading her lube all around.

Yes. He was going to do it. Salvation was at hand.

The second his mind was made up, he took charge. Everything went faster. He shifted her as if she were a doll, and wrenched his pants open. Her skirts billowed around them, voluminous puffs, like sea foam. Like a bridal gown, pale and fragile in the dark.

The stray thought startled her, but she gave into it. Who cared if this was makeshift, unplanned sex in the front seat of a car. It was also a sacred wedding night between true lovers.

The heart decided, not the circumstances.

Tears ran down her face again, at the exquisite blessing of it. The tender way he handled her, the way her body yielded to him. Eager, trusting. He deftly guided the head of his cock against her, caressing her with it until they found the perfect angle. And then, the shuddering delight as she tried to relax, to let his big, stiff cock slide into her.

It hurt, but it was also . . . oh. So. Deliciously . . . *good.*

No latex. She didn't care. She didn't feel irresponsible. The normal rules were irrelevant. Every gesture, every caress, achingly poignant and tender. Charged with significance. Magnificance.

She arched as he held her hips, thrusting deeper. Gathering her closer. He placed her hands on the back of the car seat, and started to move, surging up inside. She sobbed with each marvelous stroke. It was a constant discovery, how much pleasure her body could bear, how much emotional voltage she could carry. Every slick, driving thrust jolted her deeper into a happiness so intense, it was frightening. She was thrilling with the wonder of the violin's high note, but the intensity never subsided. It only swelled, deepened. The orchestra joined in. Jungle drums, organs, crashing percussion, sea waves breaking.

The climax ripped through her, lighting up every dark corner with the blazing light of total awareness.

As she drifted back, it was with an odd sense of relief. It was all good. There was nothing bad hiding in there. No terrible darkness that did not yield to the light. No matter what her family said, no matter their fears. She wasn't broken, or crazy.

She no longer had to bear that burden of stomach-clenching doubt. And without it, she could finally relax. The relief was exquisite.

She draped over him, panting. Almost drowsing, until it became evident that he was still hard, throbbing inside her with unabated urgency. His heartbeat pulsed deep inside, against her womb. He was rigid with the effort of staying still. He stroked her back, reverently.

She lifted her head. "You didn't come."

"No," he said.

"Why not?" she asked. "Are you trying to prove something to me? Something about your macho manly self-control?"

"You give me too much credit." He pressed a finger against her mouth. "I just figured we should save kids for when we're more settled. Let's sort things out before we make babies."

She stared at the shadowy gleam of his eyes. *Ulp.* "Ah, maybe you're right," she whispered.

"Which is not to say that I'm not into it," he said.

"Into what?"

He lifted her so that he withdrew halfway, and settled her down again, a slow, liquid stroke. He swiveled, stirring her around until she writhed and whimpered. "Into babies. With you. I'm all for it."

"I, ah . . . we just met today," she whispered.

He kissed her throat. She felt the gentle nip of his teeth, the rough swipe of his tongue. "That doesn't count," he said. "Not for us."

That could not be argued, but she still felt shy. "Most guys don't talk about babies on a first date," she babbled. "It's one of the big no-nos for girls. Quickest way to make a guy run screaming."

"I'm not running. You couldn't chase me off if you tried."

She clutched him tighter, biting her lip. "No."

"Are you running?" he asked, his voice a low rumble.

"No," she replied.

"Well, then." He lifted her up, with no effort, and slid deep inside her once again, with a groan of pleasure.

She cleared her throat, tried to organize her thoughts. "Well, I think you deserve to . . . that is to say, I think you should finish."

"Ah." His voice was velvety. "So you want my baby now, then?"

She giggled. "What I want is to watch you explode. There are ways to make that happen that don't make babies."

He was silent for a long moment. "You keep playing me."

She kissed his cheekbone, trailed kisses down his jaw, his throat. "I'm not playing you," she said, and she forced her rubbery limbs to function. She clambered off, dragging herself off that thick, throbbing prong. Then she sank to her knees in front of the seat, between his legs, in a billowing poof of pale chiffon, and grabbed his cock.

"*Now* I'm playing you," she said, and took him in her mouth.

Oh, boy. So big, so hard. He smelled so sexy. Hot and earthy, sticky with her juices. She didn't have flawless technique to boast of when it came to oral sex, but she'd never been so inspired. She was so excited, she came again herself when he exploded in her mouth.

The orgasm originated in her chest, bursting through her arms. Her fingers tingled, glowed. Flowers burst into bloom in her head, pulses of violet light. She wiped her mouth, pushed away the hair stuck to her face. Tongue-tied and sticky and shy.

Kev dragged her up onto his lap and hugged her. Tears ran down her face, and she was completely unembarrassed. It was good, it was fine. It was wonderful. Then she kissed his face, and found it wet.

Her heart opened so wide, she thought it would break, become something she never knew a heart could be. Vast and pure and fearless.

Some endless time later, she forced herself to pull away from the sweet, lazy nuzzling. "I should go," she said. "To the hospital."

He stiffened. "Why?"

She braced herself. "We should start from a position of strength. We show up at the hospital, like any concerned daughter and her boyfriend. That's not the behavior of a crazy girl and her kidnapper."

"We're not dealing with reasonable people here," he said. "Fuck them all. Let's just leave. Disappear."

She considered that seductive idea. Loving it, even though it was unthinkable, with her little sister in the equation. "To where?"

"I don't care. Anywhere. It doesn't matter. Let's tan reindeer hides in Lapland. Run an emu farm in South Australia. Herd goats in Crete. Spear fish in the tidepools of a South Sea island. I'll find a way to support us. I've got lots of skills. I'm quick with languages."

She pondered that. "It sounds great. But even if I didn't have Ronnie, it would mean giving up all hope of finding out about the first part of your life. And you'd have to give up the second part, too, that you worked so hard to build. You'd have to start out from zero. Again."

"I'd be with you. It would be worth it to me. Just say the word."

She pressed her hand to her shaking mouth. "Oh, wow. Kev. You are so sweet. I don't know what to do with you."

"What you're doing so far really works for me," he assured her.

She stifled her giggles, and refused to let herself fall into the vortex of another kiss. "Let's go to the hospital, and brazen it out."

He radiated disapproval as he drove, but when they parked in the hospital garage, he draped his coat around her shoulders, and took her hand. Everything felt different with his energy sustaining her.

They made their way down the mazes of corridors, various reception desks, wending their way towards the ICU. People kept staring. She caught a glimpse of herself in a window, and realized why.

Her hair was mussed into a voluminous mass, her eyes smudgy and huge with that after-midnight slut look. Her cheeks were a feverish pink, her lips red and puffy. Frothy frills exploded below the hem of Kev's coat. She looked like a girl who had just been nailed by a big, gorgeous guy in the front seat of his car. And Kev looked like a god. So tall, so perfect. His face was somber, his green eyes watchful. Women's eyes stuck on him and stayed, helpless to detach. Heads turned, bodies swiveled to follow. People stopped walking to watch where he was going.

And he was clutching her hand. Hers, Edie's. Pledging himself to her, offering to run away with her. Her chest felt like it would burst.

A weird counterpart to the knot of terror in her belly as they turned the corner and were confronted with her whole family.

CHAPTER
16

Having spent most of his life, or what he knew of it, in what amounted to emotional outer space had its advantages, Kev reflected. He knew who he was, insofar as a bashed up, brain-damaged amnesiac could, and he was at peace with himself. Disapproval felt like the yipping of a faraway dog to him. About as significant. People could think whatever the fuck they wanted. It didn't change reality one bit.

But that blast of icy disapproval hurt Edie. Fucking bastards never gave her a break. Or so he thought, until a slim young girl in a lavender dress detached herself from the group and ran headlong at Edie, knocking her almost off her feet in a furiously tight hug.

"Veronica!" snapped a skinny older woman with a vinegary mouth. "Come back here this instant!"

To her credit, Veronica ignored the old hag, and just buried her face against Edie's shoulder. Yay. He wanted to applaud the kid.

"Sorry," Edie whispered, over her sister's shoulder. She jerked her chin towards the others. "About them, I mean. If looks could kill."

"Not your fault." He gave her a quick, wry smile. "And I don't care." He cataloged the rest of the group. The skinny, dried-up older woman who had scolded Veronica, one chubby younger one, both in evening gowns. An older guy, with glasses. Two bodyguards. One was a big, muscular black man, the other was the ass-faced gorilla with no forehead who had driven Edie this afternoon. The one who'd spit on the ground in her presence. The one who needed to lose a handful of teeth.

The stringy older broad stepped forward. "I cannot believe this," she said. "Your father is at death's door, and you bring this person to his bedside? Have you lost your mind?"

Edie let out a sharp breath. "Aunt Evelyn, this is my boyfriend, Kev Larsen," she said. "Kev, my aunt Evelyn Morris."

Her resolute dignity made him proud. He nodded politely at the woman's empurpled face. "How do you do?" he asked, stopping short of offering his hand to shake. That would be over the top.

"I'm not enjoying this masquerade." The woman's voice was shrill.

Edie's voice remained even. "And this is Tanya Morris, her daughter, my cousin. And Marta is . . . is Marta here?"

"She's in with Uncle Charles," Tanya said. "They'll only let in one family member at a time. They don't want him agitated."

Edie forged on. "Dr. Katz, our family physician," she said, pointing at the older, bespectacled guy. She nodded toward the big black man. "Robert Fraser, from our security department." She gestured toward the Neanderthal buttface. "And you met Paul Ditillo earlier, of course."

"Ms. Parrish, are you aware that your father's security staff were attacked this afternoon by this man?" Ditillo asked. "Almost fatally?"

Kev rolled his eyes. "Fatally, my ass."

Edie blinked. "I beg your pardon?"

"One of them is undergoing emergency surgery on his knee," Paul said. "The other has a broken nose, a dislocated jaw and a concussion."

Shit. Busted. Edie looked up at him, confused. "What's this?"

He shrugged. "They jumped me. One grabbed me from behind. I didn't know they were your father's people." He shot Paul a glance. "They should be more polite if they value their kneecaps and noses."

Paul's face reddened. "This man is dangerous. It's our job to protect you, Ms. Parrish, and you are making it very difficult for us."

Edie caught her luscious lower lip between her teeth. "I doubt Kev went off deliberately looking for Parrish security staff to assault this afternoon, Paul. You told me yourself that you sent them to follow me."

Paul's nostrils flared. "That's what I expected you to say. Mr. Parrish said you were probably brainwashed."

Edie ignored that dig. "Can I go in and see him?"

"Marta's with him now," Evelyn said. "He goes in and out. I assume it was brought on by the stress. Of your little escapade."

Kev laid his hand on Edie's shoulder. No wonder she was stressed. These people were nuts. Edie's sanity was in such stark contrast, it seemed like craziness to them.

The door to Parrish's room opened. A statuesque Barbie doll in shimmering gray satin and lots of bling came out, dabbing her perfect mask of makeup with a Kleenex. She saw Edie. True to theme, her mouth tightened like a prune. It aged her fifteen years in an instant.

Then she saw Kev. Her face went blank. Not the snobbish disapproval of the aunt and the cousin. This was recognition. And fear.

Her gaze skittered away. "Have we met?" he asked her.

She shook her head. "No, no. I'm sure we haven't." She

sounded breathless. "Please excuse me. It's just that you looked a little like . . ."

"Like who?" He couldn't control the hard note of command.

Her gaze darted from him to Edie. "Um, nothing. Excuse me." She scurried, heels clicking, down the hall, toward the bathroom.

Edie gazed after her, mystified. "What was that about?"

"Not a clue," he murmured. But he and Blondie were going to be having a talk, sometime soon.

Edie kissed Ronnie on the top of the head, and murmured something in her ear as she pried the girl's arms off. She put her hand on the door, and gave him an apologetic look. "Sorry to leave you alone with that." She jerked her chin at the clot of hostility down the hall.

He smiled at her. "I'll live."

She grabbed a handful of his shirt. "Don't disappear on me," she blurted. "Don't walk back into the pages of my novel, or into the fifth dimension, and leave me stranded here alone. That would suck. Got it?"

"Fuck, no," he assured her. "You couldn't pay me to leave. I'm loving this dimension."

Her quick smile clutched his heart. "Me, too."

She went on in. Evelyn Morris strode over, grabbed Ronnie and frog-marched her out of harm's way. The girl stumbled along, sniffling.

He contemplated the scowls and poisonous glares coming his way with stoic calm, but it made him uneasy to be here at all. It felt counterintuitive, bringing Edie to a place where she clearly was not valued or respected. But probably only the big dude himself was authorized to commit his daughter to a mental hospital, and he wasn't going to be signing any paperwork tonight. Kev was almost grateful to whoever had treated the arrogant bastard's wineglass. His timing couldn't have been better.

He'd get Edie the fuck out of here and get her home, where he could proceed to convince her of the wisdom of blowing off these brainless pinheads definitively. They could be three states away by tomorrow.

Of course, she'd never leave the sister, but whatever. The effort to convince her could be a whole lot of fun. Even if it was in vain.

He found himself entertaining vivid images of various heated methods of persuasion, and remembered that he'd given his conceal-all coat to Edie. Damn. No more sex fantasies, or these people would have cause to add "sex maniac" to his list of dangerous attributes.

Edie stumbled out the door some minutes later, eyes bleak. That sadistic son of a bitch. In a hospital bed with tubes up every orifice, and still he found the energy to make her feel like shit. He hugged her. "So?"

She leaned in toward him. "He's strong enough to be pissed off at me," she said wearily. "Which is a good sign, I guess. We have to wait for the toxicology report to have any idea about drugs, or poisons."

The sphincter-mouthed aunt and cousin were still glaring.

"Babe," he murmured into her ear. "Let's get the hell out of here. There is nothing to be gained from talking to these people."

"Robert and I will escort you and Ronnie home now, Ms. Parrish," Ditillo said loudly. "And Dr. Katz will accompany—"

"She's not going anywhere with you," Kev said.

There was an uncertain pause.

"She needs care," Evelyn announced to the room at large. "She's mentally unstable. Paul, Robert, please take care of it."

The two men started moving toward him. Kev shoved Edie behind him, and gave them a thin smile. "Keep your distance," he said. "Or you'll have reason to be glad that you're in an ICU already."

The two men had enough experience to read the energy. Other people in the area felt it, too, and stopped to look. Kev just held the head bodyguard asshole's gaze, pushing back with his will. He was ready to follow through, if he had to. And hoping like hell that he wouldn't. They wouldn't want violence here. It would be undecorous, embarrassing, public. Kev didn't want it either, it would fuck them up, and make their situation worse. But these guys wanted it still less. He was banking on that. He could not let them take Edie. Not an option.

Paul's eyelids fluttered. "You will be hearing from us."

"I'll be looking forward to that," Kev said, meaning it. He turned to the cousin, and the aunt. "Ladies. With all due respect, you can go fuck yourselves." He turned to Ronnie. "Except for you, of course."

He swept Edie down the hall, as fast as she could totter.

He shouldn't have said it. It was childish, undisciplined, and it weakened his overall position, but it had been irresistible. And the shocked giggles coming from Edie made it more than worth it.

He scooped her into the elevator, silently exulting in the hysterical shaking in her slim shoulders. It would help her unload some of this tension. She took her hand from her trembling mouth.

"I cannot believe you just said that to them," she choked out.

"Me, neither," he admitted. The elevator opened, and he yanked her out. "Hurry. I want to put some distance between us and those people, before they lock both of us up."

She struggled to keep pace with his long strides. It was all he could do not to scoop her up and toss her over his shoulder. Like they needed to draw more attention to themselves right now. "Do those people have a financial reason to mess with you?" he asked.

She looked perplexed. "Ah . . . well . . ."

"What I mean is, do they get zillions if you get put away?"

"To be honest, I don't know," she said, sounding lost. "There are so many strings attached to Parrish money, I just automatically assumed I'll never see a penny of it, so I haven't bothered to inform myself."

"You need to stay away from them," he said. "Far away."

"See what I meant, about this being dangerous for you?" she said dolefully. "Just being near me is dangerous. Before you know it, you'll find yourself charged with some crime, just because you were unlucky enough to find me in a book-store this afternoon. I can't do this to you, Kev. It's irrespon-sible of me, and—"

"No!" He rounded on her, making her totter backward. "This is not your fault," he said. "You did not put me any-where. I put myself here. There's nowhere else I want to be. And I'm not leaving. That's final. So that train of thought stops right here. Everybody off that train. It is permanently derailed. Do I make myself perfectly clear?"

She stared up at him, breathed quick, and licked her lips, eyes wide. Those soft lips shone, pink and tempting. "Ah . . . OK?"

He stepped back, somewhat abashed. "Just so we're clear on that."

Edie was still owl-eyed. "Wow," she said. "That was, ah, pretty damn masterful. You're scary when you do that."

He shrugged. "So shoot me. Your freaky family stressed me out."

She looked imediately contrite. "I am so sorry about that. I told you they would attack you, and it's the last thing I wanted to—"

"Do. Not. Start." He bit the words out.

Edie cleared her throat. "Ah. Yes. So what now?"

"Home," he informed her, trying to sound masterful. "My home."

"Edie? Thank God you're still here. I was afraid I'd missed you."

They jerked around. A tall, handsome guy in a tux was loping down the corridor towards them. "Your aunt told me you just left."

He grabbed Edie, and hugged her. And kept on hugging her. And on, and on. Edie looked startled, and a little smothered. Kev counted the seconds. One. Two. Three. Four. Fuck this shit. He tapped the guy's shoulder, not gently. "Hey. That'll do. Back off."

Blue eyes looked up, from where the guy's face was nuzzled voluptuously in Edie's hair. "Excuse me," the guy said, all innocence, as he detached himself. Too slowly. "I didn't know you were, ah . . ." He glanced at Edie, waggling his eyebrows. "That he was, er—"

"I am," Kev said. "And we are. Keep your hands to yourself."

The guy lifted his hands with a chuckle that annoyed the shit out of Kev. "Whew! I didn't mean to, ah . . . whoa. No offense."

"None taken," Kev lied, after a meaningful pause. "Yet."

The man turned to Edie, reaching out to her. Jerking his hand back when he intercepted Kev's gaze. "I'm sorry, Edie," he said to her. "It's been a hell of an evening, and I was so grateful when I heard that Charles's condition was stabilizing. You must be so relieved."

"I am," Edie said quietly. "I look forward to finding out what actually happened to him. They still need to run a lot of tests."

"I hope you'll keep me in the loop." The guy stared at Kev, his eyes lingering on the scars. "This is the friend that you spoke to me about?"

Kev was startled. She'd spoken about him to this plastic putz?

"Yes, it is," Edie said. "Kev, this is Desmond Marr, the vice president of Helix. Des, this is Kev Larsen."

Marr held out his hand. Kev stuck out his own. He didn't want to shake that slobbering wanker's paw, but he didn't want any scenes, either. Not worth upsetting Edie. The guy's smile was perfect for a male underwear catalog. He couldn't bring himself to smile back. Not tonight.

"I asked Des if he might put you in touch with someone who could help you search Dr. O's old research archives," Edie told him. "I'm sorry, I meant to tell you before, but we got, um, sidetracked."

Kev was taken aback. It seemed so improbable, that just asking somebody politely could actually yield answers that might help him. And this oversexed asswipe was the last person he'd have expected help from. Maybe he just had a negative attitude. God knows, hanging out with Edie's family would bring the latent negativity out in anybody.

Desmond Marr was nodding enthusiastically, a big grin all over his face. "I've already made some phone calls. My colleague Dr. Ava Cheung in research and development is looking forward to meeting you. She's not sure what she might find, since Helix didn't exist eighteen years ago, but she'll give it a shot. I hoped to catch up with you so we could get going on this. Give me your data, OK?" Marr pulled out his cell phone, punched open the address function and waited.

Strange, that this news didn't jangle his bells more. Or jangle them in a more pleasing way. Kev just wanted to smack this guy.

"So?" Marr prompted, a hint of impatience in his voice. "Tomorrow, then? Can I have your number? Or your card?"

Kev glanced at Edie. "Have you got his number?"

"Right here." Edie reached into the bosom of her gown, and whipped a wilted business card out. Drawing Marr's interested gaze to her luscious cleavage in the process.

Kev snatched the card from her. It was warm, from being nestled against those firm, lovely tits. "We'll call you," he said. "Depends on what's happening with Edie, and her dad. We'll be in touch."

Marr's smile froze. The realest split second that Kev had sensed so far. Then the smile switched on, cheerful crinkled eyelids and overly bleached teeth. "Sure. That's great, then," he enthused. "I'll wait for your call." He made a move to kiss Edie, but Kev stepped in front of her.

"Nah," he reminded the guy, smiling real big. "None of that."

Marr's eyelids tightened. "I think you have the wrong idea. I—"

"Not at all," Kev said smoothly. "It's just late, and Edie's had a really long day. So, then, ah . . . good night."

Marr's smile faded away. "Sure," he said. "Whatever. Call when your busy schedule permits."

Kev waited for the guy to turn the corner, and scooped the sputtering Edie into the circle of his arm to hurry her the fuck up.

"Why were you so rude?" Edie demanded. "For God's sake, don't you want to look through those archives?"

The elevator to the parking garage pinged. He hustled her in and waited for the door to close. "You don't know why?" he asked. "You have no idea? Think about it for a minute. Search your memory for clues."

She made an exasperated sound. "I am too tired for games. Tell me, or else take me straight home to my own apartment. Or better yet, I'll call a car." She hesitated. "But I'll have to borrow your cell to call it."

He snorted. "That guy wants to fuck you," he said.

Edie stared up at him, her face blank. She really, truly was oblivious to all that testosterone whipping around. Granted, she was selective about who she tuned in to, but that was pretty clueless, for a psychic. And after being grabbed and kissed and groped, too.

The woman truly had no idea how gorgeous she was. The smudged makeup setting off those incredible eyes, lipstick worn off the soft pink of those cushiony, kissable lips. Tits spilling out of the dress. Any man with a goddamn pulse would want to mount right up.

He certainly wanted to, at his earliest opportunity. He dragged her out into the garage. No more interruptions, no more distractions.

She stumbled awkwardly beside him. "But he . . . but I . . . no way!" she protested. "You're way off base. I've known him since I was fourteen, and he's never . . . I just don't believe that—"

"Shhh." He lifted her up, placing her against the concrete wall of the parking garage and wedging his thighs between hers, so that she straddled the aching bulge of his cock. "Believe it. That guy wants to fuck you. But he's not going to. Because you're mine."

She stared into his face, her thighs tightening around him. Her cheeks were going pink, and the corners of her mouth were quivering.

"Actually. I'm not disputing that, Mr. Masterful," she said demurely. "On the contrary."

"That's fortunate," he informed her.

"I didn't mean to make you jealous," she went on. "I was just trying to help. In the search for your past. If you still care, that is."

"I care plenty. It's just that my brain's on override. I think it's the dress. And since you're, ah, completely in my evil thrall, and all that—"

"Excuse me?" The quiver in the corners of her mouth was becoming a genuine uptilted curve. "In your evil thrall, am I?"

"Totally," he assured her. "You're brainwashed, remember? Assface said so."

Her giggling snort made his spirits soar. "You mean Paul?"

"Yeah. So I figured to take advantage of the situation," he said. "Take you home. Show you my big bed. My big condom stash. Stake my claim, six or seven more times. Seal the deal. What do you say?"

"Oh. Mmm," she murmured, her sooty eyelashes sweeping down.

She steadied herself on his shoulders, and he stared down at the perfect curves and angles of her. He couldn't wait to let those perfect tits bounce tenderly, free of restraints like God intended. "I know some excellent brainwashing techniques," he coaxed, kissing her throat. "You'll be begging me to make the orgasms stop. So you can rest."

"Wow." She leaned into his caresses. "Sounds intense."

"It will be," he assured her. "Your problems will be a distant dream. You'll lie there, too tired to flutter your eyelids, and I'll deliver the final blow. Hand feeding you fudge ripple ice cream."

She hid her face against his neck, her shoulders shaking. "Make it Dulce de Leche, and I'll do your bidding for all eternity."

Yes. "There's an all-night grocery two blocks from my house," he said quickly. "All eternity, then. It's a deal."

He meant for the kiss to be a quick, glancing contact, a seal-the-bargain sort of kiss, and a promise of more to come, but he couldn't lean away. She was so soft and sweet. That tender mouth, those soft lips, that shy, sweet tasting tongue. She was delicious.

She leaned back, panting. "One condition," she said.

He took the opportunity to drag in some badly needed oxygen. "Condition? What condition?"

She stroked his face, thighs tightening hungrily around him. "That you let me brainwash you back," she murmured huskily.

Kev noticed, as he grinned like a fucking fool, that the scar tissue on his cheek was stinging a little bit less than before. He must be stretching the scar tissue out. Limbering it up.

"Oh, babe," he said hoarsely. "I was counting on it."

CHAPTER
17

"**D**o not lose them," Des hissed into his cell. "Whatever you do."

"No way." Wanatabe's breezy tone pissed Des off. "We've got him cold, heading over the Fremont Bridge. Would be easier if I didn't have to hold your hand while concentrating on doing my job, though."

Des clicked to break the connection. "Fuck you, too," he muttered, striding down the hospital corridor.

He was glad for the back-up, and Tom's men were admirably flex about changing plans in midstream after he found out about Larsen, but he'd forgotten what a pain in the ass collaboration could be. He and Ava were a seasoned team, but Tom's minions and their pumped up egos were going to be a challenge. It would have been less nerve-wracking to plant a GPS device on Larsen's car than to actually tail him, but they couldn't identify the vehicle until he took off in it.

Des was startled by how violently Larsen had pissed him off. He considered himself a very cool customer. A necessary character trait for a man who played such high-stakes games. Emotions resulted in mistakes. Mistakes were unacceptable. Dr. O had drilled that into them.

But that arrogant fucker Kev Larson was going to pay for talking to him like that. Correction: Kev McCloud. He was certain of it. He could feel that fact, humming in the air. He could smell it. That acrid, burning stink of destiny.

An Internet search to check out the face of the guy's identical twin, the one who'd slit Dr. O's throat, would confirm it. There had to be some resemblance, even with those godawful scars.

But he scarcely needed a confirmation. How Edie could fuck a man so hideously defaced was beyond him. The idea made him want to vomit. It he were Edie, he'd be flinching in horror whenever his eyes landed on the guy. Maybe she fucked with her eyes closed, or dog style.

He caught sight of himself in a window. Took a moment to check out his own impeccable, chiseled good looks. Smiled widely at himself, sucked on a tooth. Yes. Charming, dapper. Perfect.

Dickhead. Playing alpha dog with him. Pissing to mark his territory right there in a hospital corridor. Publically humiliating him. This brain damaged, fucked up, ugly, pathetic amnesiac asshole thought he could win a pissing contest with Desmond Marr, VP of Helix International, son of Raymond Marr, one of the richest men in America?

Wrong. Larsen was going to be humbled, and Des was going to enjoy the process, very much. So he felt territorial about Edie? Des would hit him where he lived. His mouth watered as he imagined going at that lithe body, pounding like an earth drill. Or having those plump, rosy lips wrapped around the base of his dick, anxiously sucking.

While Larsen watched, straining and grunting at the gag.

Yes. That would go a long way toward compensating Des for the discomfort of the preceding five minutes. And it didn't have to stop there. Ava had said that McCloud was the prototypical X-Cog subject. Tough enough to crown and fuck around with for a while. Des could probably crown the guy himself without burning him. He wasn't half bad at X-Cog crowning, no matter how Ava carped and carried on, with her insanely high standards about vestigial muscles and speech control and reverse sensory info, blah blah fucking blah. Spare him. It wasn't like he had to make the guy do cross-stitch.

Des would crown that arrogant prick. Make him grovel and crawl. He'd roll over, eat from the floor, bark like a dog, lick Des's shoes.

Yes, that would be Larsen's life. What little was left of it. Until he started bleeding out his orifices, and they sent him to the boneyard.

The phone buzzed in his hand, interrupting his fantasy. The display told him it was Ava. Her tenth unanswered call since he'd left the hotel. Controlling bitch couldn't just let him do his job. He muted the phone, stuck it back in his pocket unanswered. Av could wait.

He turned the corner to the ICU. There was Parrish's family. The stringy plucked chicken of a sister. Charles's sharp, masculine good looks did not translate well onto her face, sadly. Her daughter, Charles's thick-bodied, dull-eyed niece, Tanya. The sweet little sister, Veronica, crying in a chair, looking luminous and vulnerable. Big limpid eyes, just like Edie's. He ran his eyes down over her figure, in the modest lavender satin. Budding. Coming along nicely. He liked them super fresh from time to time. A taste he'd picked up from Tom, in their college days.

The shriveled bitch in the beaded black chiffon came hustling over. "Des! Thank goodness. Did you see her? Did you see that . . . that horrible person with her? Do you see what I mean about him?"

Des nodded, giving the woman a hug, careful not to inhale the powdery stink of her perfume. "I did, Mrs. Morris," he said. "Knowing he was one of Osterman's victims, and how he attacked Charles eighteen years ago, he's certainly both brain damaged and mentally ill. Deadly dangerous, and to Edie most of all. She's completely under his spell."

The aunt flinched, theatrically. "We know."

"I thought he seemed nice," Veronica muttered, rebellious.

"Don't talk about things you don't understand," the aunt scolded.

The phone buzzed again. Des pulled it out, expecting to see Ava again on the display, but it was Wanatabe. He hit the decode function, and smiled his apology to the ladies. "Yes?"

"We lost them," Wanatabe announced.

Des was speechless for a moment. "What?" he spat out.

"He's gone." Wanatabe sounded defensive. "I have no idea how he made us, but he—"

"Not interested." Des hung up, gave the ladies a reassuring grin. The rest of him wanted to howl like a hungry dog.

"I don't know what to think of this wild story of Edie's, about Uncle Charles being poisoned," Tanya said. "I mean, the only person we can think of who would have a motive is that man. And the person with the best access was Edie. Like, do the math. It's obvious."

Des stared at her, acting astonished at the woman's incredibly intelligent insight. "My God, Tanya! You're so right! I can't believe that didn't occur to me. You must be unusually perceptive."

Tanya simpered. "Women's intuition, I guess."

"When the lab has the results, they'll probably assign a police officer to the case," he said. "We have to make sure to explain this whole complicated situation right away. Make sure to stay available."

"Anything for Uncle Charles," Tanya said piously.

"I hate it that he's out there with Edie," Des fretted. "I'd like to question that son of a bitch myself."

The pig faced security guy started digging in his pocket. "I have his business card," he said.

Des stared. "You have *what?*"

"He gave it to Max Collier this afternoon." The idiot stared at the thing, brow knitted. "Kev Larsen, Lost Boys Toys and Flywear."

Des snatched it out of his hands. No home address, but he could pass what was there on to Tom, who could pry the necessary info out of the databases floating in cyberspace.

Then, the time consuming process of kissing, hugging, petting and reassuring the old biddy and her brain-dead spawn. He texted the data to Tom while loping to the parking garage. Ava could do the search, but she was probably in the middle of a screaming meltdown. Ava had to be kept busy. Her restless, unstable brain needed a constant source of data to crunch, the way a huge, slavering predatory animal in a cage needed constant chunks of bloody meat.

The phone buzzed again. Ava. He braced himself. No reason to put this off any longer. He decoded, hit talk. "Yes?"

"Where the fuck are you?" she screeched. "Why have you stopped answering your phone? Is this a time for adolescent power games?"

"Av, calm down—"

"Did they get her? Is she in the bag? Tell me she is."

"No. Ava, I—"

"What do you mean, no? We clearly instructed those meatheads to nab the mealymouthed bitch while Parrish was having his fit! We've already planted the vials of Tamlix-12 at Edie's apartment! And they wasted it? We stuck our asses miles out into the air for nothing?"

"Shut up, Av! They choked because I told them to choke!"

"Why? Goddamnit, Des!" Her voice was so shrill, he winced, and held the phone away from his ear.

"McCloud," he said, letting the word punch through the momentum of her tirade like a bullet.

She went abruptly silent. Ah, the satisfaction. Those fleeting moments of Ava rendered speechless. It almost never happened.

"What?" she whispered.

"You heard me."

"You mean, he's alive? You know where he is?"

"I know better than that. He's alive, and he's a fucking amnesiac. No clue what happened to him. Can you believe it?"

"Oh. Oh, my God." Her voice trembled with excitement. "Where?"

"Edie Parrish is fucking him. Tonight she asked if I could put her in touch with someone who could look through Dr. O's archives. To find this guy's family, his past. Isn't that sweet, Av? You can imagine who came to mind. Don't you feel the urge to help the poor fucker?"

"God, yes," she moaned. "I'll help him like he's never been helped before."

"So, you see? I had to leave her on the loose until we got a line on him. Now we bag them both. She left the banquet with him, and went to the hospital to check on her dad. I met them a few minutes ago—"

"Met them? You mean, you've met him? What's he like?"

"Ugly," Des said harshly. "He's an arrogant, ugly prick, and he needs to be taken down."

"That can be arranged, darling." Ava was happy again, excitement bubbling in her smoky, seductive voice. "So what's the plan?"

"Wanatabe was following them, but he lost them—"

"They can't even tail a goddamn car?" she exploded.

"But I am retrieving his home address as we speak," Des soothed. "We'll get them. Soon. We just have to figure out how to play this. The cards have changed, babe. It's better, now."

"What do you mean? What's to play? We take him. He's ours. End of story."

"No, Av," he said patiently. "McCloud has a grudge against Parrish for letting Osterman dick his brain around. Now he's fucking Parrish's daughter. If we want to mess with the Parrishes, he's our man. Suspect number one. It's beautiful. An opportunity we cannot pass up."

"You're complicating things," Ava scolded. "I need him as a reasearch subject, not a fall guy! He does me no good in jail!"

"Not jail," Des wheedled. "Give me credit. He does dreadful deeds, then he disappears forever. The case stays open. The evil scientist, the obscene mind control experiments, the murdered billionaire who financed it all. The kidnapped heiress, his innocent daughter, raped and brainwashed, carried away to an awful fate, her body never found. Juicy, sexy stuff. They'll write bestselling true crime novels about it."

"I still think it's too risky. Not when I need to—"

"Later, Av." He broke the connection, slid into his Jag, and was about to dial Tom to see if he'd found an address. The phone buzzed.

Av, again. He gritted his teeth, decoded it. "What?" he snarled.

"Edie," Ava whispered. "Did she look pretty tonight? Does fucking McCloud give her a nice rosy glow? Could you smell if she was wet for him? Tell me, Dessie. Did you like her?"

He cleared his throat, lust pumping through him, hot and immediate as he saw it happening. Edie, naked but for a crown in the lab beneath the bright, cruel white lights, eagerly servicing him. Ava watching, with her master crown, her dark eyes behind the goggles lit with unholy excitement. And McCloud, grunting and straining across the room while he waited his turn for the slave crown.

"I liked her fine," he said thickly. "She'll do."

"I think this is going to be a lot of fun, Dessie. Don't you?"

"Oh, yeah." He gripped his crotch, massaged it. "Lots of fun."

The drive through the city didn't cool Edie's buzz of arousal one bit, but her brain churned stubbornly along, independent of the buzz. It sounded so luxurious, to go to Kev's lair and play sportive erotic games in his big bed. Feeding each other ice cream. Fooling around, giggling, teasing. Having fun. What an alien concept.

But fun was not in the cards for her right now. She was the one with the controlling family breathing down her neck, and she had to protect Kev. Of course, the best way to do that was to stay away from him, but she couldn't ask that of herself. For God's sake, she'd just discovered him. It was too damn cruel.

The next best thing was just to try to keep them both as far out of sight and out of range as possible. It was only a temporary solution, but there she was. All out of bright ideas.

When he pulled up next to a big warehouse, she looked at him. "We can't stay here tonight," she said.

"I was thinking the same thing," he replied. "They'll find my address. It's not hard, even for a nonprofessional, and I assume your father has a private investigator on the payroll. Could your people come up with a piece of paper tonight authorizing them to drag you away?"

She considered it. "I'm not sure, not without my father signing it. But they could get the police to issue a warrant for your arrest. On what grounds, I don't know, but they'd think of something." She heaved a sigh. "I was looking forward to that brainwashing session."

"It's highly effective in a hotel room, too," he assured her. "We'll get good results, I promise. Your brain will be squeaky clean."

She snorted with giggles. "Then why are we here at all?"

"I need some stuff from my arsenal," he said. "Couple of back-up guns, some knives, some cash. Odds and ends."

She gaped. "Backup . . . you mean, you're armed? Now? With a . . . a gun?" Her voice squeaked on the word.

"Of course. I'm always armed. Take another look at my face, Edie. Can you blame me?"

Um. He had a point, but his matter-of-fact tone made her feel panicked. "Oh, God, Kev. That'll make things worse. They could use that against you, make you look dangerous and crazy—"

"I never said I would use them. I certainly won't display them. But I'm always armed. Lack of vigilance will get you killed."

She forced herself to accept this brutally cold assessment of reality into her mind, and not be scared shitless of it. "I'll need to stop at my place, too," she said. "I need clothes, underwear. I can hardly wander around tomorrow bare-assed in the Slut Dress of Shame."

He plucked at the wrinked flounces of pleated chiffon. "I love this dress," he said. "We keep this dress. It makes my palms sweat. I can hardly breathe when I look at you in that thing."

The air ignited. Edie had to consciously relax so she could pull air into her lungs to speak. "We'd better, um, try to focus," she whispered.

"Focus." His voice was velvet soft. "Right."

He was around the car and helping her out before she even managed to find the latching mechanism. Gallant gentleman. Ooh.

His building was a square brick block, no frills. The huge stairwell was likewise plain, with its wide, steel and poured concrete stairs and the massive steel mesh freight elevator.

"I'd rather take the stairs," he said. "I'm too spooked right now to walk into a cage. Makes me claustrophobic."

"That's OK," she assured him. In fact, the stairs with his arm around her was no effort. She just floated up. After all the stress and emotional violence of the evening, she was still giddy. Wafting.

He had an impressive number of scary looking locks, and he squinted at them all carefully before pushing the door open. He stepped in, still holding her outside in the dark entryway. Then he pulled her in and shut the door. "I don't want to turn on the lights," he said.

"That's OK. I can see it all right," she murmured, impressed.

Even with no lamps lit, the apartment was full of ambient light. It was enormous, the ceilings unimaginably high. It was simple, nearly empty. Walls of raw, exposed red brick. Huge, arched windows twice the height of a tall man marched along the far wall, letting in light that gleamed against the wood-paneled floor. Windows designed to maximize light for the sweatshop garment workers of a century ago, she imagined, but the effect was stunning. A huge kitchen was in the corner nearest the door, a center island with stovetop, range, sink. There was an office workspace. There were skylights, lit by the dull orange of streetlights reflecting off the clouds. She drifted out into the middle of the space. The far end had a grouping of couches, a TV. Then a loft, a wrought iron spiral staircase, presumably leading to a bedroom and bathroom.

"This is my place." He sounded oddly unsure of himself.

It was so perfectly Kev. Lavish, over-the-top luxury, coupled with Spartan austerity. She spun around to take it in, and a flicker caught her eye. Kev whipped his head around at the startled sound she made.

But it wasn't a fire. Candles. They stared at the table in the corner. Candles flickered, lighting up platters of roasted meats, grilled vegetables, cheeses. Rolls and baguette, stuffed mushrooms, roasted artichokes, a plate of peeled shrimp, smoked salmon, cracked crab. Heaps of gleaming fruit. A fluffy looking, goopy, creamy dessert, like tiramisu. A sweating champagne bottle perched in a silver ice bucket.

"Oh, my God, Kev," she whispered. "Did you . . . ?"

"No," he said. "I wish I could take credit for that, but it wasn't me. It must have been Bruno. This is his style."

"Your brother catered a surprise meal for us?"

He shrugged. "He desperately wants to get me laid. He thinks that getting laid is the solution to any man's problems. Common cold? Get laid. Ingrown hairs? Get laid. Pursued by an angry billionaire? Get laid."

She thought about it for a moment. "Works for me," she said. "Now that I've met you I can see his point."

"I never did manage to pound the concept of personal space into that kid," Kev grumbled. "He figures if he can pick the lock, he's invited." He wandered over to the table, gazed at the food. "I'm hungry."

"Do we have time to—"

"No." He grabbed a chunk of crab meat and dropped it into his mouth. "Absolutely not. Excuse me for a moment. I'll be right out."

She stared at the food as he disappeared into a room in the back, and went back to the kitchen to see what Bruno had done with the takeout containers. If he was like any normal guy . . . yes. Bruno was evidently a perfectly normal guy. The takeout containers were still there, littering the kitchen counter in a big, drippy, oily, garlicky mess. So was the heavy paper bag that the feast had come in. Perfect. Good to go.

She gathered up containers. She was hungry, and they weren't going to find anything this appetizing in an all-night Denny's. She forked food into containers, snapped lids and stowed them in the bag. She was boxing up the tiramisu when Kev came out. "Huh?"

"We're taking this with us," she informed him. "The tiramisu will do as well as ice cream. You know, for the brainwashing. The dessert element is essential. Otherwise the mental programming won't take."

"Ah . . . yeah," he said, bemused. "Whatever. I just have

to run to the safe in the bedroom and grab some cash, and we can go."

She dropped the tiramisu into the top of the bag, and called after his retreating back. "You promised to show me your big bed."

He looked back. "Don't distract me. I'm about to snap as it is."

She laid the bag on the floor, and swept her hair sensuously to one side, twisting it into a thick, fuzzy coil over her shoulder. "Snap, then," she said softly. "That's something I'd love to see."

He blew out a careful breath. "Oh, man. You are dangerous."

"Am I?" She drifted over in front of him. "Feels good to be dangerous. I think I like it."

"Uh . . ." His eyes narrowed, unsure of what to do.

Seconds ticked on, and she lost patience. "Show me your bedroom," she demanded. "Right now."

He blew out a sharp breath, and turned, throwing up his hands in surrender. She followed him up the swirling helix of the staircase.

The bedroom in the loft seemed as if it should be small in comparison, but it was a huge room in its own right, with yet another vast window on one side, though it had a huge black-out shade pulled down. More normal rectangular windows faced out the alley.

It was flickering with dozens of candles, too. On the dresser, on the shelves, on the bedstands. Another bucket of champagne sat there.

"Amazing that he didn't burn the place down." Kev opened the closet, reached inside, began manipulating something in there.

"It's beautiful," Edie murmured. And then she saw the bed.

It was as enormous as Kev had promised. He must have the sheets custom made. The snowy linens were turned precisely down, the textured bronze duvet cover strewn with a mass of crimson rose petals.

"Kev!" she exclaimed. "Did you see the petals?"

His head jerked around and he stared at the bed, and rolled his eyes. "Oh, for the love of Christ. I'm changing the locks. Again."

"No. It's wonderful. I'm charmed. It works."

He shot her a speculative look. "Works? How do you mean?"

"How do you think?" She scooped up a handful, buried her face in them. "I know we need to run. I understand completely. But candles, rose petals . . . it seems a terrible waste, doesn't it?"

She fell backward onto the bed, letting the petals bounce and flutter around her, settling around her shoulders, against her face.

When she opened her eyes, she stopped breathing, shocked.

The ceiling was covered with a painting of hypnotic beauty. A sensuous mandalic design, made of deep, earthy colors. Cobalt blues, rust reds, sunset oranges. "Kev!" She jerked up onto her elbows, flinging her head back to study it, conscious of the artful effect that position had on her bosom. "Did you paint that?"

"Yes."

She stared at it, marveling. She would have to get used to this. He was not a one-trick pony, like she was. All she knew how to do was draw, and have the occasional bizarre psychic episode. He had endless tricks in his bag. He would never stop surprising her. "It's amazing."

"It's one of my first stunt kite designs," he said. "Get up. We take care of business first. Then we play."

She got up onto her knees and hiked up her skirts, tossing them up over his bed so that the pleated frills frothed over his coverlet. She scooped up big handfuls of rose petals, letting them fall over her face, her head, her throat, her shoulders. Fragrant and soft. A fantasy.

He was almost in the bag, but she needed one last push to tip it, call it a victory. She saw herself reflected in the mirror over his dresser. She seemed to float on a cloud on the petal strewn bed, her hair a wild mass of tangles. She reached down, to the vee shaped base of the corset bodice, and tugged until her nipples popped over the top. That ought to get him. Worked before. He went gooey when she flaunted her boobs.

She adjusted herself, propping herself up for maximum special effect, and peeked up to check the results of her efforts.

His face was a mask of self-control, but his eyes blazed. The heat so intense, it felt almost like anger. But not quite. Oh, no. Not quite.

The velvety electric pressure of his desire against her was so palpable, she could reach out in the air and stroke the texture of it.

"You just love to push me, don't you?" he said.

"You've noticed?" She made her voice light. "If you're worried about the time crunch, keep in mind, I never did bother to put my panties back on. And I'm, ah, super ready. No need for elaborate foreplay. No need for a smooth lead-in. You could just, ah, go for it."

He jerked a drawer open, pulled out foil packets. Excitement thundered through her nerves, like a roar of applause in a stadium. She'd gotten him. It felt so good to tease him, to lure him. She barely recognized herself. So sure of herself. So sure of him. So free.

He stood behind her, gazing at their reflection in the mirror across the room. His body so tall and elegant. Her face seemed so pale in the flickering candlelight. Bright spots of red on her cheekbones, her eyes shadowy smudges, her boobs spilling over the bodice. A scene from a seventeenth-century bordello. The seductive courtesan, rouged nipples spilling out. She'd never cast herself in the role of sexpot courtesan before. Not clumsy, shy, inhibited Edie. He'd unleashed something inside her she'd never known was there. And she loved it.

Kev reached around to cup her breasts, rolling her nipples between his fingers. Sweet sensations rushed through her, making her shudder and arch against his caress, whimpering. His heat surrounded her. He slid his hands beneath her skirts, stroking his big hands up over her thighs, her bottom. Trailing his finger down the sensitive cleft until his finger stroked, and then slowly penetrated her hot, slick core.

She squeezed around him with a low cry, and her thighs unlocked, let his hand delve deeper, parting her, petting with a skill that unhinged her joints. Making sure she was ready. He didn't trust her judgment. So what. He knew just how much to touch, how hard, how deep, how fast. He was so tuned in to her.

He wrenched open his belt. She watched in the mirror as he rolled the condom over himself. Every tiny sound was amplified in her head, every tiny detail, intensely eroticized. She wanted to burn it all irrevocably into her mind. She wanted to hang on to this forever.

He shoved her forward, and she caught herself on her hands against the piled up drifts of silky crimson petals, as he tossed layer after layer of crinkling chiffon up over her back. Shifting her, spreading her into position. She arched her back, throat clutching with anticipation.

His big hands clamped over her hips, fingers digging in. "I'm taking you at your word," he said.

She met his eyes in the mirror, and gave him a smile she'd never seen on her own face. "You do that."

He did. He was gentle when he penetrated her, and each careful shove made her clutch around him. But once he was wedged in deep, he let go, let her feel his power. Every thrust jolted fresh excitement through her body. Each perfect, swiveling stroke pressed against new glowing sweet spots, blooming into existence out of nowhere.

The heavy thudding of his flesh pounding hers made her sob, her heart twisting and swelling into something vast. Her throat was so hot. She was wailing, yelling, she had no idea what, jerking back to meet him, but he kept her trembling and whimpering on the edge.

They soared over that edge together, and the mutual explosion rocked them, blasting them through inner space. And sweet oblivion.

They might have lain there, collasped and joined like spoons for hours for all she knew. It was earthly perfection. She could have lain there forever, just feeling close. So real. And so whole.

Kev lifted his head. "Oh, fuck," he whispered. "They're here."

"Who?" Edie jerked her head around. "Where?"

"Outside. Shhh, don't speak out loud. Maybe your dad's guys, maybe the cops, maybe the guys in the white coats, who the fuck knows. But there's no reason for a car to park in the alley under this window at this hour." He pulled himself out of her body and slipped off the condom as he circled the room, blowing out candles. "Get dressed," he said. "Quick. Goddamnit. What an asshole. Getting us boxed in."

Fortunately for her, all that getting dressed entailed was tucking her boobs back into the strapless bra and the bustier, and letting the filmy skirt fall down over her bonelessly soft nether parts.

Kev slid a large, scary looking gun into a shoulder holster, checked a second gun that was strapped to his ankle, and tucked a third, a big square looking thing, into the back of the pants he'd pulled on. He wore dull green cargo pants now, covered with handy pockets, not the dress pants he'd worn before.

She gestured at the gun tucked into the small of his back. "Aren't you afraid that gun will, um . . . go off?" she asked.

His flashing grin came and went. "No," he said.

No time for feeling silly. He flung his coat over her shoulders. "Wait here. I'm going to get my bag downstairs."

"Wait here?" She looked around, confused. "How's that?"

"We're going out the back way." He gestured at the side windows.

Her belly clenched. Heights were not her thing. "You think they won't notice a girl in a puffy pink gown playing Spiderman?"

"They're renovating the building next to mine. Gentrification has come to my neighborhood. It's covered with scaffolding, practically touches my fire escape. Makes my building a big security risk, but it's handy for a quick getaway. We'll go out that building."

"But . . . but you're parked right next to the—"

"We'll take a different car."

Of course. He had another car. But she dove after him as he headed out the bedroom door. "I'm coming out, too. For the food."

He whirled around so fast, she ran right into him. *"What?"*

"I'm hungry, and it's the middle of the night, and all I've got are animal crackers in my own cupboards," she whispered fiercely. "I've already packed it all up, for God's sake! All I have to do is grab the bag!"

He grumbled all the way down the stairs. She grabbed the big sack of food, tried to hang onto it when he grabbed her arm and swept her along, but he jerked it out of her hand and led her back upstairs.

He pulled the window open and helped her onto the fire escape, where she concentrated very hard on not looking down. Kev stepped with appalling calm over the three-foot gap over the four-story drop to the dark alley below, dangling his duffle and the food bag with a casual air that she found very irritating.

He leaned out from his perch on the scaffolding and held out his hand. She clenched her jaw. Goddamnit, she was a dangerous, feral, sexy wild thing now. Crawling around on scaffolding four stories up in the air was nothing to a wildcat like her. Even in Jimmy Choo peep-toes.

Kev pulled her to himself, right into his arms, but she didn't have a moment to congratulate herself for living through it before he was dragging her through the pitch-black. She followed him, since he seemed to know exactly what he was doing, but could anyone always know exactly what he was doing? They were going to break their limbs. Fall into a hole. Brain themselves on a beam. Get eaten by rats.

They didn't. He pulled a little flashlight out of one of his many pockets, and shone it in front of himself, leading her down dusty concrete stairs. When they got to the ground floor, he slung the duffel over his shoulder, passed her the food bag and swept her into his arms.

She squeaked in alarm. "What the hell? Kev?"

"No floor down here," he said. "It's all chunks of brick and broken pavement. You'd hurt your little naked painted toes. Can't have that."

He held her when they got to the door, and peered out of the building. Three dark figures stood at his front door. One of them took out a pick gun, and inserted it into the lock. A loud thudding sound echoed in the deserted street.

"They're going right on in," Kev whispered. "That's weird. What the fuck is this all about? Who are those guys?"

The door opened. Two of the men went in. "I don't want to find out tonight," she said. "Please, let's just go."

"Shh. This guy's looking our way. When he turns, we go, and run around the corner. Fast. Get ready." His voice barely caressed her ear. He ventured another peek, and wrenched on her arm. "*Now.*"

They took the corner and ran down the block, to where a silver Volvo was parked, and leaped in. Kev drove slowly at first, barely rolling, without turning on the lights for a couple of blocks.

When he picked up speed, she started breathing again. "Wow. Breaking and entering. I had no idea Dad's guys would go so far."

"Live and learn. Would have been a lot better if you'd listened to me. We'd have been gone a half hour ago. Don't think I like dragging you over four-story drops and into an unlit construction site for fun."

She shot him an outraged glance. "Excuse me? You appeared to be enjoying yourself on our little detour."

His eyes gleamed. "I never said it wasn't good," he said. "Just that it wasn't smart. But it's a mistake I won't make again."

"Mistake? You call sex with me a mistake? You graceless clod."

His grin flashed in the dark. "Tell you what, Edie. You win this argument. You fucked my judgement. You won, I lost. And I learned a valuable lesson. You won't win again."

"Oh, no?" She made her voice very sweet. "Is that a challenge?"

"If you want to take it as one," he said. "But we don't have sex unless we are locked inside an environment that I have judged to be one hundred percent safe. Get your head around it."

"Ah." She chewed on that. "A secure sex zone."

His grin flashed. "Exactly."

"Get ready for sexual torment," she told him cheerfully.

"Whatever. Just keep in mind. Every second of sexual torment, you pay for ten times over. I will have no mercy. None."

His voice sent a thrill through her. He didn't let her glimpse his hidden intensity very often, his iron control was so complete.

But when she caught a flash of it; his depths, the power that the severe conditions of his life had forged in him, it stole her breath.

It would have been terrifying, if she hadn't been crazily

head over ass in love with him. She felt like one of those girls on the covers of the fantasy comic books and novels she'd read as a teenager, on her knees, clutching his muscular leg. Checking out his furry loincloth at lovingly close range. Helpless love slave. Mmm. Sign her up for sexual torment.

She pressed her thighs tight around the flush of excitement.

But her pride stirred, too. He could radiate all the sexy macho charisma he wanted. She would radiate right back. Ka-pow.

"Threaten all you like, you big brute." She made her voice light. "We'll see who's begging on his knees in the end."

He laughed, delighted, and jerked to a stop at the curb. She was startled that they'd already arrived.

He got out first, surveying the street for a long moment before he let her door open. "This has to be quick," he said. "This will be their next stop, too. Three minutes. Preferably less."

She scooted and scurried to keep up with his long strides. He made impatient noises while she rummaged in the silly little clutch bag for her keys. The keys dropped, with a rattling clink. He shoved her aside, picked them up and opened the door. "No lights," he growled.

Great. Packing in the dark, with trembling hands, and a huge, impatient man breathing down her neck. She rushed around, grabbing things off her drawing table by feel, shoving them into her sketch bag.

"Hey. Didn't we come for clothes?"

"I need my sketchbooks!" she shot back. "I need pencils and pens and charcoal, and my pencil knife, and—"

"Just get them," he said, resigned. "Don't waste time explaining."

She tossed the art bag at his feet and dove into the closet, hissing unladylike expletives until she found the suitcase.

Then she blundered into her bedroom, bumping her shins hard enough to make her gasp.

"Two minutes over," he said.

"I'm going as fast as I can in the dark!" She wrenched open drawers, grabbed stuff at random. Underwear, T-shirts, something that she hoped was a sweater. Next drawer, jeans. She kicked the ridiculous shoes off her abused feet, and pulled on her red high-tops, with a sigh of relief. Though they would look very special, with the dress.

"Grab a coat, and let's go," Kev rapped out. "Now."

"But my toiletries, and my—"

"We'll buy some." He grabbed the suitcase.

Edie scuffed her feet on the ground and caught the door jamb, blocking him. "Kev, I need to leave a note for Jamal!"

He froze, dismayed. "You can't turn on a light."

"But I can't just disappear on him," she pleaded. "Please. Kev. He's only eight. He depends on me. He's my friend."

Kev was silent. "Edie, I'm sorry," he said gently. "But I have a bad feeling. Other people will read any note you leave for him. I don't think you should draw attention to Jamal. He has enough problems."

He'd hit on the one argument that could scare her into sheeplike compliance, and she still fought it. "But . . . but—"

"You'll have to make it up to him later." He slung the book bag over her shoulder, grabbed her suitcase. Shut her door, locked it.

Kev went ahead, making no sound, even on wooden boards that always groaned. He pulled her out onto the rickety landing of the staircase that zigzagged down the side of the building.

Black figures fell silently from above, a heavy rain of death.

Thud, thud . . . thud. One landed on top of her, crushing her to the stairs. Knocking out her wind before she had a chance to scream.

CHAPTER
18

Kev blocked the blackjack, grabbed it, torqued it round the arm of the bastard, and launched him headfirst down the stairs, but the second one was at him before he could draw gun or blade. A club whipped down. He blocked, lurched back out of range of the kick that would have gotten him square to the groin, but didn't have enough stair. A nanosecond out of balance, and the bastard scooped his legs from under him. Kev jabbed an elbow into the guy's face, felt teeth clack. Garlic breath. The man yanked him off his feet. Down they went, rolling like a many-limbed thudding octopus down the stairs. Pink chiffon flashed by the corner of his eye.

Edie screamed. The sound cut off to a squeak.

He struggled to control the terror while he wrestled with the muscular, python strength of Garlic Breath. He'd never fought in these conditions, his mind divided by fear or emotion. He'd always been cool, detached, a perfect fighting machine. Free of fear, guilt, anger.

Not now. He'd put her in danger for a goddamn fucking *suitcase*.

A roar of fury ripped out of him, helped him flop Garlic

Breath onto his back and pummel the guy's cheekbone, his nose. Blind impulse whipped his head to the side and down, just in time for a booted foot to swoosh over where his head had just been. A finger jab up into his attacker's exposed groin, and a gurgling howl of pain ripped the night.

His hand chopped down to the bridge of Garlic Breath's nose—

"Stop, or she dies."

Kev's eyes flicked up. The third masked man was above him on the stairs, clutching Edie. Her breasts popped out over the pressure of his big arm. He was bigger than the others, bulkier. His knife pressed her jugular. Her throat worked. The knife dug in. Red trickled down.

Kev shifted away from the guy who lay panting and limp on the landing, and rose to his feet. This wasn't Parrish security staff. Parrish's lackeys would not hold a blade to the boss's daughter's throat.

These guys were something else. Something worse.

"I'll tell you what's going to happen now, so we all understand each other," the fat guy said. "You're going to turn around, real slow, and put your hands together behind your back. Ken, get off your ass and put the cuffs on this piece of shit."

The guy named Ken groaned and grunted as he struggled to his feet. The one who'd gotten the scrotum stab. He was still reeling. Good. He'd learn all about what pain meant, before Kev was done with him.

Kidnappers. They wouldn't kill her yet. They would need to demonstrate that they had her, that she was alive, to get their money. She probably wouldn't survive a kidnapping, though. Edie's best chance for survival was concentrated in the next few seconds.

He couldn't move enough to draw the gun, not with the knife to Edie's throat, but the weighted dagger in the sheath stitched to the side of his thigh was near to hand. "Don't hurt her," he said.

"Don't make me," Fat Guy taunted.

"Get your hands off her body. And I'll accept the cuffs."

"Accept?" The guy chuckled. "Fuck you. What makes you think you have anything to bargain with? I can do anything I want with her."

To illustrate his point, Fat Guy dropped his hand to Edie's crotch, grabbing a handful of chiffon, digging with his fingers. Edie gasped.

Kev stared into her eyes, willed her with all of his strength. *Fall forward, Edie. Fall now. Now!*

She swayed, sagged forward. The knife at her throat shifted as Fat Guy dropped his hand across her chest to block her forward tumble.

Kev whipped it out, let the knife fly. It lodged, quivering, in Fat Guy's thigh. He let out a huffing grunt of shock.

"Now!" Kev bellowed, already spinning. The kick caught the guy named Ken on the side of the head. He whapped against the banister, sagged. Edie wrenched away, fought. Fat Guy struggled with her as Kev bounded toward them.

He shoved her forward, and she tumbled into Kev's arms. He reeled beneath her weight, slight though it was, slammed against the banister, slid, struggling to catch her as Fat Guy thundered past them.

The men had dragged themselves to their feet. They hurled themselves down the stairs. Kev set Edie down and leaped to the bottom of the landing, pulling his SIG 220, but he couldn't get a clear shot through that dark zigzag of stairway, and didn't want to risk shooting through a wall and hitting someone innocent. He heard thudding, stumbling, their furious muttering, but by the time they staggered out and he had a clear shot, they were out of pistol range. He needed a rifle.

The attackers limped through the gate and piled into a black SUV. Lights flashed. It roared away. Too far to make out plates.

He tucked the gun into his pants, turned to Edie. "You OK?"

She looked up, owl-eyed, from where she sat in her cloud of dirty, torn chiffon. Bright red shoes peeked out of the bottom of the skirt. "I . . . I . . . Oh, my God," she squeaked. "My God. That was . . . that was—"

"Let's get the fuck out of here," he cut in.

"Yes," she agreed fervently, but she flung herself at him when he pulled her to her feet. Her book bag had fallen to the foot of the flight of stairs, as had the suitcase. He retrieved them, and pulled Edie behind him. She walked drunkenly, stumbling. Wrecked. Fucking bastards.

He stared at Chiliker's Volvo with unfriendly eyes as they got into it. He was relatively sure he'd taken off from his place unobserved, and nobody knew the car belonged to him yet. He'd parked here, and those guys hadn't been here when they arrived. Maybe Edie's house was their next stop. Or maybe someone had let the men know they'd arrived. Her apartment could be under physical or video surveillance, which meant the car could've been compromised, with a bug, a GPS device. He'd have to take it apart piece by piece to be sure. Who the fuck had the time?

He got Edie settled, and roared away from the curb, punching the number of his car service into the cell. He set the meeting place for the passenger drop-off zone for international flights at the Portland Airport. If someone was following a GPS tag, let the search end there, and fuck you very much. He kept his hand on Edie's knee.

He couldn't tell from her frozen profile just how wonky she was. If he should be rushing her to the hospital. That was probably the responsible thing, but nothing in his life was cut and dried. He couldn't secure her in a hospital. He didn't trust Assface and his men to do it. They were just another thing to protect her from. Whenever Parrish got his shit together to sign the piece of paper that authorized them to lock her up. To keep her away from dangerous lowlifes like himself.

Her breathing was shallow. He could hear her teeth chattering. By the time he got to the airport, he'd come to a decision.

He spotted the car he'd called, and pulled in behind it. He took her hand. It shook in his. So delicate and slender, like a baby bird. But she was anything but fragile. No matter how delicate she seemed.

"Hey," he said. "I need your input."

She dragged in a jerky, hitching breath. "Me?"

"Yeah, you." He petted her trembling hand, trying to sooth it. Aw, fuck this. He shoved the center console up, slid over and seized her, pulling her into his arms. Hugging her tight.

It helped. Her heartbeat started to calm from a frantic gallop after a few minutes. He could feel the effort she was making to breathe deeper, pull the shattered pieces of herself together.

"My input," she said, her voice tight and strangled. "So tell me."

He popped the door. "Let's get out of here. Car could be bugged."

She followed him out, swaying, clutching her purse to her chest. He wrapped his arms around her, scanning the people and cars that came and went as he whispered into her ear. "There are two ways we could go. We could get into the car I called, go to a cheap roadside motel outside the city where I pay in cash, and leave no trail. We chill, get some sleep, think about our options. Or I take you to an emergency room where you can be examined and treated for shock. Your call."

"Ah." She gulped. "Um . . . I think I'm OK. A few bruises, maybe."

"If I took you to the hospital, I would worry about security," he went on grimly. "We'd have to call the police, make a report, get smeared all over the grid. Your people would have you in a fucking vise. And they would have some serious, indisputable reasons to keep you locked down. Christ, I could hardly blame them, at this point."

"Yes," she whispered. "Yes, that's true."

"Any clue who those guys were? Not your father's people, I assume."

A fresh shudder racked her body. "No idea," she said. "It was no one I knew. No voice I recognize."

"A kidnapping attempt, then," he said.

"Oh, my God." She buried her face against his chest.

"We didn't even see their faces," he said. "If I took you to the hospital, one of those guys could dress as a doctor or a nurse or a tech, and walk right past me, and I wouldn't have a fucking clue. But I can't drag you off to some hotel to hide if you need medical treatment. So tell me, Edie. But tell me quick, because staying still makes me nervous."

Her fingers kneaded his chest, like a kitten's claws. Her breath bloomed, warm and quick and frantic against his collarbone.

Kev was disgusted with himself when he felt his dick throb in reaction to her scent, her softness. Talk about bad timing. "Decide," he said. "This car is compromised, and we have to get moving."

Edie kissed his chest. "I opt for the hotel. I feel safer with you."

Relief flooded him, triumphant joy. Lust, too, roaring up like a fire doused with kerosene. *Cool it, dickhead.* She'd just been threatened with rape and murder. The famished little head could wait for its fun.

But the look in her eyes made his heart thud. Back straight, head up. Those scumbags hadn't flattened her. They wouldn't get a chance.

She'd chosen him. His eyes fogged, his throat clutched up.

Fatuous asshole. He had to toughen up, be strong for her,

to do the hard thing. Which was to clamp down on soft feelings, lock them in the vault for later. That was how it had to be, to keep his shit together.

"Let's go."

Edie let him settle her in the taxi. He tossed the suitcase in the trunk, book bag onto her lap, the big shopping bag of food in at her feet, and slid in next to her. "Cascade Locks," he told the guy.

"You didn't say you were going that far! It's four A.M.!"

Kev pried out his wallet and pulled out some bills. He shoved them into the grizzled man's hand. The guy looked at them, slid them into his shirt pocket, then peered back at the car they had just abandoned.

"You gonna leave that car parked there?" he asked.

"Yeah," Kev said.

"This is an airport drop-off zone, man. They'll bill you up the ass."

"We've got worse problems," Kev said.

The guy glanced over his shoulder, took in Edie's torn dress, the mask of smudged makeup, the bruise on her cheek. The scrape on Kev's cheekbones, the blood on his knuckles. They looked like hell.

"I don't want to know what your problems are," the guy said.

"That's good, because I wasn't going to tell you," Kev said evenly. "Get there in less than thirty minutes, and you get another hundred."

The car leaped away from the curb with a muscular surge of gas. Kev leaned back and wrapped his arm around Edie.

His mind raced. Three on one, but they'd almost taken him. So they were pros. He'd felt it, in their training, their style, their silence.

So if they were pro, why the fuck hadn't they just shot him? It would have been so much easier, quicker. Why the cuffs? Any of them could have blasted him with a silenced gun. Edie was the valuable one.

It didn't make sense. He should be dead. Something important was missing from the puzzle. It scared him, and being scared made him angrier. They'd hurt her, struck her, scared her. His beautiful Edie, who deserved to be treated like a goddess, who deserved none of this shit.

He would hunt down those scumbags, and inflict such pain as they had never known existed. But for now, he had to chill.

He closed his eyes, put it all in the deep freeze. After a few moments, he could breathe again, unclench his fists. No more red fog in his vision. With one significant difference.

The harder he tried to force it into the deep freeze, the harder his dick became. That particular door wouldn't lock anymore.

Edie had blown it right off its hinges.

She must have slept. As soon as she was in contact with Kev's big, warm body, his arm wrapped around her, his heartbeat thudding beneath her ear, she'd crashed. But ten miles past Gresham, she shook awake. The headlights lit up I-84 East, through the Columbia Gorge. The mountains of the Cascade Range towered up, steep and dark, covered with conifers. She tried to make sense of what had happened that night, but she could only think of one tiny piece at a time.

"I wonder if those guys had something to do with what happened to my father tonight," she murmured.

He glanced down. "Thought you were asleep. We're almost there."

"Do you think that—"

"We'll talk at the motel." His voice sounded as if he were angry.

Kev kept her glued to his side when they got to the motel. They registered with a bald guy who looked like he'd been dragged out of his bed and was anxious to return to it. Finally, the door closed behind them. She looked around the cramped room that smelled of cigarettes and room freshener, and was so grateful, she could have wept.

Kev looked around. "Sorry it's a dump. Mike lets me pay cash. I don't know what kind of reach these guys have, but I'm guessing it's long enough to track my credit card purchases."

"The room is fine," she assured him. "I'm grateful for it. So do you think that this could be about Dad? The attack he had tonight?"

He shook his head. "I think this is more about you than it is about him. What I'm wondering is why I'm still alive at all."

"What are you talking about?"

"Why they didn't kill me," he clarified. "I can't think of a reason."

"Uhh . . ." She struggled with that. "Could it be because you fight like a maniac? Could that have something to do with it?"

He dismissed that with an impatient jerk of his hand. "I'm not bulletproof. If I'd been kidnapping you, I'd have just shot me in the head straight off, saved myself a whole lot of trouble. But these guys went at me with blackjacks. They had cuffs ready. They seemed to be expecting me. They had an agenda, and I can't guess what it is. But I'm alive, so it's something more than just money. Or just you."

"And . . . and this means?"

"I have no idea," he said. "Nothing good. I'm sure of that."

"That I could have guessed for myself," she murmured.

He tossed down the suitcase, laid the bag of food on the dresser, the duffel on the chair. "I need to secure the room, and assemble one of these guns. You lie down. Get some rest."

She stood there staring at him. Feeling bereft and dismissed. The helpless girl in the poofy dress with nothing to contribute. A dead weight around his neck. Her throat clutched. "Won't you lie down, too?"

"Bad idea."

"Why?" she asked. "Isn't this an SSZ?"

He looked blank. She rolled her eyes, sighing. "Secure Sex Zone, doofus," she reminded him patiently.

He grunted, grim and unsmiling. "Things have changed."

Oh, shit. Didn't they always. She steeled herself to ask it. "Um . . . and how exactly have they changed?"

"*I've* changed." His curt voice made her wince. "I'm not in a playful mood. Seeing a knife to your throat really killed that buzz."

She bit her lip. So much for her hopeful fantasies of snuggling and comfort. "So you, ah, don't want to anymore?"

He stared at her like she'd gone nuts. "Fuck yes, I want to. I've got a combat hard-on that would drive steel spikes, but I'm revved up to rip out someone's throat, Edie. That's not the energy to take to bed with you. Not after what you went through. Keep your distance. It's better."

Well, hell. She'd never followed advice about what was better for her in her life. Why start now? At least he hadn't decided to ditch her and find some less problematic girl to be with. She peeked at that steel-spike-driving hard-on of his with appreciative eyes. Mmmm.

"I'm, ah, actually pretty brave," she offered, hopefully. "I won't break. I want to be close to you, and I don't mind if you're a little—"

"I sleep on the floor, if I sleep at all, which is doubtful. Drop it." He jerked his gaze away. "And wrap the coat around yourself. It's cold in here, and watching your tits pop out of your dress is not helping me."

Ah, yes. That put her on solid ground again. She shrugged the coat off, let it fall to the floor. Lifted her rib cage, to accentuate the tit-popping action. "I'm not interested in helping you resist my wiles."

He groaned, a sound like cardboard ripping. "Don't, Edie. Just don't. This is no time for games."

"But that's just the thing," she said quietly. "I'm not playing."

"You've just been attacked, threatened with rape and death," he growled. "Now is not the time for rough sex. Back off."

She walked over to him and grabbed one of his hands, pulling it up. His fingers were curled into a big fist. His knuckles were bloody and torn. She kissed the scabs, gently. "You're hurt," she crooned.

He glanced at them, flexing his hands. "I hadn't noticed."

She kissed his hand again, each finger, then the back of his hand, then his wrist. "I'm not in a playful mood either," she told him. "Oh, and by the way. Thank you. For saving my life."

He was silent, throat working as she dropped careful kisses on his hand. "Don't thank me for that. I was the one who put it in danger."

She looked up, baffled. "How did you come to that conclusion?"

"I should have known better, when I saw them going into my place. I shouldn't have risked stopping at your apartment. That was stupid. Hell, if we want to talk stupid, I shouldn't have gone to my place at all. Let alone taken time out to fuck you there."

"But you still thought all we were dealing with were Dad's guys," she argued. "How could you have known that there was a—"

"You were almost killed! For some fucking socks and panties!"

She flinched, covered her mouth with both hands, fighting tears.

Kev's face contracted. "Aw, shit. Sorry. Just please. Don't try to soothe me. Not after seeing that guy hold a knife on you. It won't work."

She grabbed his hand again, pulling it back up to her cheek.

"Kev," she said. "It occurs to me that every time we've made love, I've had to fight you for it. It's been whips and chains every damn time. It's enough to start making a woman wonder about her sex appeal."

He grunted. "Are you trying to lighten the mood?"

"Um, maybe," she ventured.

"Don't," he said. "It bugs me."

She sighed. "You are such a hard-ass."

"Getting harder by the second. You have no idea."

He tried to pull away, but she just dug her fingernails into his wrist. "You're trying to scare me," she said. "But you might as well not bother. You can't. I know you too well."

"Yeah? After one day?"

"One day, my ass. I've been in your dreams for eighteen years. You've been in mine, too. You don't fool me. I know who you are."

A muscle in his jaw pulsed. "That's great. That makes one of us."

She ran her hand over his chest, dug her fingers into the hot, thick muscle moving beneath the cloth. "Shhh," she crooned, pulling his face to hers. "Just try to relax. Come here. I need you so much."

He closed his eyes, and swayed forward, letting his forehead barely touch hers. "I would never hurt you," he said.

"Of course you wouldn't," she whispered. "I'd bet my life on that."

He jerked like he'd been struck. "We don't play for those stakes."

"God, you're twitchy," she complained. "It's just a figure of speech."

It felt good to hug him, but he was still as tense as a drawn bow. "It's strange," she mused, petting his shoulders. "I'm usually so afraid of making people angry, but I'm not afraid with you. Even when you bite my head off, I still feel completely free to speak my mind. Go figure."

That got a brief smile. "I can't scare you into good behavior?"

She snuggled closer. "You're scary, all right. But in a good way."

He looked doubtful. "There's a good way to be scary?"

"I've discovered that there is," she informed him.

"Don't bullshit me," he growled. "I'm not in the mood."

"I don't care about your mood," she replied calmly. "It's a strange feeling. Like there's no end to you. Being with you is like looking out over mountains that go on forever. Looking at the stars. You know that falling away feeling, like you're about to fly, or fall, and you're not sure which? And your chest won't let in air, and your belly tightens up?"

He nodded. "Yeah, I know that feeling," he said quietly. "You scare me, too, Edie. You scare me to death."

Hope blossomed. "Well, great, then," she said, encouragingly. "So it's settled? Let's get into bed and scare each other out of our wits."

He jerked her close. "If I start, I'm not stopping," he warned.

She rolled her eyes. "Thank God for that, at least! I don't want to have to go to all this trouble again!"

But he refused to respond to her teasing. His face was tense, stark. "What you see is what you get," he said. "I'm pissed off, jacked up. I need to slash throats and break heads. I will not be gentle."

He was still trying to scare her. Rescue her from himself. How sweet. And how futile. The last thing she wanted was rescue from him.

She craved him. Even in this mood. No, especially in this

mood. It was the perfect complement to her own. The menace in his voice made her chest clutch, with thigh-clenching, toe curling delight. She nodded.

To her surprise, he shoved her away. "I have to secure the room, and assemble this gun. Get the dress off, and get in bed."

She was taken aback at his coolness. "I should, ah, wash."

"Why?" he demanded.

"I'm not, er, fresh," she floundered. "After the last two times we had sex, I'm wet practically down to my knees."

A feral smile flashed over his face. "That's great. More lube."

She giggled. "Maybe, but there are limits. I think I should—"

"Lie down." He advanced on her. "I love lube. Lift your skirt. Let me see. I love how you shine. Your scent. Juicy and hot. Mmmm."

She backed away, giggling like a ninny. "Um, no. I'll just . . . wash."

"Suit yourself," he said. "But be quick."

She fled to the bathroom, pulled out the saline solution and took out her contacts before getting into the shower. She stalled under the hot water for a long time. She'd gotten nervous. How silly was that.

After, she dug a brush and a mini bottle of hand lotion out of her purse, used it to remove what she could of the raccoon mask, and combed her wet, snarled hair. With her face naked and free of makeup, and her hair slicked back, the siren bubble she'd been floating in dissolved. She was plain old naked Edie, looking nervous and stressed.

She marched out of the bathroom, pretending not to notice Kev's immediate and intense attention. She draped the dress over the back of a chair, and stretched out on the bed, pretending not to feel the weight of his gaze against her shivering body. Without her glasses, he was a soft focus blur, but that changed nothing. Her face was pink. Her lips tingled. She was getting all excited, just from being stared at.

She struck a sideways mermaid pose, to accentuate the curve of her ass. She didn't have long to wait. Kev had already kicked off his shoes, undone his holsters. He slid a clip into a large pistol, snapped it gently into place, then laid the gun on the bedside table. He tossed a string of condoms on the sheet. Throwing down the gauntlet.

He wrenched loose the buttons on his cuffs, and proceeded to strip, with sharp, efficient jerks, wasting no movement. Never taking his eyes off her. His body took her breath away. So strong. So perfect.

He stroked his big, thick erection absently as he grabbed a condom from the string on the bed. He climbed onto the bed, straddling her as he rolled it on, leaning over her, arms on either side of her head, his cock pressed to her belly. He stared down, eyes roving until they stopped at her breasts. He touched the angry, purplish marks that the masked attacker had left with his fingertips. "Does this hurt?"

That was the last thing she could think about, with this man all over her, his phallus pressing hotly against her. His force field drove everything else out of her head. Even the flesh-creeping horror of that attack on the stairs gave way to Kev's intense energy. She loved that about him. She loved everything about him.

She struggled to remember what the hell they were talking about. Bruises, on her boob. She shook her head. "I'm OK," she whispered.

"When I find him, I am ripping his guts out for doing that to you."

She recoiled. "Oh, God, Kev."

"I told you," he said, unapologetic. "What you see is what you get. This is how I feel. Deal with it."

She reached up, trying to hug him. "I will deal with it. It's fine," she soothed. "But let's just forget about him. Let's just think about us."

He slid down her body, seized her ankles and spread her wide. Then he settled himself with his head between her legs.

She wiggled in his hard grasp. "Hey! What's this? I thought you were in the grip of a mad, frenzied desire!"

"I am. But you need lube to deal with my mad, frenzied desire. And I need my dose. I'm strung out. Have to have it. Right now."

She struggled up onto her elbows, but one hard jerk of his big hands on her bottom yanked her onto her back again. "Don't fight me. Just get used to it." He put his mouth to her before she could reply.

She could hardly bear it. Each skillful lap and swirl made her whimper and thrash, until her pleasure crested and broke, waves that pulsed from someplace so deep, she'd never known it existed.

She was so ready when he slid up her body and mounted her. Slick and soft enough so that he could drive inside, in one seamless lunge. Her pleasure-drugged languor vanished, instantly. She was a wild thing clutching, straining to pull him deeper. Rough sounds wrenched out of her. He grabbed her hands, pinned them against her knees. Each thrust jolted her farther up the mattress. Her chest was going to burst. Harder, faster. The bed jiggled and shook. The mattress squeaked. Their bodies slapped together. It was wild, hard, ungentle. Exactly what she craved. To be pushed beyond all fear, all thought.

The explosion ripped through their bodies, fusing them. She was weeping when she opened her eyes. Whatever she needed he gave to her, with an instinctive generosity that came straight from his soul.

And she loved him for it, violently.

CHAPTER
19

Kev buried his face against her hair, struggling for air. Fried, melted, totally fucked up. He dragged himself out of the clutch of Edie's damp, quivering body, peeled off the condom. Stared down at his dick, bemused. All that sweating and pounding and thrashing, and look at him. As hard as he'd been before they started. Son of a bitch.

He grabbed a fresh condom, applied it, and rolled on top of Edie again, daring her with his eyes to try and refuse him. Edie moved beneath him, gasping softly with each shove. He grabbed her knees, folded her up high so he could see every detail. Incredible, those luminous, soft pink pussy lips distended around the shaft of his cock. Kissing his whole length as he slid inside. Every slow, aching outstroke a protracted, milking caress. Her eyes shone with tears.

And he didn't want to deal with that. He looked away, seized the base of his cock, angled it to hit the spots that melted her. Petting the secret pink pearl of her clit with his thumb. So tight and taut.

He tried to take it easy, to be slow and gentle, but his efforts were useless. Sex with her had its own huge, unstoppable agenda. It was what it was, it became whatever it had to be, and he was just a helpless puppet, panting and desperate. Clutching her, driving her until he got what he craved—a long, pulsing orgasm that lingered on and on. Her snug pussy, squeezing his cock. So fucking sweet.

He was a slave to that. Had to have it. He wanted to lose the latex. Feel her heat, her slick juice bathing him. Skin on skin.

The no latex fantasy kicked up the pace, and he was slamming into her, so deep and desperate, it scared him, but he couldn't resist, couldn't control it, but she was . . . oh. Yeah. Oh, God, *yeah.*

There she went. He let go, lost himself along with her.

He lay there afterwards, shaking. Every time they made love, he felt more naked. More out of control. Carrying on like a crazed barbarian warlord, waving his dick around like a club. But it was all bullshit. The power dynamic between them was brutally clear.

He was on his knees to her. She owned his ass.

This time, it took him ten, maybe fifteen minutes of sprawled panting before he was ready for another go at her. Throwing himself back into the trap, but this time, he'd make it less personal.

"Roll over," he ordered her.

Edie's eyes popped open. "You have got to be kidding," she said faintly. "I'm exhausted."

"Too bad," he said. "You were warned."

Edie jerked up onto her elbow. "You can't possibly still be . . ." Her eyes dropped to his dick. "My God. Are you on some weird drug?"

"Yes," he said. "My endocrine system pumped it into me when those bastards jumped us on the stairs." He flipped her onto her belly, then grabbed her hips, pulling her back until she was in the perfect position. Damp hair clung to her slender back. The arch of her back, the rounded perfection of her ass. Shadowy beckoning wonders of her secret sexy female parts. He caressed them, his mouth watering.

She looked back at him as he rolled on the condom. "Attila the Hun. Ghengis Kahn. Those guys have nothing on you."

He gripped her ass cheeks, petting their luminous perfection as he nudged his cockhead between her slick folds. "Don't even try to make me feel guilty about this," he said. "I warned you. Repeatedly."

"So you did." She sucked in a broken breath as he slid into the plush perfection of her body, wedging himself to the hilt. "So, um, Kev?"

He pulled out, hypnotized by every perfect detail of her flesh clasping him, and surged in again. His body helpless to it. Locked into that beautiful, wet, rocking ebb and flow. "What?"

"How many times do we have to have sex before I can tease you again?"

He choked on a bark of laughter. "Let me get back to you on that. I should have an answer for you by midday." He gripped her ass and started to move.

This time, it was slower, lazier. They'd taken the edge off. In fact, after a while, time warped out of shape. They could have been at it for hours or days for all he knew. The sun rose outside, curtains lightening. He made her come a few more times before she collapsed facedown on the bed. Pressing back against the slow rocking surge of his body. She couldn't speak, couldn't move. She just lay there, panting. Clutching the sheet.

She was done. She needed rest. He rode the crest and let go, letting the long, violent blast of pleasure wrench through him, and drifted back very slowly, holding her jealously tight. "You should be able to tease me, now," he said. "I could probably take it, at this point."

Her giggle was feeble. "Who has the energy? Or the air?"

He slid out of her, letting her roll onto her back and breathe.

"I was thinking," she murmured. "If you really were trying to brainwash me, this would be the perfect way. My brain feels like it's been through the spin cycle. To say nothing of the rest of me."

Her sweet smile made his eyes fog up. And after his selfish, controlling adrenaline tantrum, too. Her generosity made him feel abashed. "Me, too," he said gruffly. "I'm sorry I was so—"

"Don't," she urged. "Shhh." She put her finger to his lips, tapped them gently, stroked them. "It was wonderful. It's always wonderful."

He kissed her fingers. "*You're* wonderful."

She cuddled closer. "Did you work out your combat adrenaline?"

"I'm maybe halfway there."

She peeked up. "Halfway?"

"Maybe," he said. "Close to halfway. We'll see. Hard to tell."

She checked out his still-turgid dick. "I don't think that's normal."

"Nothing about me ever has been," he admitted. "And it's your fault, anyhow, for being so beautiful and sexy. So don't blame me."

"Oh, please."

He disposed of the condom, and in the process, caught sight of the bag Edie had insisted on bringing, packed full of Bruno's catered food. His stomach rumbled with interest. He laid the bag on the bed, tearing it open and digging for forks, spoons, napkins. "Breakfast?"

"God, yes." Edie dragged herself up. They sat cross-legged on the bed and attacked the food, reducing it to smears and crumbs in minutes. She tucked slices of rare filet mignon into his mouth, he countered with big, fat prawns, chunks of juicy crabmeat for her. The baguette was crisp outside, soft inside, and excellent spread with cheeses and piled high with grilled veggies. Portobello mushrooms were heaped with some sort of rich stuffing full of bacon and cheese. The roasted artichokes were tender, dripping with butter and lemon. Big, sweet chunks of fruit were melting and juicy. All of it. Damn good.

He checked the address of the place on the ripped bag, memorized the phone number. He'd be calling them again. He hoped, anyway, that his and Edie's lives might return to such a normal pitch that they could hope to order in takeout sometime and feed it to each other in bed. Between sweaty bouts of mind-bending sex. What a fantasy.

Bruno had racked up some big, big points, Kev reflected, fishing for a napkin to wipe his mouth. The punk might even be excused for this latest break-in. He reflected on Bruno's antics with uncharacteristic generosity as he loaded up another chunk of baguette with—

Pop. The loud sound shocked him off the bed. Bread and cheese flew, landed facedown on the floor. He snatched up the SIG 220, looking around frantically for the threat.

"Oh, God, Kev. I'm sorry," Edie said apologetically. "It's just this." She lifted the champagne bottle. "The cork hit the ceiling, and you weren't looking at it, and I . . . I didn't think."

He let out a shuddering sigh, easing down his thudding heart. "Christ, Edie," he muttered, through set teeth.

"Really." She bit her lip. "I'm so sorry." She lifted one of the plastic glasses. "Do you want some? It's warm, but it's also Dom Perignon."

He lay the gun down, and thudded heavily on the bed. His hands were still trembling. "No fucking way. I'm not touching alcohol until this situation is completely resolved."

She looked worried. "But aren't we safe here?"

"We're not safe enough anywhere that I would voluntarily drink something that could slow down my reflexes."

"Ah. I see." She put bottle and glass both on the bedstand. "That's, ah, very rigorous, Mr. Super Hardass."

"Fuck, yeah," he muttered. "Do the hard thing."

She gave him a considering look, her head tilted to the side. "The hard thing? What's the hard thing?"

He shrugged, uncomfortable. "Just a figure of speech."

"But what does it mean to you, exactly?" she persisted.

Shit. He wasn't feeling all that articulate today. "I don't know," he said, his voice surly. "It's just a thing I say. Don't know where it comes from. I guess the hard thing is usually the right thing. Or vice versa."

She pondered that. "And the corollary is that the easy thing must be wrong. Or lazy. Self indulgent. Dangerous. Right?"

Irrational anger surged. It felt like she were criticizing him, though her tone was very gentle. "Yes! It is! Like fucking you in my apartment while those kidnappers were closing in, for instance! It'll take years of being a hard-ass for me to get over that!"

"That wasn't your fault!"

"Doesn't matter," he said. "Results matter. Outcomes matter. I'm still responsible. And I might have known that something like this would happen. I might have known that it was too good to be true."

He forced himself to choke off. He was overwrought. Babbling stupid, senseless shit that would only get him in trouble.

"Too good to be true?" she repeated slowly. "And how is that?"

He was in for it now. "Yes! Too fucking good to be true! There's no way that I could just meet the perfect woman who's haunted my dreams all my life, and just have it be normal. Just have it go smoothly."

She blinked. "Clue me in as to what's smooth and normal, Kev."

"Like other people!" he yelled. "I meet you, I charm you, I date you. We go see movies, concerts. We go to bed. We leave toothbrushes and underwear in each others' places, we start unofficially living together, I meet your parents, I buy a ring, we set the date, get married, etc., etc. That's normal. That scenario, for me? No fucking way! The day I meet you, the killers close in on you! The very same day, Edie!"

"Kev," she breathed out softly. "Sweetie—"

"What am I supposed to think?" he roared. "That I'm cursed, right? That I just can't have this! I can't have you! It's just not in the cards for me, not in this lifetime. That's the truth. That's the hard thing that I have to face, but I can't face it, Edie! I just can't face it!"

His voice cracked. He turned away from her, suddenly afraid he was going to cry. Oh, God forbid. Please. Not that.

"You don't have to," she said. "I won't let you face it. I can't face it either." She leaned closer to him, pressing her face to his shoulder. Kissing it, as if she were kissing a baby. Her hand drifted up to stroke his cheek. The scar tissue was weirdly oversensitive there, but his screwed up nerve endings accepted her light touch, and amazingly, translated it as pleasure. Not the nervous tickle that he usually felt.

"Edie," he started, feeling exhausted. "I just can't—"

"Shhh," she soothed. "You think you'll be punished for anything too good, don't you? And who could blame you. You've been punished so much." She kissed his shoulder, moving her warm, soft lips tenderly over the scars. "There's something that we need to do."

He watched her rummage through the wreckage of their feast until she found a spoon, and the white cardboard container that proved to have a goopy, unidentifiable dessert, once she popped it open.

It still smelled good, despite being battered into goop. Coffee, cream, custard, soaked cookie crumbs, God knew what else.

She scooped some up onto the spoon, and shuffled closer to him on her knees, holding up the spoonful. She had that fey, magical glint in her bright eyes. The one that stopped his breath right in his lungs.

"Uh, wasn't that stuff for the brainwashing session?" he asked.

"This *is* the brainwashing session, you big silly. Get over here."

She waited patiently while he scooted toward her on his knees, and grabbed his hand tightly, like she thought he might bolt.

"Now. Repeat after me," she said. "None of this is my fault."

He sighed. "Edie. It's not that simple, and I can't just—"

"Repeat it!" Her voice had a ring of command that zapped his spine up to military drill straightness. And made the scar on his cheek sting, from the smile spreading there.

"Fine," he grumbled, rolling his eyes. "None of this is my fault."

She smiled her approval, and put the spoon of sweet goop into his mouth. The sugar orgasm jolted him hard. But Edie wasn't done with him yet. "Repeat after me," she commanded. "I deserve to be happy."

A strange, irrational tension gripped him. "Edie—"

"I know it sounds silly. I know it feels false. That's exactly why you need to say it. Don't fight me on this. Indulge me, OK? Remember what a hard night I've had. How fragile I am."

He grunted. He was being blatantly jerked around, but whatever.

"I deserve to be happy," he said, grimly acquiescent.

She put the spoonful of goop to his lips. He accepted it. They stared at each other, sobered. Something was happening. Something subtle and mysterious, vibrating in the air. It almost scared him.

"Another one," she said. Her voice had a little quiver in it. "Repeat after me. I deserve pleasure."

He swallowed. He was uncomfortable with this weird game, but there was no way out but through. "I deserve pleasure," he muttered.

Edie nodded, and gave him his spoonful of goop, with the ritual air of a priestess offering holy communion. "One last thing," she said softly. "Look me straight in the eye, and repeat after me. I deserve love."

Kev stared at her. His throat was petrified. There was big cold rock where his voice box had been. Edie just waited, merciless.

"Come on, Kev," she prompted gently. "You can do this."

He cleared his throat. "I deserve love," he said hoarsely.

She gave him the spoonful. It was all he could do to swallow it.

His throat burned. His chest, too. Her eyes were wet, shining.

He grabbed the dessert and the spoon out of her hands. "OK," he said. "Your turn now. Say it, Edie. All of it."

Edie quietly repeated the exact phrases that he had said, accepting spoonfuls of the dessert after each assertion.

At the end of the solemn ceremony, they gazed at each other. Raw emotion vibrated between them in the deafening silence.

"I love you," she said.

He swallowed. "I love you, too."

He put the container and the spoon down, and took her hands. Lifted them to kiss them, slowly and reverently. Edie pulled her hands free, put them around his neck, pulled his face down to hers.

He meant for it to be a holy, sacred kiss. Gentle, respectful, in keeping with the gravity of the moment, but no. The kiss flared instantly into something frenzied. Like he had to crawl inside her soul to survive. Like they'd both die if they didn't get closer, kiss deeper.

He pulled back, gasping for air. "You keep doing this to me, and you know I'm going to fuck you again," he blurted. "I was trying to be reasonable and civilized. Trying to give you some time, let you rest. But you keep messing with my head."

She undulated against him. "The food gave me a second wind."

He swept the containers off the bed with his arm, and seized her.

"I cannot believe it! Aren't you hardened professionals? Decades of experience? I read your brochures, gentlemen! It's all bullshit!"

Ava's shrill voice was making Des's head ache. He rubbed his temples. Tom and his men were slumped in their chairs in the big luxury trailer outside Ava's lab that Des had procured for them, in varying stages of bloody disrepair. Richard's face was turning color, both eyes swollen shut, his mouth was distorted and torn, nostrils still caked with dried blood. Ken was hunched in his chair, curled around the ugly black hematoma in his scrotum, whining about a ruptured testicle. Tom's pant leg was cut off, his thick, hairy leg bandaged with blood-soaked gauze. In short, they were a whimpering, pathetic mess.

"Ava, please," Des soothed wearily. "Calm down."

"We handed them to you! On a silver platter! And you let them get away!" Ava's voice rose to a shriek. "Imbeciles! Incompetent *dickheads!*"

"You sent us out there with incomplete intel," Tom threw back. His face was beaded with sweat, pupils dilated from the pain meds. "We weren't aware that he had a high level of combat training—"

"He is a *McCloud!*" she hissed. "Did you not read the files? His background, his father, his brothers? Did we not tell you what Sean McCloud did to Dr. O? Did you not do the cognitive enhancement program? Can you think for yourself? Is the concept foreign to you?"

"You told me he was a brain-damaged amnesiac!" Tom snarled.

Ava snorted her disgust. "In the future, remind me. Thinking is a process that you and your people need to have outsourced."

Tom's eyes went very cold. "Shut up, you mouthy cunt."

Ava's eyes lit with battle fury. "To think I facilitated orgasms for these losers." Her voice was a thread of sugary poison. "If I had it to do again, I'd compel Keira to bite their shrinking little pink penises off."

"I'm done." Tom looked at Des. "Deal's off. I cannot cope with your venomous bitch of a girlfriend and a knife in my leg at the same time. And I want McCloud for myself. I want to take this"—he held up the dagger that had been embedded in his leg—"and fuck him with it."

"Not McCloud," Ava snarled. "He's mine."

"Wait, wait, wait. Just hold on," Des broke in. "Everybody just take a deep breath." He leaned over Ava, gripped her shoulders. "Shut up," he whispered. "Or we lose everything." Ava's breath hissed through bared teeth like a cornered animal, but he held her gaze. "Everything we always wanted," he coaxed. "You with me? You'll be good?"

Her eyes dropped. She gave him a sharp nod.

Des turned back to Tom. "Ava's sorry she was rude to you."

Tom snorted his disgust. "She can suck my dick."

Ava's smile dazzled. "Wouldn't risk that, if I were you, Tom."

"Stop it! Everyone!" Des snapped. "Throwing insults is inefficient. We need a new strategy for taking McCloud without injuring him."

"Drugs," Ava said. "Trank gun. I'll load it with something special."

"Or Tasers," Ken offered.

"That's what you should have used last night!" Ava snapped. "You risked damaging his brain even more! Blackjacks? Stupid *idiots*."

"Ava! Shut up!" Des massaged his temples. "So, Parrish is no longer in the ICU," he said briskly. "I called Marta. His status has been upgraded to good, and he's leaving the hospital to look for Edie. We start making arrangements as soon as he's home."

"I thought McCloud in the bag was key to that plan," Tom said.

"We'll get him in the bag," Des assured him.

"Yeah? And how do you propose that? He's off boning the girl in a hotel somewhere. Why should he come back at all?"

"He'll come." Des held up his cell. "I've got his number, and I've got something that he wants. He'll come. So will Edie, when Daddy croaks all over the evening news. We've got them both cold, Tommy."

Tom's nostrils flared. "Could have suggested this possibility before you had me stick my neck out last night."

"I'm sorry, man. I didn't know about his combat skills, either, but I did know about yours, and they're flat-out amazing," Des soothed. "It seemed simpler to have you take him. At the time. Forgive me, OK?"

Tom grunted. "Leave the cock licking to the girls, Des. They do it better." His eyes flicked to Ava. She smiled, showing off her white teeth.

Des rushed into the breach before things could degenerate further. "We need to put surveillance cameras in McCloud's apartment, and Edie's. If either one of them should drop by, we'll grab them. Are you gentlemen, ah . . . fit for that?"

"Fuck you, man," Ken Wanatabe growled.

Richard just opened one eye halfway, closed it, and groaned.

"It'll get done," Tom muttered.

"One more thing." Des braced himself. It was a piss poor time for this particular conversation, but it had to be gotten through. "I meant to ask you about this yesterday, but things got crazy. The disposal issue."

"We took care of it yesterday," Tom cut in brusquely. "Before the banquet. It's done. Don't micromanage."

"I'm not talking about Keira," Des said. "I'm talking about what's backed up in the cooler already. I know it's a bad time, but Parrish was supposed to croak last night, and he didn't. And he's breathing down our necks. We have got to take out the trash."

Tom's mouth hardened. "How many?"

Des shrugged. "I think there's about eight, last time I checked."

"Twelve," Ava corrected. "He hasn't checked in a while."

Tom stared at Des, then at Ava. "Twelve," he repeated. "You send us out with bad intel to get fucked by that hopped-up McCloud maniac, and *then* you tell me you want us to get rid of twelve cadavers for you?"

Des gazed apologetically back at his friend. "I know, it's a lot to ask," he said. "But consider this. For an exclusive contract with—"

"No!" Ava shrieked. "An exclusive is wasted on these idiots!"

"For one year," Des went grimly on. "Shut up, Av."

Tom chewed the inside of his cheek. "Two years," he said.

"No!" Ava wailed.

"One," Des repeated patiently. "Only one."

"Eighteen months, and the bitch sticks a sock in her mouth."

"Done," Des said, giving Ava a quelling look. "We've set things in motion, Av," he said softly. "We can't go back. It's too late. Eat it."

Ava looked away. Her face was a white mask of fury.

Des pulled up the number, and hit CALL.

CHAPTER
20

Kev tried to ignore it, but the buzzing was relentless. He dragged his brain up to the level of consciousness, with the uncomfortable sense that he'd been way too far under. That phone could have been ringing for hours. He could have opened his eyes and found himself looking into a gun barrel. With Edie's lithe body draped all over his dominant gun arm. He had to sharpen the fuck up. Fast.

But he didn't want to sharpen up. Or even to get up. Fuck the phone. He was fine where he was, with Edie wrapped around him, her hair swirling over his chest, her tits pressed against him.

Who the fuck was calling him, anyhow? Someone persistent.

He stumbled out of bed into the cold, kicking through scattered clothes until he found the coat. It was on the floor, where Edie had dumped it last night. He crouched, rummaged in the pockets until he found the thing, squinted at the display. Not a number he knew.

Edie was sitting up now, looking worried. "Who is it?"

"We'll see." He sat down on the bed, and hit TALK. "What?"

A pause, and a male voice asked. "Is this Kev Larsen?"

The voice was familiar, and annoying. He fished through his databanks, trying to match it. "Who the hell is this?"

"This is Desmond Marr. Good morning!"

"Ah." Kev summoned what courtesy he could for that slobbering hound. Calling at this ungodly hour. He peered at the clock. Ten-fifty.

Shit. Not so ungodly. So what. He'd fish for something else to be rightously pissed about. "How'd you get this number?"

"Excuse me for taking the liberty." Marr's charm oozed through the electronic freqency, as unpleasantly viscous as it was in person. "Edie borrowed my phone last night at the banquet to text you, so I had the number in my records. Hope you don't mind. Did I wake you?"

Like that was his fucking business. "What do you want, Marr?"

Marr's fruity chuckle set Kev's teeth on edge. "Actually, this was about what you wanted. Weren't you interested in re-searching the—"

"I told you I'd get in touch," Kev said. "No need to call me."

Marr cleared his throat. "Ah, yes. Well, I've been in touch with the Parrishes, and they're terribly upset about Edie being, ah, kidnapped. By you. Sorry, but that's how they see it."

That gave Kev a jolt. So far, nobody knew about last night's kidnapping attempt except for himself and Edie. "She hasn't been kidnapped," he said. "We'll call them, and tell them. No big deal."

"Oh, that's great news," Des said heartily. "That'll be a big relief to everybody. So I suppose you wouldn't mind putting her on the phone?"

Kev handed Edie the phone, mouthing "Marr."

Edie took it. "Hey, Des. What's up? Any news of my Dad's condition?" She listened, nodding. "Good. I wish he'd

stay longer, but if he's feeling strong enough to launch a crusade . . . yeah, he's tough . . . that's problematic, Des. They
don't approve of me being with Kev, so it would be best if
I . . . yes, I know, but . . ." She rolled her eyes eloquently at
the tinny burst of verbal diarrhea coming from the cell. "I'm
not coming home right now. I'm safe with Kev, and . . . no.
We'll be leaving soon anyway. Don't worry about it."

Nosy shithead. Trying to pry their coordinates out of
Edie. Kev reached for the phone, cut off Des's pompous
tirade in midsquawk.

"Marr. It's Larsen. We'll talk later. Give Parrish our re-
gards."

"Don't hang up! You know those archives? Charles asked
me about them this morning. If you wait, Parrish is going to
know a lot more about you than you know about yourself,
and he is not going to leave any crumbs. If you want that
info, you have to move fast. Today."

Kev's jaw clenched. He had to find someplace to stash
Edie, and a human pit bull to guard her while he got his
hands on a car and a computer. So he could track down those
fucking kidnappers and get started on the task of grinding
them into a fine pink paste. Fuck the Osterman archives. He
was busy. "Tomorrow," he said. "Can't, today."

"It may be too late," Marr warned. "I can't guarantee
that—"

"So be it," Kev said. "I can't do anything until tomorrow."

"I'll try to hold them off until tomorrow." Marr's voice
sounded long-suffering. "I need to contact Ava. What time
will you be able to—"

"I'll let you know tomorrow. Don't call. I'll be in touch."

"Fine." Marr's voice was markedly cooler.

Kev almost hung up on the guy, but paused, gripped by an
odd impulse. "One question," he said. "Why are you doing
this?"

Marr grunted, sourly. "To be honest—"

"Yes, please be honest."

"I'm not doing it for you," Marr said. "You're a rude, un-cooperative asshole. I'm doing this for Edie, because she asked me to. And because I want to know exactly what we're dealing with, too. Like Parrish does."

"Ah." Kev listened with all his senses for more.

"If one hair on Edie's head gets hurt, it's not just Parrish who's going to be after you," Marr threatened. "I'll be coming after you too."

Ooh. Terrifying prospect. Kev sternly did not permit himself to say anything sarcastic. He'd indulged in enough childish behavior lately.

"OK," he said. "Fair enough. Tomorrow, then."

He hung up, and looked at Edie. "Is that guy carrying a torch for you? Did you turn him down, or something?"

"Good God, no." Edie looked bewildered. "Des Marr's barely ever spoken to me until last night after the banquet. He's ignored me all my life, even back at the Haven. I have no idea why he's suddenly so focused on me. It's weird."

Kev arranged himself so that his gun arm was free to lunge for the SIG 220, and tucked Edie into the crook of the other arm. "Did you look in the mirror last night before you went to the banquet? He saw you, and he had an epiphany. Can't say as I blame the guy."

"Please. Spare me. Is it my magical pink evening gown, again? It transformed me into a siren who melts men's brains?"

The woman still didn't get it. Kev decided not to bother arguing. Time enough to convince her later. "We should call your dad. Let them know you're OK. And tell them about the kidnapping attempt."

She looked pained. "He'll be hysterical."

"It's information that his security staff needs," he said, grimly stoic. "For your sister's sake. That's the only reason I'd do it."

She rubbed her face. "Let me wake up, first. Maybe some coffee."

"The longer you wait, the harder it will get," he warned. He stroked her hair for a few minutes, staring at the ceiling panels. "You said that Marr did Osterman's cognitive enhancement program, too?"

"Yes, he was one of Dr. O's favorites. In fact, it was his dad's raving about the massive improvement in Des's grades that gave my dad the idea to sign me up, too."

Kev dragged her closer. "What did Osterman do to you kids?"

A frown marred her forehead. "It was different for everyone," she said. "Dr. O's thing was about finding the perfect balance between the negative and positive approaches to releasing latent brain power."

"Positive and negative," he repeated. "Sounds ominous."

"It was," she agreed. "The positive techniques were the drugs and the behavioral training, and negative involved the removal of barriers. Inhibitions, complexes, fears, self-defeating beliefs. It boiled down to pseudo-psych motivational lectures, a heavy drug regimen, daily brain training sessions and hand tailored pinpoint electroshock therapy."

He whistled. "Holy shit. That's scary shit."

"Oh, yeah. To free us. 'From the chains that bind our brains.' Dr. O's catchphrase. I hear it in my dreams. Or nightmares, I should say."

Edie stared at the wall, lost in her unpleasant memories.

Kev gave her a squeeze and nudge. "Hey. Hello? Come out of it."

She shook herself. "He sure freed something," she murmured.

"You mean the psychic thing that happens when you draw?" he asked. "You think that's because of what Dr. O did to you?"

She met his eyes. "I know it was," she said simply. "It started there."

"What was the effect on the others?"

Her eyes looked haunted. "Hard to say. There's not many

of us left. Except for the success stories, like Des. And the high achievers don't talk about Dr. O in negative terms. I tried once to get in touch with people, do an informal survey of their experiences of the Haven. I got frozen out like you would not believe."

"So there are non-success stories, too?"

"There are a lot of non-success stories," she said quietly. "Suicides. Homicides, too. One guy killed his girlfriend, then himself. Another killed his family. There's the drug ODs, the alcoholics. There's some incidence of brain cancer. And the ones in the mental ward. Not a real high percentage, but higher than it statistically should be."

He was taken aback. "The families never protested? You'd think there would be lawsuits right and left."

"Dr. O had his ways of protecting himself," she said. "I think he implanted post-hypnotic imperatives, or something like that. Maybe I'm nuts for thinking this, but for years after the Haven, every time I tried to tell my parents what happened there, I got a blinding headache. After a while, I just gave up. They weren't interested, anyway. Not at the time. And the success stories were impressive. Like Des. He's amazing. Only three years older than me, but in a couple years, he'll be running Helix."

Kev illustrated his opinion of Des Marr's amazing qualities with a succinct hand gesture, and pulled her into his arms, as if he could protect her retroactively. "Wonder what part of Marr's brain got zapped." He could guess, but he'd keep that speculation to himself.

"Me, too," she admitted. "For me, I think it must have been some natural protective filter. Thank God it's not worse. I only have these episodes when I'm in an alpha state, and I only go into that state when I'm drawing. Or, ah . . . when I'm having sex with you." She turned pink. "I tune into you then, too. But that's the only exception."

His cock began to twitch and throb. He bore down on the impulse to roll onto her and take the plunge. Not while she was making halting, painful confessions. "Interesting," he said, his voice strangled.

"Yes," she agreed. "If that kind of info came at me full bore all the time, I'd be in a padded cell. Or dead. Maybe that's what happened to some of the unsuccessful Haven alums. I just got lucky."

"Or maybe you were stronger," he suggested.

She flinched. "I never felt particularly strong. On the contrary."

"There's all kinds of strength. You're very strong." He nuzzled her shoulder. "Hard to believe all the parents allowed it."

"The parents didn't know," Edie said. "Dr. O was good at playing us. Making each kid feel crucial to Dr. O's plan for a better world. Don't tell your parents! They'll never understand the new, powerful super-you! Don't distress them with things beyond their comprehension! Only the elect few are capable of undergoing my ultra-secret mind techniques, and so on and so forth. What teenager could resist that?"

He stared at her. "You did, evidently. You never bought it."

She snorted. "Nope," she admitted. "He froze my blood, even before he did the electroshock stuff." She stroked her cheek against his chest. "I got the sense that Dr. O really didn't know exactly what he was doing," she said. "He was just fucking around with us. Because he could, just to see what would happen. Calling it science."

He shook the sickening image away, and sat up, pulling a number up on the phone.

"Who are you calling now?" she asked.

"Backup. We're stranded here with no wheels. We need help."

She tilted up her elvish eyebrow. "From who?"

He felt the stretch on his facial scars as the grin started to spread. "Our relationship is about to get a big fat status upgrade." He pushed CALL. "Watch out. You're about to meet the Ranieris."

CHAPTER
21

A ham and cheddar omelet, English muffins and orange juice plus several cups of coffee at the Char Burger restaurant overlooking the Columbia River went a long way toward restoring Edie's courage. Even so, when she took Kev's cell and entered her father's number, her belly fluttered as if she were about to jump out of an airplane.

In a sense, she was. But she'd jump holding hands with the most special, unique, sexy, incredible guy she'd ever dreamed of. She could do this. Self-administered pep talks aside, her finger quivered, not connecting with the button. "Can he track us with this cell phone?"

"Yeah," Kev said. "There's no GPS tag in it, but they could have the signal triangulated and get a fix on us. I should have turned the thing off last night, I guess, but I had no idea you'd given the number out to anyone until Marr called."

"Sorry about that," she said. "Giving the number to Des, I mean."

"No one could have guessed things would get so weird so fast."

"Brace yourself," she said grimly, and pushed CALL. "They're about to get weirder."

Her father picked up on the first ring. "Who is this?" he snapped.

That was a good sign. He was better. "Hey, Dad. It's me."

"Edith! Where are you?" he barked.

She hesitated. "I'm fine. How about you? Still in the hospital?"

"Of course not! How could I stay there when my daughter's been abducted? Where are you? I'll send someone to pick you up right away!"

Edie stared out the restaurant's huge windows. Stray shafts of sunlight lit the shreds of fog draped across the high, dark mountains' shoulders. Green and gray swirled and spun as she blinked tears out of her eyes. "No, Dad," she said quietly. "Thanks, but I'm fine where I am."

She could hear the gears grinding as he contemplated his next strategy. "Ronnie needs you, Edie. She cried all night. She's not eating."

Guilt was a classic, but he'd used it on her before. Betrayed her with it, too. She wouldn't do Ronnie any good once they'd pumped her full of drugs and locked her up. "I need her, too," she said, her voice thick. "You're putting me in an impossible position."

"I? I'm the one? Oh, for God's sake, Edie! Don't get me started! I cannot believe how self-absorbed you are!"

That touched off his tirade, but Kev was making a finger slicing over the throat gesture. She forced herself to cut over the stream of angry words. "One moment, Dad. I have to tell you something important before I end this call," she broke in. "About an attempted kidnapping."

"Attempted? Hah! It seems that he succeeded quite well!"

"Not Kev," she said. "That's not a kidnapping. That's just me, hanging out with my new boyfriend. Which I have every right to do."

"It's all in the labeling, then?"

"Please, Dad, listen to me! Three guys jumped us outside

my apartment last night! One of them held a knife to my throat!"

Her father was silent. "Forgive me for pointing out the obvious," he finally said icily. "But if you hadn't deliberately eluded my security staff, they would have been there to protect you. How many times have I told you about how dangerous that neighborhood is?"

"Can we put aside the scolding and concentrate, please? They didn't get me, but I wanted you to know about it, because the staff needs to be especially on the alert, to protect Ronnie."

Dad clicked his tongue in that thoughtful way that never boded well. "A knife to your throat? How on earth did you manage to escape?"

"Kev saved me," she said. "He fought them. And they ran."

"I see. Really. A surprise attack, in the dark, from three brutal professional criminals, and he scared them all away singlehandedly? My, my! He must be quite the warrior, hmm?"

She didn't understand her father's tone. How could he be so sarcastic and cavalier about this? "Yes, in fact, he is!" she said heatedly.

"Bet he didn't get a scratch, did he? Very impressive."

"Dad, please. I'm telling the truth. I'm not trying to—"

"Don't talk to me about truth, Edith. I'm sure you've been carefully coached in everything you say to me."

"No! I haven't! I was attacked, and it wasn't a mugging! I'm telling you so you can be on the alert! This was a courtesy call, understand?"

"Courtesy? Hah! God, Edith! You are so innocent, you must be a changeling! You were never in any danger from those attackers! They would have killed him if you had been!" her father yelled. "They would have shot him! How stupid can you be? Don't you see it?"

"But . . . but I . . . but he—"

"It was staged!" he roared. "This man is playing you! And you are making it so easy for him! I'm sorry if this hurts you, but this is not about you, Edith! It's about what he's trying to do to me! To punish me for what he perceives are my crimes! Whether I'm guilty or not, I don't know and frankly, I no longer care. Do not let yourself be used in this way! It is so painful for me to watch!"

"Dad, stop." He had it wrong. He hadn't been there. He couldn't know.

"I am embarrassed for you!" Charles Parrish raged on. "I can imagine your gratitude, hmm? What a bonding moment it must have been. It makes me nauseous just to think of it."

"Then don't think of it," she said.

"Ah. So that's how it is. I'll add that to the long list of things I can't bear to think about. Like my firstborn child, trying to poison me."

Edie was speechless. She finally forced air through her vocal apparatus, and squeaked, "What? What are you talking about?"

"You heard me, Edith. The toxicology tests aren't back yet, but Paul searched your apartment this morning. He found two vials of something called . . . Tamlix, I think it was? God knows where you got a designer poison like that. I certainly don't want to. Dr. Katz did some research. He tells me the effects of a small dose are consistent with my symptoms last night. The amount that you splashed in my face would have sufficed. And a larger dose would have stopped my heart."

She shook her head, as if he could see her. "I would never—"

"I know you're angry with me, Edith. But I did not know how angry. I would never have thought you were angry enough to kill."

"B-b-but I wasn't!" she stammered. "I haven't! I would never—"

"I would never press charges. I hope you know that. Particularly since you tried to stop me last night. I suppose I owe my life to that crisis of conscience."

"No! Dad, I—"

"All I want is for you to get the help you need. For you to be safe and well, Edith. And away from that . . . that person. I know you would only do such a horrible thing if someone else put you up to it."

She swallowed back the desperate, bleating denials. He couldn't hear them. "Good-bye, Daddy," she whispered. "I'm so sorry that you believe this of me. It's not true. Please tell Ronnie that I love her."

She let her arm drop to the table, and stared at the phone, still issuing a tinny squawking of frantic orders. She pushed the END button, and made it stop. Would that it were always that simple.

Kev took the phone from her without a word, and turned it off. Then he grabbed her hand, and held it. She pressed her other hand against her shaking mouth, as if her face were about to fall off.

"He thinks I was the one who poisoned him last night," she whispered. "They found vials of poison in my apartment this morning."

"Oh, shit," Kev said quietly. "That's bad."

"And the kidnapping? He says you staged it," she said. "Those guys, last night. To lure me into your wicked trap, don't you know."

His hand tightened around hers. "I would die before I would deliberately hurt or scare you," he said. "You know that, right?"

The sincerity radiating from him was impossible to fake to her, with her kinky talents. But it wasn't like she could explain that to her father. "I know," she whispered. "Thank you. For being so truehearted." The phrase was old fashioned, but so was Kev. It fit.

He kissed her hand again. "This is getting really wierd,"

he said. "Who would set you up for that? The kidnappers? And why? Why would they give a fuck about framing you to kill your dad? His death would only complicate their ransom negotiations. It doesn't make sense."

She shook her head, hiding her face in her hands.

"I can see why he thinks the kidnapping was staged, though," Kev mused. "I don't get it either."

"Well, I'm just grateful for it," she flared. "So stop saying what a big head scratcher it is that they didn't blow your brains out, because I don't want to hear it again! Be grateful, OK?"

"OK." His smile was wary, uncertain. "Sure, I'm grateful. I don't think I've ever enjoyed being alive so much." He turned her hand over, kissed her palm. "I want it to go on and on. Forever."

She sniffed back tears, and stared out at the river. Trying to process it. Her father thought she'd tried to murder him.

"Funny," he murmured. "About me staging the kidnapping."

"Funny?" She snorted. "Oh, yeah. It's just a big laugh riot."

"No, about me luring you into my wicked trap. I was doing fine without going to insane lengths like staging a kidnapping." Kev sounded disgruntled. "He thinks I'd have such a godawful time getting a date?"

His aggrieved tone set her laughing, but the laughter turned to tears. She grabbed a napkin. "He'll never let me see Ronnie again."

"I'm so sorry, babe," he said. "I don't know how to fix that."

She shook her head, grateful for him for not offering false encouragement. Some things weren't fixable. They had to be swallowed, and simply endured. She was sorry he'd suffered, but it was good to be with someone who understood that. So much didn't need to be said.

She flung her head back, lifting her glasses to dab the tears out of her eyes. "We need a plan of action."

"We've got a couple of options," he said. "I'm still in favor of falling off the grid. It would be hard, but we could do it."

"Reindeer, emus? Or goats in Crete?" She gave him a wobbly smile. "I can't give up hope of ever seeing Ronnie again. I'm just not ready to do that. I feel like I'm betraying her already. And if we ran, it would make me feel guilty. Even though we've done nothing wrong."

Kev gazed at her for a moment. "OK. That leaves plan B."

"Which is?"

Kev gazed into his coffee, apparently reluctant to go on.

"Just lay it on me, OK?" she begged. "Don't leave me hanging with the significant silences. I can't stand it. My nerves are shot."

He nodded. "Last night, a strange thing happened to your dad," he said. "A strange thing also happened to you, and to me. So let's take a closer look at what all three of us have in common."

There was an odd inevitability to it, as the name popped out of her, like it had been waiting to be let free. "Osterman," she said.

"Yes," he said.

"But . . . but he's dead," she said helplessly. "Three years ago, now. He was burned to a crisp. A fire in his lab. It's a dead end."

Kev shook his head. "Osterman murdered and tortured people for decades. I don't buy the fire in the lab. There's more to it than that."

"So you'll take Des up on his offer to look at the archives?"

Irritation flashed across Kev's face. "I don't look forward to having him in my face, but it's a start. He might be in cahoots with your dad, so that's a risk." He grimaced. "I'll call him. I guess."

"Call him," she suggested. "Call him now. Let's get started."

Kev shook his head slowly back and forth. "I get started, Edie. Not you. You stay guarded in a safe, remote place."

She stared at him. "What do you mean?"

"What I said. No more, no less." His eyes were hard as flint.

Her spine straightened. "No," she said. "We do this together."

"Don't start." She'd never heard his voice sound so cold. He sounded like a different man. "This is an argument that you will lose."

Well, she was a different woman, too. "No, Kev," she said. "I have not exchanged one prison for another. Or one warden for another."

"I'm sorry that you see it in those terms."

"Those are the only terms there are to see," she said. "Consider this. To make this work the way you want, you would have to genuinely abduct me. Right here and now, in this restaurant. I refuse to comply. I am done with that bullshit. Now and forever. Understand?"

His eyes closed. A muscle twitched in his jaw. "Christ, Edie."

"You can't do it, Kev," she said quietly. "It's just not in you. You're not like my dad. And thank God for that."

He buried his face in his hands. "Shit," he muttered.

Several minutes passed while she let him digest that. He finally lifted his face, his eyes blazing with intensity. "A compromise," he said.

"I'm not compromising about this," she told him.

"Please," he said. "I can't tell you why I feel this way, but I sense it so strongly. You're in danger. You, specifically. Those men were trying to abduct you. Your father is trying to control you. Somebody's trying to frame you for murder. Des Marr wants to fuck you. Everyone is after you, babe.

Just let me do this one thing alone. The archives. Just that. Just stay off the screen for just a couple of days, while I get a clearer sense of what we're dealing with. Please, Edie. I love you."

"That's not the issue!" she snapped. "Do not use that against me!"

"I just found you!" His voice was rough. "Let me keep you safe for a couple days, at least! I'm so afraid of losing you. I came so close last night. I can't stand it. It would kill me. It would fucking destroy me."

"What about my fear of losing you?" she yelled back. "Isn't that just as valid? This is not fair! Why aren't we arguing about me giving you permission to traipse around alone, huh? Explain that to me!"

His mouth hardened. "Sure, I'll explain it. Extensive martial arts training, three guns, five knives, and a roll of garotte wire. Sorry, correction. Four knives, since I left one in that fucker's leg. That's why I go, and you stay. Just a couple days. That's all I'm asking, Edie."

"And then? What happens then?"

"Then we renegotiate," he said smoothly.

She tilted her head and regarded him through slitted eyes. "Like hell we do. You think you're so slick, don't you?"

"Slick ain't even the word for it," said a harsh, gravely voice from behind them. "Watch out for Kevlar, the mystery man, honey."

Their heads whipped around. Three people were arrayed near the table. An older man led the phalanx, about seventy, broad and thickset, with a scowling bulldog face, a grizzled crew cut and glinting silver stubble. A woman of roughly the same age built like a large brick flanked him. Same downturned scowl, same bulldog face, but her hair was a bouffant helmet of curls dyed matte black, and she wore a paisley polyester caftan and lots of clashing plastic jewelry.

On the other side of the old man was a muscular, dark,

extremely handsome guy who was grinning crazily, from ear to ear. She recognized the dimples from the Lost Boys magazine article.

Wow. This was Kev's adopted family.

Kev let out a sigh of resignation. "Edie, meet the Ranieris."

Kev would never have dreamed that he could be grateful to that motley crew for interrupting, but he could've kissed them. Even Tony.

"I coulda shot your ass up ten times over for how you wasn't paying attention, kid," Tony scolded, and then he and Rosa trained squint-eyed stares on Edie as if she were a heifer being considered for purchase. Bruno just scoped her shamelessly, waggling his eyebrows.

"Nice, Kevlar," he said, in admiring tones. "Sweet."

Tony sat next to Kev. Rosa sat next to Edie. Rosa's fixed, hungry stare made Edie squirm in her chair. Bruno took the last chair.

"So this is her," Tony said heavily.

"Edie, this is Tony Ranieri, Rosa Ranieri, his sister, and Bruno, their grand-nephew," Kev announced.

Edie nodded with a shy smile, and murmured a greeting.

"So you're the billionaire's daughter," Tony announced.

Fucking *ouch*. Kev hissed through his teeth. Tony had the grace and subtlety of a jackhammer. "Tony, goddamnit—"

"You ain't what I expected," Tony sounded faintly miffed.

"What did you expect?" Edie asked, bemused.

"A fluffhead socialite," Bruno offered helpfully. "Gidget goes to Paris. You know, pearls and heels and ringlets and a big dress."

She laughed. "I've got the big dress, at least. It's at the hotel."

Kev thumbed the cell on, and pulled up the photo he'd taken of her in the dress. He handed it to Tony. "Get a load of the dress."

Tony peered over his glasses, staring into the little display screen, and let out a grunt of cautious approval. "Hmmph. That's more like it."

Rosa grabbed the phone, and let out the exact same satisfied grunt. "Nice dress. Now that looks like a billionaire's kid."

They stared at Edie again, trying to cross-reference the big dress billionairess image with the flesh-and-blood girl, but he could see that they were struggling with it. Edie had dressed down again, bigtime. Back were the dark rimmed, awkward glasses, the long mop of concealing hair, the faded jeans, the loose, knee-length button-up sweater. Strange, though. Trying to disguise her beauty made it all the more poignant for him. It also made him want to grab her, peel it all off. Wallow in her splendor. God. So pretty. She glowed.

"I actually don't have anything to do with the billions," she blurted out.

Tony and Rosa looked at her blankly. "How's that, honey?" Tony asked.

She looked uncomfortable. "I was cut out. I'm just your average starving artist now. No billions. In fact, my bank account's overdrawn."

Tony grunted. "Yeah, we heard your daddy was a real hard-ass."

She slanted Kev a glance. "Yeah, there seems to be a lot of that in my life lately."

"So what's wrong with you? Why'd he cut you off?" Tony demanded. "What did you do?"

"That's Edie's private business, Tony," Kev said.

"No, it's OK," she said. "There are a lot of reasons, actually. I embarrass him. I say whatever I'm thinking at the wrong times, I don't dress appropriately, I chose the wrong occupation, and I, ah . . . I don't follow orders well." She shot Kev another hard look.

He gazed back. She wanted a challenge? He'd let the

Ranieris loose on her. Let them tear and rend. He'd be damned if he'd intervene.

"And now he's pissed because of Kev," Bruno concluded. "It's a real Romeo and Juliet scenario. Super romantic. Man, I go for that."

"I wasn't expecting all of you to come out here," Kev complained.

"You weren't thinking," Bruno said. "Fortunately, you've got me to think for you. Zia Rosa's the person least likely to be associated with you in a cyber-search, so we had her rent the car. And once she knew, you think she was going to stay behind? With a new girlfriend to grill?"

"I guess not," he said, with ill grace. "Jesus. What a circus."

"So me and Tony and Rosa go back to the city in my car, and I go back to work this afternoon, since some of us poor slobs actually have to work. Remember work? Or has it been too long, for you?"

"I know all about work," he muttered.

Bruno snorted. "And I come up to the cabin tomorrow morning bright and early to spell you and do my pit bull imitation, so that you can go do your Osterman archives searching bullshit *in santa pace*."

"Ah! Really!" Edie's tone made Kev's stomach sink. "So you two have already organized everything! How helpful of you!"

Everyone promptly found something else to look at. Bruno looked up at a wall full of Indian artifacts, whistling. Tony and Rosa became deeply absorbed with the tugboat going by on the river outside.

In fact, Kev had taken great care to discuss this aspect of the plan with Bruno while Edie was in the shower. For simplicity's sake.

"This stuff takes some advance planning," he muttered lamely.

Her elvish eyebrow tilted up to a dangerous angle. "It would have been nice to be invited to the planning session."

"So, ah, Edie!" Bruno broke in, his voice big and fake and hearty. "How'd you like the rose petals and the candles?"

Edie couldn't help but smile at that transparent, bouncing clown. "I loved them," she said softly. "It was wonderful. The food was marvelous, too. Thank you. It was a lovely thought."

Well, hell. Bruno's instincts and timing were better than his own, but that reflection just irritated the shit out of him. Sweet-talking punk. "Breaking into my apartment was somewhat less wonderful, though."

Bruno gave him an indignant look. "Just trying to help you out, buddy. You would never have thought of rose petals on the bed in a million years. Watch and learn." He waggled his eyebrows again. "A guy gets amazing mileage out of a little gesture like that."

Kev was so grateful for the giggle that burst out behind Edie's hand, he decided not to come down on Bruno after all. For now.

Edie turned her attention to Tony. "I've been so curious to meet you, after what Kev told me," she said.

Tony looked intensely suspicious. "What did he tell you?"

"How you saved his life," Edie said. "And chased that guy away who was beating him, and left your job to hide Kev. That was brave."

Tony grunted. "Stupid, more like," he said gruffly. "Real nice '83 Cadillac Escalade I had to get rid of after I put him in the backseat. He was more like raw hamburger than a man. Shoulda seen that damn car. Had to bribe someone to bury the sorry piece of shit in a landfill."

Kev winced. "Jesus, Tony! Too much information!"

But there was no stopping Tony. "It ain't like you can take a car to an auto detailer and say hey, man, can you get a cou-

ple a quarts of human blood outta this thing? Fuck, no. Had
to ditch the whole car for this crazy punk. He cost me money
from the start. Shit, he still does."

"And sewing him up, ah, *madonna santa*," Rosa flapped
her hands expressively. "His face. Like sewing wet tissue
paper."

Kev slanted Edie an apologetic glance. "Sorry," he muttered.

"It's OK," Edie replied. "I saw you in that condition, too."

That was a shocker, and required lengthy explanations
about Edie's presence at her dad's office that fateful day
eighteen years before. But Kev was getting antsy. "We need
to move," he broke in.

Tony and Rosa hovered next to Edie while he paid for the
meal, eyeballing her as if she were some exotic animal. They
were going to embarrass the shit out of him. The price he
had to pay for their help.

Zia Rosa opened fire. "You want babies, honey?" she demanded.

Edie turned pink. "Yes," she admitted. "Very much. Someday."

Zia Rosa snorted. "Someday? What's this someday crap-
ola? You ain't getting any younger." She glared at Kev. "He
certainly isn't."

"You don't even know how old I am, Zia," he reminded
her, as he stuffed his change into his wallet.

"Old enough." Zia Rosa dug in her imposing shiny black
plastic purse, and tossed him the keys to a rental. "Old
enough."

"Edie's twenty-nine," he informed her.

Rosa was unimpressed. "My nonna back in Brancaleon
was a grandmother by the time she was twenty-nine!"

"You can't be recommending that as family planning,"
Kev said.

Rosa gave his good cheek an admonishing pat. "You wait
too long, your sperm's gonna get old."

"My sperm is fine, Zia. Back off."

Edie embraced the older woman, and gave her a kiss on the cheek. "Give us a little time. We need to work out some things first," she said. "But we're already talking about it."

"Talk?" Rosa's mouth quivered as she sternly refused to smile. "I know what makes babies. It ain't talk. You don't start now, Tony and me'll be too feeble to be good *nonni*. The babysitting, the diapers—"

"I ain't changing no fuckin' diapers," Tony said darkly.

Zia Rosa spat something at him in that language Kev often cursed in. Edie glanced at Kev. "What did she say?"

Kev hesitated, but Bruno leaped into the breach. "She said, 'shut up, dickhead,' he translated cheerfully. "Very grandmotherly, huh?"

"Good-bye, Zia," Kev said loudly. "Thanks for the car. I owe you."

Tony and Bruno each took one of Zia Rosa's elbows, and hauled her toward the door.

"Eat my pork tenderloin!" she called. "Rice pudding, too! It's in the trunk!" She jerked her chin at Kev. "Strong sperm! Eat meat!"

Tony and Bruno led Rosa out to the parking lot. When Bruno's BMW pulled away, Kev looked over the garish yellow Nissan Xterra that had been parked beside it. An eye-jarring, memorable color, but what the fuck. That was Zia Rosa for you. "Sorry about that," he said.

"Don't be sorry," Edie said. "She's impatient. She wants grandbabies. She thinks of you as her son. I think she's great. I think they're all great."

He glanced over at her, startled. "Really? You do?"

"So direct," she said. "You know where you stand with them."

It was the God's own truth, but it had certainly never occurred to him to be grateful for it. "Huh. Glad it works for someone. Let's move."

CHAPTER
22

Tony's cabin was in the middle of nowhere. Kev crossed the river at Cascade Locks, drove east on the Washington side to White Salmon, and then headed north up into the mountains around Mt. Adams. The roads grew progressively smaller and rougher, winding higher until they were teetering on crumbling, washboarded gravel tracks barely wide enough for the vehicle's axle. Bumping over washed-out creeks, crawling past collapsed shoulders, rockfalls, cliffs. Heart-in-mouth driving. Kev stomped upon all attempts at conversation, so she stared out the window, fuming as the miles crawled by.

If he'd wanted to trap her up here, he'd done a great job. It would take her ages to hike out of this place. If she didn't freeze to death or get eaten by a hungry predator first.

When he finally parked, she slid out, startled at the sweetness in the air, the vast silence that contained infinite songs and sounds. The trees at that altitude were a shaggy, short collection of hardy conifers, interspersed with dead white skeleton trees and choked with gray undergrowth. There was a shallow, trembling lake, a cold wind whiffling across its reedy surface, the water as transparent as glass.

Kev grabbed her hand and her suitcase, and pulled her

through a thicket of trees. On the other side was a tiny clearing, with a cabin. It was humble, just a box made of weatherbeaten wood. Kev undid a heavy padlock and went inside, throwing open the shutters. Inside was a tiny kitchen, bathroom, a sleeping area with a curtain to divide it. One bed, covered with a canvas drop cloth and a plastic tarp. A sealed plastic bag full of bedding sat on top of it.

"I'll get a fire going, and light the propane for the water heater," Kev said. "In a couple hours, it'll be warm enough for a shower."

She looked around, charmed. "Did Tony build this?"

Kev grabbed a handful of kindling from a box by the door and crouched in front of a potbellied stove. "No, this isn't Tony's style. He bought this place about twenty years ago. The widow of a friend of his who got killed in Nam needed the cash. Tony's not much of an outdoorsman, but he used to bring me and Bruno up here, just to get us out of the city. I've been keeping the place up, last ten years or so."

"It's beautiful," she admitted. She didn't experience the grandeur of nature very often. But she loved it, when she got the chance.

"Yeah, I love it up here." His face was thoughtful, as he lit the crumpled paper inside his tower of kindling and watched the flames take hold, licking at the twigs and bark. "I feel more comfortable here than anywhere else. Maybe . . ." His voice trailed off.

Edie finished his thought. "You came from a place like this?"

"It's possible," he admitted. "I have dreams. A house in the woods. Mountains, trees."

"People, too?" she asked, hesitantly.

He nodded, his face somber in the dimness. "I can see their faces in the dream, and hear their voices, but it all slips away when I wake up," he admitted. "Like a wall slamming down. I can't hang on to it."

"So the memories are there," she mused. "Just blocked."

"I don't know how to pry them out," he said. "There was no physical trauma to my brain. The people who did this to me didn't cave in my skull. I think the block is self-inflicted."

She sat down on the bed. "You did it to yourself? How?"

"I don't know. It's protective, to keep Osterman out. It's just that I can't undo it. That's just my hypothesis, though. Who knows what really happened. I'll probably never know. I just have to accept that."

She looked around the tiny cabin. Kev followed her gaze. "It's pretty basic," he said. "No cable TV, phone, cell or Internet. It's one of the reasons I like the place so much. But I'm sorry if you get bored."

She snorted. Bored. Hah. As if she could get bored, with her life in a centrifuge, and Kev Larsen constantly boggling her mind.

"You know, I could stay here alone tomorrow," she said. Kev started frowning and shaking his head, so she hurried on. "Really. Don't make Bruno skip work and drive up to babysit me. It's a big hassle, and he'd be stuck making nervous conversation all day with some girl he barely knows. I'm used to solitude. I have my sketchbooks."

"Don't worry about conversation with Bruno," Kev said. "The problem is in getting him to shut up. Feel free to tell him to zip it, by the way. He won't get his feelings hurt."

So much for that attempt. "I hope you know what a huge concession this is, on my part," she said darkly. "You guilt tripped me into this, Kev. Don't make a habit of it. I already regret having given in."

He lay a couple of larger sticks on his fire. "Too late." He was making a big effort, but his voice wasn't quite apologetic enough to be convincing. "I'll make it up to you."

She put her hands on her hips. "Really? How?" she demanded.

He rose to his feet. "I'll think of something good."

"What bullshit." She flung the plastic bag full of bedding at him. He caught it, tossed it back. She was swinging the bag of pillows at his head when he seized her.

"Thank you for agreeing to this." He kissed her with such intensity she had neither time nor breath to say anything snarky. Heat kindled, flared, and the embrace took on the usual urgent, twining desperation. He lifted his head, panting. "Edie—"

"Exploring ways to keep me entertained without TV?"

He looked agonized. "Actually, not right now. I have to make that phone call to Marr. Should have done it before, but I was in such a hurry to get some space between you and the city. I won't have time tomorrow morning, because we have to hike up to the bluff to get a signal, and it takes forty minutes just to get up there, and we have . . ." He glanced at his watch. ". . . a scant hour of daylight left."

"You'd go faster without me," she suggested.

He gave her a look. She sighed. "I'll come. Goddamn tease."

"I'm sorry," he said. "I didn't mean for it to take off like that. It was supposed to be just a kiss. But a kiss is never just a kiss with you."

She shoved at him. "Fine. Let go. Stop stimulating me."

Following Kev up to the bluff was hard at the pace he set. They thrashed through undergrowth, clambered over tree trunks, slipped and slid across rockfalls. Edie's flimsy sneakers were up to the walk even less than her legs were, but when they cleared the crest where the trees petered out, the view of snow-covered Mt. Adams blindsided her.

She forgot about her burning lungs and legs, and stared, slack-jawed. At such close range, the power radiating from the slumbering volcano was overwhelming. And oddly familiar.

It was like Kev, she thought. This awestruck feeling was familiar because Kev was just like that lonesome, snow-covered volcano, its rounded top wreathed in clouds. Secret fire in its depths. Austerely beautiful, potentially deadly, mysterious. Magnetic.

She couldn't resist the pull. She couldn't imagine ever wanting to.

The comparison brought tears to her eyes, but the raw, blustery wind blasting over the bluff was a good enough excuse, and Kev wasn't paying attention. He wandered the boulder-strewn hillside, looking for a signal. He finally crouched down in the lee of a towering black rock face.

Edie sat beside him, clutching the oversized jacket he'd insisted she wear. She was used to Portland's soggy, temperate weather. Her ears hadn't been this cold since that trip to Aspen years ago, when her dad tried to teach her to ski. She'd ended up in the hospital with a broken leg. Painful, but Dad got the message. No more skiing for Edie.

Kev was shouting into the phone, but the wind whipped the sound away. He was arguing with whoever he was talking to. He flipped the thing closed and grabbed her arm, frowning. "Let's get down the hill before you freeze." He sounded grim.

Edie scrambled to keep up with him, stumbling with weariness. Darkness had fallen when they reached the shelter and quiet of the trees. "So?" she asked him. "You set it up?"

"Tomorrow morning, at the library of the new Parrish Foundation building. With Cheung, the neuroscientist. Marr's upset that you're not coming. He thinks you're hanging from a hook by your hair someplace."

"So let me come," she suggested. "I'll put his mind at ease."

He shot her a look. "I don't give a shit about the ease of his mind. And even if there weren't kidnappers and guys in white coats gunning for you, I'd sooner drown myself than let that slobbering dog anywhere near you. Hurry up, Edie. I don't want us out on this slope if it fogs in."

She was hurt by his brusque tone, but too busy scurrying to protest about it. She was relieved when she finally caught sight of the cabin below, and the smoke that issued from the chimney.

Kev was still grim and silent once they were inside, though the cabin was deliciously warm, the fire in the pot-bellied stove crackling. He yanked the stove door open, stirring and stoking while Edie peeled off layers and rubbed her numb fingertips. She was accustomed to this tense, walking on glass, not-daring-to-speak feeling. She'd spent her whole childhood like this. She would not tolerate it from a lover.

"Why are you angry?" she asked flatly. "What the hell did I do?"

He was silent for a few moments. "Nothing. I'm sorry I appear that way," he said, his voice stiff and formal. "It's not directed at you."

"I'm the only one here," she told him. "I can feel it, on my skin. Is it Des who bugged you?"

He waved his arm, dismissively. "Not him," he said. "He's insignificant. I'm just . . ." He stopped, swallowed. Closed his eyes.

Edie didn't dare breathe. "What?"

"Scared." He forced the word out, as if pushing it past a barrier.

Edie sighed, relieved. Familiar ground. Scared, she could relate to. She'd spent most of her life scared. "You'd be a fool not to be. Half your life, your lost family, everything you were. It's terrifying."

"No, it's not that," he said. "I'm not afraid of what I might find out. I'm afraid of what might happen when I remember. Because when I remember something . . . it's ugly, Edie. It's a bad scene."

The trapped look in his eyes made her ache to embrace him, but something held her back. He would not be able to bear her touch.

"Tell me," she said softly.

He stared down at clenched fists. "When I woke up from the coma, after the waterfall, I started to remember. That mechanism I told you about . . . the head injuries must have jarred it loose. And the pain, and fear, when things started coming back . . . Jesus, it was like being burned alive. I went nuts. I almost killed an innocent man. When I saw Osterman's face posted on Facebook, I blew a blood vessel in my eye and went into a self-induced coma. For lack of a better term. I was awake, conscious. But stuck."

"That was your protective mechanism?" she said.

"Yeah. A hole inside my mind." He sounded haunted. "No way out. And I was hiding in it. That's how scared I was. Just from seeing that man's face, in a fucking photograph. That's what it did to me."

"You think sparking your memories might trip the switch again?"

"Bruno stopped me from killing Patil." Kev said. "He dragged me to the emergency room the second time. At least tomorrow, if I should attack someone, it'll just be that butthead Marr in the crosshairs."

Kev sounded more cheerful about that possibility than was strictly appropriate, but Edie was in no mood to judge him for it. "Why don't you send someone else to check the records for you? I'd do it."

He shot her a hooded glance. "Nice try."

She sighed. "Well, Bruno, then!"

He stabbed at the fire with the poker until sparks scattered onto the floor, and shook his head. "Doesn't feel right. It has to be me."

That pissed her off. Stoic, pompous, self-sacrificing jerk. "You are so arrogant," she snapped. "Such a hard-ass. You have to take on all the danger singlehandedly. Because nobody else can handle it, right? It's all for you. All the risk. All the responsibility."

He rose to his feet. "For as long as I can take it."

She shoved at his shoulder, barely budging him. "Well, I

can't take it!" she yelled. "I think it's stupid, and selfish, and unfair!"

"I'm sorry you feel that way," he said.

"Shut *up!*" She shoved him again, but he felt rooted to the ground. "Condescending *bastard!* Do not ever say that to me again!"

He grabbed her waving fists, and yanked her close. "You want to know how I came out of that hole in my mind?" he asked. "I always use the same technique. My magic secret weapon. Want to know it?"

"Why not," she snapped. "Blow my mind, Kev. It's your specialty."

"OK," he said. "I used you, Edie."

She stared at him, the pressure rising until it felt like the top of her head would blow off. "What the hell are you talking about? I didn't even know you! We hadn't even met! Don't bullshit me!"

But Kev was shaking his head. "It's true," he said stubbornly. "That image of you, the way I saw you at Flaxon. You were my talisman. I told you that, in the coffee shop, remember? You were my angel."

"No!" she yelled. "Don't start with the angel, because it freaks me out. She's not me, and she never was me! I'm glad if she helped you, but she's just a concept in your brain! Get it through your head!"

"When I was stuck, and panicking, you were my last resort," he persisted. "When nothing else worked, I pictured you in my mind's eye. And it chilled me out. It focused me, just enough so that I could find my way through the dark. Maybe it lit up neural pathways that I'd blocked. I don't know, but you were the only safe way through that wall I'd made for myself. I don't know how it worked. All I know is that it *did* work. *You* worked. You saved my life. I wouldn't have made it without you."

"No, Kev. Stop," she begged. "I can't take this."

"I can't! I will not say it wasn't real, that it was just a

cheap mind trick. It was a miracle, Edie. That's how I
learned to talk again. I was mute for years after Tony found
me. Scraping plates, mopping floors. Living in a hole behind
that fucking diner. I was going crazy, trapped inside my own
head. I couldn't even write. I couldn't reason, or plan. I
couldn't think a straight thought. I was confused, disoriented.
Because most of my brain function was blocked, in that fucking oubliette."

"Oh, Kev—"

"It was a living death," he said savagely. "Like one of
those nightmares where you're running through tar. But you
know all about it. You drew it in your comic books! I don't
even have to tell you!"

"But Kev, I didn't—"

"Even trying to talk brought on the fear," he forged
grimly on. "It hurt my head, every time I even tried. The
headaches were so bad I almost slit my wrists. But Bruno
kept at me and at me. So I kept trying. And finally, I got
through that wall. Using you. You led me through it. It was always you." He grabbed her shoulders, gripped them hard. "I
learned to talk again, to live again, because of you, Edie. Or
I'd still be there, mopping floors. Or crazy. Or dead, most
likely."

She flung his hands off her and backed away, feeling frantic. "I'm not an angel!" she yelled. "I'm just Edie. I'm
flawed, screwed up, freaked out! I've never saved anybody
from anything, not even myself. I'm totally flat fucking average in everything, except for maybe drawing pictures, and
getting myself into trouble on a regular basis. I bitch, and I
mope, and I feel sorry for myself. I have pity parties. I'm not
your angel!"

She was yelling, but she could see from his eyes that she
wasn't getting through to him. It made her want to scream.
He started toward her again. Her back hit the cabin wall.
There was nowhere else to go.

He stopped in front of her. "Trying to protect you is not

just me being macho or arrogant or controlling," he said. "It's me covering my ass. Because if something happens to you. I am fucked. I am finished."

She covered her face with her hands. "Kev, please—"

"I can't do it without you," he said simply. "I can't face it."

She let out a shriek of frustration. "OK! I appreciate that I'm important to you, yes, and thank you! But you're . . . you're deluded about me! You've got this idea that I'm this . . . this magical celestial being with all these special mystical qualities, and I'm not! The only special thing I have to offer is that I love you! That's it! That's all!"

He stared, incredulous. "That's it? That's all? You think that you loving me is something small? Something paltry?"

She shook her head. She couldn't make him understand how profoundly this scared her. The danger in it. The trap.

"Edie." His voice was soft. "It's everything to me. It's huge." He grabbed her hands, leaned down to kiss them. They trembled with tension. "I want you to consider something radical."

"Yeah?" She laughed. "I've reached my limit for radical concepts."

"You can take one more," he said stubbornly. "Consider the possibility that I see something beautiful and special in you that you can't see. Something that's never been honored, so you haven't honored it, either. But it's not just my imagination. I see it in you. Plain as day."

She shook her head. "Don't create some shining myth for me to live up to. It'll turn out badly. Don't set me up like that."

"I'm not. It's something you don't recognize, because no one's ever bowed down and honored it before. So how could you know it existed? How could you imagine how rare it is? How perfect?"

She was intensely uncomfortable, and sarcasm was her only refuge. "And what might this mysterious quality be?"

He cupped her face. "I have no words for it," he said quietly. "It can't be reduced to words. Just let me honor it. Please."

She closed her wet eyes, to block out his gaze. "Damn you," she whispered. "You're setting us both up for a huge disappointment."

"Nothing about you has ever disappointed me."

She let out a bark of mirthless laughter. "We've known each other for all of one day and a half. Give me time, Kev. Give me time."

"I will," he said simply. "How about forever?"

"Oh, God." She hid her face in her hands. "Please, stop torturing me. What planet are you from, anyway?"

He was silent for a moment. "Damned if I know," he said. "Maybe the planet's listed in Osterman's archives. I'll let you know."

He waited for her response, but she was frozen with dismay at what he wanted. The moon, the stars. Some perfect, idealized Edie Parrish who didn't even exist. Who could never exist.

Plastic crackled, boards creaked. It took minutes, just to unlock her neck muscles enough to turn to see what the hell he was doing.

He was making the bed, in the dim light that issued from the open door of the cabin. Smoothing a mattress pad over the mattress. Digging in the big plastic bag of bedding for sheets.

The prosaic task broke her paralysis. Edie went to the other side of the bed, and caught the corners of the fitted sheet as he tossed it. That, she could handle. She could help make a bed.

"I don't have flower petals to scatter over the bed this time," Kev said. "But you will have clean sheets and warm blankets, at least."

Tears started into her eyes as she tucked the sheet around

the mattress corner. She blinked them away. "You do too have flower petals," she said, her voice wobbly. "They fall out of your mouth whenever you speak. You are so sweet to me. It's just unreal."

"No," he countered. "It's absolutely for real."

"I believe you," she said. "You're not the one I have doubts about."

"I don't have doubts about you."

He smiled at her, and that didn't help her silly, soggy tear fest one bit. He was just so damn beautiful. So lovely, it was killing her. She didn't know how to take it. But she was damn well going to try.

Kev tossed the comforter onto the bed, flung a couple of pillows on top. "There," he said. "Not a worthy bower for the shining celestial being who's the holy keeper of my heart and soul, but—"

"Don't you dare make fun of me," she snapped.

"But it'll have to do," he finished quietly.

They stared at each other, over the bed, and the emotion vibrating in the air got terribly loud. His throat bobbed as he swallowed. "Ah . . . Zia Rosa made some food," he offered. "You want to eat?"

"After," Edie said.

The invisible flames between them roared in the stillness, as if she'd thrown gasoline on them with that statement of intent.

Edie knelt to unlace her hightops, which was hard, since the knots were slimed with mud from the walk to the bluff. Kev dug into his bag, pulled out a condom and tossed it onto the bed, and began to strip with his usual stark economy of movement. He was already naked while she was still prying the shoes off. He came over to speed things up.

He pulled the knit wool hat that held the thick, fuzzy coil of her hair at her nape, and unwound it, bending to kiss the tangled skein. He unbuttoned her sweater, wrenching down jeans and panties. In moments, she was shivering and naked, wearing only the thick, red striped gray wool socks. That felt pretty silly and undignified, so she sat on the edge of the bed to pull them off.

"No." Kev grabbed her ankles. "Leave the socks. They're sexy."

She giggled. "Oh, come on! They're ridiculous!"

He just grinned, and pinned her feet to the edge of the bed, knees wide, thighs open. Blatantly erotic, splayed out and offering him her muff. She forced herself to breathe, to relax. To give in to it. She had to trust him. He deserved trust. He deserved everything.

"I like the socks. They're sweet." He stroked his hand tenderly down the soft, sensitive skin of her inner thighs. Cupped her vulva, as if it were something miraculous. Tears slid out of her eyes, leaving chilly, meandering trails down her cheeks, soaking into her hair.

She had to stop bracing for the moment that he discovered the awful truth about her, or she'd bring that moment down upon them herself. She did not want to ruin this good thing.

Aw, hell with it. If he wanted to believe that she was a shining goddess, fine. She would just grit her teeth, and pretend to be divine.

For as long as she could keep it up.

Kev slid his thumbs up the length of her damp seam, and lazily down again. Easing her lips apart and playing with her slick pink folds. She was so wound up, every teasing touch made her gasp and bite her lip. He opened her. Leaned down to boldly kiss, and lick, and taste.

She fell back onto her elbows, flung her head back, giving in to his lavish, skillful tongue laving. She could feel the intensity of his desire to please her, how badly he wanted to make her feel precious and worshipped, and that made some inner resistance finally gave way.

He took his time, and she let him take her anywhere he wanted to go, surrendering to his instincts. He drove her over and over to the edge of bliss; swelling up, easing down, finally nudging her over the top of the crest. When she opened her eyes, he was pulling the condom out of its foil package, making ready to roll it onto himself.

"Wait," she said, on impulse.

He looked startled. "You need more?"

"Something occurred to me, while you were turning me into molten goop. How you created this angel in your head. How you want to worship her. But I did the same thing to you, you know?"

"What thing is that?" he asked warily.

She gripped his cock, gave it a swirling pull. "Fade Shadowseeker," she said. "Noble, righteous superhero, demigod, staunch protector of the weak and helpless. If I have to live up to your angel, then you have to live up to Fade. It's only fair."

He looked vaguely alarmed. "What does this mean?"

She slid off the bed, and pulled him onto his feet. "It means you get worshipped, too. It means you get to take your goddamned turn."

She took a moment, just to stare at his beautiful body, the look in his eyes, running her hands over his shoulders, his chest, feeling the texture of the scars beneath her fingers. She sank down to her knees.

The floor was cold, strewn with pine needles and grit. She didn't care. The stove scorched one side of her like a blast furnace and left her other side shivering. She didn't care. She gripped his thick, broad cock and went at him, worshipping every inch with the same enthusiasm that he had lavished on her. She lapped the broad, velvety surface of his glans, licking away the salt-slick glaze of precome, sucking him deep, milking and squeezing, with long, sleek, hypnotic pulls. She dug her nails into his ass, deep throated his whole length, something she'd never even known she could do, but with Kev, all assumptions were off, all misperceptions revealed. He flung open doors in her mind, in her heart, to a wealth of wordless treasures, astonished revelations.

She loved the metallic tang of his engorged phallus beneath her tongue, the throb of his heartbeat against her lips. His hitching gasps. She wanted to make him explode, swallow his salty, hot male essence.

"Wait," he choked out, holding her head still.

"Mmm?" She pulled away, with a swirling, voluptuous lick around the rim of his glans, just to feel the shudder of pleasure rack his body. It made her feel like a goddess, with divine power to grant pleasure. It was all hers to bestow, a vast abundance to rain down on him.

"Don't move." His voice was strangled. "I'm right on the edge."

She waited, obligingly, and felt the dry orgasm jolt through him. Such control. Mmm, sexy. She rubbed the purple, silk-smooth flesh of his cock tenderly against her cheek when they faded away. "Now?" she asked. "Can I? I want to make you come. I want to taste it."

"Not yet," he pleaded. "Let me save it. I want to be inside you."

As if he needed to beg. She let him haul her to her feet, and shove her toward the bed. She landed, bouncing on the mattress as he rolled on the condom. "How do you want me?" she asked breathlessly.

"Don't ask me to pick. We've got all night. We can try everything."

"Great," she said cheerfully. "Everything. Sounds excellent."

He landed on top of her, the bed squeaking. "Let's start with the classic missionary," he said. "I want to kiss you while I fuck you."

Every inner part of her relaxed and rejoiced at the contact

as he mounted her, his heat, his weight, his salt and metal scent. She opened for him, and they sighed as he entered her, gazing into her eyes. Every stroke was unbearably sweet. He gave her everything she craved with every swirl of his hips, every liquid thust, until the hard clasp of his arms and his devouring kisses were all that held her together.

And finally, even that could not keep her from exploding into blinding sparks, and dissolving into the shining infinite.

CHAPTER
23

Kev was stuck. He'd been stuck before, by brain damage, pain, fear, all that bad shit. But he'd never been frozen into immobility by pleasure. He'd never imagined how potent it could be, to lie there in the bed, and just stare at her face. He could hardly drag air into his lungs.

He couldn't have imagined how badly he could crave a woman. He would crawl on his knees until they were raw to get some of this. So amazing, so bright. Every cell of his body. Glowing with . . . happiness?

Yeah. And the dark underside, too. Fear, that someone would take it from him. Fear that would morph into terror if he gave it attention, so he wouldn't. He knew how to push fear away, hold it by the throat and pretend it wasn't there. Snarling and snapping.

But the big question now was just how to break his paralysis. His body would not respond to central command. Edie lay on top of him, her slight warm weight like a constant kiss along the length of his body.

The scent of her hair, the curve of her eyelashes. The softness of her skin under his hardened hands. Like daisy petals, butterfly wings. It was so sweet. Holding her, feeling her, smelling her. Fucking her.

His morning hard-on tightened and swelled with hungry urgency. After the kind of night he hadn't known was physiologically possible for a man. He'd lost count. They'd broken it up by talking, kissing and cuddling, intermittent dozes. Devouring pork tenderloin, baked potatoes drowned with butter, grilled vegetables. Zia Rosa's rice pudding, which had proven to be a highly effective brainwashing tool in its own right.

But she had to be sore. And he didn't want Bruno to catch them in bed, or the shower. He'd kill or die for his adopted brother, but let him see Edie in a towel, damp and flushed? No way. That was private.

Kev wanted to be up, bathed, dressed, the bed made up with tight, military corners, decorously sipping coffee on the steps outside when Bruno drove up. That meant getting up. Damn it. *Move.*

Edie stretched against him. Her eyes fluttered open, and she gave him that shockingly gorgeous smile that wiped his hard drive clean. She felt his hard-on prodding her hip, and petted it. He arched, gasping with pleasure at the languid swirls of her hand. Moist, slick. He'd been weeping precome, and she was spreading it voluptuously around.

"Edie. Stop it," he hissed, through his teeth.

Her eyes widened in mock dismay. "Oh, no! Is it Mr. Hard-ass? So early in the morning, too! Do I have to coax and beg again?"

"Bruno will be here soon, and I don't want him to walk in on us," he said. "And we finished all of the condoms."

"Oh, dear," she murmured. "Really? That's just terrible."

"Really," he growled. "Be good. Stop that. Now."

Her hand tightened. "We risked it yesterday, after the banquet. I liked it. Feeling you, naked inside me. Skin on skin. It was wonderful."

His cock jerked at the very thought, but he shook his head. "And you have got to be sore. We overdid it last night."

She wiggled, sighing with pleasure as her hips pulsed against his thigh. "A little, but I'm fine." She clambered on top of him, flinging her leg over his and sat up, letting the blanket fall. She gripped his cock, stroking. "Just a little bit? Please?"

He gripped her swirling hands, held them still. "Get real," he growled. "Since when have we ever stopped with just a little bit?"

"It seems like a terrible waste," she murmured.

"You'll get more when I come back." Kev stared into her smiling eyes, and grabbed her shoulders. He pulled her down so that their eyes were inches from each other. "You think we've got only counted minutes until your dad locks you up, right?" She stiffened, her gaze flicking away, but he held her fast. "Look at me, Edie," he said harshly.

She looked trapped. "What does it matter, what I'm afraid of? What'll happen will happen. It doesn't make any difference, whatever pronouncements we make about it. Let's just live in the moment."

Kev forced her to look into his eyes. "He won't," he said. "We'll find a way to be together. You know that, don't you?" He waited for an answer, didn't get one. "Know it, Edie," he added.

She stared back at him, swallowing. Lips trembling.

It took him by surprise, the unreasonable surge of anger. At feeling so powerless to reassure her, with the weight of her life history set against him. Years of private betrayals and abandonments that he could not fix or heal, or even reach. It drove him . . . fucking . . . *nuts*.

She gasped, and he realized that he was gripping her shoulders too hard. He let go abruptly, horrified. There were red marks on her arms. He petted them, in hasty apology. "Sorry," he muttered, abashed.

"It's OK." She propped herself against his chest again, but she wouldn't meet his eyes.

"Jesus, Edie," he exploded. "'Don't look that way. It's going to be OK. We're going to be together. What do I have to do to convince you?"

Her mouth twitched. She shot him a sidewise look from under her lashes. He'd played right into her hands. "Well. Since you asked . . ."

He shook his head, and kept shaking it, but she just fixed him with a limpid gaze, undaunted. "Please," she coaxed. "Let me feel you inside me, just one time. Before you drive away and leave me to listen to the wind screaming around the cabin all day. Let me feel you, way down deep. I love how it makes me feel." She leaned forward, raining pleading kisses over his cheek, his jaw. "I need to feel that way."

She had him by the balls. His body was betraying him. "Just inside," he warned. "No lap dancing. If we start to move, I'll come inside you. And now's not the time for the consequences. Got it?"

"Of course," she promised quickly. "Still as a statue."

He'd believe it when he saw it. She positioned herself above him, his heart practically exploded for how fucking beautiful she was, those graceful thighs parted to ride him, a flush staining her face, her chest. The bruises on her breast had darkened, bluish, finger-shaped splotches. But the fury that had gripped him at the sight splintered into sweet agony as she gripped his cock and nudged him into her slick, hot crevice, undulating to find the angle that would permit him to wedge inside, to start that long, slow slide.

She found that angle, and oh, man. He was in trouble.

She sank down, enveloping him, whimpering and gasping with each squirming shove. A slick, tight agony of pleasure. He had to fight to keep from howling, grabbing her hips, ramming upward. *No.*

Finally, she'd seated him inside, as deep as he could go,

his cockhead wedged against the mouth of her womb, his heartbeat throbbing in tune with hers. He lay there, gripping handfuls of the sheet, teeth gritted at the naked, shaking, scalding perfection of it.

She leaned down to kiss him. Her petal-soft lips grazed his, her tongue stole into his mouth, every strand of her hair caressed him. Nerve endings all over his chest jumped and crackled with delight.

So sweet, so stubborn. Always pushing him, breaking rules, shoving him out of his comfort zone. She always would. It would be a constant struggle between them, but what the fuck. He was what he was, unlikely to change. A hard-ass, bred in the bone. Hard wired to resist pleasure, to be suspicious of anything too sweet, too good.

But she would fight that, until she took him down. Red-hot love goddess, jerking him around by his dumb handle. What the fuck. She'd dragged him this far. He'd damn well do his duty and make her come.

He pulled together what was left of his tattered self-control, and reached down to her mound, lifting the top of her slit with the vee of his fingers until her clit popped out, taut and full. She writhed, eyes closed. She'd forgotten her promise to stay still, surprise surprise.

He jerked her down and kissed her hungrily, pulsing his cock inside her. No thrusting, or he'd lose it in a heartbeat. He was barely keeping himself together with this deep pressure as he caressed her clit. Coaxing that trembling tension that gripped her body. Slow and easy, pushing it further, and further . . . until it snapped.

He held her as she convulsed, arching back with a cry almost like anguish. The hot gush of girl-come inside of her bathed his cock. Her pussy squeezed him, deep rhythmic pulses. She sagged, holding herself up against his chest, opened her eyes. They shone. Tears, glittering, flashing down her pink stained, glowing cheeks. So open, so unguarded.

"I love you," she said.

It grabbed his heart, twisted. And something went *pop* inside him.

Suddenly, he'd flipped her onto her back, pinned her legs high, was fucking her like a man gone crazy. She was yelling, clutching, coming around him. Her climax called his own orgasm down, with an absolute authority that he could not contest.

It crashed down like a rockslide. He barely managed to jerk his cock out in time. He grabbed her hands, wrapped them around his cock. Hot semen spurted up, sobbing in rhythmic gushes, oozing down over their locked, trembling hands.

He sagged over her, pressing his hot face against the damp, tender skin of her breasts. Feeling her chest heave, her heart throb.

The worst had happened. What he'd always feared. Overthrown by something deep inside himself. Something beyond his control. He'd never thought that it would be love. He'd spent all his energy worrying about the demons from his dreams, the secrets of his past. But it was love that had laid him low.

He felt her struggling for breath beneath his weight. Their hands were glued together.

"Satisfied?" His voice came out rougher than he'd meant it to. As if he were angry. Though he wasn't. Not exactly.

Edie didn't look intimidated. She licked her pink, gleaming lips, looked at the sticky white liquid all over her hands, and cleared her throat. "That ought to hold me," she said demurely. "For a little while."

He slid off the bed, grabbed her wrist and pulled her into the bathroom. He set the shower running without letting go of her. The sex had rendered him down to something primitive. He didn't try to collar it. Fuck it. She'd melted his self-control with her sex games. She could damn well deal with what was left of him after.

He muscled Edie into the shower and washed her himself, touching every inch of her with proprietary hands. Massaging foamy soap onto every sweet curve and swell and crevice, kissing her until she was breathless, gasping. He soaped her up between her legs, detached the shower head and caressed her pussy with the stream of water, then sank to his knees. Shoved his face into her muff, seeking that sweet pink clit with his tongue. He had to kiss it, lick it . . .

"Please! Kev!" She was clawing at his shoulders, his head.

"Huh?" He dragged his face away, panting. "What?"

"The water!" Her lips were blue. "It's icy! And I hear a car outside."

"Shit!" He turned the water off and leaped out. "Sorry I froze you."

She laughed, shivering violently. "You didn't notice?"

"With my head between your legs? Hell, no. I don't care. Cold water, hot, I barely notice. Stay here. I'll get your clothes."

He rummaged through her little suitcase, and shoved some clothes through the bathroom door at her. "Here."

He yanked clothes on, and was missing only his boots when Bruno knocked. When had Bruno ever knocked? He pulled the door open, to confront his brother's huge, self-satisfied grin.

"Good morning!" Bruno crowed, peeking past him into the dim interior. "Where's Edie?"

"Bathroom," Kev said sourly. "Stay out here til she's decent."

Bruno stamped his feet. "It's freezing out here. Let me come in. I'll close my eyes if she comes out in her unmentionables."

Kev stepped aside with bad grace, and Bruno pushed past, hauling a couple of big bags. "What've you got?" Kev asked.

"Breakfast. Zia Rosa dropped by at five A.M. to leave this for you. Egg and cheese casserole, fresh bread and sausages, to feed your sperm. The phallic shape of the sausages is meant to be a fertility aid."

Kev groaned through his teeth, but the odor coming from the bags made saliva burst into his mouth, so he couldn't really muster the energy to get annoyed about it. "I'll make the coffee," he muttered.

He put coffee on, laid the casserole on top of the wood-stove, and set to stoking the flames. Bruno perched on a stool by the table, jiggling his foot. Whistling tunelessly, drumming his fingers. A storm of nervous energy. The kid never calmed down. Wired to be wired.

"So," Bruno said, carefully. "You, ah, ready for the big revelation?"

The question took Kev by surprise, braced as he was for sexually charged teasing. "As ready as I'll ever be," he said.

"You sure you want to do this?" Bruno's face was unchar-acteristically solemn.

"Why wouldn't I?" Kev asked. "Are you having another jealous snit?"

Bruno waved that away, irritated. "Fuck, no." He slid off the stool and crouched down to stare into the stove, at the flames licking around the kindling. "I just don't think you should rock the boat."

Kev was baffled. "What boat? I'm drowning, here. I'm looking for a rope, forget a fucking boat!"

Bruno made an impatient sound. "You're not drowning. You're Kevlar. No one messes with you. But things are look-ing up for you. I mean, you had a date the other night. You're getting laid. You've got a hot girl who's crazy for you. Does now seem like the time to—"

"You think?" Kev cut in.

Bruno blinked, confused. "What? Think what?"

"That she's crazy for me?" He felt stupid, but it just popped out. His face reddened.

Bruno let out a bark of laughter. "Focus, dude. As I was

saying. Your life's not bad. Who you are works. What you've made of yourself works. Why mess with it? Forget the past! Go forward!"

Kev let out a slow, silent breath. "I can't," he said.

"Why not?" Bruno demanded. "Whatever you find, it might be a big disappointment to you! You might have parents like mine."

That grim possibilty hung in the air while the flames took hold.

Kev finally stood up. "Two nights ago, someone held a knife to Edie's throat," he said. "She's under suspicion for attempted murder. Her father tried to have her locked in the psych ward to keep her away from me, because I'm such a pus lowlife. Things are weird, Bruno. Now is not the time to relax, or take anything for granted. We have a long way up to crawl before we even hit flat zero."

Bruno looked glum. "What does your past have to do with this crap?"

"Probably nothing. But I can't keep driving blind. I have to know what happened. If I want any chance for a future, for me and Edie."

Bruno sighed. "Oh, fuck it," he said wearily. "Whatever."

Edie came out of the bathroom, fully dressed, wet hair combed primly back into a tight braid. She smiled and murmured a good morning. Bruno seemed oddly subdued. If Kev didn't know better, he might have actually thought that his little brother was feeling shy.

Thanks to Zia Rosa's bounty, they stuffed themselves with cholesterol-laden food for breakfast, with more than enough left over for Bruno and Edie to have for lunch later on. Kev would deal with dinner plans after he saw what was in the archives.

Time pressed, with the long drive back to the city ahead of him. Edie followed him out of the cabin, and he could think of only one more reason to procrastinate. He crouched to unbuckle the ankle holster that held his revolver. "This is a SP 101 Ruger. I'll show you how to use it, real quick. Come here."

Her eyes went wide. "No way. I don't want to touch that thing."

"Too bad. Get over here. Five minutes, that's all I can spare."

Edie shook her head. "I'm not comfortable with—"

"I don't give a shit what you're comfortable with. Kidnappers out looking for your ass makes me pretty goddamn uncomfortable!"

Her mouth flattened at his tone. "I don't think five minutes is nearly enough to learn how to safely use a firearm!"

"Are you worth defending?" he demanded.

"Yes!" Her chin went up. "Jesus, Kev!"

"Then be prepared to defend yourself," he said flatly. "And if you've got five minutes to learn how to do it, then learn fast."

"But . . . but I thought . . ." Edie's gaze cut to Bruno.

"You thought I called him up here to defend you?" he finished. "Yeah, I did. And so? What of it?"

He gave Bruno a look. Bruno promptly rose to the occasion.

"They could kill me," his brother said. "And then you'd be fucked. But if you're armed, you've still got a shot. Or six shots, to be exact."

Edie looked trapped.

"You got more ammo for that around somewhere?" Bruno asked.

"In the cabin," Kev said. "Top kitchen drawer."

"Great." Bruno looked cheerful at the prospect. "We'll have shooting practice this morning. Fun activities. The time will fly by."

Good. So Bruno would do the tutorial. Kev knelt, jerked up the wide, tattered leg of her jeans. Great style for concealing an ankle holster. He buckled the thing around her slender leg, and took a moment to curl his hand around the curve of her calf. She still wore those fuzzy striped socks, which made last night's erotic escapades dance through his brain.

He rose to his feet. She stared up, furious at him for his lecturing. He grabbed her, kissed her furious face. Parted those lovely furious lips, and drank her in, until a shudder of surrender cracked her angry tension, and she softened, bending, arching back. Hanging on. The heat swelled, like a flower blooming.

Bruno cleared his throat. "I'll, uh, just give you guys a moment."

Kev barely heard the cabin door swinging shut. He was too busy tanking up for those long, bleak hours with no Edie in them. They stretched out before him, a flinty desert of boredom and thirst.

But he couldn't tank up. He was thirsty for her the second he dragged his face away. Kissing her only made it worse.

"You be good," he said, hoarsely. "Be careful."

"Me? I'm just kicking my heels like an asshole." Her words were snippy, but her voice wobbled. "You're the one who needs to be careful."

He got into the car. "I'd call you, but I can't," he said. "Call me from the bluff. One o'clock, on the hour. Don't make me wait. I'll be watching the minutes. OK?"

She nodded as he slammed the door, fired up the motor, buzzed the window down. He leaned out. "I love you."

She pressed a kiss to his forehead, and shoved his head back into the car. "Go get this done, and come back quick. You're killing me."

"Yeah." He maneuvered the vehicle around and roared away without looking back, or else he'd do something unspeakable, like burst into tears. For Christ's sake, he was going to stare at computer archives, in the company of a wanker businessman and a geek neuroscientist. He was not charging up Dong Ap Bia in the battle of Hamburger Hill. He was not heading out to storm the fucking beach at Normandy. Get a grip, already.

He did the whole drive on autopilot. It was the first time he'd ever driven that road without noticing if clouds were riding the shoulders of the Cascades, or if the massive Columbia had whitecaps on its churning slate blue surface. He drove through the city, looping through the snarl of rivers, bridges and freeway ramps that divided Portland, and connected with Highway 26 toward Hillsboro, the location of the new Helix complex. Then SE Montrose Highway, an interminable strip mall, and he made the turn onto Highett and wound through green, manicured grounds. Plenty of parking in those big lots, in spite of it being Monday morning. He went to the building Marr had designated, the unfinished future seat of the Parrish Foundation, right across the grounds from the main Helix building. Two handsome six-story mirror-glass structures faced each other across a park, reflecting the silver sky.

The entrance was unlocked, and almost deserted. The lobby looked unfinished, but even so, there was a security guard behind a desk, a dour Asian man with a ponytail. He looked at Kev, "Larsen?"

"That's me," Kev said.

The guy picked up a phone. "He's here," he said into it. "Yeah." He hung up. "Dr. Cheung told me to expect you. Go on up. Take the stairs. Fifth floor. Suite 5000."

Strange place for a rendezvous to study archives, he reflected, as he ran up the stairs. They'd have had to be moved from wherever they'd been before. Why bother with that, if they were slated for disposal? He could easily have come to them. The door to Suite 5000 was open. Light flooded through the picture windows that looked out over the swathe of lush lawn, and the Helix building. Trees waved and bent in the breeze.

There was a big pile of white plastic file boxes, heaped

with paper files in the middle of the otherwise empty, unfurnished office suite. Someone had hauled all this stuff in here. Twenty-five, thirty big boxes, brought up into this empty space. His what's-wrong-with-this-picture sensors were pinging, but he still had no clear idea of what the picture actually ought to feel like. He had no template for this situation.

He slid his hand into his jacket, brushing his SIG. The Glock was in the back of his jeans, harder to access.

Tik tik tik tik. High heels against the slate-black granite floor tile, glittering with tiny mica sparkles. A woman appeared, framed artfully in the doorway, hip cocked like a fashion model. "Mr. Larsen?"

The what's-wrong-with-this-picture vibe kicked up a notch. He stared at her, bemused. This chick did not look like a neuroscientist. She looked like a high-end call girl. Not that neuroscience and feminine beauty were mutually exclusive, but what were the odds? Her face was shockingly pretty, skin flawless, full lips red and pouting, tilted eyes painted with artful charcoal smudges. Her glossy black hair was swept up in a smooth roll. Her smile of welcome was bright, like a painted doll. She wore a navy suit, flared at the waist, short skirt showing off long, perfect legs, four-inch heels. Her low-cut white silk blouse frilled out of the severe vee of the jacket, showing lots of cleavage.

"Are you Dr. Cheung?" he asked.

She held out a slender, pale hand, tipped with long, crimson nails, and shook his hand, then hung on to it. "I am."

He pulled his hand back in the pause that followed. He sensed her waiting for some nervous schnook comment. *Ya sure don't look like a neuroscientist, heh heh heh.* "How do you do?" he said simply.

Her eyelids swept down, her smile widened. "Fine, thank you. I'm facinated to meet you. Des told me your story. What he knew of it, anyway." Her eyes took on a shimmering glow of sympathy. "It's amazing. That you were victimized like that. Losing all your memories, too. How horrible. I can only try to imagine how you must have felt."

"Don't," he said.

She blinked. "Excuse me?"

"Don't try to imagine it," he said. "You can't."

"Can't I?" Her face locked. Freeze-frame. Then the eyelash flutters and the glowing smile started up, like she'd pushed PLAY again. "I'm so sorry. I didn't mean to offend you."

"You didn't." He glanced around. "Where's Marr?"

"Oh, Desmond? He'll be back around a bit later. He had to meet with Parrish this morning. Actually, his meeting is an effort to give you some time to take a look at this stuff, before we have to fork it over to old Eagle Eye." She waved her hand at the heap of boxes. "So here it is. Des is covering for you. This afternoon, it would have been too late."

And you are not being anywhere near appreciative enough, was the silent accusation that Kev could feel burning against his skin.

Well, fuck him. Guilty as charged. He hadn't begged them to stick their necks out for him. So Marr wasn't here. He felt a twinge of unease about the dangerous, potentially violent stress flashbacks that could accompany his memories, if he should recover them.

He hadn't wanted Edie anywhere near him, if he should go into another fugue state, but this chick didn't deserve that kind of trouble, either. She couldn't be more than twenty-five. She was bent over her desk, digging in her purse at a ninety-degree angle that showcased a truly spectacular ass. She straightened up, smiling like a game show hostess, and he'd just won a prize. She held a jingling set of car keys.

"I was wondering if you could do me a favor," she asked. "Des had to run out to get to his meeting, and we weren't able to get the last couple of cases out of the car. Would you mind running down and grabbing them for me? I've been waiting because I didn't want to risk missing you. In the meantime, I can set up these laptops, and make a double workstation, so we can both scan files. It'll save us hours."

"Hours?" He was unpleasantly surprised at the thought of being hung up for that long "How long do you think this is going to take?"

She shrugged. "Could be hours. Could be days. I took all the hard files I could find from that time period, and all the electronic files I could download. I had to convert them, too, because the software was ancient. Would you mind, getting those last two cases?"

Kev tried to analyze the prickle in his neck. What could this chick do to him, anyway? Stab her stiletto heel through his eye? Blind him with her pearly whites? She could have nothing to do with his story. She would have been a tiny child when whatever had happened to him happened. Five, six years old. Eight at most. Like Edie, who'd been eleven. And yet, so unlike Edie. He couldn't help compare Cheung to Edie, since Edie was his most important point of reference. This woman was objectively stunning, but her beauty bounced off him. Whereas Edie's grabbed him by the vital organs. Edie was wrapped around his brain, braided into muscle and nerve. Edie was the air he breathed.

He kept coming up blank. There was no danger here. The worst this woman could do to him would be to waste his time, which would still suck, because he had more serious shit to attend to. But that was not her fault. So he'd try to keep a civil tongue in his head.

Cheung's smile vanished. "I could go down myself, if you can't be bothered," she said. "The cases are extremely heavy. But I'll manage."

Aw, what the fuck. "I'll get them," he said. "Where's the vehicle?"

Her face lit up. "Oh, thanks. It's a white Hummer." She tossed him the keys. "It's parked on the south side of this building."

Butch car, for such a feminine woman. She didn't look

like the off-roading type, but you never knew. He texted a message to Bruno and Edie as he ran down the stairs. They wouldn't get it until they hiked up to the bluff, but texting made him feel closer to her. He wished he didn't have to go through Bruno's phone. It made him feel self-conscious about being as romantic as he'd like to be with her.

arrived at PF Bldg library. Big pile of boxes. Love u

The Hummer was right where she said it would be. Two large metal sided suitcases were in the back. He hefted them, surprised at their dead weight, and at the absence of any sort of rattling or shifting of the contents. He tried to open them, just for the hell of it, but they had combination locks. He could have opened them, given time, but he was sure Cheung was watching the seconds tick by. And there was no point. The mystery would be revealed soon enough. He locked the car, loped back through the lobby. The security guy was gone.

Cheung turned when he walked in, and gave him a big smile. His cue to pant and wag. He did not. Her smile faded.

He set the cases down beside her desk. "Here you go."

"Oh, thanks! Here, you sit down at this computer. I've converted the first five discs and loaded them, so you can just start scrolling through the documents. See if anything rings a bell."

He leaned forward, peering at the screen. "What is this stuff?"

"These are Osterman's research notes from 1990 onward. He was developing a series of drugs to treat learning disabilities at the time, if I'm not mistaken."

Kev stared at the heap of disks. This could take forever. He needed to excuse himself from this brain-sucking bullshit and go work on finding Edie's kidnappers. Sooner would be better than later.

He had to think of some way to phrase it, but any way he

put it, it was going to sound rude. But fuck it. Rude wasn't fatal.

Cheung rose from her chair. "I'm going to grab a Diet Coke from the kitchen," she said. "Care for anything? Coffee, tea, soda?"

"Nah, I'm good, thanks."

That was when he saw the spider, crawling out of the box of disks. A tiny thing, creamy white. He leaned closer. Allatal stripes on her carapace. A silver abdominal dorsum median dark band flanked by silver commas on the abdominal venter distinguished her as an immature female *Tetragnatha laboriosa*. He let her crawl up onto his finger, lifted her up to take a better look. She should be in a forest, or at least on a shrub, out on the grounds. Not crawling around on barren beige plastic. He'd take her outside when he left.

Dr. Cheung passed behind him. The spider picked her way daintily along his forefinger. Cheung's footsteps slowed behind him. A rustling sound. His neck prickled . . .

Edie's spider drawing exploded into his mind. He twisted, but the needle stung his neck before the warning message could reach his limbs and launch him up out of the chair.

The icy burn spread through his core, crawling out to his limbs. Clutching at every muscle. *No.* Those sneaky fuckers. They'd morphed into newer, younger, prettier bodies, lain in wait for two decades . . . and gotten him. How could he have been so stupid? So complacent.

His automatic response was starting up, he could feel it already. Systems involuntarily shutting down, like a power grid going black. Into the oubliette, where they couldn't reach him—

No! He clamped down on the reflex. He couldn't go into the oubliette. He had to stay sharp. He had so much more to lose now.

He held Edie's face in his mind, the way he'd held the angel. She kept him conscious, though his body was a rictus of burning pain.

Ava Cheung leaned down into Kev's face. "Too easy," she complained, and she swayed forward and kissed him passionately. She stuck her tongue into his mouth. He could taste her lipstick. The sweet taste of her mouth, like saccharine. His gorge rose, but he couldn't move, couldn't speak. It was all he could do to stay conscious.

"Des told me you were ugly," she confided, petting the scars on his cheek. "But you're not ugly. The scars don't bother me. We all have our scars." She reached down to his crotch. Let out a croon of approval at what she found. "Substantial," she murmured. "We are going to have a lot of fun, Kev. You can be my special pet."

He stared into her eyes, stayed conscious by sheer, raw force of will. He used everything he had: the anger, the desperation. *Edie*. He couldn't believe he hadn't seen the madness in Cheung's eyes. It was so clear now. That glow, like a drug high. Now that he saw behind her illusion, he could hardly believe he'd ever perceived her as beautiful. She was grotesque. Her brain rewired into something terrifying and strange.

Edie. He clung to her image. Her beautiful face, as he's seen it that morning. Pale and clean. Tears shining in her eyes. Unspeakably beautiful and pure. So real. *Edie*. He hung on to her. Darkness was closing in around him. The edges were blurring.

The Asian security guy from the desk downstairs appeared before him, blurred around the edges, but the concentrated malevolence in his face punched through Kev's perception. Amazing, that he had not sensed it before. *Lack of vigilance will get you killed*. Too late. The man crouched, so that his face was inches from Kev's. His lips curled back from his teeth. Enjoying himself. "You gave him the shot?" he asked.

"Of course," she said. "He's good for a half an hour. Work fast."

The guy pulled on some latex gloves, produced a little

spray bottle and a chamois cloth, and began to rub down the outside of the cases Kev had brought up from Cheung's car. He took Kev's numb, stiff hands, and systematically pressed them all over the surface, paying particular attention to the handle and the locking device. He flicked the combination into place, and opened the case.

Kev's belly thudded down a couple of stories. A sniper rifle. An Arctic Warfare Super Magnum. Disassembled, packed into a case. The guy took out a Schmidt & Bender PM II telescopic scope, pressed Kev's prints all over it. Then he pressed Kev's numb fingers against a few .338 Lapua Magnum bullet casings. He disassembled the inner trigger mechanisms, pressed Kev's prints over those, too. Over the buttstock, the barrel, the bipod, the mount, the bolt, the trigger. Everywhere.

They were setting him up for something awful. Pressing his hands onto all kinds of other stuff, but he could no longer see clearly, his hands too numb to identify the objects by touch. He was fading.

Then the guy grabbed him by the shirtfront, and lifted him up. "I got a bone to pick with you, shithead," he said. "This is payback for the night before last." His knee slammed up into Kev's groin.

White hot pain exploded in his testicles. He pitched into the dark.

CHAPTER
24

"You're sure this is the address?" Liv gazed at the unprepossessing building on NE Helmut Street, the chain-link fence, all the more dingy for the drizzling rain. An overloaded Dumpster had a mattress propped up next to it. Bags of garbage were being nosed through by a knuckle-assed dog. "Charles Parrish's daughter lives in this place?"

Sean referred once again to the sheaf of printouts Davy had given him. "That's what it says here."

"But didn't you guys say Parrish was a billionaire?"

Sean shrugged. "Apartment Four F." He eyed her belly. "Fourth floor. I'd suggest you wait in the car, but not in this neighborhood. How about I take you back to the hotel?"

"Oh, shut up," Liv snapped. "Come on."

Sean stayed right behind her as they went through the gate and started to climb, matching his pace to her slow one. She was breathless by the end of the second flight, and he tried to grab her arm, to give her support, but she snatched her arm back, shooting him one of those blazing Amazon goddess looks. "Do not hover. I am *fine*."

"I'm not hovering," he said, hurt. "I'm being a gallant, attentive, caring, sensitive guy."

Liv snorted eloquently.

"Would you rather have a grunting Neanderthal pig? Pick up the pace, babe, and carry this case of beer while you're at it, OK?"

"You were hovering," she said, snippily.

"No. *This* is hovering." He swept her into his arms, and held her while she wriggled and squawked. "Worked for Scarlett and Rhett."

"Scarlett had a sixteen-inch waist!" Liv yelled. "Scarlett was not seven months pregnant! Put me down, before you throw your back out!"

"Sure," he promised, striding up the stairs. "Just as soon as I get to the fourth floor. And here we are. Madame, if you please." He set her on her feet. "Just trying to make myself useful. Earn my perks."

"Perks? Hah! What perks? Don't even get me started!"

He grabbed her, and kissed her, putting his hands under the taut swell of her belly. "Shhh. I just want to carry this weight for you, when I can," he crooned. "I wish I could do it all. The hard stuff, the scary stuff. I wish I could bear it all for you. But I can't. Biology is cruel."

She was still stiff, so he pulled her closer, petting the curve of her back. "Please, don't be mad. I love you so much. I can't even stand it."

That did the trick. The steel in her spine softened, and she bent her head to let him nuzzle her neck. He sighed. Disaster averted.

Marriage was complicated. The emotional equivalent of a game of pro basketball. Lots of sweat, lots of effort. But when he sank that ball into the hoop, oh, man. The payoff was so sweet. He lived for that.

Sean paused to stare at the scarred, flimsy looking door of Apartment 4F for a moment, and reached out to knock.

The door yielded to the pressure of his knuckles, and drifted open with a creaking sigh more suited to a gothic mansion. Sean shoved Liv behind him, and peered into the room. It had been destroyed.

"This place has been tossed," he said. "Wait one moment. I'll make sure no one's home."

"Sean!" she hissed fiercely. She grabbed at the back of his jacket, but he slipped through her fingers, already inside.

It looked like someone had torn the dingy little apartment apart in a killing rage. He peered into the bathroom, scattered with broken glass and crockery, mirror shattered, shower curtain slashed. In the living room, furniture had been overturned, the place was littered with paper. Red paint was sprayed over the walls, which were covered with pictures, photos, sketches. It formed a word, he realized, in bleeding, dripping letters. FREAK. He tugged Liv inside. "No one's here," he said.

Liv made a distressed sound in the back of her throat as she stared around at the wrecked room. "Do you think she was hurt?"

He stared at the dripping scrawl. "They wouldn't write insults on the wall if she was there for them to deliver them in person," he said. "I hope, anyway. We must be the first ones to see this. No crime scene tape. Door not locked. She hasn't been home since it happened."

Liv looked pained. "She's in for a shock. We should call the cops."

"In a minute. Let me look around. I won't touch anything."

Liv made an exasperated sound. He tiptoed around the wreckage, peering at the scraps of paper tacked to the wall. The chill that fluttered over the surface of his skin was just like the chill breeze that swept in, fluttering all the scraps of paper attached to the wall.

Kev was everywhere in those sketches. One in three, maybe more. Portraits, line sketches, studies. Fully developed action scenes from the graphic novel, complete with dialog balloons. But it was his brother. He'd bet his life on it. "This woman is obsessed with Kev," he said.

"Maybe she's simply in love with him," Liv said with a haughty sniff. "It's a fine line, when you're dealing with McCloud guys."

Sean evaluated that remark, and concluded that it was a trap. He kept his big mouth shut, so as not to risk a tempest of pregnancy hormones. They blew up with no warning, downing trees, knocking out communication lines. He hated that. The marital disaster area. He unleashed it often. It was his special talent.

The door was slapped open. He leaped to get in front of Liv.

"Edie! You're back!" A kid burst in, a huge grin on his skinny brown face. The smile blanked out when he saw them, and the apartment. He spun, took off like a bolt from a crossbow.

Sean caught the kid's thin, trembling arm before he cleared the door. "Stop," he said. "You know Edie?"

"Who the fuck are you, man?" The kid struggled with desperate strength, kicking savagely at Sean's shins. "Let me go!"

Sean blocked an admirably quick uppercut, wrenching the kid into a clinch under his arm. "Calm down. Just a couple of questions."

"Fuck you!" The kid flopped, kicked, squawked.

Liv looked horrified. "Jesus, Sean! Let him be!"

"You fuckers hurt Edie!" the kid shrieked. "You messed up her place! I'll kill you. Fucking bastards!"

"No, that wasn't us," Sean said. "But we're going to find out the guys who did it. And you can help us do that."

The kid twisted around to peer up into Sean's face. He went limp in Sean's grasp. His jaw sagged. His eyes popped. Sean knew that look. Excitement surged inside him. He clamped a careful lid on it. "What?" he demanded. "Do I look like somebody you know?"

"F-f-f-fade," the kid stammered. "Holy shit. You look exactly like Fade! Except you don't have the scars!"

Disappointment sank the swelling excitement. Of course.
The fucking comic book. Who could blame the kid. "You
mean, the character in the Shadowseeker book series? I look
like him?"

"No, I mean the real guy! I met him the other day. He
came home with Edie! I think they had sex." He frowned,
disapproving. "Gross. And she was mad at me about saying
that Fade was real, 'cause people see Fade all the time! He
gave money to the runaway shelter, and the homeless shelter,
and the soup kitchen!"

"You saw him?" Sean interrupted the kid's babbling. "You
saw a real guy who looks like me, except with scars? Not a
guy in a story?"

"Yeah! I told Edie he was real! And she gave me all kinds
of shit about it, but see? I was right." He scowled. "But she
didn't have to have sex with him. That was gross. Hey, could
you stop squeezing my neck?"

"If I let go, you won't hit me, or run, right? We can just
talk?"

"Sure," the kid said. "So you know Fade?"

The sadness that swept over him was huge. Sean set the
kid down. "Yeah, I know him," he said heavily. "He's my
brother."

"Sean!" Liv's tone was nervous. "You can't know that,
not until we meet him and talk to him!"

"I know." He let the weight of his words cut off her lecture. He watched it play across her expressive face. First the
argument, just because she was Liv, opinionated and bossy
and protective. Then guilt, as she remembered her big fat
crusade to validate his instincts. Then stern self-control
kicked in, when she wisely decided to shut up and let him do
his thing in his own weird way.

God, he loved that woman. And he was such a trial to her.
He resolved for the millionth time to be good. Not so hyper,

so oversexed, such a relentless smart-ass. A guy could only try to fight his nature.

He held out his hand. "My name's Sean. That lady's my wife, Liv."

She gave the kid a smile. The boy smiled shyly back, eyes darting to her rounded belly. "That's our kid, inside Liv. And your name is?"

"Jamal." The boy shook Sean's hand, gingerly.

"You're Edie's friend?" Liv asked.

"Yeah. Edie's cool. She lets me use her computer. And sleep on her couch. She makes great scrambled eggs, but she always burns the hamburgers. She's not much of a cook. But she's still nice."

"She sounds nice," Liv murmured. "Points for Edie."

"This guy who looks like me, did you talk to him?"

"A little," Jamal said. "I told him he looked like Fade, and Edie got mad, said Fade didn't exist again." Jamal looked rebellious. "But he was right there! I mean, shit! Who's she trying to kid?"

"Did he say his name?" Liv asked gently.

Jamal pondered that. "Uh, yeah. I think she called him Kev."

That felled him. Convinced though he'd been, his belly hit the ground, and kept on going. Down, and farther down. Liv covered her mouth with her hands. Her face was bone white.

Son of a bitch. So he called himself Kev. He still used his own goddamn name. So he still knew who he was. Where he came from.

Did he ever think about his brothers? It would seem that he did not. Had he ever wondered how much his brothers had thought about him? Had it ever crossed his fucking pea brain? Now and again?

This was bad. Being angry and hurt at Kev was even worse than missing him, grieving his death. Being furious and vengeful.

And to think he'd thought he was hip to every kind of pain this could inflict upon him. There were always brand new depths to sink to. Fresh new agony buttons to push. He let a slow breath hiss out through his teeth, and forced his voice flatness. "Did he mention a surname?"

Jamal had sensed the weird pain vibe. His eyes were big. He shook his head, edged closer to the door.

"Or where he lives?" He tried to soften the drill sergeant tone, but it was involuntary. Dour old Eamon, speaking through him.

Another nervous, scared head shake from Jamal. Great. A lead that led nowhere, except for the mental ward.

"Jamal," Liv asked gently. "Do you know any other people who might know this man Kev?"

"You mean, besides Edie?"

She gave him an approving smile. "Right! Since Edie isn't here right now, and since we don't know where she is. Anybody else?"

Jamal considered it. "Well, Valerie met him, but she's in jail right now. Fade punched out this asshole john for her. The dickhead stiffs her, and starts hitting her! Fade kicked the living shit out of the guy." Jamal mimed kicks and punches. "Ka-pow, whack! Fucking asshole."

"How awful for poor Valerie," Liv said gently. "Anyone else?"

Jamal's face lit up. "Maybe the people at Any Port would know! It's the shelter down on Stark Street. He gave them lots of money. They might know. That's where he took Valerie, 'cause she needed stitches."

Sean and Liv looked at each other. "Where's this place?" he asked.

"I'll take you there," Jamal offered eagerly.

They closed the door of Edie Parrish's ravaged apartment, and followed the scampering Jamal down the stairs. Sean unlocked the car, and watched, bemused, as Jamal clambered into the backseat, chattering about live superheroes kicking the shit out of bad guys. Sean slid into the driver's seat. Liv got in. They looked at each other.

"Uh, Jamal?" he said. "You sure you want to climb into a car with strangers? It's not really a smart thing to do. You know that, right?"

"You guys aren't strangers! You're Fade's brother!"

"Could you run up and ask your mom?" Liv asked gently. "If I were her, I'd want you to ask. I'd want to know where you were."

"She doesn't care." Jamal's smile faded to a sullen mask. "She's asleep. She works nights."

"Ah." Sean drummed his fingers on the steering column. "All right, then. How about your dad?"

Jamal rolled his eyes, and yanked the door shut. "Get real."

Sean sighed. "Put on the seat belt, then. And swear to me, on the souls of all the greatest superheroes of all time, that you will never, ever climb into a car with a stranger again. Ever. Got that? Promise?"

"Sure, no problem," Jamal promised.

Jamal's breezy tone sparked a lecture from the two of them about stranger danger that lasted the whole short ride, leaving the kid sulky and defensive. His good spirits rebounded promptly when they got to the brickfront building with a rainbow painted sign.

Jamal bounced up the stairs and rang. "Yo, Tracee!" he yelled into the intercom. "It's Jamal! Some people need to talk to Dorothea!"

They were buzzed in, and followed Jamal up a narrow staircase and down a hall lined with small offices. A door at the end of the corridor opened, and a middle-aged woman with bushy salt-and-pepper hair leaned out, examining them as they approached. Jamal ran to her and gave her a hug. She touseled his hair as she studied them, her eyes flicking to Liv's belly. "What brings you folks here? You don't look like you need emergency shelter."

"No." Sean offered her his hand. "We're looking for information."

"He's looking for Fade Shadowseeker!" Jamal broke in, his voice shrill with excitement. "He's Fade's brother!"

Dorothea's eyelids flickered. She stared at Sean's face. Then she stepped back into her office, and gestured them in. "Let's talk."

Jamal tried to come in, too, but she grabbed the kid by the scruff of the neck and scrubbed at his wild, curly mop with her knuckles. "You go find Tracee, and tell her to give you some of those brownies we got from the bakery this morning," she said. "Soft and fudgy."

Jamal was off like a shot. Dorothea closed the door, waved them into chairs, and studied them from across her desk, which was heaped with battered file folders and diverse rainbow tinted Post It notes, scribbled with numbers, reminders. "So?" Dorothea asked. "Ask your questions. I'll see if I can help you."

Sean stared down at this hands, refusing to let them clench into fists. "My brother disappeared eighteen years ago," he said. "We have reason to believe that he was abducted, and badly injured. We never found him again. A few days ago, we found this." Liv pulled the Fade Shadowseeker book out of her purse. Sean handed it to the woman.

Dorothea flicked her eye over it. "I'm familiar with it," she said. "Jamal has showed me. The resemblance is uncanny."

Excitement exploded inside him. "So you've seen him?"

She stared at him. "I mean, to you," she said stiffly.

Sean's throat tightened. "Have you seen him, or not?"

"If I had, I certainly wouldn't be doing him a service by advertising that fact, now, would I?" Dorothea replied. "A man like him, with those scars? It's clear he has enemies."

"We're not Kev's enemies," Liv said." She opened her purse, fished for the envelope, and pulled out the handful of battered photographs.

Kev and Sean together, at eight, at twelve, at sixteen, and nineteen, at Sean's high school graduation. The few pictures that existed. Crazy Eamon hadn't been big on capturing the memories.

Dorothea fanned the photos out, and stared at them. A very long couple of minutes ticked by. She sighed, sharply.

"Your brother is the most generous private financial donor that Any Port has ever had, since we opened our doors in '91," she said. "He's given us one hundred and fifty-one thousand dollars. Over the past three months alone. Manila envelopes stuffed with cash started showing up in the mail slot. I was worried that something strange was going on. Drug money, I don't know. So I had a camera installed, and I was just about to hire a private investigator to follow the man who left the envelopes when he rang the bell one morning, at five A.M."

"Valerie, right?" Liv said.

Dorothea blinked. "Why, yes. He'd defended her from a customer who'd gotten violent. He wanted to make sure she got help. I recognized him, and confronted him about the money. He gave me an envelope then and there. Told me not to worry, that he'd won it at poker, but didn't need it. He wanted to spread it around." She hesitated. "He seemed like a very decent man."

"Huh," Sean muttered. "I'm glad he doesn't have financial problems, at least. That's something. But poker? Jesus."

"How was he?" Liv asked softly.

Dorothea face went cautious. "He did not seem very happy," she said. "And he did not look . . . well. He looked kind of lost."

"He is lost," Sean said. "But he's getting found. Once and for all."

The tone in his voice made Dorothea look alarmed, but Liv reached out across the desk, and took the older woman's hand. "We would never hurt him, in a million years. You remember his scars?"

Dorothea nodded.

"He got those scars saving my life," Liv said quietly. "We love him, and we miss him. That's all. I want my son to know his uncle."

Dorothea nodded. She rubbed at her eyes, and dug into her desk for a big address book. She flipped through it, grabbed a pink Post-It, scribbled. She held the note out to Liv, shooting worried looks at Sean. As if he might leap across the desk like a rabid dog.

Sean looked at it. There it was. His brother's surname. Larsen, of all things. Fucking bland. NW Lenox Street. His address. Check it out. Kev's location, in time and space. After all these years. Hot damn.

His stomach flipped, churned. His glands fired out bizarre conflicting messages, joy, terror, fury, hope. He barely made it through the chitchat, the thank-you's. He heard Liv asking Dorothea to make sure Jamal got home safely. Thank God for her presence of mind. He'd spaced that detail completely. Then Liv was towing him down the stairs, and out toward the vehicle. "Give me the keys," she said, sternly.

He looked at her belly as he pulled them out. "But you—"

"Can drive pregnant." She plucked them from his hand, and shoved him toward the passenger side. "Shut up. Get in."

They sat for a moment, locked in their own thoughts, but after she put the keys in the ignition, Liv reached for him, threading her fingers through his own. Squeezing. He squeezed back, gratefully. Warmth, support, love. It flooded into him from her in comforting waves. She set the GPS, asked it to lead her to Kev's address.

He concentrated on just keeping it together. Sure, he could yank Liv off her feet, he could carry her up a few flights of stairs. But when it came to the stuff that mattered, oh, man.

She carried him. Every damn time.

CHAPTER
25

"I just can't thank you enough for making time in your busy schedule this morning, Mr. Parrish." Ava's breathy voice hitched with emotion. "Des mentioned that it's a difficult period for your family, so I'm all the more grateful for your time."

Charles Parrish shot a look at Des, and leafed through the thick binder that lay on his desk in the massive, luxurious office in the Helix headquarters building. "It looks like a fascinating project," he admitted, in grudging tones. "My compliments."

Ava murmured her thanks, clearly flustered by attention from the big man. Able to bestow or withhold his blessing. How the bastard must get off on his power over people, day after day. Prick.

"She's made amazing strides in cerebral interfaces," Des added. "The neuroprosthesis controllers have amazing ramifications for the treatment and therapy of patients with brain and spinal cord injuries. This research will give Helix an explosion in value and in prestige."

"Yes," Charles Parrish said fretfully, rubbing his temples. "That's very impressive, but it could just have easily have gone through the normal channels for requesting grant funding. Frankly, I don't understand the urgency of bringing this to my attention this morning, Desmond. We have a meeting next month. We could have handled this then. Why the big fuss about meeting with me today?"

"This is special," Des said stubbornly. "I didn't want it lost in the shuffle. It's explosive, Charles. Time sensitive, too. We need to stay ahead of the competition."

Ava touched Parrish's hand, and yanked it back, as if overcome by her own boldness. "Maybe I'm pushing my luck," she said. "But I would be honored to give you a private demonstration of my work. Any time. " She leaned over the desk, letting the dangling frill of her blouse brush Parrish's sleeve. Giving him a clear view of the shapely tits dangling inside. Braless, springy, dewy, soft. "Could I?"

Parrish's eyes flicked to the bounty she offered, and darted to her full, glossy parted lips, her highly accentuated lumbar arch. "Well," he muttered. "Ah."

"I know you're a very busy man." *But never too busy to want a little more of this.* Ava ventured a breathless giggle. "I'm being greedy with your time, but hey. Can't blame a girl for trying, right?"

"Ah, no." Parrish coughed. "I'll . . . take a look at my schedule."

Ava lit up with delight. "I'd be so honored."

Des shoved the paper in front of Parrish, on his desk. "And if you would just sign off on this? That way, at the next meeting, the board won't even have to deliberate, since they see that you already approved it. You know, just to speed things along."

Parrish frowned down at the paper. His gaze flicked up to Ava, sweeping over her body, her wide, hopeful dark eyes. He signed.

"Oh, thank you!" Ava's hand whipped up, and she squirted the inhalant into Parrish's face. He went still, eyes staring.

"Quick, Des." The breathy giggle was gone. Her voice was as hard as glass. "This will metabolize in just a couple of minutes."

Des knelt, yanked off Parrish's Ferragamo shoe, peeled off his sock. Ava crouched down, poised on the stiletto heels, and held up the hypodermic needle, smiling into Parrish's frozen face, his horrified eyes. "I'm so glad you found time in your schedule for me," she said sweetly. "I'm about to give you a demonstration of my current research project that will blow your mind, Mr. Parrish. And I mean that quite literally."

With that, she jabbed the needle between his toes and pushed in the plunger. Parrish jerked, but could not scream. Ava briskly put Parrish's sock and shoe back on. She tied the laces of Parrish's shoe and leaped up, rummaging in her purse. She pulled out the mesh slave crown, and shook it in Parrish's face. "Your foundation has plowed two hundred million into this thing over the past ten years," she told him. "It's time you gave it a whirl." She swung her leg over his, and sat on his lap, straddling him. "Here," she murmured tenderly. "I'll fix you up."

"For God's sake, Ava! We don't have time for depraved games!"

"I'm just placing his crown," she said, wounded, leaning forward so that her breasts were shoved into Parrish's face, smothering his nose between them. "Here, honey. Come to Mama."

Des snorted. "Are you wearing underwear, at least?"

"Why, yes! A lovely red lace thong. I picked red on purpose. Don't you think it's appropriate? It's the theme of the day. Red."

"As long as you don't lube all over his suit, you crazy bitch. God knows what the forensic techs would make of that."

"Trust me, baby." She placed the crown on Charles Parrish's head, and pulled out one of her hairpins, which she used to pluck locks of Parrish's thick, glossy silver hair through the mesh. The hair covered the contact points nicely. Thank goodness the man wasn't bald. Not that it made that much difference. The security cameras at the Parrish Foundation building that would catch the scene would be very far away. But even so. It was best to be careful. Attentive to every detail.

"Hurry," Desmond fretted. "You need to adjust my crown, too."

"All these years, and you still can't adjust a master crown by yourself," she bitched. "Idiot. I should tattoo the contact points on your scalp." She leaned back, admiring the effect on Parrish. "You look beautiful," she told the man, archly. "I could just kiss you."

"But she won't," Des cut in. "Because she's not stupid enough to leave lipstick and saliva all over you."

Ava pouted. "You're such a spoilsport, Des. Come here, let me fix you up. Sure you don't want me to crown him instead?"

"We've been through this," Des said defensively. "I know you think I suck, but this is not a particularly complicated operation."

"Fine." Ava slapped the crown onto Des's thick mahogany hair, used the pin to pull locks of his hair through it, adjusted the sensors over his skull. Almost invisible. Then she hurried over to Parrish, adjusted him in his chair, placed his hands on his desk.

"Try him," she directed. "He should be ready by now."

Des closed his eyes, and concentrated. Charles Parrish stared, in stark horror, as he lifted his hands, clapped them awkwardly. He clapped again, more clearly, more loudly. He stuck his thumbs into his ears, waggled his fingers. "Peter P-p-piper p-p-picked a p-peck of pickled p-p-pepper," he said, his voice thick and slurred.

"You have to do better than that," Ava scolded.

Des tried again. "P-peter Piper picked a peck of pickled

peppers," Parrish repeated, more clearly. His eyes were full of stark horror.

Prick. He thought he owned the world. That everyone in it was his flunkey. And to think he'd fondly fancied that he would be bending her over a lab table today, pumping away like a beast in rut. He would suffer for having even dreamed it. Randy old boar. Ready for the slaughterhouse. His time had come.

"Close his mouth, Des," she said. "And see if you can do something about his eyes. They look like they're about to pop out."

Des had a hard time wrangling Parrish's facial musculature. The result was marginally better. The best she could expect of Des, anyway. She should have insisted on crowning herself, but it was too late now. Their window of opportunity was shrinking fast. A drop of blood was edging out of Parrish's nose. It broke its surface tension, flashed down the side of the man's mouth, began to drip off his chin. His eyes began to dart. He was a poor interface subject. Too old, too male, too rigid.

"Get the papers he signed. Fast." Desmond's voice shook with strain. "He's about to pop."

Ava grabbed the papers. Parrish was sagging over his desk, gasping and hitching. Blood plopped onto his blotter. His lungs had locked. The drug was paralyzing him. He could no longer breathe unassisted.

For the love of God, did she have to think of everything? "Make him breathe, you idiot!" she hissed. "He's suffocating!"

Big heaving breaths shook the older man, his chest jerking.

"Don't make him hyperventilate," she warned. "You hack. This is the last time I let you crown, you hear me?"

It was time for the blessed event. Ava's heart began to pound.

"Have him light up a cigar," she told Desmond. "Let the pompous bastard die puffing a fat cat Cuban cigar."

Des jerked open Parrish's desk drawer, and pulled a cigar out of a box. He trimmed it, lit it. Dickhead. He could have compelled Parrish to do it himself. Would have looked better for the crime scene analysts. Then Ava saw rivulets of blood running over Parrish's mouth. Maybe that scenario was no longer feasible. Meltdown was at hand.

Des stuck the cigar into Parrish's hand, grabbed Ava's hand, and dragged her to the far wall of the room. They stood there, backs to the wall, hearts tripping. Ava opened her purse, pulled out a plastic bag, the kind used to isolate medical waste. "Have him turn around. Back to the window," she instructed, breathless. "We want the exit wound to take out his face."

Their fingers twined together. Des's jaw twitched. Sweat stood out on his forehead as he compelled Parrish to rise to his feet, puff on the cigar. The older man's lungs seized up, and he coughed.

"Forget the cigar. Just get him over to the fucking window!" she whispered furiously. "Quick!"

"Shut up and let me concentrate!" Des snarled back.

Parrish stumbled like a zombie. Blood was trickling out of his ear, but he did not fall. He lurched over to the panoramic window that showed the Helix complex, the Parrish Foundation building, the Portland skyline. Mount Hood towered in the distance. He turned around, back to the window, swaying.

Ava lifted her purse to shield her face. Seconds ticked by. Three. Four. Goddamnit, Ken, *hurry*. She needed air, but didn't dare breathe. A scream was forming inside her, a throat-ripping, head-splitting scream.

She struggled to keep it on a leash. Time enough for screaming later, when it would serve their cause. Eight. Nine. Ten—

Crash. They'd been braced for the shot, for the shatter, but the hugeness of the sound still rocked them.

It took a moment, to take stock of the new, revised uni-

verse. The walls, furniture, all spattered a bright arterial red.
Parrish, sprawled on his cream-colored rug, a hole where his
face had been. His brains, spread out in a pinkish fan around
him. The bright, cruel glitter of broken glass.

Fresh, cold air rushed into the room.

Ava and Des picked their way over to Charles's body. She
fell to her knees, plucked the crown out of the corpse's
blood-soaked hair. It was intact. Ken's bullet had not damaged it in the slightest. Good.

Her knees were getting lacerated by broken glass, but she
forced herself to ignore it. It would look good when the
emergency medical personnel got there. She dropped the
slave crown into the bag, passed it to Des. Des shoved it into
his coat. Her clothes were too tight to hide it.

Ava dabbed Charles Parrish's blood artfully onto her face,
then over her white blouse, on the ruffly silk frill. She tasted
it. So hot.

The metallic taste of blood unleashed her. She gave in, let
go. Once she started screaming, she knew she wasn't going
to be able to stop, not until they gave her a shot of Demerol.
But that was all right. She lived for these moments. Sweet
relief.

She let the screaming carry her away. Thundering through
inner space to that extreme, wordless, mindless place far beyond herself.

The only place that she could rest.

Miles was immensely pleased with himself. He glanced
at the cell phone on the passenger seat of his car. Twitching
to grab it and punch the speed dial. He had to tell somebody,
or he was going to pop a vein.

He stopped himself. Not yet. This was too good to waste.
He was going to do a personal show-and-tell, and be right
there to see Con and Davy's jaws thunk onto the floor. Sweet.
When did he, geeky old Miles, ever get a chance to surprise

or one-up a McCloud guy? Short answer: never. They were always ten steps ahead of everybody else. Always.

He pulled up in front of Con's house, where he was meeting Cindy and the rest of the McCloud crowd for lunch, and was gratified to see Davy's SUV outside. That meant little Jeannie would be wrapped around his head along with Kevvie, but what the hell, Unkie Miles was already toast. Their personal kickball, squeeze toy and body servant. He'd even been known to change a diaper in emergencies, though he'd become highly skilled in evasive maneuvers when it came to baby poop.

He grabbed the box from his back seat, ran into the house. Sure enough, he was ambushed and felled by a screaming three-year-old ninja warrior. As he lay twitching and gurgling in his death throes, Jeannie dove onto his head with a screech of blood-thirsty triumph, practically fracturing his skull. *Shit, that hurt.*

It took a while to let the grisly, choking and writhing death drama play out to its conclusion, and even longer to gently but firmly convince Jeannie and Kevvie that he wasn't going to go outside, come back in and let them attack him again. He usually did, six or eight times. Not today. He was on fire to show Con and Davy what was in that box.

The kids were dragged off him and plunked in front of some fuzzy puppet cavorting on TV, and Miles proceeded into the dining area with his prize. He was the last to arrive, and the table was heaped. Self-satisfaction gave a guy a real appetite.

"Hey, Miles. A beer?" Con handed him one.

Miles took a swig, eyeing the platter of fresh char-grilled salmon steaks with lemon and coriander that Margot was laying on the table. But even great food and ice cold brew couldn't distract him from his presentation. It was bursting out. "Got something for you guys."

"Yeah?" Davy popped a red potato into his mouth. "Let's have it."

"It's a visual thing," he said, digging out his pocket knife and tearing into the box. "A kite. Found it in a sports catalog this morning. Got online, made some calls. Found a local sports retailer in Tacoma who carried the exact design. So instead of having it overnighted, I just drove down to Tacoma and bought it." He slapped a folder of computer printouts onto the table. "Found the outfit who designed it, too. Lost Boys, based out of Portland, run by Bruno Ranieri. Ever heard of him?"

Davy and Con exchanged glances, and shook their heads. "Never," Davy said. "Let's see it."

Miles pulled the fabric section of the unassembled kite out of the box, and let the big, octagonal piece of fabric unroll. "Look familiar?"

The room went dead quiet, except for the babbling from the kiddie zone. Davy and Connor stared at the thing he was holding. Their faces were stiff. Deathly, grayish masks.

And Miles got it. Too late. A punch, right to his solar plexus. How childish and selfish he'd been, not to break it to them gently. He'd brought a bomb into Con's home and lobbed it in his face, just to get a reaction. To punish them, for being smarter, stronger, faster, cooler than he'd ever be. Forgetting that they could be hurt, too.

Oh, man. Oh, what an asshole.

Davy got up, and walked out of the room. Margot got up, scurried off in his wake.

Miles stared at the piece of nylon fabric draped over his arm, and started to roll the thing up. Make it disappear.

"No," Con lunged for it, snatched it out of Miles's hand. "No, let's hang this up. I've got all the rest of Kev's artwork up. Why not this?"

He stalked out of the room. Terrifying vibes were throbbing off the guy. Erin stood up, looking worried. Cindy looked scared.

Con came back, kite in one hand, hammer and nails in the other. He pulled framed Kev drawings off the wall, dropping them onto the dining table with loud, rattling thuds that made glasses, plates and silverware vibrate in sympathy. When he'd cleared a spot big enough, he held up the top of the mandala, placed the nail, slammed that hammer down.

"Connor!" Erin said, shocked. "Calm down!"

"Oh, I'm calm." *Bam. Bam.* The hammer left ugly scars in the white painted wall. He wrenched the fabric taut, poised a nail at the bottom of the kite. *Bam. Bam. Bam.* They flinched at each blow.

Then Con held up the right side. *Bam. Bam.* Miles felt desperate. He'd unleashed this nightmare singlehandedly. He had to do something. *Bam. Bam.* "Con? Are you OK? Please! Chill out!" he begged.

"I'm just fine." *Bam. Bam.* "I'm just great. Just hanging up my little brother's latest artwork. What's wrong with that?" Only the left side remained. Con stretched it out, placed the nail. *Bam. Bam.*

Miles winced at each blow. "You don't have to crucify the thing!"

Con stopped, breathing hard. His teeth were clenched in a grimace. He gave the nail one last brutal whack. Paint flakes exploded, showering onto the hardwood flooring. The nearest framed drawing that was still hanging fell to the floor and broke. Glass shattered everywhere.

"Connor?" Erin's whisper was tiny in the sudden silence.

"Where in the fuck has he been all this time?" Con's voice was harsh, breaking. "Where the *fuck* has he been?"

He laid the top of his head in the center of the kite, his shaggy hair dangling down to hide his face. The hammer dangled, forgotten in his scarred hand. His shoulders shook.

Madeline woke from her nap in the bassinet at the foot of the table, and started to cry. Erin started toward her, faltered, and ran to Connor, slid her arms around his waist, pressing her face between his shoulder blades. "Cin, get Maddy, please." Her voice was choked.

Maddy's cries rose in volume. Miles just stood there, like an asshole. Wishing he could just disappear into the floor.

Cindy got up out of her chair. "Miles? Get Maddy, and take her into the living room." Her voice quivered. "Make sure Kevvie and Jeannie stay in there til I get all that broken glass cleaned up."

Miles was grateful to her for taking charge, though holding the wobbly-necked Maddy scared the living shit out of him. But anything was better than staring stupidly at the mayhem he had wrought.

He gathered up the squirming, purple-faced bundle of screaming indignation, draped her over his shoulder, and fled to the kiddie zone. Which was exactly where he belonged, with his sub-zero maturity level.

It took a long time to get Maddy calmed down, but some endless minutes later she was finally asleep again. Con and Davy came into the living room, and sat down. No one seemed to know quite what to say.

"I'm sorry," Miles said simply. "I shouldn't have done that to you."

"It's OK," Davy said.

"It's not your fault," Con said. "It's mine. I didn't believe Sean's dreams and visions and kite sightings. I was too damn tired to believe them. Too tired to hope. Tired of the whole roller-coaster ride. I just wanted to move on." He dropped his head into his hands and sighed. "Jesus," he whispered. "I let my brother go . . . because I was *tired*."

Miles could think of nothing to say. "I'm sorry," he said, helplessly.

"Not as sorry as we are. We're the ones who let him down."

That pissed Miles off, unexpectedly. He saw the scene, from three years ago. That hellish day, fighting that drugged up, bloodthirsty ogre Gordon, who'd almost killed him. Sean lying there with brain bleed. Liv soaked with blood, swinging a tire iron. Cindy lying terribly still on the ground after trying to defend him. Stinking smoke pouring from the burning laboratory. "It's not your fault!" he yelled.

Con and Davy shot glances at each other. "How do you figure?"

"I saw these people. I fought them! They fucked with you!" Miles said hotly. "They hid things from you, lied to you, tricked you! It's not your fault if you fell for it! The fault belongs to those murdering assholes, not to you! So don't take it on yourselves. That's just stupid!"

Maddy woke at his impassioned speech, yawned, and projectile vomited predigested milk all over Miles's sweater. Aw. Cuuute.

Connor's mouth twitched. He reached out. "Here, give her to me."

Miles handed the infant over, and Connor slumped onto the couch and draped the kid over his broad chest, where she promptly went back to sleep. Davy fished up an urp rag from the back of the couch, tossed it to Miles. "Put one on before you pick them up," he advised. "They'll get you every damn time."

"Thanks for the tip." Miles dabbed the curdled goop on his chest.

Davy opened the file Miles had compiled on Lost Boys Toys and Flywear. "Want to road trip down to Portland today?" he asked.

Miles was disoriented. "You still want me to go with you guys?"

They looked blank. "Hell, yeah," Con said. "Why wouldn't we?"

Miles jumped up off the couch. So they weren't mad at him. He was so relieved, he could cry. But he wouldn't. "Let's go," he said. "I want to talk to this Ranieri guy. And I want some goddamn answers."

Con and Davy exchanged grins. "That's our boy," Con said.

CHAPTER
26

"You didn't eat enough," Bruno complained. "There's some sausages left." He heaped more food onto Edie's plate.

"No! I swear! I'm stuffed!" she protested, laughing. "Really!"

"Shooting's hungry work, and we've got that hike up the bluff ahead of us," Bruno scolded. "Eat, eat! You worked hard this morning. I can't wait to tell Kev how the target practice went."

Edie waved that away. She'd grudgingly enjoyed herself that morning. Bruno was a good teacher, breaking down each step in a way that made sense to her. And she hadn't done too badly. She was no longer viscerally afraid of the gun itself. She'd even begun to almost, well . . . enjoy it. As a mental exercise in concentration, of course.

"You're a great teacher," she conceded.

"Oh, that's because of Kev," Bruno confided. "He's the ultimate teacher. He taught me how to fight, how to shoot. Tracking, hunting, all that stuff. He knows it all. And way more. More than he taught me, that's for sure. All that stuff doesn't fit into my head."

"Which stuff?"

"Oh, God, pick a topic at random. Ask him about quantum physics. Ask him about Roman military history, or the evolution of invertebrates, or any animal, bird or insect you ever heard of. Geology. The movement of the planets. Astrophysics. He explained the theory of relativity to me once, when I was in high school." Bruno shook his head wistfully. "I almost understood it, for a couple minutes. God, it was beautiful. Couldn't retain it for shit, but it was great while it lasted."

She laughed, as he clearly meant her to. "That's wonderful."

"And if he doesn't know something? He goes to the library, comes home with a stack of books, reads them in one night. Processes every damn word. And knows it all when he's done. He can lecture about it, has informed opinions about it. His brain is freaking out there, in deep space. Turbocharged. I kid you not."

His tone made her smile. "I never thought you were kidding."

"He learned Calabrese dialect just from listening to Rosa and Tony, and they say he speaks it like a Brancaleon native, *stretto stretto*. And look at these." He leaped up from the table, and flung open a battered wooden cabinet, rummaging inside. "Here." He pulled out a couple of objects, and presented them to her. "Look at these."

She turned the odd objects in her hands, fascinated. They were sculptures, as far as she could tell, made of whittled twigs and acorns. One was a floating spherical form, with long floating arms, the other was a spiraling helix shape. Both were beautiful. "What are they?"

"This one is a carbon structure," Bruno said. "Don't remember which molecule. He does this with no reference to books. Just sitting out on the steps with his knife. This is a fragment of human DNA. He explained what part, but it all blew out the other ear. I got no place to put that kind of data. Look how he joined the twigs, see? No glue."

"They're beautiful," she said softly.

"Damn right, they are. This stuff was what gave me the initial idea for Lost Boys. That and the kites. He got heavy into stunt kites a few years ago. You saw that mandala painting on his bedroom ceiling?"

Images from that scorching incounter on Kev's petal-strewn bed danced through her mind. "Uh, yeah."

Bruno averted his eyes from her blush with great delicacy. "That kite was our first product. It's in sporting goods catalogs all over the country. These are the models he painted for the other ones." Bruno pressed a sheaf of pieces of cardboard into her hand. She spread them out onto the table, admiring the colors, the subtle geometrical designs. They seemed to move as she looked at them. "Wow. These are great."

"And look at the pictures. Animals, flowers, leaves. Me, too, but he bitches because I won't stay still. I'm twitchy. Look." He tossed notebooks on the table, like a little kid showing off his toys.

Edie was charmed by his eagerness to demonstrate Kev's abilities. She leafed through the notebooks, struck silent. They were so spare, and so beautiful. Stark economy of line and detail. Every pen stroke essential and perfect. Why should she be surprised? It was so Kev.

"It's not fair," she said. "He doesn't need to have all these talents. One or two are enough for any one person. It's not fair to the rest of us."

"Tell me about it," Bruno said. "He's a freak. We got used to it, over the years, but every now and then he still blind-sides us. Like with the Vietnamese. Man, that one came out of fucking nowhere."

"Vietnamese? What's that?"

"It was incredible." Bruno's eyes shone with enjoyment. "So, Kev's finally learning to talk again, right? This was years ago. I must have been fourteen or so. He's starting to force out a few words, just to please me, I think, even though it makes him sweat buckets. And one day, the Vietnamese grocer and his son come to the kitchen at the diner to make a delivery of vegetables and fruit, and they're chattering away, and out of the blue, Kev starts talking to them. In perfect Vietnamese. Not just choking out one word at a time like it's going to make him puke, either. It flowed right out. He had a whole polite conversation with them. Once they picked their jaws up off the floor, that is."

Edie forced herself to close her own mouth. "Vietnamese?"

"Yeah. Like, what the fuck, right? Tony about had a heart attack. But anyhow, people talked, and a few days later, this speech expert from Oregon Health Science University comes by the diner, wants to talk to Kev. Turns out her niece goes to the local high school with the Vietnamese grocer's son. She was intrigued. Tony tried to freeze her out, but she got huffy, started threatening to report Tony to Adult Protective Services for abuse, slavery, taking advantage of a handicapped person, yada yada. Tony was afraid whoever was gunning for Kev would find him if she made a big public stink about it, so he caved. Only time I've ever seen Tony cave. It just about killed him."

"Wow," she murmured. "That's an incredible story."

"Boy, did Tony ever complain about that uppity bitch," Bruno recollected fondly. "She thought she was God's gift. Blond, long legs, long fingernails, high heels, eight Ph.Ds."

"So did she do speech therapy with him, then?"

"Damn straight," Bruno said. "Came to see him a couple times a week. Didn't charge him, either, although I think she definitely got some compensation for her professional services when she started renting those hotel rooms for their sessions. So they could have, you know, peace and quiet to concentrate, right? He made progress real fast once they started that phase of his therapy. Probably started talking out of self defense." Bruno stopped, looking dismayed. "Oh, shit. Too much information, right? I shouldn't tell Kev's former sexploits. Girls hate that. What a fucking schmoe I am. Sorry. Forget I said it."

She suppressed a smile. "To be honest, I truly did not think that Kev was a virgin before he met me. So you can relax."

Bruno looked relieved. "Good. I just want you to have a clue, just how special that guy is."

"I think I know," she assured him. "I've gotten lots of clues."

But Bruno barged on. "You can't know, because he never blows his own horn. It would never occur to him to show off. And he's so generous. He'd give away every penny he had. Never thinks of himself." His eyes froze wide. "This is not to say that he wouldn't be, you know, a good provider. I didn't mean to imply that he's unreliable, or that—"

"You don't have to sell him to me. I'm sold. I am so convinced."

A radiant grin spread over Bruno's face. "Really? You are?"

"You're preaching to the choir," she assured him.

Bruno looked away quickly. "Well, hell," he muttered, his voice thick. "That's great. He deserves for something excellent to happen to him. He's taken so much shit, and he's, like, the best guy. The very best. He saved my life. He let me be his brother. Fuck it, I don't know. He deserves the moon and stars."

That gave Edie a twinge of unease, thinking of Kev's angel fantasies. "I'm not the moon and stars. I'm a normal woman, as hung up as the next person. Maybe more. I'll drive him crazy soon enough."

"Oh, that's OK. He'll drive you crazy, too. And I highly doubt that you're normal. Normal girls have been throwing themselves at him for years. He nailed a few now and again, but he never fell ass over head in love with any of them. So you got something special going for you."

Hmmph. Special wouldn't be quite the word she would pick, but whatever. She didn't want to bring Bruno down.

"Am I talking your ears off your head?" Bruno asked. "Kev told me not to do that, or he'd flatten me. Am I?"

She laughed. "I don't mind. How else am I going to learn all the details about him, since he won't show off?"

"Thank God," Bruno said fervently. "I hate it when I have to not talk. It builds up in my head like steam." He glanced at his watch. "If we head up to the bluff now, we'll get there right on time. We can see if Kev has discovered his perfect fucking TV family of origin."

Bruno caught her startled expression, and looked embarrassed. "Sorry, can't help myself. I think he should let go of his past. He's got me and Tony and Rosa for family. Who has the energy to cope with more family than that? You'd choke to death on more family than that!"

Edie laid her hand on his shoulder. "No matter what he finds, I know he feels lucky to have you for a brother," she said. "He said so."

Bruno stared at his feet. "Well. Um. Come on, then. Let's go."

The climb up the bluff was more pleasant at midday, with Bruno's cheerful monologue to accompany her. He set a slower pace than Kev, and never ran out of breath, just meandered beside her, occasionally giving her a hand to clamber over tree trunks, regaling her all the while with Kev's exploits, Kev's freakish intelligence, Kev's fighting prowess, Kev's various and sundry astonishing qualities. She lapped it up to the last drop. Yum. Like any woman out of her mind in love. Wallowing in her favorite topic. All Kev, all the time. How great was that?

When they got to the top, the mountain was fogged in, but the wind blew holes into the clouds occasionally, and the starkly beautiful white and black shoulder of the mountain would appear before ragged layers of gray swept across and concealed it again.

Bruno found a signal. "There's an SMS," he said, showing her.

She stared at the way he had closed the brief, terse text message. love u. Amazing, how those five characters could made her heart thud, her eyes tear up.

Bruno called Kev's number, and frowned at his phone. "It's ringing," he said. "But he's not answering."

His face had changed. Before, she'd have drawn him in a playful retro cartoon style, flashing grins and dimples. The way he looked now, she'd choose a different vibe. Starker, harder. "Not answering?"

Bruno tried again. A third time. He looked at his watch. "That's strange. He was expecting us to call. He'd be dying to talk to you, after being Edie deprived for, how long? Four hours?"

"Five hours and sixteen minutes," she corrected.

The wind moaned around the rocks. They stared at each other, and then down the long mountain canyon that lead to the Gorge, and from there west along the river, to Portland. The food Edie had eaten congealed into a cold, inorganic lump in her belly.

Bruno tried again. He shook his head. The silence felt thick and strange, after all those hours of Bruno's easy, cheerful talk.

Neither of them was willing to give up so soon, after slogging up that hill, so they found a place that was out of the worst of the icy wind.

"Can I borrow your phone?" she asked. "I'd like to call my little sister. Chances are she's being policed, since my dad forbade me to contact her, but I have to keep trying. Someday they'll get sloppy."

"Be my guest." He handed the phone over. "We'll try Kev after."

Edie punched in her sister's number, and texted:

hey ron. yr sis. gd time 2 talk?

She sent it, and held the phone in her hand, willing Ronnie to be casual, sneaky. Connecting with her little sister was the only thing that could possibly comfort her, now that she was in the down cycle of this manic emotional roller coaster of love. Terrified to death for Kev.

The phone rang, and she almost jumped out of her skin. Bruno leaned to check the number, but it wasn't Kev. It was Ronnie.

Edie clicked open the line. "Hey, sweetheart! You free to talk?"

"Edie?" Her sister's voice was high, wobbly.

"Ronnie?" she asked sharply. "What's going on, baby?"

"Oh, my God. Oh God, Edie. Daddy, he . . . he . . ." Her sister's voice broke, and her words were unintelligible, with the static, the poor connection, the whistling wind.

"Ronnie? Sweetie? I can't hear you," Edie called, desperately, crouching down out of the wind. "Try again, please, OK?"

"It's Daddy," Ronnie sobbed out. "It's Daddy."

"What about him? Is he hurt? In the hospital again? What is it?"

Ronnie started to answer. Her voice was cut off. "Edith? Is that you?" cut in a louder, clearer voice.

Edie's heart sank. Busted. Aunt Evelyn, and sounding more shrill than usual. "Yes, Aunt Evelyn. What's wrong? What happened?"

"It's Charles," her aunt said. "He . . . he's been murdered."

Edie waited for her aunt to take back the words she had just said. Those unthinkable, unsayable words. It wasn't possible. Not her father. He was invincible. A rock. Unchanging. Immortal.

"He was shot," her aunt quavered. "In his office. A sniper. Ten-thirty this morning. It's so horrible. So horrible."

She'd been crouching against the rock, but her legs gave out and dumped her on her butt. Bruno's lips moved, but she couldn't hear what he said. Just wind screaming. Or maybe the screaming was inside her head. *Daddy.* She saw his face in her mind's eye, the last time she'd seen it, in the intensive care unit. She'd drawn it so many times. Longed so hard for approval from him, for her entire life. Tried so hard to convince herself that she no longer needed his approval.

It took the certainty that no approval would ever again be forthcoming to reveal how hollow all her efforts had been.

Her aunt's shrill prattle rose and fell, scratching ineffectually against Edie's mind. She forced herself to tune in. ". . . there? Edith? Answer me! Are you still on the line?"

"I'm here," she gasped out.

"Come home." Her aunt's voice cracked. "Ronnie needs you."

"I'll be there as soon as I can," Edie replied. "Give me Ronnie."

Her aunt hesitated. "I don't think that's a good idea," she said. "You can talk to Ronnie when I can supervise you. And I'll call Dr. Katz, of course. Ronnie's very fragile, and it's not a good idea for you to—"

"Goddamn it, let me talk to my sister!"

Evelyn gasped. "Edith! How could you! At a time like this!"

Edie bit down on her frustration. The more she let them goad her, the more justified they felt in dismissing her as flaky and unbalanced. The important thing now was to get close to Ronnie, and hang on to her. Like superglue. She modulated her shaking voice. "Sorry, Aunt Evelyn. I'm just terribly upset. I'll be there as soon as I can. I have to go now."

"Edith! Wait! Where are—"

She hung up, passed the phone to Bruno, and lurched away just in time, or she would have lost her lunch in his lap. Everything she'd eaten that day came up. The heaves went on long after anything was left in there. Just dangling threads of bitter snot mixed with tears.

Bruno was waiting, his hand on her shaking shoulders, when she finally dared to stand up. He handed her a tissue. She mopped her face, let him lead her away from the mess. She no longer felt the icy wind. She felt . . . nothing. It was retreating. Miles away. In another universe.

She dragged herself together, forced her voice to function. "My father was murdered this morning," she told him.

It felt like someone else was saying the words. Her body was a numb puppet, quacking nonsense into the wailing wind. The words had no meaning, no weight. She couldn't get her mind around them.

Not her father. He was such a presence in her life. Such a mountain, a rock, a powerhouse. If he was gone, there was nothing left to fight against, define herself against. She felt disoriented, adrift.

In spite of Dad's relentless coldness, the world without him was unthinkable. She swayed, and Bruno clutched her elbow, as if she might fall. Swoon away like a southern belle with the vapors.

"I'll try Kev, one last time," Bruno said. "He should know about this." He dialed, waited, shook his head. "Let's go on down."

The walk down the mountain was an exercise in mute endurance. Her legs were numb, her knees jellyish. She kept falling.

When they got to the cabin, she went straight toward Bruno's car. "Let's go. Take me back to Portland. I need to go to my sister."

Bruno looked hunted. "I promised Kev that I—"

"I don't give a shit who promised what to who," she said.

"Those promises were all made before my father got shot to death."

"I understand completely, but you're in danger," Bruno protested. "Let me get in touch with Kev first and run it by him before I—"

"It's his own goddamn fault he didn't answer his phone." She was being unfair, but she did not care. She held out her hand. "Give me the car keys."

Bruno's mouth hardened. "I can't do that, Edie."

Well, there it was. The moment of truth. She'd been working up to this the whole way down from the bluff. Trying to find the nerve.

She was done with being controlled, policed. She would not permit it. From anyone. Not from Kev, not from anyone Kev designated.

She leaned down, pulled the Ruger out of the ankle holster, and straightened, locking her wobbling knees. She trained the gun on him.

"Throw me the car keys, or I will shoot you," she said.

Bruno looked somber. "No, Edie."

She swayed, brandished the gun. "Don't try to talk me down. I am not crazy. I am not an idiot child. I am dead serious."

"I know." His voice was low and gentle. "But you're not a killer."

"I can learn," she warned him. "Don't push me."

Bruno took a step closer. Another. She made a show of aiming, but she couldn't pull the trigger. Not even when he reached out, and clasped her hands, swinging the barrel around so it pointed into the forest. Loosening her white-knuckled grip gently with his fingers.

He clicked the safety back on. "Don't do that again, Edie," he said quietly. "Not unless you're willing to follow through."

"Fuck you." Tears blinded her eyes. She felt like such an idiot.

He turned the gun in his hands. "I know how you feel."

She let out a shaky bark of laughter. "How do you figure?"

"My mamma was murdered," he said, his voice flat. "The guy she was shacked up with was a woman-hating psychopath. And a mafioso thug. He beat her to death. I was twelve."

Oh, God. She shoved that information away from herself. She could not take it in. It was too much. "I'm sorry," she said woodenly.

"I'm not looking for sympathy," Bruno said. "I just want you to know. That I know. For what it's worth. That's all."

She squeezed her eyes shut, and nodded. "Thanks."

Bruno crouched, hiked up her mud-soaked jeans, and slid the revolver into the holster. "Kev's going to pound me into hamburger."

"For what?" she asked.

He yanked out the car keys, rattled them. "For taking you home."

CHAPTER
27

*K*ev *was running through a tunnel in the dark. Stumbling, slamming into dead ends, feeling his way. Trying to reach something, but he couldn't remember what. He had to hurry, but he couldn't remember why. Fear, teeth-grinding frustration. A rock sitting on top of his mind, blanking out everything in its blind spot. Crushing him.*

Splash. Cold water slapped his face. He gasped, tried to open his eyes. Light pierced, burned. Hurt. He closed them again.

Slap, slap. Someone was hitting his face. He was disoriented. All he felt was pain. Every muscle was locked in a state of unbearable tension. He could barely breathe, his lungs were so tight. Every breath was like lifting a ton of crushed rock with his chest. Eyelids, too. So heavy.

He forced them open, blinked. Eyes stung, burned. A woman's face swam into his vision, along with sparkles, halos, colored lights.

No sound. His ears hadn't come back from never-never land yet.

It was the chick from before. Cheung. She'd changed her clothes. Was wearing tight jeans and a T-shirt. Hair down.

Shiny, blue black. The black widow spider who stung him. The hellbitch neuroscientist.

She was talking, her tilted eyes sparkling with glee. He couldn't hear her. He tried to shake his head, let her know that the audio was off. Couldn't. Whatever she'd pumped into him had paralyzed him. Semi-voluntary systems barely functioning. He'd smother if his strength ran out. Or if he no longer cared to fight for breath.

Smack, smack. She hit him again, with evident enjoyment.

"Wake up, you lazy slob." Her voice roared suddenly, volume turned up horribly loud. Sonar shock almost made his head explode.

"You should be able to talk by now," she said. "I wanted a chat before I play with my new toy. I like when they know exactly what's happening. The inner resistance gives me a bit more traction."

He formed the word carefully with stiff, trembling lips. "Wh-who?"

She tittered. "Who what? Who are you? Nobody, now. My new toy. Do you mean, who am I?" She smiled. "I am exactly who I said I was. I had no reason to lie to you, honey. You'll never tell. I am Dr. Ava Elaine Cheung, to the rest of the world. But to you, I am God. Get used to it."

He squinted at her. "Os . . . ter . . . man?"

Her eyes glittered. "Oh, yes! Dr. O! Your old friend, right?" She patted the scars on his face. "He really left his mark, hmm? Upon me, too, I have to admit. He was my mentor, my guru. Taught me everything I know. I miss him, you know. Since your brother murdered him."

Brother? Kev's mind choked on that. His first thought was of Bruno, but that didn't fit, didn't compute.

Then the blinding realization racked him, like an electrical shock. Too thrilling to be fear, too painful to be joy. "B-b-brother?"

Cheung's eyes widened with mock surprise. "Oh, my. I

almost forgot. You don't know, do you? It's the amnesia! Oh, that's so funny." She leaned closer. "To think that I know all about your former self," she crooned into his ear. "Your family. Your history. And you know nothing. How awful, for someone else to have that information . . . and withhold it. Out of pure spite." She giggled, tapping his lip.

He dragged a breath, and formed the word very carefully. "Name?"

She waggled her finger. "Ah, ah, ah! The dancing bear doesn't get his treat until he's performed his tricks." She leaned close, kissed him wetly. Her tongue thrust deep into his numb mouth.

She was blocking what little air he was managing to get. When she finally leaned back, panting with excitement, he sucked in air, wishing he had enough saliva in his mouth to spit out the strange, bittersweet taste of her. He formed the words more easily now. Motor control was coming back. "Do that again, and I will bite off your lip and spit it on the floor."

Her eyes tightened to glittering slits, as she raised her hand. *Smack.* Fireworks exploded behind his eyes. "Wrong thing to say. You'll pay."

"I'm used to that," he said.

She crossed her arms below her tits, shoving them higher. "Your precious Edie will pay, too." Her voice was a mocking singsong.

Edie? Terror clawed at his guts. His fists were clenching, now that he was starting to feel them again. Where the fuck was he?

His head could just barely turn. He took in his surroundings. The room was bright, white, like a doctor's examining room. Crowded with electronic equipment, bottles, vials. A table with several syringes was close by him. A pile of plasticuffs. A set of shears.

He was suspended from something, couldn't bend his neck far enough to see what. Hanging by a set of plasticuffs.

His hands were cold, numb, but quasi-functional. A short foam-and-plastic-covered bench was under his ass, which took some of the pressure off his wrists. There was a plastic band across his throat. It cut into his voice box whenever he swallowed. He couldn't move his legs, or even feel them, but his balls throbbed, hard. A deep, sickening ache.

She sensed the second that he registered that pain, and reached down to grip his crotch. All he could see as he stared at her perfect smiling face was the grinning skull beneath. A death's head.

"You have me to thank for the fact that your testicles aren't a thin pink soup inside your scrotum," she told him. "Ken was going to crush them. I stopped him, just in time." She waited, as if expecting him to express gratitude. He said nothing. She squeezed his balls until he gasped. "I want you intact, for our games. When we have Edie. Mmm."

He shoved that image away, negated it. "You won't get Edie."

"Oh, certainly I will," she said. "She's on her way home right now, as we speak, to the bosom of her family. Des told me. He was there when she called them. Edie's little sister was sobbing on his shoulder."

He hung there, air frozen in his lungs, staring at her triumphant smile. "What does Marr have to do with this?"

"Everything," she said. "He's my partner. My lover. Des is offering emotional support to the bereaved Parrish family right now, in their time of shock and grief. Oh, wait! You didn't know, did you? How silly of me! You were asleep for that part! Charles Parrish is dead. Foully murdered. Poor Edie is now an orphan." She clicked her tongue. "Sad."

He tried to breathe, to fight the sickening waves of fear. "Dead? How? Who . . . who—"

"Who killed him? Oh, it's an incredible story. It starts eighteen years ago. This mysterious amnesiac with a grudge, one of Osterman's victims. He fixated on the CEO of Helix as the author of his woes, and boom." She mimed shooting a rifle, and shook her head sadly. "It's tragic," she mused. "I mean, who is really to blame, here? That poor man never got any help. The system failed him, and everyone else, in a tragic chain reaction. A sort of modern Hamlet. Everybody dies." She giggled. "Or will die, by the time we're through with you all."

Kev shook his head. "You can't pin that on me."

"He kidnapped and raped Edie Parrish, too," she went on. "He brainwashed her, sequestered her, and then he set himself up in a construction site, and waited for his chance to take Parrish out with a sniper rifle. And today, he succeeded. Thank God poor Edie was spared. Who knows what sick, twisted stuff was happening in the poor guy's brain. It makes one just shiver to think of it, doesn't it?"

"You won't get Edie," he repeated, desperately. "She's gone."

"We already have her," she taunted. "She's on her way home, to comfort her sister. When she gets there, Des will be there to greet her."

"No." Denying it made it no less true, but he couldn't stop bleating out the word, pushing that truth away from himself.

"Don't worry," she said. "Des will be gentle. He'll hold her while she cries. If she needs comfort, maybe he'll even fuck her. Lucky Edie."

That made his muscles tighten up with a jerk. He regretted his lack of control when her eyes lit up, thrilled to get a reaction.

"That wouldn't bother you?" he asked her, hoarsely.

"Oh, not at all." She petted his crotch again. "I give Des free rein. We have space in our relationship. Just as long as he brings her to me eventually. Like a dog, bringing a dead rabbit back to his master."

"Let her be," he said. "Forget about her. I'm the one you wanted, right? Nobody gives a shit if I disappear. She's a

Parrish. The whole world's looking at her. She'll be nothing but trouble for you guys."

"Oh, you're wrong, you're wrong. Oh, where do I even begin." Cheung waved her arms. "Edie's special. Like you. Like me. She'll be my missing link. We have something in common, you know. We can take an X-Cog slave interface more than once without dying of brain bleed. And it's my hypothesis that Edie can, too, based on her Haven test results and MRIs. I'd bet an exclusive X-Cog contract that she's got the stuff."

His soul shrank from the thought. "And . . . if you're wrong?"

She shrugged. "If I'm wrong, I'm wrong. She dies in twenty minutes, bleeding out her orifices, and so much for that fantasy."

"And they'll be after you to the ends of the earth."

"I'll cross that bridge when I come to it. If she works out, we'll control her completely. She'll do anything we want, and when we don't want to play anymore, she'll conveniently drive off a cliff, or swallow a bottle of bleach. Whatever tickles my funny bone."

Kev stuffed the fear into a small place in his mind, and fished everything she'd said out of his memory, looking for the sense, if there was any to be found. "Your missing link. Like you were for Osterman," he repeated slowly. "You said he left his mark on you, too. Were you one of those kids that he experimented on?"

"The only one who survived." Ava Cheung's face froze into a mask. "I am a distinguished, prizewinning neuroscientist. I publish in professional journals, I produce multimillion dollar patents. I am the reason Helix stock is sky-high. Everyone in my field knows of me."

And you mind-rape and murder people for fun. He thought it, but years in the kitchen with Tony Ranieri had taught him those moments when smart-ass sarcasm was not

called for. Hanging from the ceiling with your balls in somebody's fist was definitely one of those times.

"What did Osterman do to you?" he asked.

Ava Cheung's brow tilted up. "You want to know? You
can watch me do it to Edie. She'll be my obedient, docile
whore. And so will you."

Kev tried to listen to her with his body. To see past his
fear and revulsion, to catch a flash of the girl that she had
been before she'd been broken, twisted into something
barely human.

That girl was as lost to Cheung as his own boy self was
lost to him. Even more so, because he had protected himself.
He'd blocked that part, kept it safe. Safe even from himself,
ironic though that was.

This woman had been wide open. Gutted. She was dead
inside.

He looked into her eyes without wavering. "He hurt you,"
he said. "He used you. That was wrong."

"Don't pity me. Or I'll rip your entrails out before your
eyes."

"All right," he said quietly. "All pity withdrawn."

"I'm a million miles beyond that stupid shit," she told him.
"I'm a different order of human being. I've been forged in a
crucible."

He didn't respond. There was nothing to say that wouldn't
result in testicle squeezing, or a tooth-rattling slap.

The wild glow was fading from her eyes. What replaced it
was trapped, confused. Frantic. "How did you do it?" she
blurted. The words sounded like they were forced out under
tremendous pressure.

He stared into her eyes, feeling his way. "Do what?" he
asked.

"Get away from Dr. O, and Gordon. Nobody got away
from them, except for you. And your brother. Your goddamn,
fucking brother."

Gordon. The name conjured up nightmare flashes, rapid

and elusive, but horrible. A thick, reddened gloating face, pale blue eyes close to his own face. Helplessness, humiliation, terror. Pain, as the red-hot-tipped iron came closer, closer . . . and—

Oh, Jesus. He winced away from the harrowing inner scream echoing through his memory, and grasped on to another thought, the only one that could keep him afloat. "Tell me about my brother."

"Shut up! You're never going to see him! You'll never see anyone! Answer my questions! How did you do it? How did you break away?"

He considered his very limited options in that split second, and concluded that the truth couldn't hurt him. No more than lies could help. Though he could very well be wrong. "I don't know," he said.

She slapped him. Sweat stood out on her forehead. Her eyes were wide and staring. "You lying bastard! You prick! Tell me!"

"It's true. Those memories are blocked," he confessed. "I did something to myself to block them, but I don't know what it was. I blocked my own self out, too, in the process. I've never gotten back in."

"Did you break the dominance?" Her voice rose to a shriek.

"I don't know," he repeated quietly. "Swear to God."

She panted. "Don't do that. I am God, for you. I'm a jealous, vengeful God. I'm going to make you crawl and lick the bottoms of my feet." She socked him, splitting his lip. He licked it, tasting blood.

"I don't know," he repeated, having nothing else to say.

"Fine, then." The whites of her eyes showed all the way around. "We'll move on to the next item on my agenda. Maybe this will jog your memory." She held up a syringe. "New, improved X-Cog. You've already tried some, at the Parrish Foundation. I wanted to see how you took it, and I'm pleased at the results. Just a supplemental dose, nothing like what I gave Parrish today. His dose would have felled a bull elephant. Probably had hundreds of broken blood vessels. Good thing his brain was liquefied, or the autopsy would be a big puzzle for the coroner."

He stared at the syringe as if it were a venomous insect.

"You'll be amazed, how much more effective the drug is now," she said. "Dr. O worked hard all those years. It was X-Cog 2 or at most X-Cog 3, back in your day. This is X-Cog 19. There's a world of difference. I'll show you the trick you'll be performing today. Wait here."

As if he could wander away. He followed her as far as his head would turn, which wasn't far with that hard plastic band cutting across his throat. A few minutes later, she reappeared, pushing a wheelchair.

A girl was in it, her hands plasticuffed to the arm rests, her ankles to the footrests. Gagged. Young, no more than eighteen. She wore a gray sports bra and shorts on her slender, curvy body. Her face would have been beautiful if it had not been distorted by terror.

The sick feeling of creeping horror intensified. Whatever she had in mind for him and that girl, it was sure to be bad. There was no end to how bad it could be. He knew about bottomless pits. He lived in one.

"Kev, meet Yuliyah. Fresh out of Latvia. She's a musician. Plays the oboe. I have her audition CD in my car. I listen to it every day. A Mozart concerto. Stunning. She is going to be your new little friend."

Kev stared at the girl. She stared back, eyes wild.

He wondered if he could consciously trigger the oubliette. He never had before, but Jesus. He had to find a way, if Cheung tried to make him hurt that girl. "What the fuck are you doing with her?"

"Oh, nothing terrible," Cheung soothed. "We have big plans for Yuliyah. She's destined for the next X-Cog slave interface the next time my client needs a big job done. We finally got a reliable supply line of subjects, but every single one of my girls is spoken for. I certainly don't intend for you to hurt Yuliyah, or even leave a single bruise on her. I just want you to, ah . . ." She winked. "You know."

Fear clutched nastily at his guts. "You can't make me do that!"

"Oh, no?" Cheung's smile thinned. "I can make you do absolutely anything. I don't have a lot of experience in crowning men into sex, but it sounds like fun. And I love a challenge. Don't worry, if you're shy. I made arrangements for no one to disturb us."

"It won't work," he told her. "You can't regulate my blood flow, or hormones. You can't control my glands with that shit. And violence and rape are a huge, dick-wilting turn-off for me. Don't waste your time."

"So you think being a man protects you from sexual compulsion? Typical male arrogance. The connection between master and slave crowns is more complex now than it was in your day. There's more give and take, more exchange. And violence may not turn you on, but it sure does it for me." She giggled. "My heart is racing, already. I'm breathless and hot. And once I put that crown on you . . . you will be, too."

Yuliyah writhed against her bonds. Kev closed his eyes. He had to block Cheung out. He had no idea how he'd done it with Osterman. All he knew was the price that he'd paid for it. For eighteen fucking years.

"You know, I picked Yuliyah out of my stable on purpose, just for you," Cheung said. "She looks kind of like Edie, don't you think? I thought that might make it, you know. More exciting, for you."

His guts churned. He had to stall her somehow, keep her talking, preening, gloating. "A stable? How many girls are you holding?"

"I just got a delivery last night," she confided. "I was so excited. I have six, counting Yuliyah. All talented, all beautiful. They're already booked up, though. Lots of jobs to do. I have ten more on order."

Six now. Ten more to come. Jesus wept. "You're like Exhibit A in Criminal Psych 101," he said. "Dr. O tore you to pieces, didn't he?"

She giggled. "It's like Dr. O used to say about research ethics. If you want to make an omelet, you have to break some eggs. The bummer is if you happen to be the egg, right? Right?" Her giggle got higher, shakier. She couldn't make herself stop.

She slapped him again. The sharp *smack* cut off her own hysteria, **and** she swayed, mouth dangling open, panting. "Everybody takes their turn to crawl," she said hoarsely. "You're turn's up." She came up close to him, and whispered into his ear. "And if you're good at your interface . . . if you're very good at fucking Yuliyah . . . if you·make me come in my pants . . . I might even tell you your real name. Think about that."

She stabbed the needle into his arm. He gasped, arching.

The effect was immediate. Like a wasp's sting. The monstrous mother of all wasps. A rictus of cramping, agonizing pain.

His face was locked into a staring grimace. His teeth ground. His tendons stood out. He felt blood pulsing in his temples, pressure in his eyes increasing. As if he were screaming inside, but no sound came out.

Ava Cheung lifted up a silver mesh cap, set it on his head, and leaned close to set the little dangling sensors at various points over his scalp. The contact points had adhesive on them. She put a set of goggles on his eyes. She set a similar device on her own head, placing the sensors on herself without taking her eyes off him. She put a pair of goggles on, and grinned. "Now we'll see who's the victim, Kev. Now we'll see who's in control." She dragged in a deep breath. Her lips peeled back, her eyes closed. He was reminded of a mummified corpse.

She slammed into him. Oh *Christ*. Like being hit by a truck.

He fought, instinctively, as he felt her trying to make him move. But he soon realized that she couldn't. That connection was severed. His will to move was located someplace else, a place she could not reach. Of course, he couldn't reach it either. So what else was new.

He could feel her, flailing around in his brain. It hurt, but she couldn't get a grip on him. The block still held. *Yes.*

The emergency rewiring he'd done eighteen years ago still worked. Thanks and praise to the great Whoever. She could cut him into pieces, but she could not make him rape that girl. Pressure built, but that armored part of his brain was like a nut she could not crack.

She stepped back, eyes bulging with rage. "You son of a bitch," she spat. She grabbed another hypodermic from the table. Held it in front of his eyes, let him see the drop of liquid ooze out and shimmer on the tip of the needle. "Big, strong boy, huh? I guess you need more help than I thought. Let's see how a double dose affects you." *Stab.*

Another wasp sting. Incredible, that it could actually get worse. He hung there, rigid, enduring it. The realization formed, oddly calm. This shit would kill him. When the pressure got high enough, pop.

His only chance was the oubliette, but he'd always gone into it involuntarily. He'd never actually tried to get in.

Now was the time to figure out a way.

Of course, he might never come out. He might stay there in the dark until he wasted away, body atrophying, muscles and tendons shortening into the fetal position. Horribly conscious, waiting for death. Which would be long and slow in coming.

No good option. So be it.

He didn't know how he'd gotten into the oubliette, but he knew how he had gotten out. His little angel. Maybe she could lead him back in, too. So hard to concentrate, to still his mind, with Ava crashing around in there like a maddened bull. He called up Edie's image, her shining eyes full of

light. He let it fill his conciousness, and the violence retreated into the background. Ava could flail around however
she wished, in a room that was now empty. He took his
leave, floated away.

Edie took form before him. She stood in the dark rocky
tunnel that he knew very well, and beckoned to him. She
glowed like a pearl.

He followed her into the darkness, letting her shining
form lead him through the labyrinth. Ava pounded away, behind him. He no longer cared. He followed his love. Trusting
her without question.

She lit up the tunnel with her inner light. She was his sun.
He had no idea how far they went into the twisting darkness,
but it was far.

And then, the door. Like something out of a medieval
castle. Massive, made of heavy dark iron. Fastened with
huge square bolts the size of a man's head. Fortified, spiked,
speared, armored.

A key appeared in Edie's pale, slender hand. It gleamed
in the light that came from her lambent form. She put it in the
lock, turned it.

The door opened inward. She stepped back, beckoned
him in. Inside was only darkness. Her eyes were so sad.

Grief clutched him. He was afraid to go in alone. He
asked with his eyes if she could follow him in. She shook her
head. *No.*

Do the hard thing. He steeled himself, walked past her,
through the door and into the darkness. The door began to
creak shut. Soon would come the hollow *boom*, locking him
in the dark.

He turned to look back, though he knew he shouldn't,
that it would only weaken him, torture him. And saw it, transfixed with horror.

The enormous black widow spider stood behind Edie in
the tunnel. Her huge gleaming black abdomen reflected back

Edie's light, distorting it. The fluttering shreds of its web clogged the rocky tunnel.

The way back was blocked. There was no way out for Edie.

Her eyes met his. Dark liquid dripped down her face from her eyes. A medieval madonna, weeping blood. The result of an X-Cog slave crown. She knew there was no escape from this trap. She was doomed.

Her eyes said good bye. The doors slammed shut. *Crash.* Dark.

Horror exploded inside him with the sound. Guilt, for dragging her into this, for not protecting her better. Terror and denial and fury.

He'd fucked up. The hard thing was the wrong thing. The worst fucking thing he'd ever done. Holing up in here to cower like a trembling mouse in a burrow, while Edie was in danger. What craven bullshit.

This was worse than death. He'd thought only of himself, leaning on her, counting on her to lead him through his darkness like the ferryman of the River Styx. Using her, when he should be saving her.

Those monsters would eat her alive.

He couldn't stay in here. At the cost of blowing every last fucking capillary in his brain into mush, he had to get out of here. Right *now*.

The charge built inside him, and he stoked it, threw everything he had into it. All the nameless horror that he'd blocked from his mind, but not his body, or his heart. All the yearning and the loneliness, the mad frustration, those years of mute confusion. The towering rage.

The energy rose, like the gas pressure in a volcano about to blow a mountain miles into the air. Building, swelling—

Boom. The force of the blast knocked him out.

When his eyes opened, the pressure of the plastic band across his throat was throttling him. He was drowning. It

took a minute to realize that it was blood, streaming from his
nose down into his throat, clogging the air. Ava was on the
floor. She, too, had a nosebleed. She pushed herself up into a
sitting position, touching her head. Dazed.

Something was different. Night and day different. He was
still locked in the jaws of cramping pain, but his mind . . . it
was as light as a balloon. Like a huge rock had been lifted
from it. The blind spot.

It was . . . gone. *Gone.* Oh, Jesus.

Images began trickling into that numb space. He saw Osterman, crowning him. Osterman, trying to force him to tell
him something. But X-Cog compulsion was essentially useless for the purposes of extracting information, so Osterman
had given him to Gordon to play with.

Gordon. Oh, Jesus. He remembered Gordon's torture
now, and he wished he didn't. The burning, the cutting, the
gloating. It floated back, chunk by chunk. Fragments of a
screaming, bloody, endless nightmare.

Gordon hadn't expected him to fight back, that last day.
Gordon thought that he was played out. He'd told Kev that
was the day they'd finish him. Put out his eyes, cut off his
ears, cut off his tongue, his hands, his feet, his balls, his
dick. If he didn't tell them where Liv was.

Liv. Liv? Who was . . . he struggled, groped for it. Liv . . .
Endicott.

Oh, God. *Liv.* Yes. He saw her, in his mind's eye, outside
the library, her gray eyes full of fear. He remembered telling
her to take the notebook to Sean, and to get out of town before they—

Sean? Who the fuck was . . . *Sean?*

His brother. His twin brother.

Images unfolded, full color, full feeling. Sean. Davy.
Con. Dad. The house, the mountains. The Midnight Project.
His life. His self.

Tears streamed down, mingling with blood. One memory
triggered a hundred more, crashing down on him. An

avalanche of memories, feelings. The formless longing he'd curled around, tried to ignore for years, it finally had a name. It was for them. Brothers. Family.

He'd found a burst of strength that day, in Osterman's lair. A lucky nerve pinch put Gordon down long enough to run, hotwire a car. He'd driven to Flaxon, God knows how, to blow the whistle on the Midnight Project. Bad call, choosing Parrish, the Flaxon rep. He should have gone to the cops. To anyone but Parrish. He hadn't been thinking clearly.

They'd put him down. And Gordon came, to retrieve him.

Osterman had been furious. He'd tried to compel Kev to mutilate himself in punishment. In his desperation, Kev had done . . . something to his own brain. He'd triggered the block. Hidden in the oubliette.

That was all he could remember, but the rest was easy to reconstruct. Osterman got bored with an unresponsive chunk of meat. He sent Gordon off to dispose of him. Tony found him. And that was it.

Ava was slapping again, had been for a while, but he was too overwhelmed by memories to notice. She swayed, blood streaming from her nose. ". . . do that to me? You *bastard!* You *hurt* me!" *Whack.*

He flinched, blinked. Tossed in a heaving ocean of feelings, memories. He couldn't process them all. Half a life had been more than enough weight for his brain, his heart, to bear up under.

"Don't do that again!" She wagged her finger at him, and he would have laughed, if he could. As if he chose this crazy shit. He was driven by a herd of buffalo, all running off a sheer cliff. Story of his life.

Cheung slammed that truck into his brain again . . . oh, *fuck* . . .

It was all different now. He was naked in there now. He'd blown his protective mechanism all to shit. And now she had him. Her claws sank deep, into nerves, will. She made him move, jerking against his restraints. The harder he fought, the greater her control. She grinned, gleefully. Her teeth were blood streaked.

"That's better," she panted. "Now we're talking."

He couldn't fight. He was a shambles, and she was loving it. Touching him from within, moving him, making the muscles in his groin clench and tighten against his will, as if he were aroused.

And he was. It was true. She really could make him hard, and he hated himself for it. His heart raced, his dick tingled and throbbed.

She reached down to pet it, well pleased. "Ready now, Kev?" she taunted. "Yuliyah is waiting." She petted his penis, her hand lingering, squeezing. "Nice. I see why Edie's so taken with you."

Mentioning Edie stung him, sharpened him. Rage stabbed deep, dragging him into focus. His passive defense was no longer operational. She'd backed him into a corner. All that was left was offense.

That heinous bitch was going down.

He held Edie's image in his mind, in case it was the last thing he ever thought of. Her shining body like a candle flame.

And stopped all resistance.

Cheung faltered at the sudden lack of purchase as he sagged in her mind, the mental equivalent of dead weight, and in that instant of disorientation, he leaped at her.

Ava flinched. She'd never been challenged by a slave-crowned subject. He followed up, drove her backward into her own self. No idea what the fuck he was doing, or how. Just clawing onward.

Her eyes bugged out. He was inside. Controlling her. The contact felt hideous, unclean, and horribly easy, too. She'd been groomed for years by Osterman for submission to mental dominance.

He felt echos of what she felt. Her self-loathing, which

was so normal, so everyday, she no longer even perceived it. The distortion of the world seen through her mind; full of spite and danger. Stinking with corruption. Everything ugly, hated, despised, mistrusted.

It was like having his head in a vise. He forced her to move her arms, her legs. She was toppling. He forced her to catch herself.

There was a pair of clippers on the table next to the syringes. He forced Ava to stumble, stiff legged, to the table. To pick up the clippers.

She dropped them. He made her pick them up.

It took eight tries. Finally, she got a grip, lurched toward him. Her eyes darted crazily. Her mouth hung open, bloody mucus hanging off her slack lips.

First, the throat band, or he'd hang himself. He compelled her to lift the clippers to the plastic that bound his throat. He missed. Tried again. Missed again. Overshooting. Then he almost made her stab him in the throat. Narrow miss. Wouldn't that just be as ironic as all hell.

Got it. He forced the muscles in her hands to contract. *Snip.* His head sagged forward, limp, but he could swallow again, and gasp in air.

Then the hands. He had to do it blind, because his head was hanging down on his chest, but he finally got the blades around the plastic cuffs that held one of his hands. Squeeze. *Snip.*

One hand flopped down like dead meat, swinging uselessly. He wished he could jerk the clippers out of her hand and snip the last cuff himself, but Ava's arms were the only ones around here that worked.

Another long struggle, and *Snip,* his second hand fell free.

He fell, crashing full length, rigid as a toppling fir tree. He hit, bounced, teeth jarring, helpless and stiff, muscles rigid. He could see Ava out of the corner of his eye. Table.

Syringes. With his last bit of strength, he forced her to pick up the syringe. Her hand. So clumsy, so numb. They fumbled, struggled, to get the device into position.

He/she stabbed it down into her thigh. Shoved in the plunger with her thumb. He could feel the echoes of the icy cold burn through her. Screaming despair, tearing her mind apart.

He stayed conscious, until he felt her fall, right on top of him.

Darkness closed in around a shrinking fading circle of light, until it was a shining pinprick—and then it winked out altogether.

CHAPTER
28

"You sure about this?" Bruno braked outside the wrought iron gate that marked the entrance to the luxurious Parrish home in Beaverton. He looked uncomfortable. "I'm not. I think this sucks."

"Completely sure," she assured him. "I have to go to my sister."

"You're aware of what this will cost me, right? Kev will redesign my skeleton. I'll be short a head, or missing a couple of limbs the next time you see me. And I loved being bilaterally symmetrical."

She appreciated his attempt to lighten the moment, but any laughter would tip her down that slippery slope into a hysterical fit. "Don't make me laugh, or I'll freak. I can't cry in front of these people."

Bruno looked puzzled. "But aren't they family?"

She thought of the embarrassment that had always greeted any displays of emotion in her family. The pills she'd taken over the years, to medicate those embarrassing feelings away.

"No," she said quietly. "I can't. It's complicated."

A tall, uniformed black man came to the driver's side of

the car. Robert Fraser. She liked him better than any of the others on her father's security staff. He was always courteous to her, in spite of the example set by both his boss and his direct supervisor.

Robert murmured into his walkie-talkie. Bruno rolled his window down. Robert peered in at her. "Miss Parrish? You all right?"

"As far as I can be, under the circumstances," she replied.

"I'm sorry about your loss," Robert said.

She nodded. "Thank you."

Robert scrutinized Bruno. "Who is this person?"

"He's a friend of mine," she replied. "He gave me a ride home."

"My name's Bruno Ranieri," Bruno supplied. "I'm going to put my hand into my coat pocket to get my wallet and show you my ID, OK? So don't get all twitchy and shoot me with that SIG of yours."

"Do it slowly," Robert said.

Bruno plucked a wallet out of his pocket. He flipped it open to the license. Robert studied it. "Wait here," he said.

He muttered into his walkie-talkie, walked to the front of the car, studied the plates, recited them.

Oh, for God's sake. Edie leaned out the window. "Robert, can't he just take me up the drive?"

"He can't go into the house without a body search and a background check," Robert said.

"He's not staying," she said. "He won't come inside."

"I'd be terrified to," Bruno commented dryly.

"Really, it's OK," she urged Robert. "He's a friend. He's safe."

Another muttered exchange, and finally Robert nodded. The gate began to grind open. Robert leaned to the window and met Bruno's eyes. "Do not get out of your car," he said.

Bruno drove through. "It's like visiting a maximum security prison," he said. "Where's the razor wire and the control towers?"

In my mind. She cut the words off. They were only true if she let them be true. She stared at the house as it came into view, chilled by it. It had never been home, like the rambling Victorian in Tacoma where she'd grown up, near Helix's previous headquarters. She'd never bonded with the modern, glassy house her parents had chosen. It seemed cold, lacking in a human dimension.

Maybe that was why her parents had liked it so much.

Guilt stabbed deep, for thinking spiteful, unworthy thoughts at such a time. A suite had been designated as hers, though she'd never slept in it. Her bathroom alone in this house was larger than her entire Flanders Street apartment.

And yet, she felt so cramped here, she could hardly breathe.

Bruno braked when two members of the security personnel stepped out into the road. His brow creased with worry. "You have my number, right? Call me if you have problems."

Right. What had she ever had but problems with these people? She forced a smile. "Don't worry. Tell Kev I'll be in touch." Which was an understatement. She was going to have some choice words for Kev Larsen, when he finally crawled out of the woodwork. For not telling her and Bruno he was OK. If he *was* OK. She pushed that thought away, and waved at Bruno as he swung the car around the circle that bounded the big cluster of exotic ornamental shrubs.

He drove away, disappearing around the driveway's curve. She turned to face the house, and whatever she might find there.

Tanya was in the dark, mahogany paneled foyer. Her face looked gray, her eyes pink. Genuine grief sliced through Edie's numbness. Her throat seized up. She hurried towards Tanya, arms out.

Tanya stepped back, chin jerking up. *Don't touch.*

Edie let her arms drop, breathing down the sting. So there was to be no coming together in grief, then. Her father had mandated her status as in the doghouse, and that status would endure.

Not important. She was here for her sister. Not comfort, support, or acceptance. The rest of them could go to hell. "Where's Ronnie?" The voice coming out of her was so cool. Remote-controlled robot girl.

"In the solarium. Nice, that you finally decided to show up."

That didn't even penetrate. Edie walked past her cousin, and toward the solarium, the only room of the house that she liked. It was faced with warm, rosy cedar, and had banks of high windows that let light stream in over plush beige couches, cream wool rugs. Outside was one of the two huge, magnificent spreading oaks that adorned the sloping lawn, carefully pruned to let light into the huge windows.

Ronnie was slumped on a couch, head limp against the cushions. Aunt Evelyn's head turned as Edie walked in. Ronnie's did not.

Edie immediately understood why not, when Dr. Katz stood up. Her belly clenched with instinctive dislike. He'd drugged Ronnie.

The man seemed harmless, with his round face, graying hair, round glasses, impeccable credentials. But he loved to medicate. He was always ready with pills, so that the powerful people that paid him would not be bothered by unpleasantness, like tears, anxiety attacks, depression, psychic episodes, bad grades. Dr. Katz had the solution always ready in his hand. She hated his guts. "How is she?" she asked.

Evelyn's mouth flattened at Edie's hard tone. "She's resting. She couldn't stop crying."

"I gave her something to help her rest," Dr. Katz added.

"Of course you did." Edie walked around to the front of the couch and knelt. Ronnie's tearstained face was pressed against the cushions, her mouth squashed open. She grabbed Ronnie's hands, squeezed.

"Baby?" she whispered. "Are you still awake? I'm here."

But Ronnie was out. Edie stared at her sister, fighting her anger.

"She kept asking for you," Aunt Evelyn said.

"I told you I was coming," Edie replied. "You could have waited."

"You could have hurried," Evelyn countered.

"Before letting him bash her over the head with his pharmaceutical baseball bat?"

Evelyn gasped. "Edith!"

"It's all right, Evelyn," Dr. Katz soothed. "It's normal for her to feel this way. In fact, I expected her to react with hostility. Anger is an integral part of the grieving process. It shouldn't be suppressed, or—"

"Shut up." Edie chafed Ronnie's cold, clammy hands in her own. "I don't need to hear it. Not from you."

"Edie, you're shocked and grieving," Dr. Katz said. "I'm here for you, any time you need to vent. Or cry. Don't be afraid to let it out."

"Yeah. Right," she muttered. *Fuck you, too.* She stiffened when he laid his hand on her shoulder.

"Relax," he soothed. "Let me give you something for the—"

"If you want to keep that hand, get it off my shoulder." Edie's voice was not loud, but something in it made the room go very silent.

Dr. Katz lifted his hand away, very slowly. "Ah. There's, er, no need for that kind of language."

"Edith!" Evelyn's voice cracked with horror. "What's gotten into you?"

"Nothing," she said. "I just no longer give a shit what anyone thinks. I'm here for Ronnie. How long will the junk you gave her last?"

Dr. Katz's chest puffed. "It's hardly junk! Just a mild sedative that will help her to—"

"Just answer my question."

"An hour and a half to two hours," he said, tightly.

Edie headed toward the door.

"Where do you think you're going?" Evelyn demanded.

"I don't know," she said. "To the kitchen, for a glass of water. To the bathroom to pee. I'm improvising, here. Leave me the hell alone."

She slammed the door behind her on their indignant muttering, and set off, wandering at random until she stopped in front of a family photograph her mother had commissioned many years before.

It was an old-fashioned composition; her father in a chair in the front, as hawk-nosed and patrician as a founding father from an old daguerrotype. Her mother stood at his side with the adorable little baby Ronnie in her arms, looking beautiful and perfect in her pink twin set and pearls, dark hair gleaming in a perfect bob. And Edie, curled up at her father's feet, looking like she wanted to disappear no matter how the photographer had posed her. That had been two years after the Haven. Back when she was horribly convinced that she was going crazy.

The photo had been one of her mother's desperate attempts to sculpt the outward appearance of a perfect family. Often she'd thought that her mother's decision to have another baby was an attempt to, well, just try again, from the top. With fresh materials. Not that it made her love Ronnie any less.

Her younger face in the photo looked pinched, big eyes haunted.

She'd come a long way since the bad old days, she thought. She was making real progress. Just look at her. Threatening Dr. Katz with dismemberment. That had to be a step in the right direction.

Another few steps took her to the door of her father's study, the scene of so many lectures, so many admonitions and ultimatums. All of them useless in the end. They couldn't change who their daughter was.

Nor should they have wanted to. She was fine. She liked herself the way she was. And Kev liked her, too.

Thinking of Kev sent a knee-weakening stab of fear through her. She breathed it down, pushed on the door of the study. Went in.

It was a dark room, wood paneling, leather furniture, teak desk and bookshelves, teak filing cabinets. She wondered at the heavy, nervous feeling, as if she might be caught, scolded, punished. But by who? The only person whose opinion mattered had died that day.

Somehow, his murder had to be related to what was happening to her, and what had happened to Kev. Osterman's lingering legacy.

So why not start looking? What else was she going to do with herself while Ronnie snored away a haze of sedatives? Chat with Aunt Edith? Play Parcheesi with Tanya? She might as well get off her ass.

The computer was on. Edie slid into Dad's leather upholstered desk chair. Some part of her expected at any moment for him to burst in on her, furious at her for invading his privacy.

She clicked on his daily appointment log, scrolling through it.

Wow. For a man who had been discharged from the ICU one day before, he hadn't cut himself much slack. He'd canceled the raquetball match at the health club with one of his colleagues, but that was his one concession. He was booked solid with meetings, from eight o'clock on. At ten-fifteen, he'd typed in DES.

Ten-fifteen? Wasn't that when Des was meeting Kev? And wasn't it . . .

Oh, God. That was right about when Dad had been killed.

That made it so horribly real. She shuddered, and leaned down onto the desk, trying not to see it in her mind's eye. But she had an excellent capacity to visualize.

Her eye fell on the dagger-shaped letter opener, the one

her mother had commissioned from Cartier, for her father's sixtieth birthday. It gleamed in the box. She picked it up, turned it over in her hand. Remembering. Fifty guests, and her parents watching her like a hawk lest she blurt out something shocking and wreck the party.

She pulled herself together, wiped her eyes, and kept poking. Nothing seemed interesting or significant in her father's e-mails of the last couple of weeks. Neither was anything else she clicked on in the desktop. She left the computer, and set to looking at the hard files in the cabinets behind. Helix stuff, Parrish Foundation stuff. Reams of it.

In the Parrish Foundation stuff, she found lots of correspondance generated by her mother. Linda Parrish's graceful, flowing signature made Edie's throat seize up. There was a sheaf of files dedicated to the Osterman scandal. Memos to the Board of Directors of the PF. Many hysterical iterations about the necessity of rigorous control measures in place for every penny of research money to prevent such a disgrace from happening again. All in the months leading up to her mother's death.

Edie's eyes stung as she read them. That was Mom, all over. So rigorous, so upright, so self-righteous. Both her parents had been so proud to be part of a charitable organization that helped the world to combat pain, disability, and disease. They had considered themselves the good guys, the white hats. Crusaders, on a holy quest.

Both of them had been horrified by the Osterman scandal. They had done everything they could to distance themselves from it, to safeguard the Parrish Foundation from future disgrace. Stiff necked as any wild-eyed religious zealot. It was their best quality. And their worst.

Then she found an unlabeled file just stuck into the drawer. It was a sheaf of memos, notes, scraps, business cards, thank-you cards, invitations to events, publicity materials, magazine subscriptions, printed out e-mails. All dated around the time of her mother's death.

Edie leafed through them. This was the result of her mother's secretary going through her boss's desk after the funeral, throwing everything she didn't know what to do with into a catch-all file. Her eye stuck on an e-mail from Des Marr. The text read:

> Linda,
> Last night, I read through your new protocols to increase scrutiny and accountability for PF's future research spending. Congratulations for being as tough as nails. It's exactly what this board needs. You're just the woman to shake them up.
> I want to drop by and discuss a couple of points before we go into the board meeting. Free at eleven? It'll only take a second. Des.

Edie looked up at the date of the e-mail again. A cold skeleton hand snaked around her vital organs . . . and squeezed.

It was the date of her mother's death.

Ah, come on. No need to get the willies. What was so strange about that? It had been a day like any other day for Linda Parrish. E-mails, protocols, meetings.

But her mother had collapsed at that board meeting. She'd been dead before she reached the hospital.

Edie realized that she was doodling on the the e-mail from Des. Covering it with tiny hearts. Like she'd done on the napkin, at the restaurant. With her mother, the last time she'd seen her.

Edie's little closet full of compulsions. Her mother's voice sounded in her head, so vivid, she felt as if she'd heard it with her waking ears.

"Ah! So you're home from your little sexual adventure? And now you're spying for him?"

Edie leaped up, her heart pounding. Marta was framed in the doorway. She was almost unrecognizable, with her hair down, no makeup on her face. Her eyes were red and hollow, but they still glittered with intense dislike.

Edie forced herself to slow her panicked breaths. "No," she said. "I have a right to be here, looking at anything I choose to look at."

"Do you? More than I do? Is that what you're saying?"

"You said it, not me." Edie gazed at the other woman. Marta's haggard face indicated that she might have cared more about Dad than Edie had given her credit for. But perhaps she was grieving the prospect of marrying a multi-billionaire. Those were scarce on the ground.

A thought flashed through her mind. "Marta, were you there that day at Helix in Tacoma, when Kev's brothers visited Dad?"

Marta's face tightened. "Yes, I was. I met the McClouds, and they were animals. They physically attacked your father, did you know that?"

"McClouds?" She was startled. "Was that their name?" So her father had known Kev's real name and background all along.

"God, Edie, is that all you care about? I said they attacked Charles! Physically! He had bruises! Aren't you listening to me?"

Edie thought about the marks that Kev carried on his body, and then quickly concluded that any comparison would be both irrelevant and offensive. "And they were asking about Kev?"

"That's putting it mildly," Marta muttered. "They wouldn't give up. They just could not accept the fact that they'd killed the only two people in the world who might have possibly given them the information that they wanted. It was their own goddamn fault, and they thought that we should clean up their mess? Idiots."

Edie was bewildered. "Killed . . . how? What two people?"

Marta made an impatient gesture. "Osterman, of course!

And Gordon, his . . . oh, I don't know what you'd call him. Osterman's wet-work man. The mess was kept as quiet as those McClouds would allow. They would have destroyed Helix completely, if they'd had their way."

Edie was at a loss. "But . . . but the fire in the lab . . . ?"

"It happened, but not before these McClouds slashed Osterman's throat and bashed in Gordon's skull," Marta said harshly. "That's the evolutionary level of people we were dealing with, understand?"

Edie sucked in a sharp breath. "Oh. Ah . . . wow."

"Yes, I told you. Wild animals. I still cannot believe that in this day and age, that an organization like Helix or a man like your father could be held hostage by violent thugs like those McClouds."

As if the McClouds had been the ones systematically killing runaway kids for decades. But Edie kept that comment to herself.

"And now, the worst animal of all has finally gotten his revenge. I guess it was just a matter of time," Marta said.

Edie stared at the other woman. "What do you mean? What revenge? They already know who killed Dad? Have they got the guy already?"

"Don't be disingenuous," Marta snapped. "Don't tell me you don't know. You were in on the whole plan. His little brainwashed errand girl and fuck buddy. You practically poisoned Charles to death at the banquet the other night, so don't pretend to be sad that your lover finished the job! You should be in jail! You disgust me! How dare you come here, and pretend that you didn't know what he was going to do?"

Edie's mouth opened and closed, helplessly. "I . . . he . . . but what do you . . . how can you even—"

"Marta." Des stepped into the office. He looked pale, weary. "I know that you're grieving, but this is not how I wanted to tell her."

"Tell me what?" Edie's voice cracked. "What are you talking about? If it's what I think it is, then don't bother. I don't want to hear your poisonous bullshit! I am done, hear me? I am done!"

Des and Marta looked at each other. Des beckoned. "Edie. We need to talk. And I need to show you a couple of things that are going to open your eyes."

"My eyes are wide open!" she yelled. "I am going to Ronnie now! Everyone else just shut up, and leave us alone! Go to hell!"

"We can't, Edie. Not yet." Des took her by the arm.

Edie jerked it violently away. "Do not touch me!"

"Edie." He sounded exhausted, and sad. "Let's get this over with."

Oh, whatever. She could go humor them, listen to their lies, and tell them to fuck off afterwards. When she knew exactly what she was dealing with. Whatever they said would not change reality. They could not change what Kev was. They could not destroy him with lies.

He was too strong, too real. Too pure.

She followed Des out of the room, her arms wrapped across her chest. Protecting her heart, and what she knew was true.

Something crackled in her hand. She was still clutching the crumpled printout of the e-mail that she'd taken from her mother's catch-all desk file. Another thought occurred to her.

"Des, what about this morning?" she asked. "Did you meet with Kev? Did you show him the archives? Did you guys find anything?"

Des's eyes slid away. "That's part of what we have to talk about."

"So? Talk, then!"

Des opened the door to the library. "There's someone you need to meet," he said.

A thin, graying woman in a severe navy blue suit sat at the table, scribbling on a legal pad. She stood up when they entered.

"Edie, meet Detective Monica Houghtaling, of the PPD. Detective, Edie Parrish."

Edie shook the detective's hand, accepted her murmured condolences, and stared at the chair that Des pulled out for her, as if sitting down in it would give them some obscure power over her.

"Des." Her voice felt high, thin. A cord about to snap. "What happened this morning? With the archives?"

"Nothing happened. With Larsen, anyway. He didn't show."

"Didn't show? What do you mean, he didn't show? He told us that he'd arrived. He said—"

"I waited at the meeting place for him for an hour. Then I had to leave, because I had an appointment, at ten-fifteen. With Charles."

"This morning? You were . . . there?" Her voice choked off.

Des passed his hand over his face. "Yes." His voice was gravely and thick. "I was there, Edie. When it happened. I saw it all. Me, and my colleague, Dr. Cheung. She's still in shock."

"But that's . . . but—"

"We'd just finished presenting a new project to him. Discussing funding possibilities. And then he lights up a cigar, and walks over to the window as he's talking to us . . . and . . ." He stopped, swallowed. Looked away. "I can't . . . talk about it."

The room was silent, but for Marta's hitching sniffle behind them.

"Edie, we have to talk about some hard things now," Des began.

"Don't start," Edie held up her hand. "Don't even start."

"We have to," Des said, heavily. "We don't have the luxury of denying reality. Detective, can I show her the film footage?"

Houghtaling pulled a slim silver laptop toward herself, and typed into it, her narrow mouth tight and grim. "This is security footage from outside the Parrish Foundation building this morning, at nine-nineteen A.M.," she said. She spun the laptop so that Edie could see it.

The image was stationary, just tree branches waving gently outside the door of the new Parrish Foundation building. For a few moments, nothing happened. Then, a tall, familiar form strolled into view. Kev. Edie stopped breathing.

Kev stopped, turned slowly in a circle, eyes narrowed as he studied his surroundings. Then he went on into the building.

"There's an eight minute gap," Des said. "May I?" he asked the detective. She nodded. Des fast-forwarded, and set it to play again.

Kev walked out of the building again, brisk and purposeful.

"There's a three minute gap." Des leaned to fast forward again. "Now, watch carefully here."

Kev appeared again, this time carrying two large, metal-sided suitcases. He shoved the door open with his shoulder, turning to sidle the cases inside. She saw his scarred face very clearly.

"Your father was killed one hour later," Des said. "From an unfinished suite on the eighth floor, one that faced your father's office suite across the grounds. This was the time it took for him to set up his gun, and wait for his moment."

Edie shook her head. "No. You've got this all wrong," she protested. "How could he have possibly known where Dad would be?"

"He knew, because I told him," Des said heavily. "I told Larsen he had to be on time, so I could make my meeting with Charles. At his office, at the Helix complex, at ten-fifteen. He knew exactly where Charles would be. And when." Des passed his hand over his face. "I told him," he repeated.

"I am going to have to live with that for the rest of my life." He dropped his face into his hands.

Marta made a choking sound, laid her hand on Des's shoulder.

Edie felt horribly cool, cut out of the sob fest.

Des lifted his head, grabbed her hand. She was too numb to shake it off. "Edie. I know this is terrible for you." His voice broke. "But I have to ask. Can you think of any place the police might be able to find him? Anyone they could question? Who was the man who brought you to the house, for instance? Was he one of Larsen's associates?"

She shook her head. "Just a friend."

She was doodling again. Without knowing it, she'd pulled the pen from her pocket, laid out the e-mail, and was scribbling frantically, as if the contact of pen to paper was a lifeline to her sanity. "I can't think of anything," she said, as she felt the eye open up. Her pen moved faster.

"Edie! Stop that!" Marta snapped. "You're acting like a child! Drawing your little comic book pictures at a time like this?"

Edie stopped, feeling vulnerable and exposed as she looked into the closed faces, the staring eyes of the people in the room.

Des reached out to hold her pen hand still. "Edie. Stop drawing, and concentrate. Consider this. If he's innocent, he has nothing to worry about. By helping the police find him, you clear his name that much faster. Fingerprints can't lie, Edie. And if he's guilty, then who are you protecting, Edie? And why?"

"Stop repeating my name," she said.

He blinked. "Huh? Excuse me?"

"I know they probably taught you in some people management seminar, that people like to hear the sound of their own name, but I just find the repetition incredibly annoying," she said.

Des's face hardened. "Edie, that's not very . . ." He stopped himself. "So. You can't help, then? You can't think of anything?"

She shook her head.

"I can't believe the staff just let the guy who brought her here go without questioning him," Des grumbled.

"We have his name and plate number," Houghtaling said.

"He has nothing to do with any of this!" Edie protested.

"I hope that you're right," Houghtaling said. "And that you won't end up charged with aiding and abetting. Accessory to murder. Think about that, please, while you see if you can remember anything else."

"Please, Detective, don't put it in those terms," Des pleaded. "She's fragile, and she's been through a harrowing experience."

That annoyed the piss out of her. Kev hadn't harrowed her. These days with Kev had been the best days of her entire life, bar none, until three hours ago, with that cell phone call on the bluff. "I am not fragile," she snapped, staring at the freeze frame of Kev's thoughtful frown, looking up. Her heart cramped with love for him. "Des," she said. "What do you mean he never showed up for the appointment?"

Des looked confused. "I mean what I said. He never showed."

"But here he is," Edie said. "Right here. On the video."

Des hesitated, blinking rapidly. "Oh! The Foundation building wasn't our appointment location. We were supposed to meet in a warehouse over at the Graystone Business Park, where the boxes are being stored. There didn't seem to be much sense in moving them, so I was waiting for him there."

"That's not what he told me," Edie said. "He told me he was meeting you at the Parrish Foundation. He texted us about the pile of boxes." She turned to the detective. "Did you see the library? "

"Edie," Des's voice was long-suffering. "Of course he

told you that. Think about it. He knew you would see that video sooner or later."

"Did you see the library?" She repeated the question to Detective Houghtaling, her voice wobbly and high.

Houghtaling's lips pursed. "We did not have any reason to look on the fifth floor. The sniper's perch was on the eighth floor. I was under the impression that those floors weren't even finished."

"They're not, but I just gave you a reason to look there," Edie said. "Kev sent us a text. He saw the library. He saw the pile of boxes."

Des dropped his head into his hands. "Edie. Don't make this harder than it is. There were no boxes of files. There never have been."

"Send someone." Edie directed the plea at Houghtaling, ignoring him. "Please. Send someone to check. Right now."

"I'll put someone on it, as soon as possible," Houghtaling said.

Edie got to her feet. "Thank you," she said.

"One moment." The detective dug in her pocket, and handed her a card. "Just in case anything else comes back to you."

Edie stuck it in her pocket, and stumbled through the house like a sleepwalker. Ronnie was no longer in the solarium. She went up the curving staircase, down the corridor to Ronnie's suite.

Her sister lay on the antique four-poster bed. Edie sat down on the bed, stroking her sister's tangled hair.

Edie kicked off her shoes, and climbed onto her sister's bed. Uncomfortably aware of the weight of the Ruger around her ankle, the mud spattered jeans leaving brownish smears over Ronnie's pure-white eyelet lace coverlet. She breathed in the scent of Ronnie's hair, taking comfort from the closeness. Reminding her heart of its own truths.

She'd drawn Kev. She'd seen inside him. She'd been inside him. There was no faking that frequency, that vibration. No possibility of lies.

But how many levels to Kev might there be? She had no idea what was hidden behind that barrier in his mind. He might not know, either. There might be a good part of him, utterly sincere and honest, and at the same time . . . there might be something else. Something different.

She shivered. *No.* She had to trust herself. And him. If she let them shake her faith in Kev, she was finished.

She nuzzled Ronnie's hair, tried to make her mind blank.

She failed, of course, but the effort kept her busy.

CHAPTER
29

Kev was buried under a ton of crushing rock, but someone was worrying his feet. Kicking, scratching. Driving him mad.

Fuck this. If he was going to be buried in rock, let him die in peace, at least. Maybe he'd died, and this was hell. *Nudge. Scratch. Shake.* Like rats, at his ankles. A whimpering, muffled, squeaking sound. Desperate. He clawed his way closer to consciousness. Tried to open his eyes. Failed, the first hundred times.

Brutal flourescent lights blazed. The world was tilted wildly askew. *Nudge, nudge.* What the fuck . . . ?

He tried to see who was tormenting him. Ava Cheung was sprawled on top of him, body rigid, face a frozen grimace. Eyes blazing with unabated malice, inches from his own. Paralyzed, but conscious. Her face was striped with dark, dried rivulets of blood from her nose.

It was like waking to find a scorpion on his chest. He tried to move. His most violent efforts yielded feeble twitches.

After an interminable interval, the twitches were forceful enough to shove Ava's body off of his own. He rolled her onto her back. She gazed up, eyes glittering. The syringe still poked out of her leg.

Her finally saw who'd been worrying his feet. The girl in the wheelchair. The Latvian girl. He cudgeled his brain for her name. Yuliyah. She'd stuck one foot out just far enough from its ratcheted plastic cuff to kick at his feet. Her ankle was bloody and raw from her efforts. He wondered how long she'd been at it.

Their eyes met, and she writhed, mewled against her gag. *Hurry up, you goddamn slug* being the clear nonverbal message.

Right. Yeah. Good thing she'd wakened him. Ava had only taken one dose of the X-Cog. She'd given him two. He was roughly double her weight, but she could easily have come back to life before he had. And he and Yuliyah would have both been meat.

Not that they were out of the woods yet. By no means.

He rolled over, tried to get to his hands and knees, but he wobbled like a newborn foal. He stayed down, crawled to retrieve the clippers. Dragged himself over to the wheelchair. It took for-fucking-ever to remind the muscles in his hand how to contract again, they were each so busy trembling individually.

He went at Yuliyah's bonds. The bloodied leg, then the other one. Then her arms. He peeled the gag out. She spit out a rubber ball, coughed, and launched herself out of the chair. She yanked the clippers out of Kev's numb hand and flung herself on Ava with a shriek of rage.

His reaction time was so damn slow, the blades of the clipper were already flashing down toward the woman's carotid artery by the time he caught her wrist. "No," he said.

Yuliyah looked betrayed. He didn't understand the stream of words, but her eyes asked the question clearly. *Why the fuck not?*

Damn good question. He didn't really have an answer. Just a vague sense of it being wrong, to execute a drugged, helpless woman, no matter how much she deserved it. Plus, he was in a shitload of trouble, and Ava's death would not necessarily help him out of it.

On the contrary. They'd already fingered him for Parrish's murder. Watch them accuse him of slaughtering a beautiful young female neuroscientist, too. He'd spend his life on death row.

Besides, a quick death was too good for her. But he couldn't explain that to Yuliyah. He pried the clippers from her hand. Yuliyah burst into tears, spit in Ava's face, and slugged her.

He grabbed Yuliyah's fist before it could land again, picked up a plasticuff, mimed putting it on Ava. "We'll tie her up."

An impassioned explosion of words burst out of Yuliyah. He shook his head, grabbed more plasticuffs, fastened Ava's ankles. Then he rolled her onto her belly, fastened her hands behind her. He cinched the loop together with a third cuff so that she was arched backward like a bow. Uncomfortable as hell, but hey, so was being a mind-raped zombie slave for the rest of his miserable life. And she'd threatened Edie.

That steeled him to retrieve the rubber ball that had been in Yuliyah's mouth. Ava's eyes bugged with horror as he tied on the gag.

He stared down at his handiwork, at a loss. Great. And now?

He peered out the door, into a larger laboratory room. Still and quiet. She hadn't been kidding when she said she'd arranged not to be disturbed. Another burst of words from Yuliyah. She mimed turning a key in a lock, then pointed to Ava. She got onto her knees, scrabbling in Ava's pants pocket. Pulled out a wad of keys. The girl was sharp.

He grabbed Ava by the armpits, and dragged her trussed body out into the other room. No windows. Various other doors. He opened them at random. One was a closet full of supplies. He dropped Ava on the floor, and went in to the back, yanking boxes away from the wall until he'd created a hole. He wedged her into it and replaced the boxes.

She might asphyxiate. She might squeak and thump for days without getting anyone's attention. So her fortune was bound to his. If he got out of here alive, he'd alert the authorities to her whereabouts.

If they killed him, they would find her when she started to smell.

It was a better death than the one she'd planned for him, or for Yuliyah. He could live with that. Or die with it, as the case may be.

Now they had to find a way out. He went back to trying the doors. Many of them were locked. He held out his hand for the keys Yuliyah had taken. Finally, one of them opened. He peered inside, and found a sealed door that looked like a huge refrigerator. A string of colored lights blinked along the top. His flesh began to creep. He turned to Yuliyah.

"Stay back," he told her. "I'll take a look in here."

The girl shook her head, and clung to his arm. He didn't have the strength to argue with her. He shoved the door open.

A blast of icy air and a foul odor floated out. They shrank back, gagging. Yuliyah moaned. He pushed her back toward the outer door again. She dug her nails into his arm til they broke his skin. The two of them stepped inside together.

The room was full of metal tables, the tables covered with bodies shrouded in black zippered plastic bags.

Holy shit. He stared around, his mind wiped blank with horror.

He counted. Twelve bags. He looked at the body bag closest to him, and lowered the zipper just a few inches.

A young woman. Blood-soaked blond curls. Her face was frozen in a grimace, lips pulled back from teeth, eyes staring, spotted with burst capillaries. Blackened blood from her nose streaked her face.

Yuliyah began to scream. Kev spun around, clapped his hand over her mouth. "No!" he growled.

She choked it off, shaking with sobs. Shivering in the frigid icebox, which highlighted another problem. Yuliyah was almost naked. Even if they did get out of this place in one piece, he couldn't take a girl in her underwear out into the November air. Ava's clothes would have fit her, but he'd already stowed Ava, and the thought of peeling the clothing off that horrible thing turned his stomach. It would be about as attractive as looking in those body bags. Nobody home, just the living dead. A piece of meat, animated by rage and hate alone.

He dragged Yuliyah, still sobbing, out of the charnel house, where she promptly vomited all over the floor. Kev jerked away from the splatter. Clothing. He kept searching through the lab, yanking open doors, cabinets. Finally he hit the jackpot; lab coats, clean and pressed. For when Ava wanted to dress up and play scientist.

He wrapped Yuliyah in one of them, and pulled her behind him out into the corridor. This lab had to be underground, considering the nature of the work. Windowless, airless. The hallway was painted cinderblocks, a snarl of insulation-wrapped pipes on the ceiling. A subbasement. No points of reference. A featureless maze.

He locked the knob lock of the laboratory, used all the keys til he found the one for the dead bolt. Listened again, letting all his senses reach out, open up. Nothing to orient him. He grabbed Yuliyah's arm, put his finger to his lips, and pulled her behind himself through the long corridor. Every time they reached a corner, he would stop, listen, feel the stillness of the air, the quality of the silence, before they dared to creep around the turn.

They finally reached a stairwell. They started to climb, and reached a floor that appeared to have natural light. He leaned on the push bar from the stairwell. Poked his head into the corridor.

It was a big, empty warehouse. Yuliyah grabbed his arm and started babbling. He shushed her desperately. "We have to go," he whispered. "Shhh! We have to go! Now!"

Yuliyah pointed at herself, held up one finger. Then she held up five more fingers. "Oksana, Margaritka, Olga, Katyushka, Marya!"

Oh, excellent. As if saving one terrified, traumatized foreign girl in her underwear wasn't enough of a challenge. Why not six of them? If he weren't so desperate, it would almost be funny.

He slashed his finger over his throat, an international symbol if there ever was one. "Police," he said. "We'll get the police. The police will help Oksana, Margaritka, Olga, Kat . . . Kat—"

"Katyushka, Marya," Yuliyah finished impatiently. "Poleese?"

He shushed her, and dragged her out the door, into the warehouse. She was clearly unimpressed with him for being a lily-livered wuss, but fuck it, he wasn't even armed, except for Ava's clippers. They'd stripped him of his gear. He was only one guy, and he was tired, and scared, and Edie was out there, being stalked by some huge metaphorical arachnid from hell. Enough already.

A big metal door right in front of them burst open. Kev was already in the air as big guy leaped out, took aim—

Bam, the shot went wild as a front kick to the point of the guy's chin sent him spinning, thudding against the wall. The gun dropped.

Another guy leaped out at him with a club. He ducked the swing, grabbing the man's arm and using the momentum of his swing to fling him headfirst into the door. He whirled just in time to kick the gun from the groping hand of the first guy, who had revived.

An elbow smash to the temple, and Kev grabbed him from behind and put his thumb to his carotid artery, pressing until he went limp.

Both men down. A splotch of blood on the door matched a corresponding splotch on the second guy's head. Blood poured in rivulets over his slack-jawed face. Too easy, once again. He assumed they'd been saved by the fact that the guys were under orders not to kill them, should they escape. They were worth more alive than dead.

Kev pulled out the cuffs he'd put in his pocket, and peered into the room the guards had come from. It was full of security screens, showing the corridor he and Yuliyah had been creeping through, the doors and various vantage points from outside. The author of their strange luck sat there on the table, wrapped in brown paper; two big paper-wrapped deli sandwiches.

The dickheads had been focused on their meal. The sight of all that sliced lunch meat turned his stomach, after what he'd seen downstairs.

Kev dragged the two men into the room, and used the last plasticuffs to bind them to the radiator. He gathered up their weapons. Two guns, a knife. Car keys. He grabbed an over-sized black sweatshirt he found on a table for himself, and draped a leather jacket off the back of a chair over Yuliyah. It hung down to midthigh.

He grabbed her hand, pulled. "Let's get the fuck out of this place."

As soon as they walked in to Lost Boys, Miles knew Con and Davy were going to be useless. They stood there, staring up, mouths open. Flabbergasted.

Even for someone who wasn't hunting a long lost brother, the Lost Boys reception area was pretty special. The room had a high ceiling with lots of glass, and the entire space was filled with kites strung on wires, wild colors, crazy designs. The walls were painted with blown-up details of the mandalas. Kev's mandalas.

Miles left the McClouds to their gawking and walked

over to the cute receptionist, who flashed him an I'll-just-be-a-sec smile. He pondered his opening gambit as she concluded her conversation. It was a curious challenge. *We're looking for a guy whose name we don't know who looks like a goth comic book hero.* Hmm. Or he could hold up a Fade Shadowseeker book and say *have you seen this man?*

Yeah. Right. That would go over great.

"Hi, can I help you?" she asked brightly.

"I hope so," he said. "We're looking for information about the man who designed these kites." He gestured toward the aerial display.

The girl's smile vanished. "Oh. I can't give you any information."

She probably took him for a headhunter. "Who can?" Miles asked.

"Our CEO, Bruno Ranieri, I guess," she said.

"Can we see him?"

"Nope." She looked triumphant. "He's out of the office. All day."

Miles groaned, inwardly. "Can we make an appointment to see him tomorrow?"

"I'll check with his assistant." She dialed an extension, covered the phone with her hand and shot him sidelong glances as she muttered into it. A moment later, she looked up. "Sorry. She has no idea if he'll be in tomorrow. He's taking some personal time."

Davy and Con sauntered over to the receptionist's desk, doing their silent looming routine. Her eyes got big as Con leaned over the counter.

"Personal time?" he said softly.

Davy pulled a business card out of his wallet, put it on the counter. He tapped it with his finger, and shoved it toward her. "Our business with Mr. Ranieri is very personal," he said. "It is also extremely important. Please have him call. As soon as possible. In fact, if you have a number where he can be reached, you might call him right now."

She stared at the card. Her eyes darted from Davy to Con. "Um. I, um . . . don't?" she squeaked. "Have any number. I mean."

They gazed at each other and turned to go. Thwarted by their own macho manly code of conduct. There was only so far a McCloud guy would go to intimidate an innocent woman. Miles certainly couldn't do it. He sucked at intimidation. He couldn't even intimidate his girlfriend Cindy's jealous cat into not pissing in his shoes.

They headed for the door, but Con stopped, blocking their way, to peer at a framed magazine article. Big color photos. A black-haired guy flashed an ain't-I-cute smile from the pages. Lots of dimples, movie star teeth. Con pointed. "That's Ranieri."

They stared at the face, memorizing it. The receptionist started muttering nervously into the phone again. Calling the cops, maybe.

They went down the stairs. As they reached the lobby, an angry male voice was suddenly amplified as a man shoved the door open.

". . . was I supposed to do, for the love of Christ? Hold her at gunpoint? Her dad just got offed! I had to take her home!"

It was Ranieri, without the dimples or the smile, dressed in a fleece shirt and jeans and growling and snapping into his cell phone.

". . . sure, if he'd ever answer his fucking phone, so get off my case!" He walked past them. "How should I know? He didn't tell me where he was going! He has to face the monsters alone and all that macho shit . . . if you have a better suggestion, I'd love to hear it!"

"Bruno Ranieri?" Davy said.

Ranieri spun around. "Gotta go," he muttered into the phone. "Call you later." He clicked the thing shut. "Who wants to know?"

"I'm Davy McCloud. This is my brother, Connor McCloud, and our friend, Miles Davenport," Davy said.

They looked for a reaction to the name, but Ranieri didn't exhibit one. He just stared, slit eyed. Sizing them up. "What do you want?"

"We're looking for the guy who designed your kites," Davy said.

Nothing changed on the surface of Ranieri's face, but Miles could feel the temperature plummet. "Can't help you. Sorry."

Davy looked like he was grinding his teeth. "Just his name."

"Nope." Ranieri turned toward the stairs.

Connor grabbed his shoulder and spun him, blocking the punch Ranieri aimed to his midsection, and shoved him against the wall.

"We're not fucking off until you give us some information," he said.

"Wrong," Ranieri spat.

A quick, slashing flurry of tight blows and blocks followed, only a fraction of which Miles caught, they were so fast, and then Ranieri did something quick and twisty with Connor's arm, followed up with an elbow whack to the point of his chin that Con barely evaded. He hooked a leg around Con's bad leg, jerking him off balance. Con stumbled back.

Ranieri backed toward the exit, panting, still on guard. "You assholes want some more?"

Con waved his hand. "That's OK," he said. "I've had enough."

Ranieri backed out the door. Miles stared after the guy as he loped away, and at Con and Davy.

"What, you're just going to let him leave?" he squawked. "Why the hell aren't we following him? We know he knows Kev, right? Don't we know that he knows Kev?"

"Yeah, we know." Con held up a little square of gray paper. The backing off one of the slap-on tags, the Squeaker.

The smallest of the battery operated tags from the Safe-Guard catalog. It had a limited amount of juice, but it was flat, light, hidden in a square of dark mesh fabric with an adhesive back, and could be swatted onto someone's back and not noticed for hours. "And you bet your ass we'll follow him. Did you see those mantis moves? And the white crane?"

"Saw it," Davy said. "He's good, too."

Miles was sick of not getting the mysterious significance of all the monosyllables. "What does this guy's technique have to do with Kev?"

"That's one of Kev's favorite strikes," Con said. "Kev trained that guy."

"Ah . . . oh." Miles's mouth snapped shut.

"I want to attack him again," Con said. "See what else he likes."

"You're starting to sound like Sean," Miles observed.

Connor lifted his eyebrow. "Miles. You wound me."

"And we're wasting time!" Miles yelled. "Let's go run that son of a bitch to the ground! Let's squeeze him like . . . like a lemon!"

Davy's laugh sounded freer than Miles had ever heard it, in all the years that he'd known the guy. He gave Miles a slap on the back that jolted all of the organs inside his rib cage into a new alignment, and they took off running, as fast as Con's limp would allow.

He and Yuliyah pushed out the door, unchallenged. It was some industrial warehouse complex out in the middle of nowhere, chain-link fences, buildings. It was cold, raining. Apparently deserted.

He looked down at Yuliyah's bare feet, gritted his teeth, and dragged her behind him. Cars were parked behind the building. He held up the pop locks he'd stolen, tried them. Lights flashed on a Mazda CX-9. There was a GPS device mounted on the dash. He ripped it out and loaded Yuliyah into the SUV. It seemed strange, how easy their escape had been, but their opponents had no reason to think anyone could beat an X-Cog crown. Ava had been confident of her supremacy.

His mind raced as he maneuvered the car through the complex, looking for an exit. Yuliyah's pale, bare legs were goose-bumped. He ramped up the heat, gestured at the seat belt, but she was shivering, lips blue. He leaned over, yanked out some slack in the belt, fastened it.

He couldn't leave her at an emergency room. Too dangerous. The paperwork, the questions, the cops. He couldn't afford an encounter with the police, either, if what Ava said about Parrish was true. That was a tarpit he could drown in. Stay away from bureaucracies when people are trying to fuck you, frame you or kill you. But he had to get Yuliyah someplace safe. Zia Rosa? But Zia was compromised already, having rented the car for him. The police might even have already followed that trail of bread crumbs to its source. Rosa, Tony, the diner.

In which case, God help them. The police, that was to say.

He had to stay free, armed, off the grid. He needed cash, a new vehicle. To wash the crusted blood off his face. To save Edie. And he was responsible for Oksana, Margaritka, Olga, Katyushka, and Marya, too. To say nothing of that freezer full of dead girls.

Ah, man. And the day was still young.

He got out onto the road, and drove around until he saw signs for 26. He headed back to Portland, trying to keep it under ninety, but he was so jacked up, it was impossible. He jerked the car to a stop outside Any Port. Yuliyah fumbled with the seat belt, hands shaking. He circled the car, unhooked her, set her pale bare feet on the curb. He pulled her to her feet, but her knees buckled under her. She was done.

He tossed her over his shoulder, ran up the steps, buzzed.

"Who is it?" someone asked.

"It's Kev Larsen. I've got to speak to Dorothea, quick," he said. "It's an emergency. A life or death situation."

The door lock popped open. He pushed into the foyer, up the stairs. Dorothea hurried toward them. "Good God! Who is this girl? What happened to her?"

"Got a bed I can put her on? Some warm blankets, hot fluids?"

"Come in." She led him down a maze of corridors, into a cubicle with a dorm-style bed. Kev laid Yuliyah on it. Tracee, Dorothea's assistant, hurried in, arms full of blankets. Tracee appeared to be fussing competently around Yuliyah, so he pulled Dorothea out into the relative privacy of the hallway. He grabbed her hands, squeezed them.

"Her name is Yuliyah," he said, cutting off the excited stream of words. "She's from Latvia. Find her a translator. She's been kidnapped, abused. She's in danger. You have to keep her hidden. Her enemies are very powerful. Get her a doctor if you have to, but keep it quiet."

Dorothea blinked. "I take it her enemies are your enemies, too?"

"You got it. Look. I'm being framed for something bad. Yuliyah could prove my innocence." He paused. "If she survives."

"I don't need any proof," Dorothea said stoutly. "I'm convinced."

"I appreciate that," he said, meaning it with all his heart. "Just keep her safe."

"Count on me," she said.

He squeezed her hands. "I'm putting you and your organization in danger. I'm sorry, but I didn't know what else to do. I have to go."

"Already? Sure you don't want to rest too?" She patted his unscarred cheek anxiously. "A cup of tea, some soup?"

"No. There are other girls where she came from. I have to help them." He grabbed her hand, kissed it. "Thanks, Dorothea."

"Well, take this, at least." She pulled a small packet out of her pocket. "You look terrible." It was a package of Wet Wipes. He pocketed it with a grin of thanks and bolted for the exit.

"Kev! Wait!" Dorothea huffed behind him as he took the steps four at a time. "I just got this visit from this guy who claimed to be—"

"Later, Dorothea!" He let the door slam, his mind miles ahead.

If they hadn't yet discovered that he and Yuliyah had escaped, then they had no reason to guard his place. If they had discovered it, they would be sending someone to wait for him. Just in case he was actually so ass-wipe, dick-brained, asinine stupid as to go back home.

Which he was. He had no choice. He needed those alternate identities he'd grown. Too bad he hadn't had time to grow one for Edie. It took years to establish an identity that held up to official scrutiny.

But if he had at least one, he could work, and they would be able to travel, rent cars and housing while he grew ones for Edie and Ronnie.

And he needed weapons. He felt naked without them.

The tires squealed as he yanked the car around and accelerated in the direction of his home. In and out, hard and fast.

He had to risk it. It was their only chance.

CHAPTER
30

"Someone's been at this thing with a lock gun." Sean leaned forward to take a closer look. "Recently, too. The lock is new. And so are these marks." He looked up at the blank, unadorned brick building, stark against the white sky. "Wait in the car, Liv."

She made an inelegant sound. "Don't be ridiculous."

He didn't even bother to start that battle. He just pushed right on in. The lock had been so damaged, it no longer functioned at all.

They climbed the stairs, finding no clue as to which of the doors on those landings could be Kev's until the top floor, where there was only one, the others having been bricked up. That door hung open.

"Someone broke in here, too," he said.

"What a coincidence," Liv murmured.

Sean poked his head through the door, listening. It was dead still in there. Liv threaded her fingers into his. He kept listening, until Liv started tugging impatiently. He walked in, pulling her behind him.

Huge, open spaces. Vast windows. Raw brick. Wrought iron. Gleaming expanses of teak flooring. Huh. Kev had not done too badly for himself. As if giving fortunes to the runaway shelters wasn't enough of a clue. That metal-toned kitchen with the big tiled central island including sink, gas range, oven . . . wow. After redoing a kitchen and bathroom in his condo with Liv, he was keenly aware of just how much money he was looking at. His brother had one hell of a decorating budget. Son of a bitch.

The mobiles hanging from wires on the ceiling made his breath catch. They twisted and turned gently in a draft from some open window. Like the ones Kev used to carve from twigs and acorns back home. Models of molecules, from when he was twelve years old, reading post-graduate-level books on organic chemistry. For fun.

Yup. This was Kev, all right. This place was Kev all over.

"What do you want to do?" Liv's voice sounded hushed and nervous as she looked around. "Wait for him?"

Sean stuck his fingers in his pockets. "I have a funny feeling."

"Funny feelings are the norm for you," Liv pointed out dryly. "If you weren't having one, you wouldn't recognize yourself."

"No. I mean, about him being gone. The locks being forced. The graphic artist's place being tossed. Something's wrong. Something's off."

"What a surprise," she said dryly. She spun around, gawking at the high ceilings, the vast windows. "Think there's anything wrong with looking into the other rooms? It seems, I don't know. Invasive."

He laughed. "No more invasive than letting us think he was a corpse rotting in the ground for eighteen years. That really invaded my peace of mind."

"Sean—"

"I wouldn't worry about it, babe. Really. Root around in his underwear drawer. Let's see if he's a boxers or briefs kind of guy. And while we're at it, let's just see . . ." He grabbed an unopened envelope from a mesh basket on the desk, ripped it open. He peered at the bill. "Whoa. Look at all those extra cable features for his fifty-two inch plasma TV. Cushy, for a guy who grew up hauling water in a bucket and crapping in a hole in the ground. He's forgotten his humble roots."

"Sean, stop it," she said.

He strode into the kitchen. "I'll check out the fridge, while we're being invasive." He yanked it open, pulled out a bottle of Dos Equis. He twisted the cap off. "About time that bastard stood me a drink."

She draped her crossed arms over her baby bulge, her soft lips gone thin with disapproval. "You're losing it," she snapped. "Cool it."

"Oh, I'm cool. I'll just chug this beer on down, and when it works through the tubes, I'll go take a nice, long piss in his bathroom. Then I'll use his toothbrush to freshen up." He sauntered back to the studio. An envelope had fluttered to the ground. He scooped it up. "What's this? A phone bill. Let's take a look!" He ripped it open, peered at the balance. "Huh. This one's pretty contained."

"He probably mostly uses his cell," Liv said.

"Or maybe he just doesn't have any friends," Sean said. "Maybe he has nobody to talk to. Must be hard to maintain relationships when you go around faking your own death. Puts a real crimp in your social life. Goddamn fucking lying *bastard.*"

"That is enough!" she yelled. "You are indulging yourself, and I am tired of this tantrum! Get your head back in the game!"

Sean let the trapped air escape from his lungs, in a long, thin wheeze. "It's not a game."

She took his hand again, tugged it. "I know that, baby," she said quietly. "I know it better than anyone. Come on. Let's keep looking."

* * *

"Alarm's tripped, at the Larsen place," Wanatabe said.

Tom whipped his head around. "What?"

"You heard me." The guy's voice was sullen. After three days, his balls were still aching. Fucking sissy baby. Tom was losing his patience.

He stomped over. "You got a visual?"

"They've just moved out of range," Wanatabe said. "Looks like Larsen and some chick. But not the Parrish chick. A different one."

"Larsen?" That jolted him. "That's not possible."

Wanatabe shrugged. "Looks like Larsen."

"Let me see." He leaned over while Wanatabe selected the footage, ran it back, and set it to play.

They watched Larsen poke his head in the open door and look around for a long moment, those weird, pale green eyes glittering with concentration. Holy shit. Tom's jaw dropped. How . . . ?

The guy looked behind himself, murmured, and crept through the door, pulling a woman behind him. Not the Parrish woman, as Ken had said. This one was shorter, chubbier. Long, curly dark hair. Pretty, vividly colored, curvy. Pregnant, he noticed suddenly. He could see the swell under her sweater. Larsen clutched her hand, keeping her close—

No. Not Larsen. This guy's hair was longer. The man turned, three hundred and sixty degrees, to look at the apartment, lips pursing in a silent whistle. The right side of his face was smooth. Unscarred.

Fucking shit, this was the twin! Sean McCloud. The one they'd read about in the files. The one who slit Dr. O's throat.

Rage gripped him. A desire to tear out the guy's throat. Intellectually, Tom knew it was the conditioning Dr. O had instilled in his elite cadre of star pupils. But knowing didn't lessen the urge.

McCloud was lucky it wasn't public knowledge who'd slaughtered Dr. O. If it had been, every member of Club O would have been after him, to rip him into bloody pieces. Wipe out his entire gene pool.

He eyed the bulge under the sweater of that pretty woman. Yeah, actually. His gene pool would be a fine place to start.

"Contact the rest of the team. Tell them to rendezvous outside Larsen's place immediately," he said. "We'll meet them as soon as we can get there. We're taking that son of a bitch. Alive. He is mine, got it? The woman, too. Don't kill them. Use the dart guns, or the Tasers."

He lifted his com device, since duty dictated that he keep the crazy bitch in the loop, and punched in Ava's code. "Come in, Ava. We have a situation at Larsen's place."

No reply. Fury burned in his belly. He hated dealing with self-indulgent civilian pussies with no concept of teamwork, order, or discipline. Fucking him up, slowing him down. Drove him nuts.

"Ava! Come in, goddamnit!" he roared.

Nothing. He tried the guards he'd posted above Ava's snakepit lab. "Janowizc? Hackman? Come in! Come in!"

Nothing. What the *fuck?* He had to waste precious time to compensate for incompetence. He was going to personally crush Janowizc's and Hackman's balls for dicking around on the job. "Go ahead," he snarled to Wanatabe. "I'll meet you there. Have to go check on Marr's bitch. Block them into Larsen's place. And do . . . not . . . hurt . . . them!"

Wanatabe got to it with gratifying speed. Tom left the big trailer that they'd been bunking in, and jogged, panting, through the warehouse complex til he got to the one that concealed Ava's lab.

He peered into the guardroom. His jaw sagged with dismay. Aw, fucking shit. Both guys unconscious, bleeding, and tied to the radiator, useless bags of shit that they were. He left them, and ran toward the room where Larsen had been shackled. It would be just like that crazy bitch, to go have fun with the guy, gloating and taunting.

Sure enough. The room was empty. The chair where they had fastened him was empty too. The shackles lay open. Larsen was gone.

What the *fuck?* That arrogant bitch wasn't supposed to touch him. No one knew how Kev McCloud had gotten away from Dr. O and Gordon. No one knew how Sean McCloud had beaten the crown and managed to kill Dr. O. Until they knew, the plan was to proceed with extreme caution, and a loaded gun to the guy's head at each baby step.

He keyed open Ava's lab. A nasty stink and a cold draft came from one door. Fridge was open. He closed it, shoved the other doors open.

The mess told its silent story. The bench, plasticuffs hooked to the top bar. Chunks of plastic cuffs lying around on the floor. An empty wheelchair on its side. Syringes on the floor. Ava had muscled that guy in here all by herself, and crowned him. And McCloud had taken her.

Good fucking riddance.

Tom pulled out his cell. The call to Des had just connected when he heard the muffled thudding sound, choked whimpering.

Oh, man. No way. This was too sweet.

He cut off the call, followed the sound to the supply room. He flipped on the light, clambered over the boxes, peeked down into the suffocating crack of space where Ava was wedged.

She was arched backward, red faced, choking for air. Her purple face, broken blood vessels, wild eyes, and tangled hair made her look like the ugly hag that she actually was.

He started to laugh. Time was tight, but he held up his cell phone and snapped a picture. "Sorry, but I just had to immortalize this," he told her. "You look like ten kinds of shit, sweetheart."

She mewled, thumped with her feet.

Tom shook his head. "You let him go, you dumb cunt.

Now I have to go find him. You can wait until Des comes to get you. I don't have time for this tedious shit. Sit tight, babe. Think good thoughts."

He pried himself out of the tumbled boxes, still laughing, and flipped the light off before letting the door of the utility room slam shut.

Sean and Liv took their time wandering through Kev's apartment. Everything Sean's eyes fell upon made his guts clench up with weird recognition. They studied the kitchen, the desk, the studio, the artwork, the bookcases, the living space. They stopped short on their appraisal as they approached the dining area, assailed by a horrible smell.

"What's this?" Liv said. "Yikes. That's vile."

"My brother has become a slob?" Sean postulated. "That's weird. Kev was always superclean. Even worse than Davy. I was the only one in the whole family who ever approached slob status."

They stared at the mess on the table. Someone had laid out a romantic feast, complete with candles, and left the remains to ferment.

"No one's been in here in . . ." He sniffed. "Four days. Or three. There was fish in that meal. Fish is the secret incredient that gives unwashed dishes that special olfactory oomph, you know?"

"Spoken like a true ex-bachelor," Liv said primly. "I wouldn't know, myself. I do my dishes as I use them. On the spot."

"Yeah, yeah. I know. You're perfect, and all that." Sean held up one of the candle holders, sniffing it. "Scented candles? Pink? Jesus, has he gone over to the other side? What the fuck is that about?"

"It's about her," Liv said quietly. "It's about Edie Parrish."

He gaped at her. "Nah. Really? You think?"

"Didn't you see the way she draws him? Did you see those graphic novels? How over-the-top romantic they are? She worships him."

Sean picked up another candle, this one a deep crimson. "Well, hell. Looks like he worships her back. So they were too overwhelmed with passion to come down and do their dishes. For three whole days?"

Liv looked thoughtful. "We're talking a McCloud guy plus true love, remember. Three whole days in bed is doable. I can visualize it."

Sean squinted at her. "Don't visualize it with anybody but me."

She started to reply, eyes sparkling. He clapped his hand over her mouth. "Get your head back in the game," he whispered, and gave her a kiss. He pulled her across the expanse of floor, and up the spiral staircase. The bathroom was on the loft. Not opulent, but nice. After their remodel, Sean could price the materials with his eye. Ching ching.

They opened the door to the bedroom. It too was large and simple. Wooden venetian blinds over the windows, swaying in a draft.

Then they saw the mandala painting on the ceiling.

Sean was helpless to reel his jaw back up into place. His throat was tightening, like screws were turning. His hands had gone numb. He put the beer down on the dresser with a trembling hand.

The mandala was identical in every detail to the painting on the ceiling of their bedroom, the one Kev had done the year after Dad died, except magnified to the tenth power. It seemed to expand out to infinity, far beyond the confines of the room.

The twelve-year-old Kev had lost himself in that painting for weeks, putting all his unspoken grief into it. None of them had talked about how they felt after Dad died. None of them knew how. It wasn't done in Eamon McCloud's house. They swallowed it down, clenched their teeth and their bellies against the sickening ache, pretended that everything was normal. When the bottom had fallen out of the world.

Kev's mandala brought it back. Those strange, silent meals in the first months. Davy looking tough and tightlipped at the head of the table instead of Dad. Eating Davy and Con's cooking. Burned meat, squirrel stew. Flat, unyeasted bread, crunchy undercooked rice. Dirt in the vegetables. Not much else. In a holding pattern of uncertainty, afraid to take a breath, make a move. No fucking clue how they would survive without Dad. What they were supposed to do, alone and broke.

Then Davy had shouldered the duty of the firstborn. He'd found a job on a construction crew. As soon as Con had followed suit and was earning money too, Davy had joined the army and gotten shipped out to Iraq. The world in constant flux. All those unexpressed feelings were tied up in the swirling shifts and shadings in that painting.

As a twelve-year-old, Sean had lost himself staring up at Kev's painting, as he lay on his bed. He had let the image swirl him up into its vortex and carry him away, washing his mind blessedly clean, so that he could breathe. Even sleep, sometimes. Kev's special gift.

Kev had not forgotten them, Sean realized abruptly. His brothers were there, in Kev's head. They loomed large. He couldn't cancel them out. And looking at that ceiling, it didn't seem as if he wanted to.

"It was a message, you know," Liv said.

"Huh?" He tried to fish her words out of his short term memory, but the task was too much for his boggled mind. "What?"

"The kite," she said. "It was a message to you. He's been calling out to you for years." She let out a shaky breath. "And you finally heard him." Her voice choked off. She pressed her hand over her mouth.

They stood staring. Then Liv gasped, let out a delighted laugh.

"What?" he demanded. "What is it?"

"The bed! Look at that!"

He looked at the rumpled bed. The duvet and sheet were turned down, and . . . horror exploded inside him. "Jesus, is that blood?"

"No, you silly!" Liv sat on the bed, scooped some of the withered dark spots up into her hand, and sniffed them tenderly before letting them flutter back down. "Rose petals. Oh, God. How romantic."

Sean let out a sharp sigh. "Jesus Christ. You scared me."

She sniffed the petals clinging to her hand. "I'm so glad. He can't be too bad off. Not if there are rose petals on his sheets."

"Yeah, right. He's getting laid, at least," Sean said grumpily.

"Don't be crass," she said. "Rose petals are not about getting laid. They're a tribute to a woman's hunger for tenderness. Sensitivity. Wordless understanding. You know. Those things that girls like."

"What's this, Liv?" he demanded. "Are you telling me I'm not tender or sensitive? That I don't feed your womanly hungers enough?"

Her sexy, rosy mouth quivered as she fought hard not to smile. "I'm just happy, for Kev and his lady friend. That he gets it. That's all."

"Oh. I see. You mean, it wasn't enough, the time that I got the paintbrush and the chocolate and caramel swirl sauce and did that great Postimpressionistic artwork all over your—"

"Absolutely not the same thing," she said crisply. "That was extremely enjoyable, and you get points for using sugar and chocolate, but there is no comparison."

"And the time I spent eight hundred bucks on sexy lingerie for—"

"Do not even mention sexy lingerie to a woman well into her third trimester," Liv warned. "It will break her heart."

Sean bit back a snarl of frustration. "When I get my

hands on my brother, I'm going to have hard words with him. About making trouble between me and my wife. Creating unrealistic expectations. Rose petals? My ass, Liv. It's a fucking circus trick. That's all!"

"Is it? Well, you go ahead. Have those words with him," she suggested. "Maybe you'll even learn something. Wonders never cease."

He crossed his arms over his chest. "Soon as we get back to the hotel room, we're going to have a long talk about your womanly needs, babe. And just exactly what it is that you think you need to fulfill them."

Her eyes glowed with sensual promise. "I think that sounds like an excellent idea."

The air combusted. He was so turned on, he wanted to use Kev's bed then and there, to show Liv just how deep his commitment to fulfilling her womanly needs went. That was to say, to the hilt. All night long. And forever, while he was at it.

But through the fog of lust, another thought pricked him. How smoothly she'd wrangled him through this encounter with his brother's home and life. Not letting him hit the ceiling. Soothing, lecturing, scolding, teasing. And when all else failed, she just seduced him.

He was such a goddamn puppy. Sit, wag, roll over and beg. Eating out of her hand. Or better yet, eating chocolate caramel off parts of her that were even more sensitive. Any time. Any damn time.

But now was not that time. He looked away from the sultry glow in her eyes, the flushed lips, her absolutely lickable, suckable tits, and cleared his throat with a harsh cough. "So. Let's be methodical."

"Oh, yes. Please, let's," she murmured.

"Stop it, Liv," he warned. "Let me concentrate. The elements fit together. The doors were forced. Pink scented candles, rose petals on the bed, so sex happened. The dishes were left undone for days. And there was no apparent sign of violence. Nor has anyone reported a break-in. So they haven't been back. Like the Parrish chick's place."

"So?" Liv said. "Conclusion?"

"So they come here, and Kev's prepared a big romantic meal, with candles, etc. They chow down. Then, they go up to the bedroom, and do whatever it is that they do with their magic fucking flower petals."

Liv cleared her throat, stifling a giggle.

"But while they're up in the bedroom, they hear someone coming," he said. "Kev has to protect her, so instead of going down and getting into it . . ." He walked over to the window, the one whose blinds were blowing inward, and peered out. "They crawl out on the fire escape, step across onto the scaffolding, and flee out of that building."

"Leaving the dishes to fester," Liv said. "Very good. I like it."

"But where are they now?" Sean mused. "And who is after them?"

A gust of icy wind swept through the blinds. He shivered with a strange foreboding. Suddenly he had yet another reason to add to the long list of compelling reasons to get out of Kev's place and back to the cozy bed in their hotel room. "Let's go," he said. "This place is not safe."

Liv followed him, with no back talk. She'd caught the same spooky vibe. He slunk out the bedroom door, pulling Liv behind him.

The vibe was building up into something approaching panic. A sense of having miscalculated, fucked up. Missed something important.

Of course, at that moment, the cell phone vibrated in his pocket. Thank God he'd turned off the ringtone. He yanked the thing out.

It was Davy. Movement down below caught his eye. The front door, silently swinging inward.

He yanked Liv to the floor beneath him, clamped his

hand over her mouth. *Company,* he mouthed, jerking his gaze toward the door.

Two men, peeking in the door. Big guns. They moved in, tippety tapping like ninja cat shadows, and here he was, like an asshole, all alone with his wife, with the precious little space shrimp paddling around inside her, and one dinky fucking six-shot emergency revolver.

He eyed the bedroom door behind them. The room with the escape route. Too far. That much movement to the end of the loft would catch the eyes of those men, even slithering. Liv was wearing a bright red sweater coat. He was wearing drab gray and jeans, but she looked like a peony in full bloom up there, against the red brick walls. A pregnant peony. God help them.

He shoved Liv toward the bathroom door, hanging blessedly open from his previous inspection of Kev's choice of bathroom fixtures. She slithered in on her side, face pale, mouth clamped, teeth digging into her lower lip. Not a peep out of his Amazon queen.

He followed, feet first, crawling backward over the slate-colored bathroom tiles. He tapped in a message to Davy.

kev's apt. 46 NW Lenox with liv. company. help.

Sent, he shoved the phone in his pocket. His brother's apartment was so fucking huge, he'd need a rifle to take those guys from here. And now they were trapped. Far-fucking-out. He might have known.

Kev was a McCloud, after all. This crazy shit was inevitable.

Kev parked on the far side of the building next door to his own. His sixth sense was screaming, so he figured his chances of getting in and out without tripping an alarm were slim. Then again, they would have watched for his return until this morning, but after they'd taken him, there was no reason for them not to turn their eyes away.

Unless they'd found Ava. Always a possibility.

The safe with the ID info was built behind a hidden sliding panel inside his bedroom closet. He had various other caches in other parts of the house. He'd installed them as he remodeled the place from the naked bricks some years before. He even had a few outside the building. Ten thousand bucks and one of his fake IDs were shrink-wrapped in impermeable plastic and stowed in a fake utility box that was mounted on the light pole outside the building.

He shimmied up, pried the box loose with a rock, retrieved it. Another cache was tucked behind a loosened brick outside his bedroom window, puttied up to seal out the damp. He'd get that one, too.

He'd known he was being paranoid to the point of urgently needing medication when he prepared the hiding places and their contents. He hadn't understood the impulse, and he hadn't tried to. He just wanted to be able to get the necessary basics, and be able to cut and run without entering his building, should he ever find the need.

But there was Edie to consider, now. The sister, too. He needed more resources to evade a kidnapping charge and stay on the lam. It would be insanely complicated to go on the run with a woman and a child both. Probably impossible. It was hard enough alone.

So? What the fuck? What else did he have to do with himself? Without Edie, his life was worth nothing. He could only try.

He picked the padlock of the deserted building across from his, and slipped inside into the darkness. Thankfully, the construction site was deserted today. He slid like a shadow through the gutted building, trying not to leave any footprints on the walkways, and crawled onto the scaffolding, stepping across onto the fire escape. He pried out the putty, collected the cash behind the brick, and shoved it into the big front pocket of the black hoodie he'd taken from the guard.

The window was still open a crack. It would be funny if he'd gotten robbed in the meantime by normal thieves. After all the crazy shit going down, something so banal would be almost refreshing.

He slithered through the window, letting the wooden blinds slide across his whole body as he dropped down to the floor in a crouch.

It was silent, but his inner alarms were clanging. He went to the closet, glad he took care to keep doors and hinges oiled. No squeaking as he slid the panel down and tapped in the electronic combination.

Lack of vigilance will get you killed. He finally understood where that came from. Dad's phrase. And he was just as crazy as old Eamon.

There was a fat money belt, all prepared, with documents inside—birth certificates, voter registration cards, credit cards, bank cards, credit histories, property tax records of his various alternate selves. It was complicated and expensive to keep them current and viable, and Bruno had thought he was nuts. But hey. He felt vindicated as hell today.

Two loaded pistols were inside, with extra clips, a Beretta Couger and a H&K USP. He loaded up the side pocket of his cargo pants with the Couger, shoved the H&K into his pants. Shoved the clips and a box of ammo into a bag, which he slung over his shoulder.

Still more weapons were in the safe on the other side of the closet, but that would be even more greedy and dumb than he'd been already. He felt around, checking to see what he'd forgotten, and his hand brushed the thing, spinning in the empty safe. A detonator for the M18A1 Claymore antipersonnel mines he'd wired into niches in the brick wall downstairs, covering them with artwork. Angled to destroy intruders coming in the front door. He pulled it out, gazed at it, wondering what dark impulse had prompted him to install them.

He slunk back toward the window. He had more caches around the house, but he'd pushed his luck far enough. One more shove, and it would snap. And he and Edie would be fucked.

Then he saw the beer.

A Dos Equis, from the six-pack Bruno had ordered from the Mexican restaurant. A ring of condensation was forming around the bottle on the dresser top. He had not left it there.

He crossed the room, touched the bottle with his fingertip. Half drunk, and ice cold. Just out of the fridge. It was still sweating.

Someone was here, in his apartment. Right now.

But who would come in, open a beer and wander around his place drinking it? Not any of Des and Ava's goons. The times he'd seen them in action, they had been very focused and professional. It was more like something that Bruno would do. But over the years he had trained that insolent slob of a brother to use coasters when he laid beverages on Kev's hand-finished wooden furniture, or risk broken bones and ripped cartilage as a consequence. And Bruno wasn't here. He was with Edie.

Oh, please, God. Please, let Bruno still be with Edie.

He yanked up the dark hood, pulling the cord tight around his face, and got down, wiggling through the bedroom door on his belly to peer through the wrought iron railing of the loft.

Oh, fuck. One guy, armed, poking through his studio. Another, staring at the dining room table. As he watched, two more slithered through the door, dead silent, gesturing at each other with prearranged signals. Looking for someone or something specific. Tense, focused.

Not the beer drinker. Whatever. Fuck it. Let it remain forever a mystery. He was out of here, this name, this place, this life. A blank slate once again, but at least this time, he'd have Edie. If God was kind.

God often wasn't, though. And there were his brothers, now. How could he not contact them, now that he knew who they were?

Not now. He slithered back into his room, and pushed those confusing, unhelpful thoughts away as he pushed the switch.

CHAPTER
31

The Squeaker led them to Tony's Diner, off Sandy Boulevard.

Davy parked across the street. Through the windows, they saw Bruno Ranieri perched on a stool at the counter, talking to an old guy with a jarhead haircut. An older lady with big hair was participating in the conversation, waving a spoon as she did so. The people eating watched as if it were some sort of dinner theater in the round. It looked like the conversation was degenerating into a shouting match.

"Shall we?" Miles asked.

Davy looked dubious. "We'll be taking our lives in our hands."

"That's where they usually are," was Con's wry observation.

They waited to enter while a file of nervous, whispering customers pushed their way out, throwing nervous glances behind themselves. Plates with half-eaten burgers and fries lay on the table. The decibel level swelled when the door swung open. Most of the screaming was impossible to decipher, since the two older people were screaming in a foreign language that sounded vaguely like Italian, but not quite.

Miles, Con, and Davy walked in. Bruno Ranieri looked dumbfounded. "What the fuck are you assholes doing here?"

"We told you already," Davy said. "Looking for information." He directed his words at the older man. "Are you Tony?"

The old jarhead reached under the counter. "You want some information?" He whipped up a sawed-off pump action Remington 870 shotgun and aimed it at Davy's chest. "I'll give you some fuckin' information."

The customers started collectively freaking out, and the old man waved the gun around. "Everybody out of here!" he bawled. "We're closed! Come back another day and I'll give you lunch for free. Clear outta here! Move it!"

The old man's tone reminded Miles of the way the McCloud guys talked when they were under stress. When the last customer scurried out, Davy and Con and Miles stood there, staring at the shotgun.

"These those bozos you told us about?" the old man asked Bruno.

"Yeah," Bruno said. "The very ones."

Con made a strangled sound. Miles turned. He was gazing at the wall. "The drawings," he whispered.

They looked. The framed drawings on the walls were not the usual horrific restaurant art. Miles recognized the style instantly. It was like the stuff displayed in Davy's and Con's houses. Kev stuff.

"I think you guys oughtta forget the fuckin' artwork, and look at the gun," the old guy growled. "You think I wouldn't shoot you with it, you're dead wrong."

He looked sincere. Miles took a deep breath, and hung on hard to his guts. A skill he'd learned from hanging out with McClouds.

"Now you pussies got a couple of choices," the old man rasped. "You can turn your asses around, fuck off and disappear, permanently. Or else, I can shoot you dead. Your choice. You got five seconds to make up your mind. Five. Four. Three. Two—"

"I propose a third option," Con said. "Put down the gun, and tell us where you've been hiding our brother Kev for the last eighteen years."

The old man squinted at them, studying Con's face, then Davy's. Then Miles's. A look that seemed almost like fear came over his bulldog face. "What the fuck . . . ?" he whispered. "Who?"

"Don't fall for it, Tony," Bruno Ranieri hissed. "These guys are the assholes who attacked him and Edie. There were three of them, remember? And he said they had training."

"Someone attacked Kev?" Con's voice sharpened. "When? Why?"

"Shut your fucking mouth, and mind your fucking business." Tony swung the shotgun up and aimed at Connor. "I know who you are. I been waitin' for you for years. Eamon McCloud sent you, right?"

Davy and Con were too surprised to speak. Tony shook the gun to break their spell. "Am I right?" he yelled. "Answer me, goddamnit!"

Bruno looked baffled. "Eamon who? Who the fuck's Eamon?"

Davy cleared his throat with a harsh cough. "Eamon McCloud was our father," he said. "Kev's father."

Tony's face turned a strange shade of eggplant. "But that's . . . that's bullshit," he sputtered. "I know about that guy. I know what he was, what he did. I heard the stories!"

"Then you knew more than us," Con said. "What stories?"

"About McCloud! That he was a killer for hire!" the old man bellowed. "About his trophy collection. Ears, tongues, balls! That he'd slit your throat as soon as look at you! That he could snipe somebody at twenty-five hundred meters, right through the eye! The kills weren't certified, because it happened deep in-country, but everybody knew!"

Davy and Con looked at each other. "We don't know about that," Davy said. "Could be true. Except for the trophies. That wasn't his style. He didn't talk about Nam. But it haunted him until he died."

"Died?" Tony sounded personally insulted. "Whaddaya mean, died? He ain't dead! I looked around, I informed myself, and I didn't hear nothing about him being dead! Or about him having kids, neither! Nobody said anything about that!"

"Nobody knew," Davy said. "We weren't entered on any public registries when we were born. He wasn't entered on any when he died. We buried him ourselves. Kev was twelve."

Tony gave Miles a long, slit-eyed look. "Who's this kid? He ain't your brother, or Kev's, neither. Not with that long honkin' schnoz."

Miles forced himself to take that with his habitual saintly patience. He'd learned to live with his nose, and everything that came with it. "I'm just a friend," he said.

The gun did not waver. "Give me one good reason why I should believe you guys."

"I'll give you more than one." Con pulled an envelope from his pocket, and shook the photographs into his hands, gleaned from his walls before they'd left his house that afternoon.

Tony held out his hand. "Lemme see those."

The old lady crowded close. Bruno leaned over their shoulders. The family resemblance came into focus. They all had the same furiously suspicious frown on their faces.

"This one is right before my mother died, in '75," Con said, pointing. "The two little ones are Kev and Sean, his twin. They were four. I don't know which one is which in that picture."

The old lady clapped a beringed hand over her mouth. "He was a *gemellino*? So blond. So cute," she crooned. "*Che piccino carino*."

"Twin," Tony said, his voice heavy. "He had a twin?"

"Identical," Con said. "This one is where they were both eight. I was twelve here, and Davy was fourteen. And this is Kev, doing one of his drawings. I think Davy snapped that when Kev was about sixteen. And this is when Sean graduated from high school. All of us together."

"Oh, *madonna santissima*." Tears welled up in the old lady's eyes. "Just look at him. Without the scars. *Mio povero bambino*."

"What scars?" Davy demanded. "Who scarred him? And what the hell has he been doing for the last eighteen years?"

Tony lay the gun slowly back under the counter. Bruno kept shuffling through the pictures, his face screwed up in fierce concentration. As if he were convinced that they were somehow fake.

Tony moved slowly, turning to pull down a ceramic keepsake in the shape of the Roman Colosseum. He pulled a rubber plug from the bottom, and shook something small into his hand. He paced around the counter. It dangled from his hand. Dog tags, darkened with age.

"This was in his jeans pocket, the night I found him," Tony said.

Davy snatched the thing. Con leaned over his shoulder. "Oh, Jesus," Con said softly. "I didn't even know Kev had those."

"Found him where?" Davy asked, his voice hard.

"In Renton. Behind the warehouse where I was working. August twenty-four. Ninety-two. This big sonofabitch was beating him to death. I was a working a night shift as a security guard. Watched it on the camera for a while, but it bugged me that the other guy was too messed up to fight back." Tony shrugged. "Went out with my Beretta, took a few shots at the dirty motherfucker. And there Kev was. Almost dead."

"But he lived," Miles prompted.

"Yeah," Tony said. "He lived. I didn't know what the fuck to do with him. Couldn't take him to a hospital. I figured they'd be waiting for someone to do that. So I took him with me. He was wrong, up here, for the longest time." Tony tapped his temple. "Couldn't talk, or write. Like a retard. Whoever cut him up and burned his face did something to his brain, maybe. Who the fuck knows."

Davy and Con both flinched at that. "Burned?" Davy asked.

"Tortured." Tony said bluntly. "It was real bad. He didn't remember anything. Couldn't talk. I kept him here, with us. He worked here, ate here, slept here. He was safe. We took care of him."

"But you had this." Davy shook the dog tags. His voice rocked with tightly controlled anger. "You could have found us with this. You could have brought him home. We could have taken care of him. He was our brother, goddamnit. Ours to keep safe. Ours to take care of. Why the fuck didn't you find us?"

"I made a bad call," Tony said stiffly. "I thought McCloud was a killer. When I saw how Kev could fight, I figured the kid had been on Eamon McCloud's team, and he'd gotten on the guy's bad side. I figured looking for McCloud would get him killed. So I sat on it."

Connor blew out a harsh breath. "Oh, God," he muttered.

"Your daddy taught you boys to fight, right?" Tony asked.

Davy nodded. Tony grunted. "That would explain the way he fought, the stuff he knew. I figured him for SF, or exSF. How else would he know all that knifework, all that survival shit?"

"Being Eamon McCloud's son," Con said. "Part of the curriculum."

Miles tried to get the conversation back on track. "He lost his memory? Did he ever get it back?"

"Not really," Bruno said, reluctantly. "A few months ago he went over a huge waterfall, bonked his head. He knocked some of that stuff loose, but just a little bit. Just enough to drive him totally bugfuck with frustration. That was what started all this crazy shit."

"A waterfall?" Connor's voice cracked. "What in the fuck?"

"Don't ask us to explain the stunts that guy pulls," Bruno growled. "He has no fear of death. Drives me bonkers. So anyway, he remembered Osterman, and the torture. And he's been trying to get more of it back ever since. He was obsessed." He threw up his hands. "And see? He starts making progress, and all hell breaks loose. People start attacking him, people get shot to death—"

"What?" Connor and Davy yelled in unison. "Who got shot?"

"Charles Parrish," Bruno explained glumly. "A sniper blew his head off this morning. And now Kev's missing."

"What do you mean, missing?" Miles demanded. "Now he's found, right? How the hell can he still be missing?"

"Missing is missing," Bruno said. "He left this morning to meet some Helix fat cat who promised to show him the Osterman archives. He had this thing about recovering his past. To find his lost memories at all costs." He looked them over and grunted, clearly unimpressed with the representatives of Kev's past that stood before him. "He was supposed to check in hours ago. He never did. And he won't answer his phone. Not even for Edie. That's not like him."

"What was the name of the fat cat?" Connor demanded.

Bruno looked irritated. "Who the fuck knows. He's Kevlar, the mystery man. He doesn't talk unless you put a gun to his head, and sometimes not even then. Edie'd know, but she has no phone."

"Edie the graphic artist?" Davy asked.

"Yeah, Kev's new true love," Bruno said. "She lost her dad today, to that sniper. Everything's all fucked up. I just knew that if he started poking around in his past, it would blow up right in his face. And sure enough. Ka-boom. What a fucking mess."

Miles rubbed his hands together. "So? We came here to find him, so let's go find him."

Bruno pulled out a phone, punched buttons. "I've got Edie's little sister's number." He waited, and shook his head. "Nobody's answering."

"How about Kev's house?" Miles suggested. "We might find, I don't know. Clues. Right?"

Davy and Connor's faces lit up. They looked at Bruno. "You got keys to his place?" Con asked.

Bruno gave them a devilish grin. "Who the fuck needs keys?"

The blast knocked every cell of Kev's body loose. He lay there, stunned. Struggled to his feet.

Someone hurtled through the door. Kev delivered a bruising kick to the bastard's face, knocking him back into the drifting billows of dust. The guy fetched up hard against the wrought iron railing.

Kev followed up, landing a jab to the kidney. Someone was screaming. Female, far away, words impossible to hear. The guy blocked the chop he aimed to the bridge of the nose and snagged the fleshy part of Kev's thumb, twisting it over in a manner calculated to induce agony up the twisted tendons. But not to him. He held himself apart, detached from screaming agony. He had lots of practice.

His twisted hand was useless, trembling, but he jabbed up with the other, trying for a stab to the pancreas. The bastard twisted like an eel, took it on the ribs, but Kev managed to snag his hand. He grabbed the back of the guy's jacket, and heaved him over the railing—

The man's face came into focus, in an endless, eternally dilated instant, turning, somersaulting, staring straight into Kev's eyes.

Sean.

His brother. His twin. Their fingers tightened around each others' hands, an iron death grip. He broke Sean's fall. The weight of his brother's dangling body almost wrenched Kev's arm out of its socket.

Kev hung over the railing, coughing and choking on the smoke. Sean dangled from his hand, like fruit from a branch.

His reflection, staring up at him. Blood streamed from Sean's nose, his cut lip. He swung there, backlit against billows of dust, eyes bright and sharp. Kev tightened his muscles against the dead weight dragging at his muscles and tendons.

"Sean?" His lips formed the word, but no sound come out.

"So you know me," Sean said. "You know my name." Each word was bitten off, cold and hard and separate.

Kev's mouth worked, uselessly. That voice. *Yes.* His brother. He'd heard that voice in his dreams, every damn night. The dream memories tumbled down on him, like rolling logs. Crushing him with their weight.

"You lying snake son of a bitch," Sean said. "Let go of me, and get your sorry ass down here, so I can kick the shit out of it."

Bam. Bam. Muzzle flashes flickered in the murk behind them. So there were more coming in the door. A woman's voice, shrill. A hand, tugging at his arm. Her words sank in. ". . . pull him up, you stupid asshole!" she shrieked. "You two can have this fight later!"

Fight? What fight? More muzzle flashes. Bullets whizzed and whined. He was disoriented, confused. He hauled on Sean's arm—

Fire flicked across his forearm, and the bullet drove into

the door behind him. Wood shards splintered, flew, and his hand gave way—

Sean fell. A bellow of denial built in Kev's lungs, cutting off when his brother landed like a cat, and flung himself behind a couch for cover. Someone was pulling, dragging him down—*Liv!* Jesus, that was Liv Endicott! Recognition lit up his brain like a blinking Christmas tree. So sweet, to recognize her, even if she was scowling, yelling.

Bullets whined and zinged over their heads. He jerked back into focus, yanked out the H&K and squeezed off shots while he barked out directions. "Right side of the bedroom closet. Safe in the wall. Combo is 'thy fearful symmetry,' with a star, an asterisk, and a pound sign after each word. Three pistols, six clips. Get them all!"

She wiggled through the door on her hands and knees. He squeezed off shot after shot, peering into the murk. A shriek of pain from the direction of the front door rewarded him. Liv was back with an armful of hardware, clips sliding from her arms. That was when he saw that she was pregnant. Holy shit. He gestured shyly with the gun at her belly. "Is that . . . uh . . . did Sean—"

"He did," she said crisply. "This is Sean's son. Your nephew. Eamon. Do you suppose we could catch up on our lives another time?"

He pointed to the guns. "Can you handle one of these?"

"Hell, yes." She grabbed a big PX4 Storm subcompact, and positioned herself while he changed clips. Sean was looking up, gesturing frantically. Kev let drop a Para-Ordnance P-14-45. Sean plucked it out of midair and dropped back again as bullets punched into the gray plush couch. Stuffing flew. Fuck. Kev hoped the wooden structure inside the thing would provide enough cover for him.

"Hold your fire!" someone bawled, from the direction of the front door. The voice was familiar. "You assholes! We need them alive!"

Furious protests and obscenities from the direction of the kitchen. Kev aimed a shot toward the voice. *Bam.* A hoarse shout of rage.

Nephew? Son of a bitch. She had his nephew floating in there, and his name would be Eamon? He'd gone from zero to a hundred, in seconds. It made him giddy, to have his family back in his head.

A bullet whiffled through his hair, snapping him back into focus. He wouldn't have anything if they all ended up dead.

"Goddamnit, hold your fire!" the rasping voice bellowed again.

"Get back up here!" he yelled down to Sean. "I'll cover you!"

He blasted away while Sean made a dive for the spiral staircase, but the attackers weren't returning fire. They had yielded to the authority of whoever had been bawling those orders.

Sean jerked. Stopped halfway up, and stood still, as if he'd forgotten what he was doing. His head dropped back, eyes locked on Liv's, his eyes pleading as he reached up, clawing at his chest.

A tiny dart protruded from it.

Sean fell, tumbling head over ass. He ended up sideways, head down, arms dangling from the railings.

"Sean!" Liv pumped bullets furiously into the featureless cloud of dust and hurled herself down the stairs.

A man stepped out of the smoke, grinning, and Kev suddenly remembered where he'd heard that rasping voice. That big, awkward body, the strange frequency of the man's fucked-up brainwaves.

This was the guy who had held a knife to Edie's throat. The one who'd left bruises on her breast.

Click. Click. Kev's clip was empty. He groped for a fresh cartridge, but the guy was walking in slow motion through the apocalyptic, dusty murk toward Liv and Sean, laughing like some goblin from hell.

The dart would fly before his gun could be loaded and fired. The guy took aim. Kev crouched on the railing like a panther. He screamed as he leaped. Pink-rimmed eyes flicked up, the dart gun swung up—

Gravity smashed them together. They rolled, sprawled, through shards of brick and glass, flailing and wrestling. The guy was horribly strong and agile. His eyes glinted with wild empty light that made Kev think of Ava. Dead, but run by something else, something alien and evil.

The guy's extra fifty pounds of bulk almost pinned him, and he took a nasty punch to the ear. He saw stars, but wrenched an arm free to block just as the man's hand slashed down clutching a sharp shard of glass. He jerked it back into the fat guy's face, and the flinch gave him the opening he needed to flip the man off his body. He slammed a brick toward the side of the guy's head, but he blocked it with a shout and stumbled back, rolling up onto his feet, panting heavily.

Kev followed the flit of the man's eyes, and dove for the dart gun at the same moment that the other man did. A kick spun it out of Fat Guy's reach, and it skittered closer to the spiral staircase—

Bam. Bam. Liv was trying to shoot at the goblin now that they were no longer grappling, her face tense with concentration. Fat Guy's hand swung up to let a dagger fly, but Kev turned, letting it whoosh by and bounce harmlessly off the bricks.

The guy leaped, hit the ground to seize the dart gun, and aimed from the ground up at Liv. Kev leaped between them with a shout.

The gun spat. He felt the blow like a fist to his stomach, stumbled back against Liv, knocking her heavily onto Sean's limp form.

He stared at the dart sticking out of the black hoodie, a few fingers above the level of his navel, while Liv was shoving him aside, struggling to bring the gun up, screaming.

The thing was sticking out of the fucking money belt.

Bam. Bam. No time to appreciate the joke. He struggled to heave Sean over his shoulder. His brother was as heavy as fucking concrete.

Up the stairs, legs shaking, Liv backing up behind him. Fat Guy came after them. She finally trimmed the bastard, and he jerked back with a shout of anger, grabbing his shoulder. Lucky shot, because her clip emptied as they reached the top of the stairs.

They ran for the bedroom. He laid Sean down on the floor, ran back to lock the door and wedge the dresser in front of it. Then Kev lifted the blinds of the window—

Zing, a bullet clipped the window frame. Splinters and paint flew.

Fuck. They were trapped from below, too.

Davy tried to call Sean to update him as they followed Tony, but got no answer. They pulled up abreast of Tony's pickup in an industrial district. Bruno rolled down his window and gestured up ahead. "Second building on the next block. The one with all those SUVs parked right in front of it." He frowned at it. "Weird. Nobody lives in the building except for Kev. There's usually nobody who—"

Boom. Windows blasted out of the top floor. The power of the explosion vibrated through their bodies.

Car alarms started to squeal. There was agitated activity around the SUVs parked in front of the building. Shouts, yells.

"Holy fuck." Miles's voice was shaking.

Ping. Davy's phone signaled an incoming text message. He stared at it. "Sean was in there," he said, his voice dead flat. "Liv, too."

There was about four seconds of blank horror, and Miles felt the atmosphere shift. The McCloud dudes were ice cold, all business. A trick he had not learned yet. He shook where he sat, thinking of Sean . . . no. Not Sean. Not Liv. And the baby, too. Not thinkable. He shoved it away. Twisted his hands, clenched his teeth. Hung on to his shit.

Davy jerked a compartment up from the floor of the SUV, and pulled out a gun case. "I have my Glock, and a Colt Cobra. What have you guys got?"

Miles shook his head. He'd never gotten a license to carry concealed. Who was he trying to kid? Davy grunted his disgust, and tossed him the Glock, and three clips. "Take this."

"I got my Beretta, and the pendant and earring set that Tam wanted delivered to her client," Con said. "A hundred and fifty K worth of custom designed platinum, diamonds, Composition B, and frag."

"Oh, man," Miles said. "Tam'll kill you if you cost her that much money." Tam still scared the living bejesus out of him.

Con wrenched open his shoulder bag and pulled out a crimson tooled leather jewelry case. He flipped it open and pulled out the shimmering handful of loot inside. "Jesus, that woman is crazy."

"Her psychosis is useful in a pinch," Davy slid a clip into the gun.

"I'd prefer regular old grenades, thanks. I don't need the bling."

Davy pulled a pair of binoculars out of the center console. "Three guys going in, at least one is armed—no, all of them armed, with Uzi's, it looks like. What did Kev get mixed up in, fucking World War III?"

Bruno leaned out of the window. "I'll circle around," he said, in a tight voice. "We'll park behind the building next door."

They made a loop around the big warehouses, and heard the gunshots begin. "That's good," Davy said.

"Good?" Miles's voice broke. "How can that possibly be good?"

Davy and Con exchanged thin smiles. "Somebody's still alive to shoot back," Con said.

Tony got out, with his shotgun and a Beretta Cougar. Bruno leaped out of the pickup, brandishing a Taurus Millennium. He was spitting angry words at his aunt, pushing down on her bouffant hairdo. Trying to make her get her head down. The pouffy jet-black curls sprang right up like a jack-in-the-box, plump hands waving. Bruno flung his hand up in eloquent disgust, and loped along the side of the building.

They hastened to follow. Miles's heart was lodged in the place where his Adam's apple ought to be, thudding in its tiny prison. He clutched the gun in a sweaty hand, hung on to his guts. To think he could be leading the life of a tech nerd. Cowering under a rock like a pallid, lovelorn grub in his parents' basement. No life, no sex, no Cindy. No mortal danger, either. Suffocatingly safe as a bug in a rug.

But no, here he was. Gunshots were building into a storm of apocalyptic intensity, and he was running toward it. Not away.

Bam, bam. Miles jumped, squeaked. That was closer. Outside the building, not inside. Bruno peered around the edge of the building, jerked back, gestured them closer. "Two cars, six guys," he whispered. "Kev's trying to get out the back window. They've boxed him in."

Davy's grin was feral. "So let's distract the bastards."

Con stared at the fleet of black SUVs pulled up in the alley beyond the Dumpster, his eyes slitted. "If I take the car and loop around, I'll get behind them to toss the diamond doodads."

"Be careful," Davy said, as Con pelted away so fast he forgot to limp. They crouched amid piles of garbage behind the Dumpster.

"Cover me," Bruno whispered. "I'm going into the building next door. Going to get up to that window. To help them out."

"I'm with you," Davy said. He slapped Miles on the shoulder. "Keep those guys busy."

Davy and Bruno ran for it, and all hell broke loose.

Miles's head rang with gunfire. He squeezed off shots, biting his lip til it bled. Keep those guys busy? Leave that life or death job to the shit-scared, worked-over tech nerd with the borrowed gun? Great.

Tony seemed to read his thoughts, and slapped him on the shoulder. "Concentrate on the two guys in back," he yelled into Miles's ear. "Keep those fuckers down. I'll take the guys in the front."

Direction helped. He did has he was told, but the noise made his head ring, and everything felt grotesquely bright and surreal. But he kept on until the clip was empty, and reloaded with shaking hands.

Keeping those fuckers down.

CHAPTER
32

Kev's muscles quivered with strain as he laid Sean down gently, letting him slump against the wall. Kev sank down beside him, panting.

He was all out of ideas. The walls were closing in. The front windows were a sheer four-story drop with a gauntlet of bullets in between; whoever was still pissed and shooting inside, plus whoever was pissed and coming up the stairs, and who the fuck knew who waited outside. The stairwell was the only way on to the roof, another dead end. And even if he did pry Sean out this bedroom window alive, he had no idea if he could clamber across that gap one-handed, with his twin brother draped over his shoulder like a two-hundred-and-sixty-pound scarf. To say nothing of the idea of Liv stepping over it, too. She might as well have a bull's-eye painted all over her pregnant belly. Jesus. The very thought made his joints loosen with horror.

Liv gathered Sean's limp body up, supporting him with one arm. Kev gestured toward her bulge. "Are you, ah . . . is it OK?"

She gave him a look that made him wish he hadn't asked.

There was no need to even say it, their imminent doom was so obvious.

"I'm glad he got to see you. At least once," she said. "Even if it was through a hail of bullets. Before . . . whatever happens now happens."

"Yeah." He reached out to touch Sean's carotid artery. His brother's heart pumped away, strong and steady. "I'm glad, too."

"Glad he got to bitch you out, too," she said, with more heat. "Not as much as you deserve, though. You bastard, Kev. How could you?"

She clearly expected him to say something. To defend himself. But nothing came out. There was too much to say. It was bottlenecked.

"Why the hell did you stay away all this time?" The words exploded out of her, voice shaking. "All that time wasted! And it hurt him, you know that? It hurt them all, but it hurt him the most!"

It hurt me, too. He cast around for a starting place, but the story was too huge, too long, too crazy, and he was so rattled, he wouldn't make any sense. "It's not my fault," he said helplessly.

Her lips tightened. Not good enough. Try again, asshole.

But he was speechless, clueless. All tapped out. "I'm sorry."

And oh, God, he was. He should have broken down those inner walls before today. Years ago. Guilt ached and twisted. He had no fucking clue how he could have done it, but he should have, somehow.

Gunblasts started up again, but they weren't landing up here on the window frame. He ventured a peek, ducked down as he saw glass shatter in the windows of one of the SUVs. Shouts.

Excitement surged inside him. He tamped it down. It was nice, and heartwarming, that somebody was on their side, but it changed nothing. They were still fucked. He took another peek—

Crash. Glass shattered inward, all over them. He reeled back. Liv shrieked, cowering, holding her arms over hers and Sean's faces. More bullets tore through the slats of the window shades. They dangled, twisted and broken in the silence that followed, swinging in the cold wind that swept in.

"Kev? Yo! You in there?"

Holy shit, that was Bruno! Kev leaped up to see, staying well back and out of range. His little brother was framed by the scaffolding in the building across from him. Grinning madly, eyes alight.

"Bruno?" His voice came out in a hoarse, croaking whisper. "How the fuck did you know—where's Edie?"

Bruno flung up his hands, a gesture he got from Zia Rosa. "Later for that." He heaved a big plank through the air. It landed heavily on the fire escape, jittering the shards of glass that covered it. "Come on!"

"Liv, first," he said.

Bruno looked blank. "Who's Liv?"

"Liv's OK?" Another guy appeared behind him.

Their eyes met. Kev's knees almost gave. That face, so hard and craggy. So much like Dad, it hit him like a club. "Davy?" he whispered. All that was missing was the long hair, the bushy beard, the wild, staring look in his eyes. Davy was the living image of their father.

"Hello? For fuck's sake?" Bruno brayed through cupped hands. "Stop before I puke, OK? Can we save the violins for later? Please?"

Shots whined off the scaffolding, ricocheting off the building outside, as if to illustrate his point. Bruno leaped back, cursing.

Kev hauled Liv to her feet. "You, first," he said.

"No!" she yelled. "Sean is injured, and—"

"And you're pregnant. I have to cover you from this side

while you go. I'll carry Sean over after, but I won't go until you're across."

She made a grumbling sound deep in her throat. "Typical."

"When I start shooting, go fast," he ordered. He wrenched the blinds away from the adjacent window and rammed it up and open.

Bang. Crunch. Someone was kicking in the door, jarring the furniture he'd blocked it with. *Bam,* a gunshot smashed the lock. Wood splintered. *Bang.* It was the fat guy, beating his way through the door.

The dresser shifted. One of the fat guy's mad, glittering eyes shone through the crack. Kev took a shot. *Bam.* The eye vanished.

Crunch, another powerful kick. The door opened a little wider.

"Hurry!" he howled at Liv. He leaned, hanging out the window and shooting down at those bastards with a long, blood-curdling yell.

Liv crawled out, wobbled on the warped board for a few heart-clutching moments, tumbled forward to catch Bruno's outstretched hands, and was yanked to safety. Kev dropped back inside the window, breathing hard. Still alive, and so was she. He was dizzy with relief.

Crunch. The bedroom door jolted open farther. He pumped a few shots through the crack in the door while trying to figure out a way to get his unconscious brother out the window and onto a tiny fire escape.

His imperfect solution was to slide out backward, leaving his back as a shield and his ass as a tantalizing target, while reaching in to grip Sean under the armpits, dragging his brother's limp body out onto the fire escape. There was barely room for one, let alone two, but he wrestled Sean into place over his shoulder and forced his trembling legs to unfold. Balance. Every muscle shook. Sweat dripped off his chin. Bruno's face was a blur in the background, Davy's and Liv's beside his.

He pulled them into focus. Big mistake. He let them blur into the background again. The raw fear on their faces did not help him at all.

Something bigger than a gun exploded below. Shouts, yells. He didn't dare look to see. He swung his leg over the fire escape, set his foot on the board. Balanced on that quivering leg on the warped plank while he lifted the other foot off the relative stability of the fire escape.

It would be three or four shuffling steps before he could pass his burden to the outstretched hands on the other side. *One.* The plank jiggled and bowed under their combined weight. He waited for a bullet to punch into him from below. Not yet. *Two. Three.* Davy and Bruno leaned forward, reaching desperately to grab Sean—

Bang, a bigger explosion. *Whump, crash. Crack,* a bullet from the window behind him scored the side of Kev's shoe. He did a wobbling dance step as the board shuddered loose of its place on the fire escape.

He heaved Sean to Bruno and Davy with the last instant of purchase he had left, and then he was dancing in midair, legs flailing—

He caught himself on the scaffolding, and hung there, by the same damn hand that had caught Sean over the railing. The same arm that had been smashed by the tree trunk in the waterfall incident.

Fucking *ouch.* He struggled to breathe. Looked down at his feet, waving over the blur of lethal activity beneath.

Davy and Bruno were squeezing off shots at the guy in the window. He was shooting back. Kev thought of the waterfall. Crazy laughter bubbled up from deep inside. This felt so familiar, somehow. What the hell he did to deserve this crazy shit, he did not fucking know.

A hand clamped over his wrist. Davy had braved the fat guy's bullets and climbed down the scaffolding to pull him up while Bruno covered him, spraying bullets into Kev's bedroom window. With some grunting and straining and excrutiating pain, he hooked a knee, then a foot. Davy hauled Kev up by his sore arm and tossed him face-first into the dim building. Kev fell to his knees, gasping and coughing.

"We don't have time for this!" Bruno yelled. "You shot? Wounded?"

"Fine," he gasped, choking and coughing. "I think."

"Then move your ass! Fast! Now!"

They dragged him along. He stumbled, running where he was led, thudding through forests of pillars and steel cables. Davy carried Sean without apparent effort. The situation looked dire as they peered out of the bottom floor. Then a car horn began to blast. Tony's old Chevy pickup appeared around the corner, Zia Rosa at the wheel, mouth open in a battle yell. She leaned out the window, screamed, *"vaffanculo, you stinkin' sonzabitches!"* and laid on the gas, heading for a black SUV.

Men leaped to get out of her way. *Crash,* she rammed into them, and put the truck in reverse. *Bam.* Zia's windshield shattered. Tony and a lanky guy that Kev didn't recognize leaped out from behind the Dumpster and dove into the bed of the pickup. Tony screamed at Rosa to drive, drive, drive. Another guy came running with a limp from behind the smoking ruins of the SUVs.

Tall, long hair. *Connor.* That was Connor. They were all here.

The Chevy slowed. Zia Rosa howled for them to hurry. A bone rattling thud as he jumped? fell? was pushed? into the pickup bed. Sean thudded in after him. Liv, Davy, and Bruno followed. The tires squealed as Zia Rosa reversed, braked violently, and took off.

Some moments later, he hoisted himself up, and looked around.

Liv lay on her side, cradling Sean's head in her arms, staring at him. Davy stared at him. Con stared at him. Bruno and

Tony and the dark-haired guy stared, too. All of them were staring at him.

Oh, shit. He was in for it now.

Tom looked away, stoic as the EMT dressed the wound on his shoulder. His teeth were clenched so hard his skull ached. But not against the pain. It was the anger that he could hardly control.

That sneaky son of a bitch Larsen had fucked him up the ass. Seven men dead, four in the explosion in the apartment, three in the firefight. Three more injured, one with a crushed pelvis from being rammed by the pickup, driven by that crazy hag, whoever the fuck she was. Tom would find out, soon. Oh, yeah. She would pay. Larsen and his fucking motley band were going to see what happened to people who messed with Dr. O's army.

Detective Widome of the PPD was talking. His jowls flapped. Tom breathed down the impulse to rip the man's slack, ugly face off his skull. Before throwing him facedown and crushing his vertebrae into pebbles, one by one with his boot heel. "Excuse me," he said, through his teeth. "I was woolgathering. Would you repeat that?"

"Certainly. I was just saying that we need a formal statement as soon as possible about your involvement in—"

"I told you! Charles Parrish contracted my security firm to deal with Kev Larsen, aka McCloud. I'll demonstrate that accord at my earliest opportunity. Tragically, we were unable to protect Mr. Parrish from his killer, but when we got a tip Larsen had returned, we came down on the bastard." Tom waved his arm at smoking vehicles, the shattered glass, ambulances, body bags. "This was the result. The story is straightforward. There won't be any surprises in my statement."

Widome chewed his lip as he surveyed the carnage. "I'll

still be interested. Quite a fight, hmm? Bit off more than you could chew?"

Tom swallowed back killing rage. "We underestimated his resources," he ground out. "We weren't aware that his brothers were already backing him up. It was just a manhunt before. Now it's a war."

"I don't think so." Widome gave him a big smile. "I think you'd better step aside and let us deal with this, Mr. Bixby."

"I have to fulfil my professional obligations." Tom smiled back, even bigger. "I'm sure we can work together. Help each other."

"Of course," Widome said. "Within the confines of the law."

"Of course. And now, if you'll excuse me. I need to see that my employees are getting the care they need. And contact the widows of the men who died today. Later. OK?" He crunched through the broken glass, nose stinging at the stink of burning rubber, and called Des.

Des picked up, and started to babble. "I've got a problem. I need your people to go to the Parrish building to dismantle the boxes we put in the library for Larsen this morning. The Parrish bitch is flapping her jaw. No one appears to be listening, yet, but just for safety's sake—"

"You call that a problem?" Tom let out a harsh laugh. "I'll tell you problems. Seven dead guys. A fortune spent on their recruitment and training, lost. Claymores exploding in our faces. Two armored vehicles, essentially destroyed. Three men in the hospital, with bullet wounds. One rammed by a fucking truck. The press nosing around, the police three miles up my ass. And Larsen, gone. Because of your little fuck buddy. Ava the wonder cunt."

"Gone? How?" Des's voice cracked. "How the fuck did you—"

"I didn't! Your girlfriend was jerking herself off, and she muffed it. He cuffed her, gagged her, and locked her in the fucking supply closet. I left her there, by the way. In the closet. To reflect upon her personality flaws. You go let her out. I didn't have the stomach."

"Holy shit," Des muttered. "Where's Larsen now?"

"Who knows," Tom said. "He blew up his apartment with my guys in it, shot up the rest of my men with his psychotic brothers, and now they're gone. Off to plot how best to fuck us next, no doubt. So if you've got your thumb on Edie Parrish, keep it there. We end this tonight."

"Tonight? But I—"

"Tonight. We get the big family bloodbath all over with. I do not want this fucking freakshow to drag on and on. I am done."

"But Ava needed Edie for—"

"I don't care," Tom told him. "My profit margin just took a fucking nosedive twenty minutes ago. I won't stick my ass out any further just because your girlfriend wants to diddle herself some more."

"Tom, listen."

"No. *You* listen. Finish it tonight, or the deal is off. I withdraw my support, and you deal with the McClouds yourself." He focused on a body bag being rolled onto a truck. "Trust me, you don't want to do that. Go get your girlfriend out of the closet before her head explodes."

Tom hung up. He hoped the dickhead managed to wrangle that crazy bitch into shape fast, because Ava would need to put in some serious X-Cog crowning action soon to sell this fucked-up scenario to the law, and the press. It was spinning out of control.

But Tom was itching to get his hands around McCloud necks. To feel veins throb, eyes pop. See faces turn purple. His heart pounded.

A final gift, to lay on that dark altar. In honor of Dr. O.

CHAPTER
33

Dusk faded to dark while Edie lay there, cuddling Ronnie, who slept like a rock. She herself couldn't hope for sleep, not unless she asked Dr. Katz for some in pill form, and she'd sooner drown herself than do that. Besides, she had to stay sharp. Not that she felt sharp, except in the sense of jittery and jagged. Fragile as crystal.

Kev hadn't called. Of course, he wouldn't have Ronnie's number unless he'd gotten in touch with Bruno. So he'd been missing all day.

Or he wasn't calling her on purpose. Because he'd gotten what he needed, and he was done with her now.

No. She rejected that voice nattering in her head. She wouldn't be fooled. Not by fear. But neither did she want to cling to a sweet lovely lie, and hide her face from the painful truth. That was no good, either.

There was a TV on the dresser. Edie grabbed the remote and turned it on, just for a little chatter. The silence was so heavy, she felt like she would asphyxiate under it. Local news started to play.

She stared at it, zoning out. The crumpled e-mail was still

clutched in her fist. She took a look at the paper, smoothing out the wrinkles.

It was a picture of Des. His eyes glowed, as if a light shown out of them. The effect was chilling. She studied every element, mixing them up, turning them upside down. She wished her psychic ability came with a glossary handbook. Her subconsious mind was so damn convoluted. She had a hell of a time figuring this stuff out.

Des wore a crown in the drawing. Not surprising. She'd always perceived him as the crown prince of Helix. But that empty glow, brrr. He looked like someone possessed. And there were hearts. Bunches of them, like something a lovestruck thirteen-year-old would draw all over her school notebook. Around the signature word of the e-mail, *Des*, she had drawn a larger heart, and behind it, two crossed bones.

The symbol for poison, but with a heart, not a skull. Hmm.

Hearts, like the ones she'd drawn all over her mother's portrait.

Odd, that her mother and her father had both received visits from Des on the days of their deaths. But then again, they probably had both received visits from Des on a daily basis. She was being fanciful.

An image on TV caught her eye. She did a double-take, and jolted upright, upping the volume. It was a photo of the red-haired girl. The one who had come to the book signing. The one she'd drawn.

". . . at large, but a manhunt is underway for Craig Roberts, prime suspect in the murder of Victoria Sobel, a Portland University student who was found strangled in her dorm room last night," said a female newscaster. "Sobel had been involved with Roberts, a local radio disc jockey, for the last few months, according to friends. Roberts was last seen in the Clackamas area . . ."

The words faded away, drowned out by the roar in her head. So telling Vicky about Craig hadn't saved her. No escape for Vicky.

She flipped off the TV. Better to face the smothering silence than get slapped in the face with how ineffectual she was. She saw Vicky Sobel's freckled, laughing face in her mind's eye, even with the TV off. Tears slid down her cheeks.

She thought about Kev's lurking spider, and her stomach flopped.

But Kev wasn't like Vicky. And neither was she. The thought stirred in the depths of her, beneath the pain and the fear. A quiet voice, not the scolding one. Reminding her of the flat, undeniable truth.

I was right about Vicky Sobel. I always call it right. Always.

It wasn't particularly comforting, but it straightened her slumped spine, even while her chest shook. Tears streamed down her face.

She slid down, butt sliding off the bed and onto the braided rug, shaking with sobs, which was better than that hard, bruised ache in her chest. She hadn't shed tears all day, except for that first shallow explosion, with Bruno, and that had been more shock than anything.

It had finally started to flow. She cried for the father she'd never had, the one she'd never have. No chance to redeem herself now.

She didn't know poor Vicky Sobel at all, but that distant, awful tragedy unlocked the floodgates of her own. By the time it all worked through her system, she felt deeper, softer. Calmer. And very clear.

She was going to trust herself. She was worth trusting. And she was going to fix this mess. She was not going to sit around and meekly swallow this evil, lying, ridiculous bullshit down. No way. No more.

She got up, paced restlessly around in the twilit room.

"Hey." Ronnie's voice, soft and whispery. "You're here. Good." She rubbed her bleary eyes.

Edie spun around, dove for the bed, and the two of them

lay there, hugging tight. The knowledge twisted and ached inside her, that she was going to have to leave her sister alone again to solve this problem. Some malevolent entity was at work, someone who wished her ill. She had to fight it. She could not be passive and just hope for the best. Truth would not prevail unless it was helped along, vigorously. By her, personally.

She thought about the kidnappers. The banquet. The vials of poison inexplicably planted at her apartment. And now, this. Kev's disappearance. Kev, on that video. Her father, killed. Kev framed.

Just as she'd been framed.

Somebody wanted . . . what? Money? A mess this big, violence this awful, it could only be about money. Or revenge. Kev was the only candidate for revenge that she knew of, and she had ruled him out.

That left money. Ronnie ostensibly had it, now. But whoever was making this happen was probably not going to leave matters that way.

She buried her nose against Ronnie's shirt, and pondered the spooky sketch she'd drawn of Des Marr, with his empty eyes and his crown. The e-mail to Mom, from Des. The hearts. Poison.

If Ronnie died . . . the bulk of her father's multibillion dollar fortune went to the Parrish Foundation, to support medical research. Des was on the board of the Parrish Foundation.

But Des? What could he have against her father? The Marr family was immensely rich in its own right. Des was successful, admired, adored. Charles Parrish had liked and respected him. Had mentored him since business school. Something was so strange about it, so twisted. She shivered. Thought about the boxes Kev had mentioned in his text message.

Either Kev was lying, or Des was. She knew who she wanted to believe, but wanting wasn't enough. Certainly not for the police.

"Ronnie? Baby? I'm going to have to leave you for a while," she whispered. "There's something I need to check on, before it's too late."

"I'll come with you," Ronnie said.

She considered it, and regretfully shook her head. Ronnie had to be safer here, surrounded by security personnel, than wandering around with her bumbling sister Edie, with her empty wallet and her borrowed Ruger six-shot. "You can't," she said, helplessly. "Things are too dangerous. I don't have a plan, or any money. I can't keep you safe."

"I'd rather be with you than be safe." Ronnie's arms tightened.

"Please, baby. Just for a while. Somebody's setting Kev up, and me, too. I have to go check some possible evidence. Before it's too late."

"You?" Ronnie's eyes got big. "Setting up you? For what happened to Dad? But that's nuts. Nobody who knew you would believe that!"

Edie was intensely grateful her father hadn't told Ronnie about the planted vial of poison. "Marta believed it," she pointed out.

Ronnie rolled her eyes. "Yeah, well. Marta is Marta." Her eyes sharpened. "You look more guilty if you run, you know."

"I'll look guilty no matter what I do," she said.

"This is so they can't put you in the nuthouse, right?"

Or worse. She thought of the kidnappers, the cold blade at her throat. "Yeah," she said. "Something like that."

"If you run away for good, I want to go, too," Ronnie said, with quiet intensity. "Don't leave me here. Promise you'll come back for me."

Edie grabbed Ronnie. "I promise," she said softly. "I don't know how, but I promise. If you'll promise me something, too."

"What?"

"Be careful with Des Marr."

"Why? He's always been so nice." Then Ronnie's eyes widened. "Oh! I see. Did you do one of your special drawings? Can I see it?"

Edie hesitated, and then pulled it out and unfolded it. Ronnie stared at it for a few moments.

"Yikes," she said slowly. "Spooky. You don't have any idea what—"

"Nope," Edie said. "Not a flipping clue. Just please, be careful with him. Don't ever be alone with him. Don't go anywhere with him. OK?"

"OK." Ronnie pulled a cell phone out of her pocket, and a charger off the desk. "Take this, all right? I won't tell anybody that you have it."

Edie took it, and realized that it was turned off. Duh. Of course Aunt Evelyn would have turned it off, after they'd dosed Ronnie.

Kev could have called while it was off. Her heart leaped, her fingers twitched to turn it on, check for missed calls. But not now. She slid it in her pocket, stuffed the charger in the other. "Thanks, sweetie."

Ronnie sniffed. "I'll charge up my old one. You still remember my last number, don't you? I'll program it in, OK? And call me. Call soon."

Tears grabbed them by the throat, and it took a good fifteen minutes of hugging and sniffling before she could start to plan. Though plan was really too kind a word for it. This was a blind impulse. A suicidal dive out of the frying pan and into the naked flames.

But it was all she could do. There was no excuse for cowering here like a bunny in a cage, waiting for the walls to close in on her.

She convinced Ronnie to wait in her room, so that she could think a straight thought without blubbering. She stood in the corridor, gathering her wits, her nerve. What to do. Money. Car keys. A way out of here. A place to go. Her list of goals. She hurried to the room earmarked as hers, and rummaged through the jewelry box. She'd opted to keep her valuables here, and there were costly pieces, with good stones that she might be able to sell. She shoved pendants, earrings, bracelets, rings into her pockets. Funny how the jewelry was hers, but she still felt like she was stealing it.

At the bottom of the stairs was Dad's studio. She went in, opened the desk drawer where he'd kept keys. Three of his four cars were parked downstairs, but inside the compound. One set of keys was to a Porsche that was acutally hers on paper, being one of Dad's string-attached gifts. She'd never gotten an opportunity to drive the thing. It was also inside the walls, though, and she was never going to be able to convince the security personnel to open the gate for her to drive out.

She saw a set of keys she remembered Dad using one day when he'd taken some philanthropist friend of his to look at the Parrish Foundation building. A building master key. She thought about the boxes in the library, and slid it into her pocket.

Her next blind impulse compelled her down to the security room. She stood outside the door, which was slightly ajar.

Paul Ditillo's voice floated out. His back was to the door. ". . . told you that crazy rich bitch hated her dad! She's in it, up to her neck! And if you ask me, she's even more dangerous than that . . . huh?"

Robert nudged him, eyes darting toward the door as Edie pushed it open. Paul turned, stared. Funny, how that hostility used to bother her so much. Now it was so insignificant. She stared at the banks of TV screens that showed all the vantage points of the security cameras.

Paul cleared his throat. "What can we do for you, Ms. Parrish?"

She groped for a coherent answer as she studied the screens. Four images on each screen. Four different screens. Five seconds for each screen. God, how she sucked at multitasking. "Ah . . . I was just, um, wondering what your security procedures were, tonight," she said, lamely. "I wondered what, ah, precautions you were taking."

Paul exchanged can-you-believe-this-chick glances with Robert while she checked the clock on the computer screen against the watch she had on her wrist. Her watch ran thirteen seconds ahead. The north view appeared when the minute hand was at twelve. Five seconds. Then the south view. Then east. Then west. Back to the top, twenty seconds later. Three cycles of each direction of views each minute.

"We're taking all due precautions," Paul said. "You have nothing to worry about. Why not just go take a nice little pill and lie down?"

She blinked. Wow. Gloves off. Not that Paul had ever been particularly polite to her, but zowie, that was harsh. Contemptuous.

At the right of the entry were hooks for hanging coats. She recognized the one Paul had worn the other day when he picked her up to go to the salon. Charcoal gray, lined with puffy silver down. Funny, how vivid every little detail was. "Actually, I was wondering if one of you gentlemen would drive me someplace," she improvised wildly. "I need to run a couple errands, and obviously, it's better if I'm not—"

"No," Paul said.

His response was certainly no surprise, but she bristled and put on an affronted look. "What do you mean, no?"

"No, meaning you're staying right here, Ms. Parrish."

She lifted her chin. "You have no authority to keep me here. My father thought he did. But he's not here."

"Yeah, and isn't that convenient," Paul sneered. He circled the desks and backed her up with the force of his hostility, right up to the row of coats. She sidled until she was pressed against Paul's coat in the corner, recoiling at his hot, smothering tobacco breath.

She groped delicately behind herself for his coat pocket. Found it. Dug, found nothing. *Shit.*

"I'll be honest with you, Ms. Parrish. I'm not real sure who's in charge around here right now." Paul lifted a thick forefinger, tapped her collarbone with it. "But one thing I am sure of. It isn't you."

Edie glared back as she scrabbled in the other pocket. There. Zipped halfway up . . . but the zipper gave. Her hand slid in. Car keys. A wallet. She seized both, slid them into her jeans pocket. Grateful for the corner she was wedged into, hiding her criminal activity.

Paul was getting off on his intimidation show. "Go on upstairs, Ms. Parrish." His lip curled in an unpleasant smile. "Be a good girl."

She backed out, trying to look cowed, and ran up the stairs, back to Ronnie's room. She slapped the door open. "I'll need help to get out," she said breathlessly. "Do you have some firecrackers left?"

"The ones Dad had a fit about? That I was supposed to get rid of?"

"You didn't, did you?" she asked, anxious.

Ronnie's eyes lit up. "Oh! You want a diversion? Super cool!"

"But I don't want to get you in trouble," Edie fretted.

Ronnie shrugged. "With who? With Aunt Evelyn? Get real."

Ronnie pulled the cardboard box of firecrackers out of her closet and began to scoop out her favorites while Edie puzzled through the logistics. The escape had to be meticulously timed. Since there was not room inside the enclosure for the vehicles of security and domestic staff, they parked in a covered structure outside, parallel to the west wall. The oak tree in the middle of the west yard had branches that would get her to the edge of the eight foot wall, and foliage to hide her while she climbed. They decided that Ronnie should start throwing firecrackers from the terrace five seconds before the second hand clicked on twelve.

"But how many should I throw?" Ronnie asked.

"Just enough to get me over the wall," Edie said. "I'll have a fifteen second blind spot from when the first firecracker goes off to do it."

"It would be more believable if I lit them all," Ronnie mused. "Like, I flip out, and just keep throwing and screaming and crying until they come running up there to stop me. A total, frothing at the mouth freak-out fit. Actually, that sounds kind of nice. Cathartic."

Edie harrumped. "Don't push it. It's bad enough that they think I'm bonkers. Trust me on this. You don't want to fall into that trap."

"Hey." Ronnie sounded hurt. "I'm high-strung, I have an artistic temperament, plus I was orphaned today. I think I'm entitled to a screaming nervous breakdown, like all the other overprivileged brats."

Edie grabbed her. "You know what? I love you," she whispered.

"I love you, too." Ronnie squeezed her breathless. "Of course, Dr. Katz will zap me again, but I wouldn't mind being knocked out for a while longer." She pressed her hand against her belly, and blew out a breath. "It would be nice. To take a break from this feeling."

That made Edie nervous. "Ronnie. Don't even say that. That's no way to deal with your feelings. Promise me you won't start—"

"Shhh." Ronnie gave her a sad smile. "Give me some credit. I'm not stupid. And I'm not a coward, either."

"I know you're not," Edie sniffled. "Thanks, baby. I love you."

One last hug, and they crept up to the terrace. Edie waved to her sister, and dropped down onto the slanted shakes of the solarium roof.

She slipped on the deep slant and grappled for purchase, heart thudding. Falling off the high side of this roof was certain death. She steadied herself, crept across the roof of the solarium. Ronnie watched anxiously over the railing while

Edie dangled off the edge, and dropped out of sight down onto the lower roof of the huge kitchen space, hoping that no one was in there to hear the thump. She was glad she had the high-tops. Once across that, it was only an eight foot drop or so off the eaves and down to the patio below.

The oak's branches nearly touched the kitchen roof, so she slunk beneath its cover into the yard. Her heart raced so fast, she felt faint.

Part of her begged for the rest of her to go back, to where things were safe and certain. Where someone else made all the decisions.

But that safety was just an illusion. It always had been. She leaped up, grabbed the biggest branch of the oak, and scrambled into the tree. Light slanted through the ragged leaves clinging stubbornly to the branches. She held her wrist up to it, and peered at her watch.

Oh, God. She had to get up into place and hop onto that wall in only thirteen seconds! Thirteen desperate, sweaty, face scratching, knee wobbling seconds of climbing through a tree, in the dark—

Pop, pop, whiz, bang, the first firecrackers exploded before she was in place. She scrambled faster, feeling her tiny fifteen second window ticking into nothing. More fireworks on the other side of the house. Ronnie yelled, in a thin, high voice. Hissing, bangs, pops. The scent of sulfur drifted over. Men, shouting. Doors slamming. Hubbub.

Edie lunged for the top of the wall, slipped, grabbed, caught herself by bloodied fingertips. Scrabbling for traction with her rubber-soled sneakers. *Pop, pop.* She could see bursts of light flickering. Ronnie was screaming. It sounded very believable. Someone else screamed, too. Maybe Evelyn, maybe Tanya, or both. Shrieking like tin whistles.

A final, desperate burst of scrambling, and she heaved herself up, got her leg over. Lowered her body down as far as she could, hanging by shaking arms. She dropped, landed painfully on her wobbly legs, and took off sprinting. Fell headlong, landing on her face. Mouth full of dirt and grass and woodchips. She struggled up, and took off again.

She dove for the shadows between the parked cars under the shelter. She'd run several seconds over. If anyone had the presence of mind to watch the screens during that scream-fest, they would have seen her. And if so, so be it. She was done, for the moment. She panted, letting that twenty seconds of security camera shots cycle through, and then another, and another. If they'd seen her, let them come for her.

No sign of it, though. She checked her watch for the next blind spot, peeled herself up off the asphalt, and pulled out Paul's car keys, creeping along until she found his dark green Saturn. She let herself into it. Ronnie was still scream-ing, but the fireworks had stopped.

She fired up the engine in the next blind spot, pulled out and accelerated down the long drive, turning out and onto the main road. She pulled out the phone, called the nearest car service she knew of on Ronnie's cell. There was a GPS device mounted on Paul's dash. She had to get rid of this car as soon as possible. They'd nab her in a heartbeat.

"Clark Car Service, can I help you?" said the bored voice.

"I need a car to meet me at the outlet mall on Montrose Highway," she said. "In front of the Shari's restaurant, please."

"Ten minutes," the man said, and hung up.

Edie parked Paul's Saturn at the Target lot on Montrose, and searched through Paul's wallet as she jogged through oceanic parking lots to the Shari's. Eighty-three bucks. Not bad. Car fare. For tonight, anyway. She stayed away from the restaurant until she saw the car pull up, and eyeballed the logo. She sprinted over, got in. The plush leather seat of the limo felt like a lover's embrace. "Evening," she gasped out.

The guy glanced over his shoulder, did a double take. She looked down at herself. Jesus. Blood, dirt, leaves. Yikes.

"Where to?" the guy asked, sounding nervous.

Edie took a deep breath. "Take me to the Parrish Foundation building. Five hundred Highett Drive, off Montrose Highway. Toward Hillsboro."

The place was deserted when they pulled over in front of the main entrance. There was crime scene tape over the door, but everyone had left. "Can you wait for me here?" she asked the driver. "I won't be long."

The guy nervously eyed the yellow tape stretched across the entrance. "Meter's running," he said.

"That's fine." She fished the master key out of the snarl of jewelry stuffed into her pockets. She could see the gaping hole in the glass on the fifth floor of the Helix building, like a gouged-out eye. Dad's office. It made her dizzy. She had to dangle her head, let the blood run back in.

It didn't matter if the security camera saw her. She walked in with her head high. There was no shame in trying to protect the man she loved. She wasn't going to get anywhere near the actual crime scene on the unfinished eighth floor, where the sniper had set up his perch. She wouldn't touch anything, move anything, mess anything up for the forensics people. Her conscience was clear. She took the back staircase in the dark. The door to the library suite was wedged open.

She switched on the light. Tears overflowed in her eyes. Heavenly choruses sang. The boxes. They were there, as Kev had said.

It wasn't that she had doubted him. Never that. But oh, God, it was sweet relief, to have physical reality back up her own instincts.

She pulled out a tissue, and examined their contents without touching them. There were no archived files, no computer discs. Just accordian folders, stuffed with paper culled from the recycling bins outside the Helix mailroom. Memos, newsletters, junk mail. The dated stuff was no more than a month old. And under the top layer, not even that much theater. The boxes below were stuffed with shredded paper.

It was a stage set, but a very shallow one. They'd had no intention of keeping him here more than a moment or two. This had just been to make him relax, assume things were normal, and then . . .

And then? What the hell had they done to him then? She pressed her hand against her belly, fighting not to cry. She would call him again, but first, Detective Houghtaling. Clearing his name, protecting his freedom, was more important than indulging her shaky nerves.

After all. He had all those missed calls on his phone. If he was reachable, he knew damn well that she was thinking of him. The dog.

She took pictures of the boxes from every angle with Ronnie's super-duper smartphone. She shot a mini movie, panning from the pile of boxes to the view outside the window, the gaping broken window of Dad's office. She struggled until she figured out how to attach the photos to a text message, sent them to Houghtaling's phone, and called.

The detective picked up quickly. "Houghtaling here," she said.

"Detective, this is Edie Parrish."

"Hello, Ms. Parrish. What can I do for you?"

"I found some information that might be of interest to you," Edie said. "It's about the boxes at the library. The ones that Des Marr said didn't exist. They do exist. I'm looking at them right now. I took pictures, and sent them to your phone. Did you receive them?"

"Yes, I did. You're at the Parrish Foundation building right now?"

"Please come and verify what I'm saying for yourself," Edie said. "As you promised that you would."

"And I would have kept that promise, if you'd given me time," the detective said.

"I don't have time," Edie replied.

"Ms. Parrish, you are aware that you are violating a crime scene?"

"This isn't the sniper's perch. You said yourself that no one has looked at the library until now. I took a movie of the broken window of the Helix building, to date the photo, and I didn't touch anything with my bare hands. The boxes are filled with scrap paper and shredded paper. It was a trap, for Kev, Detective. They lured him here."

"I'll send someone to pick you up right away," Houghtaling said.

Edie felt a maddeningly familiar frustation crush her lungs, her throat. Those pauses, that silence. She knew the vibe. The realization grew, blooming into frantic disbelief. "You don't believe me, do you?"

"It's not that I don't believe you," the woman said carefully.

"Come and see for yourself!" Edie begged. "Des was lying through his teeth! Doesn't that change things? Point to other inconsistencies?"

The woman was silent. Edie's brain raced ahead, trying to anticipate her. "Oh, God. You're thinking that I set it up? Aren't you?"

"No, not necessarily," Houghtaling said. "But you're stressed, confused, and grieving. You have access to that building, which begs the question as to who else had access to it. You are also in serious danger. Please stay exactly where you are, Ms. Parrish. Someone will be there to get you in a couple of minutes. We'll keep you safe."

Edie let the hand that held the phone drop, swinging limp at her side. The woman's voice chattered on, tinny and far away. She thumbed the line closed, staring out as . . . oh, dear God.

Headlights were coming up Highett Drive.

CHAPTER
34

"I can't do it tonight," Ava repeated, for the tenth time.
"You'll do as you're told, Av."

Ava's teeth rattled violently as she stared out the windshield at the city lights, raindrops beading the glass. She couldn't stop shaking.

She'd shaken the whole time she'd been locked in that stifling hell of a supply closet, and she still shook. Some mechanism in her brain, concussed by that horrible mind-to-mind encounter with McCloud.

Rape, she amended silently. What he'd done to her was rape. Feeling him in there, jerking around, feeling her feelings, knowing them intimately. Her shuddering intensified. She couldn't bear to feel her own feelings. Much less could she bear for a hostile stranger to feel them.

She was never crowning the treacherous bastard again, but she would love to tie him to a chair and crown his precious girlfriend. Sign her up for that. She felt a squirmy rush of sexual heat at the very idea.

Odd. She'd been with so many men, she did not even consider sexual contact particularly intimate. She was so accustomed to using sex. First for survival. Then she'd been compelled with X-Cog. Then she'd used her beauty and her body for advancement, and convenience. Finally, out of sheer habit. She barely noticed the sex, except insofar as she had to keep up a pretense of enjoyment.

Sex was nothing. But mental rape, oh God. Shame throbbed through her. She felt soiled, foul. Her feet drummed, her hands twitched, thinking of those years with Dr. O. How he would crown her, and then force her to—

"Goddamnit, would you stop that?"

The harsh edge of Des's voice jolted her. She stared at him, hurt.

He glared at her. "Stop twitching and jiggling! You're acting crazy! And you look like hell. What do you need, coffee? A drink? A pill?"

"Fuck you, Des," she replied.

"Pull yourself together. Tonight's going to be complicated, and you need to be at your best." His eyes swept over her, dismayed.

"But we can't do Edie tonight! Edie's the only one who—"

"Yeah, I know about your Edie theories, and her perfect brain."

"You promised me I could have her! Why not change the scenario? Have her kill the little sister, and then just disappear! We'll take her! No one will ever find her! It's no more risky than what we're already doing!"

"Things have changed," Des said. "It's too complicated. I agree with Tom. We're cutting our losses. We can't afford a big manhunt, an ongoing investigation. They'll never stop looking for her after what we've got planned, Av. Tom and his men will take care of the McClouds, we take care of Edie and Ronnie, and it ends here, tonight. And I, for one, will be grateful. This fucking thing is starting to get on my nerves."

Ava clenched her teeth to keep them from chattering. Curled her toes, pressing them hard against the floor. Her fingers twisted together.

"It's a waste," she said rebelliously. "All the things I could have done, the things I would have learned. The fun you and I could have."

"Sometimes you just have to make personal sacrifices, Av."

"We could have played with the little sister, too, Dessie," she coaxed. "If we bought some more time. She's so young and tender and virginal, hmm? Fresh as a daisy. Just imagine it, hmm?"

"Stop it, Av," he growled. "Don't even try. It's a done deal."

"Now that I think about it, I could have compelled Edie to marry you," she mused. "We didn't think this thing through at all. God, the possibilities, Des. The crown would be easy to hide under a wedding veil. Or I could design a nuptial crown, with decorative dangly bits. A wedding headress. I'd be the bridesmaid. Wouldn't that just be a hoot?"

Des pulled a master crown out of the bag on the center console, and tossed it on her lap. It was followed by a cap made of stretch velvet.

"Get it on," he said. "You might not have time when we get there."

Ava pulled down the visor, and flipped on the light, wincing when she saw her bloodshot eyes, the broken capillaries in her eyelids. Yuck.

It took her shaking fingers twice as long as usual to situate the crown. She pulled the cap on, noting that the red color accentuated her pallor and all the imperfections on her ravaged face. At least it hid the wild snarl of hair. Des had been in such a goddamned hurry after he dragged her out of the supply closet, he hadn't given her time to splash her face or comb her hair. They'd been off like a shot, to do that fat pig bastard Tom's bidding. Licking his toes, like good, obedient doggies.

They pulled up at the gate. The security guard looked at Des. "Good evening, Mr. Marr. Who's your friend?"

"This is Dr. Ava Cheung," Des said. "She's the lady who . . .

well, she was with me this morning, in Charles's office. When it happened." Des gestured the guy closer. "I want to be here for Ronnie and Edie, but I couldn't leave Ava alone," he said, in a stage whisper. "She's been traumatized, and she doesn't have any family of her own here in town. I thought we could all . . . grieve together. Of course I'll understand if Evelyn or your head of security has a problem with that."

The guy peered in at her. Ava did her best to look lonely and pathetic and traumatized. It wasn't much of a stretch, actually.

"Just a moment." The man stepped away from the car, muttered into his walkie-talkie and waved them through. "Go on in."

"You really are an amazing liar," she told Des as he parked.

He killed the motor. "We all have our gifts," he said.

They were met at the door by Evelyn Morris, Charles Parrish's lemony older sister, and Tanya, her cowlike lump of a daughter. Des introduced them and sketched out Ava's heart-clutching trauma.

Their eyes brimmed over. "Oh, you poor girl," Evelyn quavered.

Ava let her lips tremble, her chin begin to shake. Then her throat, her chest. Soon she was sobbing wildly. The older woman embraced her, weeping. The younger cow got into the action, blubbering and snorting. Ava was stuck in a damp, snorting, sniffling group hug. Dear God, when would it end? She met Des's ironic gaze over the women's heaving shoulders, and tilted her eyebrow. They all had their gifts, yes.

But some people simply had more of them.

Once through that tiresome ordeal, Ava felt a gentle touch on her shoulder. A pudgy, bespectacled middle-aged man was smiling at her. "Excuse me, Dr. Cheung. I'm Dr. Katz, the family doctor. I wondered if you would like for me to give you something. Just to help you rest."

Not. Drugs would fuck her ability to crown, which would

be disastrous. She honked into a tissue and gave him a brave, tremulous smile. "Thank you so much, doctor. But I just have to face it, head-on."

"You're very courageous," Dr. Katz told her solemnly.

"Thank you," she murmured demurely.

"How are Edie and Ronnie doing?" Des asked. "Are they resting?"

Evelyn shook her head, pressing her knuckles against her shaking mouth. "Edie's gone."

The two of them stared. "Gone?" Des demanded. "Gone where?"

"We have no idea." Evelyn's voice sharpened. "She manipulated poor Ronnie into creating a diversion that terrified us all out of our wits. Then she jumped over the wall, stole a car and disappeared."

Ava blinked. She hadn't expected such spirit out of mopey Edie, everybody's favorite scapegoat. "She's out there all alone?" she gasped. "With that murdering lunatic at large? Des, we have to go after her!"

"Yes, we certainly do! Evelyn, can I speak to Ronnie?" Des said, his voice urgent. "If she's gone out to meet that man, we have to hurry!"

Evelyn looked doubtful. "I couldn't get a thing out of her. But go up, do what you can with her. Third floor, second door to the left."

Ava stifled her giggles at Evelyn's choice of words as they started up the stairs. They would do what they could with her. Oh, yes indeedy.

Des gave her a hard stare. "Keep it together, Av."

They knocked on Ronnie's door, and it cracked open. Ronnie's hair was a rat's nest, her face blotchy from crying. "What do you want?"

"Can we come in and talk to you, Ronnie?" Des coaxed.

The girl's face was sullen. "No." She pushed the door.

Des wedged his foot into it. "You have to tell us where Edie went. She's in danger."

Ronnie rolled her eyes. "No shit, Sherlock."

"Then you should be helping," Ava scolded. "Before she falls into the hands of the people who murdered your father!"

Ronnie's eyes flashed. "Edie will be OK. She's going to clear her name, and her boyfriend's name, too. Then you'll all see what dickheads you've been. So why don't you all just piss off?" She kicked Des's foot out of the door. *Slam.* The door lock clicked.

"That mouthy little shit," Des whispered.

"Want to reconsider the plan?" Ava cooed. "Shall we wait until you have a chance to teach that uppity brat a lesson?"

Des's eyes flashed, tempted. "Don't distract me," he warned. "I have to hurry. She's gone to check on the boxes in the library suite."

Ava's eyes widened. "Oh!"

"Yeah. Thirty boxes of scrap paper won't look good. But if I get there before she does, or at least before she calls . . ." Des trailed off.

"So? Let's go!" she prompted.

"No, stay here. Stay close to her." He jerked his head toward Ronnie's door, and handed her the bag that held the slave crowns and the syringes loaded with X-Cog 19. "Don't let her out of your sight."

Des left her in the padded lair of the Parrish princesses. Ava stared at Ronnie's door for a while, then sauntered up the corridor.

She peered in the next suite, flipped the light switch. Track lighting tenderly swelled in brightness, illuminating a luxurious room lined with bookshelves, carpeted with a costly cream wool rug. A four-poster, covered with a pouffy comforter. An en suite bathroom. Huge shower, hydromassage tub. Her eyes flicked away from her own image in the mirror. She looked so young and vulnerable. Hard-used.

Like she'd been when Dr. O had found her. Fourteen years old, living in flophouses and brothels. She'd run away from her mother's live-in boyfriend, who'd been pimping her out to his drinking buddies, and from a mother who'd been too depressed and alcoholic to care.

Ava looked at the opulent room, thought of the foul places she'd slept. The things she'd done. The things that had been done to her.

Destiny was a heinous bitch. She and Edie were so similar. Eerily so. Same age. Identical test results. And yet, Edie was the princess, sitting on the silken pillow, while Ava huddled in the stinking shit.

There was a jewelry box open on the dresser. Ava poked through it, but there wasn't much. Edie must have taken the fine jewelry to pawn. So she wasn't planning on coming back. Hmm. Des better hurry up.

Ava looked through the drawers. The top ones were stuffed with lingerie. Pretty. She pulled some of it out, considering. Nylon stockings, silk stockings. Scarves. Those would come in handy later on.

She went to the closet, flung it open and gasped, awestruck. Floor length designer gowns. Gorgeous. She peeked at the labels. Dior. Dolce & Gabbana. Milla Schön. Versace. She stroked them. Satins, featherlight silks. Crinkly puffy expanses of taffeta. The sexy heft of lavish beadwork on chiffon, the glitter of brilliants, sequins.

Awww. And nobody understood the poor little pathetic princess poopsie. She had to act out. Run away. Live in a cheap hovel and pretend to be a starving artist. When she had all this. It was offensive.

That stupid, hypocritical, lying, self-indulgent little *cunt*.

The ripping sound took Ava by surprise. She stared at the skirt of the off-the-shoulder Armani tea gown done in dull bronzy gold chiffon. Rosettes of fabric adorned the gather between the breasts. The empire waist hung loose from the bodice, in tattered swags. She'd torn it off. Her hands were trembling. She forced herself to breathe, backing away from the closet. Her legs shook. Her feet. The earth was shaking beneath her. The bed swung up, broke her fall.

A heavy *whump* of air escaped from the puffy down coverlet.

She lay there, hugging the leather bag to her chest, wishing that the bed would stop rocking and whirling. She stared up at the night sky through the skylights on the roof. Maybe she would dress Edie in one of these gowns. Something pale, bridelike, that would really show off the blood. Too bad she didn't have any ropes of pearls to dress the princess with. Or a tiara. Like a princess Barbie.

Ava smiled dreamily as she pictured it. Wild hair, big skirt, pale dress. Screaming. Scarlet up to her elbows, clutching the long knife.

It tracked, beautifully. After all, Edie was nuts. Everyone said so.

"So we wipe out the light-sensitive photochips in the security cameras with a laser. Then we toss a few grenades while you jump the wall, run in and get Edie. We blast a hole in the wall so you won't have to climb it on the way out. We have a getaway car ready. Simple. Right?"

Kev lifted his head, and gave Miles a considering look, trying not to let his lips twitch. "I like your style," he said. "Bold, flashy. The only problem with your plan it is that half of us would get killed executing it, and the other half would go to a maximum security prison for thirty years. And they would be justified in sending us there."

"Oh." Miles's shoulders slumped. "Well. Excuse me for helping."

Kev shoved back sweat stiffened hair. "I just wish she'd pick up," he said, rebelliously. "What, are they napping? Today? Jesus."

He dropped his face into his hands again. Unable to tolerate being the focus of so much scrutiny. So self-conscious about the scarring. Intensely conscious of the way that visceral reminder of past pain made his long-lost brothers feel. He'd gotten past it years ago, himself, but they had to process it as if it had just happened.

And they were struggling with it. That was clear to see.

They hadn't talked much since the battle at his apartment. There was a tacit agreement to let Kev off the hook, at least until the imminent threat of death and dismemberment was over. But when that time came, ah God. The weight of it, the enormity. Eighteen lost years.

His brothers understood about the amnesia, intellectually. But they were still pissed at him in their hearts, and he didn't blame them.

It didn't help that the world had blown-up in their faces, quite literally, the second they'd found him. Piss-poor way to kick off an intense, emotionally charged family reunion. But it was just his style.

Every time he looked at Con or Davy, he started to shake. All those years. All those layers of grief and anger and doubt. All the things he didn't know about them, the stuff he'd missed, the stuff he'd never know. It blew his mind. He wasn't coping. The only thing he could do was to keep his head down, his eyes shut. Avoid it all.

Fortunately, they were all good at pushing emotional stuff aside to tend to a job of work. True sons of Crazy Eamon McCloud. But then again. It was that very gift that drove Dad bugfuck, in the end.

Dad. It gave him a dissonant jolt, to have instant, blinding access to his childhood memories again. And they were so vivid. Unfaded and untarnished by time or wear, like normal people's memories. They'd been preserved in pristine condition in that fortress in his mind. It shocked him, to see Con and Davy's faces, two decades older.

And then there was Bruno, seething up there in the front seat. Kev had had sharp words with him about letting Edie out of his sight. His little brother had gotten his feelings hurt. He was sulking, bigtime. Kev didn't have the energy to deal with that, too. Later for Bruno's snit.

The first thing they'd done after getting Sean and Liv to the hospital was to go back to the warehouse complex outside Hillsboro where Kev and Yuliyah had been held, and mount vidcams at the exits, hoping that they weren't being observed by existing security. They'd stuck repeaters to trees and lightpoles at regular intervals, extending the signal to a place where the van could be discreetly parked, and huddled inside it, quiet and tense. So far, so good. No one had bothered them, or appeared to notice them. Davy had found WiFi coverage, and was tapping away at a laptop, making calls, pulling in favors. He'd found the make and model of Ava Cheung's car, and Des Marr's.

Now they just had to figure out what the fuck to do.

The smoke-colored Chevy Astro van they were in belonged to Alex Aaro, a tight mouthed, taciturn Army Rangers buddy of Davy's who had recently moved to Portland and was developing his own security consultancy. Aaro was at the wheel, Bruno was beside him. Miles, Con, Davy and Kev were shoehorned into the back, fighting for remaining oxygen molecules, smelling each other's rank stress sweat.

Marr had showed up shortly after they'd set up. He drove a silver Jag, and pulled into the entrance, turning toward the building where Kev had been held. They watched him park, go in.

Kev stared at the screen, wondering what to do. Block the vehicle when the bastard drove out? Follow him, or yank him out from behind the wheel and beat the shit out of him? Demand the location of the captured girls? If he clammed up, Yuliyah's companions were screwed.

And Jesus, Mary and Joseph, why the fuck didn't Edie call? How could her little sister turn her cell phone off on a day like today?

Unless she'd been forced to turn it off.

He shuddered. Con, who had been talking into his cell phone, felt it. He patted Kev's shoulder until he raised his head and forced himself to look into his older brother's searching eyes. "You OK?" Con asked.

He gave his brother a speaking look, and slumped again.

Con kept on with his conversation, but kept his hand on Kev's shoulder. ". . . OK, whatever, but tell Nick and Becca to get their asses up there, fast. I want someone else besides just Val . . . yeah, yeah, I know, but those guys are deadly, and they've got serious resources."

He hung up, met Kev's questioning look. "That's Seth," he explained. "Friend from way back. Brother of my ex-partner in the FBI. My partner got killed by a mobster. Seth helped us kill the mobster."

"And married the mobster's daughter," Davy added laconically.

Kev was taken aback. "Really? She didn't mind? About her dad?"

Con and Davy exchanged looks. "It's complicated," Con hedged. "A long story. You'll meet him tonight. Raine and Jesse, their baby, are going up at Stone Island tonight, up in the San Juans. Along with Erin and Margot, and the kids."

"Kids?" He looked quickly, back and forth. "You both have kids?"

"Two," Con said. "My youngest is two months old. Madeline. My oldest is three." He cleared his throat. "His name is Kevin."

Kev tried to swallow. His throat was swelling.

"And I've got one. A girl, two. Named Jeannie, for Mom," Davy said. "And, ah . . . maybe . . ."

Heads turned. "No way," Miles said. "Really? Wow! You guys breed like bunnies!"

"It's too soon to talk about it," Davy muttered. "But we think so."

Kev's heart was pounding. Jesus. Little kids, babies

everywhere. And his crazy shit was putting them all in jeopardy.

"Seth's going to guard Liv and Sean at the hospital," Con said.

Kev let out a dry laugh. "So you think Tony and Rosa aren't enough protection for them?"

Davy snorted. "Tony and Rosa are hell on wheels. Literally. She broke the truck's axle. There's blood on the grill. But more guns never hurt. Tam's on her way down, too. So watch out."

Miles whistled. "Oh, Lord. That means you have to tell her about her earrings and necklaces."

Connor looked defensive. "So? I used them! They saved our asses! That's what they're for! They're supposed to be used, right? Isn't that the idea? Shouldn't she be glad they helped us survive?"

"They weren't yours to use. They were encrusted with diamonds," Miles reminded him glumly. "She's gonna kill your hairy ass."

"She can take a number and wait in line," Con said testily. "Val's going to the island, with Nick and Becca. To cover the kids and wives."

Davy rolled his eyes. "Great," he muttered, sourly. "Awesome."

"Val? Who's he?" Kev wanted to know everything all at once.

"An ex-spy. Tam's boy toy. Guy looks like a fucking cover model." Con looked as disgruntled as Davy. "Not the kind of man you put on top of the list to guard your wife while you're away, but everybody else is busy. So what the fuck. He's damn good with a gun. At least."

"Tell Erin to have him change Maddy's projectile-crap diapers," Davy suggested. "Make him babysit Jeannie when she hasn't napped."

"Ex-spy? Who's this Tam?" Kev asked. "She sounds interesting."

There was a burst of nervous laughter, quickly smothered.

"Tam can't be described in words," Con said. "She can only be experienced. And she cannot wait to meet you. Oh, boy."

This cagey, evasive bullshit was starting to get on his nerves. "This is another one of these stories that's too long to start?"

"Right on," Davy said.

Kev sighed, and addressed his next question to Bruno, who had been muttering into his cell. He reached up to pluck at his brother's sleeve. "You talked to Zia? How are Liv and Sean?"

"Better, they think," Bruno said. "The ultrasound looked OK. She had some spotting, though. They shot her full of anti-spasmodics. She's asleep, now. Limp as a noodle. Sean's awake, though. Zia says he's torturing the nurses, yanking out his IV. He wants to come join us. She's working him over but good. Nobody messes with Zia Rosa."

"I'll feel better when Seth gets down there," Con muttered.

"Marr's car's coming out the entrance, and he's not alone," Davy rapped out. "There's a woman in the car."

Kev lunged to look. His guts twitched as he recognized the delicate profile of the woman in the passenger's seat. "It's Ava."

He'd explained the X-Cog events as they had put the surveillance of the warehouse in place, and it had been a blessed relief to find them all hip to the bizarre situation. Sean's wild adventures with Dr. Osterman and Gordon three years ago had made long explanations unnecessary.

Aaro moved the van to follow at a discreet distance. They got onto the main strip, and it became clear that Aaro was an old pro at tailing, so Kev sagged back and left him to it, trying to ignore how exhausted he was. The lights of the strip malls flashed by. It had started to drizzle.

Bruno turned his head after a few minutes. "They're turning onto Cedar. I think they're headed to the Parrish place."

Kev's tired body jolted straight up into the air. "With Ava?" he yelled. "He's taking that psycho bitch to Edie's family's house?"

"Relax," Davy soothed. "Come on. Realistically. What can he or the psycho bitch do to her there, in front of her family?"

"You don't know that family," he said. "Or that psycho bitch."

Bruno's guess was dead on. Marr's car turned at the private drive that led to the Parrish home. Aaro pulled over and killed the engine.

"I cannot let him take that woman into the house where Edie is." Kev muscled his way toward the door. "I'm going in."

His brothers dragged him back down.

"To do what?" Con's harsh voice jolted his raw nerves. "Don't be a fucking idiot. If you get anywhere near that place, they will grab you, and fuck you up. Let this be your mantra, buddy. Repeat after me. I cannot help her from behind bars. Come on. Say it. Know it."

Kev groaned. "Oh, God," he muttered. "This is killing me."

And it kept killing him, second by bone-grinding second. They ticked by, with agonizing, silent slowness. No one had the heart to speak under that crunch of fear and constraint.

Then headlights cut through the night once again. The streetlights gleamed on the silver Jag as it paused outside the gate.

"Just the driver," Aaro said. "He left Psycho Bitch at the house."

Everybody looked at Kev. "Your call, buddy," Aaro said. "Do we follow him? Or do we stay with her?"

Kev stared at the taillights. He felt pulled tight, part of

him following the car as Marr pulled away. Stretching like a rubber band.

It was the tug that did it. He was afraid to let the cord snap.

"Follow him," he said. "We can learn something from him. We won't learn anything staring at a street sign."

The van surged to follow. They followed the distant tail-lights, and landmarks came in and out of focus. He knew this road. He'd seen it this morning. Eons ago. Montrose Highway. "He's going to the Helix complex," he said. "He's going to turn left, here. On Highett Drive."

Des's left turn signal began to wink. Kev rubbed his eyes, and when he opened them, Davy was holding his cell phone out.

"Try her again," he said.

Kev stared at the thing, dispirited. "I've tried twenty times."

"Try again," Davy urged. "You know you want to."

Oh, what the fuck. He took it, punched in the number.

It rang. His heart flipped. The thing had finally been turned on.

"Hello? Ronnie?" Edie asked. "Is that you? Is everything OK?"

Her sweet voice made tears of competing relief and fury spurt out of his eyes. "Edie? It's Kev."

"Oh, my God, Kev! Where have you been?"

"Later for that. What about you?"

"I'm OK. Did you hear about my dad?"

"Yes," he said, thickly. "I'm so sorry."

She cleared her throat. "I know. Well. Um. Later for that, too. Look, Kev. This thing is a huge set-up. They think you killed Dad. You have to run. And I mean now. I mean, right now."

"Edie, never mind that. Listen to me. I just—"

"Never mind?" Her voice rose. "Do the words 'death

row' mean anything to you? Does 'life in prison if you're really lucky' ring a goddamn bell?"

"Calm down," he begged. "I'm just trying to tell you about—"

"Don't tell me to calm down! I have had the shitty day to end all shitty days, and I am not calm!"

"If you can't calm down, just shut up! Listen to me!" he bellowed.

The guys in the car shrank back instinctively.

There was a startled pause from Edie. "I'm listening," she said.

"The short version is, there's a woman in the house with you who is extremely dangerous. She—"

"I'm not in the house right now."

"What?" he yelled. "What do you mean, not at the house? Where the fuck are you? Where did you go?"

The other guys made frantic *calm down, cool it* gestures, but he was freaking out as he watched Marr park in the lot where he had parked this very morning. It looked deserted, but a single light was on, on the fifth floor. Maybe some forensics types were still working.

"Please, don't scream," Edie said. "It flusters me. I'll tell you everything, OK?"

Davy leaned forward with his binoculars, peering out the windshield. "He's out of the car," he announced grimly. "He's going in."

"Just tell me where you are," Kev begged.

"Well, I sneaked out of my dad's house, which was harder than you might think. Now I'm at the Parrish Foundation building—"

"What? You're where?" He sprang up, knocked his head against the van's ceiling, hard enough to make his vision darken.

"The Parrish Foundation building," she repeated. "I'm in the library. I wanted to show the detective the boxes that Des—"

"She's inside the Parrish building," he said to the van at large.

Aaro floored the accelerator. The van leaped ahead. Kev lost his footing, fell headlong across Con's and Miles's laps.

"Run!" he yelled into the phone. "Christ, Edie, run out of that place, right now! Des Marr is in there, looking for you!"

"Des? Here?" Her voice was uncertain. "No! You're kidding."

"Yes, and he's a sociopathic killer! And so's his crazy girlfriend! So shut up and run! Is there an exit out the back of the building?"

"Yes, but I—"

"We'll be there in a few seconds! Run! Look for a gray van!"

"Oh, God," she whispered. "I love you, Kev."

She hung up. Kev pounded his fists against his knees. "Faster!" he yelled. "Can't you get any more speed out of this piece of shit?"

The tires squealed, fishtailing. They took the curve on two wheels. Centrifugal force tumbled everyone into a struggling tangle of limbs.

The van jerked to a stop. Kev dove out the back, stumbling to his hands and knees. He got up and sprinted for the door. Serious door. Made of thick, solid metal. Pushbar on the inside. Just a small window which showed exactly nothing in the darkness.

Of course, it was locked.

CHAPTER
35

Edie's legs felt hollow as she flipped off the light. She wondered which stairwell Des would take, and peered out into the hallway—

Whack. Something slammed her to the ground, on her back.

"Gotcha." It was Des, breathing hard. There was just enough light filtering from the two stairwells to make out his gloating expression.

She sucked in a desperate teaspoonful of oxygen. "Des?"

His expression morphed into concern. The transformation was bizarre. "Edie, what are you doing here?"

Edie coughed. "What are you doing on top of me?" she croaked.

She struggled, but he was big, heavy. Shock was replaced by fear, which grew sharper every second that passed. God, how she needed air.

"Protecting you!" His voice was self-righteous. "You're a danger to yourself, Edie. You need to be back home, where you're safe."

The lecturing tone was dissonant with the nasty, breathless intimacy of his body. She struggled. He rolled his weight more squarely on top of her. His chest was so rigid. Like he was encased in steel.

Body armor? Oh, God. The fear ratcheted up.

"Let's try this again," he said, as if he were talking to a stubborn child. "What are you doing here, Edie?"

He knew. No point in lying. "I wanted to see if the boxes were here," she rasped out, breathless.

"So? You see that they're not. Satisfied now? Can we go home now, and have cookies and tea?"

What the hell? She doubted, for one horrible instant, that she actually had seen them. Wondering if she really was wrong in the head.

But that quiet voice whispered, *stand firm. He's fucking with you.*

"The boxes are there, you lying bastard," she said. "Get off me. I took pictures of them, and sent them to Houghtaling. The game is up."

His first reaction was to look hurt, but as they stared at each other, she felt that eye open up. The one that opened when she drew.

For the first time, she used it, instead of letting it use her. She had no idea how. The wild intensity of the last few days had taught her.

She let that eye open deliberately, and looked at him with it. And oh, God. If she'd been scared before, it was nothing compared to now.

There was no one in there. Nothing that she even recognized as human. That spark, the heart. He didn't have it. No one was home.

He knew, the second she realized what he truly was. His smile widened grotesquely as all pretense of normalcy fell away. He shifted, pressing against her, and his penis swelled against her belly.

She stiffened in revulsion. And he liked that. Her disgust actually turned him on even more. His pulsing and grinding intensified.

"Edie, Edie. What am I going to do with you now?" he
mused. He pinned her hands above her head, yanked the
neckline of her stretch T-shirt until her breast was exposed
and clicked his tongue. "Bruises! Your lover's so rough. That
mean, nasty brute. But don't worry . . . Des will make it better." He slid down her body, and licked her breast.

She fought not to scream at the horrible wet swipe, sensing that would make things worse. She had to be cold, indifferent. *Hurry, Kev. Hurry.* "What did Dr. O do to you?" she
asked.

Des lifted his face from her breasts, distracted by the
question. "Exactly what he tried to do to you," he said. "It's
just that in me, it worked. In you, it didn't. Simple as that.
You weren't strong enough."

Delay, delay. "I wasn't?" she squeaked. "Strong how?"

Des chuckled. "If you have to ask, there's no point explaining, but I'll indulge you. Dr. O set me free. Before the
program, all my instincts, impulses, desires . . ." He empha-
sized the last word with a hard pulse of his hips. ". . . were
blocked. By fear, guilt. Stupid inhibitions. Dr. O took the
fear and guilt away. And I took off. Like a rocket."

Memories of those horrible sessions strapped into Dr. O's
special chair swirled up. "You mean, the electroshock treat-
ments?"

Des looked offended. "It was much more sophisticated
than that."

She was so appalled, she forgot to be diplomatic. "You
mean he burned the part of your brain that can tell right from
wrong? Morality, ethics? He made you into a . . . a so-
ciopath?"

"Oh, please." Des rolled his eyes. "Your slavery to unconscious programming is showing. He altered the part of our
brains programmed to believe that X is right, and Y is
wrong, but who's to say? It's relative. It's random. Once you
understand that and really experience it, you're free. The
world has no limits, except for those you make yourself.

You're free to do anything . . . if you can get away with it. And I always can."

He appeared to be so utterly convinced of what he said. It was surreal. "What about love? Loyalty?" She was afraid to know the answer, but she couldn't help asking.

He looked vaguely baffled. "What about them?"

"You don't care about them? You don't feel them?"

He shrugged. "Feelings are just hormonal squirts, brought on by unconscious programming. They don't last. They're good for nothing except for momentary physical satisfaction." He licked her breast again, and grinned. "We don't worry about feelings. We're past all that."

"We? Who's we?" Her teeth were starting to chatter. *Hurry Kev.*

"The successful ones," he explained. "Club O. Dr. O's army."

That sparked a fresh, brand new stab of pure horror. "Oh, God. You mean, Dr. O did this to other people? Not just to you?"

"The strong ones," he repeated, emphasizing the words. "Every brain responds differently. He tried to do it to all of us, but some of his subjects weren't, well, you know." He sniggered a little. "Worthy."

"Like me," she whispered.

"Like you," he agreed. "Although you've managed better than most of Dr. O's duds. At least you're still alive, and not in a padded cell." He paused, significantly. "So far, anyway."

She struggled to shove him off again, but he was horribly strong, and held her in place with his weight. "We're everywhere," he said, his face gloating. "Our abilities are expressed in different ways, but we all like power. Doctors, scientists, business people, politicians, military. But all of us have something in common. Freedom." He leaned, until his hot breath filled the air between them. "Too bad it didn't work on you."

"I'm glad," she said. "I'd rather be dead than like you."

He jerked her face toward his. "You're tougher than I

thought. I wasn't expecting this kind of resistance. It's sexy." He kicked her legs open, settled himself against her. "This is all for you. Lucky girl."

Her gorge rose. "Don't, Des."

"Why not? I can do anything I like. All I have to do is find a way to spin it. And sell it. I'm so good at that. Like with your mother."

"My mother? What does she have to do with—"

"You never asked yourself why a woman in such perfect health would drop dead on a sunny September day, hmm? It was so easy."

She gaped at him, so shocked she didn't even try to raise his bulk to drag air into her chest. "You killed my moth—"

He cut her off with a smothering, bruising kiss. His muscular tongue thrust deep, making her gag. She fought for air. Her vision dimmed. Her feet drummed. Des had murdered her mother. He'd murdered both her parents. The weight of the Ruger banged the floor.

The Ruger. She pulled her face away, with huge effort. "L-l-let's go into the library, at least," she gasped out. "There's a rug in there."

"The princess likes her comforts? Works for me. Easier on my knees. I like to fuck from behind." He got up, yanked her to her feet.

She yelped with pain, and stumbled, sagging. Groping desperately at her ankle for the gun. Des roared at her, tried to drag her upright.

She lolled, as limp as a doll, swinging by her arm. Des kicked the side of her thigh. She screamed with pain, but by then she'd loosened the gun snapped into the holster, swung it up, squeezed the trigg—

Bam.

The force of the shot knocked her right back down onto the floor. Des stumbled back, arms pinwheeling. He thudded to the floor, but rolled instantly up to his knees, pulling out a gun.

She shot again, from the floor. He flipped backward.

She staggered up onto her knees. Shot again, again, aiming for his head, but her hands shook, and the shots went wild. She felt no righteous satisfaction, just horror that it should fall to her to put that subhuman thing out of its misery. Someone was screaming, high and thin. *Bam. Bam.* Her eyes blurred with tears. She squeezed the trigger—

Click. Click. Empty. All six shots, gone.

She backed away, wobbling on rubbery legs, brandishing the useless gun as if it could still protect her somehow. She heard sobbing, hiccupping. Huge, rasping gasps for breath. That was her. She ignored herself, focused on that monstrous, inhuman thing on the floor.

Des moved, sat up, clutching his arm. His hand was red. Blood dripped down onto the pale floor tiles. He grinned, his teeth amazingly white in the gloom. His gun swung up. "Is that all you've got?" He jumped to his feet, without much effort. "You bad girl. You winged me. You'll pay. Nasty little bitch."

Bam. She screamed, stumbling back against the wall.

It took a couple of shocked, confused seconds to realize that she hadn't been shot. It was Des who'd been slammed backward and off his feet again. Someone was yelling, but she was deafened by the gunshots. Des crawled up, onto his knees—

Bam, again. Des flipped over sideways, howling with fury.

". . . all right? Edie? Edie! Can you hear me?"

Oh, dear God. Kev, shouting from the end of the dark hallway.

"Kev!" she wailed, and took off toward him.

Bam, a bullet clipped the wall beside her head, gouging into naked drywall. Dust and particles flew in a stinging cloud.

"Edie! Get down!" Kev bellowed.

She dove, bounced, slid. *Boom,* a muzzle blast flashed in

the dark as Kev returned fire. "Stay down!" he yelled. "Crawl like a snake! Move!"

Bullets sang over her head, a whizbang thunderstorm. She wriggled, snakelike, over the shard covered floor.

Bam. Kev grabbed her arm and yanked her through the doorway. They plunged into the stairwell. Two other man crouched there with him. She dove into space. The staircase slammed into her stumbling feet when gravity caught up with her. Kev steadied her, pulled her on.

She glanced at the two men. Unfamiliar. One was murmuring into a cell phone. ". . . got her. We'll be around to meet you, ten seconds."

"Is he still . . . did you get him?" she asked Kev.

He glanced back. "Don't know. I thought so, but he—"

Bam. Bam. The stairwell rang with shots. The thudding of feet.

"That answers that," Kev muttered. "He must have a vest."

The back door was wide open, glass smashed. A gray van idled there, back doors yawning. Bruno ran toward them, grabbed her other arm, pitched her inside like a sack of grain. The guys dove in after.

Bruno leaped into the driver's seat. The van surged before the doors were closed. They braked moments later, and another guy jumped in the front, another into the back. The van took off, tires squealing around curves as they headed back for the turn-off to Highett Avenue,

Lights, flashing. The red, pulsing strobe of cop cars approaching.

"For the love of God," Bruno moaned. "Who the fuck called them?"

"I did," Edie admitted, through stiff, numb lips. "Sorry."

Bruno hissed something savagely through his teeth. "Is there a road on the other side of the park grounds?"

"Ah . . . I think so," she said. "There's a new subdivision over there, but I think there's a—"

Bump, bump, whump. The Chevy Astro lurched and corrected as Bruno drove over the curb and thudded through the
ornamental hedges. They bumped and thudded over the
landscaped garden, wooded greensward, swerving around
trees. The tires wallowed in drifts of woodchips, thudded
over rocks and walking paths. With no headlights they narrowly missed an ornamental fountain in the dark.

In the back, they bounced and rocked, slamming into
each other. There was a grinding crunch and lurch, throwing
them all against one side. Bruno switched on the headlights,
cursing.

"Oh, Christ, please. Don't kill my van!" one of the guys
begged.

"You Ranieris are freaking maniacs at the wheel," another
one commented.

"It's genetic. He learned to drive from his wacko aunt."

Edie cleared her throat. "As I was saying," she called out,
more loudly, "I think there's a subdivision over there, but
there's a creek at the other end of the—"

Splash. The van plunged into the creek, spewing great
fans to the side as it wavered . . . tipped . . . righted. Moved
forward. The water rose, gurgling. The bank ahead was horribly steep, shiny with mossy mud.

The tires wallowed desperately, digging, fighting. The
motor roared, whined, roared again—and they found traction, lifted up. Out.

They bumped and rocked over the rise, and thudded
down onto asphalt. The street soon opened out into a loop of
orderly new single-wide and double-wide manufactured
homes. Pebble or woodchipped lawns. Bruno swept around
the loop, and found the road that led back to Montrose Highway. A snarl of cop cars blinked at the Helix complex.

They turned onto Montrose Highway, merged with traffic. Outback Steakhouse. Shari's. Target. Hampton Inn. No
one could speak, for a few minutes. Edie couldn't believe
they'd really gotten away.

Kev had really come for her. Somehow.

One of the men flipped on a light. A van full of battered, exhausted men all stared at her so intently, it made her cringe.

Kev stared, in particular. He looked awful. Bruised, pale.

"Edie," he said wearily. "Meet some more of my brothers."

Des leaned against the stairwell. He pressed his bleeding shoulder to the wall and slid down, leaving a dramatic strip of crimson. He ripped open his shirt, staring at the bullet holes in the vest. Between Edie and Larsen, they'd gotten him nine times—seven of them caught by the vest, but he was going to have some ugly bruising under there. One had dug into his deltoid. Another had trimmed his thigh.

One of the dimples in the vest was a scant inch from the top. It had almost gone through his throat. It hurt like hell, and he was so angry. *Emotions are hormonal squirts,* he reminded himself. *Use them. Don't be used.* A direct Dr. O quote. She wouldn't get far, the stupid, dirty whore. Not with that smartphone she'd been yapping into. The service provider would give the GPS coordinates to Parrish's head of security in a heartbeat, after what had happened today. And if they didn't, he'd just start making phone calls. His father, to start with, who had given piles of money to the current senator's election campaign. The Governer. The Attorney General. It wouldn't take long.

He dialed Houghtaling's number. "Hello, Mr. Marr," she said.

"Detective, you were just on the phone with Edie Parrish?"

She paused, startled. "Yes? And?"

"She just shot me, Detective. Larsen shot me, too. Would you . . . send an ambulance to the Parrish Foundation building, as soon as possible? South stairway. Fourth floor landing. I'm not sure . . . that I'll have the strength to make another phone call. But I had to . . . to tell you . . . about . . ." He made his voice fainter, slurring. "About Edie."

"Mr. Marr? Are they still there?" Houghtaling yelled. "Mr. Marr!"

"I knew Edie would come here," he muttered hoarsely. "She'd prepared that scene in the library, probably days ago. I was hoping . . ." he paused, panted for a few beats, "that I could get her back. Before he took her again." He coughed, choked pathetically. "But I failed."

"Send an ambulance to the Parrish Building asap!" Houghtaling bawled out to someone. "Mr. Marr?" she spoke into the phone again. "Mr. Marr? Are you still there? How badly are you wounded?"

"Sorry," he whispered. "I go . . . in and out. I had to . . . tell you. That they had her. Before it's too . . . late. Find her. Please. Find her."

"Yes, of course, Mr. Marr. I'll get right on it."

"Hurry," he begged. "I can't . . . I . . ." He let his voice trail off, left the line open. Listening to her shout his name.

He relaxed on the stairs, dabbing blood onto his face, for effect. Psyching himself up for the next act.

BJ Meyers was nervous, bored, and scared. Fear did not make the boredom any easier to bear. Surveillance sucked. He fidgeted in the car seat. He kept thinking about all his dead colleagues. Blown up, shot up.

Christ, he'd thought he was done with that, after those tours in Iraq and Afghanistan. Right on the streets of Portland, Oregon. He hadn't expected that in a stateside gig. Bixby Enterprises was supposed to be an interim job. The pay was frickin' great. Eight months of this, and he'd have a stake for his own business. If he didn't get killed first.

His fingers drummed the steering wheel. His feet tapped at the plastic floor mat. He stared up at the third-floor window—

Holy shit. There was a beam of light moving up there. It

disappeared, but he was sure he'd seen it. Shifting shadows. But no way could someone have gone in the main entryway without him seeing. Whoever it was hadn't turned on lights. So he was alert for surveillance. Which meant he was dangerous.

Yeah. Whoever could wipe out over half of a ten man team from Bixby Enterprises was plenty dangerous.

BJ steeled his nerve, and darted across the street to the diner's awning. He sidled along the building, into the alley, where the Dumpsters festered. Someone had pulled the ladder of the fire escape down. There was a hook, rope. Son of a bitch. He'd gone in the window.

As he watched, a man crawled out again. Short, wide. The older guy. He had a duffel. He'd returned for weapons, money, documents.

BJ shrank back behind the Dumpster as the guy climbed down, surprisingly nimble for an old fart loaded with a heavy bag. He dangled off the bottom of the sliding ladder, dropped to the ground with a grunt, and loped toward an aging Taurus sedan, registered to his sister Rosa Ranieri, the crazy bitch who had smashed Jarold's pelvis and hip.

BJ dove down into the garbage just before headlights sliced through the night and revealed him. The car roared past the Dumpster and sped away. BJ brushed garbage off himself and bolted for his car, pulling up the boss's number. Tom picked up promptly. "What?"

"Tony Ranieri just came home and got his stuff and his sister's car." BJ's voice shook with excitement. He fired up the ignition, booted up the laptop.

"There's an RF tag on the car?"

"Of course." BJ checked the monitor as he pulled out into the street. "I'm about eight hundred meters behind him."

"Stay on him," Tom said. "Stay tight. He might ditch the car."

BJ laid on the gas. "I'm on it, boss."

CHAPTER
36

"Detective, I'm not asking you to believe me. I know that you won't. All I'm asking is for you to protect Ronnie." Edie pleaded. "Get her out of there. I'm begging you. Get her someplace safe, someplace secret, with police protection. She's not safe with those—"

"Not safe?" Houghtaling snorted. "With her aunt, her cousin and a four-man security team? Ronnie is fine. It's you we're worried about."

"She's with Des Marr and Ava Cheung," Edie said again. "They are killers! Cheung tried to kill Kev before he got away! She's killed before, and so has Des Marr! They killed both my parents! And there's that cold room full of cadavers at that warehouse in Hillsboro—"

"I'll have someone check out this alleged room of cadavers," Houghtaling said. "But so far, I've seen no evidence that Ava Cheung or Desmond Marr are anything but law-abiding citizens. Mr. Marr's lucky to be alive. You're lucky he's alive, too, Ms. Parrish."

Edie shuddered, remembering that empty glow in Des's eyes. "He was sexually assaulting me. I have a right to defend myself."

Another snort. "Who put that gun into your hand, Ms. Parrish?"

Edie fought for control of her voice. "Someone who cares about me," she said. "Someone who gives a shit."

"Huh. The hole you're digging for yourself keeps getting deeper. Please, put down the shovel. Before it's too late to help you."

Edie hung up. Alex Aaro tapped on his computer, doing something to the signal that made it impossible to trace. He was a big guy, muscular and craggy. Dark hair, pale, grim mouth.

They were hiding out at Alex Aaro's place, a few miles out of the little town of Sandy. Hidden deep in a huge, hushed evergreen forest.

She stared down at the phone in her hand. It wasn't the one Ronnie had given her. Kev had taken hers back in the van, pried out the SIM card, and thrown it out into the gutter. This one belonged to one of the McClouds. She didn't know which. Tired as she was, it was hard to keep multiple big blond guys straight. Sean had arrived an hour or so after they got to Aaro's place, so there were three new exhausted, grim McCloud guys staring at her with intense curiosity. Plus Bruno. Even Tony was there. He'd arrived shortly after Sean. She glanced at Aaro. "One more call? To see if I can get my sister? I have to try to warn her."

He nodded. "Go for it."

She dialed her sister's old cell phone number, the one she'd promised to keep turned on for Edie's call, and crossed her fingers.

"Parrish residence," said a man's voice. "Who is this?"

Great. Paul Ditillo, of all the luck. He'd taken Ronnie's phone. "Paul, it's Edie," she said, resigned. "Can I talk to Ronnie?"

"Not in this lifetime. Where's my fucking car?" Paul asked.

"Parked at the Target on Montrose Highway," she said,

heart sinking. This was futile, but she had to try. "Paul, that woman Des brought to the house, Ava Cheung, is a killer. She shouldn't be around Ronnie. Neither should Des. Please, find a way to get rid of them."

Paul made derisive sound. "Des is asleep on the couch, zonked out on pain meds from getting shot up by you and your sniper boyfriend. And Cheung, this deadly killer who must weigh, oh, maybe a hundred and ten pounds, tops? She's sitting on the floor, holding his hand crying into her chamomile tea. Spare me."

"Paul, I know it seems—"

"Do yourself a favor, Edie. Take your fucking meds."

She hung up and pressed her knuckles against her mouth. "I struck out," she whispered. "Bigtime."

Kev took her hand. "You've done everything you can for tonight."

"But I can't just leave her there with those horrible people!" she burst out. "That asshole Des is asleep on the couch! And Ava's with him! Drinking . . . goddamn chamomile tea! It's so screwed!"

"That's good news." It was Tam, the McCloud brothers' mysterious, shockingly beautiful female friend, who had also shown up shortly after they arrived at Aaro's lair. "They're taking a break from slaughtering and mind-rape. A nap, some tea. Everybody needs a breather."

Edie rounded on her in outrage. "How can you joke about this?"

The woman's slender black-clad shoulders lifted in an indifferent shrug. "Coping mechanisms differ."

"Take your coping mechanisms and shove them up your ass!" Edie snarled. "This is my little sister! You don't know what it's like!"

"Yes, I do, actually," Tam said. "I had a sister once."

Edie turned to stare into the woman's fathomless amber eyes. She was afraid to say it, but she'd been neatly maneuvered into it. "Once?"

A tiny nod. Then Tam made her wait. And wait.

"And?" Edie prompted, her voice getting sharper.

"I was not able to protect her." Tam's low, smoky voice went crystal hard. "She died."

Edie closed her eyes. Sick nausea rolled in her belly.

"It happens," Tam went on mercilessly. "You deal with it."

"What the fuck is this shit?" Kev demanded. "Is this supposed to help? Is this useful? Shut up, lady! Back off! We don't need this!"

"Excuse me for being a walking worst case scenario," she said. "But I survived. " She poked Edie's shoulder. "You're a survivor. "Maybe your little sister is a survivor, too. We can only hope."

"But she's only thirteen!" Edie wailed.

"Thirteen. That's old enough. Is she smart? Tough?" Edie swallowed, and nodded, and Tam went on briskly. "Well, good, then. She's got a shot. A long one, but that's better than nothing."

"Jesus!" Kev glared at her. "That's supposed to comfort her?"

Tam looked blank. "Certainly not. Why on earth would I do that? Stop coddling her. It's irritating me, and it doesn't help her."

Kev turned to his brothers. "Where did you find this crazy bitch?"

Davy and Con looked uncomfortable. "It's a long sto—"

"Say that once more and I rip out somebody's throat," Kev said.

Everyone in the room but Kev and Edie exchanged quick, nervous glances. Tam just chuckled to herself. Her own little private joke.

"Try not to let her bug you," Sean offered. "She's just that way. We're so used to it, we don't even notice anymore. We just hear blah, blah, blah when she comes out with her spurts of vitriol."

Con jumped in. "She makes up for her horrible manners and her bitchy remarks and her piss poor attitude—"

"It's called blunt honesty," Tam interjected. "Be refreshed by it."

". . . by saving your ass from a horrible fate from time to time," Con concluded doggedly. "She saved mine once. And Erin's."

"Yours, too, indirectly," Davy said. "Those guys at your apartment were hammering us. If Con hadn't blown up their armored SUVs with Tam's jewelry bombs, we'd all be meat."

"About that." Tam crossed slender legs and swung a high-heeled foot. "Let's discuss my lovely diamond bomblets, which you were charged to deliver before you exploded them for your own selfish—"

"Selfish?" Con snapped back, defensive. "They were killing us!"

Tam laughed. "So easy to bait. Be cool, Con. We'll work out a payment plan. Little Kevvie and Maddie will have to give up their college funds, maybe, but higher education is overrated, you know? I never had any, after all. I had, well . . . lower education, I guess you might call it." She lit a ciga-rette, winking at Edie. "Very, very low."

"Everybody ignore her," Davy said. "Tam, shut up and behave."

Tam made a kissy-face at him, and puffed out a smoke ring.

But Edie kept looking at Tam. Tam gazed back, cool and direct.

She couldn't stop wondering how it felt to be a walking worst case scenario. And if she was about to find out. She folded herself in half, hugging her knees to her face. The fear made her feel so sick.

"Edie? Won't you at least try to eat something?" Kev pleaded.

Edie looked at the trestle table, heaped with fruit, deli salads and sandwiches, and shook her head. "System's down," she said.

Kev looked exhausted. His eyes looked almost bruised, the shadows were so deep. They were crowded into the big, drafty future basement of the house that Alex Aaro was in the process of building for himself. There was only an outer frame for the upper stories so far, though he was starting to work on the floor of the level above.

Aaro was camped out in what was clearly going to be a huge storage basement and work space, but he'd set it up with the basic essentials of living: a table, one battered recliner facing a flat-screen sixty-inch TV mounted on the wall, a few kitchen essentials, gas range, microwave, sink. A sleeping space and bathroom were out back, in a separate cabin. The fragrance of the trees blew in through the open door. One of Aaro's cats slid in like a shadow through the open door, and hopped onto Edie's lap, rubbing its ears against her hands.

"Shouldn't you close the doors?" she asked, hesitantly.

"The cold helps keep me awake," Aaro told her. "And a locked door won't make us any safer." He pointed at the monitors mounted over the desk where he sat. "I set up thermal imagers, so we'll see anything warm blooded that gets within a hundred meters of us. There are motion detectors, too. Anything taller than a rabbit or a squirrel will set off the sensors. We're covered. You can relax."

Relax. As if. The place felt lost, like Kev's cabin. A narrow, winding dirt road led from the highway through the Cascades to this place. No light penetrated the heavy roof of spreading pine and fir branches. No sounds of civilization, just the enormous rustling of wind in the trees.

She was barricaded with high-tech security, surrounded by guys with guns, but safety was a state of mind. And it was one that Edie could not achieve with Ronnie under the same roof as Des and Ava.

Aaro got up, and cast his eyes over the guys sprawled around the tables and chairs in various attitudes of exhaustion. Bruno's head was cradled in his arms. Miles was asleep in the recliner, snoring.

"We've got to get out of here," Kev said. "They'll find us here."

"You've got to rest for a couple hours." Aaro opened a cupboard, and yanked out an armful of sleeping bags and tattered blankets. "You guys go bed down on the tatami mats in the exercise room." He cast Tam a cautious look. "But I don't know what to do with you, babe."

She smiled. "Do nothing. Always the safest policy. I'm not camping out with a bunch of snorting, malodorous men. I'm checked into a charming little B&B in Sandy. Sweet dreams, gentlemen."

Aaro jerked his chin at Kev and Edie. "Take her to my bedroom. Towels in the cabinet, sheets in the bottom drawer if you're squeamish."

"What, Aleksei?" Tam purred. "No rose petals to scatter on the sheets for her? How churlish of you."

The guys turned, casting hostile glances in Kev's direction.

"About those rose petals, man," Con said. "That stunt really fucked us up."

Kev looked around, utterly bewildered. "What? Fucked who up?"

"All of us," Sean said darkly.

Kev looked at their frowning faces. "But . . . who knows about—"

"Liv saw them." Con sounded aggrieved. "Liv told Margot and Erin on the phone when they called her at the hospital. Margot told Tam and Raine. Erin told Becca and Cindy. And now all of the women are busting our balls about oh, how sweet, and oh, how sensitive, and oh, how fucking romantic. Thanks, man. Thanks. Real helpful."

"But I—"

"I mean, for Christ's sake, I'm dealing with diapers and colic, and tantrums, and Kevvie's screaming night terrors," Con bitched wearily. "I've forgotten what sleep feels like!"

"I've got a two-year-old kicking me in the face all night, plus I'm dealing with morning sickness," Davy butted in, not to be outdone.

"Suck raw ginger root for your morning sickness, Davy," Tam offered sweetly. "I'm told it does wonders."

Davy ignored her. "It's not enough to keep your shit together, deal with your kid, make a living, throw your underwear and socks in the right basket and hang on to your temper. It's not enough to be willing to take a bullet for her. Oh, no. A guy has to twist his brain into a knot to figure out how to keep the magic alive. It's hard enough just to keep the bodies alive around this crowd of crazy fools!"

"It's enough," Edie put in, quietly.

Davy cut off in midtirade, disoriented. "What's enough?"

"Being willing to take a bullet. That's really enough," Edie said.

Davy looked gratified. "I appreciate that."

"But the petals were nice," she added demurely.

Davy rolled his eyes. "Yeah. And so, like I said, Kev. Thanks for raising the bar for all of us. At the worst possible time. What a get-to-know-you-again present. A big, fat, hairy issue with the wife. Long, emotionally charged conversations deep into the night, when we could be sleeping, or even having sex. Hooray."

"Hey! Don't pin that on me!" Kev pointed at Bruno without hesitation. "That was him. That was all his idea. He did that!"

Bruno dragged his head up, blinking sleep-reddened eyes. "Like, what's the big goddamn deal?" he asked crabbily. "You buy some cheap roses. You throw the petals on the sheets. They look pretty. The chicks go wild. It's not rocket science."

Edie winced. "Don't spoil it for me, Bruno."

"So it's like we thought!" Davy said triumphantly. "It's just a cheap carnival trick. It's all about getting laid, right?"

"Well, yeah. Isn't everything?" Bruno looked perplexed. "What matters is how the chick reads it. That's what you got to manipulate."

Edie covered her ears. "I don't want to hear this." She was shaking with laughter, though the frequency was too high, too thin. Laughter only dogs could hear. She covered her face, and fought not to let it become tears. Not in front of Tam, the walking worst case scenario.

Kev tugged at her arm. "Come on. Let's go rest."

He led her out into the night. The soft, rustling chill of the forest surrounded them. Her shoes crunched on the spongy carpet of pine needles, but Kev's feet made no sound. She didn't have the strength to wonder how he did it. It was all she could do not to fall on her face.

The cabin was simple and spare. Inside was just a big king-sized bed with a comforter and a few pieces of furniture. Kev locked the door, peered out the windows, threw open cabinets until he found a pile of towels. He tossed one to Edie. "Want a shower?"

She wondered if she could stay on her feet that long, and decided being clean and fresh was worth it. Once under the stream of hot water, she took longer than she'd meant to and when she came out, her hair twisted into a tangled wet rope, Kev was stripping the sheets off the bed.

She was startled. "You have the energy to change sheets?"

"You think I'm going to let my woman sleep on sheets that another naked man has wallowed in? No fucking way."

She snorted with laughter. "Mr. Rigorous Hard-ass is back. I was wondering when he was going to show up."

"He's never far away," Kev said curtly. "And I'll warn you. It's not going to get better. I'll probably get worse with age. And the more I care, the worse it gets. So brace yourself."

If we live that long. They both left it unsaid, but it rang in the silence like an iron gong.

"Shouldn't we be coming up with some sort of plan?" she asked.

He shook his head. "I'm done in," he said. "Maybe you'll have a psychic vision that'll give us an idea. We need all the help we can get."

"It doesn't work like that," she said snappishly. "I told you. It's not a precision instrument. It's more like a kick in the head."

"Whatever." His voice was thick with weariness.

She moved to help with the bed, and they worked together silently. Kev tossed the comforter on top, and grabbed another towel. "I'm as rank as a goat," he said. "Get into bed, so you don't get chilled. And be ready to talk, when I get out of the shower."

"About what?"

His blazing gaze rocked her backwards. "About why you sneaked out of your dad's house and went to the Parrish Foundation building all by yourself," he said. "I'm real interested in your motivation for that."

The bathroom door clicked shut behind him.

Edie sat down on the edge of the bed, chilled to the bone by his tone of voice. She waited, her back very straight.

He finally came out, and carefully did not look at her. She waited, while he dried off. He was covered with scrapes, bruises, scabs. He checked the gun he'd laid on the bedside table. Peered out the window. Sidestepping the can of worms he'd opened.

"Stop stalling. Finish what you started," she said. "You asked what I was doing at the Parrish Foundation. It's not obvious?"

"No," he said. "The rest of the world thinks that I'm a kidnapper, brainwasher, and killer. What I want to know is if you thought that, too."

She stared at him, incredulous. "But I . . . no!"

"Then why did you go to the Parrish building? You didn't know about Des and Ava. We hadn't even spoken yet. But you knew there was a killer out on the loose. So why run out into the dark by yourself, just to verify what I said? Were you having doubts about me?"

She shook her head frantically. "No! I just wanted to see for myself that the boxes were there, like your text message said!"

"So my word wasn't enough for you?"

She bristled with outrage. "Well, it certainly isn't enough for the police! I wanted proof I could show to Detective Houghtaling! I wanted her to see that it was a trap! I sent her fifteen pictures, much good it did me. Now she thinks I set up the scene myself."

But Kev was not to be sidetracked. "Were you relieved?"

She tightened the towel and stood up. "Yes," she said flatly. "I was. I was so relieved, I cried. OK? Happy now? Satisfied?"

"So you did doubt me."

Edie felt lost. The look in his eyes, so faraway and cold, made him seem like a stranger. Hard and closed to her. She shook her head.

He took a step toward her, fists clenched. "You actually thought that I would seek you out, fuck your brains out, lie to you, use you, and then murder your father. Oh, and don't forget the violent kidnapping attempt I arranged, to terrify you into bonding with me."

"If I thought that, I wouldn't have gone anywhere," she told him crisply. "I certainly wouldn't be here with you now. I'd have stayed home, and done as I was told. How dare you criticize me?"

He let out a harsh bark of laughter. "Imagine how I felt when Bruno told me he'd left you at your dad's house. How I felt while I was being mind-fucked by Cheung. While she was telling me what she had planned for you. How much fun it was going to be."

"I had to go to Ronnie. That was not a bad decision," she insisted. "That was necessary! You'd have done the same!"

He ignored that. "Then I find you in the Parrish building, alone, with Marr stalking you. Yeah, Edie. I do dare to criticize that decision."

She flung her arms up. "So sue me! I'm doing the best I can! I wanted evidence to clear you, for the police! I was trying to help, and if that isn't enough for your hard-ass rigorous high standards, then fuck you, too, Kev! Fuck you too!"

They stared at each other. Both were breathing hard.

"So here it is," Edie said, her voice tight. "Our first real fight. The moment of truth. I warned you, Kev. I told you from the top that I'm not a shining angel. I'm a normal person. I make bad calls, dumb decisions, but I'm doing my best, and I deserve a goddamn break!"

His mouth twitched. "So I'm not the righteous superhero, either?"

"You certainly are not," she said sharply. "You're unfair and suspicious and negative and mean and horrible."

His face was a hard mask. "Yeah, well. It's been a tough day."

"Tough?" She laughed. "That's your excuse? You want to do a tough day one-up-manship? Go ahead. Shoot the starting gun, Kev. Let's see who comes out ahead."

He snorted. "That could get ugly."

"It's already ugly," she replied.

Kev sat down on the bed, and dropped his face into his hands. He stayed there, motionless, until she wanted to pound on him. "Goddamnit, Kev. Stop that," she begged. "Look at me. Finish this!"

He looked up. The raw pain in his eyes made her chest seize up. "How could you think that about me?" His voice was thick. "I thought you knew me. It was the first time I ever . . . ah, fuck it. Never mind."

Manipulative bastard, wringing her heart like a dishrag. "Don't you dare make me feel guilty, on top of everything else!" she yelled.

But he kept looking at her as if she'd just driven a knife into his chest. "Stop it, Kev!" she yelled. "Just . . . stop looking at me like that!"

He broke eye contact, looked at the floor. Which was no better.

"I will say this much," she finally offered, her voice wobbling. "I do know you, Kev. All except for that part of you that nobody knew. The part you didn't know yourself. I wondered if that hidden part might . . ." She dragged in air and forced herself to finish. ". . . might have another agenda. I thought it for, oh, a minute and a half. Then I got over it."

"What, like a split personality?"

"It occurred to me," she admitted. "Briefly. That's all."

"I'm not a killer," he announced. "I remember everything, after what happened with Ava. I broke that wall down."

"I believe you," she said. "Do you think I'd be here if I didn't?"

He lifted his head, and stared past her, like he was bracing himself. "My father was a paranoid schizophrenic," he said.

She was taken aback. She struggled with it, her mind blank. "Ah. Wow. I'm, ah, sorry about that," she faltered.

"I'm not asking you to be sorry. I just thought you should know. In case it's a problem for you. There's a genetic component, you know. I was raised by him, with my brothers. In complete isolation. Homeschooled. He died when I was twelve. It was a bizarre upbringing."

"It can't be much more bizarre than my own," she said quietly.

His chest jerked. "That's a generous way of looking at it."

"We're not to blame for our parents' insanity," she said. "It's hard enough to take responsibility for our own."

"I've been trying to do that for eighteen years," he said.

She let out a careful breath. "You did a fine job," she ventured.

"You think so?" He raised his eyes to hers, bright with challenge. "Then draw me again. Draw me right now."

Her legs gave out. She sat down, heavily. "Kev. Please. I don't know what you're trying to prove, but you don't have to—"

"Do it, Edie." His voice had that metallic edge it got sometimes, when things were dangerous.

"I don't even have paper or pencil," she hedged.

"There's paper on the dresser," he said. "There's a ballpoint pen next to the phone. Make do with those. Just do it."

She stared at his masklike face. "What do you want from me?"

He held out the paper and pen, with a clipboard that lay beside the printer. "Trust," he said.

The anger in his voice made her shiver. She took the clipboard and the pen, and sank down onto the cold floor, cross-legged. The towel fell from her body. Icy water dripped from her hair. She was careful to position the paper so it wouldn't get wet. Wet paper sucked.

"Get dressed first, if you're cold," he said.

"Oh, how generous," she muttered. "Let's just get this over with."

She gazed at his face, and began to draw. The image took form swiftly, the stark bones of his face, the shadowy intensity of his eyes.

But her inner eye did not open. The mysterious harmonics did not swell and come into focus. She kept drawing, waiting. It didn't happen.

Her pen paused, as a flash of insight suddenly revealed what the problem was. She almost laughed, but it just wasn't funny. "You're too angry," she told him. "You're jamming the airwaves."

He didn't reply. His throat bobbed, as he swallowed hard.

"You want trust from me, but you don't trust me back," she said.

She got up, laying the drawing down on the dresser. The cold space between them felt vast. This was stupid, and she was having none of it. She walked over to him. Touched his face, tenderly.

He turned away, avoiding her touch. "Try fucking me, then."

She jerked her hand back like she'd been stung. "Excuse me?"

"You said once that your psychic communion thing happened when we had sex," he said. "So let's try it. I'm all for that."

He was. It was impossible for him to hide, being stark naked. His cock had swelled out, long and reddened. His eyes were hot with lust.

She took another step back, oddly unnerved. "I don't think so."

He gazed at her body. The heat of his hunger licked across her skin, like tender flames. She could feel its buzzing, ticklish electric pressure against her skin. His energy was so powerful, even when he slammed his doors shut. And in spite of the violence and death and danger, she wanted him, too. Angry as he was, he was real and warm and solid. He was Kev, behind that thick wall, and she ached for him.

But she'd be damned if she'd make it easy for him. Arrogant dog. How dare he. She turned her back on him, walked around to the side of the bed, and slid under the coverlet, turning her back to him.

Silence stretched for several minutes. She lay there, eyes frozen wide. The weight of his gaze was like a hot hand on her body.

"Freezing me out?" he asked softly.

"No, Kev. That's what you did to me. This is the result."

The bed shifted as he got into it. He slid across the mattress, and grabbed her, pulling her back against his body. "I'll melt you, then."

She stifled a moan of delight at the contact of his body. So warm. Her skin shimmered with pleasure, everywhere that his skin touched hers. She shook in his arms, racking spasms, as if she were coming.

Kev nuzzled his face in her damp hair. His cock pressed against her thigh, hot and insistent. "This is a switch," he said. "Usually I'm trying to resist, and you're coaxing me. Against my better judgment."

"It's time I stopped acting like an eager little puppy," she said. "Those days are over. No more begging and pleading."

He parted the hair on her neck, pressed his warm lips to the back of her neck. "I can beg and plead, too."

"Beg away. See how much I care."

His lips were so soft, moving over her nape. His hand stole around to cup her breast, and the other slid underneath her, in the curve of her waist, sliding over her thigh to cup her mound. His fingers stroked the seam of her vulva, delicately seeking out her clit.

She shivered, trying not to whimper. Not fair. He came at her from every direction. Overwhelming her with his hot, urgent embrace, his soft kisses, fingertips caressing and circling, teasing her open.

She was racked with unreleased tension, thighs locked, but the hot liquid rush of arousal betrayed her. Kev slid his finger into her slick well of lube, thrusting, petting. A growl of triumph vibrating his chest.

He dragged her closer, so his glans touched her labia from behind, an urgent, pleading caress against her softness. Sweet, coaxing kisses to her nape made her shiver and squirm, softening even more.

She didn't mean to let him do it, but a little pushing and

wiggling, and his cockhead nudged just inside her slick folds, rubbing and caressing, bathing in her liquid warmth while his fingers worked her from the front. She was wound so tight, like wires about to break, but he was tender, relentless. Insisting.

When she finally snapped, the strength of the orgasm wrenched her into a blinding red oblivion that she had not asked for but could not resist. It stampeded over her, practically knocking her unconscious.

When she oriented herself in time and space once again, he'd thrust two of his fingers deeper. They made wet, silky sounds as he petted and stroked. "You're melting," he whispered. "You're ready."

She reached out for him with her mind, but he wasn't letting her in. He was still jamming the frequency.

"You're not," she replied. "You're still as hard as ice."

He nudged his cockhead deeper, rocking, pressing. "I'm supposed to be hard," he said. "Just like you're supposed to melt. Biology."

"Don't play word games. You know damn well what I mean."

He caught her clit between his fingers, squeezing tenderly, and swirled his cock against her sweet spots, making her light up, squirming and shimmering for him. "Let me in." His voice was rough, like a command, but she could feel the rigid control of his body. He wouldn't move until she opened for him. And she was dying to give in.

He knew it. He was counting on it. Arrogant, complacent bastard.

She turned, looked over her shoulder. "Let me in, too."

His eyes narrowed. The air hummed with tension.

"You, first," he whispered. "Then we'll see."

A final instant of resistance, and hell with it. They didn't have a chance in hell of a future together, and she wanted this. Pride and dignity be damned. They wouldn't do her much good in the grave.

But he had to look her in the face. "Let me turn around."

He let her flip onto her back, and settled himself between her legs. He paused, as he ran his hand down her body, from throat to thigh. His face was grim and tense. He reached out, switched off the lamp.

"Hey!" Edie jerked up in protest. "That's a dirty trick! I wanted to see your eyes! Turn that back on, right now!"

"No." He folded her legs up, high and wide. "I can't look at your bruises while I fuck you. It bothers me."

She propped herself onto her elbows. "They're not your fault!"

He nudged himself against her tender folds, easing inside. "No? The day I met you, you didn't have a single bruise. I know, because I inspected every last goddamn square inch of your body myself. You hang out with me for four days, and now you're covered with them. Conclusion?"

"But I—"

Her voice cut off as he surged inside her, in one hard thrust.

She forgot what she was going to say, clutching at his chest, wiggling to find the perfect angle that let him slide deeper.

He began to move, arching over her. He started slow, but not for long. They were both too desperate for that. They picked up speed, force. Heaving and rocking. It wan't their usual shining fusion of souls. He was so far from her, but his desire and hunger were no less because of that. If anything, he was more desperate.

They fought to get closer, clawing for each other on every level. Thunder and lightning. Pounding and gasping. He drove deep and hard. Her nails dug into him, lifting herself. Slamming thrusts, frenzied kisses, clutching hands, whimpering and gasping.

Both earned more bruises. Neither cared. She turned herself inside out for him as the blinding orgasm blasted through them—

He cracked open. His guard fell, and she saw everything.

This time it really was a kick in the head, like the early, bad old days, when the unwanted visions would blindside her. Images, impressions, shocking and horrible. Merely the echoes of what he'd been through that day, but they jolted her to the bedrock of her being.

Fear, horror, grief. A dead girl, staring out of a plastic bag. A live one cuffed to a wheelchair, weeping. A hideous, bulbous black widow spider with a woman's gloating face and long black hair, laughing as she wrapped sticky fibers around her prey, strangling it to immobility.

Then, the breaking of that ancient inner fortress. Memories flooding in. Faces, places, feelings. So vivid, the tears flooded her eyes.

Brothers, bullets, bombs. It had all exploded in his face. He'd been broken to pieces, again and again that day. And still, amazingly, he was whole. Shining and whole. And so beautiful. God, she loved him.

She wound her arms around his shaking, sweaty shoulders. Holding him as close as she could. Tears flooding down her face.

She tried to make him turn his face, but he resisted, pulling out of her. He fished around on the floor for his clothes, pulled on his jeans. She shivered in the wall of cold air that rushed between them.

"Kev?" She reached for the bedside lamp.

He batted her hand away so violently, the lamp fell off the table. It broke against the floor. "Don't," he said savagely.

She sat up startled. "Kev? What's wrong?"

"If you have to ask. I'm finally getting it."

"Getting what?"

"The disadvantages of having a psychic girlfriend."

She was bewildered. "But . . . but I thought you wanted—"

"I changed my mind," he said. "Or came to my senses, more like."

She shrank in on herself. "You mean, you're ashamed?" she whispered. "At what I saw? What you let me see?"

"I just mean I want some space." He picked up the gun, shoved it into the back of his pants. "You stay here. I'll go out, keep watch——"

"That's not fair!" she yelled. "You asked me to! You bullied me!"

"Life's not fair. Haven't you noticed that? Look, Edie. I'm sorry about this crazy shit. I'm sorry about . . . what just happened." He gestured toward the bed. "I shouldn't have done that to you. I won't do it again. You and Liv and Tony and Zia Rosa will go up to that island in the San Juans with my brothers' friend Seth today. I'll get the fuck out of your face. And who knows, maybe you'll have a chance at survival."

She launched herself at him, and swatted at his shoulder. "I don't want you out of my face! You bastard!"

"Too bad. I'm going out," he repeated, stonily. "Stay here."

Cold air swirled and gusted in as he jerked the door open. It swung shut behind him, shutting out air, noise, the night. And him.

Edie sat down on the bed, her hands pressed to her face. She wanted to find him. Start slapping and screaming like a fishwife, but it would be childish and embarrassing. He was counting on her natural horror of making a scene in front of his newfound family. She was Charles and Linda Parrish's daughter, after all.

Let him have his precious space, then. Let him choke on it.

It occurred to her, as she washed herself up again, that neither of them had thought about contraception. That edge-of-doom vibe. Neither of them expected to live long enough to deal with consequences.

She dressed, and fished the cell phone out of her pocket. The sky was getting lighter. She stared at the phone that one of Kev's brothers had lent her, thumbing it on just to see if Ronnie had managed to steal her phone back and send a message. She should go see if Aaro would help her call Ronnie again with his magic signal bouncer.

It rang the instant she turned it on. She stared at the display, heart leaping into her throat. It sank back down immediately, when she saw the number. Not Ronnie's. And so? There was no one else on earth she wanted to hear from. Not on this telephone.

But the ringtone jabbed, like a needle in her brain. *Who?* She answered. "Yes?" she whispered.

"Good morning, Edie." Des's voice. There was an oily smile in it that made her stomach flop horribly. "Do you want to live?"

She sank down onto the bed again. "Yes," she said.

"How lucky for you that you answered this call," he said. "Do you want your lover and his band of merry men to live, too?"

"Yes," she said again.

"We know where you are. We're looking at you, out there in the forest. There's a clear vantage point for our thermal imaging. You and Larsen were fucking in the cabin about, oh, twenty minutes ago. The rest of them are in the big house. My finger is resting on a button that will blow you all instantly into fine, vaporous particles. Unless you do exactly . . . and I mean, *exactly* . . . what I say. Understand?"

She swallowed over a knot of terror. "Tell me what you want."

"I'm going to give you simple, clear instructions, Edie. If you disobey any one of them, I will push the button. Is that clear?"

"Yes. Listen, Des—"

"The first instruction is to say only 'yes.' Say it in a low, obedient tone of voice. If you say anything else, I push the button. Got that?"

She swallowed. "Yes."

"The second direction is that you keep this phone connection open at all times. If you should drop the phone, push the wrong button with your cheek, if we should suddenly lose coverage . . . I cut my losses, and push the button. Bye-bye. Ka-boom."

"But Des, I don't know if—"

"Remember the first instruction, you stupid bitch," he snarled.

She bit her lip, forced it out. "Yes."

"The third instruction is to make no unneccesary movements. I'm looking at your cabin wall through a powerful thermal imaging device. You're sitting at the foot of the bed. You need to work on your posture."

Pride and anger stiffened her spine, involuntarily.

"Ah, that's better! And watching you screw Larsen, whew! I had no idea you were so passionate! It was like watching a forest fire." He chuckled. "Did you come? You can tell me." He hesitated. "Say it, Edie."

Her gorge rose. She steeled herself and whispered. "Yes."

"That's good! So. Do anything I didn't tell you to do, and I will see you do it. And I will push that button. Understand?"

"Yes." Tears flashed out of her squeezed shut eyes. She reached up to brush them away.

"Get that fucking hand down until I tell you to raise it!"

Edie stood, hand in midair, and slowly lowered it. "Yes," she said.

"Get up. Come out the door," Des said. "Act natural. Walk directly in front of the house."

She stared down at the ballpoint pen that lay on the floor. The crumpled piece of paper that had wafted to the carpet when Kev left the room. "Can I put on my shoes?" she whispered.

Des hesitated. "Be quick," he said. "And no more questions."

Edie slid to her knees. She scooped up the pen with one shoe, the paper as she grabbed the other, and sat down on the bed again, the paper spread out on the floor between her feet. She held the pen as she did up the laces of the high-tops, and scrawled in huge letters,

BOMB

"You're done tying your shoes," Des said.

"Yes." Edie stood, and stepped outside the cabin door, leaving it gaping wide. The icy wind whipped at her wet eyes, her still-damp hair. She let the piece of paper flutter out of her hands, to the frosty ground.

Des said nothing. He had not seen it. Tears of relief trickled out of her eyes. *Please, Kev. Or someone. Anyone. See it. Find it.*

"Now what?" she asked.

CHAPTER
37

The wind swept up the canyon, sharp and raw, hitting Kev's face like a slap. He welcomed it. He deserved a slap.

He slogged through the undergrowth up to the craggy cliff face that was upslope from the drafty, half-built house. The house was perched on that same cliff, he now saw. The foundation was sunk into a chunk of volcanic rock. A big bank of picture windows had already been put in on the floor above the basement where Aaro lived now, probably to block the weather from the slow, one-man construction site. They would look out over a stunning view, over a sheer cliff to a riverbed canyon below. Very dramatic.

Kev couldn't believe how far things had gone. It was bad enough that he'd used her for two decades as a talisman and navigation device, before even knowing who or what she was. And now that he knew her, he was using her even more. He craved her. He was strung out on her, out of his head. Her body, her mind, her way of talking. The way she made him feel. Being seen by her. Being known.

He'd put her life in danger repeatedly. He'd known, in his skin, his guts, his balls, that he couldn't have this. That being with him was a death sentence for that girl. And he'd pretended not to know it.

And tonight, Jesus. He was appalled at himself. Bullying, scolding, blustering. Coercing her into rough sex, after a day like today.

And now she could end up doing time. If she survived at all.

He had to muzzle this beast. Damage control. If he had to confess to a crime he didn't commit, murder and rape and brainwashing and abuse and God knows what else to clear her, he would. He would.

It would have to be enough, that Edie existed someplace, safe and whole, even if she was not happy. Maybe he could read her graphic novels to pass the time while he rotted in prison. It was exactly what he deserved, he reflected grimly. Let the fucking punishment fit the crime.

"Hey. Kid."

He turned. It was Tony. He'd aged ten years in the last twenty-four hours. His lines were seamed even deeper, the pouches heavier.

He cupped his hand against the wind to light a hand-rolled cigarette. It glowed as he sucked in smoke. His grizzled stubble glinted silver in the pale half-light of dawn.

Kev couldn't make his voice work. The thought of Edie hating him, after what he'd said. It compressed his larynx to the hardness of a diamond. "What are you doing out here?" he finally said.

"Came out to take a piss," was Tony's laconic reply.

Kev tilted his eyebrow. "Aaro had indoor plumbing, last I looked."

"Don't get mouthy with me," Tony said. His eyes were slitted, measuring. "Thought you'd be in with your lady, makin' the best possible use of your time. What you doing out here in the cold?"

Kev coughed, to clear the way for words. "She's not my lady."

Tony blinked. "What the fuck? You're head-up-the-ass in love."

"She keeps narrowly escaping death. Now she's looking at prison time, if they pin Parrish on me. I'm bad for her health. And reputation."

Tony folded his arms over his chest. "What does she think?"

Kev looked back out over the canyon. "It doesn't matter what she thinks," he said. "My decision's made."

Tony coughed. "You haven't had much to do with women, kid."

Kev grunted. Like he needed love advice from Tony Ranieri. Every woman Tony had ever been involved with hated his guts.

"Shouldn't you be inside, getting some sleep?" he asked.

"Hard to sleep in that place," Tony said. "Temperature's subzero."

"It's got to be warmer than it is out here."

"I'm talkin' about your brothers," Tony said. "They think I'm lower than dirt, for sitting on you for eighteen years. Like a fuckin' hen."

Kev shrugged. "Well. It is what it is. Can't change it now."

Tony smoked, and waited. Kev felt the weight of his expectant pause, and turned his head, staring at the old man.

"Let me get this straight," Kev said. "You want me to tell you that it's all perfectly OK? That I understand?"

Tony's nostrils flared. "I had my fucking reasons for what I did."

Right. Like getting unpaid slave labor, twelve hours a day for years. "Sure you did, Tony," he said sourly.

"You can't tell me that if I'd gone off looking for these McClouds Osterman and his goons wouldn't have gone for you. Back when you was practically a drooling vegetable," Tony growled. "They would've gone for all four of you! You'd have been meat, kid."

"Maybe," Kev said. "We also might have exposed that

bastard and finished it back then, eighteen years ago. Before he went on to murder and brain damage dozens of innocent teenagers."

"You're blaming me for that, now, too?" Tony hunched his head down into his shoulders.

"I'm just saying that we can't know. So cut the pronouncements and the justifications. It's a waste of time. What's done is done."

"You are one righteous hard-ass." Tony pinched the cigarette, and sucked in the last drag. "You think I fucked you up bad, huh?"

Aw, Christ. Tony was wanking away at the self-torture. Kev sighed, watching his breath curl. "No," he said wearily.

"You think I shoulda taken you to specialists, at two hundred bucks a pop? Sold some crack cocaine to pay for it, maybe? You think I shoulda got a bunch of candy-ass social workers to fuss over you, feel sorry for you? Jerk you off?"

"No, Tony," he said, tonelessly.

"Or shelled out money for private speech therapy? I had to take care of Bruno, too, goddamnit! Nobody ever gave me a fucking dime to pay for that kid's expenses, and you expect me to—"

"I didn't expect a goddamn thing, Tony. You could have left me at the warehouse to die if you felt like it," Kev said. "It was your choice."

Tony hawked and spat over the cliff. "So I'm an ice cold, egoistic, opportunistic bastard, huh? Right? Go ahead. Say it."

Kev shrugged, mercilessly. "You said it, not me."

Tony wiped his mouth, scratching the stubble under his chin. "Just keep in mind," he said. "If I had a son of my own, I'd have treated him the exact same goddamn way. And he'd be just as pissed as you."

Kev was startled. He stared at the old man, bemused. Trying, and failing, to decode that cryptic statement.

"You get me?" Tony demanded. "You get what I'm saying?"

Kev cleared his throat. "Ah. I think so."

"So don't take it personal."

"OK," Kev said. At a total loss.

Tony stubbed out his cigarette on the rock, muttering. He dug in his pocket, and pulled something out. Small, tarnished oblong discs that dangled on a chain. He handed it to Kev. "Better late than never."

Kev took it, stared at the tags. *Eamon McCloud.* His chest hurt.

Tony turned, and stumped away.

"Tony," Kev said, on impulse.

Tony did not turn. Kev groped for something coherent to say. Something to answer that backhhanded, rough moment of grace.

"Thanks for saving me," he said.

Tony didn't look around. "You're worth saving, kid." His voice sounded heavy and sad. He walked back to the house.

Kev's hands closed around the dog tags, looking inward as the memory unfurled. Of that day his overblown hero complex had convinced him it was his job to singlehandedly get proof for the cops that the Midnight Project was something foul and criminal. He knew more kids would die if he asked someone else to do the job. There had been no one to ask for help. Davy was in Iraq, Connor off on a stakeout for his new cop job. Sean had been out of his mind in love with Liv Endicott, and her dad had gotten him locked up in jail to keep him away from her. So no back-up from that quarter. He was on his own.

But it couldn't wait. He'd gone to his father's bedroom, which none of them had touched since his death eight years before. The room was thick with dust, but the bed was still made up with military neatness, the drab green wool blanket pulled as tight as a drum. He'd taken the dog tags out of a tin cup that sat next to a photograph of his mother, and sat on the bed, holding the metal discs in his hand, staring at Mom's smiling face. Silently begging for courage. To do the hard thing.

Then he'd shoved them into his pocket—and gone off to fucking Armageddon, all alone. His head shoved six miles up his ass.

Only eighteen years later was he finally even physically capable of pondering the massive consequences of that decision. His stupidity, his arrogance, it took his breath away. But he'd paid for it. Paid in full.

Sean came out on the porch. He caught sight of Kev up on the bluff, and gestured him down. As soon as his voice would carry over the scream of the canyon wind, his twin shouted, "What's with Edie?"

Kev's guts locked up. "What do you mean?"

"You have no idea why she would suddenly decide to take an early morning stroll and walk out of the security perimeter?"

Dread slammed into him. He looked at the cabin. The door hung open, banging on its hinges. A piece of paper fluttered and danced on wind gusts. "Oh, shit," he whispered.

"Aaro saw her, but she was in front of the house, so he thought nothing of it. Then he poured himself a cup of coffee, went over to the door, and she was gone. Halfway across the meadow already. She's not even wearing a coat. It's fucking freezing out here."

"Which way?" he demanded.

Sean pointed. "Straight north, toward the highway."

Kev leaped off the rock and onto the path, across the clearing—

Bam. Bam. Guns blasted, woodchips flew. Kev hit the ground and started crawling for cover. The piece of paper swirled and spun in the wind, closer to him. He snagged it out of midair.

His own grim face stared out of the paper. A line draw-

ing. Grim features, flat mouth, fulminating eyes. And above
it, a scrawled word.

BOMB

Then he heard her scream.

Edie hugged herself in the frigid dawn. She clutched the
phone to her ear under damp, half-frozen hair. Her ear
burned with the toxic contact of that falsely gentle voice.

"Look down, Edie. There's a beam sunk into concrete, in
the foundation of this building. Do you see something?"

She jerked back in revulsion. "Oh, God, it's a—"

"Shut up! No sudden movements! Look again, you idiot."

She looked again. She did not like snakes, but she forced
herself to stare at the thing, until . . . Wait. This was not a
real snake.

A mechanical snake. A robotic thing. Dark, metallic.
Wound around a beam that supported the house. The narrow
end of its tail was lifted, like a rattlesnake's. The robotic
snake slowly, gracefully lifted its head, and looked at her,
cocking its head rakishly.

She recoiled. Its face was a recessed camera lens. It
looked like a wide-open, voracious silver mouth, like a gigantic tapeworm.

"Isn't it amazing?" Des asked, in a conversational tone.
"Two meters long, and it can get anywhere. Past a thermal
imager, a motion detector, infrared. It slithers through rocks,
rubble. Sends back sounds and images. Even thermal images. That's how we saw you through the cabin wall, see?
And best of all . . . it carries ordnance. It's less maneuver-
able with a load of explosives, but it manages fine."

The snake unwound from the four-by-four beam and
slithered in a smooth, back-and-forth swishing S movement
over to Edie's foot.

It lifted its head, wound itself around her ankle, and

squeezed. The camera snake head looked up, wagging. Taunting her.

"Aw," Des murmured. "It likes you. Don't move, Edie."

Edie fought to stay still. "Stop it," she whispered.

"Listen carefully." The snake detached from her leg, and coiled itself up. "Turn your back to the house. Lean down, pick up the snake."

She hesitated. Des clicked his tongue.

"Edie," he chided. "You're being thick and slow. That snake is a bomb. If I push the button, you will all die. Is that what you want?"

"No," she whispered, in a tiny voice.

"Well, then. Pick up the snake."

Edie clenched her gut, and did so. The robot snake was extremely heavy. It writhed in her grip like a living thing.

"Stroll away from the house . . . slower. Straight ahead. Slow down, Edie. Yes, that's the pace. Slow and steady. Casual. Look up at the trees. Enjoy the beauty of nature, hmm? Keep going."

Her feet crunched over the frosted pine needles. One mud-stained red high-top in front of the other, staring down so she wouldn't trip. Clutching that abominable thing in one hand.

Out of the trees. Into a meadow. Pushing through long, folded wads of frosted dead grass. She shuffled forward, her arm burning with the effort of holding that awful thing out.

She reached the end of the clearing. Men rose up silently at the edge of the trees, like pale shadows in white and gray winter camo, bristling with guns and hardware, thick with body armor, faces hidden by ski masks. Guns, pointing at her. A lot of guns.

She stopped, shivering violently. Waited. Six, seven . . . eight men.

One of them jerked the snake away from her. She let her burning arm drop. Her other arm, too. She slid the phone into her pocket.

The one who had grabbed the snake tossed it over his

beefy shoulder, and cuffed her arms in front of her with plastic bonds, ratcheting them brutally tight. He grabbed her by the arm, made a signal to the other seven men. They dropped to the ground, started slinking towards Aaro's house. She turned to watch, but the man wrenched her along beside him. "Not a sound," he hissed.

They stopped at a clearing. She could hear the highway not far away. Logging trucks roaring by. Several cars were parked there. One was the car that Kev's Zia Rosa had rented. The one Kev had driven to the Helix complex the day before. The yellow Nissan Xterra.

Des sat next to a stump with a laptop. He held his phone to his ear, but when he saw them, he made a show of closing the connection. His smile was so normal. As if they were meeting for coffee.

The big guy shoved her uncomfortably close, sandwiched between the two men. Des was dressed in a winter coat, black hat. He was pale, with circles under his eyes, and very bulky under the coat. Edie reached out with her cuffed hands, and poked at his chest. Rigid as steel.

"Nervous, Des?" she asked. "Are your painkillers working?"

Des slapped her, knocking her back against the other man. Then he frisked her, his hands lingering on her breasts, her ass. Crouching down to feel her ankles. She saw stars, tasted blood in her mouth.

The man who'd cuffed her crouched in front of the laptop, and manipulated the joystick. There was a video image on the screen.

"Look at this, Edie," Des taunted. "Your snake bomb wasn't the only one who went adventuring. Look where this one's gotten to."

The big guy lifted his ski mask, and showed her his fleshy face. His eyes lingered hungrily on her chest. "Remember me, beautiful?"

She shook her head mutely. He jerked down her shirt,

until her breast was revealed, and fitted his fingers over the bruises around her nipple. He squeezed, hard. She jerked back, but Des blocked her.

The pain made her want to vomit. She gasped for air.

"Remember me now, bitch?" the man growled.

"Focus, Tom," Des snapped. "Show her the snake's-eye view."

Tom spun the laptop so she could see it better. Her breath caught. The screen was divided into four images. Each was a different perspective of the exterior of Aaro's house, except for one, which was an interior. A muddy, fish-eye view from a corner of the inside. She could see a cat's food dish in the foreground, a forest of chair legs. A muddy, booted foot. Noise, men's voices speaking. The sound was distorted, but she could distinguish voices. Tom manipulated the joystick, and the camera panned around. Up, down. Right, left.

"A swinging cat door. That's how I got it in." Tom sounded pleased with himself. "I could've planted the thing in the space under the house, but this way, I can physically see when they're all inside. The other snakes will tell me when the men should drive them all in, and then boom! All gone at once! Problem solved in one blow. I love that."

"Tom likes to streamline," Des explained.

"These babies are fun to play with." Tom sounded like a kid with a new toy. "And so discreet. I took my time this morning, finding the perfect placement at my leisure. And look." He grabbed the one draped over his shoulders and pushed a button. A device detached itself from the snake's lens eye. "A retractable infrared periscope. We use them in the dark, too." He lifted a black plastic device, like an ergonomic remote control. "This is the detonator. Slick, huh? I love this shit."

He sounded like he expected her to be pleasantly impressed. She looked around at the vehicles. "That's Kev's car," she said inanely.

"Oh, yes. We've fixed it up for the police," Des assured

her. "We've thought of everything. It's all about the spin, remember? Selling the story. There's C-4, and the AWM sniper rifle that killed your father. We covered them with your boyfriend's fingerprints when we took him yesterday. And now, the cherry to put on the top. This!"

Tom held up the mechanical snake she'd carried. "A snakebot bomb, covered with Edie Parrish's fingerprints," he said. "That'll be in Kev's car, too. What will they make of that, I wonder?"

Des clicked his tongue. "You bad girl. What did Charles do to you when you were little that made you so angry? Everyone will wonder."

"Why did you . . ." Edie's throat seized up. "Why not kill me along with them? Why draw me out? You just wanted to gloat?"

"No," Des said absently. "We've got other plans for you. Shut up."

Like hell. She dragged in a breath, and screamed. "Kev! Bomb!"

"Fuck." Tom lunged for her, clapping his hand over her mouth. "Should have gagged the bitch," he snarled, grabbing the walkie-talkie.

Edie struggled, and kept screaming. He whapped her on the side of the head, dazing her.

"Positions?" he rapped into it, and listened to a terse, staticky reply that she could not make out, because she started screaming again, even though it hurt her head. She couldn't make herself stop.

"Pin them down," Tom yelled, over her shrieks. "Nobody leaves the house! Drive them in! Des, shut that dumb bitch up before I shoot her!"

Des grabbed her from behind. Guns blasted across the meadow. She used Des's body for ballast, and jackknifed, kicking the laptop off the stump. It flipped, spun, cracked to the ground, screen side down.

Tom roared in outrage, launching himself at her—

Thhtp, the muted sound of a silenced gun firing, and Tom was knocked backward with a shout, thudding heavily to the ground.

He gasped for air. *Thhtp*, another shot. He squawked, writhing on the ground, cursing viciously.

Edie twisted to look. Tam stood among the trees, a stark silhouette, elegant and cat-slender in quilted black nylon, holding a huge, squared off pistol. Her face was pale and set.

"Let go of her," she said. Her smoky voice was menacing.

Des backed away, holding Edie in front of himself as a shield.

Edie writhed and flopped. "Tam!" she shrieked. "It's a bomb! A bomb in the house! A snakebot loaded with explosives! Tell them!"

Tam's eyes flashed. A com device appeared in her hand as gunfire crackled across the meadow.

"Aaro?" she shouted. "Come in, Aaro? Anybody? Anybody?"

A staticky hiss. Then a voice, tense, shouting, "Tam? Tam!"

"Con!" Tam yelled. "Bomb! A snakebot! Watch out!"

"In the corner!" Edie shrieked. Des tried to cover her mouth with his hand, but she tore her face loose, writhing. "By the cat dishes! And the detonator, it's here! That black thing! Quick! Tom had it, it fell down over—"

Des slammed the side of her head with his fist, tossed Edie aside and dove for the detonator. Tam's gun spat again. *Thhtp.*

Des yelped, jerking on the ground. Edie hurled herself at the detonator, grabbed it. Des's hand shot out, clamped her throat, hard enough to grind bones. Her heartbeat got louder, roaring in her head.

She could hardly hear Tam screaming into the com device. Tom was struggling up onto his elbow, face distorted with rage. Taking aim.

get rid of it . . . going to blow . . . goddamnit, now, right now . . .

Bam, bam, bam, bam. Tom fired his gun. Tam's voice cut off.

Tam lay flat, gasping, clutching her shoulder, her thigh. Tom swung his gun, bashing Edie's elbow, jarring her grip on the detonater.

Des snatched it. She screamed, in horror, despair—

Boom.

The sound was huge. The woods shook, the trees quivered.

In the numb, dreadful silence that followed, Edie looked at Tam, sprawled on the ground. Their eyes met. Tam's were full of stark grief, and a knowledge that they shared, now. There was no bottom to that hole. A person could keep falling forever.

Des and Tom struggled to their feet, panting. Des jerked Edie up, cursing as she wobbled and sagged. "On your feet," he snarled, and turned to Tom. "Are you shot?"

"I'll live," Tom muttered. "The vest caught them. Just a flesh wound. Hurts. That dirty little cunt. I'll teach her."

"I'll take Edie, then," Des said. "You go do clean-up." He gestured toward Tam, aiming a vicious kick at her wounded thigh. Tam jerked, gasping, but made no other sound. "Kill her."

"Oh, yeah," Tom said, with relish. "It'll be my pleasure."

Edie held Tam's gaze for as long as she could while Des dragged her to his car, which was parked behind Kev's rented SUV. He lifted the remote, popped the trunk, and the world flipped and spun as he tossed her in. She landed with a jarring *thump*, a gasp of pain.

Des stared down, lips drawing back in a quivering parody of a grin. "This is where the fun starts. Bitch." He slammed the trunk shut.

The smothering darkness of the grave closed in around her.

CHAPTER
38

Kev writhed on his belly toward the house. The woods offered cover, but he had only one clip. If they cut him off outside with no ammo, they'd slaughter him, and the house was an arsenal.

Bullets whizzed, digging into the packets of cedar shakes Aaro had planned to side his house with. Another gouged into the future deck, a raw framework of four-by-fours. He scrambled around to the back, then leaped up on top of the half-constructed porch. A bullet scored a red line of fire across his thigh as he slithered in the door.

The front windows on the basement level had been shattered. Everyone was flat on the floor. Aaro was tossing guns and clips around from a big metal locker that lay on its side.

Another barrage hit, punching through walls. Glass and wood, drywall, chalky chunks of sheetrock showered down. A walkie-talkie lay on the floor. It was squawking. A female voice, shrill and urgent.

Con crawled over, shouted into it. His head jerked up, eyes wide with alarm. "Bomb!" he yelled. "Snakebot! In the house!"

The writhing caught Kev's eye. A one-eyed, mechanical

boa constrictor, heavy and thick, clothed in a sack of winter camo canvas. Flipping and flailing like a crazed whip. He flung himself at it.

"Drop it! It's going to blow!" Con screamed. "Everybody out!"

Kev looked around. Exits blocked. Guns blasted outside. They'd get torn apart if they ran out of here. Even if he tried to jump out with the bomb into a hail of bullets, the blast would knock him back inside.

The other direction, then. The picture windows on the second story of Aaro's house, the ones that looked out over the sheer cliff. He leaped for the scaffolding that led up to the unfinished loft.

Time dilated. Bruno and Tony leaped at him, mouths working in grotesque slow motion. Screaming at him to stop. But he couldn't.

He'd be silhouetted against the sky for the marksmen outside. So be it. Neither of his families would get blown up today, for having tried to save his sorry ass. Not if he could help it. And Edie. Oh, Edie.

Something grabbed his foot, wrenched. He was hanging with the injured shoulder, reaching with the other. He yelled at the brutal yank, lost his grip. Howled, in rage and despair as he fell, hit the ground.

Tony yanked the snakebot away, and started climbing up before Kev could move to stop him. He looked down as he stepped onto the loft, his eyes meeting Kev's. His face hard, with grim acceptance.

Bullets shattered the windows, punched into Tony. Lifted him and the flipping snakebot up, back, out, and into the void outside. Arms and legs wide, sprawled backward, suspended, falling . . .

Boom.

The huge explosion stunned them all. Kev lay open mouthed. Struck stupid. Time stopped. That hadn't just happened. Not possible.

Not Tony.

Bruno's face jolted him into the time-space continuum again. His mouth open, yelling something that Kev couldn't hear. Tears streamed down Bruno's face. He leaped up, hung out the shattered window, screaming incoherently as he sprayed bullets from an M-16.

Miles seized him by the waist and yanked him back down again. A volley of bullets thundered through the space where Bruno's torso had been, leaving a pattern of holes in the opposite wall. The light shone through them, the wind blew through. The smoke swirled, stank. The place was a fucking sieve. Ah, God. Tony.

You're worth saving, kid.

He was sobbing. Someone tugged on his arm, finger to his lips. Aaro. He tried to stop his chest from shaking, tried to close his mouth.

Aaro shoved an Uzi and a spare magazine into his hands, and beckoned, gesturing to stay down. Wrenching up boards with a hammer, they slithered through the ragged square torn into the floor, down into a crawl space. It was part solid granite bedrock, part poured concrete. From there, they writhed out into a narrow trench which had been dug through a thicket of sapling pines. They could crawl through the forest without making the branches shake, and giving away their position. Aaro had built his house on a cliff, and dug himself an escape hatch. The kind of paranoia that would make Crazy Eamon proud.

Ahead of them, there was a rustling of branches, a cracking of twigs, a choked cry. Then Sean appeared, his hands red. Kev was too numb to be startled by the face of the dead man when he crawled past the corpse. The guy's white and gray camo was bloodsoaked, his eyes wide with surprise. Mouth wide. Throat slit.

Sean had done that. Kev tried to get his head around it, then stopped trying. They wiggled in single file. Circling wide through the forest, to get behind the guys who were still shooting at the house.

Time warped as they crawled. He stopped when he saw Davy, sprawled on his belly, a Ruger 10/22 semiautomatic rifle poised on a rotten log, taking aim. Davy was a crack shot, the best of the brothers. He'd inherited the ice-cold inner stillness that had made their father a legendary sniper. The rest of them had not. They were good shots, but not on Davy or Dad's level. They waited, all holding their breaths. Three hundred meters or so. The distance was nothing for Davy.

Bam. Half the man's head exploded. Davy barely flinched. Deep in the zone. Kev envied him. He himself was a fucking shattered mess.

Then another belly-to-the-ground slither through bushes and dead leaves and pine needles. Three of the guys in winter camo were crouched behind Aaro's battered, mud-splattered gray van, conferring angrily in whispers. Con popped up and lifted a long tube with two telescopic ends onto his shoulder. It took Kev a few seconds to place it.

Holy shit, that was an AT4. An anti-tank weapon. Those guys were toast. Aaro had some serious shit in his toy box. In fact, Aaro's eyes were wide as he silently gestured at Con to stop, stop, stop—

Kaboom. The vehicle lifted up with strange, aerial grace, bashing down onto its side. Glass, shattering. A column of greasy smoke. Flames licking.

Aaro clapped his hands over his eyes, cursing in some thick Slavic language. "My van," he moaned. "Did he have to kill my van?"

Deathly silence, then nervous muttering. A guy desperately trying to raise someone on the com equipment. He was huddled behind Zia Rosa's Taurus sedan that Tony had driven, talking into a com device. From his desperate tone of voice, he wasn't getting a reply.

Davy had a clear shot. He positioned the rifle, but Kev

waved him down. The guy was alone. The tone in his voice indicated that he wasn't a threat on his own. He'd panic, and bolt.

Sure enough. The guy dove into the trees and fled.

Kev rose to his feet, and started running. It wasn't a decision. He just couldn't wait anymore, no matter who might be shooting at him.

The others came after him, merging with the last path Edie had taken. He saw them from across the meadow, and began to sprint. Two bodies on the ground. A big guy, sprawled on top of a long, slender woman, dark hair spread out in a fan. The wet gleam of blood beneath her. He ran faster, breath jerking, heart thundering, chest burning and cramping with anguish, denial—

That hair. Too straight, too shiny. The hand. Those fingers were longer, olive gold, not the pale pink tint of Edie's. This was Tam.

Kev hurled himself to his knees, and heaved the big guy off her. She'd been shot. In the leg, and the shoulder. It looked bad. Her face was gray, her lips blue, but she as still alive.

The big guy, Tom, was very dead. His eyes were blank, his mouth wide open. His bowels had loosened. He smelled foul.

Davy, Con, Sean, Miles, and Bruno crouched down around her while Aaro circled, gun out, on the lookout. Davy and Sean yanked off their belt pouches, and got going with bandages, tourniquets.

"Jesus, Tam," Davy growled. "What did you do to that poor guy?"

Her lips twitched. She lifted her fingers, fluttered long gold nails at them. "Cat scratch fever," she whispered. "Nerve toxin."

Kev focused on the tiny needle that stuck out from under the nail of her index finger. Her down coat was soaked with blood.

Davy looked up at Sean. "Call Val. Tell him to charter a private plane from Friday Harbor to the Hillsboro airport," he said. "Tell him to hurry."

Sean got on it. Kev stared down into the woman's grayish face. Blood spatters at the corner of her mouth. Jesus. She looked like she was dying. He felt like a user, but he had to know. "Tam." His voice shook. "I know you're hurt, but please. Where did they take Edie?"

Her eyes fluttered open. She dragged in air, face contracting in pain at the effort. "Des Marr," she said. "Car trunk. All I know."

Davy dug into the dead man's pockets and pulled out a wad of car keys. "Take the bastard's rig," he said. "He doesn't need it anymore."

"To where?" Kev snarled. "In which fucking direction?"

Davy's lips twitched in a short, grim smile. "She's got my cell phone, little brother. At least, I hope she still has it."

"Yeah? And so?"

"So you're set." Davy jerked his chin at Miles and Sean. "Con and Aaro will get Tam to the hospital. And the rest of us will show our little brother the wonderful world of X-Ray Specs and SafeGuard beacons."

"We don't have a handheld," Sean said.

"Call Nick. Have him spot you from Stone Island," Davy said. "He has all our codes."

Sean punched in another number. Started muttering to someone about beacon codes, coordinates. Kev stared at Tam, panting. Blood soaked into the leaves beneath her. The woman had been so strange, so rude to them the night before. But she'd tried to protect Edie. Maybe at the cost of her life. He inclined his head, respectfully. "Thank you."

She nodded. "Edie's tough." Her golden eyes were slitted with pain. "Hang on to her. That's . . . rare."

"I mean to," he said.

He took off running. Toward the end of the world, probably, but it no longer mattered to him. As long as he could see Edie.

Just one more time, before he went over the brink.

Ava leaned closer to the bathroom mirror, struggling to repair her face into something she could use as a weapon. It was hard, tonight.

She'd slathered on foundation to cover her sickly pallor and spots, but it wasn't the right shade for her skin. Several coats of old, lumpy mascara made her eyes big and kittenish. Lip gloss, and that was it. She left the master crown on, and ran a brush through her hair. Good thing she had the cap, because her hair was wretched. And no time for a shower. Des and Edie would be there in a half an hour.

The blessed event was at hand.

She shoved plastic cuffs up her tight, fitted sleeve. Wadded the flexible slave crown into the waistband of her jeans, which were looser than usual. Stress made her slimmer. More room for the gun. That went into the back. She gave herself a critical once-over.

Lost sex kitten left in the rain. But that look had its uses.

She put an ear to Ronnie's door, heard the thump of headphones. The girl was sulking, listening to her iPod. Ava descended the stairs and peeked into Parrish's study. She spotted it instantly. A silver letter opener in a fine leather case. CWP. Parrish's monogram. She pulled out a scarf she'd gotten from Edie's drawer, wrapped it without touching it.

She slid it into the pocket on the side of her pants. The monogram gave the murder weapon that personal touch that meant so much.

Then she headed down to the security room and peeked in. Big eyed, self-conscious and shy. "Um, excuse me?" she said softly.

Two security guys looked over. The other two were out

making the rounds. "Dr. Cheung," the older, senior one said. "Can we help you?"

Paul was his name. She pulled in her lower lip, leaving half to dangle, plump and enticing. Fluttering with the gummy eyelashes, waif-like. "I couldn't sleep," she said. "Have you heard from her?"

"From Edie, you mean?" Paul's lip curled. "Don't count on it."

Paul wouldn't do. Too big, too fat, too old. Robert was more like it. He was fifteen years younger, maybe thirty-five. A big, handsome black man. No wedding ring, she noted. He'd be more believable as Edie's patsy. That poor fool Edie fucked into dazed submission, along with the promise of the moon, and billions of dollars. Yes, Robert was her man.

"There's something I need to show one of you gentlemen," she said timidly. "In Edie's room. Nothing urgent. I don't want to, you know, bother you, or take up your valuable time. But I want someone to see."

"Just tell us what is it that you saw, Dr. Cheung," Paul suggested.

"You have to see it to understand," Ava said. She gave Robert a pleading smile. "Would you . . . ? Please. It'll just take a moment."

"Go check it out, Robert," Paul said grimly. "And hurry back."

Robert walked her out, polite doubt on his face. She pulled him into the kitchen, looked around to make sure they were alone.

"Dr. Cheung?" he said, baffled. "I thought you said—"

"Shhh," she whispered. "Just a moment." She heaved her chest, arching her back. Pressing on her bosom in just such a way as to tug down on the stretchy shirt, and simultaneously shove up her enhanced breasts. "I just . . . wonder if you'd just take a second to . . . to . . ."

Robert looked almost afraid, staring at her tits. "To what?"

She blinked her heavily mascaraed lashes. "Hold me," she blurted. "P-p-please. I feel so lost." She pressed her face to his chest, grabbed his hand, brought it up to her breast with a pleading whimper.

His hand shook. She struggled not to smile. She had him. So easy. They were always so easy, the filthy fucking pigs.

Stab. The needle went into his arm, the plunger came down.

Robert stiffened. His jaw stretched in a taut grimace. Air rasped into laboring lungs. Poor Robert. She was almost sorry for him. So cute.

She got to work with the crown, attaching sensors quickly. Robert's shaved brown head made it easy. She braced him against the wall, confident that his locked knees would hold him upright.

She looked into his staring, white-rimmed eyes. Sweat stood out on his brow. She grabbed a paper towel from the kitchen counter and dabbed it tenderly. Stood on her tiptoes. Gave him a light kiss.

"Showtime," she whispered, and sank in her mental claws.

Surprisingly, after the first shocked resistance, it was an excellent interface. As high as seven, on a scale of one to ten. Granted, she'd given him an enormous dose, but he was also a macho man, probably ex-military, certainly not the usual optimal interface profile. She was pleasantly surprised to find lots of fine muscle control after just a few moments of manipulating him. But with such a high dose, her window of opportunity was tight. She compelled him to pull his gun, staying a few steps behind as he paced back to the security center.

She didn't go inside, having ascertained that there was a security camera in there. Excellent, for her purposes. Very convenient.

Paul turned when he came in, but turned away when he saw who it was, so Ava didn't even have to deal with the iffy proposition of aiming the gun without the X-Cog goggles.

She just walked Robert over, compelled him to put the gun to the nape of Paul's neck, and fire.

Paul slumped over the keyboard, a dark hole in the nape of his neck. Blood spewed all over the keyboard and computer monitor.

She forced Robert to shut off the computer that ran the surveillance program on the blood-spattered keyboard. Just in time.

The others came running, having heard the shot. She brought Robert back out into the corridor, and slunk behind the open door of the kitchen to keep eye contact. Surprise and quickness was key, here.

"Robert?" one of them gasped, huffing. "What the fuck was—"

Bam. Bam. Both men fell. She stepped out, watched the arterial blood spread from death wounds in the forehead, throat. Silence. Just the labored sound of Robert's breathing. Evelyn and Tanya were screaming. She had Robert walk into the room where they huddled on the couch. Dr. Katz cowered there, too, begging incoherently.

No one noticed her lurking in the corner behind the door. Robert trained the gun on them. Ava tried speaking through him.

"Sit down in the chairs," Robert said. His voice was thick and hollow, but comprehensible. What a nice, deep voice he had.

A little gun waving got them twittering and squeaking, rushing to obey. She compelled Robert to cuff them to the chair, hands behind them. They let themselves be trussed, without resistance, begging and squawking. Stupid geese. Already dead, and they just didn't know it yet.

Then Robert was done, and a good thing, too. Robert was played out. A short-termer. She could feel the pressure building up in his eyes. Blood was flooding out his nose already. He was drooling, too. Bloody drool. God, how she hated it when they drooled.

He made it to the entrance hall, thudded to his knees, then fell heavily on his face. She rolled him over with her toe, grimacing as she plucked the slave crown off. She'd make Edie shoot him in the face, to cover up the mess. X-Cog metabolized quickly, but the broken blood vessels would look suspicious to an attentive coroner.

Though she doubted it would occur to anyone to ask questions.

So far, it had gone beautifully. Relatives trussed and sniveling, awaiting their doom. Des and Edie should be arriving right about now.

A chime announced someone at the gate. She giggled as she realized that it fell to her to open the place up. Oops! Of course! Everyone else was dead, dying, or handcuffed to a chair! She found the button to open the gate, and a flash of movement on the stairs caught her eye. The girl's eyes were wide with shock and terror. Fucking brat.

Ava smiled, and aimed. "Don't move, Ronnie."

The constant scream of the motor had eased off. Some ten minutes ago, Edie felt the highway off-ramp, and now, city streets. Traffic lights. An unnatural calm settled into her. She was past the worst. She was trying to keep a clear sense on how much time had passed, the velocities they were going, but she kept zoning out.

We have other plans for you. She shuddered, longing for the Ruger at her ankle, but it was lying on top of Aaro's dresser. Des would have found it when he frisked her anyhow. No tricks up her sleeve now.

The car slowed, idled. Another traffic light? A lurch, and the engine stopped. Her calm evaporated.

She heard the door pop open. Des, walking away. Time passed, interminable, impossible to measure. She counted her heartbeats.

The trunk popped open. Trees towered overhead. Des

grinned down at her. He grabbed her by the armpits, yanked her out of the car. She realized where she was. Fear multiplied, tenfold. The Parrish home. *Ronnie.* Oh, God. They still had the power to crush her heart. Even now.

She sagged. Des grabbed her by the hair, dragging her after himself. "None of that," he growled. "On your feet."

The pistol barrel pressed under the point of her jaw. She'd almost be relieved if he pulled the trigger. Where was everyone?

A woman stood in the front doorway. Small and delicate. Asian. A velvet cap hid her hair. The first impression, from a distance, was that she was beautiful, but as Edie approached, the illusion of beauty faded.

She stared at Edie, black eyes hot with predatory hunger.

"You're Ava Cheung?" Edie asked.

"So happy to meet you at last, Edie," the woman said. "Do you remember me from the Haven?"

Edie shook her head. Ava's lips drew back. "Of course you don't. Why would the lofty princess notice one of the lab rats?"

Edie didn't have any answer to that. "Kev told me about you."

"Did he? By the way, my condolences. I heard he got blown up."

Edie couldn't hide the flinch. "Where is the security staff?"

"Oh. Them." Ava's smile thinned. "You'll see. Come take a look."

Des forced her forward, jabbing with the pistol. She jerked back with a gasp when she saw Robert's long body stretched out on the marble floor. Blood pooled under his head. "Oh, God. Is he . . ."

"Dead? Not quite, maybe, but he will be soon. We'll just leave him to it. Come on to the dining room, and I'll show you what we've—"

Edie dug in her heels. "I don't want to see."

Smack. Ava slapped her face, hard. "I don't give a shit what you want!" the woman shrieked. "Do as you're told, you stupid bitch!"

"Ava!" Des scolded. "No marks! She's the aggressor, remember?"

Ava waved that away with a hand that was covered with a latex glove. "We can do whatever we want," she said airily. "They'll attribute all that to Larsen. Rough sex, punishment. Maybe they'll think Larsen found out about her dirty affair with Robert, do you suppose?"

"Affair . . . ?" Edie looked back at Robert. "My *what* with Robert?"

Ava giggled. "Or maybe Larsen himself forced her to seduce Robert. Oh, that's even dirtier. I love it." Edie stared at her, confused. "To persuade him to be your accomplice, of course," Ava explained, impatiently. "To take out the security staff, the cameras and all that."

"No." Edie shook her head, frantically. "No one will believe that."

"You'd be surprised," Ava said. "People are foul and filthy, you know. There's nothing they love more than thinking that other people are even filthier and fouler. Oh, look! Your favorite people! Say hello!"

Edie struggled to focus her eyes in the dim room. The sounds clued her in. Mewling, muffled weeping, squeaks. Aunt Evelyn, Tanya, and Dr. Katz, in bathrobes, pajamas. Cuffed to the dining room chairs.

"Why?" She turned to Des. "They have nothing to do with this!"

Ava's giggle was shrill. "I gagged them with panties that I found in your drawers. It's those depraved details that make the story work. Oh, while I'm thinking of it." She grabbed Edie's hair, and yanked. Edie gasped. Ava dropped Edie's hairs on the carpet, on Aunt Evelyn's lap, Tanya's slipper, over Dr. Katz's arm. He flinched at her touch.

"Where's Ronnie?" Fear strangled Edie's voice into a squeak.

"All in good time," Ava chided. "First, the costume. You can't slaughter your entire family dressed in that. You look awful, Edie."

Faintness welled up, threatening to pull her down. Ava slapped her face, and bent her double. "No way, bitch. Get your head down. You can't faint. That's not in the script." Ava hauled her back up by the hair, and smacked her again. "Try that again, and you'll be sorry."

A senseless desire to laugh seized her. "I'm already sorry."

Smack. "Sorrier, then. Come on, Des. Get her up the stairs."

"There's no time for costumes," Des groused. "Don't be childish."

"Why not? It's only five forty-six. The next shift of security guys won't be here until eight. We can take a few minutes to dress her. And I'm not being childish. It's called 'attention to detail.' Idiot."

Des sighed, and prodded Edie with the gun. "Whatever."

They didn't stop at Ronnie's room, but pushed right on past to her own. It was topsy-turvy, the drawers tugged out, clothes dangling. Shoes were scattered over the floor, dresses lying everywhere in bright pools of color. Ava picked up one of them. It was pale peach, strapless, with whimsical lacy ties up the front of a tight, fitted bodice, and a full skirt. She swung the thing around, humming. "I like this one," she said, almost dreamily. "A princess dress. Take off your clothes."

Edie froze solid with disgust, at the thought of being naked in front of that pair. It took the bruising force of Des's gun, prodding beneath her chin to get her moving. High-tops, first. The muddy laces were impossible to undo, so she just wrenched them off. She peeled off jeans, shirt, and that was it. Her underwear was long gone. Abandoned in Aaro's cabin, along with her life, her heart, her hopes. Her future.

Ava and Des stared at her body, horribly interested in it.

"Dessie," Ava said softly. "Look at those tits. Lovely, hmm?"

Des cleared his throat, his face flushed. "We don't have time to—"

"To do anything about your erection? Awww. So sad."

"Put on the fucking dress, Edie," Des rapped out harshly. "Now."

Ava tossed it to her, and Edie stared down at her filthy, scratched hands holding the delicate fabric. Leaving smudges, mud, bloodstains.

She unzipped it, and struggled for a few minutes before managing to fasten the zipper up the side. It was tight. She'd been a few pounds thinner back when her mother had gotten her this dress.

Memories floated back. This dress. Her parents thirtieth wedding anniversary dinner. A black tie affair. Two hundred guests. She'd done something that made her mother furious. Some ill-timed, prophetic blurt, to some extremely important guy. A politician, maybe. It seemed so trivial, now. Her mind was racing around like a headless chicken, trying to flee the reality of her immediate future. Still a mystery. But not really. Not so much. Some variation on pain, horror, and then death.

"Pretty as a princess," Ava said softly. "Now. Out the door. Move."

"Aren't you going to crown her?" Des asked.

"I'll wait til we get to Ronnie's room," Ava said. "If she's a dud, I don't want to have to move the body. Saves on mess."

Des wound his hand into Edie's hair and yanked her head back as he prodded her with the gun. The lights in the corridor made her eyes water as she stumbled, barefoot over the carpet runner. She saw the frame of Ronnie's door. Des let her head drop, shoved her through.

A thin sound escaped her when she saw Ronnie, gagged and tied to her four-poster. Her eyes met Edie's, wide with terrified entreaty.

Edie's heart thudded. Sickening hammer blows. The big box that held the rest of Ronnie's firecrackers sat next to the bed, with puffs of red tissue paper sticking out.

"Behold, your murder weapon." Ava Cheung held out the gleaming letter opener, nestled in another silk scarf. "You'll stab everyone to death, but you won't know about me being here, because I came here after you left last night. I'll be the one witness, hiding behind a curtain. Terrified for my life." Ava was purring with satisfaction. "Des will be gone before the cops come. The security shift will find you dead, and me, catatonic with shock. I'm not quite sure how you'll kill yourself yet. But I'm taking suggestions, if anything juicy occurs to you."

Edie looked into Ava's glittering eyes. The question rose up from deep within her, from beyond even fear. "You don't even know me," she said. "Why do you hate me so much?"

Ava lifted the syringe. "Because you are what you are," she said. "You have what you have. And still, you dare to feel sorry for yourself."

Reactions fought inside her. Indignation. The hot desire to defend her right to be miserable, too. And then, the clear, almost crystalline realization of how strange, how stupid, how silly it all was.

"I regret that," she said quietly. And strangely, she meant it.

For what it was worth. She knew that it would change nothing.

"Don't be," Ava hissed. "I don't need your regret. I need . . . *this*."

Ava stabbed the needle in.

CHAPTER
39

Bruno drove, which was good, because Kev would have driven them right off the road. Fortunately, the highway was empty at this hour. Sean had been on the phone nonstop with the guy named Nick up in the San Juans who was following Davy's signal on the satellite map. The signal was still moving, but they were a good twenty-five minutes behind it, and they weren't gaining. Marr's Jag only had two people in it, and did a hundred and ten without breaking a sweat.

The fat dead guy's Mercedes G-Class had a powerful engine, but it was carrying five big men, and Bruno wasn't getting more than ninety.

Bruno's eyes and nose were still streaming, but he just wiped them on his sleeve and drove grimly on.

"Hey," Sean announced to the vehicle at large. "He's turning off onto Highway 26. Must be heading back to the Parrish place."

Kev felt a sick horror clutch his innards. "He's taking her to Ava," he said dully. "Like a dog taking a dead rabbit to its master."

The others exchanged looks. "Hey, come on," Sean encouraged. "It might not be that bad. The Parrish house is a fortress, full of security and domestic staff, and her family. He can't possibly—"

"Ava Cheung has been in that house for six hours," Kev said. "She has an X-Cog crown. They could all be dead by now. Easily. Do you know what someone with a fucking crown can do?"

Sean stared at him coldly for a second. "Yeah, brother," he said. "I remember what a crown can do. I almost murdered my wife with a blow torch the last time I wore one. So watch your fucking tone of voice."

Kev muttered an apology, remembering oblique references to Sean's own adventures with Osterman and X-Cog. One of the many stories that there was no time to tell. Who knew if there ever would be.

Minutes ticked by as Bruno coaxed speed out of the Mercedes. Sean's phone rang again. He listened. "Marr's car has turned off 26. It's going south on Cedar," he said. "Six minutes to the Parrish house."

And they still had so far to go. "Goddamnit, Bruno!" Kev roared. "Can't you kick some more speed out of this thing?"

The motor roared as they sped through the pale gray dawn.

The sting. Like a spider bite. Edie's mind freewheeled as the cold numbness spread, and in its wake, a tension that pulled her tighter and tighter. Every muscle was contracted, tearing at all the others, stretched to the screaming limit. She was arched, grimacing. She'd snap if she made a move. Her bones would break, her tendons pop. Her lungs struggled to expand. Oh, God. Air. *Please.*

Ava came closer, bracing her against the wall as she attached a device to Edie's head. Sticking the dangling metal sensors against her skull. The frantic need for air built and built. She was smothering.

The room was going dark. Blessed unconsciousness.

"Need to breathe?" Ava asked. "Want some help?"

The woman slammed into her mind, and Edie reeled under the onslaught. Like corrosive gas. No way to block it out.

Ava expanded Edie's lungs for her. Her chest jerked and shuddered. The air hurt, forced into her tense, locked lungs.

Kev had told her how the X-Cog crown worked. But she'd had no idea. She felt death around her. A wasteland of foul, poisonous hatred. The pressure in her eyes, in her brain. Her heart, laboring frantically.

Des lunged for the window. "Car, outside the wall," he said.

Ava looked startled. "It's too early for the new security shift."

"I'll go take a look." A gun appeared in Des's hand. "Can you handle this alone? Remember what happened today. Don't get cocky."

"Are you kidding?" Ava tittered. "She's no McCloud. She's just a poor little dumb rich girl. I'll just diddle around with her for a while, get a feel for her. Be quick, Dessie. I wouldn't want you to miss the show."

Des chuckled. "No way." He disappeared out the door.

Ava leaned closer to Edie's face. Her laughter echoed, strangely metallic, in Edie's ears. Ava's eyes were white rimmed, like a mad horse. Splotches of makeup on her sallow skin.

Something cold and hard touched Edie's palm. Her fingers closed around it. The letter opener. Her rigid arm rose up, stabbed violently down. *Yes, that's a good girl . . . walk over here now . . . that's good . . .*

That mocking voice was getting farther away, her ears roared, her heart galloped. She tasted blood. Her body convulsed—

She took a step forward. Another. And another, more smoothly.

She floated back from herself, watching it like a movie. Reflecting with detached irony, what a shame it was that she hadn't realized the true wealth she'd had. Not until it was being torn away.

She'd had Ronnie. Kev. She'd seen beautiful things. She'd spent so much time in that timeless, blissful place where she went when she made art. Drawing, painting. Utterly happy and at peace. That was wealth. She only saw it now, when it was all being destroyed.

The way this woman had been destroyed.

With that insight, her inner eye opened up. Lights, going on everywhere. She didn't want it to, she hadn't asked it to. She didn't want to see what was behind that woman's tormented eyes.

But she saw it anyway. With an awful sense of recognition, as if she were looking in the mirror. Rage, shame, self-hate. Crushing her.

Grief. She dragged in air, willed it away, fighting for breath—

Ava's eyes widened. They realized at the same instant that Ava had not initiated that breath.

Edie's arm dropped. The knife fell to the carpet. Terrified joy warred with disbelief. Ava was screaming at her. Edie felt drops of hot spittle hitting her face. A thin thread of blood trickled out of Ava's nose.

Edie tried to move. Her euphoria was quickly deflated. She was still immobilized. Pulled so tight, her body was about to snap. But her will to move was out of Ava's reach, as long as that inner eye stayed open. The part of her mind that Osterman had stimulated, or eliminated, or whatever the hell he'd done . . . had created a blind spot.

The only catch was that in this state, she was connected to everyone. The barriers were gone. That was why she knew things about people when she drew them. She didn't want to know Ava, to fuse with Ava, but she had no choice. She was one with Ava's torment. She saw it all, felt it, owned it. She'd have screamed, if she could. This made the X-Cog rictus seem like nothing. This was pure, burning hell on earth.

Ava was wailing, screeching. Blood streamed from her nose. Mascara dripped. Mouth stretched wide. Hitting Edie's face, swatting, punching. She knocked her back against the wall.

Ava's mind was shaking apart, and Edie's along with her. A screaming hurricane inside them both, destroying everything.

Edie drew in another shuddering breath . . . and embraced the storm. Getting bigger, softer, wider. Expanding. Like ripples spreading, until the disturbance was just a small, frantic movement in one part of her consciousness. She regarded it while the rest of her expanded into a serene vastness. She could just keep going. Expand into infinite space.

Maybe she'd even find Kev out there. The thought made her heart clutch with hopeful joy . . .

And she saw Ronnie, far below her. Curled up like a little, huddled comma on the bed. All alone, terrified. In hell.

Ronnie. She couldn't float away. Ronnie needed her. Kev would have to wait. Grief cut deep, again. She had to leave this peace now, and claw her way back down into that hellhole of violence and fear.

Thwack, thwack. The pain came back into focus. A front hand whack, then a backhand one. Hard, jaw rattling slaps. "Goddamn you! Goddamn you!" Ava shrieked. "Don't you dare die, bitch!"

Oh, I wish, Edie thought, almost wistfully.

A spate of gunfire thundered below.

No one had challenged them at the gate, which turned Kev's stomach with fear. His brothers and Miles yelled at him, wait, stop, hang on, but he crawled up onto the top of the Mercedes G-Class, catching the top of the wall, scrambling up. A brief moment to take stock of the ominously dark, quiet house, and he leaped, thudding onto soft grass. He pushed through some rosebushes. Thuds sounded behind him. The rest of them crept up behind him, cat silent and wary.

The front door was unlocked. It swung silently open to his gentle push. They stared at the long body of the man who lay there, face down, a pool of blood forming under his face on the gleaming marble floor.

Kev slid inside, sidling by the wall. Miles and Sean drifted like shadows toward the wing that opened off to the right. Bruno gestured silently in the direction of the stairway. Kev slunk through the arch to the left, Davy following him.

A bizarre tableau. Three people, gagged, tied to chairs, all in a row. Staring, their purple faces mad with terror. But still alive.

Kev recognized the older one as he darted closer. The aunt from the hospital. The cousin. The butthead doctor. He plucked away the gag from the older woman's mouth, which appeared to be a filmy lace bra, and yanked a wad of cloth from her mouth, which proved to be a pair of matching thong panties. "Where's Edie?" he demanded.

The woman coughed, hacked, and began to scream.

"Oh, shit," Kev muttered, and shoved the panties back into the woman's mouth. "Not now, lady."

Davy crouched behind the old woman's chair, sawing through her cuffs. The younger one's rolling eyes and terror sweat didn't bode well for time-sensitive information gathering, so he left her for Davy's tender mercies too, and tried the older guy. He got to work on the gag. Pink tap pants. A matching satin bra. "Where's Edie?" he demanded.

The man coughed, sobbed. "She . . . she . . . ah . . . Des Marr—"

"I know about Des Marr. Tell me where Edie is!" he roared.

"Drop your gun, Kev." A familiar soft, hateful voice from

behind him. "And you, too, whoever the fuck you are. I never did learn to tell you McCloud assholes apart. You all look alike to me."

Kev spun. Bruno's reddened eyes stared up at him from a hammerlock against Marr's chest, in mute apology. His chest jerked, trying to get air. Marr's gun was shoved up under his chin.

"Drop it," Marr said. "Now. Or his head explodes."

Kev's gun dropped. Davy's thudded down soon after.

"You bastards were supposed to be dead." Marr sounded piqued.

"Yeah, well," Kev muttered. "We're funny that way."

"Take a look at my gun, Kev," Marr said. "Recognize it?"

Kev took a look. It was a SIG 220, like the one he'd taken with him yesterday, to go to Helix. "That's my gun?"

"Registered to you. Covered with your prints. Inside and out." Marr sounded complacent. "I'm wearing a latex glove, of course. Edie will hold it when she blows her brains out, after killing all of you. And you still take the fall. From the grave."

In the silence that followed, they heard the whining of police sirens. Alarm flashed in Des's eyes. He looked at Kev, at the weeping women huddled on the floor, the doctor curled into the fetal position.

"I don't think you have time for that scenario," Kev said slowly. "I think there are too many people to kill, Marr. And too little time."

"Oh, yeah?" Marr laughed, harshly. "You think?" He yanked Bruno's head back. The gun barrel whipped around to point at Kev.

Kev dove to the side. Bruno convulsed, like a huge fish flopping—

Four guns thundered, all at once. Des jittered, suspended against the wall. He slid down, his face a pulpy red mess, and thudded on top of Bruno, sagging forward. The screaming from the ladies got louder. The doctor joined lustily in.

Bruno crawled from under Marr's corpse, spattered with blood, looking pale and shaken.

Miles and Sean rose up from their positions crouched at the door, but Kev raced past without looking or hearing.

Edie.

More gunshots rocked the house. Ava looked almost frightened. Edie could smell the stench of the other woman's fear sweat.

"OK," Ava panted. "We have to do things a little differently now. See this? Watch." She grabbed an orange candle from Ronnie's shelf, and grabbed the book of matches beside it. She lit it.

She leaned close to Edie, holding the lit candle close enough to Edie's face so that the burning sensation became uncomfortable, then painful. Awful pain. But she could not flinch. She was frozen stiff.

"I'd like to do to your face what Gordon did to your boyfriend's," Ava said. "But I guess I really should do Ronnie's. After all, she's the one you're jealous of, right? Daddy's little favorite?" She lifted the candle. "I'll make a deal with you. You stop blocking me . . . and I'll have you slit her throat, nice and quick. It'll be all over in twenty seconds. If you don't stop blocking me, I will burn her face for a long, long time, while you watch. And then, I slit her throat. You decide."

"Edie?" A voice shouted from downstairs.

Kev. Oh, dear God, that was Kev's voice. He wasn't dead!

Excitement, disbelief, shattered her detachment, her mind-mode wavered, and Ava's control slammed into her again. Ava laughed triumphantly, and forced Edie's arms to raise, her hands to flex. She placed the burning candle in one of Edie's shaking hands, the knife in the other. "Now we're talking," she said. "Party-time, Edie. Walk."

And she did, toes clenching on the thick carpet. Her mind

raced. She was paralyzed. The only way to move or walk at all was to have Ava move her. And so . . . and so. She padded toward Ronnie's bed. Focused on the candle flame in the foreground, Ronnie's flailing body in the background.

Eyes wide, Ronnie watched her big sister lurching toward her like the living dead, with a blade and an open flame.

All Edie could do was hope that the trajectory Ava chose would take her right over to the box by Ronnie's bed. And time it just right, or else the candle would ignite the bedclothes.

Closer . . . closer. Knife in her right hand. Candle in her left. One more step, but she needed lead time. She concentrated . . .

. . . and sank deeper within herself. Softening. Drawing back, letting that inner eye open. Let it take in everything. Accept everything.

She stopped. The knife fell from her slack hand. The candle clung a moment to the sweat on her palms, but then it fell, too.

It thudded into the box, with its protruding clusters of crumpled red, orange, and yellow tissue paper. The paper caught fire.

Ava let out a shriek of rage, and launched a front kick that caught Edie in the head, and knocked her off her feet. She sprawled full length.

Ava yanked the box closer, batting at the flames. A Roman candle went off, spitting a fountain of sparks into her face.

Ava screamed, tumbling backward as the fireworks all went off.

Kev took the stairs three at a time, boots thudding heavily down the corridors, following the sounds of the explosions. The smell, too. Hot, stinking sulphurous. The smell of the pits of hell. Smoke poured from under one of the doors in the corridor. He yanked it open.

Ronnie was tied to the bed. The canopy was on fire. He ripped it down, stomping it. Cut her loose, shoving her off the smoldering bed.

She yanked out her gag. "Edie!" She pointed toward the window, coughing and spitting. "Edie! She took her! Out there!"

The third-floor window was shoved open. Outside the gabled window was the steep, pointed roof of the three-story high solarium.

Ava was perched on the apex of the roof, her back to the very edge. Her face was black with soot. She'd dragged Edie out with her.

Edie's legs dangled limply down against the roof, her pale, filmy dress snagged on the wooden shakes. Her dirty feet were bare. Her eyes fastened on his. She wore a crown. Not a muscle moved in her face. She'd been dosed with X-Cog, and crowned, but Ronnie and the rest of them were still alive. So Ava hadn't mastered her. Behind the heaving ocean of terror, he felt fierce pride. So tough. Sweet and modest, but inside, where no one could see, the woman was tempered steel.

He heard Ronnie's gasp behind him. "Edie," she whispered.

"Get back." He pushed her away from the window. "Don't watch."

But Ronnie popped back up. She wouldn't be pushed away.

Ava laughed. "The amazing Kev McCloud. He defies death, spits at an X-Cog crown, laughs at weapons-grade explosives. But he's not laughing now." She cradled Edie against her chest, a sickening semblance of affection. "Go ahead," she urged. "Shoot me. Dr. O used to get nostalgic about how brilliant you were. You could probably calculate the position her broken body would land in, if I let go of her right now."

"I know," he said.

She tittered again. "So?"

"So let me come out there and get Edie, Ava."

"Oh? Are we on a first name basis? Don't get fresh with me, dog. I'm holding her. I have the power, remember? I have the power."

"You have the power. You have the power to stop this, too."

A strange light blazed from her eyes. "Don't condescend to me."

"I'm not," he said. "Let me come get Edie. It's over. Des is dead. All of them are. The cops are coming. See the lights? Hear the sirens? They're surrounding us. If you cooperate, Edie and I will explain to them what Dr. O did to you. You'll get the help you need. I promise."

Her laughter wheezed out. Tears streamed from her eyes. "You think this promise of life in a locked psych ward is so appealing?"

"Consider the alternative," he said.

"Oh, but I do," she said. "I've considered it every fucking day of my fucking life. You have no idea."

They stared at each other. "If you hurt Edie, I will rip you to pieces," he said, but he could feel the slack emptiness of the threat.

Ava felt it, too. "Whoo! I'm so frightened, I'm simply shaking. Shaking so hard I just might . . . oh my God! I almost dropped her!"

"Ava." He forced himself not to yell. "It's over. The cops are—"

"It's Larsen!" a voice on the grounds bawled out. "In the window!"

Running, shouts. "He's got them trapped out on the roof! Hurry!"

Ava looked down, then back at him. A bloody smile split her blackened face. A searchlight was trained on the women, then on Kev.

"Drop your weapons, and put your hands in the air!" a man blared, through a megaphone. "Or else we will shoot!"

Oh, Christ on a crutch. But what the hell. His gun was useless anyway. Kev lifted his gun, dropped it. Held his hands in the air—

Thwhangg. A bullet ripped out a piece of window frame. He stumbled back, reeling, and shoved Ronnie to the ground. "Stay down!"

Ava shook with laughter. "We're surrounded by cops, yes, but they're on my side! It's so funny!" she gasped out. "Oh, Kev, you mean, bad boy. Trapping us poor helpless girls out here on the roof!"

"Let me get Edie," he repeated, desperately. *Thwinggg*, a bullet dug into the roofing material. He flinched back, cursing.

"You and your girlfriend are just alike." Ava struggled onto her feet, dragging Edie's body up. "The one thing I can't stand is for someone to feel sorry for me. So this is what I have to say to you."

Thwanggg, another bullet carved out wood chips, made paint chips scatter. Kevin jerked back. "What?"

"Fuck you," Ava said. "All of you."

The hand clutching Edie's chest did a graceful farewell finger flutter. She fell back, taking Edie with her. Over the edge. Out of sight. She made no sound, but Kev's howl of anguish accompanied her down.

CHAPTER

40

Six weeks later . . .

K ev got out of the car, checking the address on the scrap
of paper, though he'd memorized it the second Ronnie
dictated to him. Forty-two Lake Circle Road. The paper was
limp and creased from being carried around in his pocket like
a love token. It wasn't. It wasn't even a message from Edie
herself. But it was all he had. He clung to this fragile link to
her.

He hadn't seen her in weeks. At first, he'd been arrested,
locked up. He'd spent the better part of twenty-four hours
writhing in the flames of hell before someone finally took pity
on him, and informed him that Edie Parrish was still alive.

Ava Cheung was dead. She'd broken her back and neck
on the boughs of the oak tree outside the solarium—and in
the process, she'd broken Edie's fall. Edie had broken her
leg, cracked some ribs, knocked her head, had some organ
damage. She'd spent some dicey time in the ICU. But her
family had whisked her away before he was free to go to her.
To hide her from the glaring light of the press to convalesce.
A decision he understood perfectly. He approved of it, too.
Except that they had hidden her from him, too. And that
sucked ass.

It had taken tedious days of hashing out the details before the police were convinced that he was innocent of any wrong-doing. Ronnie's testimony, and that of Evelyn Morris, her daughter Tanya, Dr. Katz and Yuliyah, the Latvian girl, had freed him. Richard Fabian, the only one of Bixby's team to survive the battle in the forest outside Sandy, had led the police to the place where Yuliyah's companions had been held captive, so all six girls were safe, and free.

They'd let him out just in time for Tony's funeral. That had been hard. But no one would tell him where Edie was, or even how she was. He begged, bullied, guilt-tripped in vain. By now, the Parrish staff wouldn't even take his calls any-more. They'd sent a big bouquet to the funeral home for Tony, though. Gee. How very fucking nice of them.

The weeks crawled by. He began to try, in agonizing bits and pieces, to wrap his mind around the possibility that Edie'd had enough of the crazy shit in his life. Improbable, deadly, disgusting things, like X-Cog, like Des, like Ava. She'd had a belly full of it, and she was done.

He could hardly blame her. But she could find the courage to tell him to his face. She could cut him loose. Just let him just fall out of the fucking airplane, and be done with it. Not dissolve him in acid, inch by goddamn inch. Tortured by conflicting doubts and hopes.

He wouldn't have thought that she could be so cruel.

A wooden walkway snaked around the rocky lakeside, forming bridges over huge fallen logs, swampy areas. The air was bitterly cold. Snowflakes drifted down to dust the dark rocks. He climbed the stairs to the glassy house perched on stilts right on Franklin Lake. No security staff was in evidence, though he was sure he was being watched.

Christ, he was so scared.

Ronnie opened to his knock. She looked thin, pale. Taller, too, if that was possible in only six weeks. She'd made the jump from girl to woman since he'd seen her last. She gazed at him. "Thanks for coming."

"Thanks for calling me," he replied.

Tanya appeared in the foyer, her eyes bugged out in alarm. "Ronnie? What's he doing here? How did he find this—"

"I told him, Tanya," Ronnie said quietly. "I invited him."

"But Mother told you to wait! You know Edie's fragile right now! The last thing she needs is for some crazy—"

"It's time," Ronnie raised her voice and cut her cousin off. "I can handle this, Tanya. Thanks. You can go."

Tanya subsided, sputtering protests. Kev followed Ronnie's slim, straight back through the house, impressed. Huh. The chick took after her sister. Not to be messed with.

"How is she?" he asked.

Ronnie led him through a glassed-in porch along the side of the house. "Not great," she said. "She's healing, physically. She doesn't use the crutches anymore. But she can't sleep. She can't stop shaking. She can barely eat. She has stress flashbacks, bad ones. She feels awful."

"Did she ever . . ." He stopped, afraid to hear the answer.

Ronnie glanced back, her gray eyes shrewd. "Ask for you? Only in her sleep. When she manages to sleep. Which isn't often."

"Ah." He had no idea what to make of that.

"That was why I called you," Ronnie said. "I figured, in your sleep, you don't lie. When you're awake, you can fool yourself, or chicken out, or spout all kinds of bullshit. But not when you're asleep."

"I see," he said. "So she's spouting bullshit by day, then?"

"No," Ronnie said crisply. "She's having a hard time by day. And by night, too. And you better be careful."

Or else was the silent addendum. Not necessary, though. He'd be careful. Oh, God, yes. It was only his whole life hanging in the balance.

Ronnie opened the door out onto the back deck. A set of stairs connected to another wooden walkway that led to the lakeside.

Sharp wind blew across the dark, slate-colored water, ruffling it into chopping whitecaps. Dead white skeletons of tree trunks and white tangled root systems snaked around the shore.

Edie sat on one of the huge dead logs. She wore jeans, a thick down coat. A fur-trimmed hood was pulled up over her head, but her long hair streamed out of the hood, fluttering in the wind like a flag.

His knees were so weak, he felt like he'd sag down to the ground. His stomach churned. No more wondering. Christ, he wasn't ready.

Ronnie gestured for him to go. "Don't make me regret having called you," she warned, again.

Kev tried to respond, but his voice wasn't working. He set off in Edie's direction. The wind was roaring in her ears off the water, and he made no sound as he walked. It was second nature to him, after Dad's training. And still, she heard him. She turned when he was thirty meters away. He stopped, transfixed by her gaze. Heart thudding.

He was astonished again, by how damn beautiful she was. She was translucent. Deep, endless. Light shone through her. His angel. And her eyes, God. He wanted to fall to his knees.

At least, he hoped she was still his angel. No man could claim an angel for his own. It was greedy, selfish. Too much to hope.

He hoped anyway. But he couldn't move. He was scared stiff.

And now? He had no idea if he was welcome. He would do any desperate thing, if only he could figure out which. Should he kneel, beg, prostrate himself? Take charge, embrace her? He didn't have the nerve.

She looked like she might shatter like glass if he touched her.

One thing was sure. The message better be nonverbal because if he tried to talk, he was going to burst into tears, and who knew when he'd stop crying. A guy had his limits, his poor dignity. Such as it was.

He had to get closer. Closer and closer to her ethereal beauty. Those bright eyes, so beautiful. So faraway. Infinitely far.

But the closer he got, the more faraway they seemed.

Edie rubbed her eyes, looked again. It was him. But she could be dreaming. Or hallucinating. Wouldn't be the first time. Though she'd found that waking hallucinations were always horrible, violent things, not the good happy ones. Which was freaking unfair, in her opinion.

She'd been struggling to separate dreams from reality. The stress flashbacks kept her zinged, which killed sleep, which drove the whole cycle deeper into a bottomless downward spiral. She'd be stirring a spoonful of honey into a mug of tea, and suddenly feel Des's pistol jabbing into her throat. Or dressing in her bedroom, and whammo, there was Ronnie, tied and gagged on the bed, flames dancing around her. She'd actually feel the knife, clutched in her shaking fist.

She had attacks of violent cramping. Her wrists felt chafed and burned, even though the scrapes from the plastic cuffs had healed. Her head hurt all the time. She was dizzy, disoriented, depressed.

And the dreams of Kev. Striding toward her over a blasted landscape, his long coat billowing behind him. Wind in his hair, light in his eyes. Love in his face. Then he disappeared. Vanished, which instantly turned the beautiful dream into an aching nightmare.

She blinked experimentally. He didn't disappear. He made her eyes sting. Since it happened, the world had been mostly in black and white. A dull gray pall over everything. Even the lake, which she loved in every season, seemed dead, lifeless. A sere wasteland where nothing would ever grow again. But not Kev. He was in full, vibrant color.

He was waiting for her to speak, but her voice was locked in her throat. She had no idea how to unlock it, so she did the only thing she could think of. She held out her hand.

His eyes flashed. He approached in a few wide leaps, grabbed her hand, and clutched it, like he was afraid she'd pull it back.

"Hey," he said hoarsely. "How are you?"

She wiped away more tears. "I pretty much suck," she admitted.

"But you're alive." His voice was rough.

She gave him a little nod. "Yeah," she whispered. "So are you."

"So am I," he echoed. "Couldn't tell from the way you've been acting, though."

She gulped. "What do you mean? How have I been acting?"

"Like you're dead," he said harshly. "Like I'm dead."

She shut her eyes against the anger blazing out of his eyes. "Oh, God," she whispered. "Kev. Please. Just don't."

Kev muttered something, in that strange, harsh dialect. "Sorry. I didn't mean to come at you like that. I promised Ronnie I wouldn't."

Her eyes popped open. "Ronnie told you where to find me?"

"It was about time someone told me something!" His hurt and anger punched through again, making her flinch.

"I'm sorry," she said, miserably.

"Me, too. Again. Fuck it. I can't help it," he said savagely. "Six goddamn weeks. I could understand it at first. You were unconscious, in the ICU, whatever. I was locked up. Everybody had more important things to worry about than my poor hurt feelings. I know that. But six weeks? Why did they all stonewall me? Did you ask them to do that?"

"Kev—"

"Because if you want me to disappear, I will." He pushed on, determined to get it all out. "If you want me to fuck off, I swear to God I will respect your wishes. But just this dead silence, shutting me out . . ." He turned away, looking out over the water. His throat worked. "I'm sorry," he said. "Let's try this again, from the top. I asked you how you're feeling. You said you feel like shit. Where do we go from there?"

"I could ask you how you feel," she suggested, timidly.

He slanted her an eloquent look. "Don't."

There was an awkward silence, and he looked away, digging in his jacket. He passed her a folded piece of paper. "This is for you."

She stared at it, nervously. "What . . ."

"From Jamal," he explained. "I've been keeping an eye on him."

Tears sprang into her eyes as she unfolded the page and read the almost unintelligible note. "Thank you," she whispered. "How is he?"

"He's OK," Kev said. "He misses you. We bonded over that."

"Oh." She swallowed. "So. Um. How is Tam doing?"

"Better. She cut it close. One bullet punctured a lung, another almost nicked her femoral artery. One more milimeter, and she would have bled out on the ground in thirty seconds. But she didn't."

"I'm so glad," she whispered.

"Me, too," he said. "Even though I had to watch her man, Valery, hanging around her hospital bed. You know, combing her hair. Rubbing her feet. Trying to make her eat. Annoying the living shit out of her, in general. You can just imagine how that made me feel."

"Oh. Ouch," she murmured.

He shook his head. "Here I go again. Oh, by the way. Tam told me you were tough. She said I should hang on to you, before she fainted. Could have been her final words. Hell of a compliment, considering."

"Wow," Edie said faintly. That jarred with her current

self-image. It almost made her laugh, but that would make her sob. Bad idea.

"I'm trying to hang on to you," Kev said starkly. "I want to, so badly. But you're like a curl of smoke, Edie. I can't get hold of you."

She looked at her hand, enveloped in his big one, and gave his fingers an encouraging squeeze. "You've got ahold of me now."

"Do I?" He turned the force of his bright, challenging eyes on her.

She looked squarely back. "Yeah."

"Then you won't mind if I do this." He cupped her face, kissed her.

The kiss was gentle, but not timid. It was intensely intimate, knowing. His hot, tender mouth slowly, mysteriously sought out her response, calling it forth with his slow, patient, irresistible magic.

And out of nowhere, ah, God. There it was. That rush of heat raced through her body. She leaned into him. The kiss got deeper, sweeter. Their embrace tighter, hungrier. His energy flooded through her. Filled her up. Sweet, sweet relief. Her chest started to shake.

They hung on to each other, swaying, while the wind whipped and swirled her hair around their heads, while the water sloshed and gurgled on the rattling pebbles of the lakeshore.

After a timeless interval of perfect bliss, Kev kissed her cheekbone a few dozen times, and spoke. "My brother Sean, and his wife, Liv. They had their own run-in with Dr. O, a few years ago."

"Yes?"

"I won't tell you the details, because it was awful, as you might imagine. But they lived. Afterwards, Sean freaked out. He ran away."

"From what?"

"Liv," he said simply. "He was afraid he might hurt her.

Because of being crowned, compelled. Possessed. The stress flashbacks scared him to death." He brushed his knuckles tenderly over her jaw. "So, I just wondered if maybe something like that was happening with you."

The delicacy of the question moved her. He was so sweet, so careful. Even as angry and abandoned as he felt.

She pressed her forehead against his. "Yes, and no," she whispered. "At first, I was just out of it. Everything hurt. I didn't even want to come back. And when I did . . ." Her voice petered out.

"What?" he prompted gently. "Please. Tell me."

"Ava," she blurted. "I felt guilty. I felt bad for her."

He didn't reply, just stroked her face and waited.

"I resisted the crown by opening up my inside eye," she told him. "The thing that happens when I draw? It created a blind spot. She couldn't move me. But to do it, I had to . . . to fuse with her."

Comprehension lit his face. "Oh, God. That had to be bad."

"Very bad." Her voice wobbled. "I poisoned myself. Because I got her, you know? Her pain, her sickness. I *was* her, for a little while. Long enough. And I can't seem to . . . oh, shit. I can't even explain it."

He hugged her tighter. "I felt her too, when she crowned me."

"I couldn't hate her," Edie whispered. "Not after I knew how she felt. What she'd suffered. It was just . . . too close to home. It broke me. I just don't know if I can be fixed. So I stayed away. From everyone."

He stroked her hair. "I'm not everyone, Edie. I'm me. I'm Kev. Remember me? I can handle it. I'm not scared of this. Not if I have you."

She threw her head back, blinking away defiant tears. "You think? I'm a mess, Kev. I cry all the time. I wake up screaming any time I get to sleep. I get stress flashbacks every day. And the psychic thing. Remember how that eye only opened when I drew? Now it never closes."

He blinked, impressed. "Wow. That must be interesting."

"To say the least," she muttered.

He waited for a few moments. "And? Is that all?" he prompted.

She laughed, startled. "What, isn't that enough for you?"

"No," he said. "Not enough to justify running away from me."

Edie pressed her face against his jacket. Still strangled by that noose that had held her back from reaching out to him. The fear, the shame, the hopeless exhaustion. All her boundaries, smashed to trash.

"It's like I have no skin," she explained, haltingly. "I'm blasted by info all the time. I have to stay alone until I learn how to block it, and who knows if I ever will. Maybe it was the crown, maybe the head injury. I've been hiding out. Hoping it'll get better. But it hasn't yet."

"And? So? Can't I help? Can't I be with you while you learn?"

She shrugged. "You've seen the disadvantages of having a psychic girlfriend. You wanted space, right? You won't get it hanging out with me."

His eyes blazed with outrage. "You can't throw that in my face!"

"I'm not throwing," she replied. "I'm just quoting."

"Yeah, out of fucking context! I was trying to get you away from me! Trying to keep you safe! That space was meant to save your life!"

Edie pulled him closer again, dragging his resistant body toward hers. "Thank you for trying so hard," she whispered. "Don't be mad."

"Go ahead," he said hotly. "Examine every unworthy thought, every impure impulse! I don't give a fuck. Hell, my impure impulses are all about you, anyhow. All you'll see if you look inside me is how much I love you. How shit scared I am of losing you. That's the content of my waking consciousness. So if you can stand it, please. Have mercy."

"Oh, Kev," she whispered, brokenly.

She dragged him nearer. He groaned and gave in, his arms closing around her. "I was wondering why you seemed even more beautiful than I remembered," he mumbled into her hair. "It must be the psychic thing. You're like a flood-light now. You blind me."

She shook with soggy giggles. "Aw. That's so romantic. Have you been taking lessons from Bruno?"

He snorted his disgust. "That superficial, manipulative punk? Hell, no. How can you say that? These are the truths of my heart."

They swayed together, their bodies shaking with unbe-lieving joy.

"So, your brother Sean," she said, finally. "He ran away from his girlfriend? How did it play out?"

Kev lifted his head, and gazed into her face. "He came to his senses," he said. "He decided to trust himself, and her, too. He threw himself at her feet. Begged her forgiveness. She finally gave in."

She hid a smile. "Ah. I see. Is that what you want from me?"

"I want everything from you," he said, forcefully. "I want it all. Nothing held back. The good and the bad. Now, for-ever, always."

She wound her arms around his neck even tighter.

He nuzzled her neck. "They just had their first kid, four days ago," he said. "Eamon Seth McCloud. Named after our father."

She lifted her head. "Really? Oh, wow, that's great," she said warmly. "Congratulations, Uncle Kev! It all went well?"

"Yeah, it went great. They were worried, because they thought he was early, but he came out at almost nine pounds. Big bruiser. Sean's nuts about him. Zia Rosa's up there with them. Feeding them hand-rolled pasta and beef broth. To make milk."

"Really? Zia Rosa, up there? With your brother? Wow!"

"Yeah, she's adopted my brothers and their wives and kids. They're good sports about it. The awesome food helps. Finally she's a grandma. Nonna Rosa. She's in hog heaven. It's good that she has something else to think about right now. It really helps her."

The memory crashed back, and guilt, for being so self-centered. "Kev. I'm so sorry about Tony. I'm sorry I wasn't there for the funeral."

He leaned his head on her shoulder, hiding his face. "It's OK," he murmured. "You weren't even conscious."

"I wish I could have been there for you. Holding your hand."

"We got through it," he said. "And you can hold my hand now. Just don't ever let go of it."

"Never," she said.

They came together, fusing into a single being. A blaze of perfect happiness. She blinked back tears, and saw Aunt Evelyn, Tanya, and Ronnie standing up there on the deck, watching them. Ronnie was crying. Tanya looked oddly wistful. Aunt Evelyn just looked worried.

She made her way down the stairs and the wooden walkway.

"Excuse me for interrupting," she said stiffly. "But it's time Edith came in out of this terrible wind. She's delicate, you know."

Kev turned and nodded politely. "Hello, Mrs. Morris."

"Hello, Mr., er . . . should I call you Larsen? Or McCloud?"

A slow smile started over his face. "How about you call me Kev?"

Aunt Evelyn turned a dull red. "Hmmph. Should I let the staff know there'll be another for dinner?"

Kev wound his arm around Edie's waist. "Let's go out," he whispered into her ear. "I want you all to myself."

Out? Wow. She hadn't gone out in weeks. But with Kev at her side, she might be able to face it. It might even be, well. Fun.

Giggles started welling up, like bubbles, wonderful and effervescent. "We're going out," Edie announced.

Aunt Evelyn spun around, horrified. "Out? Out where?"

Edie shrugged. "I don't know. The steakhouse on Highway 16, maybe, or the pizza parlor. Or the drive-in. Big Jim's has good burgers."

"Are you crazy?" her aunt squeaked. "You're ill, Edie! You're injured! Emotionally fragile! You need constant care!'

Crazy. Yeah, maybe. But she didn't care. Not if she had Kev. She was a ship in full sail. She could go anywhere, do anything. No limits.

"Don't expect her back early," Kev added.

"Ah, actually, don't expect me back at all," Edie amended. "We'll probably get a room at the motel on the highway."

Aunt Evelyn threw up her hands and stomped away. Ronnie chortled behind her hand, but her eyes were wet.

"What do you say we go discuss our honeymoon itinerary?" Kev said into her ear. "The Galapagos Islands have always looked really interesting. Or the ruins of the Incan Empire."

She giggled harder. "I'm game. But what about the reindeer in Lapland? And the goats in Crete, and the emus in Australia?"

"Fine with me," he said promptly. "We'll put them on the list. And Paris, Rome, Venice, Athens? Prague? New Delhi? Katmandu? Kyoto?"

"All of them," she said rashly. "Let's go everywhere."

"Oh, God, yeah."

They grabbed each other, forgetting anyone was watching. Not caring. Kissing each other until neither could tell whose tears were whose. Just that the kisses were salt-sweet and delicious and perfect.

And that the love would be forever.

If you enjoyed *Fade to Midnight,* you won't want to miss Shannon McKenna's next thrilling romantic suspense novel featuring Bruno Ranieri and the McCloud Brothers. Read on for a special preview!

A Brava hardcover on sale in October 2011.

Portland, Oregon

I have many important things to do. You are not one of them.

The non-verbal message vibing off the hard-ass brunette's haughtily turned back was impossible for Bruno to misinterpret. But perverse, self-flagellating idiot that he was, it went straight to his dick.

She'd walked into Tony's Diner at 3:45 A.M., and he'd swear to God, he'd felt her coming before she even turned the corner and moved into the light under the awning outside. He was primed for her, after the last two nights of torture and titillation. Begging Fate to bring her back.

Fate had been kind. After hours of waiting, finally the follicles on his body tightened, lifting hairs on end in a breezy, ticklish rush of animal awareness. The bells over the doors jingled. And there she was.

His hair follicles weren't all that lifted and tightened. Good thing he wore an apron over his jeans. When the chick with the black pageboy sashayed into Tony's Diner, no matter how blitzed from lack of sleep he was, his glands

promptly pumped a substance into his body that made him
want to break into an old-time dance number. An incredible
rush. A tingling sense of infinite possibility, combined with
a mega-boner. A huge, awestruck "wow" from the depths of
his being.

She'd chosen a table today, rather than the counter. Each
seating option offered different viewpoints, with varying advantages and disadvantages. He hadn't yet settled on his favorite. The back view was nice for legs, ass, the graceful
nipped-in curve of her back, the nape of her slender, soft-
looking neck, and he could get a lot of easy, blatant ogling in
while hustling around behind her back. When she took a
table he got more frontal scoping action, but had to resort to
old tricks from adolescence, developed before he'd discovered the ease and simplicity of mirrored sunglasses. Take it
in, in one sweeping glance, and then pore over the gathered
data in the privacy of his own dirty mind. He could never
gulp enough of this girl in a single glance, though. He
wanted to sit down across from her. Fix her with an unblink-
ing, predatory stare.

Not that she'd notice, of course. She probably wouldn't
even look up. Her powers of concentration were world-class.

He kept trying to pin down what it was about her that got
to him. It was a thorny problem, requiring detailed, up-close
research and analysis, he decided, preferably conducted in
bed. Maybe the sharp, up-tilted angles of cheekbone and
eyebrows, maybe the big, mysterious greenish-gold eyes, set
at an exotic, catlike slant, accentuated with bold eyeliner and
long, curling lashes, heavy with mascara. She wore bizarre
red cat-eye glasses with fake gems in the corners that
should've made her look grotesque, but they didn't. They
looked quirky, sassy, bold, playful. They threw her startling
beauty into sharp relief. She could wear anything and look
great. Anything or nothing. Nothing would be fine, too. She
needed no tricks. But she could pull off any she wanted.

And that mouth. She'd painted it a bright scarlet that was

supposed to make her look super tuff, but it didn't work worth a damn. He wondered if she knew that. It didn't seem deliberate. The lush fullness of the upper lip made her look secretly vulnerable, almost childlike. And the severe, shiny jet black hair was all wrong for her skin.

Which was glowing, luminously pale.

The look was Salvation Army sexpot. Shabby black stretch lace shirt, designed to showcase an enticing nipple hard-on. Frayed denim miniskirt, just a little too tight for a luscious ass. Tiny bulge of sweet, snowy pale muffin top coming out the low-slung waistband where her shirt rode up. Made him want to grab and squeeze and stroke. Scuffed, shiny red fuck-me peep-toes with three-inch heels. Shapely rounded legs, clad in black stockings with so many rips and runs, it had to be on purpose, but who knew? He was usually good at decoding what girls were saying with their clothes, but he couldn't read this chick. She dressed like she wanted attention, and yet she stared into that netbook like her life depended on it, black-tipped finger-tapping in a ceaseless, buzzing blur of sound. A bluish glow illuminated her face. Eyes frozen wide. A million miles away. Denying Bruno's very existence upon this earth by the massive force of her indifference. Even while ordering food.

She was a bad tipper, too. But the low-cut shirt and nipple hard-on made up for that sin most abundantly.

There was that other quality, too. The one he barely knew how to articulate to himself. An intangible glow that hung around her, a sparkling cloud you could only see if you weren't looking at it. He knew it existed because he'd grown sensitive to it hanging out with his adopted brother, Kev. Who, mellow and gentle as he was, always carried a disquieting aura of danger about him. A sense of things about to happen. Good things, bad things. Big things.